"WHAT DID YOU SAY, BOY?"

"Yes, my lord," came the peculiar rasp.

Antonio stepped forward. "I promise you whatever pleasure you might get in babbling about what you saw would be undone by the thrashing I will give you if I hear the story from some stranger in the street. Is that understood?" he asked, gripping the youth's shoulders to give him a good shake.

At the touch of his hands on her body, rough as it was, a bright current flashed through Veronica, making her gasp aloud. Abruptly, he released her, shoving her against the wall as he stepped back himself. Veronica's head came up and her eyes met Antonio's. She felt a wild elation at the confused mix of emotions she read there. He had experienced it too, that surge of power between them. This magic flowing through her was flowing through him as well, and no disguise could conceal it. She almost laughed aloud then, in giddy joy, seeing the astonishment on his face at war with desire and annoyance, seeing him struggle to mask all three behind his courtier's cool detachment. He still thought she was a boy, and he was utterly bewildered at his response. . . .

The
Prince
of Cups

GAYLE FEYRER

A Dell Book

Published by
Dell Publishing
a division of
Bantam Doubleday Dell Publishing Group, Inc.
1540 Broadway
New York, New York 10036

ISBN: 0-440-21777-6

Printed in the United States of America

Published simultaneously in Canada

July 1995

10 9 8 7 6 5 4 3 2 1

RAD

To Richard,
for unending support and encouragement.
To Tashery,
for shared critiques and shared fantasies.

Prologue
— The Foretelling

 LUCIA Danti waited. She sat alone in the top room of the tower, the ancient Roman watchtower she had made her home. Isolated at the edge of the Danti estate, it stood stern and benign, surveying the countryside surrounding Florence. She had chosen it for its solitude, its centuries. The age of the stones comforted her, the past held within the gray granite breathing its own deep quiet, encircling her with peace. But Lucia was not peaceful, though she was patient. The sight was not her gift, but she did not need it to know that Veronica would come to her today. Before her, in preparation, the round oak table was spread with a velvet cloth the deep blue of lapis, its edges heavy with golden fringe. As she waited, her arthritic hands slowly sifted through her *Tarocco* pack, shuffling and reshuffling the hand painted cards, her eyes glancing now and again at the vivid stylized images. Each picture offered a message of reassurance. If it were not for that, the advice she was about to give would be different indeed.

Lucia lifted her head, then turned to the single large window, its rounded arch framing a view of clouded sky and gently swelling hills sketched with the supple shapes of parasol pines, of cypress and olive trees. Their soft grayed greens were accented by the dark clusters of mulberry groves. Lucia gazed on the landscape intently, but it was her ears, not her eyes, which told her Veronica was coming. Outside there was the sound of hoofbeats, their swift approach reined in abruptly, then footsteps racing up the narrow stone steps of the tower. Lucia set the cards aside and turned to face her great-granddaughter as she arrived, flushed and breathless at the door to her room.

Veronica paused there, gathering control, her whole body taut with suppressed emotion. "Mama Lucia, do you know? Did Uncle tell you?"

"Yes, child."

Lucia watched as Veronica searched her face for some shred of hope, the possibility of reprieve. Lucia knew there was none to be found there, and knew also that if Veronica did not find some release for the turmoil within her, she would be tempted to do something rash. Despite her serious demeanor, a streak of wildness ran deep in the girl. Lucia opened her arms. For a moment Veronica hesitated, then she flung herself across the room and into those arms, kneeling on the ancient stone floor, sobbing her heart out.

Quietly, Lucia stroked the smoky red hair that lay in disarray across her lap. It was such a pleasure for her crabbed old hands to touch, thick, springy soft, and the color . . . only the leaves of the flowering plum trees were such a color. It was a sadder pleasure that Veronica trusted her with this grief. She had been so open as a child, her summer visits from Siena one of Lucia's greatest delights. Since her parents' death by drowning a year ago, Veronica had kept her sorrows too much to herself. Was it worse that she lived now in the city where they had died? No, Lucia knew it was nothing so simple. It was the *Tarocco* Veronica shunned—that and her own gift.

Ah, the sobs were quieting now. They could begin to talk. Lucia placed her faith in the cards when she spoke of this new trouble. "It will not be so terrible, Veronica."

Stormy gray eyes lifted to meet her own. Lucia saw anger and despair warring there as Veronica cried out, "Roberto della Montagna is an idiot! Uncle means to marry me to a mindless fool! I cannot bear it!"

It was a callous thing, to choose a twenty-year-old simpleton as husband for a girl who loved the quiet magic of books, the delights of the mind, as much as the wilder joy of galloping her little mare across the hills outside the city. True, not all clever men wanted clever wives, even in progressive Florence in the year 1493, but this was a travesty of judgment. Veronica's guardians had looked not for a husband to please their niece, only an alliance to please themselves. Lucia fished a handkerchief from the pocket of her *camorra* and handed it to Veronica, who scrubbed away the tear streaks, her fair skin mottled from crying. Lucia stroked her cheek. "I knew his mother, and I have met Roberto too. He has the mind and the heart of a child, without a child's meanness. You will come to no harm from him.''

"But. . ." Veronica paused, on the verge of tears again. She bit into the full flesh of her lower lip, letting the small, sharp pain cut against the urge to cry. Her chin firmed, and Lucia saw her own strong jawline, her own courage, impulsiveness, and stubbornness in the face that confronted her. "He will be my husband and share my bed. Then there will be children . . . ."

"A secret—between you and me, child?" she asked, and Veronica nodded. "I doubt that he will carry the defect in his seed. Roberto's mother came to me when he was still young in her womb. She was full of fear and bitterness. Birthing the last child she bore Luigi della Montagna had almost killed her. This one had been forced upon her. There was no love lost between her husband and herself. Luigi was handsome in his youth, but looks were all he had. A shred of kindness would have served her far better. She was full of fear and anger and begged me for herbs to rid herself of the child, but I would not help her.''

"Would you do such a thing, Mama Lucia?"

"Perhaps . . . a woman should not have to give birth to hatred, or to her own death. But she was too far along for the herbs I knew to work without harm, and the *Tarocco* also warned against it. She would not listen to me, though, and went elsewhere, to someone less knowledgeable or less scrupulous. She had gold to pay for the drugs she wanted, and someone sold them to her. So she took her potions. They made her very ill, but despite that she did not lose the child.''

"But he was born flawed," Veronica finished.

"Yes. His mother returned to me a year after he was born and told me the story. She was no fool, she knew why he was not normal.''

"What did she want, when she came to you again?"

"Forgiveness. Peace."

"Did she find it, Mama Lucia?"

"I read the *Tarocco* for her. It was a simple reading and the outcome card was the Ace of Cups. I told her that all the child would ever ask from her was love. It was the peace she wanted, for she had that to give him. Her last two years were happy ones, caring for her Roberto.''

"I will not be able to love him, Mama Lucia.''

"Not as a husband perhaps, but as a child you can love him, a great, sweet, gentle child. You will be his protector, Veronica, as he will be your freedom. The movements of a married woman are not so circumscribed as those of a maid.''

"Aunt says I should be grateful to marry into such an aristocratic family. Mama and Papa were not even from Florence, and I have Gypsy blood as well. But I am proud of you, Mama Lucia, and Siena was more beautiful than here, where everything seems so flat and grim. Sometimes I feel I have been shut away inside a dark box, and galloping outside the walls is my only escape." Veronica's eyes narrowed. "Aunt says all Florence knows I am nothing but a *selvaggia,* a wild little heathen, riding my horse astride like a boy.''

Lucia smiled. "It's true you're more pagan than Christian at heart. None but the followers of that silly monk Savonarola will care one fig about such antics, not with your beauty and the dowry that goes with it.''

"Aunt says no one will want me and I shall be a spinster.''

"Nonsense, but you will be seventeen come fall, Veronica, and that is late to be marrying.''

"Not late enough for me," Veronica said rebelliously, her strongly marked brows drawing together in a frown. "It is Uncle's fault, with his stupid, snobbish ways. He has always idolized the old families.''

Lucia nodded. Her grandson's fawning was sillier than ever now, with Florence struggling to reassert its republican heritage, but he had always been a foolish boy. Success, wealth, personal accomplishment, these were the true measures of worth in Florence, not lineage.

"We were small merchants and artisans only a generation back, so I should be grateful to marry the idiot son of a great house," Veronica said sarcastically. "Our money is good enough for them, is it not? We are as rich as they are now.''

"Richer. Your family has had great success. You've had the advantages of the finest ladies, for all your mother and father indulged the free spirit in you. You are as good as they are, dear child. Better. Luigi della Montagna may come from a once noble bloodline, but he has no nobility of soul. He is a greedy man, weak, selfish, and cruel.''

Veronica shivered, and Lucia brushed away her own sudden sense of foreboding. ''It's not the father you're marrying, child.''

''I told them I would rather not marry than wed Roberto. I told them I could live with Cousin Daniele. He loves me better than they do, but they will not let me stay with him.''

''They are your legal guardians, Veronica. Daniele offered to take you in after your parents' death, but they would not hear of it. They are too proud of their new wealth and status not to be embarrassed by having a member of the family who chooses to be an artist when he might be a gentleman. An old fortune teller like me was bad enough.''

''Mama Lucia—I can run away if you help me. I will join the Gypsies. They will take me in if you ask them to do it. You have taught me enough of your herbal lore that they will respect me. I can be useful as something other than a wife.''

''You have a talent for healing, child. The touch of your hands can ease pain, but your practical knowledge is still too small. You can soothe, but you cannot safely cure.''

''I have some understanding of the cards,'' Veronica began, then faltered. Before her parents' death, she had studied the *Tarocco* eagerly whenever she visited. Since that painful day, Veronica had avoided the cards whenever possible. Instead, she had concentrated on developing her healing abilities, helping Lucia whenever she tended the sick at the convent hospital.

''Your looks would be your dowry to the Gypsies, rather than these fledgling skills you claim.'' Lucia waited to see if there was aught else Veronica would offer. Her great-granddaughter had another talent, the gift of second sight, and for it alone the Gypsies would welcome her in their midst. But that gift Veronica would not volunteer, even in her desperation. It was that very ability which had troubled her so, this whole year past.

''You must . . . .'' Veronica pleaded.

''No, I must not,'' Lucia said, refusing to succumb to the temptation of offering that talent to her troubled people. That way would not be right for Veronica. Lucia had romanticized that roving life far too much, spinning tales for her great-granddaughter's pleasure. To be raised within the Gypsy culture was one thing; to try and join it from outside quite another, even with Veronica's abilities. The life was a difficult one, for her people were persecuted. The girl might well be happy for a time, reveling in the adventure, but she'd lose far more than she gained. Too much of what Veronica loved would count for nothing among the Gypsies, not her learning, nor her gentle civilized graces. She should not abandon those. They were the jeweled chalice that contained and shaped the wilder elements within her.

"The world keeps a tight rein on women, Veronica. What escape would it be, when some man would claim you there as quickly as here? There's nowhere to run, child. Little pagan that you are, you're not fit to make a nun of, even if your uncle would let you enter a convent. That would be the tightest prison of all for you. Witch, wife, nun, or whore, there's not many choices for a woman in life, and trouble comes with every one of them."

The smoky eyes glared at her. "I will not marry him," Veronica whispered. "I will not."

Mama Lucia searched the accusing face before her. They had not spoken of it aloud, but now they must. "Veronica, have you had forewarning against this marriage?"

Veronica's gaze held her own for a second, then fell. "No. Nothing. Neither before Uncle told me or after. I would have told you if I had, Mama Lucia."

"I know you do not desire your gift, child, but you possess it nonetheless. Denial will avail you nothing."

"I have no choice. It cannot be denied. It comes as it will, but rarely, and seldom for anything but ill. My gift is so much less than you think, Mama Lucia. My little knowledge of herbs has more worth than these uncertain imaginings."

"You say you have no choice. But you have chosen to shun the *Tarocco*, Veronica. Why, unless you fear that gaining skill there will open the doors to the sight?"

"Yes, that's true." Stricken, Veronica gripped Mama Lucia's hands in her own. "When I ran to you the day my parents died, I was full of fear. I knew they would die, but not how. Then when you laid out the cards, I saw it all, clearer than any vision before or since. The bridge collapsing, water everywhere, that wet suffocating darkness.''

"Ah, yes, child, I know . . . ."

"But what I saw changed nothing, Mama Lucia. Nothing I have ever seen has been in time for me to affect the event, only suffer it."

"Painful as it is, you must return to the *Tarocco*," Lucia chastened softly. "The gifts are linked for you. You must open your mind and your heart to this power. When you achieve that, perhaps then you will find more joy."

"If it brought me more—more joy or more power to change the misfortune it shows me, then I would seek it though it brought me suffering." Veronica met her eyes in a fierce challenge. "It is nothing to envy me for, Mama Lucia."

Lucia felt her cheeks flush, but she held her great-granddaughter's gaze. It was true, but she pitied Veronica as much as or more than she envied her. The *Tarocco* was dark as well as bright. The cards had shown Lucia grief and fear, violence and horror. Looking at them, she perceived their hidden meanings, she felt their power, but she never *saw* anything but the painted images themselves. The exquisite surfaces revealed the truth to her, but they were also a protective barrier. Never had she plunged through the symbol into the reality itself. Part of her longed for the gift, but Lucia knew she would not have wanted to see, to feel, the death of her loved ones with the shattering anguish that Veronica had experienced.

"Perhaps," Mama Lucia said, looking at the pain, the anger, in her great-grandchild's eyes. But she knew she would never choose to relinquish the powers she did possess and that, somehow, Veronica must embrace her own.

"No premonition has come to me, but there is still the *Tarocco*. Read the cards for me, Mama Lucia," Veronica said, defiance and fear mingled in her voice.

"I hoped you would ask." She handed the cards to Veronica. "You know what to do."

Lucia watched as her great-granddaughter shuffled clumsily, as awkward as Lucia had ever seen her. With her left hand, Veronica cut the pile she had shuffled into three smaller ones. As Lucia reached to stack the cards with the first cut on top, Veronica said, "Mama Lucia . . . once . . . when I was little, and you were not here in the tower, I asked the cards who I would marry. I picked one card.''

''Yes?'' Lucia waited, and the *Tarocco* waited with her. Holding it she felt anticipation within an enveloping stillness, the cards she held in her hands full of warmth and potency, pulsing with their own subtle heartbeat.

''They told me I would marry the Fool. I thought they were scolding me for touching them. I never asked again.'' She laughed bitterly. ''I did not think they would be so literal.''

Lucia only nodded, there seemed nothing to say to that. Picking up the *Tarocco,* she dealt seven cards facedown, choosing a simple layout forming a horseshoe shape. When she was finished, she turned the cards over, one by one.

''Only two Swords, a single Coin, and all those Cups,'' Veronica exclaimed, as the cards were revealed. ''And nothing but Minor cards—not a single Major Trump. It does not make any sense to me, Mama Lucia!''

Lucia was puzzled too. Because of the way the cards had vibrated as she held them, she had expected more figures from the Major Arcana to appear in the reading. But aside from the absence of Major Trumps, the spread made absolute sense. ''It is because you are too upset, Veronica. You expected something different, so you won't see what's under your nose. Look here, the first card, the Five of Cups, is the past—the cup of happiness is overturned. There's your melancholy and bitterness, your frustration and your tears. And over here, the sixth card is the Six of Cups. The worst obstacle is your own nostalgia for what's gone and can't be brought back. Nothing has gone well for you since your parents' death, though you have, to your credit, made use of what is left you.''

''I miss them terribly, but I always loved you just as much, Mama Lucia,'' Veronica said vehemently. ''I could not have borne it without you.''

Lucia eyes grew moist. Sniffing imperiously, she pursed her lips and returned to her scrutiny of the cards. ''Here is the present situation. The Eight of Swords is a card of great difficulty. The circumstances here are dictated by fate—you cannot escape them.''

''Strength comes through submission,'' Veronica said, her wide, full mouth thinned with resentment.

"Pay attention to the cards, child! That's the rule of the Nine of Swords, not the Eight. No sense in playing the martyr if you don't have to do it," Lucia snapped. "Sometimes you must surrender, and sometimes you just snatch up what's at hand and whack away at whatever's after you."

"Yes, Mama Lucia," she answered, but her voice was edged with hostility.

"Well, you were right to begin with, much as you hate the idea. Fighting will do you no good whatsoever, nor running away. What changes you can make will come through care and effort, not struggle and defiance. Not through tears, either. The trouble can't be changed, so you'll need all your spirit to face up to it. Here, the fourth card, the Five of Swords, says the same. You feel humiliated, defeated, but it's best to swallow your pride and move on."

Veronica poked the next card with her finger. "The Ten of Coins. That is the attitude of those around me—aunt and uncle concerned with family wealth and bloodlines and nothing else."

"You're determined to dwell on the bad, aren't you? Look at the Four of Wands. This event will lead to a time of growth for you, a blossoming forth of your skills and graces."

"A blossoming." Her voice was flat and scornful. "I do not want this marriage. It does not have to happen. You have told me over and over that the cards deal with possibilities, probabilities. I can change what is happening, make it different."

"And throw away this perfectly lovely outcome card? The Nine, one of the sweetest of all the Cups. Contentment and kindness, generosity of spirit and great affection."

"I do not believe it," Veronica cried furiously. "How can I?"

"You can believe your eyes. It's right there in front of you." A storm of temper would do the girl no more good than a storm of tears.

"The reading cannot be right. There are only the Minor Trumps here, none of the Major Arcana, not the Fool nor the Tower. Nothing. This is one of the most important, one of the most terrible things that has ever happened to me. My whole life is changing."

"But you see it is not such an upheaval as you thought," Lucia replied. "Have the cards ever lied to you?"

"No." A dark whisper. "No. No. No."

Lucia wondered if the *no* was continued denial or the beginning of acceptance. She doubted that Veronica herself knew. Lucia would have taken it no better if her family had tried to force her to marry such a husband, however gentle and childlike. But Lucia trusted the *Tarocco*, and the prediction was encouraging. She was aware of the pulse in her hand again. The cards were not finished.

"Is there something you want clarified, Veronica?" she prompted.

"All of it," the girl said miserably.

Lucia followed her instincts and laid another card atop the outcome card.

"The Wheel of Fortune," Veronica said, relieved to see a Major Trump at last, but confused as well. "Change, a new phase of life? That card should have been at the beginning, not the end."

"No, your marriage is not the change of which it speaks. The Nine of Cups is the initial outcome of the reading, and the turn of the Wheel follows on that time of contentment." Lucia laid her hand across the Wheel of Fortune and closed her eyes. "This change is far future, not near. Years, Veronica, not days or months." She opened her eyes to her great-granddaughter's stricken face. "No matter how overwhelming it seems to you now, this marriage is less a new beginning than a time of preparation. There is growth, yes, maturation, but it is all in anticipation of something greater. It is a time of ripening, a time of waiting."

Veronica studied the layout, puzzled that the powerful trump, the outcome card, offered no resolution, only a greater mystery. "Waiting?" she asked. "Waiting for what?"

To answer the question, Lucia turned over yet another card and laid it overlapping the Wheel of Fortune. The dark elegant male face of a Court card stared out at them with commanding arrogance. "Not for what, child, for whom. The Prince of Cups."

"Oh," said Veronica softly. "Yes."

At the sudden change in tone, Lucia lifted her head. Veronica's gaze was still fixed on the compelling figure of the Court card, embracing the Prince in some intense inner vision of its own. She seemed to glow, filled with a soft flame of joy that illuminated her face from within and spilled forth into the very air about her. Lucia had seen that flame within her only once before, and then it had been a burning agony. The *Tarocco,* and something more than the *Tarocco,* had given Veronica an answer she could accept, one that she desired. She watched as her great-granddaughter touched the card lightly. Veronica had lovely hands—long fingered, with a strength that only emphasized their grace—and the brush of her fingertips across the painted figure was a delicate caress. As swiftly as it had come, the poignant, sensuous mood was gone. In its place was something at once calmer and fiercer.

"It is all right then," Veronica said with absolute certainty, standing up from the table. Lucia saw determination in her face and body, her gawky adolescent coltishness gathering into something slender and commanding. *Yes,* she thought, *the woman begins to emerge from the girl.* Irrelevantly, she wondered when the girl had grown so tall.

"I am going back now, Mama Lucia, to tell them I will marry Roberto della Montagna. If it has to be, I want to get it over and done with."

"Yes, child. I think that's best."

Veronica reached out and touched the pasteboard image of the Prince of Cups again. The woman's command was still there, fused now with that tender dreaminess and an inner, vibrating passion. "I would do anything for him, Mama Lucia. I have been in love with him from the moment I saw him, and I never had him in a reading before. It was the Prince of Cups I wished for when the *Tarocco* told me I would marry the Fool. If I cannot have him for my husband, then I must be content to have him for my lover. I only hope I do not have to wait too long." And then Veronica was gone, running down the stairs as quickly as she had run up.

When she had gone, Lucia picked up the last card, surveying the painted face, so arresting even in miniature. The exquisite insolent features captured all the intensity of the card's

Scorpio rulership. "The perfect courtier," she muttered, "handsome as Satan and too clever by half."

Once again, the cards seemed to throb as Lucia held them, and the uneasiness she had felt before Veronica's arrival returned to vex her. Abruptly, she placed the Prince of Cups in the center of the table and pushed the cards of the first layout aside, not bothering to reshuffle them. This reading would proceed from the last one. "You can be passionate, but you can be cruel as well. What changes come with you?" she asked the Prince. "What do you bring the child I love?"

Choosing a new layout, the Cross, Lucia began to deal. Her hands were oddly reluctant to release them, but the cards themselves were eager, and as she turned them over, the Major Trumps blazed forth among the Minor. Here was the foretelling of destiny her great-granddaughter had expected. The Lovers were there, of course, at the very heart of the reading. The figure of the Devil lurked beneath them, all cruelty and lust and dominance. And over here was the ominous Moon, with its miasma of illusion and self-deceit, leading one on dark and twisted paths. And the Major Trumps were surrounded by angry Swords, powerful cards that predicted not only sorrow but violence and treachery.

Lucia had a moment of dizziness, of fear, a dreadful vertigo that seemed to pull her into that obscure and turbulent future. Would she have encouraged this marriage if she had seen what lay beyond it? There was danger here, mortal enemies and the possibility of failure both from without and within. She compressed her lips, scolding herself. "You're no better than that chit of a girl, Veronica, reading doom into everything. Look at the cards. There's no need to see only the strife, the grief and suffering." She reached out and touched the Ten of Cups, the promise of perfect consummation in love. And the last card, the outcome card, was a Major Trump, the glory of the World. The fulfillment of destiny.

Still, the sense of foreboding remained with Lucia. With so many obstacles, the outcome was not guaranteed. The cards were optimistic. More optimistic than she was. She frowned at the haughty figure of the Prince of Cups, with his sumptuous robes and his gem studded chalice. "Looks to me as if you're more trouble than you're worth," Lucia grumbled at him. "I never did like you brooding, secretive ones, all smoldering sex and arrogance. One thing I'll tell you, young man, if you don't love my Veronica, it's you who'll be the fool."

1 The Summons

NIGHT. He was in the cell. Torches flickered through the barred window in the door, a candle stub guttered by his pallet. It was cold, a dank, moldy chill that sank through the flesh and permeated the marrow of the bone. The clammy air was heavy with the smell of old straw, spoiled food and filth, of iron and rust and despair. Despair was the subtlest stench, a pervasive miasma sweated into the stone by the countless prisoners who had lain here before him. Saturated, the walls sweated it back into the air. Antonio learned the color of despair, along with its scent. It was the same color as the stone, dull gray oozing darkness at the edges. Air of stone. You breathed it in, air so thick it clogged. Sighed it out, weary of holding the weight of it. The darkness gathered, pooled in the lungs, a blackness within. You coughed it up. The smear shone wetly in the faint circle of candlelight. Not black but red.

Silently, the cell door swung inward, a golden oblong of light opening within the darkness. Fighting his weakness, Antonio forced himself to stand. He stared at it, knowing he was not free to go. Not yet. He was waiting. Waiting. A figure appeared, ominous against the torchlit portal. Dread swept through him as the form slowly approached. Then the nebulous body, the shadowed face took form, and Antonio saw it was his mother. He felt a sweet, giddy rush of hope leavening the fear. Close now, she lifted her arms to embrace him. Jewels fell from her hands, all the glorious jewels he had seen her wear as a child. Luminous ropes of pearls spilled between her fingers, and delicate glittering orbs of silver filigree, golden chains linking gleaming precious stones, sapphires and amethysts, diamonds and emeralds. Rubies dripped to the floor, bright as blood.

He reached out for the jewels, the price of his freedom. They poured over him, a shining rain of gems and metal, light at first, then heavier and heavier as they wrapped around him, tangling him in their cold, thin metal strands. He felt the pressure of them tighten around his throat, strangling him. His fingers jerked against the chains, fighting to break their hold. As he fought, his mother stood before him, watching silently, her empty hands extended, her eyes wide and pleading, her breast heaving with his own struggling breath . . . .

Antonio woke abruptly. He sat up in bed, shivering in reaction to the dream. His head ached abominably, and his guts seethed. Hangover as well as nightmare. Wretched as he felt, at least he was wretched in Rome, of his own devising, not chained in an English prison cell. Those months of misery were long over. It was 1496, near a dozen years since the Battle of Bosworth and the death of Richard III. Not that he had cared then on whose side he fought. He had been courting death, not glory, in that alien land.

Glancing about him, Antonio did not recognize the ornate room he had slept in, but it must be somewhere within the Borgia palazzo. Lavinia's blond hair was spread out on the pillow next to him. He lay back and closed his eyes, forcing his body under control and gathering his wits. It had been a long time since he dreamed of that damp malodorous prison. Death had responded, belatedly, to his ardent wooing. He had almost died there, stretched out on his grimy pallet, coughing his lungs up in bloody clots. Perhaps if death had been quick, he would have welcomed that dark consummation. But the long time alone, sick and deserted, had taken him to a deeper core, down to a ferocious will to survive buried under the grief and guilt that plagued him. Dying, he found he still wanted to live. Had he been well, he could have redeemed his life with his sword, a skilled mercenary fetched a good price. But he was ill, worthless in himself. It was Giacomo who had told them Antonio di Fabiani came from a rich family. An heir's ransom was set on his head, and a messenger sent to demand the gold.

His father had refused to pay a single ducat. His father would rather see him rot.

Then Giacomo had reappeared, bearing the jewels his mother had sent to ransom him. No one except his mother would have dared to cross his father's command. And Giacomo, who might easily have vanished with that wealth and bought a new life for himself, had paid the ransom and tended him back to health. Antonio remembered the house of the sympathetic English widow Giacomo had found to board them. He remembered waking clean and warm beneath the down coverlet, the back window showing him a sunlit garden blooming with purple crocuses and yellow daffodils, the early lilies rising tall and white on smooth green stems. Remembered his mother's brooch of garnets and pearls nestled on the widow's ample black silk bosom as she leaned over to plump his pillows.

Remembered Giacomo, who no doubt shared the bosom with the brooch, spooning hot beef broth down his throat while he prattled nervously about his adventures, ". . . . pirates on the seas and brigands on the roads. I'll wager I've hidden behind every bush between Italy and England, shaking in my boots the whole while. A fine time I had too, trying to find different places to hide those jewels, to keep them safe. There had to be enough for the ransom here and bribes there, not to say something left to get us back home again. Didn't know what shape you'd be in, did I? And I was right. About at useful as a newborn kitten, you are." Antonio had not begrudged the widow her prize—better to see it adorning her than think of it shut in his captors' treasury—but he had been furious to be reminded of his weakness. "Don't glare," Giacomo had scolded. "You'll waste your strength."

In his dream it had not been Giacomo but his mother who appeared carrying his ransom. Well, that was obvious enough. He did not need some Gypsy fortune-teller to unravel that thread of meaning, nor explain the choking weight of the debt he owed her. He felt trapped, as trapped as he had been in prison. But it was not a debt he could refuse to repay. Sighing, Antonio rubbed the ruby ring he wore on his little finger, all that was left of the treasure she had given freely for love of him.

He opened his eyes. The bleak hell of the dream cell made a vivid contrast with his present luxurious surroundings. Patterned marble, intricate tapestries, and scrolled woodwork lavished the walls and floors of this opulent room. The gilded chairs and tables were inlaid with ivory and ebony. The vast bed in which he lay was draped with scarlet satin and plush velvet fringed with gold. A handspan of openwork embroidery bordered the fine linen sheets. The last guest room he had occupied in the Vatican had not been half so impressive. That realization was his first warning, but his first effort to sit up was spoiled by the magnitude of his headache. He could hardly bear to look at the pulsating red of the hangings and the mingled scent of incense and perfume was sickening. He had not drunk this much—had not been drunk—in years. He liked his wine well enough, but not being out of control. Much of last night was a blank. Gingerly, Antonio raised himself on his elbow and turned to look at his companion.

As he now suspected, it was not Lavinia who lay beside him. True, the courtesan bleached her hair to exactly this flaxen shade, but the adolescent body was not Lavinia's, nor the delicate lines of the profile. Not even the sweet violet cologne. Those belonged to Lucrezia Borgia. Rolling onto his back, Antonio groaned. For weeks, he had bent his diplomatic skills and courtly graces to avoiding just this dangerous situation. Now, sotted to insensibility, he had thrown away his efforts in a night of heedless debauchery. With luck, he would escape with his skin, but that was not the point. He was disgusted with himself.

There was movement beside him, then a light, honeyed voice said, "Good morning, Antonio."

When he looked, Lucrezia was sitting up in bed, the sheet raised modestly to her bosom, the embroidered openwork artfully arranged to reveal her pale pink nipples. She was a clever little creature, all malleable acquiescence on the surface and all connivance underneath. Well, she had to be clever to manipulate men as dominating as the Borgias. And she had obviously had her way with him as well. A just reward, for both of them. Lucrezia giggled and licked her lips, looking as innocent as a baby fox glancing up from its first kill.

"Good morning," Antonio muttered in return. He lay back and closed his eyes, dispensing with courtly graces.

Lucrezia snuggled closer. "Don't be annoyed. You are so handsome, Antonio, it was worth it to have you at least once. I want to choose for myself sometimes, instead of always being told who I must have."

Antonio considered the various implications of that. There were rumors the Pope was hunting for a new husband for his daughter. Certainly, he had the power to annul the first marriage he had arranged for her, and there were more promising prospects on the horizon. Antonio doubted that the other rumors about Lucrezia and her father were true. Roderigo Borgia, now Pope Alexander VI, was lustful and corrupt, but not depraved enough to commit incest. Lucrezia's two older brothers were another matter. Golden, rotten Juan had no doubt lured Lucrezia to his bed. The Pope's second son enjoyed beautiful women almost as much as he did pretty young men, and the perversity of possessing Lucrezia would have been an irresistible temptation. Nor would Antonio have been surprised if Juan had offered his sister's favors to him. It was the sort of twisted power the man liked to wield.

Then there was Cesare, the eldest. Antonio did not believe the two brothers shared Lucrezia's favors. There was a similar erotic intensity in Cesare's relationship with his sister, but not the same aura of secret complicity. Cesare was no doubt capable of the act, if only to prove himself better than Juan. Most of the Vatican Court were well aware of his superiority, but the Pope and his daughter were significant exceptions. Juan was their favorite. But Juan had not been there last night, and it was Antonio who had bedded Lucrezia. Whether Cesare's feelings about his sister were fraternal or something more, the young Spaniard was certainly possessive. He would probably be mortally offended at not having been consulted about Antonio's mating with his sister. Which put Antonio's own life at risk, despite the fact that he had once saved Cesare's in a tavern brawl.

The rescue was one of the vagaries of fate, for their skill at arms was equal—so far as they could ascertain. Part of the relish of their acquaintance was leaving that skill untested, as they left unspoken but understood the knowledge that they would enjoy killing each other. So far, they had both been wise enough not to provide the other with an excuse. Antonio was more cautious in his vices than Cesare, and bloodlust was not one he indulged casually, as the Borgias were wont to do. He was content to savor the pleasure of the temptation rather than the act. He hoped this midnight folly would not prove too much provocation for Cesare.

Bending over his ear, Lucrezia murmured, "Cesare is with Lavinia. He did not see us together."

He regarded her through narrowed lids. She was smiling her vixen's smile. Appreciating the irony, he found himself returning it. They understood each other well enough. They both had a strong instinct for survival. As for Lavinia, Cesare was welcome to her. She had no wit and he was bored with her already.

"We had a lovely time, did we not?" Lucrezia asked coyly, running a fingernail down his chest. "I like men who have a streak of wildness in them."

"Mmmm," he responded dolefully. His own memories of the night were far more nebulous than he wanted to admit. He had behaved like an idiot. Bad dreams and debauchery, the cause was one and same. He knew what he was going to do, had known it since the letter first arrived. There was no escape in this frantic revelry, no point in postponing the inevitable any longer. It was, on the whole, a good time to leave Rome. Strife between the Borgia brothers was escalating, and it would be wise not to be involved.

Sucking her lower lip and toying with his navel, Lucrezia was eyeing an area under the covers that Antonio knew would not rise to the occasion. He gritted his teeth into a smile and sat up. Holding Lucrezia's hands so they would not go exploring, Antonio kissed her politely. "I shall never forget this, *grandezza*," he told her quite truthfully. The morning, if not the night, was emblazoned on his brain. "But I must leave now. There are things I cannot postpone, even for so pleasant a prospect as your embrace."

He got out of bed and began to dress, pulling on his hose and fitting his *braghetta* over his sex. She was not a foolish child, to wheedle where there were no sweets to be had. With a coy pout she reclined among the pillows, still well pleased with herself for having finally managed to seduce him. "What things might these be?"

"Travel preparations," he answered, reaching for his doublet. "I am leaving Rome and returning to Florence."

Lucrezia's eyes widened with surprise. Antonio never spoke of it, but his history was no secret.

He answered her unspoken question. "At long last the exile returns home. By invitation."

"How lovely for you," she commented without enthusiasm.

"Yes." That was presuming, of course, that he survived his welcome.

—

Standing by the desk, Giacomo hesitated, filled with trepidation. It had to be the letter that was upsetting Antonio—he'd been in a black state ever since it arrived three days ago. His master was intensely private, and if Giacomo were caught snooping, he'd be in disgrace for days, perhaps for weeks. Still, this was his best chance to discover the letter's contents. Antonio had spent last night with that witch Lavinia, and would probably not be home for another hour or two. Giacomo smoothed back the fine brown hair that had flopped forward over his eyes and set to work. With care and delicacy, he fitted a bit of wire into the lock of the desk and wiggled it about. There was a tiny but quite satisfying click, and he gently lowered the lid, revealing the folded pages tucked into a cubbyhole.

Opening the letter, Giacomo recognized the writing as Antonio's mother's, though it looked tight and cramped. She would not mind his looking at it, at least not very much. After all, Madonna di Fabiani was the one who'd arranged for him to learn to read. And she'd entrusted Antonio into his care. Making his way through the opening lines, he moaned aloud: "Oh no, it's worse than I thought." Choking back the lump in his throat, Giacomo began the letter again.

December 12, the year of our Lord, 1496
Antonio, My Dearest Son,
There is something I must tell you. Something of which I did not write before, hoping to spare you grief. I am dying, Antonio. It is a wasting sickness, one which waxes and wanes in its power over me, but which steadily encroaches. I am resigned to death, but not to my life as it has been for these twelve years since you left Florence. In his love and

respect for me, your father has agreed to rescind your banishment from this house and to reinstate your inheritance. I cannot say that this is the choice of his heart, as it is mine, but he is a man of honor and will make the effort now to heal the breach between you. Perhaps if you had married again and had children, he would have taken this step earlier. I know you assumed your cousin Stefano would have the estate. But I believe your father always planned that your inheritance would pass to your children, even when he still chose to deny it to you.

As your father has granted me this wish, Antonio, I ask one of you as well. You have not remarried. I beg you to put the past behind you and accept a young girl of Florence as your bride. We have found a maiden of excellent family, and your father has made tentative inquiries which have been favorably received. Of course the alliance would benefit both our houses, but the girl herself is a pretty child, docile and exceptionally religious. I cannot help but believe one so devout would be both a dutiful wife and a good mother to your children. Perhaps I will live long enough to hold your son, my grandchild, in my arms.

There could be no more providential time for your return. Florence, under the guidance of the divine inspiration of Savonarola, is now . . . .

Filled with a sudden foreboding, Giacomo raised his head from the letter to find Antonio standing not six feet away. Giacomo had time to note that Antonio's usually impeccable attire was faintly rumpled, and the glossy black hair was actually disheveled. He was, however, perfectly furious.

"Forgive me for interrupting, Giacomo." Antonio pronounced each word with frigid courtesy, though his face was livid, the dueling scar by his mouth suddenly conspicuous, a glimmering little half moon. "I do hope you found my letter enlightening?"

Startled, Giacomo said the first thing that came to his mind. As was often the case, it was the wrong thing. "You weren't supposed to be home yet."

"No? Granted, my arrival is unfortunate . . . for you. But it is my room, my desk, and my letter," Antonio said, and then he smiled. The last time Giacomo had seen him smile like that, there had been an assassin's blood on his sword. Of course, Antonio would never hurt him, but the look alone was enough to skewer him where he stood.

With instinctive restraint, Giacomo refrained from collapsing in a heap with his arms over his head and begging for mercy. While such a theatrical ploy had been known to diffuse Antonio's anger into exasperation and amusement, in the present circumstances it was more likely to provoke disgust, turn the anger cold and unyielding. Giacomo simply could not bear a fortnight of Antonio's ice-edged scorn. The very thought made him shiver. Therefore, he must produce some explanation.

"I shouldn't—I know I shouldn't have. But what did you expect me to do with you acting as you have been for three days now, my lord?" Giacomo began at his most breakneck pace. "I'm supposed to take care of you. It's my job, my duty, my privilege to tend to your needs. Obviously something is wrong, and if you're not telling me what's upsetting you, I have to find out one way or another, or how am I to know what to do to make it better . . . ."

Giacomo gulped for breath, watching as Antonio's eyes continued to darken with outrage. They were quite beautiful eyes really, eyes the ladies sighed for, a deep glowing mahogany fringed with straight dark lashes. You wouldn't know it now. They looked black as fate, a tiny pinprick of light glowing in them like the glittering tip of a dagger. Of course his master was tall, but he did not ordinarily loom. Giacomo gulped again and lowered his eyes from the controlled fury of the face to the hand extended out to him. He stared blankly at it for a second, the pilfered letter all but forgotten, crushed in his fingers. Antonio's fingertips flexed once, an imperative command that made Giacomo twitch in response. Gingerly he refolded the crumpled parchment and placed it in Antonio's hand.

"You are my valet, not my physician or my confessor. Is it too much to ask that you let me tend to my own problems?" Antonio asked with glacial sarcasm.

"Yes, my lord. Too much to ask. Entirely too much, since you're becoming more unhappy rather than less unhappy.

You've been to visit the lady Lavinia three nights in a row now. That always means trouble . . . ." He paused in his babble, watching as Antonio's eyes widened in astonishment, then narrowed in suspicious assessment.

"What?" Antonio's lips formed the question almost soundlessly.

Giacomo pounced on this tiny breach. "You only visit the lady Lavinia when you are very angry, my lord. And your mood is seldom improved afterwards. I had to take matters into my own hands and find out what was bothering you."

Giacomo was gratified to see the surprise return to Antonio's face, and the dark anger fade to baffled affront. Then surprisingly, Antonio's lips quirked in one of his secret smiles, remembering a private joke or some new erotic gambit of Lavinia's. But the smile was brief and Giacomo's sins were not forgotten. Eyeing him balefully, Antonio grumbled, "You should be strung up by that prying proboscis of yours."

"True. Entirely true, my lord. Definitely true. A magnanimous judgment, in fact . . . ."

"Ahhhh!" Antonio made a strangled sound and raised his arm in mock gesture of threat. "You are impossible. You have the courage of a rabbit and the morals of a weasel. I would get rid of you, but I would have to replace you with both a valet and a fool."

"Yes, my lord. A trained valet will cost you dear these days, and a good fool is hard to come by. For that matter, even a bad fool is hard to come by."

"Get out of here," Antonio ordered, "and do not let me see your wretched face for the rest of the day. Make yourself useful. We have to start closing the house. As you may have surmised, we will be leaving for Florence at the end of the month."

"Yes, my lord."

Giacomo ducked out the door and scurried up the stairs to the servants' quarters. At least he'd managed to exasperate Antonio and intrigue him a little. It was good distraction from the anger, though he'd had to offer up that rather precious tidbit about Lavinia to achieve it, and it was one he'd rather not have surrendered. Antonio was very clever about other people . . . but quite naïve about himself sometimes. The ploy was only partially successful. He knew Antonio's wrath was still simmering at the invasion of his privacy—as if masters had any privacy from their servants. A good servant had to know his master backwards, forwards, and inside out. Antonio had come to expect this, was even properly grateful on occasion, but he didn't like to have his nose rubbed in the ways in which it was sometimes achieved.

Giacomo had to confess he did feel a bit chagrined, since the sentiments of the letter were so very personal. But Madonna Leonora had entrusted Antonio to him ever since the ghastly day of the funeral, when Antonio's father had told him he was banished, and he'd ridden away with only the clothes on his back. She had begged Giacomo to ride after her son. That was the only time his master had ever hit him, trying to make him turn back to Florence. He'd had to dog his trail for a week before Antonio had grudgingly accepted the inevitable, though he would barely speak to Giacomo—unless it was to tell him to keep quiet. "I thought exile was my punishment," his master had said. "Must I suffer the slow torture of being talked to death?"

Giacomo had kept chattering, partly because he couldn't help himself, partly to try and help Antonio. Talking about everything and nothing until one night around the campfire Antonio had started yelling at him, screaming at him, then burst into tears. A seventeen-year-old boy learning a man's despair. Giacomo had been silent then, just holding him while he wept, terrible body-wracking sobs that went on and on, until he was too exhausted to do anything but sleep. Morning came, and they never spoke again of that night. Giacomo knew well enough about Fabiani pride. The men were all proud as Lucifer, and there was no help for it. But things were a bit better after the storm of emotion. The black grief lifted a little, enough for Antonio to pretend to act like a man who was not utterly wretched, and nothing was ever said again about Giacomo returning to Florence alone.

Giacomo slipped into his room. He was lucky—it was early yet, and there were a few morning embers alive in the grate. Still shivering a little in the aftermath of the confrontation with his master, Giacomo added some straw and bits of kindling, working up a cheery blaze. He had to stay out of Antonio's sight today, so he'd start his own packing now, and begin making arrangements with the kitchen for the food they'd take. They'd want things that would keep on the road: bread, dried meat and fruit, some sweets. But first he needed a bit of a talk to clear the air.

Giacomo poured himself a glass of wine, then set up his chair and footstool in front of the hearth. He pulled off his boots, stretched out his legs, and prepared to have a conversation with his feet. It was one of his favorite bits of personal philosophy that feet were the most noble of life's servants, humble, obedient, and long-suffering. Not his virtues, of course, but ones he could appreciate. When he wanted good counsel, he often conferred with them, like two little wise men. Lifting his counselors onto the footstool, Giacomo tugged his hose to fit more comfortably, and let the fire begin to toast his soles.

"Feet," he informed them, "we're in trouble."

At the end of the day they would have more to say for themselves. There would be twinges of dismay, throbs of concern, sighs of assent. Now they simply waited, toes tilted towards him expectantly.

"It's truly strange, Feet. It's become like a dream of Heaven, to be forgiven, to return to Florence. I always pictured it as a time of celebration—in spring, with lots of budding and blooming in the air, or during fall harvest, with big bunches of juicy purple grapes on the vine, ripe and ready to be squeezed into wine." He sighed. "Instead, we ride in the dead of winter and go home to grief.

"But even if it weren't for the sadness, I'd just as soon not go. We've been doing quite well for ourselves the past few years. Merchant prince suits Antonio better than mercenary, though he's wicked with a sword when he has to be. Remember the time he sliced up those three nasty thieves in Naples, with me sitting on the fourth? We've had a lot of adventures together, and seen a lot more of the world than we would have otherwise. There's not many such as me that've seen such exotic sights as Constantinople and Damascus—though I'm just as happy the master decided not to set sail for the New World everyone's talking about. We're not as rich and power-

ful as we'd be with the family money and influence, but we're
a lot more free than we'd be in Florence.''

His feet were in perfect accord—they wanted to stay right
here. In fact, they wanted him to add more twigs to the dying
flickers of heat, but he told them no. ''We've got to be up and
about. Start planning the packing. There's no way out of it.
We'll have to go home, but I'm telling you, Feet, there's nothing but misery there for Antonio. His mother is dying, and that
will tear him apart. His father will never forgive him, never,
because he never really loved him, and that will tear him apart.
And there are others, Feet, who'll never forgive him. The tearing they'll do will be with steel in their hands.'' His toes
curled in trepidation. ''To tell you the truth, the swords and
knives are the lesser danger. At least he'd let me tend to
wounds they made. But whatever pain his parents give him,
he'll lock away inside himself, let it eat at his innards while he
puts more armor on the outside, turning himself colder and
darker and deadlier than ever.

''To crown it all, Feet, they've picked out someone for him
to marry,'' he cried out in exasperation. ''I hope they've done
a good job of it. Religion's no way to judge. Look at the first
one. Beatrice was convent raised, with the face of an angel—
and the heart of a whore. Truth be told, Feet, I think she was a
little mad and couldn't help herself. I never told Antonio I saw
her eyeing everyone from the stableboy to his father. With her
beauty they all had to look back too, even those that wouldn't
act on it for fear or honor. It was like the gates of Heaven
glowed all golden before you—for all you knew there'd be
Hell to pay in the end. Mad or sane, she was clever enough
about it. I never saw her witching anyone else when Antonio
was there to see. Then she had eyes only for him.''

Giacomo shook his head and his hair fell forward again.
Annoyed, he smoothed it back restlessly. ''The talk of how
devout this new one is makes me squeamish. Believing in
God's all well and good, but a man needs a wife with her
fervor in the right place. Antonio especially. He needs someone good, but good as in honest and kind, good as in warm and
passionate. Someone who can unlock all those dark places
inside him. Who'll love him more than the sun and stars put
together, so he can love her back the same way.''

He'd hoped Antonio would find what he needed before some circumstance like this trapped him. But Antonio had shunned marriage, had shunned even the usual affairs of the heart with married women of quality, never offering them more than friendship. For amorous satisfaction, he confined himself to the embraces of accomplished courtesans, sampling the voluptuous wares of the most renowned Goddesses of Love. There was always a Lavinia around, but she never lasted long. Women like that were fevers that burned in his blood and left him parched and wasted. Sometimes Giacomo thought Antonio couldn't, or wouldn't, find a love to match the physical passions in him. Sometimes, vexed, he just thought Beatrice had given Antonio a taste for bitches in heat.

"And now the family's going to marry him off to another stranger. I wonder what it would take to get him to turn her down? She'd probably have to be demon spawn with two heads and pointy hooves." The fire was almost out, and his feet, grown chilly, cramped in annoyance. Giacomo leaned forward to knead the stiffness. "No point in complaining, I don't like it any better than you do. I tell you, Feet, it's going to be a catastrophe."

2 *Luigi*

HUNCHED in a corner of the room, Roberto was still crying but not as fiercely now. Veronica knelt beside him and stroked his hair back from his face, forcing herself to calm her own inner turmoil. Roberto drew a deep sobbing breath, then rubbed his head against her hand. Relief washed through her, and she wrapped her arms around him, hugging him close. When his father upset Roberto, it often took much longer to quiet him. Veronica was grateful the upset was no worse than this. she had been coiled tight with tension all day, waiting for some catastrophe. Benito opened the door, nodding to let her know the path was clear. With the storm

waning she could offer her tempting distraction. She rocked
Roberto a little, comforting him, then kissed his cheek. "We
have found some kittens for you to play with," she said softly.

"Kittens?" he asked, lifting his swollen face and sniffing
loudly.

"Outside," Benito promised. "You must stop crying now
and get up on your feet."

Roberto immediately scrubbed away the tears with his fist
and clambered to his feet, looking about him with pleading
eyes. "Outside?"

Benito smiled at Veronica and winked. She thought again
what a blessing he was, with his boundless patience and wry
good humor. Benito had been Roberto's much beloved servant
for fifteen years before Veronica was married to Roberto. She
knew she would never have adjusted so quickly to her strange
situation without his help.

"In the stable, Roberto," Benito said. "Come along."

"Bombol's outside—can he come too? I'll tell him don't
bark."

"Yes, he can come into the stable, but not too close to the
kittens. The mama cat will scratch his nose with her claws,"
Veronica said.

"Ouch." Roberto rubbed his own nose.

"Yes, ouch. Here, let me help put your jacket on you. It is
cold outside, and the sky looks like snow."

"Like snow? The sky looks like snow?" Roberto started
laughing at this strange idea. Lifting his hands, he fluttered his
fingers down like snowflakes.

Veronica laughed too, delighted with his image. "The sky is
smooth and white, just like a snowbank. When it looks like
that, it is so full of snow that all the flakes will soon burst out
and come floating down."

She buttoned up the quilted wool jacket and put a warm cap
on Roberto's head, his favorite red one, then led him to the
door. As always, Luigi della Montagna had placed them in the
shabbiest set of rooms, underneath the back tower. Veronica
did not care that their lodgings were plain and almost as small
as the servants' quarters. Tomorrow she would be back at
Daniele's, in her own room where painted green vines climbed
the corners to blossom at the ceiling. For now, she was quite

content to be set apart from the rest of this family, and the isolation served them well. Opening the door, she checked the hallway, but there was no one in sight.

"Tiptoes," she whispered, making a game of it. Together, the three of them crept down the corridor and made their way to the kitchen. Her father-in-law had ordered Roberto to stay in his room until he stopped "that wretched sniveling." Roberto had stopped crying so he should be allowed to visit the kittens, but Veronica did not intend to ask Luigi's permission. Not in his current mood.

The cook waved them through his domain with a ladle, intent on basting the roast of lamb for the evening meal and not wanting any intruders. He looked the other way when Veronica snatched four warm *biscotti,* fragrant with the scent of toasted hazelnuts. Outside in the courtyard, the big yellow dog joined them, barking happily until shushed, then cavorting around them, all muddy paws and thrashing tail. Veronica passed around the crunchy sweets, giving Roberto an extra one to feed to Bombol. Roberto gobbled the *biscotti* and pointed excitedly to the stable. Smiling, Veronica let him forge ahead, the dog romping beside him, while she and Benito strolled more slowly. She shivered slightly in the December chill, wishing she had worn her fur lined mantle.

"Madonna Veronica?"

"Yes, Benito, what is it?"

"I don't think I should go see the widow Elizabeta tonight. This visit is so difficult for Roberto."

"Of course you shall," Veronica assured him quickly, though in the furor she had forgotten the request he had made when they arrived yesterday.

"I'm grateful, my lady. She's taking a trip to visit family in Siena, and I won't see her for a while. But I'm worried about Roberto. His father has frightened him with all this yelling."

"I think he will be all right. I wish we could go home today, but I am afraid to make Luigi even angrier."

"Maybe the master will order us to leave." Benito gave her a small, conspirator's smile. "He has before."

Veronica smiled back, then sighed. "I doubt that we will be so lucky. I think that this time Luigi needs an audience for his

grievances. I will endure his harangues gladly, if we can keep
him from tormenting Roberto.''

The cause of the great uproar was Roberto's half-brother
Frederigo, who had appeared for the Christmas festivities
dressed in the habit of a Dominican monk and announced to
his father that he had joined Savonarola's order. He was Fra
Frederigo now. Luigi was furious. Frederigo was his only sur-
viving male heir other than Roberto, and Luigi despised his
defective son. Frederigo, though younger, was to have inher-
ited control of his estates. Maria, zealous in her devotion to
Savonarola, was glowing with the victory of having her son
join the ranks of the pious Friar. Her spiteful rapture only
aggravated Luigi's wrath.

"It is difficult," Veronica continued, "but we are leaving
tomorrow afternoon. I can stay with Roberto tonight if he is
lonely or upset. Right now, I am more concerned Roberto will
be up till all hours playing with his new kitten. We will have to
give him one, you know. He misses the old cat so.''

"Yes, I was thinking that too. I made sure the kittens were
old enough. I didn't want to see him cry again.''

Still talking, they entered the dimly lit expanse of the stables, the air pungent with the scent of horses and hay, oil and
leather, dirt and dung. There was the occasional muffled clump
of a hoof as the animals shifted in their stalls, and soft wickers
and snorts as Roberto peered into each successive stall. Even
these marvelous beasts did not distract Roberto from his hunt.

"The mama and her *bambini* are in the tack room," Benito
told him, and smiled as Roberto hurried forward. "Gently,"
Benito called after him.

"He is always gentle," Veronica chided.

"Yes, my lady. Still, it's good to remind him. He's over-
excited, no?''

"Yes," she agreed.

"Remember, Bombol must sit outside," Benito called out
as Roberto reached the door of the tack room, the dog padding
at his heels.

"He won't hurt the kittens," Roberto pleaded. "Bombol
likes kittens.''

"But the mama will not like Bombol.''

"Scratch his nose," Roberto remembered. "Ouch." He

then explained this carefully to the dog, who settled into a dejected heap outside the door.

"And ask the mama cat's permission before you pick the kittens up," Veronica called, as Roberto vanished into the tack room.

Bombol whined softly as the two of them approached the tack room, beating his tail in the dust. Benito knelt to pet him. "You don't want scratches on your big nose, believe me, Bombol. I'll scratch your ears instead, and that will feel good."

Looking in the tack room, they found Roberto happily sprawled on the floor, his back propped against the boards and his lap full of fat mewing kittens, who were beginning to climb onto the new perches he provided. The mother sat at his knee, purring as she watched her brood protectively.

"Pretty . . . pretty," Roberto repeated softly to himself as he stroked each one in turn, lifting them to his face to feel their prickly little pink tongues lick at him. He hugged them carefully, and made happy crooning noises as he rocked back and forth. A black and white kitten with a white mustache scrambled up his arm and attempted to crawl inside his collar. Roberto giggled happily. There was a bench along the wall, and Veronica and Benito sat on it, joining in the praise and petting. A fluffy gray kitten attacked the curled toe of Veronica's slipper, and the mustached one ventured over and began making its way up Benito's leg. "Those are my good hose, kitten," he told it, removing it by the scruff of its neck.

Veronica held out her hands for it and carried it to her lap, watching as Benito plucked at the snag in his knee. "Your good hose. And is that your best jacket, as well?" she teased him.

"Elizabeta isn't sure how long she will be gone. I want her to remember me at my best." He grinned at this, then shrugged, "I'm not handsome, but that can't be helped."

Benito had an ugly yet oddly endearing face. The features were squashed together, set off with big, brimming eyes and a wide, lopsided smile. "She likes you very much, I think," Veronica smiled.

"Yes, I think so too. She won't marry me till next year, after her last son is wed. She is a strong woman, but she worries

about her children, worries about the business. I don't want to
be another worry, so I wait.''

Elizabeta is a lucky woman, Veronica thought, tempting the
black and white kitten with the end of her long braid. Benito
would be a sweet and caring husband. *Husband.* Married, she
almost never thought of Roberto as her husband. It was a
strange life she had been leading, more mother than wife, and
a virgin mother at that. The irony made her smile a little,
though no doubt Fra Frederigo would find it blasphemous.
Mama Lucia had been more right than she realized about Roberto, for he had remained a child in body as well as mind.
And the *Tarocco* cards had been right as well. Once married,
her life had changed very little, except for the better.

Barely a month after the wedding, Veronica had taken Roberto to visit the secluded house her cousin Daniele had inher-
ited on the far side of the Arno. Roberto had instantly fallen in
love with its ramshackle loveliness, frolicking in the orchard
and hiding himself in the branches of the ancient weeping
willow that grew outside the high stone walls. He cried when
they left, and begged everyone for days afterwards to let him
live there. After initial misgivings, Daniele had invited them
both to stay there for a few days. The days had stretched to
weeks, the weeks drifted into months, then years. Luigi,
pleased to have Roberto out of his sight, even paid Daniele a
subsidy to take them into his home. Her aunt and uncle were
suitably scandalized by the arrangement, but Veronica was a
married woman now and outside their control, if not outside
Luigi's.

So she and Roberto and Benito occupied a wing of
Daniele's house. Roberto was blissfully happy, away from the
house where he had known no tenderness except for Benito's
since his mother died when he was three years old. The artist's
villa was an escape to an enchanted palace. He was always
careful not to disturb Daniele in his studio without being
asked, and Daniele, understanding Roberto's fascination, had
paints made specially for him. He spent hours playing that
way, entranced with his colors or enraptured with the flowers
in Daniele's exquisite garden. Veronica loved nature, and Roberto taught her to share his own special contemplation, that
magic quiet he found with animals, flowers, the bright flicker

of sunlight on water. More than anything else, that present of tranquil absorption endeared him to her.

But for all his sweetness, it was difficult at times to tend a giant child and Daniele's home was a refuge for Veronica as well. Her questing intellect had been scorned within Luigi's household. Here it was encouraged and richly nourished. Daniele always ordered copies of the latest folios and sent for books fresh from the newly established printing presses. Veronica eagerly devoured these treasures and discussed them with her cousin. The walls were hung with Daniele's work and the innovative paintings he bought or traded with his friends. Many of the most interesting people in Florence came to commission him or simply to while away the afternoon in talk, and neophyte though she felt herself to be, Daniele and his friends made her welcome in their discussions. "You are good for us," Daniele said to her. "We like to dress our ideas up, embellish them with fancy embroidery, with gold bullion and feathered plumes and make them prance about. You want to see how they look standing naked before us, stripped not just to the skin but to the heart."

Veronica would never be a creature of the mind alone. When her high physical energy made her restless, she rode her mare in the woods and fields outside Florence, reveling in the speed of her mount, the wild rush of the wind. She would gallop to some secluded knoll where she could enjoy an hour of perfect solitude, savoring the scents of grass and trees. Other days she guided her mare along the road to Mama Lucia's tower, carrying a gift of dried fruit, tender cheese, or a freshly baked loaf for lunch with her lessons. She had increased her knowledge of herbal cures, but her main focus was once again the *Tarocco*.

She had gained no greater control over her gift, if gift it was. Despite Mama Lucia's hope, there had been no fusion of the *Tarocco* with her own fickle talent, nor any premonitions that approached the power of her parents' death. Veronica could only be happy that it was so. She had foreseen a small fire, a harmless boating accident, the sad death of the old blind ginger cat who had known and walked every stone of Daniele's house. He, at least, had not died before she could find him and offer some shred of comfort. More often than not, there were no images, only heightened emotions, at once intense and nebulous. Sometimes it was impossible to separate her own normal anticipation or apprehension from a forewarning. She had dreaded coming here today, sensing some confrontation with her father-in-law. Luigi had been vile, but his drunken tantrum had not warranted the panic that had seized her this morning. Veronica thrust those memories aside. The unpleasantness was over, and no great ill had come of it.

All in all, she was grateful for her new world. The shredded edges of her life had knitted together. She no longer pined for the hillside streets of Siena, for she had a family again— if a rather oddly assorted one. They lived comfortably, within their means even, since Veronica had begun to manage the household. Good food, good humor, an extravagance of books and art to pleasure the mind and spirit—these were more valuable than the grudging riches and cowed servants of Luigi's palazzo. There was little to complain of except the duty visits to her less congenial relatives. Blessedly, most of these took place on special occasions, lavish balls, or rich holiday feasts that provided entertaining distraction from the family squabbles. She was almost content.

There was only one thing lacking. The Prince of Cups.

Three years had passed since the *Tarocco* had promised him to her, since she had felt with such certainty that he would come. Holding that surety in her heart, Veronica had not asked the cards about him since, only about the small everyday problems of her life. She supposed it might be years before he appeared. The thought filled her with loneliness and a growing frustration. Lately, she had begun to hunger for him, in a way she hardly understood. Thoughts of him filled her with a physical yearning edged with an almost painful anticipation. By day, she found herself searching for him in the faces of the handsome young men of Florence. At night, her dreams had been filled with him, always recognized in whatever guise he appeared.

Last night as she had lain in bed, he had come to her just as she drifted into sleep. The vision of him seemed to emerge from the midnight sky itself, like some terrifying and exquisite demon of the night, trailing the darkness like vast wings. He hovered before her, a figure of shadows, his face, his body frosted by moonlight, his eyes glowing with an infinite blackness that burned to the very core of her. His voice, velvet and steel, whispered her name as he gathered her in his arms. His mouth, his body covered hers as if it were the night itself embracing her, and the enveloping darkness of him kindled in her body the blazing fire of the sun.

"Madonna? Madonna Veronica?"

Veronica felt a faint flush tinge her cheeks. She drew out of her reverie and answered smoothly, "I am sorry, Benito. I was thinking about a promise the *Tarocco* cards made me once."

"Well, they'll keep their promise, I'm sure. I've never known Mama Lucia to read the cards wrong."

"Neither have I," Veronica said loyally, though her heart was still aching. Her stomach growled, a more prosaic ache, reminding her she had only picked at her afternoon meal while Luigi ranted at them. There had been no pleasure of mind or body in this holiday feast, nothing but trepidation before, during, and after. "You stay with Roberto, Benito. I am going to beg more food from the kitchen. I am famished."

"Yes, Madonna. I'd like an apple, if there's one to spare."

"An apple!" Roberto sang out. "Sweets!"

Veronica's mission was partially successful. She had to wait while the cook bawled out the new scullery maid, who had drained away the chicken stock and saved the bones. This disaster left him in a bad mood, and he had refused Veronica any more of the pastries. He did, however, relinquish three polished apples, and wrapped a small wedge of cheese and a chunk of bread in a napkin. Gratefully, she stuffed them in her pockets and went outside.

Back in the courtyard, Veronica saw Fra Frederigo standing by the outside gate, talking to his mother and his little sister, Dorotea. They were Maria's only children, and both resembled her rather than Luigi, slight in build and fervent in spirit. Frederigo had Maria's dark coloring, and Dorotea, Luigi's lighter brown hair and blue eyes. Both had their mother's features. The straight nose and thin lips that looked pinched and grim on Maria were ascetic on Frederigo. On Dorotea the small features looked delicate and prim, giving her the prettiness of a tightly budded rose.

Veronica crossed over to talk to them. Together, they regarded her approach, a common expression of censure on their faces. All three of them were difficult to be around, for they always looked to draw offense from what she said, when she would have been content with indifferent courtesy between them. They disapproved of her family—her disreputable artist cousin on the one side and her fortune telling great-grand-mother on the other. *My Gypsy blood,* Veronica sighed inwardly. Not only the simple fact of it, but its "spiritual" manifestations. Frederigo was convinced Mama Lucia was a witch, her healing herbs and her gift with the *Tarocco* tools of the black magic she surely practiced. He was suspicious of Veronica as well. Astrologers and people with Mama Lucia's talents had long been an accepted and popular part of Florentine life, interwoven with its Christian worship. Any major event demanded an augury as well as a prayer. But recently Savonarola had preached fiercely against the divining arts, and things were not as easy as they had been.

"I wanted to wish you well," Veronica said to Frederigo.

Frederigo scowled at her, looking to find some ulterior motive. She had none, but since he despised her beliefs, he was convinced she must despise his. "Am I to believe you approve of my choice?"

"You have chosen to follow what you believe in, Frederigo. I respect that." It was true enough, and she understood part of what he sought. Much in the Church touched her. There was inspiration in the joyful singing of the psalms, comfort for sorrow offered in the scriptures, awe and delight in the pageantry. Though there was beauty to be found there, Veronica was more moved by the eternal resurrection of spring after winter, by the transformations of the earth—seed and bulb unfurling their array of flowers, grains, and trees, all the boundless miracles of life itself. She could find no heresy in the belief that divine wisdom could be imprinted in the *Tarocco,* or found encoded in the stars. To her the boundaries Frederigo set on his faith were narrow and cruel. He seemed always to choose what closed his heart rather than opened it. "I hope you will find the peace you seek."

"It is an honor to serve Savonarola," Frederigo proclaimed. "He is a prophet of God, walking among us. In the pulpit he is a figure of glory, crowned with holy fire, yet within the walls of San Marco he is the soul of humility. His clothes are the coarsest cloth, and he takes only the poorest food from the plates. Fastidious as he is, he sets himself the meanest tasks, even cleaning the latrines. He is our example, our ideal. Not once have I heard him raise his voice, yet all obey him eagerly." Frederigo's voice faltered for a moment, then he continued, "Fra Girolamo is a saint. We will follow him into the flames of Hell itself, in this holy war he wages."

Savonarola's war was with the Borgia Pope, but Frederigo's, Veronica thought, was still with his father. She disliked her brother-in-law, but she also felt sorry for him. Luigi was overbearing and abusive. Frederigo had often suffered from his violence, verbal and physical. She suspected Frederigo viewed the role of Christian martyr as more noble than that of Luigi's helpless victim.

Suddenly, a great commotion assaulted her ears, the sound of Bombol's frenzied barking mingled with shouting voices. Roberto's voice rose above them all, screaming in fright. Picking up her skirts, Veronica dashed across the courtyard and into the stables. The noise was worse here, for the horses were upset now as well. They neighed shrilly, pacing restlessly back and forth, some of them kicking at the wooden walls of the stalls. She saw several figures struggling by the tack room. Two of Luigi's guards were trying to drag Roberto towards the stable doors. Frightened by their roughness, he fought them frantically. Roberto was clumsy but very strong.

Part of the fray, Benito had hold of the arm of the tallest guard. "Let him go, you are frightening him!" he yelled. "He will come with you. Let him go!" The man shoved Benito away, knocking him to the ground. Benito scrambled to his feet and grabbed at the shorter guard, saying something she could not hear over the other noise. An older, smaller man Veronica did not recognize came out of the tack room, garbed in the pink robes of a physician. He ran about them flapping his hands, obviously trying to placate everyone and obviously ineffective. Roberto shrieked when this strange man touched him, and Bombol, driven to frenzy, leaped at the little man and bit his calf.

"My leg! His teeth! My leg!" the doctor screamed, adding to the chaos.

Benito let go of his hold on the guard and seized Bombol's

collar, although from his expression he would just as soon let the dog bite. He pulled Bombol into the tack room and closed the door, but the barking continued.

"Bombol!" Roberto cried out, as if the dog were his last hope.

Roberto was so overwrought, Veronica did not know if she could quiet him immediately. First the guards must release him, but she had only a little more influence with them than Benito did. She heard voices behind her and turned to see Maria and Dorotea watching the confrontation. Maria signaled her daughter away from the dispute, but made no move to intervene with Luigi's men. Frederigo was nowhere in sight. Facing the guards again, Veronica walked up to them and spoke in her most authoritative voice, pitching it low under Roberto's shrill cries. "You will stop that at once."

"Begging your pardon, Madonna Veronica," the biggest of the men answered impatiently. He was ginger haired, with scarred and pitted skin. "Master Luigi ordered us to bring Roberto to the house."

"To drag him kicking and screaming?" she asked with cold anger.

"It looks to be the only way we'll get him there," he said insolently.

"Roberto doesn't know them well, Madonna Veronica," Benito said, coming up behind her. The deferential tone he used supported her and accused the guards. "They told Roberto he had to come with them. Then they took the kittens away from him. Yanked them out of his hands."

She was furious with their callous stupidity. "What did you expect, treating him so roughly?"

Sneering, the guard jerked his head at the doctor cowering in the corner, "The leech was there to help keep him quiet."

Given some notice, the little man whined, "Your dog has torn my gown!"

Veronica turned back to the guard. "Tell me what is happening."

"It's not for me to know, Madonna, only to obey orders."

Roberto wriggled desperately, and the guard twisted his arm behind his back till he squealed. Roberto stopped his violent struggles, but he went on sobbing hysterically. Veronica saw it

was not just exasperation that had caused him to manhandle
Roberto, it was brutality. He was a vicious bully. It was in his
eyes, in the cruel smile he now wore. Veronica wanted to take
a riding crop to him.

"Let go of him," she insisted, anger sparking her voice.

"I can't do that, Madonna."

"He is used to obeying Benito and me . . . ." she began.

"Luca, get him up to the house!" It was Luigi's voice,
rough and slurred with drink. He stood at the door to the
stable, with two other guards beside him, glaring at the scene
with bloodshot eyes. "You two help them. Now!" he bellowed.

The new men rushed forward to obey. Together they lifted
Roberto and carried him out of the stables, screaming and
struggling violently once more. The little doctor hung back in
the shadows. Luigi glared at him. "You too," he ordered.
"I've got two more of you leeches, and a woman too, if you
need her. Go find out what I want to know."

"If I can, my lord, yes, if I can." the man squeaked and
scurried after the guards. Benito started to follow after him.

"You!" Luigi commanded Benito. "Stay with that dog.
Shut its yowling snout, or I'll have it shut for good."

Benito looked at Veronica, and she nodded. He complied
without a word, joining Bombol in the tack room. The barking
finally stopped.

"I will go inside the house now," Veronica said firmly.
They would need her help with Roberto, and she could question the doctor more easily than Luigi. She moved forward, but
her father-in-law caught her arm as she passed, a bruising grip.

"You stay here."

"Let go of me!"

He only pulled her closer, pressing his face close to hers, his
breath rank with wine. "Why aren't you pregnant?" he
snarled at her. "Why've you never been pregnant?"

Veronica stared at him, shocked. She had said nothing to
Luigi before because she assumed he knew his son was impo-
tent when he betrothed them. Roberto had been twenty then.
She had thought her family had been deceived, if anyone was.
She did not want Roberto's children, and the relief she had felt
at the discovery was like a gift of fate, for she had accepted

whatever the marriage would bring when she had accepted
Mama Lucia's *Tarocco* reading. She had shared that relief with
Mama Lucia and Daniele. There had been no reason to tell her
aunt and uncle, much less Luigi and Maria. The marriage had
become a refuge rather than a trap. She would not seek an
annulment now, for it would mean abandoning Roberto to his
father's abuse.

"You aren't going to get away with this," Luigi said. "For
all I know, you've witched him!"

He shoved Veronica away from him and stomped back to the
house. Maria regarded his departure scornfully. She turned
back to Veronica, and her expression changed to one of bitter
envy. "I would not have told either."

Veronica looked at Maria in surprise. Coldly voiced as it
was, this was the first personal confidence Maria had ever
given her, a secret shared between women. Veronica shook her
head. "I thought he knew."

"He did not know because he did not want to know. He
wanted an impotent son even less than a simple one. It is a
lesson he teaches those around him very quickly, not to tell
him certain unpleasant things. For years there were other sons
to carry on his name, his seed, and he was grateful you did not
conceive. Too grateful to question why." Her eyes glittered
with triumph. "Now the others are dead without issue, and
neither of the two that remain will ever bear sons of their own.
It is God's choice to let Luigi's line wither and die."

"I have to go inside," Veronica said quickly. She was appalled at the depth of Maria's hatred, but it must be easy to
hate a man like Luigi. "There is no need for the doctors to
torture Roberto."

"Luigi will have to have their pronouncements, now that he
has decided to listen, has paid gold to listen. Stay away from
him until it is over. He will punish somebody. Why have it be
you?"

"Better me than Roberto."

She smiled thinly. "Roberto he will punish in any case. The
doctors will examine him quite thoroughly, no matter what you
try to do to prevent it. They have their instruments ready."

Veronica rushed across the courtyard, but Luca, the pockmarked guard stopped her at the door. "Let me through," she demanded.

"I've got orders not to let you inside." Luca stepped forward, smiling his ugly little smile. He was angry with her interference and obviously hoping she would provoke him. Veronica knew she would not be able to coax or fight her way past the man. Circling the palazzo, she tried the front door with no better luck, and her search for an open window proved equally futile. Anger warring with dismay, she turned around and walked back to the stable and into the tack room. She joined Benito sitting on the bench with Bombol curled up at his feet. The infuriated mother cat glared at the three of them as they sat there morosely. After a while the black and white kitten braved an advance on them. It sniffed Bombol and gave a tiny hiss. Getting no response, it scurried up Veronica's skirts and settled in her lap, purring when she rubbed its belly.

"Benito," she said, after a time.

"Yes, my lady?"

"It is already getting dark, Benito. I want you to leave now and go see your Elizabeta."

"I cannot do that now, Madonna Veronica."

"Yes, you can. Roberto will be so hysterical after this that the doctors will have to give him a potion to sleep. If you come back early in the morning, we can spend time with him before we leave for home. He can come pick out a kitten—this one, I hope. It seems the friendliest and the most playful."

"But my lady . . . ." he protested.

"Go now, Benito, before Luigi orders you to do something else. I will stay here for a while, with Bombol and the kittens. I will be all right. I would rather know you had your night with Elizabeta than have you here. Why have one more unhappy person?"

"All right, my lady. Thank you."

Benito left. Veronica found a lamp above her on the shelf and lit it. One of the grooms' dusty surcoats was dangling from a hook. Shivering with cold and distress, she slipped into the too-big garment and huddled against the wall. After a while the mustached kitten climbed down and began to play with Bombol's tail. This initiated a short period of mutual investigation, from which the kitten retired triumphant and

Bombol settled down again with a whimper and only the tiniest scratch on his nose. Veronica remembered the food she had begged from the cook. Two of the apples had fallen from her pockets. She ate the last one and shared the bread and cheese with Bombol. Two hours later, the smaller guard came and told her to come into the house.

Filled with a gnawing apprehension, she hurried to Roberto's room, but the doctors were gone and he was already fast asleep. Gently, she cleaned his face, wiping the sticky syrup of poppies from his mouth and the traces of tears from his eyes. She crossed the hall to her own room and undressed in front of the fireplace, though the flames had burned out. As her garments slipped to the floor, chills swept over her, mingled with a nausea. Fighting the sickening wave, Veronica braced herself against the mantel. When they passed, she crouched by the hearth, stirring the cold ashes with the poker, hoping to uncover a spark of warmth. Finally, she abandoned the futile chore. Still trembling with cold, she dropped the poker onto the tiles, crept under the covers of her bed, and fell asleep, exhausted.

Veronica woke into fear. Something was wrong. Someone was in the room with her. She knew it. The silence was too watchful, the air thick and fetid. Sitting up, she drew the bedclothes about her and searched the darkness, willing her eyes to identify the darker shadow within the shadows. She had not barred the door, it would not have occurred to her. Perhaps it was only Roberto, his mind bewildered with the sleeping potion, stumbling in from his room across the hall. But she knew it was not. Roberto would not bring this reek of old sweat and spilled wine, nor this suffocating dread. There was a shuffling sound, then a thump followed by a hoarse curse. "Signore Luigi?"

The hulking form stumbled to the foot of the bed, peering at her in the gloom. "Dead," he told her, his voice slurred. "All my sons . . . dead."

"No," she said, shivering a little. This was crazy. Only Roberto survived from Luigi's first marriage. One son had drowned soon after Veronica's marriage, the other had been killed in a duel over a year ago. Mourning had been laid aside, but not grief apparently. Now Luigi seemed to view Frederigo's joining the Church as a kind of death. And Roberto he wished had never been born. "No," Veronica insisted. "Frederigo is still alive. And there are Dorotea and Roberto. You have living children. You have your wife and family around you." She did not say loving family.

"Dead, or good as dead. Worthless. What's left is worthless. You know what I got left? A female, a fool, and a friar, that's what I got." He half chanted the phrase, as if he'd gone over and over it in his mind, a bitter litany. "A female, a fool, and a friar. All that's left of the first wife's the fool. This last wife whelped the friar and the female, then she dried up on me. No more sons. Not even a bastard son for me. The kitchen bitches whelped more bitches, far as I know. All my bastards are bitches." He laughed as if this were tremendously funny, then repeated again with injured resentment, "Not even a bastard son. Bastard's better than nothing, but I wanna legidimed heir. My heir."

He staggered closer, and Veronica pulled up her feet as he collided with the far end of the bed. She could see him now, his wine-stained clothes and skulking expression. He gazed down at her, and she watched the sodden self-pity harden into crude appraisal. A coaxing smile came to his face. A leer. "You're not doing Roberto any good. Roberto's no good for anything. But you could be good for me."

"No," Veronica gasped, understanding now the reason for this drunken visit.

"Two sons left. One's celibate and the other's impotent, isn't he? Doctors said so. One son won't, one son can't. Stupid pricks, both of them." He giggled in the dark. "I think the one who won't's even stupider than the one who can't. Don't you, Veronica?"

Her heart was beating wildly. She was frightened, but she did not want to scream unless she had to. And if she had to, what good would it do? Roberto was strong but clumsy. He would try to protect her, and his appearance might well shame his father enough to stop him. But Roberto was so deeply drugged with poppy he would not wake. Benito was with Elizabeta. Bombol was in disgrace in the stables. There were others who might come, but the heavy door and thick stone walls would easily muffle her cries from their ears. Luigi might be drunk, but he knew she was alone and vulnerable.

Perhaps she could elude him if his coordination was poor enough. He was a powerful man, but alcohol was taking a stronger and stronger hold on his life, degenerating his body along with his character. If she could only flee the confines of this tiny room, she would be all right. If she could not escape, there was a weapon—the heavy poker she'd dropped by the fireplace. Carefully, Veronica slid along the side of the bed, trying to make it appear that she was obeying Luigi, yet position herself for escape. If she maneuvered correctly, she could throw him off balance. She lowered one leg to brace herself and felt the stone floor a shock of cold against her bare foot.

"That's right," Luigi urged. "You come here to me."

He tottered forward, his hands reaching out for her, and stumbled against the foot of the bed. Quickly, Veronica rolled across the bed, landed on the far side, and ran for the door. With a sudden drunken wiliness, Luigi regained his balance and lunged after her, grabbing her legs and throwing them both to the floor. He dragged her towards him, laughing as she fought him. Veronica realized he must have had dozens of such wrestling matches with the helpless serving girls. The more she struggled, the harder he gripped her, not drunk enough to lose hold of his prey. Fighting down her own panic, Veronica forced her body to stillness, hoping to talk him into releasing her. That act of will he viewed as one of submission, and his heavy hands began pulling at her shift, pawing her body. When she tried to cry out, to plead with him to stop, his mouth covered hers, his thick tongue thrusting inside, gagging her with the taste of sour wine. She bit him. Squealing with pain, he reared away from her.

"Bitch!" he yelled at her. "Vicious little bitch!"

She kicked out with her bare feet, aiming for his exposed groin, but the angle was wrong and she caught his thigh instead. She shoved him away from her and scrambled for the fireplace. The poker was almost in her grasp when he grabbed her ankles and jerked her back, rage making him stronger than before and more savage. His body rose above her, then his arm. She saw the dark mass of his fist descending, felt the shock of it heavy as a club against her temple. The strength of the blow dazed her. Though she struck out at him, the flailing movement had no power now. She felt she watched from a distance as one hand ripped open her shift. Clumsy fingers mauled her breasts, then moved down to grope between her thighs. There was a sudden tearing pain as the thick fingers thrust into her body. She screamed, wrenching away from him. Her outflung hand touched the poker, wrapped around the handle. Luigi hurled himself on top of her, his legs forcing hers apart, his hardened organ jabbing at her. Desperation giving her strength, Veronica smashed the weapon against his head. Luigi groaned and collapsed on top of her.

She crawled out from under the massive weight of his body. Clutching the poker, she stumbled across the room to the door and crumpled there again, bruised and dazed. Why had this happened? He could not really want a child, not one his Church would call incestuous. Frederigo's defection and the news about Roberto had provoked this crazed attack. Luigi was driven to her by some strange mixture of rage and grief and lust. Lust? Veronica knew Luigi had mistresses, that he took advantage of some of the servants — some even welcomed his attentions for the favors he bestowed. She shuddered with nausea. How could they endure such a brute? She had always felt safe before. Lecherous as he was, Luigi had shown no interest in her. Roberto repelled him, and she had seemed to also, married to the son he despised. Was tonight an aberration, or had everything changed now that he knew she was Roberto's wife in name only? Must she fear rape every time they came here?

Poker in hand, Veronica approached Luigi's unconscious body, tempted to raise the weapon high and smash it down. Shatter his skull and all the evil thoughts within it. No one would know it had not happened defending herself in the struggle. They all hated him, but alive he was master here and his family would shield him. His death would save her and the rest of them as well. A shudder ran through Veronica, and she lowered the poker. She could not do it. Rage was still hot in her, but the thought of murder was icy cold, chilling her soul. She loathed Luigi, but she could not kill him.

She backed away from him. Her robe was draped over the

one chair, and she pulled it on over her torn shift. A pitcher of water sat on the dresser by the bed. She picked it up and poured it over him. She set it down again and renewed her grasp on the poker as Luigi struggled to his knees, groaning and sputtering.

"What . . . ?" he muttered, staring at her with bleary eyes. He shook his head, peered down at himself in confusion, one hand rubbing his exposed genitals. He focused on her slowly, aware first of the poker she brandished, then her identity. "Veronica?" he croaked.

"Get out," she hissed. "Get out of my room and do not ever come back. Beget your bastard son on someone else. I have heard there are whores who will mate even with animals if the price is high enough."

He glanced stupidly down at his limp member again, then stuffed his nakedness inside his clothing. His fingers left dark smears on the lighter fabric of his hose. He peered at the stains, then raised his eyes to her, staring wildly. "A virgin? You were a virgin?" he asked. A fit of alcohol-sodden remorse possessed him, and he fell on his knees in front of her, his hands clasped, swaying and moaning. "I have forced a virgin."

He did not even remember what had happened. He was a brutal drunk, and his maudlin repentance sickened her. "I am virgin still," she hissed at him, "though you have broken the proof of it."

Luigi stopped swaying. He licked his lips, his eyes scanning her body. His face set in a look of sorrowful petulance, regretting not the attempt but the failure. "I did not . . . ?"

Could she hate him more if he had achieved his goal? Yes, even more, for the battering, the violation of her body would have been worse, and with it the knowledge that he had found his pleasure in her pain. "No, you did not, and you never shall."

"A virgin," he repeated, befuddled.

How could he not have known or at least suspected, once he knew Roberto was impotent? "Did you think I went with the stableboys, Luigi?"

He looked up at her, and the trembling pout of his lips took on a hard edge of belligerence. "A lover. You should have a lover, some hot young gallant to service you. Do you think I expected you to be satisfied with that mindless hulk? You did not need to protect yourself. If you had gotten yourself pregnant that way, I would never have questioned it. Never bothered to have Roberto tested.''

She listened with horror and outrage to his twisted reasoning. The vile act he had attempted was now her fault. He was grotesque. "Get out," she repeated, her voice hard and cold. "Get out before I kill you."

"I had to have been drunk to go after a skinny bitch like you," Luigi sneered. He pulled himself to his feet, then lurched over to the door. Glancing over his shoulder at her, his expression grew hard and calculating, "Speak of this to anyone, anyone at all, and you'll be sorry. I can tell my own version, you know. They would go along with me, the ones that matter, the ones in court. Men run this city. Men understand things like this. The way a woman can tempt a man, drive him to wickedness."

Veronica stared at him, filled with horror and disgust. Luigi could and would do such a thing, try to lay the blame on her for his own savagery. There were those who would help him to do it, whether they believed the tale or not, because their corrupt power was interwoven with his. But there were also those who sought truth and justice for their own sake . . . .

"Accuse me, and I will say you laid a spell on me—you and that Gypsy crone. I'll say I saw you in the woods, drinking blood and coupling with Satan himself. Frederigo would like to believe that. He would see Savonarola gave the case special attention. Between that crazy monk and my friends in the courts, both of you would burn for witches." He came towards her, an evil grin spreading on his face. "They have ways to make you confess. A few turns of the wheel, and that decrepit Gypsy would be dead before they got her to the pyre."

"No!" Veronica screamed it at him, hating him, and the hand holding the poker raised up and swung down.

Luigi staggered back, grasping his arm, bellowing with pain. He leaned against the door, moving his arm gingerly. "Bitch," he gasped again, "you could have broken my arm."

"I will break your head open if you touch me again," she said. "Get out."

"You just remember to keep your mouth shut," Luigi snarled at her. Opening the door, he cast a quick glance into the hallway, then slipped outside.

With a cry of rage, Veronica swung around and smashed the china pitcher with another sweep of the poker. Then she flung it aside and collapsed on the bed, shivering and sobbing. Part of her wanted only to forget what had happened to her—part of her hungered for revenge. "I should have killed him when I had the chance," she whispered bitterly.

Now she would be pitting not only her own safety against Luigi's power, but Mama Lucia's life as well. Her great-grandmother would choose to fight, but Veronica could not help but choose to protect her. Her silence was a small price to pay to protect Mama Lucia. The decision made, Veronica sat up. She stripped off the already torn shift and ripped it into pieces, crushed the pieces into a ball. She would burn it in the kitchen fire. She would have to have a bath, a very hot bath, to scrub every trace of him from her skin, though she wondered if she would ever feel clean again.

3 *The Homecoming*

 ELEVEN gates led into Florence, City of the Red Lily, one hundred thousand strong. Antonio entered the city through the massive iron-studded doors of the Porta della Romagna. Once inside the walls, he dismissed the guards he had hired for the journey. With Giacomo chattering beside him and his own small entourage following behind, Antonio guided his black stallion through the grassy outskirts that quickly gave way to flagstone streets and blocks of shops and houses. They trotted past the stern facade of the Palazzo Pitti, more fortress than palace, following the road till it led them to the indolent green waters of the Arno. Ignoring the goldsmiths' shops that lined both sides of the bridge, they crossed Ponte Vecchio and rode on into the core of the city.

Beside them the footpaths were more crowded than ever, rich and poor moving about their business amid the buildings. Stark against the cloudy gray sky, the city looked austere, even forbidding. Granite and marble, brick and plaster, the earth tones of the walls echoed the winter landscape of Tuscany, all its variegated grays and golds, muted greens, faded rose, rust red and umber. Antonio considered himself a citizen of the world, yet surveying the buildings of his birthplace, he felt a strong sense of the vigorous, stubborn roots that had nourished him. Florence lacked the exquisite grace of Venice, the heady mix of crumbling archaic splendor and raw, expansive energy that was Rome, but it had a forthright character that spoke to him. Even in its severity, the city struck unexpected chords within him.

Following a well-remembered route, Antonio emerged into the central square and the Duomo was revealed before him. Truly a wonder of the modern world, the great vaulted dome had been visible as they approached the enclosing walls of Florence, then hidden again as they moved through the crowded streets within. Now, the vast cathedral rose up before him, a pastel dream of Heaven rising high above its earthbound neighbors. The mosaic marble walls glowed softly in the clouded winter light, the pale rose and white set off by bands of deeper green. Seeing this marvel again, the beautiful gleaming heart of Florence, Antonio felt a surge of gratitude that his father had rescinded his banishment.

He did not dismount, for he wanted to reach the estate by noon, but Antonio let Ombra meander slowly through the teeming streets, circling back the river. He was aware of changes. Some added to the richness of the city—Donatello's statue of Judith and Holofernes had been given a place of honor in the Piazza della Signoria, her upraised sword a warning to tyrants. There were new homes and businesses, but although the city had grown, it felt less prosperous. Antonio knew he marked these changes more strongly because he remembered Florence in the lavish glory of Lorenzo di Medici's reign. Some of the great buildings looked neglected, and the poor had multiplied. Everywhere he looked, small straw-thatched huts with oiled linen windows crowded in amongst the greater bulk of multistoried guilds and palazzos of granite,

ironwork and glass. Those huts belonged to the prosperous
poor. Many wandering the footpaths were obviously homeless
peasants come in from the country. At every corner it seemed
he was accosted either by beggars or groups of zealous Florentine youths demanding alms for the poor. The last was a new
sight, and a disturbing one. He did not like the edge of coercion that lurked behind their belligerent piety. Several contrib-
utors were obviously intimidated into parting with their charitable coins. Still, he supposed these boys were better than the
gangs he remembered from his own youth, who found sport in
hurling rocks at hapless passers-by.

Even with the air of shabbiness, the dark edges of tension
and apprehension, the city was prosperous. There was cease-
less bustle as the people went about their work. Merchants and
vendors abounded. From the food stalls the rich aroma of
fresh-baked bread mingled with the pungent scents of garlic
and onion, smoked meats, fresh fish, and brash red wine. The
smells of business were thick in the air as well, the sharp scent
of the tanner's craft, the smelting smoke of precious metals,
the dense, soapy odor of wet cloth. Bright accents of color
ravished the eye. The weavers and dyers of the wool and silk
trade that formed the basis of Florentine economy swarmed
through the streets, carrying their vivid burdens of yarn with
them. Antonio smiled as he rode past a boisterous argument
between two dyers. They shouted, waving their fists at each
other, one with arms blue to his elbows, the second with ap-
pendages stained a bright marigold. A third party, of a striking
scarlet hue, interposed himself between them. Giacomo
grinned at him, his brown eyes alight with mischief, and Antonio answered that impish smile. This was more like the Florence he had known and loved.

"Accorr'uomo!" The cry for help or warning went up. Immediately, all the shops slammed shut their doors and windows, and the vendors packed up their goods, guarding themselves against whatever problem, large or small, real or
imagined, had been proclaimed. There would be a quarter hour
of muffled silence before, tortoise-like, they poked their heads
from out of their wooden shells to test the safety of the street.

"Accorr'uomo!" Several voices took up the call. Antonio
saw there was some disturbance up ahead of him. Curious, he

quickened his stallion's pace, weaving him in and out of the crowd along the narrow street, until they came out into an open square and a tumult of noise and confusion. There was yelling. That proved to be another group of youths, surrounding an old beggar who crouched in the street, his arms wrapped about himself defensively as they pelted him with rotten vegetables and filth from the gutters. Protecting himself as best he could, the old beggar raised his head and bawled out his own simple cry for help.

As Antonio approached, two more boys rushed up with pockets filled with stones. Times had changed far less than he had thought. He glanced around but there was no watchman in sight, nor did anyone in the outer crowd interfere as the youths began to fling the rocks at the helpless old man. Antonio urged Ombra forward, breaking through the inner circle of the boys to reach the terrified beggar, who had sense enough to grab hold when he reached out his hand. He weighed no more than a bundle of sticks as Antonio swung him up onto the saddle. He aimed his mount at the gang on the far side, and they jumped aside in fright. Two rocks struck his back as he cantered through, but he preferred them to rotten vegetables. The reek of dirt, garbage, and garlic on the beggar made him regret his charitable impulse somewhat, but he carried the old man across the square and headed for the closest bridge. Giacomo followed behind him, yelling parting insults at the angry boys.

"Why were they stoning you, old man?" Antonio asked as the clattered across the river.

"Blasphemy, Excellency. They said I spoke blasphemy."

This poor creature's lot in life might well provoke him to some nasty exchanges with the Almighty, Antonio thought. "God's not been treating you well?"

"I'd never blaspheme against our Lord, never. It was the Friar, that Savonarola, who denounces the Pope, who I spoke against. The Pope is God's chosen on earth."

"Those boys attacked you for criticizing Savonarola?"

"Oh yes, Excellency. It's not safe to speak out against the Friar. Those boys are his minions, and they're everywhere. The watchmen fear them and refuse to help when there is trouble. Rich or poor, no one is safe from them. They'll spy on their own parents to win a blessing from Savonarola."

Antonio was disturbed. His mother had written of inspired sermons, of great crowds flinging wide the church doors to dance and sing God's praises in the streets. The Romans spoke in furious or delighted outrage of Fra Girolamo Savonarola's vituperative attacks on the Pope, and speculated on the Friar's life expectancy. With all these secondhand accounts of the Dominican monk's growing power in Florence, Antonio had never imagined it pervading the streets in this militant fashion. He found a safe corner to leave off the old man, once he was assured he had no need of a doctor, and slipped him some money to take away the sting of his bruises. He tugged his hand away, embarrassed, when the old man tried to kiss it in his gratitude.

"Bless you, Excellency. Bless you."

"Guard your tongue, old man," he warned, then spun his horse around and rejoined Giacomo.

"He'd better guard his tongue," Giacomo said, licking his lips nervously, "or they'll pierce it for him. One of those young ruffians let me know that's the new punishment for blasphemy."

"The courts here are not likely to punish a man so for speaking his mind. The city would be inhabited by mutes." Florence was given to fits of violence, but would the city enact such a vile retribution for so petty an offense? "The statutes are filled with rules and regulations more ignored than observed."

"I wouldn't put it past that lot to do it themselves," Giacomo answered, his brown eyes troubled. They rode back to the bridge in silence, waiting for the rest of the entourage to catch up with them. His sense of duty reasserting itself, Giacomo reached over and brushed at Antonio's dusty cape. "Lucky the eggs didn't get you," he said brusquely. "I hope playing good Samaritan didn't leave you covered with fleas."

Antonio gave a short laugh, but the incident had tainted his vision of Florence. "Enough of the city," he said. "It is time to return home."

———

The gravel path was new, crunching under Ombra's hooves. The dark green cypresses had grown taller, their elongated forms standing sentinel along the approach to the Fabiani estate. Overhead the sun had emerged, a cold white disc in the clouded winter sky, its bleak light glazing the pale stone walls and marble pillars of the house. Halting his horse in the courtyard, Antonio gazed around him and found it all unchanged . . . and strangely unfamiliar. *Home.* He formed the word within his mind with the deliberation, the uncertainty of a foreign tongue. *Home.* There was no revelation of meaning, only the chill silence surrounding him. Abruptly, he tossed the reins to the groom, gesturing to Giacomo and the rest of his entourage to dismount. Giacomo had said nothing for ten minutes. Grateful for small miracles, Antonio offered his valet a faint smile of encouragement, then turned back to the house.

His father appeared at the top of the stairs and stood, silent and waiting, while the steward introduced Antonio to the servants. He memorized their names and faces quickly, but his awareness was fixed on the man above him. Giorgio di Fabiani cut an impressive figure, as always. The robe he wore was unadorned, cut in the somber Florentine mode, but the fabric was the richest charcoal velvet lined with sable. His hair was gray now, the beard cut short and square as before. The silvering made his father all the more distinguished, setting off the patrician features. It seemed age had only made him more indomitable.

Antonio ascended the marble steps, watching his father's face as he did so, and his heart sank within him. There was no expression, no gesture of welcome there. He had not thought he expected it, but he must have allowed some hope to seep into his heart unawares, to feel now this cutting disappointment. His lips curled faintly in self-mockery, and when he climbed the final step to stand face to face with his father, nothing remained of that flash of pain except the arrogant disdain that it provoked in him. To judge from his expression, that emotion matched his father's perfectly.

"Antonio, you have returned to the Villa Fabiani." A simple statement of fact, nothing more, from the unrelenting face before him. What love his father had for him had died with Alessandro.

"Yes, I have."

"Rooms have been prepared for you and your servants."

"Thank you," he responded dryly.

"Your lady mother wishes to see you. Later, we will have matters to discuss."

"As you wish."

His father nodded and turned his back on Antonio abruptly and smoothly, as one man might strike the face of another with a glove. Motionless, Antonio watched his father slowly walk away, an elegant, erect figure moving from shadow to sunlight to shadow again as he passed along the colonnade.

"My lord?" The face of the servant was ever so faintly hostile, though his manners were perfectly correct, taking his cue from his master.

"Yes?"

"If you will follow me, I will show you to Madonna Leonora's room."

The servant was middle-aged, but not anyone Antonio remembered from twelve years before, when this was his home. Twelve years. Just seventeen that autumn, newly married, he had thought himself a man, with his early aptitude for business, his skill in weaponry, his fierce passion in bed. Now he saw he had been little more than a child. A blind child.

"I know the way," Antonio said coolly, dismissing the man. He entered the house and stood alone in its cool, gray-shadowed foyer, feeling memory embrace him like a shroud. He turned to the left and walked down the corridor, anticipation and dread growing with each footstep as he approached Leonora di Fabiani's room.

"Mother?" Antonio whispered, a sound so choked he had to repeat it. This time it sounded too loud within the oppressive quiet of the room.

Again, he thought he had prepared himself. Again, pain more acute than he could have anticipated pierced him, this time with no disdain or weary irony to muffle the anguish. He stifled his reaction, so his own distress would not cause the emaciated woman before him more suffering. She had written she hoped to live long enough to hold his child. How did she live now? Commanding himself to move, Antonio walked to the bed. Kneeling beside his mother, he bent his head and kissed the hand that grasped his own so weakly. Her fingers were cold and brittle, like winter twigs. When he raised his face, he was smiling at her, the most gallant smile he could summon.

"Has he forgiven you?"

"I am here, Mother. I am home."

She looked at him, her eyes huge in her gaunt face, her body wasted beneath the delicately embroidered coverlet. He hoped the words would be enough. She had always believed, too easily, in what her heart wanted. She kept staring at him. "I asked him to forgive you, to love you for my sake, and to give you back your inheritance, your place in our family."

Antonio closed his eyes and pressed his lips to her hand once more, feeling a dreadful kinship with his father. He too must have knelt here beside her while she asked of him what he did not want to give, and known he would give it because she asked. Because they both loved her, they would patch together the damaged fabric of their lives and hold it up as whole cloth to her fading eyesight.

"I have found a bride for you. A good girl, devout. She is very young, so you can mold her as you wish. There should be children here again, Antonio."

"Yes. Yes, Mother," he answered, "of course."

She sighed with relief and stroked his hand. A wave of depression washed over Antonio. He was consigning his life to ease her death, and he would have to live with what was done long after she was gone. But he could not deny her. It was the only thing of import she had ever asked of him. And only, after all, what was expected of any man of good family . . . .

She plucked at his hand, and he had to bend down to hear her speak. "It was such sadness, Antonio, to be able to put words on paper, yet never to speak to you, embrace you. I often wished that your father had forbidden me to write you, as well as to see you. Perhaps then I would have had the courage to disobey him."

"I understood," he assured her, knowing how much she loved his father as well as honored him.

"Only once did I defy him," his mother said, more to herself than to him. "He was so angry when he found I had given my jewels to Giacomo. He would not speak to me for days."

He knew his father's grim silences all too well. "You saved my life, Mother."

She frowned, her eyes focusing on him again. "When you were captured, it was still too soon after Alessandro's death. If it meant your life now, I am sure your father would pay the ransom."

He could find no answer to that. The bitterness of his father's denial ran deep in Antonio. His banishment from Florence had seemed no more than justice, but the terrible months when he had lain abandoned and rotting in the English prison cell were a torturous memory. Nor did it seem that anything had changed for his father. No, that was not true. His father was willing to suffer his presence now. Perhaps, in time, that very presence would thaw his coldness.

"That is not important now," she murmured. "You are home again, where I can see you, touch you. There is so little time, Antonio, and yet I am too tired to keep my eyes open."

"Sleep then," he said, and caressed her forehead as he remembered her doing for him when he was a child. After a while she moaned softly and closed her eyes. He felt his heart stop and hold a beat until she drew her next breath. He knew he would feel that catch in his breast often, wondering always when that final silence would claim her.

It was a civilized lunch he shared with his father. They partook of leek and mushroom soup, a savory chicken pie with winter vegetables, and fine white bread with cheese, followed by a rich compote of brandied fruits. With human perversity they spoke of his mother's illness as they ate, but in abstract terms as if she were not someone dear to them both. When the plates were cleared away, a *tisane* was brewed in the ornate tea service of gold-chased silver. As the warm scent of herbs and spices filled the air, Antonio was assailed by bittersweet nostalgia. It was his father's favorite *tisane*, tangy with lemon peel and rose hips, fragrant with precious cinnamon. The immediacy of the memories evoked by the aroma startled Antonio. He was flooded with images of his childhood, his lost youth.

He became aware that his father had paused. Antonio knew it was unlike himself to lose track of any conversation, especially one so important. Hoping no question had been put to him, Antonio posed a quizzical, "Yes?"

His father nodded and continued. "While your mother was still able, she attended the sermons given by the Friar of San Marco, Girolamo Savonarola. He preaches that he will make Florence a city of God on earth."

"In Rome they say Savonarola has changed our city into a monastery."

"Did it appear so to you?"

"The red lily is a bit wilted, and Savonarola's influence more apparent than I expected, but I did not find the changes that severe—as yet." Antonio took his first sip of the *tisane*, past and present flowing together on his tongue.

"Unfortunately, Savonarola's political aspirations appear to be as great as his religious zeal. The success of his supposed prophecies has given credence to any pronouncement he cares to make, though it did not take a prophet to guess Lorenzo di Medici would die. As for the French invasion—who knows what sources the Friar had within their court. In any case, the Friar has an ardent following, even among the great houses such as ourselves, and certainly with the uneducated masses of the Florentine populace. He had to move to the Duomo to accommodate the crowds; sometimes as many as fifteen thousand appeared."

"That I had not heard. The number is impressive."

"Evidently he is sincere in his faith, completely incorruptible."

Antonio had no doubt that his father had personal knowledge of more than one bribe offered and refused. His father would respect this brand of integrity, even if it annoyed him exceedingly. "As you can imagine, his inflammatory zeal was a favorite topic in Rome. The Pope finds him a sharp thorn in his side."

"His office is sacred. He should not permit an underling such as Savonarola to make such abusive attacks upon it."

"Alexander VI would much prefer to ignore Savonarola, as he ignores everything that does not add to his purse or his pleasure. Or directly threaten his power—either within Italy or from without."

"I fear the Friar is now the most powerful voice in Florence.

We have no one to equal him. The death of Lorenzo the Magnificent left a great gap in Florentine rulership. His fool of a son, Piero, lacked all the skills of the earlier Medici and retained all their arrogance. His family ruled this city for three generations. He threw that power away in less than three years. Because of Piero's craven treaty with the French, the Medici family is now outlawed from Florence, the three globes of the *palle* device stripped from their buildings. All in all," his father sneered, "it is a remarkable achievement."

"You must know Piero still hopes to return. Despite his paltry finances, he has begun collecting mercenaries. With the current unrest in Florence, he anticipates a violent mood swing that will reinstate him."

"It is impossible," his father stated adamantly. "Whatever problems may afflict us, the return of that betrayer will not be one of them."

Antonio continued to sip his *tisane*. His father's views were as inflexible as always. The Florentines were too unpredictable in matters of politics for such certainty. "I am surprised Piero escaped the city with his life, after surrendering Pisa to placate the French."

"Exile was not sufficient punishment . . . ." his father began, then stopped abruptly, two bright spots of color appearing high on his cheekbones.

Exile . . . . For a heartbeat they stared at each other, speechless, unmoving. The word had opened the gulf of years that lay between them, flooded it with a torrent of emotion. Antonio felt a rush of anger, its sweeping tide crossed with fierce currents of guilt and despair. Strangely, it was pity for his father's plight that gave him back his voice. "There has been a void in Florentine rulership," he prompted.

"Yes, a void," his father repeated, and then continued as if there had been no break. "There has been no individual of Lorenzo's caliber since his death, no coalition. Our own political party has lost power even as the Friar's has gained in strength. Those who follow his lead have been dubbed the *Piagnoni*, because of their pious sniveling."

"And in turn they call you . . . ?"

"The *Arrabbiati*, as if our outrage were excessive," his father sniffed imperiously. "Barely two years ago, this rabble forced through their new constitution. United under the spiritual and worldly guidance of Savonarola, they have wormed their way into every governing body, even as high as the Signoria. Unchecked, they will establish the dominance of classes totally incapable of governing the city.''

Antonio's mouth quirked ironically as he responded, ''These *Piagnoni* wish to reestablish the Republic in rule as well as name?''

His father's eyes narrowed. ''Are you mocking me?''

''No, Father,'' Antonio said, although it was not the truth. He was not seventeen and had long since outgrown the habit of deference. The endeavor irked him, and anger had taken the edge off his caution. He must guard his sarcastic tongue more carefully.

''Such vulgar democracy is like a plague which attacks Florence every century or so,'' his father said dismissively. ''The great families must strengthen themselves. Unquestionably, power should be divided among us. Florence is a Republic. Those like ourselves, who honor the old traditions, must develop our internal alliances and maintain our dominance in the Signoria. No one wants a single family to rule the city as the Medici did for so long.''

Unless it is one's own family, Antonio thought. *And all alliances must bear that in mind.*

''To this end I have begun the initial negotiations for your marriage. The young girl is of a noble line. I cannot imagine that you would have any objections to her, as she is entirely suitable.''

Antonio said nothing. He was certain his mother's dying wishes were the primary factor in this arrangement, yet once he had made his promise to her, his father sought ways to make the situation as beneficial as possible. Giorgio di Fabiani was both a practical and fiercely political man. Two hundred years before, the newly formed Republic forbade the aristocracy from every honor and office. Unlike others who renounced their noble rank and changed their name, his family had proudly retained their own and thereby lost direct participation in Florentine government. Although they could no longer vote or hold office, they had many direct and indirect ways to affect the politics of the city. Antonio's marriage was not an opportunity to be wasted.

"Their family line is impeccable," his father affirmed, "as old as our own, though they chose to abandon their ancient name and rank. Their political views coincide with ours, and their votes will give us more influence. The girl's dowry is magnificent, and it will please you to learn she is attractive as well as virtuous, albeit of tender years."

Antonio was glad she would be pleasant to look at, though her personality was more important. Tender years? "What is her age?"

"She turned twelve this past September."

Antonio was unsettled, though his mother had also told him the girl was young. The simple fact of the impending marriage had perturbed him, and combined with his greater concern for his mother's health, he had given little thought to the details. The realities of the situation were now closing in on him. A bride that young was going to require more attention and training than he wished to give. Many of his contemporaries would find such a fresh young bud all the more desirable, but he was not one of them. He was used to the companionship of women of intelligence and sophistication. He wished his father had found a wealthy widow, gracious and well-versed in the ways of the world. He no longer expected a faithful wife, only a discreet one. What he said was, "I am sure your choice is appropriate."

His father rose from the table, and Antonio did so also, "We will discuss the details tonight. I will send your compliments and arrange a meeting with the family and your prospective bride for a week from today?"

"Very well."

"Your mother will have need of your company this afternoon," his father said. "We will speak again this evening."

"Until this evening, then," he answered.

Alone once more, Antonio left the dining room and sought out the salon, where arched doors opened out onto the great terrace behind the house. The past was thick about him everywhere, but the memories of his wife, his brother, would be the most difficult to face. He walked to the end of the balustrade and looked down the marble stairs. At first there was nothing, only the mottled gold marble with no visible stains remaining. Then deliberately, he evoked them, and the ghostly images superimposed themselves at the bottom of the steps.

"Beatrice." Antonio whispered. He had not spoken her name aloud in years. "Beatrice?" He made it a question, but he no longer knew what answer he sought.

He had been sixteen when he and his friends had climbed the great oak overlooking the convent orchard, and seen Beatrice for the first time. She was climbing a tree herself, scrambling up with a flash of leg to throw peaches to her companions. Antonio had instantly fallen in love with her impossible, fragile beauty, a quality barely human. She was a pale-haired fairy's child, her enormous eyes dark and gleaming in her delicate face. The girls had seen them watching and given the expected squeals of dismay and delight before dashing for the convent. Beatrice had simply looked at him across the small space separating them. Only at him, no one else. She reached up, chose a perfect, golden ripe peach, and tossed it straight to him. Then she leapt from the tree and ran after the other girls back inside the convent. When she was gone, he had raised the blushing fruit to his lips, bitten into the succulent flesh, the sweet juice, the lush fragrance drenching his senses, more intoxicating than wine. It was as if an angel had leaned down from Heaven to gift him with the taste of nectar and ambrosia.

Antonio had gone home, unable to get the girl's face from his mind. He was haunted by visions of her melting brown eyes, her tender mouth, the veil of spun gold hair floating about her as she ran. Knowing nothing of her, he had gone to his father and begged to marry her. Then he had waited, afraid his father would find her background too insignificant. Antonio no longer cared if he equaled the brilliant match his older brother had made. Rich and well connected, Laudomia was a plain little wren of a woman. She worshipped his brother, dining from the crumbs of his affection as if from a banquet. Although his father declared Beatrice's name and dowry "little better than adequate," he indulged his besotted son, and Antonio was married to Beatrice.

Besotted indeed. His Beatrice had seemed as perfect as Dante's immortal love. The streak of elemental wildness in her only seemed to enhance the perfect illusion of innocence. Antonio had ignored the faint emotional dissonance that sounded beneath the sweet harmonies of the flesh. Caught up in her fey spell, behavior he could perceive now to be irrational, even cruel, had then seemed childlike and adorable. As for her wanton lovemaking . . . well, he still had not found its match. Perhaps that was only because he had loved no one since, and had none of love's sweetness to transform the carnal delights of the flesh. Even when the discordant notes grew louder, sending faint vibrations of fear through him, Antonio told himself the trouble lay with himself rather than with Beatrice. To doubt her was to doubt love.

Love. A cruel sweetness. One better not suffered. He never again wanted to experience that ultimate vulnerability, that ultimate folly. He had kept his heart to himself since then, and would continue to do so. He wondered now if he had even been the first with Beatrice. With her whore's wiles, she could have sold a false virginity a hundred times over and been believed. When had she found the time to betray him? It had seemed he was never out of her bed.

Alessandro. He formed the name silently, and that ghostly, leonine figure rose up to confront him.

As a child, Antonio had adored his elder brother. As a youth, the relationship had changed, taken on a combative edge, the love colored with fierce rivalry. Alessandro had always been his father's favorite, Antonio his mother's, and they had both competed for the other's measure of affection and to outdo each other in accomplishment. The tension of that conflict was drawn tight between them when Antonio married Beatrice.

He saw Alessandro's face before him, flushed with guilt and anger, when Antonio found them coupling flagrantly in the garden. "The little bitch wanted it," his brother snarled. "She came sniffing around me, all wet tongue and wagging tail. Those big brown eyes that beg you for it. Would you have turned her away, Antonio, if she had been mine?"

"Yes," he had whispered vehemently, "yes, I would." But he was not sure, then or now. He would have known she was false, yet wanted to believe whatever lies she told, as Alessandro had. Even despising her, Alessandro wanted her, protected her from the husband she had cuckolded.

"Is it my fault you are not enough for her, Antonio? She is mine now!"

"No!"

They had fought, hand to hand, along the terrace. The memory was a vivid blur with a few frozen images. He remembered still how it felt, wanting his brother dead, wanting to kill him with his own hands. It was Alessandro who had drawn the knife, his face contorted above Antonio's as they struggled, fell, rolled along the pavement. Then there was the sudden flashing arc of the blade in the sun. He had been so filled with rage he had hardly felt the sharp slash of the weapon along his arm. But he had seen the bright red blood staining the silver metal, known it was his own, seen the knife rise up again to strike. Doubling his legs under him quickly, he had kicked up. Antonio remembered the satisfying impact that had sent the body above him hurtling away. He remembered the cry he heard as his brother fell, tumbling down the marble steps, and the swift sense of doom it had brought with it. He remembered the grotesque sight of Alessandro lying twisted at the foot of the stairs. He remembered his father's face, looking down at the broken body, looking up at his own.

And then Beatrice was kneeling before him, clinging, her cheek pressed to his loins, her breath warm on his sex as she swore to him over Alessandro's corpse, "I love you, only you. There is no one for me but you." He thrust her from him, sick with rage and desire.

The servants found her body the next day, sprawled where Alessandro's had fallen, her neck broken, dark blood matting the pale spill of her hair. Crouching beside her, Antonio stared into her wide, glazed eyes, and learned the most intimate face of death. Knowing her dead, knowing her betrayal, he did not understand how it could not be over. How he could go on loving her desperately, even as he hated her utterly. Knowing there would be no release for either emotion.

Spurious explanations were given to the family and to Florentine society, explanations few believed and all accepted as a matter of course: Alessandro had died in an accidental fall. His devoted sister-in-law, wandering about in grief, had fallen down the same steps . . . .

But Antonio could not believe Beatrice's death was an accident. It was too perfect, an act of divine retribution—except he no longer believed in any deity. Then his mother had come to him, weeping, to confess the fault was hers. She had threatened Beatrice, telling her that Antonio had renounced her, that she was to be returned to her family in disgrace. Publicly repudiated, she would be scorned by society, nor would any other man take her to wife. Beatrice had been terrified, and why not? She had seen the disgust and horror in his eyes when she knelt before him. He had refused to see her when she came begging to his door. The lie his mother invented was probably no different from the truth.

And Beatrice could not live without adoration.

At the funeral there were whispers, the insinuation that Beatrice's death was not accident nor suicide but execution. Most thought that Antonio had broken his unfaithful wife's neck. With the whispers came looks, sidelong glances that rested on him in speculation, in fear, often in approval. It was his right to avenge his honor, and few condemned him for the act he had not committed. A handful of Alessandro's friends glared at him, hands on their swords. Laudomia, hysterical with grief and rage, flung herself on the corpse and screamed at him. A whore had seduced her husband, and the whore's husband had killed hers. She swore to see Antonio dead.

His father had pronounced his banishment the same day . . . .

"My lord?" The same manservant was back, his tone obsequious this time. "Your mother is awake, my lord, and asking for you. She wants you to come and read to her from the Bible."

"Yes," he said. "Yes, of course."

———

For over a week Antonio remained on the estate, dividing his time between his parents. The dinner with his bride had been delayed another week in favor of an elaborate betrothal party. The event was now only four days away, but he put it from his mind. That encounter would be less arduous than the ongoing discussions of Florentine politics and family policy, in which Antonio struggled to find points of compromise without directly challenging his father's autocratic views. There was also the task of relearning the intricacies of both the estate management and the banking concern, and there were discussions of how his own enterprises might best be combined with or left separate from his family's business ventures.

If Antonio had not expected a welcoming warmth from his father, he had anticipated a practical respect for his accomplishments. Instead, he found it was presumed his successful import business would simply be abandoned, or turned over to one of the family agents to manage. Stung by his father's disdain, he had finally balked at the incorporation, his refusal initiating their first open argument, cold-voiced and controlled though it was. Stubbornly, Antonio had refused to give way. His father had yielded instead. If his lingering animosity was unpleasant, at least it was accompanied by a modicum of grudging respect. That was more than Antonio had earned from the concessions he had forced himself to give against his own nature and judgment, hoping to build rapport between them.

The sessions with his father were draining, but nowhere near as difficult as the excruciating encounters with his mother. Leonora di Fabiani had always possessed a true Christian goodness. Now there was a missionary fervor in her which dismayed him. Antonio knew the approach of death evoked it in her, though he also blamed the overzealous influence of Girolamo Savonarola. Her religious obsession devoured her spiritually, even as the illness devoured her physically.

Their moments of real communion were rare, priceless, and he was unbearably frustrated by the pious formulas which shut her soul further away from him. Too much of the time, he had the ghastly feeling that the mother he loved was already lost to him. There was no brightness left in her. No laughter, even in her eyes. Only a desperate plea he could not answer. He realized that his mother only longed for his happiness, and believed she had found the sure and certain way to achieve this. Drugged against pain, caught up in her own fervor, she would believe for both of them, living in her future hopes for him, as he lived in his memories of her. His mother was not a fool; in her lucid moments she saw her failure and his own. He could give her love, honor, even obedience in this marriage she asked of him, but not a rebirth of faith.

This afternoon, while she slept, he had been seized with an
urge to escape even the effort at pretense. He told Giacomo to
have their horses saddled. At the stables he found his valet and
two of the best guards. He did not argue with Giacomo's precaution. Antonio knew his brother's widow might try to arrange a fatal encounter along the road. It would not be the first
time. After checking their weapons, he ordered one man to
ride ahead, one behind, then mounted Ombra and together they
left for the city. No incident marred the short journey. The day
was fine, the air rainwashed and clear, flushed with a false
spring warmth. Florence looked magnificent and Antonio was
determined to enjoy his outing.

"My lord?" Giacomo asked after they had roamed the
streets of the city for a while.

"Yes?"

"We do not seem to be going anywhere?" Giacomo questioned tentatively.

Antonio realized he must have been in an ugly temper of
late to evoke that tone of voice from Giacomo. Dealing with
his mother and father had exhausted all of his patience. For the
past week, his valet's behavior had been extremely subdued.
Giacomo was doing his very best to be helpful, no doubt, and
Antonio knew the usual alternating inundation of effervescent
babble and exaggerated complaint would have driven him mad
in the difficult circumstances. Perversely, Antonio found he
now missed it.

"Aren't you enjoying seeing the city again, Giacomo?"

"Yes." Again, the hesitant tone.

"What is it, Giacomo?"

"I wondered if my lord was perhaps on quest for . . . female companionship?"

The incident of the purloined letter still rankled, and Antonio felt a sudden spark of anger. He wheeled about in the
saddle, but Giacomo looked so abashed that it silenced the
caustic remark on his tongue. It was particularly unfair when
the thought of finding a woman had crossed his mind, only to
be pushed away. His growing sexual need had seemed an obscenity when confronted with his mother's mortality.

The proximity of death sometimes aroused him. Aroused
the need to renew life—a primal urge that was a confrontation

with survival. Sex was where life and death met, mated with each other, conceived each other. Yet the release he had sought in the past, after the peril of a battle or the lethal conflict of a duel, seemed more acceptable than the need to escape the oppressive atmosphere of his mother's slow deterioration. The contempt he felt for his reaction did nothing to alleviate it, however. He realized his sexual craving was only becoming stronger. He could ignore it, but he knew his temper would grow more foul than it already was. Giacomo already suffered from it, and while it was doubtful he would lose control with his mother, his father was another matter entirely. That could be disastrous. It would be best all around if he found some "female companionship." Florence was not as famed for her courtesans as Venice and Rome, but there would be many beauties skilled in the erotic arts.

"What do you suggest?" Since Giacomo had brought up the problem, he must have some specific solution in mind.

"I have taken the liberty of making some inquiries, my lord."

"Have you now?" he inquired ruefully. "Why am I not surprised?"

"It's not as easy as you think it might be. The fanatical Friar's put quite a crimp in all the social vices," Giacomo complained. "Look around. It's only a week before *Carnevale*. You see anybody trying out a bit of costume, feel any of the old anticipation stirring in the city? Savonarola's banned the whole thing. Too pagan. Too lewd. He's going to have some holy parade instead, singing psalms in the streets and such. The finish is a great big fire where people can burn up any bit of prettiness they've got that isn't properly religious. He's calling it his bonfire of the vanities."

Antonio frowned. *Carnevale* had been one of the liveliest times in Florence. It made him uneasy that Savonarola had succeeded in suppressing that earthy, exuberant celebration of life.

"Priests are always preaching, of course," Giacomo rattled on, "but usually people aren't listening quite so carefully, much less fixing fines and exacting nasty punishments. Life does go on as usual, but more behind closed doors, so to speak. A good gambling table is hard to find, and as for the professional ladies, they don't have a nice boulevard here like in Rome. There's no place where you can have a drink and a bit of a talk with the other gentlemen while you look over what's available.''

"The effects of Savonarola's preaching are far more negative than I realized," Antonio acknowledged wryly. "I regret the absence of the boulevard on general principle. I would, however, prefer something less conspicuous."

Giacomo cleared his throat and assumed a consequential expression. "There are two local beauties, much praised for their skills. There are rumors of a very charming, very fresh young lady from Pisa, soon to make her debut."

"Piquant, no doubt, but I'd prefer someone of experience." He waited for Giacomo to elaborate about the original two possibilities. His servant seemed oddly reluctant. "Yes?" he prompted. "Tell me what you've learned."

Giacomo twitched, and Antonio narrowed his eyes speculatively. What was wrong? He was going out of his way to be appreciative of his valet's efforts on his behalf.

"There is someone . . . special. The famous Bianca."

"Bianca of Venice?"

"Of Venice, Rome, and now of Florence."

Antonio was instantly intrigued. He had seen Bianca twice in Venice at certain rather decadent parties, noted her exceptional beauty and indulged in fleeting sexual speculation. His appraisal had been subtle, but both times she had turned and looked at him as if he had whispered these lascivious musings into her ear. She had smiled, sharing the silent fantasy with him, her gaze licking over his body. There had been a challenge, a hot flame in those ice blue eyes that aroused him. Antonio had planned to approach the blonde courtesan with an offer, but business had called him away to Rome. When he heard of her appearance there, she was rumored to be bedding one or all of the Borgias, and he had put any thought of her from his mind. Having her was not worth having his throat slit. Much good his caution did him. He had risked the same fatal effect tumbling drunken into Lucrezia's bed, without a tenth of the attraction he felt towards Bianca.

Well, now she was in Florence. She would be expensive, but he had never minded paying for excellence. Given the scandal and rumor that surrounded any famous beauty of her profession, she herself seemed to be circumspect, even secretive. She was intelligent, known for her conversation as well as her amorous innovations. For all her civilized graces, her perfectly polished beauty, Bianca had the air of some exquisite predator. There was something feral about her—something dangerous. Which made her all the more erotic. Antonio had caressed a sultan's tamed cheetah once. Collared with rubies, sprawled on a bed of satin, she had stared at him with her great golden eyes while he stroked her. She had yawned, showing her gleaming fangs, then rolled over, offering her soft, pale-furred belly. All that lethal power, purring at his touch.

Yes, Bianca was like that. Antonio found he did not even want to look elsewhere until he heard her answer. Just the memory of her stirred the coiled heat in his loins, hardened his sex. A pity that would be wasted. Suggesting an immediate assignation would be discourteous, insulting even, to a courtesan of her standing. He would send Giacomo with a note requesting a meeting and let her determine the mode of it. He would need an initial gift, something luxurious but not ostentatious. No jewels this time. A fancy box of some rich confection, honey nougats, candied fruit peels, or *panforte*. Perhaps a bottle of perfume as well, a cut-crystal vial of French scent nestled in a bouquet of silk ribbons and winter violets.

He looked up to find Giacomo eyeing him gloomily. What was wrong with the man? Antonio expected him to regard this entire episode as a personal victory. He should be exulting, bouncing in his saddle, and all but crowing with triumph at his own cleverness. At the very least he should be disgustingly smug. His valet was actually pouting. Then Antonio remembered Rome again, and the unfavorable comments Giacomo had made concerning the lady Lavinia. *Another man-eater,* Antonio thought, and smiled.

"I knew it," Giacomo grumbled dejectedly. "I knew Bianca would be the one you'd want."

He looked so glum, Antonio burst out laughing. Really, it was too much, the way Giacomo fussed and plotted over him like some crafty mother hen. The image amused him, and he laughed again. "Your mother was a broody hen," he told Giacomo, "and your father a fox with a taste for fancy feathers."

"Huummff" was his valet's only response.

"Come, Giacomo, stop sulking. I must write a note for you to deliver, and select some perfume for the lady." Antonio dealt in certain rare oils himself, as well as furs and other luxuries. This purchase would be a simple and pleasant way to open negotiations with the dealers in Florence. "White hyacinth would suit her, I think. And a confection. You may choose it, if you like, and indulge your own appalling sweet tooth as well." That promise should improve Giacomo's mood. It would have to suffice. He certainly was not going to let his servant choose the woman he bedded!

"If you need to get in or out of the city after curfew, old Leonardo still stands night watch at the northern gate," Giacomo announced, conceding defeat and gaining prestige with the same bit of advice.

"I will remember that, for midnight ventures."

The various tasks involved kept Antonio's mind occupied, and he was grateful for the afternoon's diversion. Finally, gifts and note dispatched, Antonio sat at a small table in Vesuvio's, drinking an excellent wine, rich, red, and dry as a sirocco. Giacomo would have to return soon, the café was actually supposed to close at six o'clock. Another of Savonarola's dismaying new laws. Meanwhile, Antonio relaxed and watched the other patrons engaged in typically impassioned Florentine discussion, their hands sculpting the air as they argued.

At last, Giacomo appeared in the doorway. Weaving his way through the tables, Giacomo handed him a sealed note written on heavy lavender paper and scented with the hyacinth perfume, a promising sign. The note assured Antonio that Bianca would be most pleased to see him. She suggested he accompany her on a visit to Daniele Danti on Friday. The painter, she wrote, had collected the most amusing portfolio, the work of several prominent artists, which he might find it stimulating to view.

"Stimulating, indeed," Antonio murmured, smiling to himself. Highly erotic, he was sure. Perusing the drawings would simultaneously titillate him and provide Bianca with an opportunity to observe his responses obliquely. It was an excellent way to inform herself of his preferences. Or of any perversions he might possess, for that matter. Well, she had no worries there. He trusted she would find him adventurous but not depraved. The folio would be fascinating, no doubt, and he would enjoy seeing whatever painting Daniele Danti was working on, pornographic or not. Yes, it would be an entertaining day. Especially as the lady had, in essence, promised to fulfill that evening whatever desires she happened to arouse in the course of the afternoon.

4 The Meeting

 "COME in, come into the studio, Veronica, and see my progress on the painting. I have been obsessed. Inspiration seized me and I worked like a madman. I've done nothing else for two days, three days now," Daniele said with blissful satisfaction, gesturing her towards the canvas. "You see, the arrangement of the angels is entirely different. This way the movement of the wings is more dramatic."

"You are right, Daniele, this pose makes a better frame for the other figures."

Daniele was working on an *Adoration of the Magi* for the Della Montagnas, always a popular theme for a commissioned painting. The family, prominently featured in the foreground, rode on horseback as an entourage to the three wise men, bearing their own precious gifts to the Christ child. Maria and Dorotea were there, but Veronica was glad Luigi's face had not yet been added to the procession. His figure was only blocked in, as was Frederigo's. She did not want to have to look at him, not even as a rendering of lines on linen canvas. Like Luigi, her figure and Roberto's were only tentatively suggested. Since she and Roberto were readily available but often restless models, Daniele had done a few smaller charcoal sketches on paper in preparation for the painting. The drawings were rolled up under the easel, and Veronica, suddenly curious, drew them out and sifted through them.

"I look so young," she said, feeling estranged from the carefree creature depicted in the sketches.

"Has youth forsaken you so quickly, then?"

She looked up at Daniele. The tone had been teasing, but Daniele's head was cocked to one side as he scrutinized her with worried hazel eyes, more uncle than older cousin in both his age and his protective concern. Veronica lowered her gaze, rolling the sketches up and tucking them back in position. Daniele sensed something was amiss, something beyond the stress of family trouble over Fra Frederigo and Roberto. The reason seemed obvious enough at first, for Roberto had been upset for days after their return from the Della Montagna palazzo, and her worry for him was unfeigned. But the days had became a week, the week a month. Daniele, Benito, and even Roberto had turned their attention to her, wondering at her waspish temper and dark moods of depression. Daniele had already asked her twice, directly, if anything was wrong. Perplexed and hurt, he had nonetheless accepted her evasive answers. Veronica was grateful he would never pry. She was ashamed of her own duplicity, even lying to Daniele about the bruises Luigi had inflicted on her, saying that poor Roberto had accidentally struck her when he struggled with the guards.

She had not been to see Mama Lucia, knowing that her great-grandmother would not simply poke about with cautious questions but demand to know what the trouble was. And if Veronica would not give her an answer, the *Tarocco* cards would. *The Ace of Swords, reversed,* she thought bitterly, *and the Ten as well. I have suffered violence, but I have chosen my own martyrdom.* Part of Veronica longed to unburden her troubles, to find some release for the rage that burned against both Luigi and the crippling fear he evoked in her. But she was convinced Luigi would carry through his threat if she exposed him. The best thing for all concerned seemed to be to keep silent, so she held her tongue and nursed her injured spirit in private. She felt guilty now as well, knowing that she wounded those who cared for her by not confiding her pain.

Seeing she would not talk, her cousin turned back to the painting. "I should put Frederigo among these monks, now. He would be happier there. I will put him in the center, holding the cross."

Daniele was working on a section of figures in the background behind the nativity scene, a grouping of three humble friars, who were circled in turn by the new angels with their lavish, multicolored wings. One of the friars extended a long cross over the tableau. At the moment the cross was balanced on a small table piled high with books to lift it to the angle he wanted.

"There, you see! Impossible! The effect of the angels is different, so the center figure must kneel, and I must also change the angle of the cross," Daniele indicated the teetering construct. "Cecco . . . you know my little Cecco, who modeled for the angels?" At this Daniele blushed slightly.

"Yes," Veronica replied, smiling a little. She knew all about Daniele's angelic little Cecco. The young man was very pretty, with dark tumbling curls and an impish personality. Daniele was quite smitten.

Seeing her smile, Daniele blushed a brighter pink but kissed his fingers in appreciation of Cecco's attributes.

"He sent word he cannot pose today. His mother is ill, and he must run errands."

"Cecco's mother is often ill of late." Veronica raised her eyebrows in rueful commiseration, and her cousin shrugged and sighed deeply. Cecco's mother was an ardent supporter of Savonarola and disapproved strongly of her son's relationship with Daniele. She was doing her best to thwart it without confronting him directly about his sinful behavior. Veronica doubted that Cecco's affection could survive his family's censure.

"If he does come tomorrow, it is not worth obtaining another model." Daniele yanked his frizzled chestnut hair back behind his ears in aggravation. "It is frustrating, this section should be done next. The movement of the cross, so, diagonally over the group is important, and the gestures of the friar's hands, pointing the attention inward. Cecco has beautiful hands."

She knew a request when she heard one. The work would take her mind off herself and Daniele's off his worries about his friend. "I can hold the cross for you, Daniele."

"It is a boring pose, Veronica," he protested tentatively.

"I have nothing else to do. Benito has taken Roberto, Bombol, and the new kitten for a walk by the Arno."

"It will tire your arms."

"You forget I am a good horsewoman, cousin. My arms are quite strong enough, and if I am holding the cross, I will not be able to wriggle as I usually do." She studied the rough sketch of the figures and added impulsively, "Let me put on the habit, Daniele."

She smiled at him, the pure silliness of the idea taking hold of her imagination. Veronica had always loved costume balls and *Carnevale*. She had occasionally worn some piece of a costume for him to help him in his work, but the monk's habit seemed rather daring in its very religious severity. Daniele grinned back at her. The harmless impropriety pleased them both, conspirators in mischief.

"Your sandals, Friar," he said, scooping them up from the floor. "The habit is in the red trunk."

She took the sandals and found the habit under an embroidered cloak in the trunk. Stuffed in one corner were a wig and two false beards, one a spreading mass of gray curls suitable for a prophet, the other a small, neat dark brown affair. "This too," she said, holding it up.

"*Perfetto,*" Daniele applauded. "I shall await your transformation."

Veronica gathered up her costume and left the studio. A vine-covered balcony ran along the entire U-shaped upper story of the house, and she crossed over to the far end of the wing that held the little dressing room Daniele had arranged for his models. It was a simple room with only a screen, a chair, a bureau, and a small mirror on the wall. Veronica removed her dress, hung it up behind the screen, and held up the habit. Looking at it, she had a sudden vivid image of herself escaping Florence dressed in this monk's robe, casting frightened glances over her shoulder as she fled the pursuing Luigi. She leaned against the wall, feeling queasy, realizing there was more to her impulse to don the robe than amusement and a need to distract herself from her own unhappiness. Fear had been a constant companion these last weeks, its sibilant voice hissing questions in her ear. If Luigi set his will to raping her, could she stop him? What if he changed his mind and de-

nounced them? What if he demanded her body in exchange for
Mama Lucia's safety? What if . . . ?

"Enough," she whispered vehemently. She would not do it,
it was that simple. The threat was enough to buy her silence
but not her submission. Luigi's power of coercion was limited
because he would not want to carry out his threat. Only the
dread of his own exposure would make him risk such a public
scandal within his family. Bedding her would not be worth that
risk. Her fears were exaggerated. Luigi would not try to molest
her again; he did not really find her desirable. She would never
be alone with him again in that fashion—and would protect
herself if she were. She had defeated him once, she could
again. This time she would kill him if she had to. There were
moments when all she wanted was to have the poker in her
grasp once more.

Veronica shivered, dismayed at the extremes of emotion Luigi's assault had engendered. It was her sense of helplessness
and fear that brought about these escape fantasies, her unre-
leased anger that brought the visions of beating him bloody or
denouncing him publicly, watching him grovel before the accusing eye of Florence. Well, she had chosen silence and must
make the best of her choice. The only way she would take
action against Luigi was if he approached her again, and that
was the last thing in the world she wanted.

Quickly, Veronica put on the habit over her shift, tied the
coarse rope belt about her waist, and loosely bloused its folds
to obscure her breasts as much as possible. The hood was
distorted by the way her hair was twisted up on her head, so
she undid it and tied it back with a bit of ribbon. In the small
mirror she adjusted the false beard and mustache on her face.
It fit well enough, though it would never bear close examination, at least not without a bit of glue to prevent its going
askew. But it did transform her face, emphasizing the more
angular elements, disguising some of the softness of her lips.
Her brows were rather strong, and many men had large eyes
such as hers. Very well, her escape fantasy was possible. If
circumstances were ever so desperate, she could disguise herself this way and run from Florence. A monk would not be a
wise choice, despite the ease of the robe. They were clean-
shaven more often than bearded, tonsured—and versed in reli-

gious services Veronica could not, would not, pretend to perform. But the false beard combined with a man's robe and a hooded cloak would be a way to change her appearance and cover her departure.

Pleased with her transformation, Veronica returned to the studio, adopting the docile posture of a monk on the way to prayers. "Bless you, my son," she intoned, lowering her voice.

Daniele crossed his arms on his chest, surveying the transformation with a mock-lascivious eye. "So handsome you are, little monk!"

She laughed, and was grateful she could laugh at his silly innuendoes. She was safe from Daniele. Not even this mischievous disguise could tempt him from his true preference. Only the angelic Cecco's virtue was in any danger, and he desired it so. More than that, her cousin was the kindest of souls and would never force his attentions on anyone. She felt only amusement and affection for his teasing, and no more attraction or repulsion for his male body than she had ever felt. She was glad that the disgust, the nausea she felt at the thought of Luigi, the fear that rose up in her now when some nameless stranger followed her too closely in the streets of Florence, did not warp her trust for this gentle man.

Daniele had already prepared his palette. Together they cleared away the table, and Veronica knelt in position. She took hold of the cross, extending it forward as Daniele directed. Before Daniele could even begin to paint, there was a knock at the door and one of the servants slipped inside. "Master, the lady Bianca and a gentleman, Signore Antonio di Fabiani are downstairs," he announced, then at Daniele's surprised expression he lowered his voice and whispered, "She says she wrote you to expect them."

"Bianca!" Daniele rushed to a desk at the back of the room. There were several notes piled up there. He often neglected to open his messages when he was as involved in painting as he had been with his angels. He picked up a square of lavender paper and broke the seal, reading quickly, combing his fingers through his hair. He turned back to the servant. "Yes, she did write me. Show them in, then bring some wine, the dark Roman red and the best of the dry white. Use the silver goblets." Whirling around, he saw Veronica still in place with the cross. He gestured frantically at her, indicating she should exit out the smaller door to the little dressing room. Then he smoothed his rumpled hair and went to receive his guests.

Veronica stayed in position, amused and defiant as well. She could unveil, flip back the hood, remove the little beard, and be introduced as her true self. But it was not very fitting for the lady of the house to have assumed such a role . . . and it would be intriguing to maintain the disguise. She was very curious about Bianca. She knew that Daniele wanted to paint the notorious beauty, but Veronica had never seen her, either on the woman's two previous visits to Daniele's or on the streets of Florence. The latter had seemed a more likely possibility, because Daniele had turned very prudish at the idea of introducing her to an infamous courtesan. Now she was here, and Veronica had every intention of observing her anonymously.

The door opened and the woman who stepped inside was indeed beautiful, almost frighteningly so, with the perfect features and impossible fairness of some mythic queen of snow and ice. Her white-blond hair was dressed with jewels, and the flawless skin shone pale as alabaster against the violet silk of her gown. The square cut bodice plunged almost to the tips of her breasts.

"Venus, the Goddess of Love!" Daniele exclaimed, taking Bianca's hand and leading her into the center of the room. "Venus . . . and Mars," he added, turning to the man who followed behind. Focused on Bianca, Veronica had a fleeting impression of black hair and clothes, the sweeping gesture of a bow, the graceful flourish of a hand.

"Mars—God of War," the man said, rising from his bow.

It was the voice she recognized first, as if it flowed into her blood, whispered along her nerves, spoke its secret name in the pulsing chambers of her heart. The sound was layered, textured with contrasts, a voice fluid as wine, soft and dense as sable. The smooth, deep resonance was cut with another note, a faint rasping edge like the delicate prickle of a cat's tongue. A note she instinctively knew could harden and grate like the clash of sword blades, the sliding stroke of steel against steel.

That voice spoke, and in a single instant the world underwent a fabulous alchemy, dross matter transforming to insubstantial gold. Everything that had gone before was a pale shadow to this brilliance burning her from within and without. Veronica could scarcely breathe. It was no longer simple air she drew into her lungs but some brighter, purer element, almost unbearable in its intensity. Her vision shimmered, everything she saw touched now with gilded light. Newborn and trembling, Veronica watched the small social drama enacted before her, praying her unsteady hands would not drop the cross with a resounding clatter.

Daniele was studying the stranger intently now, caught up in mercuric inspiration. "Even better . . . Pluto," he said softly. "Pluto and the fair Persephone." He turned to Veronica as he pronounced the last name and smiled. His guests were slightly confused, as the comment was no longer directed to them and made no sense spoken to the tableau with the monk. Daniele seemed to realize this suddenly and turned back to his guests with a sheepish smile. "Forgive me, I am always painting things in my head. A dozen pictures at once."

"I would be honored simply to see the one in progress," the man said, and Daniele motioned him to a chair near the easel.

From beneath her hood, Veronica surveyed the arresting figure of this stranger. Yes, Pluto, Lord of the Underworld, was even better than Mars, and better than both was the Prince of Cups. The haunting face of the painted *Tarocco* card figure was made flesh in this unknown courtier. He had even assumed the Prince's pose, lounging insolently in the chair, clasping in one hand the goblet of wine the servant had poured for him. The image of her fantasy had come exquisitely alive before her eyes.

His skin was finely grained, its fairness set off by lustrous black hair that gleamed like a raven's wing where the sunlight from the window touched it. The dark, brooding eyes were deep-set under arching brows, framed with straight lashes that cast sharp little daggers of shadow. His mouth was both severe and sensuous, the curves of the upper lip strongly sculpted, the lower lip fuller, the edges curled in a faint smile, amused and mocking. A face with everything, power and sensitivity, cruelty and tenderness mingled. He turned now to watch the courtesan, displaying high cheekbones and the arrogant nose of a classic profile. He smiled with a hint of wickedness, a sophisticated decadence half real and half assumed.

"To Venus," he said, raising the goblet in a toast. The hands were strongly veined and masculine, yet each fluid gesture was elegance itself.

"I do prefer Venus to Persephone," Bianca answered lightly, raising her cup in turn. "The charm of ravished innocence is so fleeting, do you not think so, Antonio?"

"Compared to the celestial delights of a knowledgeable Venus, most certainly."

"Antonio," Veronica whispered to herself, remembering the servant's introduction now. "Antonio di Fabiani."

He rose from the chair and walked to Daniele's painting, glancing at Veronica briefly, then comparing her pose to the figure outlined on the canvas. She studied him as he studied it. The clothes he wore were the height of fashion, a striking combination of black and silver. The lean, muscular legs were well displayed in black silk hose, topped by a doublet of shimmering black velvet and quilted satin, edged with silver bullion. The sleeves were slashed with cloth of silver and the shoulders ornamented with a scattering of white and black pearls and tiny, glittering diamonds. He carried a long *estoc* and a dagger at his side, each in a chased silver scabbard. The weapons completed the living portrait of the perfect Italian aristocrat, all his own deadly menace sheathed in rich fabric and polished manners, ready to be drawn at a moment's notice. No, this man could wait and wait. There was fire there, but it burned under ice.

She was staring, helplessly. As if he felt her watching, Antonio turned his own scrutiny upon her. She dropped her eyes instantly beneath the penetrating gaze. Only her grandmother had ever looked at her that way, with eyes that stripped every mask. She felt he must know who she was, though it was impossible, with her kneeling here in her false beard and monk's habit. That inner knowledge was too much to ask. Or was it? He was her Prince of Cups. He was promised to her, and he had appeared at last. How could he not recognize her as she recognized him? Her heart began to pound, and the extended cross teetered in her grip.

"I think your model has grown faint," Antonio said, a thread of concern woven into the deep texture of his voice.

She glanced up furtively, but his eyes were veiled now, his manner bored as if he never considered anything in life more significant than his next change of clothes. *He hides his compassion,* she thought, *even in such a small thing. It must run deep in him, give him pain, or he would not bother to conceal it.*

Daniele rushed over to her and plucked the cross from her. "Verono," he said chidingly, "did you not get enough sleep last night?"

She cast a desperate glance into his face, in which assorted emotions were dancing, exasperation, concern, and devious amusement among the most obvious.

"No, *maestro*," she murmured, keeping her voice low and husky. She wanted desperately to escape, but not as desperately as she wanted to stay.

"It is my fault, my angel. I keep you too busy, work you too hard." Her cousin continued to play out the masquerade and also took some small revenge for her disobedience.

Veronica blushed furiously. They would think Daniele meant the kind of after-hours work little Cecco contributed. "No, *maestro*," she croaked.

"No, of course not. It is a labor of love, no? Well, I do not need you any longer today. Go change your clothes and rest up. You can come back tomorrow."

"But . . . ."

"I insist."

"Yes, *maestro*," she answered, since there was no way to dodge Daniele's order.

Her legs felt shaky as she hurried across the balcony to the dressing room. Once inside she did not change her clothes, only collapsed onto the chair and waited a minute or two for her body to stop trembling. Then, mortified but unable to resist the impulse, she opened the door so she could creep back quietly and listen to the conversation in the studio. But the three of them were outside, Daniele leading them along the balcony to the central staircase that swept down into his elegant courtyard garden. They were not looking her way, so

Veronica moved forward quickly, positioning herself behind a vine-covered trellis that hid her from view.

"Please, the sun is shining. Take a stroll in my garden while I arrange for refreshments." Daniele offered, gesturing from the top of the stairs. "My cook is a sour old thing, but her pastries are marvelous. You must sample some of her delicacies."

"That is most thoughtful of you," Antonio said.

"My mouth is watering at the thought," Bianca announced, descending the stairs.

"After the refreshments, I will bring out my infamous portfolio. Do you know, Bianca, Botticelli is begging me to burn it in Savonarola's bonfire of vanities. Just toss all those marvelous drawings into the flames!"

"I do not understand," Antonio said, standing at the foot of the stairs. "I have seen Botticelli's work and find it very erotic —refined and delicate, yes, but erotic nonetheless. I cannot imagine how a man who paints with such exquisite sensuality could ask such a thing. For that matter, I cannot imagine one artist asking such a thing of another."

"It is a foolish idea, converting *Carnevale* to another dreary religious procession. The populace needs to exhaust itself with a good orgy in order to endure the strictures of Lent that follow," Bianca said archly.

Of course, Veronica realized, they had come to entertain themselves with the erotic folio. She had seen it only once. Daniele had always kept it under lock and key, another of his occasional acts of avuncular propriety. In exasperation, she had finally filched the key from him, determined to satisfy her curiosity. All of the drawings had been beautifully rendered. Many were quite lovely and tender, but others had been raw and explicit enough to embarrass her. She blushed now, to think of Antonio perusing the folio with Bianca. The courtesan would not be embarrassed. Each drawing would be offered to him like an invitation.

"It will take me a few minutes to arrange our little feast. I will leave you here in the garden. My camellias are beginning to bloom, such an alluring pink. Please, enjoy yourselves." Daniele turned and hurried into the house.

Taking advantage of the unseasonable warmth, the two,

courtier and courtesan, strolled among the greenery and early
blossoming plants, pausing by the small fountain with its
statue of a prancing faun. The garden was large, and Daniele
had designed it to be attractive in all seasons. There were
certain sections deliberately and romantically screened from
view. Smiling, Antonio led Bianca to such a sheltered island.
Where they stood, they would be hidden from the eyes of
Daniele and the servants, but they were quite visible to Veronica, concealed behind her ivy trellis at the far end of the balcony.

Realizing their intention, Veronica meant to turn away, but
just then Antonio moved behind Bianca, his hands lifting to
caress her neck. The gesture stilled her as completely as it did
the courtesan. That subtle touch, the merest dalliance of fingertips against flesh, riveted her, trembling, where she stood. For
her, the other woman hardly existed now. It was her own skin
that tingled, just there, where the fingers of one hand traced a
skimming line out to the shoulder's edge, then moved back
along the line of the collarbone to the hollow of the throat. His
hand moved down, following the shadowed line of cleavage to
the bodice of the low cut gown. Veronica gasped, feeling her
own nipples stiffen as Antonio's fingers edged inside the tight
bodice. Antonio's free arm encircled the courtesan's waist, his
hand cupping the other breast from below.

Bianca laughed, a low throaty laugh full of promise, and the
sound of it broke through the spell that held Veronica. With a
few deft gestures, Bianca unfastened the jeweled clips that
held the top of her gown. It opened easily, exposing her
breasts, a whore's garment, designed for just such easy access
and display. The other woman was very real to Veronica now,
with her insinuating laugh, her large round nipples so vivid
against the pale skin of her breasts. Surely they must be
rouged! Veronica felt a surge of shame and jealousy mingling
chaotically with the tumultuous excitement that filled her,
frightening her with its intensity. Part of her wanted to run
back into her little room and hide, another part wanted to fight
the fair-haired vixen below, tooth and nail, for daring to accept
the caresses that Veronica's body insisted belonged to her. Her
confusion must have made her careless, for Bianca lifted her
face abruptly, her eyes finding Veronica's half-hidden form.

She made no attempt to cover herself but laughed again, looking straight into Veronica's eyes. The courtesan arched her back, pressing her breasts, her erect nipples, forward into Antonio's hands, and leaning her head back a little, she whispered something into his ear.

Then Antonio's head lifted, and it was his eyes that met hers, dark and blazing, for an unbearable second before Veronica turned and stumbled back into the little dressing room.

Ignoring the courtesan's laughing protests, Antonio released Bianca and ran swiftly across the courtyard. The trellis looked sturdy enough, and it was more direct than the stairs. He was up it in three quick movements and onto the balcony. The door the boy had vanished behind was just closing, and Antonio shoved his shoulder against it, forcing it open against the other's weaker efforts to shut it. Once inside, however, he simply locked the door and leaned back against the frame with studied insouciance, eyeing the embarrassed young man who seemed to be trying to withdraw inside the hooded habit like a turtle into its shell.

Antonio smiled a little. No doubt Bianca had found the idea of a voyeuristic monk quite titillating, even if it was only an imitation monk. She'd probably make a risqué little fiction of it, changing the names and places—and the outcome. She had already displayed a gift for such entertainments. Still, he was here to prevent the lad from spreading the actual story himself, with or without embellishments. He loathed the idea of being the latest juicy bit of gossip in the city square, for his family's sake more than his own.

"No doubt you had a pretty view from the balcony, boy, a sight fair enough to warm the embers when you are in your dotage. But I want it understood, between us, that what you saw will remain a vision in your brain, rather than become a tale wagged on your tongue."

The imitation monk sank even deeper into the folds of his habit. At the moment all that was visible of his face was a wisp of beard. An unintelligible mumble emerged from the depths of the hood.

"What did you say, boy?"

"Yes, my lord," came the peculiar rasp.

Antonio stepped forward, deciding to reinforce his words with just enough threat to give them significance. "There is no harm done—and will be none if you hold your peace. But I promise you, whatever pleasure you might get in babbling about what you saw would be undone by the thrashing I will give you if I hear the story from some stranger in the street. Is that understood?" he asked, gripping the youth's shoulders to give him a good shake.

At the touch of his hands on her body, rough as it was, a bright current flashed through Veronica, making her gasp aloud. Abruptly, he released her, shoving her against the wall as he stepped back himself. Veronica's head came up and her eyes met Antonio's. She felt a wild elation at the confused mix of emotions she read there. He had experienced it too, that surge of power between them. He was not only some precious fantasy come to life, to be dreamed over as the youth he thought her to be might have dwelt on his images of Bianca. This magic flowing through her was flowing through him as well. A connection did exist between them, as vital as she could ever have hoped for, and no disguise could conceal it. She almost laughed aloud then, in giddy joy, seeing the astonishment on his face at war with desire and annoyance, seeing him struggle to mask all three behind his courtier's cool detachment. He still thought she was a boy, and he was utterly bewildered at his response, a little angered perhaps, but too honest to blame her.

Stunned, Antonio stared into the clear gray eyes, aglow now with inner fire. The little monk wanted him, not the beautiful Bianca, and his own response was unprecedented and distinctly unnerving. His body still tingled from that simple contact, from the spark that had leapt between them. He cast his eyes down over the slim figure concealed in the habit, then quickly up to the face again, his eyes narrowing in sudden realization. Antonio laughed aloud, relief dispelling the intensity of his first reaction. He reached out, plucking away the false beard and tossing it aside. He pushed the hood back from the undisguised face and undid the ribbon that tied back the mass of hair, drawing it forward. The hair was truly a marvel, abundant and the most amazing color, like a smoldering fire.

The face was unusual as well, with those large gray eyes and dark brows, the slanting cheekbones, the wide, mobile mouth. Lovely . . . and definitely female.

"You are not entirely what you seem," he said, still smiling, "but I much prefer you in this new guise, charcoal smudges and all." He reached out and stroked the smoothness of her cheek.

Veronica permitted the liberty. More than permitted it. Her eyes closed without volition, and she leaned her cheek into his hand, caressing it in turn. A moment before, he had assumed her a boy, probably Daniele's catamite. Now her true sex was revealed, but her status was no different. A little model, enraptured with the dashing aristocrat. He was obviously accustomed to such adulation and thought little of it.

Antonio did not know why he was so compelled to touch her. He felt drawn to her as he might have been to some shy wild thing encountered in the woods, that might be soothed, touched, tamed. She looked a little frightened still, flushed with embarrassment and alight with desire, altogether irresistible. The strange thing was that his hand trembled slightly as he brushed that charming smudge from her cheek, that his heart was pounding in his chest as if he were an adolescent boy full of trepidation.

The costume was an absurdity. It fastened at the throat, and Antonio undid the tie. The opening of the neck was slashed deep, deep enough to spread the loose garment over her shoulders and slip it down to collapse in a heavy pool of fabric at her feet. Her shift was finely made, sheer linen edged with satin ribbons and fragile lace. A present from Daniele or some other patron? While the design was surprisingly chaste, the fabric was enticingly transparent, revealing the rounded mounds of her breasts with their rosy centers, the long slender limbs, the shadowed triangle at the juncture of her thighs. The curling hair there looked an even darker red. He surveyed all this veiled beauty, then raised his hands to the lacy straps at her shoulders and slipped the garment off. Her body did not have the classic proportions considered the ideal of beauty, nor was it voluptuous, yet its willowy shape was delectable to his eye, the gentle flow of its lines elegant and feminine.

The girl was shivering. Surely she wasn't afraid of him? She stared up at him, her eyes huge, filled with expectation and a bewildering innocence. Her profession indicated much experience, but perhaps had she never had so rich, so sophisticated a lover. Sophisticated! What was he thinking of? He had meant simply to brush her lips with his and then leave. Now she was naked before him, her pink nipples drawn to taut little points and a seductive musk rising from the moist, secret folds of her body. He must stop this. The situation was impossible, absurd. He had one of the most famous courtesans in Italy tapping her foot in the garden while he dallied with some tantalizing sprite of an artist's model. He must leave at once. But first he would have his kiss.

"Another day perhaps, *dolcezza*, but now I have a lady waiting." He bent forward then, a small regretful smile tilting his lips.

Veronica shivered again as Antonio cupped her face in his hands. He found her, her passion for him, amusing. He was condescending to leave her a memento, a kiss to dream over. She thought she would die of shame—or perhaps of anticipation, for she wanted the kiss as much as he imagined she did and more. It seemed she had waited her whole life to be standing here, with his mouth poised above hers.

Antonio was filled with the strangest hesitation, and a growing hunger. His lips hovered above the girl's, feeling their moist silky surfaces barely touching, the warmth of their breath mingling, the promise of the delectable wetness waiting within. He did not know how long their lips poised there, asking each other these sensitive questions in the secret language of the flesh. Questions only deeper knowledge could answer. His mouth closed the space between them, and they were kissing, softly, softly, but with a growing fervor.

Veronica sighed as their lips met and clung, moving together with delicate devouring motions. The edge of his teeth caught her lower lip gently, caressed it with the tip of his tongue. Tentatively, she answered the moist, teasing probe with her own tongue. He caught it, drew it into his mouth, and sucked on its sweetness. He let his own tongue be drawn into hers in turn. A giddy delirium filled her, drinking the wine rich taste of him, a thirst she could never quench.

Her arms were around him now, and he embraced her too,

drawing her closer and closer. He pressed the length of her to fit his body, and she yearned towards him, feeling herself defined against him and melting into him both. He was fully aroused, and the hard shape of him imprinted itself like a brand on her flesh. Veronica shuddered with longing and pressed herself against his desire. He pulled her closer, rocking her body against him, then lifted her up. Still innocent, she hardly understood what he wanted of her, only obeyed the directions of his hands cupping her buttocks, stroking her thighs, raising her higher. She clung to him with her arms, her legs, instinctively wrapping herself about his body. The plaster of the wall was rough against her back, the fabric of his clothes a luxurious softness caressing her breasts and belly, but that rich texture was not as desirable as the skin she hungered to feel naked against her own.

Then, within that soft crush of silk and velvet, there was the touch of flesh, secret and unbearably intimate, the satin hardness of his sex nuzzling the warm, moist opening of hers. Stroking her, pushing up, and entering. She moaned for hurt, a bearable pain mixed with an unbearable longing which was both pain and pleasure, an ache so acute it overwhelmed that lesser pang. Antonio moaned in answer, as if he shared both sensations, his body responding to her need as he penetrated her slowly, slowly, their bodies speaking their new found language to each other in gentle whispers of movement. They pressed together in this slow, questioning dance until, finally, he came to rest fully sheathed inside her.

He whispered again, "Ah . . . *dolcezza.*"

He began to move within her, and with each sweet piercing thrust it seemed as if the tender inner darkness they shared blossomed with light. Where their bodies met and fused, a pulsing sun of sensation radiated its brightness. Time and flesh dissolved as they strove together to reach its glowing, molten heart. It seemed impossible to reach that quivering center, attain that exquisite pinnacle, then Antonio pressed forward once more, a single thrust, and they were both enveloped in exploding light. Veronica cried out as the fierce, sweet sensation shook her, soft, broken cries of amazement and rapture. Antonio's cry was a deep echo of her own, his body arching, his head thrown back as he came to climax. She felt him throbbing, alive inside her, felt the core of her body caressing him as they shuddered together in ecstasy.

———

Afterwards, still embracing, they stared into each other's eyes. His eyes burned dark, almost black, the widened pupils filling them like the gaze of eternity, full of wonder and ancient knowledge. She felt what she knew he must feel, reborn, at once infinitely new and old as time. For that eternal moment they looked into each other's eyes, while her body held him, still firm within her. Female embracing male, Veronica embracing Antonio, in a deep recognition of flesh and spirit.

Then, into the heart of his gaze came a flicker of something she could only call fear. It was gone as quickly as it appeared, but with it went everything else. Deliberately, Antonio closed himself off from her. She saw it in his eyes, felt it as surely as a door shut in her face, locking her outside him. She stared at him, stunned, her lips forming a soundless protest she could not voice. Then he was separating their bodies, a process suddenly awkward, and he would not look at her. His sex slipped from hers, and he lowered her legs to the floor, stepped back from her and deftly adjusted his clothing. Standing alone, she shivered abruptly, bereft and chilled. Antonio bent and scooped up her shift, offering it to her as if it were a dropped handkerchief, his courtier's manners encasing him like silver armor, bright, shining, and impenetrable. Defending against what? But she knew what—defending against the perfection they had shared.

He looked almost bored now, his face was so shuttered, though his eyes shifted slightly, refusing to quite meet hers. "*Dolcezza*," he repeated the endearment, his mocking voice souring the sweetness. "I trust you will forgive my . . . precipitousness. It did seem to be what we both desired."

"Yes," she said simply, and his eyes again met hers for a second, in that unguarded way that seemed to touch the deepest part of her.

He frowned and made a small sound, formed the fragment of a word, the shape of it softening, parting his lips so she longed to kiss them again. But he did not ask who she was, what her name was. The practiced mask slid over his features again. Stepping back, he reached inside his money pouch, withdrew two golden ducats and placed them on the bureau. "*Grazie, dolcezza*," he said, and closed yet another door, leaving her utterly alone.

Veronica gasped as if he had slapped her, a gasp that was close to a sob. She knew, to the marrow of her bones, that what Antonio had felt had not been as simple as lust. Now he had left her money. How could he not know what she had given him had not been a whore's offering, with a whore's price? Knowing, how could he choose to make it so? Her elation had given way to shock, almost to despair. She had not thought of Luigi once while Antonio touched her. Now the dreadful sense of violation returned to her body and soul, and a humiliating rush of shame at her own wanton acquiescence, no better than the whore he thought her to be. She had given him what Luigi sought to steal, and he had tried to buy that gift from her. Brutal as Luigi's physical assault had been, Antonio's emotional desecration seemed infinitely worse, the pain of it reaching places Luigi could never touch. Then anger began to burn through all the other emotions Antonio had left behind. The shame was his, not hers.

Liar, she thought, her outrage at his betrayal seething in her. Then, snatching up the coins, she whispered the word out loud, over and over again: "Liar . . . liar . . . liar!"

It was hours later, when she was sure Antonio and Bianca had gone, that Veronica dared to return to Daniele's studio, dressed once more in her own clothes. She found him on the floor, where he often liked to draw, sketching madly. Several quick charcoal drawings were scattered around. One or two were of Bianca, the others were of Antonio. For one fearful moment Veronica wondered if her cousin was also infatuated, but when he spoke, it was with a purely artistic lust.

"His face is marvelous, marvelous! He must let me do a portrait. Look here . . . the halves of the face are never quite the same, not on anyone. And if you cover one side so, the differences in the features, the expression, are more striking. Here you see fury, passion, here tenderness, sorrow. On him it is so vividly marked when you observe each side separately, but when you see the whole face it all comes together in that sardonic detachment, and the intelligence, the wit, gives it such life. I must paint him! He does like my work, I think he might commission a portrait.''

Her emotions still in turmoil, Veronica knelt beside him. Her hand reached out, hovering over the stark charcoal planes of Antonio's cheek, the arched line of his upper lip that begged to be traced by fingertip, by lip, by tongue. Deliberately, she gestured over to the other drawings. "What about Bianca? I thought you wanted to paint her as Venus."

"Yes, she is perfect. So erotic, but so cold. I would paint her as an exquisitely vain Venus, as self-possessed and cruel as a cat. And he would make a wonderful Mars, though he would not pose with a courtesan. A pity. These aristocrats make such silly rules for themselves."

"Mars?" she asked, her mouth dry. "I thought you preferred Pluto?"

"Yes, Pluto," he smiled up at her, "with you as Persephone. I have often thought you would make a lovely Persephone, you have the gentleness, the innocent wildness. I would paint her abduction, the dark chariot, the trampled flowers. No, Persephone a shining radiance in the darkness of Hades. Ah! do not tempt me, my mind is filling with pictures, more than I can paint in a lifetime!"

He sprang to his feet and went to the back table to pour a goblet of wine for himself and one for her. Veronica accepted the offering, sipping the wine to moisten her throat. "Thank you."

"Well, you finally got to see Bianca. I hope you were pleased with yourself, dawdling about in your costume," Daniele scolded her playfully. "I am glad they came—it was a most entertaining afternoon. I must look through my neglected messages and see what other surprises are in store."

Daniele returned to the table and picked up the three days of notes that were scattered there. "There is a shipment of ground lapis. The price is outrageous, but the blue glows like no other. Vellum. Gold leaf. Bah, bills are so boring. Ah, my new doublet is ready, the green satin damask. Can I afford to pay for it?"

"Yes, but no matching hose till next month. Wear your

black ones with it." She managed a smile, holding out her hand for the bills.

Daniele handed her the offensive objects and proceeded. "A commission to design and paint six chairs? No. True, every object should be beautiful, but for me, the surface area is too small. I will suggest a nice bench with a back of fine white poplar—or a *cassone*, a wedding chest. Even better, here is a letter from the Aristi requesting two more family portraits. They are finicky, but I can have my new silk hose and order some books as well. Don't raise your eyebrows at me, Veronica, you usually read them before I do."

"Only if you are too busy painting." Then, smiling, she added, "Or talking."

Now it was Daniele who raised his eyebrows, but it did not stop the flow of words, "Ah, here on the bottom is another peremptory summons to the Palazzo della Montagna. It is for tomorrow night. Myself included, as well as you and Roberto. Some event bound to reduce us to wretched misery for days afterwards? No, my thinking of the *cassone* was prophetic, for it is a dinner party for Dorotea's betrothal. A good banquet will be had by all, albeit their cook is no match for ours. I shall wear the new doublet. What time is it to be?"

"Dorotea's to be engaged?" Veronica asked, startled, as Daniele paused long enough to scan the note. "No one said anything. But they never tell us anything if they can help it. I hope they picked someone understanding. She is terribly young."

Suddenly, Daniele burst out laughing. "Oh, no! I cannot believe it. It is priceless! No, it is horrible, dreadful! He is going to marry her—marry Dorotea, that little snippet of a branch from her mother's bough. It is ridiculous. A man of his appetites—he will eat her in one bite for breakfast. Munch, and she is all gone!"

"What are you talking about, Daniele? Who are you talking about?"

"Antonio!" he exclaimed. "Antonio di Fabiani is going to marry Dorotea."

5 The Courtesan

 "WAKE up, mistress," Dimitri murmured solicitously.

Bianca stirred lazily as the eunuch drew back the hangings of heavy silver satin and thin white silk gauze that surrounded the bed. Then he opened the velvet drapes letting the cool winter sunlight stream in through all the windows. She breathed deeply, enjoying the sweet scent of the mint *tisane* Dimitri had already placed on the table by her bed. There was a small round of almond cake for her breakfast, as well as a crisp sweet apple, thinly sliced. Three white camellias were placed in a vase of fragile Venetian glass. The eunuch added another pillow to the pile on the bed and gave Bianca a hot steamy towel to cleanse her hands and face.

"Bianca," Dimitri said, his voice hushed and eager, "I went to the market, and then to the Villani palazzo. I have had an interesting talk with some of the servants there."

Bianca yawned, pulling the slippery bedspread of quilted mauve satin up around her chin. "I am tired, Dimitri, we will talk of it later. Villani stayed late last night. All I want is to lie abed awhile and eat my breakfast in peace. Where did you get these lovely white camellias?"

"Signore di Fabiani sent them this morning. A whole basket full of them. They must be the first blooms in Florence," he added sulkily.

Bianca smiled. "No, I saw some pink ones the other day. Go prepare a bath for me, Dimitri. Add a little of the hyacinth perfume Fabiani gave me."

"Yes, mistress, I will have the hot water readied for the tub. With the perfume." Her servant's tone was almost hostile.

"No, Dimitri, I've changed my mind. Add the rose perfume instead." The oil of red roses had been a Christmas gift from Dimitri, along with a special decoction of belladonna flowers.

"Later, Dimitri, when the tub is ready, you can help me bathe."

"Yes, Bianca," he answered, his plump Greek cherub's face glowing beneath the dark, oiled ringlets of his hair.

Bianca breathed the fumes of the *tisane*, letting the sharp mint fragrance clear her head. Then she sipped the brew and nibbled at the almond cake. Snuggling down into her pillows, she winced at the soreness between her legs. Bianca hoped there were no bruises. Ugolino Villani was impossible. She was glad to have finally decided to get rid of him. Dimitri would be pleased as well.

She smiled at the eunuch's sullen reaction to her request for the hyacinth oil. Dimitri would accept Antonio if he had to, and the camellias were an indication that he would have to. True, there was no accompanying note, no fragment of poetry to praise her. Dimitri would not have dared to conceal it. But the flowers were acceptable, if not as ardent as Bianca would have liked, for she had not been entirely certain Antonio would make contact again. It had been a vexing sensation—and nothing but foolishness, after all. Some men were always sad after coupling, no matter how exquisite the pleasure during the act. It seemed the handsome Antonio was one of them. Perhaps he would sample others, but he would return here. She knew her professional rivals in Florence, and there were none to match her, certainly not for a man of his intensity. How many times had he taken her, and satisfied her? Three? A few moments of melancholy during the interim were negligible compared to that voracious ardor.

He would make an interesting diversion from her other machinations, useful as well as pleasurable. Florence had its virtues—far too many virtues at present, with the ever increasing popularity of Savonarola creating the fashion for overzealous morality among the populace. Twice she had been publicly chastised for the opulence of her dress. If it were not for the influence of the men Bianca had cultivated, things would be even more difficult for her. Antonio had only recently returned to Florence, but his family was rich and powerful. He could prove to be a powerful patron if she remained in the city.

Fabiani was already proving to be a generous lover. They had stopped at a jeweler's after the incident at Daniele's, and he had gifted her with a necklace, a long rope of ice white baroque pearls, tinged with gray and lavender iridescence. He'd claimed they had obviously been made for her dress and that the fairness of her skin increased their luster. Holding them up, Bianca was gratified to note that the compliments he gave her were quite accurate. It was tedious to receive an expensive but unflattering present. He had begged to buy them for her quite prettily, as if there were indeed a question of her acceptance. When she had graciously agreed, he'd added a lovely jewel box of silver filigree, set with moonstones and pale, scintillating opals. He was definitely feeling guilty.

She had been quite incensed at first, when he had returned from his supposed scolding of Daniele's little pet and had the nerve to apologize for the "foolish waste of precious time" with the musk of sex clinging to him. Bianca was tempted to dismiss him on the spot for abandoning her to go fumble with that gawking adolescent boy, but Daniele had reappeared, with a servant bearing the tisane and pastries, and she had not wanted to make a scene. By the time they were back in the studio and enjoying the repast, curiosity had overcome resentment, and she decided to hold her tongue. Later, he had more than compensated for the slight.

"Shame on you," Bianca scolded herself, drawing one of the camellias from the vase and brushing it across her cheek. "If he were not so beautiful . . . and so talented . . . you would not have forgiven him."

She had chosen her bedfellows in Florence for reasons that were purely political or monetary. In Antonio's case she would lose nothing by indulging herself for more frivolous reasons as well. Antonio di Fabiani had caught her attention in Venice, and as was her habit, Bianca had immediately researched him. Nothing had come of it then, but she had reviewed her information when he approached her a few days ago and sent Dimitri to listen to the latest gossip. Bianca knew various versions of the old scandal that had sent him away, and she knew he had finally returned because his mother was ill. More pertinently, she had learned of his preference for professional companionship, courtesans of beauty, intelligence, and accomplishment. He had an eye for beauty to be sure, but it was always female beauty. There was no indication of more diverse predilections on his part, and after spending the evening in bed with Antonio, she decided to regard the episode with Daniele's model as one of minimal significance.

Bianca circled her nipples with the cool white petals of the camellia, remembering the night she had spent with Antonio. It had grown cold when the sun went down, and he had risen naked from the bed and built a blaze in the fireplace himself. Then he had flung the thick quilt onto the floor and carried her to the fire. She remembered the red shadow play of the flames across his fair skin as his body strained above hers. He had the grace of some great cat, sleek and tautly muscled. She had often imagined the luxurious peril of having a tamed panther at her bedside. An enslaved Antonio had even more allure.

Yes, she wanted him to come back. She was becoming aroused just thinking of him. Bianca tossed the flower aside, her hand sliding lower, across her belly and down, clasping the plush mound between her thighs. It lingered there a minute but then withdrew. She did not want to satisfy herself. Her own fingers were skillful, but she wanted a mouth, a hot, wet mouth covering her. And she would not have to wait very long for that.

Dimitri soon returned. She had other servants, of course, as befitted her station, but they were dismissed at night. Only Dimitri was allowed into the private sanctuary of her bedroom. As he approached, Bianca tossed the flower aside, rose from the bed, and stretched. "Come, tell me what you have discovered while you prepare me for my bath."

Dimitri slipped off the delicate silk shift Bianca wore, muttering under his breath at the torn fabric, "He has damaged it, the pig Villani."

"Better it than me."

"Did he try?"

"Any impulses he had were skillfully deflected. The shift did suffer, however."

"It is not ruined, only ripped along the seams. A seamstress can refashion it with embroidery."

"I thought it could be mended. Of course, he has promised to pay for another one, even finer."

"He will probably want to rip that as well."

"Perhaps he will never have the chance," Bianca said lazily, watching Dimitri's breath quicken, the bright, hopeful gleam come into his eyes.

"Yes?" he whispered, a secret question.

"Perhaps," Bianca repeated, teasing him. "He tore my dress too. I do not like to have my lovely things spoiled."

"The pig," the eunuch hissed. "The pink pig!"

"I think he will find association with me far more expensive than he planned."

"A high price," Dimitri said. "The highest."

If Villani's fetish had been less destructive, Bianca would have found it as entertaining as she usually did these small, personal sexual oddities. She looked down at her body and smiled to herself, caressing first her large round nipples, then the pale floss curling on her mound of Venus. The fairness of her hair there had proved a fetish for many of her patrons. The majority of the courtesans rechristened themselves, choosing classical or romantic names for the most part. Her own name was chosen to reflect her natural white-blond coloring.

"Ah . . . Bianca," Dimitri murmured. Standing behind her, his fingers joined those of his mistress, delicately carding the fluffy growth.

It was not only her patrons who were enraptured with her fairness, her wintry beauty, and none of them was as devoted, as fervent in their attentions as her willing slave Dimitri. Nor as useful. Bianca leaned back against the plump body, feeling the knowledgeable fingers slide lower, part her tender lips, and dip into their inner moistness. She gave a small murmur of approval as fingertips circled the stiffening bud of flesh within.

"He was no good for you, that pink pig Villani," Dimitri said, his voice cajoling.

"No," Bianca whispered. "No good at all."

"A lout. A clumsy oaf. Men, they have no finesse," Dimitri insisted.

"Not like you, Dimitri," Bianca assured him. It was not entirely true, but few males had the adroitness of her eunuch. Few set themselves to please her as she was expected to please them. And it was not wise to mention such exceptions as Antonio.

"They say they worship your beauty, but they desire only to pillage it."

"Lay me on the bed, Dimitri. Worship me."

Strong as many of the whole men Bianca had known, Dimitri lifted her, carried her to the bed, laying her there on her back with her hips at its edge. She knew she looked delectable, her body pale against the expanse of mauve satin.

"Open to me," Dimitri murmured huskily, stroking the silken skin of her inner thighs.

Bianca took hold of her legs, just under the knee, and tilted her hips up, holding herself totally open and exposed to Dimitri's gaze, his touch. "Like this?"

"Yes . . . wider . . . wider. You are beautiful, mistress. Soft and pink like a rose wet with dew," Dimitri whispered, his mouth nuzzling those pouting pink lips.

Bianca smiled in anticipation, feeling the eunuch's hot breath on her tender flesh.

"Please, mistress," Dimitri asked, "Ugolino Villani, we shall kill him, yes?"

"Yes, yes, I think so," Bianca laughed, then hissed with excitement as Dimitri's mouth, his tongue, his teeth feasted on everything offered to him.

The rich, heavy scent of roses permeated the room. Bianca luxuriated in her white marble bath, clouds of fragrant steam rising about her as Dimitri gently sponged her body. Together they discussed their plan of action for the Villani assassination, the servant informing his mistress of the new information he had garnered in the marketplace and from his visits with the Villani servants. Dimitri had many delicious tidbits of gossip to trade, and he was expert at random questioning that yielded up pertinent information amidst general chatter.

"Dimitri, you are invaluable. I do not know what I would do without you."

"I want only to serve you, mistress. You know you are my life." He kissed the soles of her feet.

Bianca smiled. She had bought Dimitri in a slave market ten years ago. Recently she had freed him, but the legal formality was meaningless—he was still totally her slave. In his consuming passion Dimitri could be trusted implicitly, as long as his devotion was suitably rewarded. In return, he had brought her precious knowledge. The Greek had been captured as a youth and castrated to serve in a Turkish harem. Within that guarded sanctuary of eroticism, he had learned many secret arts of love and death. He had greatly extended her sexual repertoire, and his knowledge of poisons surpassed any apothecary she had used. Bianca was much stronger than she looked, skilled in the use of sword and dagger. Dimitri was stronger still, the heavy body almost as powerful as a whole man's. Bianca used a silk scarf, a necklace of cunning design, or a swift wire garrote to strangle a victim. Dimitri had taught her this method, but he preferred to throttle his victims with his bare hands or with the pressure of a forearm against the throat.

Together they were almost a perfect team. Bianca occasionally wished for a male partner as well. As there were certain things men would reveal only to a woman, there were others they would speak of only to each other. For these things, a eunuch was no more a proper confidant than a female. Bianca had certain clever disguises she could effect that would bear close, but not intimate, scrutiny. Also, a handsome male could service the women she could not seduce herself. Dimitri would never stand for it, however, and Bianca doubted that she would ever find a male she could trust. Unless he worshipped her as the eunuch did, such a man would want to control her, and if he did worship her, Dimitri would likely dispatch him. The eunuch might scorn male clumsiness, but he was bitterly jealous, hating them all for possessing the manhood that had been cut from his body.

"You arranged a meeting with Madonna Villani?" Dimitri asked.

"Yes, secretly. An agreement has been reached."

"Did you decide to reveal your identity?"

"Yes. I think we can trust her. Although Villani has cowed her physically with his beatings, she is not small spirited. She hates him and will feel nothing but relief at his death. The first son, her favorite, inherits the estate, but she has certain jewels that would make the venture profitable for us. It is almost worth it for the practice alone," Bianca laughed. "I would not want our skills to grow rusty from disuse."

"No, one must keep an edge always, like the blade of a dagger. Sharp, very sharp."

Bianca always chose her commissions carefully. Some of her tasks she had undertaken incognito, her clients never learning her true identity. If they were aware of it, she must make certain not only of her own success, but of their continued silence. The same perception that allowed her to intuit the desires of the men who approached her, from the simplest and most banal to the most perverse, allowed her to perceive who among her other clients could be trusted to keep silent. She quickly detected those who would grow arrogant and brag of the success of the crime, as well as those who would crumble and succumb to guilt. Either weakness could destroy her. With a dozen assassinations to her credit she had misjudged her clients only twice, and both times she had been able to remedy the situation, quickly and lethally, before she herself was implicated.

"Yes, we will we take this commission. I need the diversion," she admitted. "What use is intrigue when there is nothing to discover? Continuing this Savonarola assignment Cesare Borgia has given me has become little better than a penance for the sin of failure."

It was at the Cardinal of Valencia's request that Bianca had come to Florence. Cesare's original hope was that the Friar would prove open to seduction and therefore to ruin. He had a reputation for saintliness, and reputations could be destroyed. It seemed a simple assignment.

When Bianca had first appeared in Florence, she had presented herself to Savonarola as a possibly repentant Magdalene. It was an alluring role she had found quite effective with the clergy in the past. Bianca did not expect to succeed at once with the Friar, but she thought she had chosen the perfect variation. Her approach was tentative, searching, a fragile pride masking the shame of her lustful flesh. She allowed no overt provocation of word or deed to betray her true intent, just the seductive aura of sin emanating from her, a subtle, insidious perfume.

In Savonarola's case it was ineffective, unnervingly so. Although the Friar had seemed receptive when he arrived, he had spoken with her for no more than a few minutes before rising abruptly, eyes blazing in a face livid with rage. That fire made his cold, quiet voice all the more chilling as he pronounced her a vile, deceiving harlot and accused her of being an agent of the Devil. He had ordered her out of his sight, refused to see her again despite tearful entreaties, and warned the other monks against her. There was a young novice who did not heed the warnings and provided her with occasional tidbits, but she had given up on her attempt to debauch the Friar. There had been no hidden lust behind his anger. Bianca told herself that Savonarola's own spies must have acquired some knowledge of her connection with the Borgias and passed it on to him. Knowing that, he could have guessed her appearance was an attempt to seduce him. But it had not felt like that, not at all. He had simply stared at her until his strange burning eyes had incinerated the false mask of penitence she wore.

"It is not your fault the commission the Cardinal gave you has not succeeded," Dimitri consoled her. "Savonarola has no passion. How can you seduce a man who has no passion?"

"Oh, he has passion, but only for preaching."

"That is not a lust of the flesh."

"No, if he lusts for anything, it is for martyrdom. Frankly, I hope the Pope provides him with it."

Bianca resented the failure, even though she had played her own part flawlessly. Nothing could be done with a man who considered women of her profession to be "pieces of meat with eyes." Really, Savonarola was quite loathsome. She had suggested assassination, but Cesare said the repercussions would not be worth it. The seduction would have been a coup he could brag about to his father, the murder would have had to be kept secret. Despite urgings from Dimitri, Bianca considered it unprofessional to murder simply for personal pleasure.

After the debacle, she would have preferred to return to Rome or, better still, resume the lavish life she had led in Venice. Instead, Cesare had asked her to remain and glean whatever intelligence was available in Florence. He could not safely be refused.

Caged, Bianca had begun to look around for independent work to divert herself. Dispensing with Ugolino Villani promised an end to boredom. The anticipation of danger tingled in her nerves. There was a certain satisfaction she achieved with her perfect murders that rivaled and even surpassed the most perfect seductions. Both were displays of power, and she found that they complemented each other in the most intriguing fashion. She had even managed to find some modicum of pleasure with Villani last night, knowing she was going to kill him.

Bianca rose from her bath, the water cascading over her naked body. She waited while Dimitri fetched a towel to dry her, then stepped from the tub, basking under her servant's continued ministrations, the nubby feel of the towel against her skin. Dimitri rubbed her with the oil of roses and dusted her body with fine talc.

"Poison, no?" Dimitri asked, eyeing the corner wardrobe, its false bottom concealing vials of distilled potions and lethal minerals, collections of dried herbs, barks, and berries. Wolfsbane and hemlock, thornapple and mandrake root, foxglove and deadly nightshade waited in the dark.

"Perhaps," Bianca answered, frowning. Dimitri rubbed the crease between her brows, and Bianca smoothed her expression to its usual imperturbable coolness. A goddess carved in white marble. Dimitri slipped a shift of fine linen over her head, then Bianca sat at her dressing table while Dimitri began to arrange her hair.

"Poison," the eunuch murmured again. "A slow poison that eats the belly. His cook says he has terrible gas in his entrails. Poison is good when he is already afflicted with such pains."

"Yes," Bianca said, but she frowned again. It had been necessary to be so circumspect in Florence, and she was feeling a bit restive as a result. A stiletto in a dark alley would suit her current mood more. Stealth, darkness and the sweet rush of bloodlust. "A robbery would be even better—there would be no suspicion cast on his wife or myself. There is too much talk of how he treats her." She smiled at Dimitri. "If we are certain he has not identified us, there is no reason the act need be too quick."

"A gag in the mouth," Dimitri said. "A knife in the belly."

"It should not happen after a visit here. It would be best if I were never questioned."

Dimitri began to dress her, first the lavender undergown and then the chartreuse silk *camorra*. "This is the most important

thing I discovered. Tuesdays he gambles at a house across the
Arno, he and some of the older men, Romolino and Della
Montagna, as well as several of the young *Compagnacci*, the
"bad companions" who loathe Savonarola so much. The place
is not well known, because of the Friar's hatred of gambling."

"Perfect," Bianca said, feeling her blood begin to quicken
with the thought of the hunt. "Let us hope he wins a great deal
of gold, so the purse we steal off his corpse will be a fat one."

6 *The Betrothal Party*

"HAVE you seen Signore di Fabiani yet, Pippa?"
Veronica asked the maid her aunt had sent down
to help fix her hair.

"No, Madonna Veronica, but I hear he's very
handsome, very dashing," the girl answered as
she deftly wove strands of gold through her hair.

"Are all the maids talking about the engagement too? I
imagine they must be."

Pippa giggled. "Of course, Madonna! A betrothal, a wedding is always very exciting. We'll all have a good talk in the
kitchen when the party is under way. Then I can tell the others
about it when I get back to the Palazzo Farentino."

"The Palazzo Farentino?"

"Yes. Your aunt borrowed me from my mistress because I
can do this special plaiting."

"I see," Veronica said, hoping disappointment did not show
in her voice.

Apparently it did not, for the maid chattered on. "The little
madonna is lucky to be marrying such a young and beautiful
husband, no? And I'm sure the signore's family must be very
important."

"Yes, I think they must be." Veronica sighed to herself. Gay
little Pippa would like nothing better than to gossip with her,
but she knew nothing at all. It appeared the mysterious Antonio would remain mysterious awhile longer.

Veronica wished they were not both so ill-prepared to meet each other. Feeling emotionally bruised, she had not been able to deal with Daniele's gleeful mockery at the news of Dorotea's engagement. He had wanted to talk, but she had begged a headache and gone to bed. Once there, Veronica had lain awake for hours before sleep claimed her. She wished she had her own *Tarrocco* deck. She did not want to run to Mama Lucia with this strange turmoil. Not yet. Her newfound desire taunted her, its torment renewing her anger. Anger gave way to shame, and shame transformed into desire, the sweet fearful anticipation of seeing Antonio once more, touching him once more. Round and round, an endless cycle . . . .

Waking from a brief sleep, she'd spent the morning alone, still contemplating her own tormenting emotions and attempting, futilely, to write Antonio a note explaining who she was before she saw him again. Her own confusion made the simple facts impossible. Just who, in truth, was she now? And who was he? Veronica had brooded on the mystery of Antonio's dark and tangled nature for hours before she thought to ask the question in more practical terms. Since her marriage, she had grown familiar with the families who were in the forefront of Florentine politics. Veronica had heard the Fabiani name, but though the family had wealth and power, they kept very much to themselves. She knew little of them, and she had never heard of Antonio.

Eager to acquire knowledge, Veronica had hurried to Daniele's studio. Her cousin always seemed to know everything about everybody, but he was out visiting for the afternoon. She knew Daniele would be at the betrothal party, but he had not reappeared at home by the time she left. Her other early efforts had fared no better. When she'd asked Benito what he knew of the family, he had answered, "Fabiani? I thought the sons killed each other in a duel over a woman." He could not remember what woman, when, or which sons. He was surprised when she told him that Antonio di Fabiani was very much alive.

She had even braved grim and ponderous Simona, the cook, who was baking tarts in the kitchen. Simona had only narrowed her eyes and clucked her tongue at the news of the engagement. When Veronica asked her why she was so disapproving, she'd clamped her mouth shut and said she was "a Christian soul and refused to spread slander." Worse than saying nothing, Veronica thought with exasperation. Every closet in Florence was crammed full with old skeletons, and every Florentine did his best to keep his own quiet while rattling everyone else's. Everyone but Simona, who could not be wheedled out of a single morsel of information. She was one who felt that masters and servants had best keep to their proper places, and if Daniele hadn't paid her so lavishly, she would certainly have gone to a family who showed more sense of propriety. Actually, Veronica suspected the cook was too dour and self-righteous even to gossip with the other servants, much less her employers. Veronica then further insulted her sensibilities by having no appetite for her custard tarts.

"Hold still just a moment more, please, Madonna Veronica," Pippa chided her. "I know you are late, but your hair is almost done. I promise it will be very special."

Trying to calm her turbulent emotions, Veronica forced herself to sit quietly while Pippa finished looping and coiling her hair. She smoothed the folds of her skirt, her fingers stroking the plush fabric. The gown she had chosen to wear to the engagement party was of crushed silk velvet, the color a lustrous garnet red that glowed deep purple in the shadows. The sleeves and low square-cut bodice were stitched with the same dark garnet gems, mingled with the brilliant violet of amethysts and the vivid fire of flashing red rubies. The color of the gown was so rich, so uncompromising, it had always been a challenge to wear it. Always before she had felt like a young girl dressed in a woman's elegant finery. Wearing it tonight, Veronica felt sensuous and defiant. It gave her courage, like an exquisite soft armor that drew her own strength to the surface and protected her vulnerability.

"There," Pippa declared, obviously pleased with her efforts.

Veronica lifted the mirror of silvered Venetian glass and contemplated Pippa's work. Her thick hair was swirled up, little strands of it interwoven with thin gold chains set with the same gems that adorned the dress. With her elaborate hair style and her eyes and lips tinted with cosmetics, she appeared worldly and sophisticated, exactly how she wanted to look. "It's perfect, Pippa."

"You are so beautiful this evening, Madonna Veronica. There will be no one more lovely, not even Madonna Dorotea."

"Thank you, Pippa," she said to the maid.

"Where are the matching shoes, my lady? I do not see them here."

"All the shoes were packed in one case, the green one. It is in Roberto's room."

"I'll fetch them."

Alone, Veronica gazed into the mirror, and her image stared back with a direct, luminous gaze. Pale and translucent, her skin gleamed against the rich red of the gown. Despite what Pippa said, Veronica knew she was not really beautiful. She did not have the classic features that were the ideal. Her eyes and her mouth were too large, the lines of cheek and jaw too angular. But tonight she felt beautiful. It was love that made her feel so radiant, so gloriously alive. Love that filled her with this light that shone from out her eyes, her skin. Love. Antonio. Antonio di Fabiani . . . her lover. Was that too much to hope for? So many Florentine wives had lovers; surely he would be hers. It would not be difficult to arrange meetings, romantic trysts in quiet spots. She had lived so long on dreams and duty, now real passion was within her grasp. Was it not possible to claim, finally, some happiness as a woman? To discover the mysteries of desire with this man who filled her with such sweet flame?

Veronica laughed nervously, full of longing and apprehension. She was presuming so much. She had not even found a way to warn Antonio of her real identity before he appeared here tonight. She had never sent a missive to a lover. How was it managed discreetly? So simple a thing, and it was impossible. She had tried to write a note to prepare him, but the words had seemed trite, or coy, or reproachful. Each attempt was more graceless than the last, so she had written nothing, which was the worst of all. The whole situation was so complicated, so preposterous. He was to marry Dorotea, and she felt only dismay and pity at the thought. It was not Dorotea but Bianca who was her true rival. She had to compete with the most accomplished courtesan in Florence.

But she must show some restraint, especially when she had been so wanton with him. What would he think of her when he realized she was supposed to be well bred, not some poor girl from the streets Daniele had found to pose for him? Her cheeks flushed with shame, then anger, as she remembered again the gold coins he had left. Only he had not known who she was, had assumed her status to be something entirely different. If he thought her no more than a model, of course he would give her money. A poor girl would expect some reward, even if her passion were not feigned, and Daniele's model had been rewarded extravagantly. Two ducats were as many months' wages for most. Why must she make them an insult?

No, the gold had been a deliberate affront. She had seen his face change, closing her off from him. Denying her. He had used the money to distance himself from the passion they had shared, to demean it. How could she still want a man who treated her so? Having treated her so, would he even want her again? But Antonio had felt the same passion she felt, she was sure of it. How could he not? He must—was he not her Prince of Cups? He must still want her. She could not bear it if he did not!

Veronica laid down the mirror, gasping, the rush of contradictory emotions making her feel dizzy. She bit her lips to quell the rising tears. She had not known love would be like this, sweeping her this way and that. She felt exhilarated, exalted, one instant, trembling with fear or fury the next. Yes, trembling. Her hand was shaking. She was afraid to go into the ballroom now. She would make an utter fool of herself by losing her temper or bursting into tears. Love was terrifying. This woman's passion made her feel like a lost child, but as a child she had never felt so frightened, so uncertain.

"Here are the shoes," Pippa announced, reappearing in the doorway. "The green case was not so easy to find. It was under a towel, with the little kitten asleep on top of it. What is its name?"

"Marco Polo, the explorer," Veronica said, amazed at how calm her voice sounded. She stood, only a little unsteady, and slid her feet into the gold-embroidered satin slippers.

"Perfect," Pippa said. "Now you are ready."

"Yes," Veronica replied, drawing herself straight and turning to the door. She was not ready, not ready at all, but she could not bear to wait a second longer.

———

The ballroom was brilliantly conceived, Antonio thought, looking around him. The effect was rich and festive, with the walls of deep rose accented with gilded scrollwork complementing the wide expanse of the marble mosaic floor. The marbles were the finest dark green from Prato, pure white from Carrara, pink from the Maremma, set in a complicated geometric pattern. They were the same marbles used in the facade of the Duomo and had been chosen for that reason, no doubt.

Returning his attention to the people in the room, Antonio scanned the guests for new arrivals. He had met everyone, at least briefly, and did not bother to approach anyone. Someone would come to him soon enough, and he was growing weary of the repetitive social pleasantries. He hoped supper would be announced soon. Two more hours—no, he would have to make it three—and he would be free to retire. Sleep would be more amusing than most of the company. Tomorrow he had to ride about the estate with Luigi and survey certain property that would come with Dorotea's dowry.

The voluptuous brunette in amber satin was eyeing him again. He did not acknowledge the look. He had no interest in that sort of entanglement, not even one equipped with such a magnificent cleavage. There was a sudden overabundance of females in his life, all demanding attention one way or another. There was the problem of Dorotea and all the duties that entailed. He'd almost forgotten to send the camellias to Bianca this morning, and all because of the auburn haired model. He had cursed himself since for not asking the little witch her name. It might help to dilute her power if he could simply think "Sophia" or "Diana" instead of being inundated by images of her. He was constantly remembering the way she gazed into his eyes so seriously, the way her long white limbs had twined about him when he lifted her against the wall. When he entered her, their flesh had seemed to melt and fuse into one entity . . . .

The sight of Daniele entering the ballroom pulled Antonio from his reverie. Immediately, he had to subdue the desire to go question the artist about his model. It would be the height of vulgarity under the present circumstances. If his obsession held, he could easily pay another visit to the studio. He frowned, annoyed with himself and the entire situation. An experienced courtesan was more to his needs, but neither his deliberately conjured memories of his torrid night with Bianca, nor the day's preparations for this party had been able to distract his mind for long from thoughts of the sweetly wanton redhead. She had such a striking face, with those thickly lashed eyes and strong brows, that full, passionate mouth.

Yes, her mouth was luscious, but what if she had no conversation? A brief encounter could be savored for its sensuality alone, a gift of pleasure exchanged between male and female. If he was to spend any time with a woman, he must be able to converse with her. He did not frequent courtesans for their amorous skills alone. Still, he would swear the girl was intelligent at least—her eyes had that vital spark. Perhaps she had some enrichment from her associations with the artists. He remembered distinctly the husky contralto of her voice, though she had spoken so few words to him. The accent was almost cultivated . . . . as if one could tell after such brief communication. This was nonsense. If he was going to obsess about the girl, he should find her again and let the passion burn itself out, hot and quick.

He hoped Daniele was not her lover or, if he was, that she was of no particular significance. The costume continued to disturb him. True, Daniele had been painting a monk, but why the silly beard? It seemed to Antonio that they must be playing some sort of sexual game together. Had Savonarola's preaching frightened the man so that he was attempting to act against his own nature, resulting in this bizarre compromise, a woman dressed as a boy? Perhaps he dallied with the female sex occasionally, and the monk's costume was only a tasty bit of revenge on the Friar. Daniele's oddities were no concern of his, of course. He certainly did not want to alienate the only member of Dorotea's family he liked so far by putting them in conflict over this disheveled street urchin. His actions the other day had been discourteous to say the least, ravishing his host's probable inamorata. He should simply forget the girl, but that was proving far easier said than done. There, Daniele had noticed him and was waving an arm in greeting, like an exuberant stork. Antonio smiled and gestured him over.

"So, we are to be relatives?" Daniele said, grinning at him impishly.

Antonio's smile twisted ruefully. "A fact that had not been mentioned to me before my visit. My father was most embarrassed when I mentioned I had been to see your studio." There had been several revelations in that cursory conversation. Besides the disreputable artist, his father had confessed his new family also possessed an idiot son, a Gypsy fortuneteller, and the *selvaggia*, the wild girl, Veronica. *"Selvaggia?"* Antonio had asked, amused by the situation. "Incorrigible little savage. She rides astride," his father had informed him with such disdain that Antonio wondered if it was men the girl straddled rather than horses. He was tempted to pursue these bizarre aberrations further, but his father was only concerned with Luigi Della Montagna's political influence.

Daniele heaved an exaggerated sigh. "I am one of the black sheep of the family. A humble artisan."

"You do not hold, then, with the modern theory that painting is the equal of poetry and music, rather than a purely mechanical accomplishment?"

"Of course it is the equal of the other arts, and a fit occupation for any gentleman with the talent for it," Daniele exclaimed. "It is no help that Plato, whose philosophy is so venerated, scorned painters as lowly imitators of reality. Not even the greatest minds are always right, and he was wrong in this. We are not mere artisans, any more than the poets who lay pen to paper to express the images in their minds. Many intellectual skills are necessary for our work, as well as manual dexterity. Perspective depends on precise mathematics, and what is purer than that?"

"What indeed?" Antonio asked, amused by Daniele's passionate outburst.

"Ah, I see the devious glint in your eye now. In future, I shall be more wary when you ask deliberately provoking questions with such studied innocence." He smiled wickedly. "I will tell you one of my deepest secrets, Antonio."

"Yes?" Antonio smiled in return, though he felt a ridiculous flutter of apprehension and knew he was afraid Daniele would say something about his model.

"Working out the geometry of perspective gives me the most fearful headache," Daniele moaned. "It is color I love, texture, capturing the essence of emotion—not the creation of these proportionally receding vistas that are so in demand!"

Antonio burst out laughing, then smothered his response with a brief cough.

"I do it very well, you understand. Only I do not like to do it! Ah, there is Mama Lucia with Roberto," Daniele exclaimed suddenly, gesturing to a dark wizened little woman dressed all in black. "Pardon me, I must greet her."

"The Gypsy I was also just informed was among my new relations?" Antonio asked, intrigued. The old lady managed to look both fragile and formidable. She stared at him boldly from far across the room, and Antonio thought she had the most penetrating eyes he'd ever seen.

"The blackest of the black sheep you will be inflicted with, marrying into this fold. You will have to have her tell your fortune. It will be a revelation, I assure you."

"Yes, you must introduce me. And is that Veronica then, the blonde woman standing next to her by the window?" She did not look especially wild.

"No, why should you think . . . ." Daniele began with a puzzled air, then smiled archly. "Of course, you have not been formally introduced to Veronica, have you?"

"No," Antonio replied, puzzled in turn by Daniele's odd expression. "You consider her one of the black sheep as well?"

"Of course. Veronica is the black lamb. Come, I will take you to Mama Lucia."

At that moment, Luigi appeared with a business associate he insisted on introducing. Daniele wiggled his eyebrows and left. Antonio greeted the new guest, Ugolino Villani. He was a plump, florid man who did himself no service dressing in a long, pleated *houppelande* of bright pink brocade trimmed with gold bullion. His wife, a tall, gaunt woman in gray, hovered behind him, an oppressive shadow. Luigi left, and Ugolino began to lecture Antonio loudly on his personal preference in trade routes. The man was full of secondhand theories he presented as fact. He was pompous, belligerent, and ignorant. If possible, Antonio disliked him more than Luigi, and he was pleased when the mismatched couple took themselves off again.

Glancing across the room at Dorotea, Antonio wished yet again that his father had chosen a different bride for him. There was no spark between them at all, not of mind or body. He did not really expect passion, but his marriage looked to be remarkably boring. The girl was certainly pretty in a delicate, restrained way, but shy and withdrawn, with minimal education. Most Florentine girls of good family received some instruction in the classics. Dorotea had little beyond her scripture and stitchery. He'd spent half an hour in difficult conversation with the girl and her wary, protective mother, and had been glad of the chance to circulate again among the other guests. He would have to rejoin them when supper was announced. Maria caught his eye, and he bowed to her. She turned and whispered to Dorotea, who flashed him a brief startled glance, then dropped her eyes and curtsied. Her skittish reaction looked more like apprehension than modesty. Was it fear of their wedding night—or perhaps it was tales of his scandalous past that filled her with such trepidation?

"Are you planning to kill this wife as well?" a brittle voice asked, echoing his thoughts. "Madonna Dorotea looks harmless enough, but you never know what wickedness might lurk within that childish frame."

Antonio stiffened slightly, then turned to greet his brother's widow. "Laudomia."

"You haven't answered my question, Antonio." Barely chin high, Laudomia glared up at him, her pale blue eyes glazed with malice. The little wren had become a shrike. Her second marriage must have given her no happiness, that she could carry this enmity for so many years. If anything, she seemed to loathe him more, and her loathing confirmed his suspicions.

"I did not kill Beatrice," Antonio said quietly.

"She tripped and fell, did she? Broke her pretty little neck so conveniently for us all? You expect me to believe that?"

"I expect nothing, Laudomia," he replied coldly. "I am

simply answering your question. I did not kill Beatrice. I do not murder women.''

''Not even when they mean to murder you, Antonio?''

''I have considered making an exception in that case. So far, I have only had to kill the assassins you sent after me.''

''Someone has been trying to kill you? It gives me great pleasure to hear it. But why should you think I ordered it? There must be many who hate you as much as I.''

''A friend of Alessandro's might have brought a guard or two along, but he would have been there for the kill. The first assassin came alone. When he tried to dispose of me, he said, ''Your family sends you greetings, Antonio di Fabiani.'' Upon consideration, only you would have demanded such a melodramatic commentary. The deed alone would have sufficed for anyone else.''

''How clever you must think yourself.''

''The next time there were four assassins. Rather more difficult to handle but not, as you see, impossible.'' Not with Giacomo's timely aid, but Antonio did not tell her that. ''I assumed you were overcompensating for the error of sending just one man the first time. I confess, I am uncertain if you have sent others. There are always brigands about, but there is a different flavor to the violence when your life rather than your purse is the main objective.''

''You have traveled widely. I could send my greeting only when I knew where you lived.''

''And there must have been certain difficulties. Assassins do not frequent your usual social circle.''

''I managed,'' she answered, giving no clue if she had help. ''Nor am I done yet. You will have to kill me, Antonio, to be safe from me. But I will give you a respite, for your mother's sake only. She is dying. I would not have her final weeks made wretched, knowing her one remaining son had gone to the grave before her. Mark the length of her days well, for they are your last.''

''I will remember.''

''I wish you joy in your second marriage, Antonio. The same joy I have found in mine. Perhaps you will be grateful that it will be so brief.'' Her eyes glittered wildly for a second, but Antonio did not know if it was with tears or the flashing edge of violence. Her voice was a vicious hiss as she whispered, "I buried my heart with Alessandro, buried it alive. But it did not die, Antonio. My hate keeps it alive, beating in the darkness of the grave. It will not die till you are dead as well. Only then will it rest in peace."

Laudomia turned and left him alone. Antonio beckoned a servant and took a goblet of wine from his tray, sipping at it while he regained his composure. He felt as though Laudomia had spat in his face, and resisted the urge to wipe away the invisible spittle. He still had not decided what to do about Laudomia. It was difficult, having so pitiful an enemy.

"Was Laudomia disagreeable?" another voice asked, one he did not recognize. Frowning slightly, he turned to meet this new adversary, a fair-haired young man. His countenance was handsome and vaguely familiar with its wide mouth and leaf green eyes. Quickly he sifted through possibilities. "Stefano?" he inquired, with reasonable assurance.

"You remember me, cousin Antonio. I'm flattered. I was only a boy when you . . . left Florence."

The young man's manner was amiable, but his conversation was ill-considered. Stefano was to have acquired Antonio's inheritance if he had not returned. Perhaps the loss of it rankled? Or perhaps Antonio had become too sensitive after Laudomia's malevolent greeting? He had expected to run the gauntlet of Dorotea's relatives, rather than his own.

"I'm glad you're back, truly I am," Stefano said ingenuously.

Luigi reappeared to inform him supper would be announced in a moment, and Antonio introduced him to his cousin. Stefano absented himself quickly, which was a point in his favor. Antonio was inclined to like anyone who disliked his future father-in-law. Sober, Luigi had a shrewd head for business and politics. That was all his own father cared about, that and Luigi's once noble lineage, though there was little nobility in the man. Already he was drinking too much, talking too loudly. Luigi had probably been an extremely handsome man in his youth. There were remnants of it yet, though his appearance had coarsened and he looked fleshy and dissipated, slothful despite his rich garments.

"What do you think of my little Dorotea?" Luigi leered and nudged his arm.

"She is lovely," Antonio replied honestly.

"Prim little thing, but she'll be a nice tight squeeze when you bed her. If you're lucky, she won't sour as fast as her mother."

With a surge of bitterness, Antonio wondered if his father had chosen this family with the sole purpose of punishing him for his sins.

Suddenly, he felt a compelling urge to turn away from Luigi, not in revulsion against the man but towards something else. It was the strangest sensation, almost the instinctive warning prickle of danger, yet not that either. Something subtler, softer, an awareness, an invisible beckoning touch.

Beside him, Luigi turned, his eyes narrowed intently, and he said, "Here comes Veronica."

———

She recognized Antonio instantly, even with his back to her, simply from the elegant stance of his body as he stood talking to Luigi. His clothing was silver gray, smoke to her dark red jewel fire. Aware of her regard, Antonio turned and recognized her as swiftly. He straightened, drawing back a little, a physical gesture of denial. For the briefest instant, his eyes went wide, disbelief flaring within them. Then the polished mask fell into place, though his eyes did not leave hers as she crossed the floor. As Veronica approached him, the room, the world itself seemed to condense to only the two of them. Energy pulsed like a heartbeat around her, drumming louder with each step that brought her closer to him. Face to face, she looked up into the imperturbable social mask, through it, beyond the semipolite curiosity and feigned boredom, to what it covered . . . amazement, barely suppressed anger, the flickering heat of desire. Deeper still, to the old embers of pain burning within his eyes.

"My eldest son's wife," Luigi said. "Veronica, this is Antonio di Fabiani."

Veronica saw a brief flicker in Antonio's eyes as well. So he had been told about Roberto. Cursing Luigi's obtrusive presence, she curtsied and acknowledged the introduction, "Signore Antonio."

"Madonna, this is a surprise I'd not expected. A surprise and, of course, a pleasure. Your presence is stunning . . . astonishing." His voice was cold as he paid her the courtly compliment, but his eyes raked over her with a hot flare that bordered on insult.

"I don't remember that dress." The rough edge to Luigi's voice, the shadowed emotion on his face, was the one thing that could shatter Veronica's concentration on Antonio. It was an emotion she had hoped never to see there again. Lust. Instantly, intuitively, she knew why. Luigi's mauling had roused nothing but her disgust. Antonio had awakened her sexually. She was a woman now. Luigi sensed the change in her, and it excited the animal in him. He was drunk again, drunk enough to forget both his vulgar repentance and her fierce retaliation.

"It needs some fine jewelry, a necklace for that white throat. Rubies, bloodred rubies." His slurred voice promised them to her, insinuating the cost. He stepped forward, reaching to touch her throat. Veronica put her hand there ahead of him, warding him off. Luigi's hand hovered in the air. His eyes met hers, filled with lewd cunning. He leaned forward and whispered so low only she could hear, "Do witches . . . wear rubies?"

The soft-voiced menace froze her where she stood. Luigi lowered his hand and Veronica gasped as his fingers trailed across her breast, a calculated accident. He chuckled and drew his hand back, rubbing his fingers across his lips.

"Excuse me, I must join my bride-to-be," Antonio said, his voice, his face filled with contempt as he surveyed the exchange between them. He turned and left her alone with Luigi. Veronica stood there, wanting to curse him for abandoning her, wanting to weep till her heart was washed of its pain. Dimly, she heard one of the servants announcing supper, saw the guests begin to move through the arched doorway to the room beyond.

"Come sit with me. I'll make a place for you beside me," Luigi breathed in her ear, as if offering her the seat were an honor. Veronica saw Maria watching them, her expression as contemptuous as Antonio's. Luigi slipped an arm about her waist, his fingers nudging the underside of her breast. She shuddered and pulled away from him.

"I'll sit with my family," Veronica told him curtly, and went through the door alone.

The gilded dining room was ablaze with candles, and a great feast was spread out on the table. There was honey duck with oranges, roast lamb, chicken stuffed with sausage, apples and hazelnuts. There were platters of tender ravioli filled with goat cheese and dressed with olive oil and herbs, plates of buttery cabbage and sweet anise, and a pyramid of baked onions wrapped in golden pastry. For dessert, dishes of fine *maiolica* displayed sugared almonds, preserved figs, spicy pear tarts, and an almond torte layered with apricot jam. Luigi was once again the proud father, the generous host, calling for toasts to the happy couple. Veronica could hardly force the cup to her lips, much less drink the wine. She sat between Mama Lucia and Roberto, picking morosely at the food on her plate, watching Antonio surreptitiously beneath her lowered lashes. He did not glance at her once.

She had to give him credit, his manners were perfectly polished. He chatted occasionally with the guests closest to him, and he was most solicitous of Dorotea. Her sister-in-law looked appealing in her dress of cream and gold brocade, her brown hair braided into intricate loops threaded with ropes of tiny pearls. Pretty and fragile, she still looked a child, with only the faintest hint of the emerging woman. Her demeanor was subdued, and she could barely bring herself to look at her future husband, her eyes darting to survey him as he enticed her attention with tempting pastries and fragments of conversation. Antonio managed to make it seem there were no awkward pauses, filling in the long spaces between her monosyllabic answers with his courtier's anecdotes. Dorotea had no more sense of humor than Maria, so Antonio's manner became more sedate in dealing with her.

Finally, he managed to kindle her interest. It must be talk of Savonarola. The Friar and his sermons were Dorotea's one passion. She and Maria attended every Mass that was given, events Veronica was sure Dorotea had anticipated far more than she had this party. As Dorotea's fervor grew, Antonio's attentiveness became more perfunctory. Veronica could sense it from where she sat, from the slight shifts in posture and expression. He was polite, but her zeal obviously made a poor impression. Dorotea was totally oblivious to his withdrawal. She leaned closer and placed a small pale hand on his arm.

Veronica's heart skipped a beat. She did not know if *jealousy* was the right word for the strained misery she felt now. Certainly she had been jealous the other day, fiercely jealous of the beautiful courtesan Antonio had caressed. She could see no desire in him for Dorotea—but he would wed her and take her to his bed. She would know his gentle caresses. Even now, Dorotea could reach out and touch his arm so simply. Veronica had a sense of hopelessness and absurdity in the social contract of marriage that had bound her to Roberto and would now tie Antonio to Dorotea. She understood the practicalities of fortune and property, but they meant little to her. The meshing of those two individuals was ridiculous. Marriage should be a sacrament, flesh made soul and soul made flesh. It had been corrupted to earthly uses. How sad.

Husband, she thought. No, never husband, though her heart chose to claim him as such. But lover, perhaps, if she had not lost him already. He had looked at her with such anger, such scorn. But she had seen desire in his face as well. No, she had not lost him yet and she would fight to keep him. Veronica only wished she better understood the weapons of love.

Beside her Mama Lucia said, "So, he's the one you've been waiting for, is he? Your Prince of Cups."

Veronica turned to her, startled, though that was witless of her. What had she expected? Mama Lucia always saw right through her. Was it only Mama Lucia? Veronica prayed she hadn't been making a fool of herself. She had never been in love before. How did one manage to pretend that everything was normal, ordinary?

"Don't worry, you're staring discreetly enough. Those nice long lashes of yours are a great help for spying. It would be clever of you say a word or two to the other guests, though. And eat something, don't just stir your food about." Eyeing Antonio boldly, she sniffed, "Not my type, but he's handsome, I'll give you that. The eyes alone are worth sinning for, and he knows it too, conceited devil. Not that they'll do him a bit of good with that frost-bitten bud of a girl. She's not one

who'll ever blossom. I imagine he knows that as well. He'll
sense where he's wanted, that one." She peered at Veronica.
"Got you all tied up in knots already, has he? How long has
this been going on? Is he the reason you've not been to see me
lately?"

Veronica dropped her eyes and flushed. There were two different answers to Mama Lucia's questions, and she did not
know how to begin to explain. Not here and now.

"Never mind, don't tell me. I can see just from looking at
him that he's too much trouble by half. But what's the use,
men always are. Well, no one in love ever listens to good
advice. Not even their own, much less anyone else's. But you
know where I am if you want me, child. Or the cards." Her
black eyes grew very bright, and she whispered conspiratorially, "If he hurts you, I'll make him sorry. I've a curse for
hives. I've never used it, but I'm sure it will work."

Veronica couldn't help but giggle. She leaned over and
kissed Mama Lucia's cheek. She forced herself to eat what
was on her plate. She was glad she did, for Luigi called for
another round of toasts, demanding they all drink, and yet
another, and this time she complied, hoping it would relax her.
A sweet dessert wine was served as well. Roberto drank his
own small glass and managed to steal her goblet too, when she
wasn't looking. She hadn't the heart to scold him when she'd
been giving him so little attention. He was happy enough with
the wonderful food Benito cut up for him, though the wine
soon had him nodding over his plate. She had Benito escort
him to bed before he fell asleep and had to be carried.

With a final toast, Luigi announced there would be music
and dancing in the ballroom. The guests rose from the table,
some with eager exclamations, some with groans of dismay,
depending on the amount of food they'd consumed. Luigi
spoke sharply to Maria, who was clutching his sleeve. He
pushed her hand away and approached Veronica purposefully.
Maria hastened after him, infuriated. "This is outrageous. You
know I did not want such a gluttonous feast with Lent so close
at hand. Neither did Dorotea. Better this offensive luxury
should be fed to the bonfire of the vanities. Savonarola does
not approve of such lavish entertaining, nor does he condone
profane music or dancing."

"Can't play the *Te Deum* at a betrothal party, can we?" Luigi snarled at his wife. "Go to confession if you must, and fast for a month in penance for everyone else's sins as well as your own. But suffer in silence, woman. My guests will enjoy themselves and go home well fed."

Maria scowled at him but said nothing more, drawing her thin lips into a thinner line like a pale pink scar, then turned her back on him and marched off. As Luigi stood watching his wife's stiff-backed withdrawal, Veronica rose quietly from her chair, trying to slip away unnoticed. Luigi rounded on her quickly, taking hold of her arm. His voice dripped cloying sweetness. "You're so beautiful tonight, Veronica. That color is perfect for you. Red is for passion."

"Let go of my arm," she hissed at him. He only gripped it harder, twisting a little so she had to suppress a gasp of pain. The feverish glitter in his eyes frightened her.

"Why don't you dance with me, Veronica? I was a good dancer in my day." Luigi leaned close and muttered into her ear, "You might learn a thing or two." He leered at her as if she were one of his whores. If he did not let her go in one minute, she would grab a goblet of wine and fling it in his face.

"Madonna Veronica," Antonio's voice interrupted smoothly, "you promised to dance with me."

"You should be dancing with Dorotea," Luigi growled at him.

"She takes no pleasure in such frivolities."

"Then keep her company," Luigi snapped.

"I would not want her to think that our house will be without music and dancing, though she need not participate. I am sure you can appreciate my position," Antonio answered him, taking hold of Veronica's other hand. "This lady will lead the dance instead."

For a moment they all stood in a frozen tableau that seemed at once foolish and dangerous to Veronica. The music commenced, a lively counterpoint to the tension, and Luigi released her arm. Unpredictable as always when he drank, now he looked simply befuddled, his anger muted to petulance. Antonio led her back into the ballroom and out onto the dance floor, joining the other couples who had risen when the music began. Relief filled her at his swift intervention. "Thank you."

"You should choose your lovers with more care, Madonna, and avoid the ones liable to make an unpleasant scene."

"How dare you!" Veronica gasped, shock sweeping away gratitude or even denial. She stopped completely for a second, but Antonio's practiced skill kept her moving mechanically through the intricate pattern of *La Spanga*.

"You feign indignation very well, Madonna. However, there is a way a man has of looking at a woman he has already sampled, as opposed to one he still hopes to enjoy, which tells the truth far better."

Sampled, perhaps, she thought with fury, *but not enjoyed.* He was laughing silently at her anger, his dark eyes flashing with vicious mockery. She glared at him, her pride, her sense of justice outraged. How could she give him the truth when he misinterpreted everything so perversely? Why rescue her from Luigi's bruising grip to inflict a more painful bruise on her soul? Oh, it hurt, it hurt to have him despise her, unjustly or not! She must hold on to the anger, it was her only shield against his cruelty. If she must, she could play this cynical game as well as he did.

"The same as the look on your face now?" she challenged him brazenly as they circled each other.

"That depends on the look, Madonna."

"Smug and condescending."

"And lustful?" he asked, arching an eyebrow. But his voice went deep and rough at the edges.

"Greedy, at least."

He smiled at that, a wolf's smile. "Ravenous. Insatiable."

"That was not my experience," she countered sharply. "You hardly lingered to savor what was offered."

"You forget, I had a banquet to attend elsewhere that evening." Following the pattern of the dance, he spun her under his arm, drew her close again. "Next time, I promise I shall give . . . your offering . . . my undivided attention."

"You have not been given a second invitation."

"But I know you are generous with your bounty. You would not turn me away if I appeared starving at your doorstep."

"Knowing the other banquets you might easily attend to sate your hunger? Why should I bother?"

"Why? Because I do bother you, Madonna, as you bother me. And knowing you, I know you would not turn me away."

"Would I not?" she challenged, her eyes flashing at his presumption. He did not know her at all.

"No, you will not," he said, making it a threat. A promise.

The music ended, and Daniele came over to ask her for the next dance. Antonio bowed and left. Veronica was grateful for her cousin's chatter about his day. At the moment, she hadn't the heart to question him about the Fabiani family. As they moved through the final steps, Veronica saw Antonio dancing with a beautiful brunette in a dress of dark gold satin, a glittering topaz necklace enhancing the swell of her full white bosom. That was the wrong stone, surely, Veronica thought. Topaz was worn to ward off impure love. Daniele departed, and Veronica forced herself to remain in the ballroom, to dance *Il Canario* with a young man named Stefano Simonetta, who proved to be Antonio's cousin. He flirted with her while she smiled back politely, then with an old gentleman who lamented the passing of the Medici dynasty. Next there was a friend of Frederigo's who thought Savonarola inspiring—but not enough to become a celibate monk, Heaven forbid. She was thankful that Luigi ignored her now, having found a plump widow more responsive to his attentions.

She danced with Daniele again, and in a disquieting echo, Veronica saw Antonio had returned to the brunette once more. The sharp claws of jealousy closed and tightened on every vital organ in her body, pain and fury knotted together. Stefano sought her out once more, charming and handsome with his tousled golden hair and open face. She accepted, wondering if she could make Antonio jealous. She forced herself to flirt, but it was not worth the effort. The floor might as well have been strewn with glass. Each step was agony, but she must smile and smile and smile.

7 The Confrontation

AFTER two more dances, Veronica left the ball-room. She meant to go see how Roberto was, but first she climbed the stair to the tower near her room and let the chill night air cool her fevered emotions. The aching pain was back, sharper now than anger or jealousy. Antonio's scorn wounded her, despite its injustice. He had no right to judge her, but somehow it was worse that he despised her for something that was no fault of her own. He thought her wanton. Yet how many women had known him for pleasure or for payment? The irony was bitter. He had been the first with her, but Luigi's brutal fumbling had shattered the proof of it. If he had appeared a month earlier, she would still have had that sacrificial bit of flesh to offer him along with her new-minted passion.

But what did it matter? It was as a woman she loved Antonio. It was an accident that she had kept that physical mark of innocence long after it had been bargained away without her choice in marriage. It might have been claimed by the husband she never wanted, it might have been given to another out of curiosity or affection or loneliness. She might have desired another. Only Veronica knew she had never desired anyone but Antonio. She had waited, and her Prince of Cups had appeared. The final card turned over to end the *Tarocco* reading, saying "Here is your destiny." But her destiny denied her, mocked her.

Others loved desperately and were scorned. The pangs of unrequited love were mourned in song and poem. Was it her pride that made her assume that he must feel as she felt? Or was it simply that she loved and so believed, as countless others had foolishly believed, that she must be loved in return? Well, perhaps he did care. Perhaps not. For now she would simply see to Roberto. If she could barely think of anything but Antonio, there were still other things that she must do.

Veronica went back down the stairs, opened the door to Roberto's room, and found herself in the midst of another small crisis. Marco Polo had gone exploring again and could not be found. Roberto lay on the bed in tears, while Bombol trotted back and forth whimpering almost as pitifully. Benito was looking rather frayed about the edges.

"I'm sorry, Madonna Veronica. I don't know what happened."

"It's not your fault, Benito. Perhaps the maid left the door open. You go hunt for the kitten while I sit with Roberto."

"I hope I'll find him soon."

"So do I. But between the wine and the tears, Roberto will fall asleep soon, lost kitten or no."

"Maybe I can get someone to help. I won't be able to look in all the rooms."

"I know. Do the best you can. And ask Pippa or one of the other maids to come help me undress when they're free." She sat down on the bed and put her arms about Roberto, who buried his head in her lap.

"But what about the party, my lady?" Benito whispered urgently. "Don't you want to dance?"

"That's all right. I don't really want to return. Not now. Bring the kitten back if you find it. If not, just go and enjoy yourself."

"Thank you, Madonna Veronica. I'll hunt for Marco Polo now. Later . . . well, there's a bit of gambling tonight in the stables. You can send for me there if you need me."

"Good luck," she wished him. She turned her attention back to Roberto, stroking his back, finding some comfort in comforting him. She wished she could cry out her troubles so simply, so wholeheartedly, and forget them as easily the next day.

But she knew she could not bear to surrender one memory of Antonio, sweet or bitter.

———

Antonio entered his room and stripped off his jeweled doublet. Where the hell was Giacomo? Off tumbling one of the kitchen maids, he presumed. Well, he wished him joy of it. No, not wenching, he remembered—gambling. Giacomo had asked leave to join a game of dice tonight. Antonio hung up the doublet in the wardrobe himself. The room he'd been given was one of the most lavish in the house. The walnut furniture was ornately carved. The four-poster bed, the walls, were hung with rich tapestries of hunting scenes in subdued tones of blue and gold. The richness, the comfort, should have been welcoming, but the fire had died down and the room was cold. Chilly in his shirt of thin white silk, he added kindling and a small log to the embers and went to the chair to pick up a sleeveless jerkin of embossed leather lined with gray fox. There was a squall of outrage, and a black and white kitten tumbled onto the floor. The fur must have provided a fine nest until he had so rudely dumped it forth. Antonio lifted the kitten by the scruff of its neck and surveyed it. Staring back at him with large chartreuse eyes, it reached out and batted his nose with a dainty pink paw.

"You are lucky you've learned to sheath your claws," Antonio told it. He upended the kitten and raised its tail. "You are also lucky you're male. I am not in the mood for female company. As it is, you may stay and entertain me."

Antonio put the kitten on the floor. He slipped into the warm jerkin and returned to the wardrobe. A moment's ferreting about produced one of his fringed riding gauntlets. Antonio sat on the rug by the fireplace and engaged the kitten in a vigorous game of kill-the-glove. It was a spirited little creature, and its antics did improve his humor considerably. He rolled it over and tickled its furry belly, which resulted in a brief bout of kill-the-hand. After a final valiant attack, the kitten consented to be petted, purring loudly as Antonio fondled its ears.

"I am a liar," Antonio informed his companion. "The problem is that I am most definitely in the mood for female company." His own hand offered the simplest solution to his frustration, an immediate and uncomplicated way to ease the seething tension that permeated his mind and body. The brunette in amber satin was an eager widow, not some man's wife, and she had made it abundantly clear she would be eager to alleviate any such tension he might display. It was not as if he had no options available.

"I am in the mood," he clarified to the kitten, "for very

specific female company." For the *selvaggia*, the wild girl. Far wilder, it seemed, than he had first imagined.

Antonio had to admit he was still thoroughly incensed, both with himself and with the Lady Veronica. The red-headed witch had a name now, at least. Why were women so endlessly conniving? She could have easily forewarned him of her true identity. A brief discreet note would have sufficed. But no, she had to make an entrance in her new persona, have him gaping at her like a besotted adolescent. He felt a total fool. Why should it have occurred to him that Daniele's smudged "model" was the lady of the house? Why hide her identity? It was a bizarre costume, but surely the artist could have introduced her, instead of playing silly games. Daniele was hardly a man for strict propriety. Still one never knew, it could be as simple, as innocent, as not wanting to put her at a disadvantage in front of strangers. Unless it was all part of some not so innocent game they were playing. Perhaps Veronica was mistress of the house as well as lady. Why not, living with Daniele and married to that simple child of a husband?

And then there was Luigi. What had he said to her, that she would allow him to touch her so intimately? Antonio had wanted to throttle the man when he saw his fingers caressing her breast. That would have been a fine scene, attacking his father-in-law-to-be at the betrothal party. He had not trusted himself to interfere the first time, and should probably not have done so the second, but Veronica obviously regretted the liaison. Could Luigi have coerced her? How? She had male relatives to protect her, if she wished it. Was she so promiscuous she simply could not help herself? Did she bed them all, the son, his father, and her cousin as well? His own cousin, Stefano, appeared to be next in line. For all he knew, she coupled with half of Florence. Why could he not rid his mind of a woman who was so obviously trouble?

The kitten squawked and squirmed in his grip. He must have been mauling the poor creature. Antonio lay on his back and placed the kitten on his chest. "My apologies," he told it, petting it gently once again. It eyed him distrustfully for a moment but finally succumbed to having its chin scratched.

There was a knock at the door. Antonio sat up and called out, "Come in."

Giacomo poked his head in the door. His eyes widened when he saw the kitten. "Benito, look here," he called over his shoulder, and a second head, amiably ugly, like a wrinkled frog, joined him in the doorway. The face made his valet's small neat features quite handsome by contrast. Giacomo pointed to his feline guest. "Master, I've been helping Benito hunt for that furry bit of a beast all over the palazzo, and here it is in your room. I must have let it in myself."

"Whose is it?" Antonio asked, lifting up the kitten. "A pretty bit of fluff for the pretty Dorotea?"

"No, my lord, kittens make Madonna Dorotea sneeze." Benito said. "It's Master Roberto's. It should not be here, my lord. I am sorry it bothered you. I will return it."

Antonio stood up, holding the kitten to his chest. "Never mind, I will do it myself."

"But, my lord . . . ." Benito was perplexed.

"It's all right. I like the creature. It will amuse me to return it to its lair."

"Very well, it is most gracious of you. The rooms are downstairs in the back, by the tower overlooking the courtyard. Roberto's is on the left. And . . . my lord?" His voice was tentative.

"Yes?"

"The kitten, Marco Polo, he prefers to ride on the shoulder."

"Like this?" Antonio smiled and placed Marco Polo on the designated perch, where he was quite at home. Benito smiled back, obviously reassured.

Stained glass lamps cast flickering colored shadows on the wall as Antonio walked through the hall, wondering why he had set out on this nonsensical errand. Well, the answer was simple enough. He felt it in his quickening heartbeat, in the heat, the tightness gathering in his loins. Despite his anger, his misgivings, he wanted to see Veronica again, alone if possible. It was a foolish risk, but if the opportunity presented itself, he knew he had to have her again. The only way to swiftly dissipate a carnal obsession was to indulge it to the fullest.

Antonio paused by the staircase to the tower, reaching up to fondle the kitten's ears. One inner voice urged him to turn back while another wondered at his own reluctance. True, he was breaking his own rules about sexual liaisons, but they were hardly engraved in stone. His preference for professionals saved trouble, that was all. So why did he still hesitate? Perhaps he was afraid another encounter would disenchant him? Veronica might easily seem awkward now, after an evening of Bianca's skilled and passionate embraces. Memory might already have colored the first experience, making it seem more magical than it had truly been. It might only have been the piquant situation that had kindled such a fire. There had been the delicious surprise of unveiling that lovely willowy body beneath the clumsy monk's disguise, and her obvious enchantment with him which had provoked such an excess of tenderness in his response to her. Though it was the little "model" he had thought enraptured with the dashing aristocrat.

What egotism! It served him right for being bewitched by the wide-eyed candor of her gaze that made her seem so trusting, so guileless. Antonio scoffed at his own credulity. What did looks prove? Nothing. Young as she was, Lucrezia Borgia's air of innocence was nothing more than an accident of feature combined with a skillfully practiced expression. If she was not as ruthless as her father and brothers, she certainly shared their corruption. But to look at her, you would presume she thought of nothing but psalms and sweetmeats.

And of course there was Beatrice, who had looked so angelic. Never more so than when she knelt before him, tearful, disheveled, and wanton, swearing her love with Alessandro's corpse tumbled at the foot of the stairs. Antonio shivered, thrusting the image from his mind.

Sex was a battlefield. The bittersweet peace all fought to attain was an illusion, a brief respite in the midst of eternal conflict. Women, like men, learned how best to handle their weapons. No doubt Veronica rehearsed that soul-piercing gaze daily in her mirror. He knew he could not trust her, but what did that matter? They needed each other for nothing but the pleasure they could take from each other's bodies. Why did he still resist his desire? He did not imagine she would deny him, despite his impertinence in the ballroom. There would be a bit more haughtiness, perhaps a few more wounded looks, a flare of temper hot enough to ignite them both. She burned for him, as he did for her. Or perhaps he still flattered himself. She wanted something, a certain significant portion of his anatomy. That he in particular came attached to it probably had little relevance.

———

Veronica opened the door to the light knock. Antonio stood in the hallway. All her anger and misery vanished before the devastating impact of his presence. The raw sensual power emanating from him took her breath away. Adding an incongruous note, the mustached kitten perched on his shoulder like a wizard's familiar. It mewed in greeting.

"This belongs to your household, I believe, Madonna?" he asked, nodding to his companion.

"Yes. Come in, won't you?" she said automatically, her voice barely audible, then added, "For a moment." Antonio had appeared on her doorstep, just as he had threatened, promised to do, and she had not turned him away.

Antonio's lips curled in a brief ironic smile, and he stepped inside the door. As it had in the ballroom, a field of magnetic energy enveloped them, so that the very air shimmered with excitement. Antonio's manner was courteous once more, but his eyes glittered, bright and implacable as a predator's, falcon, wolf, panther. Veronica felt like some entranced prey beneath that gaze. She was mesmerized, waiting, more than waiting, wanting to be devoured. It was irresistible, this urge to become one with him.

Antonio handed Marco Polo to her. His hands carefully did not touch hers, but even the deliberate omission seemed a caress, the only one Veronica could have borne at that instant. She moved mechanically across the room, aware of his eyes on her, intent, waiting, and placed Marco Polo on the pillow beside Roberto's head. The kitten promptly yawned widely, all pink tongue and needle teeth, stretched, and curled up in a sleepy ball. Veronica petted the kitten, then stroked Roberto's damp hair back from his forehead.

"He drank my wine at supper. A whole goblet. He has no head for it."

Antonio watched her ministrations, wondering briefly at the small shabby rooms, hardly better than servants' quarters, that had been given to Veronica and her husband. He could not view the great child asleep on the narrow bed as any sort of rival, and he found himself oddly touched by her maternal gestures. That tempered the immediate fierceness of his response to her, but did not quench it. He did not want to weaken towards Veronica—she manipulated him far too easily as it was, with her searching eyes and soft, husky voice. She had so many guises: street urchin, woman of the world, gentle caretaker. She looked far younger now than she had in her jeweled ball gown. Her hair was unbound, the wild spill of dark, smoky red billowing about her shoulders and down the back of her forest green robe. Beneath the plush velvet he glimpsed a shift of fine linen, like the one she had worn under the monk's habit. Under that, unseen but known, her tender nakedness beckoned to him.

"He will sleep deeply?" His kept his voice quiet, but there was nothing innocent in the question.

Veronica turned back to Antonio, and her breath quickened as their eyes met once more. She could see his chest rising and falling in the same fast, shallow breaths. Her heartbeat must be audible, an insistent sound and pressure thrumming through her body. "Yes," she whispered.

"And where do you sleep, Madonna?" he asked, making his intentions explicit.

Silently, Veronica led him across the hallway to her own bedroom. *He should not be here. I should not let him come in.* It was madness, madness, yet it filled her with wild exhilaration. He had to have her, she could read it in his face, that blazing hunger. He could not stay away from her, any more than she could deny him. She opened the door and went inside. Behind her, she heard the door close, the lock click. She faced Antonio, shivering slightly with apprehension and desire. He did not embrace her immediately, only looked at her with those hot, hooded predator's eyes. Eyes that held her at bay, trembling, when she wanted most to rush into his arms. She could not move, but she felt a surge of heat between her legs, sweeping fire along her veins.

"Well now," he said, and the smile was a predator's smile as well, "my little artist's model."

He shrugged off the jerkin he wore, tossing it aside and came forward slowly, stalking her. The pure white of his shirt shimmered before her eyes. His snug silk tights revealed the sculptured muscles of his legs. The protective *braghetta* barely concealed the straining shape of his arousal. Standing before her, Antonio reached out and unfastened her robe, pushing it off her shoulders and letting it fall to the floor as he had done with the monk's habit. Then he slipped off the thin transparent shift, leaving her naked before him. He did not kiss her, only watched her face as his hands stroked down to her breasts, his fingertips drawing together to pinch her nipples lightly, raising them to taut peaks. Veronica sighed. Antonio's fingers closed a little harder, and harder still, till she whimpered with the small, sweet pain. He cupped one breast, caressing it as his other hand slid down over her body, down her belly to the throbbing center of her. His fingers combed through the dark flame of hair between her legs, then pressed against her, parting her lips, opening her to his touch. His fingertips sought and found the moist hot bud of her desire. She cried out, her arms embracing him, her body melting with desire, her heart dissolving with love.

''There,'' Antonio whispered, his gasp of passion echoing her own soft cry. ''There'' he repeated, his voice, his hot breath caressing her as his fingertips circled insistently, flicking over and over the sensitive spot, until Veronica thought her legs would give way beneath her. She clung to him, moaning as his fingers slid deeper, dipping into the hot wet center of her body.

Antonio's other hand left her breast, roving over her hip to slide down her back and cup her buttocks. Pulling her closer to him, his strong fingers kneaded the soft flesh of her cheeks, pressed into the cleft between them in a suggestive caress. Veronica shivered against him. Part of her was ashamed that she let him claim her so easily, let him do whatever he chose. Part of her desperately craved his touch, wanting whatever he wanted.

''Do you find such sweet perversions appealing, *dolcezza*?'' His voice purred in her ear, sultry and provocative, but she heard a sharp thread of anger running underneath the arousal. ''Savonarola has made things a bit difficult in Florence for men of your cousin's predilections. Perhaps the next best thing to a boy is a woman dressed as a boy?''

Her response to his insinuation was a hopeless tangle of emotion mingling with the desire that pulsed with each tantalizing touch of his hands. There was anger that he should presume to judge her and pain that he did, that he gave her contempt even as he demanded passion. And there was laughter too, thinking how shocked Daniele would be at such a suggestion. Her cousin had teased her with the palest image of such a fantasy when she had emerged in her monk's costume, with no thought of ever enacting it. Antonio meant only to humiliate her.

"Such a thing was never suggested," Veronica said coolly, marveling that her voice was as calm as it was, with his hands exploring, penetrating the most secret parts of her body. "It is you, Signore, who seem bent on enacting it. Perhaps your own predilections are suspect."

The insinuation was enough to make him release her and step back, his eyes narrowing in outrage. A man more defensive of his sexuality might have struck her, even after provoking the situation. Seeing the laughter she could barely suppress, anger, then humor flashed in his eyes, a glittering spark. He smiled at her, his feral wolf's grin, acknowledging the point she had scored. She saw he was a man who honored his enemies, and Veronica realized that was what she was to him, the enemy. For Antonio this was not a love affair. It was a war.

Sudden fury filled her, fury that he forced his war to be hers as well. She had offered him the most honorable surrender of all, the absolute surrender of love, and he had abased it. He had taken all that sweetness and reshaped it, honed it to use as a vicious weapon. Well, if the conqueror had less honor than the conquered, she would learn to fight him. She saw an answering flame flicker in his eyes at her reaction, reveling in her anger, wanting that hot flame of rage to stoke their passion.

Antonio pulled her closer, lifting her against him. His arms were tight around her, shaping her body to him, letting her feel the hard tension of the muscles in his arms and legs, letting her feel the insolent male hardness of his sex pressed to her thigh. He kissed her, a kiss that was half bite, teeth as well as lips covering her mouth, his tongue thrusting between her lips, hot and swift. She tried to pull away, and he tightened his grip, arching her back. He lowered his lips to her upthrust breasts, his mouth leaving a searing imprint on her flesh. Taking hold of a nipple, his teeth teased it with their sharpness. Edging the sensation to pain, he soothed the bite with soft washes of his tongue, then sank his teeth in to taunt the tender flesh again.

Tormented with pain and pleasure, Veronica wanted to hurt him as he hurt her. She cursed him in whispers, and his voice answered hers, harsh and panting. She fought, not really to be free but to challenge his cruelty. He was strong, but a kind of frenzy claimed her as they battled. She broke free of him, but he seized her, carried her across the room, and threw her onto the bed. Then he was on her, his mouth, his teeth traveling over her as she twisted and writhed beneath him, until the twisting and writhing was no longer a furious protest but a furious response to the sorcery of his touch. Even when pitiless, his mouth, his hands were deft, sure, following their instinctive knowledge of her.

She was naked, and he was clothed still as he had been the first time. It was a further humiliation that he kept this civilized armor on while he exposed her utterly, body and soul. Veronica wanted to rip his garments, strip this false protection from him, as he had divested her of every vestige of hers. She had to reach the heart of him somehow, and his body was the only way he offered. She raised up from the bed, her fingers tearing at the fine silk of his shirt. He knocked her hands away and unfastened his *braghetta* and hose, releasing his aroused manhood, allowing only that exposed nakedness to all of hers.

Somehow it was the final insult. Veronica slapped him, struggling to escape in earnest. He caught her again, flipped her over, and pressed her face down on the bed, kneeling between her thighs. One hand held her head, his fingers twined in her hair, while the other fondled her intimately, his fingers delving into her wetness, discovering her readiness to receive him despite her fury. She shuddered, and her hips seemed to lift of their own accord as she felt not his fingers but the blunt thickness of his sex stroking her there. She moaned, reaching to meet him, to draw him into herself. Then his hardness found her soft opening and plunged into the depths of her, withdrew and plunged again, fierce strokes that plundered her. He pressed against her, one hand sliding around her waist, pulling her closer. His hand slid lower, over her belly, between her legs. His palm massaged the sensitized mound, while his fingers spread open her lips, searched and found the swollen pearl of sensation bedded there, rubbing it in time to the thrust of his hips. Veronica could feel the skillful calculation, his handling rough, but only rough enough to insult her sensibilities, not to destroy the pleasure of his touch. His cruelty filled her with anger, with fear, but her need for him was a fever, a burning hunger that obliterated all else. Her body moved without her volition now, begging for completion, betraying her utterly.

"No!" she gasped out, writhing beneath him. "No!"

Antonio let her go. Withdrew from her. Stunned, she stared at him over her shoulder. "No?" His eyes were black with passion, his arched manhood wet and glistening from her body. He laughed at her. "No? Don't say no, *selvaggia*, when what you mean is yes."

Sobbing with fury, Veronica turned to face him. Her love was with her now, in reach of her arms, but she was hating him even as she loved him. His mockery was driving her mad. She could not understand how or why everything was so twisted. Why did he torment her, arouse her ruthlessly then taunt her with her desire? But she did want him, love him. It was unbearable to have him out of her. She could no more deny him than she could deny life itself, for all its cruelty.

Beyond caring what he thought, she pulled Antonio to her, muffling that vicious mouth with her own. Her lips, her tongue, her teeth attacking him with fierce kisses. Clasping her hips, he fit himself to her, thrust in deep and hard. She wrapped herself around him, her nails raking him in desperate need as he drove into her again and again and again. Her body raged against his, sharing the fury they both felt. They coupled wildly, snarling like cats, covering each other with bites. A terrible consuming darkness grew between them, devouring them, swallowing them whole in a black pulsating void. She heard his voice cry out with hers, a cry too terrible for pleasure, too sweet for pain, as the darkness shattered into a billion glittering knife-edged pieces.

They lay together, gasping for air, their skin drenched in sweat. Veronica felt utterly drained, but only her body was sated. The physical core of her still throbbed with the dark, dreadful joy of their shared release. Her spirit ached with misery, weighed down with unshed tears and the acid dregs of anger. Slowly, Antonio raised himself off her, wincing slightly as he pulled away from her. His shirt was tattered, and she saw the bleeding scratches along his arms, the bites on his chest and neck. Memory flashed the feel of his skin rippling under her nails, the metallic iron tang of blood on her tongue. She could not believe she had acted so savagely, yet she had. She cupped one hand to a breast, covering the stinging bite on the nipple. She remembered how gentle he had been when first he touched her. She turned her face away from him, wanting to weep but too weary even for tears.

He leaned over to whisper in her ear, his voice hoarse, "Witch. You are a witch."

She flinched at the word. "Does that make you a warlock?" she asked bitterly, "Or the Devil himself?" It had been his choice, to drive her to this violence. But he had found a match in her. It seemed he did know her, after all, better than she knew herself. Even now, the dark timbre of his voice stirred her, the sound resonating in the throbbing pulse between her legs.

"Let us say we deserve each other." He stood up and straightened his torn shirt, closed the open tights, retrieved his jerkin from the floor. Drawing it around him, he walked to the door. He hesitated there, then turned back to her. Smiling sardonically, he reached into a small pocket and withdrew two more gold coins, tossing them onto the bed beside her. "*Grazie, dolcezza.* You are all that I remembered—and more."

———

The corridor was deserted. Antonio closed the door and leaned back against it. He sighed heavily, closing his eyes as the dark malaise that followed sex swept over him. Most pleasure had a price, and he had long ago accepted that he must pay for his in grief. Ever since Beatrice, it had been like this. Once it was over, all he wanted was to be alone, solitary, until the void within him healed. He was never alone, of course, and had the manners not to indulge his melancholy overlong. No, this was not quite the same. What he wanted now was to go back into that shabby little room and hold Veronica, simply hold her, until the sense of emptiness waned.

The need was so intense he shuddered, fighting it off. His anger had made him somewhat excessive, but to show tenderness now would be to arm her against him. He would be defeating himself after he had gone to such lengths to demonstrate to Veronica she could not control him with her games. It was dangerous to show her how much she had beguiled him. If he was wise, he would end this madness and return to his exquisite courtesan, but Bianca's artful caresses seemed contrived to him now. Antonio winced again as he moved away from the wall, the scratches on his back stinging. She had marked him well, his *selvaggia*.

"Damn," Antonio cursed under his breath. Between his clothes and his back, Giacomo would work himself into a frenzy of curiosity. That was the last thing he needed. He did not want Giacomo ferreting about in this affair, offering either censure or blessing. Luckily, his valet would probably be gambling until dawn. Antonio returned to his room and stripped. The blood on the jerkin was negligible, but the shirt was useless. He tossed it into the fireplace and watched it burn. Giacomo would miss it, of course, and there was no explanation for his back except a woman's nails. Antonio gave a short laugh. He would simply misdirect Giacomo's suspicions to the lascivious brunette.

His valet appeared in the morning, having managed, despite his best cowardly instincts, to get his head bashed in a fight over the dice. Alarmed, Antonio leapt to his feet and led him to a chair. Giacomo was pale as a ghost and wobbly, but the flamboyance of his moans soon convinced Antonio that the silly fool's hangover pained him far more than his injury. He was also, for the moment, blessedly oblivious to the finer points of his master's love life.

8 *The Bonfire*

THE children came, thousands of them, robed as angels. The richest wore fluttering white silk, the poorest chalked sackcloth, their heads adorned with wreaths of dried flowers or early spring blossoms woven into fragrant halos. The Friar had beckoned them forth from every dwelling in Florence and the surrounding countryside. He called, and they came out to march through the streets, singing hymns in their sweet celestial voices. For Savonarola and for the throng of enraptured believers, these young singers were a symbol of the purity that was to transfigure the heathen spirit of *Carnevale* into a holy celebration. Like the children, many of the watching men and women were adorned with wreaths and that sweet fragrance mingled with the floating smoke of incense and scented tapers, veiling the sweat of close-pressed bodies. Above them hazy clouds parted, and the sun shone down on the multitude. Taking the sunshine as a good omen, the crowd cheered, and the small figures marching in the procession raised their voices even louder in song.

A small gathering within the vast one, Veronica stood with Daniele, Roberto, and Benito. Heaving a sigh, the accompanying Bombol sat down beside them, scratching one large floppy yellow ear. Together, they watched as the parade flowed past them into the piazza, the singing children giving way to the older youths who marched as standard bearers. The multicolored banners fluttered in the breeze, baring the emblems of the sixteen gonfalons that made up the four quarters of Florence. Veronica named them all to Roberto: the Golden Lion, the Viper, the Unicorn, the Shell . . . .

"Look, look, Dragon!" Roberto cried, pointing to his favorite as the gonfalon marched past them. He loomed in front of Veronica, blocking her view, and she was suddenly struck by his resemblance to Luigi, the physical breadth and height of him, the fall of the coarse sand-colored hair. She closed her eyes for a second, fighting a queasy wave of fear and disgust. Then Roberto turned and smiled his sweet child's smile, and any repulsive resemblance to Luigi vanished. Roberto's features were rounded and soft in both shape and expression, and there was not a hint of cruelty in him anywhere. Veronica smiled back at him, shaking off the unnerving vision. Her reaction to Luigi seemed to be getting worse, not better. The humiliating encounter with Antonio had confused her, mixing shame and anger, guilt and desire. That confusion was breaking down the barriers she had built against the memory of Luigi's brutal attack. Or was it only simpler to fear Luigi than Antonio? To hate Luigi rather than herself?

Shivering a little, Veronica forced her attention back to the last of the passing parade. Compared to the old *Carnevale*, there was little to distract her here. The singing was truly lovely, but she had too much apprehension about Savonarola to be deeply moved by this religious display. She would have enjoyed the procession more if he had not used it to supplant the revels of *Carnevale*. "I miss all the splendid costumes and masks," she lamented to Daniele, "and watching everyone laugh and flirt in the streets. It might have been vulgar and rowdy, but *Carnevale* was always bursting with life. This is not the same at all."

"It is stupid to try and reform the festival," Daniele muttered beside her. "It brought the winter months alive, and people need the catharsis. Without it, they will be short on sins to confess during Lent."

Veronica remembered Bianca saying much the same thing. She felt her body tense. Even that tiny reminder of the courtesan was sharp-edged with jealousy. Veronica sighed. Her shifting moods were making her dizzy. She loathed being so at odds with herself. Raising her chin, she said stiffly, "Everyone else seems enthralled with Savonarola's celebration."

"Self-righteousness can be as heady as sin," Daniele grumbled. "The crowd is intoxicated enough with it now because it is a novelty, and because Savonarola is going to give them the bonfire of the vanities for a spectacle. How many times can he do this before he runs out of things that people will freely give to the flames, or will let themselves be coerced into sacrificing? Will he take the things by force then? Or start burning the people?''

"Daniele," she murmured comfortingly. She could hear the fear edging the anger in his voice, those painful emotions blotting out her own for the moment.

"How he loves to quote Leviticus. The same book that calls me an 'abomination' forbids men to cut their beards. Next they will be beheading the beardless.'' Daniele gestured with disgust to the waiting pyre. ''That is where Savonarola would like to see those like me, atop that monstrosity. He would light the fire himself and watch while we all sizzled to a crisp.''

They gazed at the great wooden pyramid dominating the center of the Piazza della Signoria. The ascending tiers rose step by step to the pinnacle, each row piled with the luxuries that Savonarola had condemned. Groups of the most ardent of the Savonarola youths had gone from house to house collecting these vanities of the flesh and spirit. Veronica's heart ached for the beautiful treasures about to be burned, along with all the frivolous nonsense. *Carnevale* costumes and other lavish clothing were heaped all about the base, the rich fabrics a vivid mass of jewel colors. Embedded in folds of velvet and satin, discarded masks stared out at the crowd with dark empty eyeholes. Above the extravagant garments were stacked the gaming tables and all the other trappings of gambling and sport. Veronica wondered if there were any *Tarocco* packs among them. On another tier were risqué books and pictures deemed too profane, or too lascivious to adorn the walls of properly religious homes. The piles of lutes were especially sad, and the children's dolls with their dangling arms and legs. The jumble of cosmetics and hair pieces simply looked bizarre. Cascades of pink and white powders spilled over clumps of false curls and braids, the wigs all tangled with bottles of perfume, jars of ointments, and scattered mirrors flashing crazily in the sun. Sixty feet in the air, wax and wood figures of the Olympian gods and goddesses ringed the goat-headed statue of Pan, old King *Carnevale*, who sat atop the pyre, patiently waiting to be burned.

"You are here, as I prayed you would be." A deep rusty voice spoke behind them. Veronica turned with Daniele to face the stooped form of Sandro Botticelli, peering down at them forlornly. Always temperamental, his fascination with Savonarola had turned the gentle artist morose. He seemed weighted down with sadness, this shy, awkward man who had painted such graceful and elegant paintings. "Have you changed your mind, Daniele, and brought that sinful folio to be burned in the bonfire?"

"You can see I have not," Daniele said sharply.

Her cousin seldom went anywhere without his leather case with paper and charcoal for rapid sketches. Today was no exception, but the well-worn binder he carried could not be mistaken for the large folio. "You know that Daniele would not burn those drawings or any others, Sandro," Veronica chided gently.

"I hoped against hope," the other artist replied bleakly. He unrolled a collection of charcoal sketches, studies of classical male and female nudes. "I brought these. A study for Mercury and Mars, two more of Venus. Pagan gods."

"No," Veronica whispered, staring down at the delicate drawings, then up into Sandro's mournful face. She was torn between pity and anger. Why had he chosen a path that brought him so little peace, that desecrated everything in which he had once believed? "Sandro, you must not destroy these beautiful things."

"Oh, but I must," Botticelli said seriously. He stroked their surface gently with his fingertips, then tied them up again carefully. "I was hoping you would understand."

"How could you hope I would do anything but try to dissuade you?" Daniele asked fiercely. "Anything else would be a mockery of our friendship. Your talent is a gift from God, and you defile it in the name of this pious Philistine."

"You misjudge him. The holy Friar believes art is a great source of inspiration, especially for the poor. It is only irreverent art which must be destroyed. Or religious paintings which are so poorly executed they make the sublime appear foolish."

"That Savonarola despises mediocrity is the only thing I have heard in his favor."

It was the wrong thing to say, for Savonarola was known and beloved for his endless labor among the poor. Botticelli shook his head sadly and turned away from them. They stared after him as he walked towards the pyre. Abruptly, Daniele turned back to Veronica, "I cannot bear this. I will not watch them incinerate art like so much rubbish."

"It is terrible," Veronica said. "It is sacrilege."

"Yes, that is exactly what it is. Look what becoming a follower of Savonarola has done to Botticelli. It has destroyed him as an artist. He hardly paints anymore, he is drowning in religious melancholy. It makes me ill." Daniele's tall gangly body seemed to crumple in on itself, and he raked his hand through his hair, tugging at the frizzy strands.

"Don't torment yourself by staying here, Daniele. Benito and I can manage Roberto perfectly well on our own. He does not understand what is being destroyed, he just loves to watch the flames. Roberto thinks fire is more beautiful than all the lovely things they will burn in it."

"I know," he sighed.

Still Daniele lingered and Veronica looked at him questioningly, saw the conflict in his eyes. "The artist in you wants to walk away from the destruction of beauty. But the artist wants also to stay, to emblazon the images on his mind and then paint them."

He shrugged ruefully. "It is dramatic, even if it is despicable."

"Quiet," a voice behind them hissed.

An expectant hush fell on the crowd as the song ended and Savonarola appeared at last. He mounted the platform and raised his arms to bless the vast congregation that had gathered in the piazza. As always, Veronica was amazed by his effect. The Friar had tremendous presence for such a small unprepossessing man, with his sunken chest and thin frame wasted by fasting. Ugly yet compelling, his face was dominated by a large hooked nose and thick lips. Gazing over the crowd, his green eyes glowed with a fanatical light, and his sallow skin flushed with excitement. Savonarola was transported by his own zealous passion, and it was that impassioned faith which moved others.

Veronica was drawn, despite herself, by the strange mixture of fear and fascination she felt for this man who claimed the gift of prophecy. At first, when he had still preached of God's love, she had been moved by his eloquence. That enchantment had been brief. The brighter side of his vision had given way quickly to darkness, and Savonarola spoke of hellfire and damnation more often than love and grace. But that initial experience had given her a taste of his power. Now all his sermons had a central obsession. First he denounced the depraved Pope, then the corrupt Church, threatening all those who did not follow the rigid doctrine he himself preached, or who dared to question his inspiration.

"You do not want anyone to prophesy," he cried out, his voice carrying over the entire square. "But it is God who chooses his prophets, and God's prophets will choose death before denial of such a divine blessing. I speak only the truth. Your very sins prophesy against you. It is not I but all earth and Heaven that prophesy against you. The earth is the garden of the Lord and you have despoiled it. The true Church leads men to live in simplicity and humility. It urges women to be chaste and pure. But you, you lead your flock away from the true path. You lead them into temptation. You have despoiled the world and corrupted men and women both with avarice, pride, and lust."

Even with the denunciations, the primary mood of the gathering was one of celebration. Savonarola himself responded to the atmosphere, and finished his speech by praising the glory of the day and blessing the divine sacrifice they were all making to the honor of God. "This world is but a proving ground for the next. Cast aside temptation. All is vanity, nothing but vanity. Cast off your worldly objects, and you will begin to cast off your worldly desires, the dross that weighs down your souls. Seek the eternal beauties of the spirit rather than the ephemeral beauties of the flesh. Abandon all but God, and God will embrace you all. I tell you Florence is to be His holy city on earth, and I will lead you, His chosen people."

What greater vanity than that? Veronica wondered.

At last, the Friar signaled and the music of fifes and trumpets was heard. Church bells rang out over the square. The choir of angelic children began singing the *Te Deum*. Standing beside Veronica, Roberto caught his breath as the flame bearers ran forward and tossed their torches onto the pyre. Packed full of brushwood, straw, and gunpowder, it ignited all at once, adding its hiss and crackle to the music of the instruments and singing voices. Bright tongues of yellow, orange, and crimson leaped up, spreading over the tiers, rushing higher and higher, until the pyramid was totally enveloped in shimmering flame. The crowd stood, mesmerized, while the great bonfire blazed to the heavens. Then a great cheer broke out. Roberto jumped and squealed with excitement. Within moments, the heat was intense, the pulsating breath of fire sweeping over the square, adding its own roar to the vast voice of the watching masses. As the tiers of vanities burned, the lightest of the objects were lifted into the air, drifting like flaming blossoms over the crowd.

"There go all their silly little sins," Daniele scoffed. "Burnt to nothing and floating away on the wind."

The fire burned for a long time, consuming its sacrifice of beauty, then slowly died away. When the pyre was finally nothing but ashes and embers, Savonarola gave another signal, and a giant wooden cross was brought forward on ropes and raised up in its stead. He lifted his hand, commanding the musicians to play new music. The closest of Savonarola's fellow monks and his most ardent follower, Fra Domenico da Pescia, came forward, leading bands of children and older youths. Da Pescia was widely praised for reforming the wild youths of Florence and bringing them under Savonarola's holy sovereignty. Some of the boys were truly sincere, with all the exultation of youth. But Veronica thought that too many of them had simply found a sanctioned way of harassing the helpless, tormenting whomever the Friar denounced from his pulpit.

As Veronica watched, Savonarola linked hands with the children and other monks and led them forward to form the first of three circles around the massive cross. The center was composed only of the Dominican monks and the youngest children. In the second circle were the older boys, young laymen, and clerics, and in the third old men, priests of other orders and burghers. Bedecked with wreaths and singing Savonarola's hymns, they danced around the cross. Veronica, like the other women, stood outside this privileged center of celebration. Many simply watched the men, others sang and swayed back and forth to the music by themselves. She wondered how many others resented the deliberate exclusion, and how many accepted the judgment. Savonarola often praised women's moral character above that of men, but in most ways he still treated them as inferior beings. Their presence would hardly have profaned a simple circle dance.

On the other hand, Roberto was overjoyed by dancing. He joined in on the outskirts of the far circle, lumbering about with an odd bear-like grace. Bombol and Benito gamboled beside him. The servant found a fallen wreath, scooped it up, and crowned Roberto with it. He crushed it to his head and spun about ecstatically, crowing with happiness. Succumbing to artistic fervor, Daniele wandered about, dashing off quick sketches of the dancing figures from different vantage points in the piazza.

Feeling totally like an outsider in the midst of the ongoing celebration, Veronica glanced around her. She was hungry by now, but Savonarola's implacable youths had driven off the usual batch of *Carnevale* pastry sellers before the crowd gathered. Another supposed bit of sacrilege the Friar had condemned. She herself would feel more charitable with a full stomach. Scanning the crowd with forlorn hope of discovering a defiant baker, Veronica saw her mother-in-law standing a few yards away with Dorotea. Slowly, she made her way through the crowd. Even if her mother-in-law did not care for Veronica, Maria would resent the disrespect if she did not greet her. It was difficult to be civil sometimes, but having even the most tenuous alliance with Maria would help Veronica feel safer when she had to visit Luigi's house.

It was more difficult than ever to force herself to be polite to Dorotea. She still seemed such a timid child, it was hard to think of her as a rival, but there was no way to be at ease with her either. Veronica's secret desires made her feel hypocritical, and it was not a feeling she liked. Such romantic entanglements and deceits might be common enough, but she had never had to deal with them before. One more knot in the unpleasant tangle of her emotions. Looking up as she approached the two of them, Veronica noticed that Dorotea seemed to be arguing with Maria, or pleading with her.

"I will do my duty," Dorotea was saying to her mother, her voice shrill. "Surely if I do my duty, Signore di Fabiani . . . ."

Veronica's curiosity was instantly roused by the comment about Antonio, but Maria deliberately shushed her daughter as

Veronica approached. Maria stepped forward aggressively to greet her. ''I did not expect to see you amidst Savonarola's faithful, Veronica.''

Inwardly, Veronica sighed with exasperation. She wanted to hear more about Antonio, not argue about religion, but she made herself answer courteously, ''I think all of Florence is here today. Roberto loved watching the fire. Bonfires were always a part of *Carnevale*.''

''The old bonfire represented the flames of carnal passion. Savonarola's pyre burns with the holy light of redemption.'' Maria's eyes glittered as she spoke. ''As the vanities of the flesh are consumed, the soul burns brighter. Every sinful luxury cast into the flames lightens the heart of the giver.''

''Sometimes sacrifice can be beneficial,'' Veronica said haltingly, ''like cutting back a tree to bring new growth.'' She hoped it was so for those who had surrendered their treasures to the fire.

''There is Frederigo, by the edge of the circle!'' Maria exclaimed eagerly. ''I must try to speak with him. Wait here quietly, Dorotea.'' With that repressive remark, she left the two of them standing alone together. Dorotea looked utterly abandoned, staring after her mother, then turning back to Veronica, her eyes wide. Veronica wanted to question Dorotea about Antonio, but she hesitated, feeling guilty. The girl obviously needed a confidante, not an interrogator.

Impulsively, Veronica reached out and took hold of her hand. ''You look so unhappy, Dorotea. Is there some way I can help you?''

Dorotea snatched her hand back, clutching it between her small breasts as if the touch had burned it. She stood trembling for a minute like a frightened animal, then cast a desperate glance at Veronica and blurted out, ''I do not want to marry him. He will hurt me. I know he will hurt me.''

Veronica took a deep breath. Her own inquisitiveness, as well as her sympathy, had entangled her in this, and she could not turn away from this frightened child now. She was not sure what to say. Novice herself, she had known only the extremes of sexual experience. She had escaped Luigi's vile attentions, then rushed to embrace a desire so overwhelming it encompassed brutality as well as tenderness. Desire for the man Dorotea was to marry. The last thing she wanted was to entreat Antonio's cause for him, but Dorotea's shivering panic must be reassured.

"You do not have to be frightened, Dorotea," Veronica said softly. "Antonio di Fabiani is a man of experience. He will be gentle with you." She was certain this was true, despite how ruthlessly he had last treated her. It was passion that released the emotional violence in him.

"He is drenched in sin. But all men are, all except those who embrace our Lord and keep themselves chaste. He embraces evil, wasting himself in the bodies of harlots. I heard the servants gossiping. He bought a necklace for one of them, a rope of pearls big as hailstones. Pearls are for purity, for chastity. A gift fit for the Virgin, and he gives them to a harlot infamous for her depravity," Dorotea gasped out.

Bianca, Veronica thought bitterly, picturing that frosted beauty ornamented with pale, glimmering pearls. She thought of Antonio's gift to her—the gold coins that scorched her with shame.

"Why would any woman want to do that, open her body to unsanctified lust? To suffer one man is bad enough, a duty to be borne for the sake of children. It is a just retribution for Eve's sin." Dorotea's thin voice rose, shrill and hysterical. "Marriage is a sacrament. I would never defile a bond I made before Our Lord. I would never dream of being unfaithful. He would not kill me, would he? He would have no reason."

Running out of breath, Dorotea stared at her, a rim of white showing all around her pale blue eyes. Shocked, Veronica did not know what to make of this amazing speech, half preaching and half frantic plea. "I do not understand, Dorotea. Why are you so afraid? Why ever would you think Antonio would kill you?"

"Did you not know, Veronica?" Maria reappeared beside them, her voice cutting in coldly. "I thought it was common knowledge throughout the city that Antonio di Fabiani had killed his brother and his wife after he found them in bed together. Dorotea's father has chosen to betroth his only daughter to a murderer."

Veronica shook her head, to deny even the possibility of such a thing. But Benito's words returned to haunt her; *Fabi-*

ani? I thought the sons killed each other in a duel over a woman. Her denial would not change reality. Blood feuds, duels of honor, raged throughout Italy. Antonio was capable of killing, in hot blood or in cold.

She looked up, and as if she had summoned him, she saw Antonio waiting there, only a few yards behind Maria and Dorotea, half-concealed amongst the crowd. He had not shown himself to them, but waited for Veronica to notice him. Wanting her to come away with him, alone, to some rented room, some hidden alcove. Wanting to light, in secret, their own *Carnevale* fire. His eyes blazed across the distance separating them, stripping her once again of everything but her passion for him. If it were not for Maria's words, she would have gone to him again, forsaking everything else. She thought of the violence in him, the violence he awoke in her. Fear seized her, as if she embraced not life but death. Was it love that she saw burning there, or hate? For Antonio was there any difference? This love could destroy her. Distraught and confused, Veronica turned away from him.

He did not do it.

The knowledge came to her with utter certainty, as powerful as any vision she had known. Like sunlight pouring through her, it banished the dark shadow of her fear, rushing through her with blazing light and warmth. But when she turned back, Antonio had gone.

Veronica saw Maria and Dorotea still standing before her. She laughed aloud, joy and pain and giddy relief all mingled into one. "He did not do it," she said without thinking, giving voice to her revelation. Staring into her incandescent face, Maria made the sign against the evil eye. Grabbing Dorotea's arm, she pulled her into the crowd.

Veronica laughed again, trembling with the intensity of her revelation. Impulsively, she ran after Antonio, hunting for him amid the throng, certain she must find him. Half an hour's fruitless search convinced her of the futility of her quest, leaving her footsore and weary of heart. The clarity of her belief had clouded as well. She was certain Antonio was innocent, but she wondered now if that certainty had arisen solely from her own desperate need to believe.

She must discover the truth.

9 Assignations and Assassinations

BIANCA was soaking in an herbal bath when Dimitri came in to announce in his most formal voice, "Signore di Fabiani is downstairs, mistress."

"Antonio?" the courtesan asked, startled by the swift excitement she felt, the flutter of anticipation in her belly.

Then she tightened her lips in frustration. She wanted to see Antonio—how very much surprised her—but it would not do to encourage such spontaneous visits. They could prove inconvenient. Today was, in fact, most inconvenient. There were certain significant plans for tonight. Dimitri would be very annoyed if she accepted such a distraction. Fabiani was a courtier, knowledgeable in the etiquette of professional assignations, so why had he appeared without sending a messenger to request a meeting, as he had done the first time?

She would send him away and enjoy her bath. At least the odor of soot was washed away. She had wasted hours watching that fool Savonarola's triumphal procession, even though Cesare would have a dozen other reports of the sanctimonious event. Suddenly, Bianca smiled. Antonio must have been to the bonfire of the vanities. Perhaps he too had experienced a surfeit of piety, the Friar's pyre igniting less holy fires in him. Such carnal revelry would be a fitting end to *Carnevale*. She should celebrate to spite the Friar if nothing else.

Bianca felt a sudden pulse between her thighs, a moistening. Ah, he was so tempting! So few of the men she bedded truly aroused her desire, much less satisfied it. Still, this unannounced visit was almost insulting, and by rights she should send him away. The proprieties extended to her were a measure of her worth, as well as the richness of the gifts she received.

While she vacillated, Dimitri extended a flawless white ca-

mellia pinned to a small pouch of silvered tapestry brocade.
''He begs your pardon if the time is inopportune and offers
this token of his admiration.''

She set the flower aside and opened the drawstring of the
bag, spilling the contents into her hand. An exquisite pair of
earrings this time, square cut aquamarines framed with tiny
diamonds and fringed with a cascade of seed pearls. He certainly had an eye for what suited her. If he had bought them
today, he must have offered the owner a liberal bribe to open
his shop. Dimitri wrapped her in a towel as she rose from the
tub. ''Tell Signore di Fabiani to wait in the *salotto*. I will be
down after a time.'' Even with such a generous gift, it was part
of the game that she would keep him waiting after such an
untimely impertinence. Dimitri scowled but went to do her
bidding, then returned to help her dress.

Seated before her mirror, Bianca lifted the ear drops to her
face again, examining their effect. They were perfect with the
gown she had chosen to wear today, frost blue velvet, the
sleeves slashed to show an undergown of the sheerest opalescent tissue and tied with silk tassels. Nevertheless, she laid the
gift aside and selected her large sapphire and diamond earrings
instead, and the heavy matching necklace. The dark blue gems
were from Cesare Borgia, a more opulent and expensive gift
than any Antonio had given her as yet. Bianca fastened the
jewels and retouched her makeup with deliberate slowness,
then contemplated the combined effect. Striking, if a bit excessive for afternoon, but she was determined to make a dramatic
entrance.

Bianca wished she could believe Antonio was so enamored
of her he could not stay away, but she doubted it. Not yet.
While he excelled in deft wit, in the delicate compliments
expected of the courtier, it was obviously an intellectual pleasure with him, a joy in language. She had soon perceived that
he scorned any pretense of a grand amour. His body was hot,
deliciously hot, but his head and his heart were quite cool.
Cool as her own. Perhaps they were too much alike for her to
affect him as passionately as she hoped to. Still, she had just
begun to set her mind, her body, to that challenge.

Antonio rose as Bianca entered the *salotto*. He surveyed her with a suitably appreciative eye, then bowed smoothly. "Forgive me. I have an impulsive streak."

"Indeed?" Bianca commented, her voice, her expression both aloof. She was not sure whether to take this impulsive streak as a compliment. She eyed him coolly, but admitted to herself that he was even more handsome than she remembered, dressed today in an embossed leather doublet of deep rich maroon, silk tights sculpting the muscles of his legs.

"It seemed imperative to see you. I do realize you may not be free."

Aware that she might indeed dismiss a suitor whose approach displeased her, Antonio waited, poised as always, but Bianca sensed something had changed. There was a sharper tension under the polished manners and composed demeanor. His eyes met hers suddenly and held. Bianca drew a small, quick breath as the black flame in them kindled her own inner fire. He wanted her now, this instant, needed her. The fact was not a surprise, why else was he here, but the intensity of her own reaction still shocked her. She should not give in to it, to him, so easily. A certain courtship was required. To compensate for this discourteous entrance, she had planned to demand a little stroll, a suitably elegant meal, perhaps even another small tribute. Antonio would do what was customary if she asked it. He would play by the rules and restrain the desperate hunger that had brought him to her.

Oh, she would love to watch him burn. But this smoldering fire could be smothered as easily as fanned in the waiting. Delay could dull both urgency of his desire and her response to it. Some men would not respect her or value her favors unless they paid dearly. Her intuition told her he would value her more rather than less if she did not put him through the required paces. And if she did not answer this burning need in him, she might lose him. Very well—if she was going to permit herself this indulgence, she would play her role to the hilt.

Bianca walked up to him, her face lifted to his, but not for a kiss, only to stare into his eyes and show her own growing heat. "I have a few hours to share," she murmured. "They are yours if you desire."

"Oh yes, I desire," he whispered roughly.

''Come with me.'' Bianca turned around and led Antonio up the stairs to her bedroom. Dimitri had readied the bed, she saw, drawing aside the hangings and turning back the quilt.

He undressed her skillfully, his deft fingers tugging loose the silk ties, his hands caressing the soft flesh he exposed as he quickly and carefully removed each lavish garment. Bianca did not touch him in turn, not yet, but demanded this homage as her due. She stood for a moment utterly naked except for her jewels, her snow white skin set off by their ice and midnight glitter. Antonio lifted the necklace in his fingers, then smiled ironically as he let it rest against her skin once more, leaving its challenge between them. Bianca found herself answering that mocking smile. She stepped forward eagerly, tugging at his clothes.

Antonio's face tensed momentarily, then he stepped back and stripped off the layers of leather, linen, and silk. As the garments came off, Bianca saw that his body was marked with bites and scratches, just healing. It was not her right to comment, but it infuriated her that he would come to her with the marks of another woman still on him. He arched an eyebrow and smiled again, glancing at her sapphires. They were both wearing the gifts another had given them.

Antonio lifted her up and carried her to the bed. He remembered her body well and used that knowledge to rapidly arouse her desire to his own pitch. She reveled in his skill, the way his mouth roved the slope of her shoulders, where she had such unexpected sensitivity. His hands cupped her breasts, peaking the nipples between thumb and finger, then sucking, tormenting them with tongue and teeth. Sliding down her belly, one hand twined in her pubic hair, massaging the mound of Venus till it throbbed, then the hand moved lower, the fingers teasing open her pouting lips, dipping into the waiting moistness. Wet with her own slickness, they centered on that hidden bud, circling lightly until it was taut and throbbing, then attacking mercilessly, vibrating the hot center of her till she spread her trembling legs in uncontrolled abandon, pressing herself into that torrid stimulation. She moaned helplessly as his fingers left that sweet peak, moaned again as they thrust into her, their rapid stroking working her to a frenzy.

Bianca hissed at him as he pulled his hand away from her

just as she climbed towards her completion. His legs opened hers wider, his hands caught hers and held them above her head. He held her down, his eyes black and blazing with lust, with some dark emotion between fury and laughter. Then he began stroking the open, wet fleshflower of her sex with the velvet headed tip of his own, until she wanted to scream at him, bite him, pull the iron hardness that teased behind that velvet touch into the pulsing hollow of her body. She arched up to try to draw him into her. Then she did scream as he plunged into her with one glorious stroke. He released her hands, and she closed herself around him, arms and legs imprisoning his torso, her teeth, her nails piercing his flesh so he could not pull away again. She felt the light marks of the half healed scratches that other bitch had left on him and dug into them, clawing them open with her own nails. He gasped at the fresh pain, but it did not override his pleasure, and he thrust into her deeply.

"More. Harder. Harder." Demands she usually made to excite her partner she now gave to reach her own climax.

He drove into her fiercely, mercilessly, and it was what she wanted, forcing everything from her mind but the release she craved. She cried out, her body thrashing, her nails digging deeper into his wounds in the fury of her need. Her orgasm sent him over the edge as well, moaning like a lost soul as he poured out his seed inside her.

Antonio withdrew from her body and rolled away, lying silently beside her. For a long time, Bianca did nothing, too exquisitely sated to bestir herself. Then she turned to him and stroked his temples lightly with her fingertips, then massaged his brow. He did not respond to her coaxing. The dark mood of aftermath was on him even more deeply this time. Did it correspond to the growing passion he felt for her? Bianca hoped so. It was so seldom she encountered her equal in bed. He was a man whose skill did not leave him even in frenzy, but melted and fused with that greater heat.

"I seem to want it all the time, lately," he murmured.

Want *it*, not want *you*, Bianca noted. But he was here with her. Was it a confession? Did this dark fever in him burn for her? He was too enigmatic to read. She found she wanted very much to have him as her devoted slave. Wanted to see love as well as lust brimming from those dark brown eyes. Wanted to have him succumb utterly to her power. Of course, those who were so enamored of her soon became boring, although there was a certain amusement in seeing what they could be forced to do for her. Somehow, she could not imagine Antonio ever being a bore.

After a time, Bianca rose from the bed and put on a dressing gown of oyster satin encrusted with heavy silver embroidery. She sat in front of the mirror and began to retouch her makeup, a delicate reminder that her evening was not free. Antonio raised himself on one elbow and watched her ministrations for a moment, then roused himself and dressed. He stood behind her, his hands on her shoulders, and bent down to kiss her neck, sending lovely little shivers down her back, and she murmured softly to him, a faint sigh of appreciation. She felt his hands tighten on her shoulders, an infinitesimal degree. Smiling, she raised her head to meet his eyes in the mirror, and the smile froze on her lips. Antonio's face was closed and distant. His eyes and mouth hardened. It was the face of a man who had made a resolution. *He is putting me aside,* she thought. An icicle of fear impaled her, heart and belly, terrifying in its intensity. Despite the piercing coldness, Bianca kept her chin raised, her breathing even. Perfectly poised, she stared into the mirror, seeing nothing. *What is wrong? Why doesn't he speak?* she wondered. Then desperately, *What is happening to me?*

"I do not like to inconvenience you," Antonio said. "Neither do I want to miss an opportunity to share your company. Perhaps you would set aside, shall we say, two days a week for me? Would Tuesdays and Fridays be possible for you?"

"Yes," she said, relief flooding her, and triumph. He was not dismissing her; rather he had fought his own growing need and lost. She would own him yet. "Yes, I can make arrangements to accommodate you—with pleasure."

"If I cannot come, I will send word, so you may have the day to amuse yourself as you choose. I may be impulsive, but you will not find me interfering."

For once, she would have preferred jealousy. She considered a moment and then made her own offer. "If the impulse seizes you, as it did today, it would not offend me to find you at my door. If our moods match and the time is convenient, what better way to spend the afternoon?''

"That is generous of you. In turn, you will find me generous in my gratitude," he assured her.

She removed Cesare's jewels and put on instead the earrings Antonio had brought today, and the rope of pearls. "I do not doubt it." She watched as his eyes briefly appraised the sapphires, then lifted to meet hers once more.

"Emeralds?" he suggested, his hand caressing her throat. "No, rubies I think, and a gown of white velvet. The gems would glow against your skin, bright as rose petals fallen on snow."

Bianca laughed, "Yes, that would suit me perfectly . . . ."

Dimitri was sullen after Antonio left, which only delighted Bianca more. Bringing in her masculine disguise, a charcoal gray doublet and hose plus a short hooded cape, he tossed them unceremoniously onto the bed. "Your reflexes will be off," he complained, "after idling away the day in bed."

"Oh, I wasn't idle. This afternoon has only whetted my appetite for tonight." Bianca laughed seductively, letting Dimitri's jealousy foam up since there would be a way for him to exorcise it, and not on Antonio. She lifted her hands up, arm's length from her face, and stared at them, remembering her pleasure as she had dug her nails into Antonio's back. "I will be at my best, never fear. See, I've already drawn blood."

There were few lanterns illuminating the streets, and they had taken care to pass no late-night wanderer since crossing over the Arno. Silently, they slipped into the alley by the stone wall that marked their destination. Muscles already warmed from the walk, Bianca slipped out of her cloak and stretched briefly, enjoying the ease of movement in masculine garb. The enclosure surrounding the house was smooth and high, but several great trees spread their limbs over the wall. Dimitri made a stirrup of his hands and boosted her within reach of a thick overhanging branch. Swiftly, she pulled herself up into the tree. Bianca's night vision was acute and she was glad there was only the thin curve of a sickle moon, the sharp points of stars, to light the darkness. She wanted that added

cover. There were plants in leaf and blossom within the wide
expanse of the garden, but many of the trees were still bare of
concealing foliage. She traversed the branch to the trunk and
lowered herself to the ground. Within the garden now, she
prowled along the inside of the wall, the dark gray of her
garments blending into the night shadows.

Four guards were stationed in front of the house. Bianca was
silent and quick enough to escape the attention of the two on
patrol. The others were gambling like their masters, oblivious
to trouble. Under a circle of lantern light, they tossed their
dice, cursing and coaxing the bones by turn, passing a heavy
leather skin of wine back and forth between them. The three
guards at the back were no more vigilant. Ugolino usually kept
late hours, but there was always the chance he would already
have left. Bianca was relieved to recognize his chief guard
standing sentinel in the back.

Screened by an arbor, Bianca darted across the garden and
climbed the vined trellis to a balcony, the balcony to the tiled
roof. She tried several vantage points, testing the windows that
looked into the rooms within the house. Most were dark, or so
muffled that only the faintest sound of voices penetrated the
glass and heavy curtains. Bianca moved rapidly to the one
bright window she had observed. The room was filled with
Compagnacci, the wealthy young rakes of the city who were
allied with the Arrabbiati against Savonarola. They went about
in the usual pack, drinking, gambling, and whoring together.
All three activities were in progress now. There were three
whores in the room, though they looked to be shared between a
half-dozen men. Typical. No courtesan of her quality would
deign to frequent this place, unless she came to gamble herself.
There were a couple of older men among the *Compagnacci,*
but no one Bianca recognized. On the whole, there were fewer
men tonight. Not all had brazened their defiance of Savonarola's great day. Ugolino was not visible, but she could not see
any of the other rooms, only a glimpse of the hallway as a
servant entered with bread, olives and wine. She was glad the
wine was flowing freely. Ugolino had no self-restraint.

Bianca felt more secure having checked the house and gardens. She wished she had seen Ugolino, but she knew he was
still inside. Now that she knew the number and disposition of

the guards, Bianca retraced her path to the trellis and followed the arbor back to the high stone wall. A niche on the south side housed a pious statue that provided good hand- and footholds to take her to the top of the wall again. Bianca circled back to check on Dimitri, testing his reflexes. But he was alert, expecting just such a ploy, as well as being keyed up for the kill. Silent as she was, he heard her approach and turned, sword drawn. Drawing her dagger, she saluted him briefly, then signaled him to wait. Grinning, Dimitri tossed her cloak up. Wrapping it about her, Bianca settled back against the tree trunk, all her energy coiled tightly within. They had come as late as they dared. She hoped the unknown interval before Ugolino appeared would not take the edge off their timing.

It was over an hour before Ugolino came into the garden and called to his guard. Bianca immediately gestured Dimitri to move ahead to the rendezvous point and check for any possible trouble ahead. She would follow behind their target. She and Dimitri had chosen a preferred place of attack and two alternatives, locations where any unfortunate noise was least likely to be heard. Looking back into the garden, Bianca frowned. Another man had joined Ugolino, and it looked as if they were leaving together. The two stood talking together in the flickering torchlight. No, they were arguing. The second man was Luigi della Montagna, his face sullen and hostile. Obviously, he had been drinking and losing heavily. Ugolino was flushed with fatuous pleasure, enjoying the other man's seething anger. Their voices carried easily in the cold still air.

"You never know how to lose," Ugolino gloated.

"You'll have the money," Luigi growled at him. "I'll pay you next week."

"Oh yes, I'll have it. I'll make sure of it."

"Are you insinuating I'm not good for it?"

"I know you have it, Luigi," he laughed. "I also know how you hate to part with it. I want you to send it over tomorrow, and I'm not someone you can afford to offend."

Luigi and Ugolino left the enclosed garden and set out down the street, their guards holding the torches to light the way. Bianca had taken the possibility of extra companions into consideration with Dimitri when they had surveyed the neighborhood. Her pulse quickened with apprehension, but she was still hopeful. The men's homes lay in different directions. Unless Luigi wanted to continue the argument for argument's sake, they would probably split up at the next cross street. Bianca found a soft landing and jumped down from the tree, then following cautiously, she shadowed the four men as they walked towards the river. Luigi and Ugolino were foolish to have only one guard each, who had to carry the torch as well as protect them if the need arose. It was all part of the attempt to keep the location of the latest gambling house secret. More men would draw more attention. Yes, they had paused at the cross street and were splitting up. Barely in time—the argument had grown more bitter, with nasty implications of cheating thrown in for good measure. Another couple of minutes, and they would have drawn swords. Both of them were cowardly at heart, but they were drunk enough tonight to demand satisfaction for their insults.

Ugolino lingered for a moment, calling after Luigi. He never did know when to keep his mouth sealed. At last, he turned back toward the river. Using all her stealth, she drew closer. They were approaching the overgrown alley she had chosen for the kill. There had been no warning signal from Dimitri, and the road was clear ahead and behind. They would do it here. Bianca deliberately slowed her breathing. It had been too long between kills. The anticipation was affecting her, rushing through her veins like wine. Bianca pulled out her garrote, two feet of thin wire attached to wooden handles, and stretched the weapon taut between her hands. Flexing her muscles, she prepared to strike. Her glance flicked briefly to Dimitri. Smiling, he nodded his readiness.

As Ugolino and the guard drew abreast of the alley, they attacked in concert, so the two men had no time to do more than grunt with surprise. Moving from behind, Dimitri immobilized Ugolino while Bianca took the guard. Swiftly, she looped the wire over his neck, crossed her hands, and jerked. The man was faster than she expected. Tough and sinewy, he twisted toward her even as she pulled the weapon tight, grabbing for the wire with one hand and thrusting the torch at her face with the other. Bianca saw the movement coming, and the strength of the wire gave her the advantage. She stepped to the side, her stance still firm as the torch passed by her. As the

guard lost balance, she jerked the wire harder. Helpless, he
thrashed for a moment, clawing at the wire crushing his wind-
pipe, then slumped to the ground. She moved smoothly with
the falling body, keeping the garrote drawn tight. Leaning over
him, knee pressed into his shoulder, she yanked the wire a
final time. Bianca held the man down for a few seconds more,
but it was an unnecessary precaution. He was quite dead. Smiling, she pulled her weapon free and abandoned the lifeless
body.

Dimitri held Ugolino, his arm wrapped around the struggling man's neck, choking off his air. "Let him know who
brings his death," Dimitri said. Bianca scooped up the guard's
guttering torch from the ground. Lifted, it flamed to new life,
illuminating her face for Ugolino to see. He gasped, his eyes
wide with terror and confusion. Bianca drew her dagger and
raised it between them. Deliberately, she kissed the flat surface
of the blade, ran her tongue up its length.

"Cut them off first. Cut them off and stuff them in his
mouth," Dimitri hissed, and Ugolino squirmed in terror, his
eyes bulging.

"This is supposed to be a robbery," she hissed back at him.
Really, Dimitri was becoming excessive in his urge for retribution. This was not a situation where they could afford to indulge themselves. Bianca did not want anything too unusual in
the crime, certainly not the kind of outrage castration would
provoke.

"Then do it slowly. You promised to do it slowly."

"Yes." From a deep pocket in her cloak, Bianca drew out
rags, stuffing Ugolino's mouth with one and binding the gag in
place with another. Dimitri loosened his hold on his captive's
throat the slightest amount. Ugolino struggled to escape, but
the eunuch's grip was still too strong.

"Now. Now," Dimitri urged her in a frenzy of excitement.

Smiling into Ugolino's eyes, Bianca drove the knife into his
belly, dragging it down and up again to disembowel him. The
stench of blood and guts filled the air. Ugolino's body
convulsed in Dimitri's grasp, a high-pitched whining emerging
from behind the gag. "Squeal," he whispered softly into Ugolino's ear. "Squeal, pink pig."

There was a noise. Someone stepping on a dead branch?

Instantly, Bianca tossed away the torch. She stepped to the side and slit Ugolino's throat to finish him off. Dimitri moaned in protest, but she was already running back up the hill. She thought she saw someone, something, a dark shadow drawing back behind a wall. She increased her pace, dagger ready as she turned the corner, but no one was visible on the road. Bianca ran to the next crossing, but there was no one in sight there either.

If there had been an observer, why hadn't he raised a cry of alarm? The sound could have been her imagination or the small movement of an animal. The uncertainty disturbed her, but even if there was someone, it was unlikely she had been identified. She had been reckless not to take Ugolino deeper into the alley, but she was not entirely a fool. Even in the torchlight she and Dimitri had kept themselves hooded. They should be unrecognizable from that distance.

Bianca retraced her steps and found Dimitri had pulled the guard and Ugolino deeper into the alleyway to delay discovery till morning. She helped him finish off their scheme by stripping both corpses of their purses. Ugolino's was heavy, if not as heavy as it might have been had Luigi paid his losses, and he wore considerable jewelry as well. One of the lesser rings would do for proof that they had completed their commission for Ugolino's wife.

Abandoning the eviscerated body, they moved off swiftly into the night.

10 Conversations

"Signore di Fabiani is innocent," Benito said. "At least, according to Giacomo he is."

"I hope so, for Dorotea's sake," Veronica said. Head down, her hair tumbled like a curtain, shielding her face from view. She reached out, fingers toying with the tender green stalk of an iris, and wondered at her own duplicity. She had set out to discover all she could of Antonio, both past and present, but Benito believed their talk to be nothing more than their usual bit of family gossip. She had always been private with her problems but not secretive. First Luigi's threats and then her troubled affair with Antonio had distorted her world. Fear and passion wrapped their coils about her, enclosing her in a brooding darkness, isolating her more and more from those to whom she had been closest.

"It was the night of the betrothal, you remember." Keeping an eye on Roberto, who was wrestling with Bombol in one corner of the garden, Benito leaned back against the base of the fountain and settled into his tale. "You should have seen Giacomo. He's such a lighthearted rogue, it's hard to picture him angry. We'd gone out to the stables for a bit of midnight dicing. A lot of wineskins were emptied that night, and Giacomo had finished off more than one of them. I don't think he was drinking to celebrate, though. He didn't seem all that happy about the coming wedding."

"No? He was not overwhelmed by our family's virtues?"

Benito snorted, "A little too overwhelmed, perhaps, by Madonna Dorotea's virtues. I don't think she will be the easiest mistress to serve."

"I think you are right," she whispered conspiratorially. Dorotea would resent everyone for her own weakness. But it was not her sister-in-law that she wanted to hear about. Hoping her urgency was not obvious, Veronica prodded Benito, "You must finish your story."

"There was the usual talk, of the pleasures of gambling, of wine and women, what troublesome creatures they were. Some guard, thinking himself clever, said that if Signore di Fabiani found his new lady a trouble to him, he could be rid of her as easily as he had the last one. Well, the next thing we knew, he and Giacomo were rolling about in the dust and straw, stirring up an unholy commotion. All the horses stamping about in their stalls, and the dogs barking . . . ."

Benito paused abruptly, no doubt remembering, as Veronica was, the earlier fight in those same stables. She kept her head bent, stroking the clinging lavender petals of the iris with her fingertip. After a moment, Benito went on, "The guard was a lot bigger, though Giacomo's a tough enough fighter when he's mad, and knows a neat trick or two. His feet are a marvel. He inflicted enough pain to make the guard even madder, so three of us had to drag him off Giacomo. The guard went off to sulk in the corner. Giacomo was bleeding all over himself from a cut to the head. I took him up to the kitchen to get it cleaned and patched.

"He told me then it was true Antonio had killed his brother in a fight, but that it was an accident. It was Alessandro who had the knife and murder in his heart. They fought over the wife, right enough. Beatrice her name was, beautiful as an angel and sweet as sin. More than a little mad for men, she was, but Giacomo swears Antonio never harmed her, though she broke his heart. He wouldn't have—nor could he have, Giacomo says. Knowing his master was upset about his brother, he spent the whole night wrapped in a blanket outside his door. Says he never slept a wink for worrying, and would have heard if his master had left the room. It was that morning they found the lady, and his master was more stunned than any of them, by Giacomo's account."

"You believe him?"

"I believe he believes it. No reason not to, that I can see. He's got a clever tongue in his head, and I'm sure he could tell a pretty lie if it pleased him, instead of losing his temper and getting himself thrashed. He felt foolish enough over that, said he'd not be able to tell his headache from his hangover in the morning. Why should he bother to lie? I shouldn't like to think Signore di Fabiani had murdered a woman, but there's not many men in Florence would condemn him for killing an un-faithful wife. Not many in Italy." Benito frowned, "I can see as how the story would frighten a shy pious lady like Madonna Dorotea—but it was twelve years ago, and it's not as if the signore has left a trail of dead wives and murdered mistresses behind him since. I should not think Madonna Dorotea will give him cause to doubt her, in any case. Most likely she's just afraid of marriage."

"Most likely," Veronica murmured, for that was true enough, the one fear fueling the other.

"Still, it's strange that the wife died the same night as the brother, so it's hard to credit Giacomo's tale entirely. Maybe he did fall asleep." Benito shrugged. "There's no way we'll ever know what happened. Not for certain."

———

"There is your answer."

Veronica stared down at the *Tarocco* cards. The Prince of Cups lay at the center, surrounded by a fan of scattered Cups, combative Wands and cruel Swords. The jewel colors gleamed up at her, vivid against the midnight blue velvet. As she watched, the mocking images danced before her eyes as Mama Lucia's words danced in her mind, as teasing and ambiguous as Benito's. Veronica pressed her hands to her temples, trying to bring the pictures, their meaning, into focus. When she lifted her gaze, Mama Lucia's eyes were gleaming too, and they did not waver.

"It's all there," Mama Lucia repeated, her knotted fingers gliding over the layout. "The betrayal of love, violent death, deceit, grief, and exile."

"That does not answer my question. It is a simple question. Did Antonio murder his wife? Yes or no?" There was an edge to Veronica's voice, for it seemed to her that the interpretation, even more than the cards, had been deliberately evasive.

The edge to Mama Lucia's voice was as sharp as her own. "Will yes or no make any difference to you? The man was a mercenary, I heard. His hands are hardly bloodless. There is a streak of violence in him. It glitters bright as a sword blade."

"No," she said, shaking her head. "That is war, and savage

though it may be, he would have been defending himself against another man, armed and deadly. This is different.''

"Is it? Perhaps she deserved her fate. Perhaps she goaded him beyond endurance, or tried to kill him herself.''

Veronica only shook her head again. "He did not do it.''

"Why do you ask, Veronica, when there is only one answer you will hear?''

She could not say, "I know it as clearly as I knew my parents' death.'' Mama Lucia would believe that as Veronica believed the *Tarocco*. It was her own doubts she sought to quell. Arriving at the tower, Veronica had steeled herself to ward off Mama Lucia's searching questions. But there had been no prying, though she knew her great-grandmother desired and deserved her confidence. Nor had she once been addressed as "child" today. Veronica realized they met now on new ground, not only child to great-grandmother, acolyte to teacher, but woman to woman.

"Veronica?'' Compassionate and merciless, the black eyes met and held her own.

"There is only one answer my heart will believe, but I cannot believe my own heart. Nothing is as I imagined it would be, Mama Lucia. If I am wrong about this, then I can be wrong about everything. I trust the cards, and you, to give me the truth.''

The fierce gaze softened, and Mama Lucia nodded. She reached out once more to the *Tarocco* spread, her nail tapping the center card of the fan. "The Five of Swords is reversed. The deceit follows the violence, and it is not his but another's. Your answer is no.''

"Antonio did not murder his wife,'' Veronica said quietly. It was the answer she wanted, the answer she had known was true, yet relief did not come as expected.

"You believe him innocent, yet you fear him.''

"I fear myself, perhaps.'' She hesitated. "Sometimes . . . when I am with him . . . I do not know myself.''

"It is your own death you fear. He can destroy you. Perhaps not his hands at your throat or his knife in your heart. The thrust of his sex can be as fatal as a dagger. It pierces the heart of the body, the heart of the soul. When love is good, you die of joy. The body dissolves and you emerge reborn, like a butterfly from its chrysalis.''

''It was like that, once,'' Veronica said haltingly, for even that first time Antonio had closed his heart away from hers.

''Look at me, Veronica.'' Mama Lucia waited until Veronica looked again into those penetrating black eyes. ''You have not wanted to tell me of him—not out of shyness, nor discretion, nor the secret spell that lovers weave for themselves, but because of shame, of pain. Do you want a love you are afraid to voice? A love which is the death of the soul?''

''No,'' she answered. ''But I want him and no other. I do not think, for me, there is another.''

''Then you must fight for him. You must claim all your power, and use it,'' Mama Lucia said, as if she read the conflict within her.

''The power you speak of is not something I control. Insofar as I have it, it controls me.''

''Like love, you must surrender to it, Veronica.''

She smiled bitterly. ''Antonio will not have my surrender. He has made love an endless battle between us, and he is far more skilled than I in the arts of war.''

''What fool fights a battle he has already won? For all his experience, he is fighting blind and weighted with armor. As for his precious skills, there is nothing he knows that you cannot learn. His own hands can teach you how to conquer his flesh. But flesh is only the battleground. The war is in the heart. So, like you, he must surrender. Perhaps then he will learn what victory is.''

———

''Daniele, I would like to look at the erotic art portfolio. Would you give me the key, please?''

Brush poised, bits of cerulean blue paint daubing his face and hair, Daniele stared at Veronica, his hazel eyes round with surprise. After a moment, he laid his brush aside, wiped his hands on his smock, and went to the desk at the back of the room, ferreting about in the drawer. Withdrawing the key from the hidden compartment, he handed it to her. ''If you want to see it, I suppose you're ready.''

"Thank you." She did not enlighten him that this would be her second viewing.

"Do you want me to leave, Veronica?"

It was kind of him to offer her privacy, when he was so involved in his work. "Go on painting. I'll take it over to the corner table."

Veronica unlocked the cupboard where the portfolio was kept and carried it to the back of the room. Clearing away the remnants of Daniele's supper, she sat down and opened the folio on the table. She began to peruse the drawings, seeing them with new eyes, the eyes of experience. She studied not only the images, but her own response to them, what stirred her physically as well as aesthetically. Studied them also for what she could learn, for what would please a man, please Antonio.

One of the pictures she remembered liking before now seemed coy rather than sweet. Two others still seemed truly beautiful, with their voluptuous line and tender gestures. She realized they were among the least explicit, but they were drawn so beautifully that Daniele had included them. There were others, quite explicit, that she found both exquisite and arousing. Not many of the drawings embarrassed or shocked her now, though she found a few that distressed her in their raw carnality or the darkness of their vision. Some of these she simply disliked. Another brought Luigi to mind, disgusting her. Among the rest, one or two were disturbingly compelling, evoking all the conflict of her feelings for Antonio. She understood now how hate and love could mix.

After a while Daniele came over and stood beside her. "Which ones do you like best?" he asked, curious and slightly embarrassed. Quietly, she laid out her favorites, choosing six from among the thirty or so Daniele had collected. He sat down beside her and studied her choices. Looking at the drawings together initiated them into a new acceptance and understanding. In many ways, Daniele had treated her as an adult for years. In other ways, he had protected her as if she were no older than Dorotea. For all his teasing, he had never seen her as a sexual being before. Well, she had not felt as one before. All her relationships were subtly shifting.

"You always had a good eye." Daniele glanced at her,

looked back at the drawings again, then picked up three of them and laid them out side by side. "These I understand. They are all very beautiful, very poignant. The emotion is real, the fluid line coveys the tenderness of the gesture."

"Yes, they look like they are in love. In this one you can see the emotion in the faces. Here it is in the way the man holds the woman, the way his hand caresses her."

"Why did you choose this one?"

"I loved that one because everything in it seemed so sensuous, the fabrics, the flowers are as erotic as the bodies."

He picked up another drawing, one of the dark, compelling ones she could not turn away from. "This surprises me. Or perhaps not. It is one of the best I have, very powerful. It is passionate but not so pretty."

"This isn't pretty, but it is beautiful. Frighteningly beautiful."

"Full of fury."

"Yes, full of fury," she whispered, Antonio's face rising before her.

"And what about this one?" he asked, lifting up one of the illustrations she had discarded.

"No," she shook her head. "The drawing is even better, I can see that, but I don't like it. There is passion in it, but it's the passion of cruelty, the lust for power. This first one is about the torment of desire, the pain of love. There is no love here."

"Are you in love, Veronica?"

She smiled ruefully. "Does it show so clearly?"

"You've changed. I did not think why until you asked to see the folio. You were so withdrawn for a time, then suddenly . . . . You are more vivid, somehow. Like a red rose unfurling, your color blazes out. But you are blooming in shadow, I think, not in sunlight." He picked up the last drawing, a charcoal sketch of a starkly beautiful male nude. A man lost in rapture as he pleasured himself. "Antonio di Fabiani?"

She had chosen it for the resemblance to his face, his body, the intensity of his passion. "Yes," she answered, then lowered her eyes from Daniele's gentle, questioning gaze.

"Your first love . . . and unrequited, I fear? Does he even

know? I suppose he must. He did dance with you at the party, I remember. But only the once.''

Veronica did not respond to that. She trusted Daniele. For all his frivolity, he was perceptive and kind. She wanted to tell him, to ask for his advice and learn from his knowledge of men. But Mama Lucia was right—there was too much shame, too much pain. If she started to tell it, she would tell it all. Daniele saw her as such an innocent. He would be shocked at her wantonness, giving herself impulsively to a man she did not know. He would understand that finally, because he understood and accepted human passion. But he would not understand or accept Antonio's cruelty, not to someone he loved. How could she tell him Antonio had given her money, not once, but twice? How could she tell him she still desperately desired a man who treated her as if she were a whore? Something had gone terribly wrong between them, something Veronica still hoped could be changed. Until then, she did not want to present Antonio in a negative light. And if nothing changed, then she was not sure she ever wanted anyone to know what had happened.

''Such sadness,'' Daniele said softly, enfolding her in his arms. ''I don't blame you for being enamored. He is very handsome, very compelling. But I should tell you, my dear, that you may not have a chance with him. Not because you aren't beautiful or clever enough, for you are, but the gossip is that he only beds professionals, accomplished courtesans like Bianca.''

''Women he pays,'' Veronica said bitterly. Must she play the whore to keep him? Could she bear to keep him if that was the cost?

''Perhaps it arouses him, makes him feel in control, to put a price on his pleasure. Some men are obsessed with such things. Perhaps it is only a preference for skill and detachment, sex without emotional entanglements.'' Then he shrugged. ''Perhaps the gossip is completely wrong, though my sources are usually accurate.''

''How can they know such intimate things?''

''He has traveled widely and known many women. There is more than one courtesan here from Rome and Venice. Sometimes they share such knowledge.'' Daniele paused. ''In some ways, I think you are older than I, in others you still seem to me a child. You have had no small loves to teach you the ways of such things. This man is very sophisticated, very jaded. I do not want you to be hurt, either because he makes love to you or because he doesn't. Also, there is something . . . dangerous in him.''

"Yes. I know."

"Do you? Well, sometimes danger is part of the appeal, no? I prefer the sprite, but I have also known the lure of the demon lover, on occasion.'' He smiled sadly, for his sprite, Cecco, had heeded his family's complaints and abandoned him. "We always hope those who are dear to us will love more wisely than we do.''

Veronica took his hand, her smile not much livelier than his own, "What little wisdom I possess has deserted me, I'm afraid.''

Daniele squeezed her hand between both his own and then released it. Reaching out to the drawings, he began to move them about, laying out several "Antonio liked this, I remember. Because it made him laugh, most likely. He has a wicked sense of humor. And this one . . . well, that is something all men desire. The tongue is beautifully done, no? Like velvet. And these two that you liked, the one that is 'frighteningly' beautiful, and this with the entwined bodies, so tender. He pretended to ignore it, but his eye came back to it. He admits to his darkness more easily than to his light. He is not a man that it will be easy to get close to, Veronica.''

"I know that too."

"What will you do if he gives you his body, Veronica, but not his mind, his heart?''

"That I do not know."

———

Veronica watched covertly as the cool March breeze ruffled Antonio's hair, lifting the fine glossy strands from his forehead. She longed to do the same, remembering the silky texture beneath her fingertips. He looked so beautiful today, framed against the vast tricolor mosaic of the Duomo walls. Escorting Dorotea to Savonarola's Mass, Antonio had toned his doublet and hose to the more sober Florentine mode, the

color a deep forest green, subtly accented in black and silver.
Veronica lamented her own practical gray wool, but she was
escorting Roberto and, even with Benito's help, was likely to
encounter sticky fingers at some point. As she watched surreptitiously, Antonio bent his head to catch some phrase of Dorotea's. A small smile cut his lips, precise and polite. It was not a
smile Veronica would have wanted, but he had given her nothing. Aside from his first coolly courteous greeting, Antonio
was studiously ignoring her.

It had all gone for naught. The gossip, the *Tarocco* reading,
viewing the portfolio with Daniele. A month had passed, and
in that time she had not seen Antonio once, until now, where
they were surrounded by an audience of relatives and neighbors. Thankfully, Luigi was not there, nor Fra Frederigo. Maria
was more than enough today, setting Veronica's teeth on edge
with her sanctimonious judgments. Savonarola's sermon had
been scathing, exciting the crowd and inspiring the worst in
her mother-in-law.

"The Mass was impressive, was it not?" a light voice asked
beside her. Veronica turned to greet Stefano, Antonio's cousin,
who had danced with her at the betrothal. The small smile she
gave in answer to his question was a twin to Antonio's, no
doubt. She did not want to start an argument.

"Miraculous," Dorotea whispered reverently, her small
hands playing over her ivory rosary. "Who can deny the Holy
Friar's truth?"

"Some still can," Maria accused. "Daniele Danti has not
accompanied you to hear Savonarola, Veronica. It is not surprising that a man of his shameful affections dares not brave
this holy sanctuary. It is surprising that you have once again
sought to hear Savonarola preach."

Why did she love her malice so much and nurture it as if it
were a virtue? "Ever since the bonfire, Roberto has wanted to
come, so Benito and I brought him to Mass today." Veronica
doubted Roberto understood much of the sermon, but he responded to the Friar's compelling voice and to the heady atmosphere of adoration that filled the crowded Duomo.
Daniele, of course, would have none of Savonarola. "My
cousin has gone to hear Fra Francesco di Puglia."

"The Franciscan?" Maria asked scornfully. "Every week his audience dwindles."

"Daniele prefers his sermons," Veronica said evenly, though he had complained only this morning that Fra Francesco's once elegant speeches were becoming no more than petty attacks on his Dominican rival. "There is little choice in Florence nowadays," he had muttered. "One can select ranting fanaticism or sanctimonious pique." Veronica would have enjoyed repeating that comment, but only Antonio would have appreciated it.

Maria's voice rose. "There will be retribution. Fra Francesco cannot attack the word of God unscathed. Savonarola is a holy prophet."

"It is not God he attacks but Savonarola's interpretation of His words. They both voice their religious grievances," Veronica pointed out to Maria. "Savonarola preaches against the Pope, and Puglia preaches against Savonarola."

Maria's next attack was halted by the arrival of Madonna Villani in their midst. Widowhood agreed with her, Veronica noted. She seemed a person now rather than a walking shadow. Veronica doubted if anyone missed Ugolino, he had been a dreadful man . . . but not as dreadful as his fate, his body slashed by thieves in a dark alleyway.

"My own father still prefers Fra Francesco's sermons, as does Antonio's," Stefano said to the ensuing silence. "A voice of eloquence and elegance, but no emotion. Although Savonarola's fervor carries him to extremes, I cannot help but prefer him. Inspiration, passion, and daring—his is the voice of the future. Do you not agree, Antonio?"

"The voice of the future and the voice of the past are sometimes as one," Antonio answered him.

"But you came to the Duomo today, to see him," Stefano said. "Certainly you must admire the Friar?"

"Not all eyes are friendly. You will find many of his enemies here today, as well as his admirers. He has too much power to be ignored."

"But which are you?" Stefano asked, perturbed.

"What an ingenuous question, cousin. As it happens, the answer is neither. I am here at my mother's request," Antonio said, "and to accompany Dorotea and her mother. Savonarola is a fascinating figure and his power is obvious, but it is not a power which affects my heart or my mind.''

And what power will? Veronica wondered, longing to possess it.

"I heard your lady mother was very ill. Take her my sympathies, and tell her I plan to visit. I am glad she is well again," Stefano told Antonio.

"She will never be well, but she is improved for the moment," Antonio said, his voice gone flat. "I know it would give her pleasure to see you, Stefano. You would be wise to visit soon."

"Home now?" Roberto asked plaintively, tugging on Veronica's hand. He was restless now that the ceremony was over, wanting to dance or sing or run to release the energy gathered up within him.

"We promised Daniele we would meet him here," she told him.

"Home," he insisted, a whine coming into his voice. He began to bounce up and down in distress, bored and agitated at the same time.

"Look over there," Veronica pointed. The pastry sellers were out in full force today. "Benito will buy you a *panforte*, Roberto."

"Yes, yes, sweets!" he cried to that, switching his attention to Benito, who gave Veronica a smile and a puzzled lift of the eyebrows. She saw his eyes return to Stefano and herself, and he grinned before letting Roberto drag him away through the crowd to carry out Veronica's errand of bribery.

The right reason, dear Benito, she thought, *but the wrong man.*

She was behaving like an infatuated fool, lingering here. Why had she discarded that perfect opportunity to escape this misery? There was no point in torturing herself with Antonio's impossible nearness. There would be no way, here, for them to be alone. The tension, the friction of his presence was almost unbearable as it was. Tenderness, anger, palpable desire washed over her in turn. His voice, the movements of his body, all abraded her frayed nerves. But walking away from his presence was like walking from light into darkness.

If Antonio still felt as she did, he gave no sign. He was

obviously making no effort to communicate with her at all. If he had wanted to talk, to be with her, she had not been hard to find. A visit to Daniele would have afforded him the perfect excuse to see her.

She had turned away from Antonio at the bonfire. Because of that, Veronica had resolved to approach him herself, when Maria had informed her that his mother was much worse. She waited while the date of the wedding was advanced, postponed, and set again with the vacillations of his mother's illness. With Madonna di Fabiani so sick, she felt it would be selfish and unfeeling of her to go to his home offering not sympathy but challenge. Veronica was glad, after hearing the dark undercurrent of pain in his voice when he spoke of his mother, that she had not confronted him.

Then he was gone from Florence for over a week. Daniele brought word that Antonio's father had sent him to visit certain family lands that bordered on Siena, filling Veronica with a rush of homesickness. She longed to walk the twisting cobbled streets with him, show him her childhood haunts. Those cool green hills would be ablaze with color now. They could ride through seas of white daisies, blue irises and cornflowers, wild pinks, primroses, and bright red poppies. Find some secluded tree-shaded stream and make love . . . .

But it was not she who shared his caresses. Daniele had also told her, wanting not to hurt her but to bring her the truth, that Antonio had bought Bianca a fabulous emerald necklace. Antonio had not sought Veronica out, but he had found time to visit the courtesan and deluge her with jewels. Did all these lavish gifts show her worth to him, or did they free him from the need to give anything of himself? Veronica's pride was still bruised from their last encounter at the betrothal. This news etched at her resolve, corroded it, leaving her vulnerable and uncertain. His anger, his violence had been part of an intense and intimate contact. Today he offered only a polite facade of indifference, blank and smooth as glass. If she would shatter that glass, she must find her own anger again, to armor herself against the flying shards.

Her own polished manners masking her pain, Veronica turned to Stefano. He was definitely attentive, asking after Roberto's health, Daniele's painting, as well as her impression of

Savonarola's sermon. Was it simply the polite flirtation of the moment, or was he trying to court her? He was quite pleasing to look at, a glossy, golden youth, and easy to talk to, open and unguarded in his speech. He seemed so young, so naïve, especially compared with Antonio, but even with other young gallants of Florence. He impressed her as sincere, but she wondered if his naïveté was only part of a pose he cultivated, one that suited his boyish good looks and won him sympathy, and more than sympathy, from women.

Would encouraging Stefano make Antonio jealous? He would no doubt see it for the ruse it was, but it might stir him anyway. Veronica had always despised such manipulations, sure they were unnecessary. She had not imagined that love would call for such calculating weapons. Veronica sighed, knowing she would never be as ruthless as her opponent, flaunting his bejeweled mistress. True, she had flirted with Stefano at the betrothal when her anger was high, but it was not her nature to do it now in cold blood. Nor did she want the burden of dealing with the results if Stefano took her seriously. If she wanted anything from him, it was not passion but friendship.

A wealthy couple joined the circle, standing by Madonna Villani, across from Veronica at the edge of the group. The man was ponderous, heavy-jowled and gout-ridden, his wife dwarfed by his bulk, tiny and nondescript. Yet he seemed the mouse and she the lion. Veronica found her vaguely familiar but could not place her. Her pale, protuberant eyes were her only distinguishing feature. The woman was watching Antonio with such fixed intensity that Veronica thought her infatuated. *Yet another rival,* she sighed inwardly, pitying the besotted creature. She was the only other person whom Antonio avoided with as studied indifference as he did Veronica. Then, looking more closely, she saw it was not love but hatred, that lit those pale eyes. They burned with a fire so cold, Veronica shivered in its glare.

Turning back to Stefano, Veronica continued their conversation, pleased that her voice was still level. He was asking now about her views on the recent grain riot. "I hope you have not been frightened by the violence, Madonna? You should not walk unescorted through the streets."

"There has been no trouble this month," she replied, choosing to ignore that last offer. "The violence was frightening, but one must feel pity for the people. They are destitute. The times are troubled, but surely Florence could distribute a little more grain to the needy."

"You are foolish," the small woman said loudly. "Such largesse would only make the situation worse. Even more of these innumerable troops of country peasants and beggars would flock into our city and drain its resources. They are no better than thieves."

"They come seeking a better life here, Laudomia, only to find themselves perishing with hunger," Stefano chastised her.

Veronica knew then who she was—Alessandro's unforgiving widow. During the past weeks, Veronica had learned as much as she could of Antonio's history, from the day of his birth to the name of his horse. She doubted it was coincidence that Antonio's trip to Siena had coincided with the anniversary of his brother's death. She addressed Laudomia, "Madonna, the convent hospitals are full of these poor people. Many of them have collapsed in the streets. Some have been found on the embankments, dead of starvation."

"We will impoverish ourselves and join the poor, no better than they," Laudomia said flatly.

"Savonarola, in his compassion, has implored the citizens of Florence to succor all those in great need," Maria interrupted. "Inspired by his exhortations, the city has made many provisions and the people have generously given alms. I have offered the help of my own hands to tend these wretched creatures."

Ah, yes, Maria's charity, Veronica thought wryly. Three times this past month, she and Mama Lucia had gone to the convent hospital with food and herbal remedies. Maria had come one day, with a basket of bread. Her mother-in-law had spent only a few moments with the sick, but over an hour trying to convince the convent to dismiss Mama Lucia and her dubious services. But the nuns were old friends, who valued her great-grandmother's knowledge over Maria's recriminations. Maria then refused to tend the patients, saying there was no virtue in saving their bodies if their souls were damned.

"They bring nothing but trouble," Laudomia declared,

"sowing disease and disorder throughout the city, rioting in the streets. Florence is no longer safe from this rabble."

"Even before the riot, there were deaths in the Piazza del Grano," Stefano said. "The prices there are the lowest in the city. The poor crowd in so thickly, trying to buy a little cheap grain, that some have died of suffocation in the crush."

"Have you considered that this panic may have been provoked by Piero di Medici's supporters?" Antonio asked, changing the slant of the conversation totally. "In the midst of all the furor, I am told that a chant of '*Palle, palle*' was taken up by the throng."

"Whenever there is trouble nowadays, someone always calls upon the emblem of the Medici," Stefano said, "just as though Piero had not betrayed everything his family represented."

"Hence the cry of '*Palle.*' Evoking the honor of the Medici name gilds the tarnish on Piero's," Antonio said with a cynical smile. Although he was speaking to Stefano, Veronica saw that his gaze had locked with Laudomia's. "Since the riot, the rumors of his return to Florence have doubled. And these tales have a new twist, that Piero plans to distribute grain before he rouses the city to follow him. His supporters may hope to provoke a popular revolt in his favor. If it succeeds, they will step forward to claim the victory and reinstate Piero. If it fails, they would fade quickly back to the safety of the gray shadows."

Veronica saw Laudomia bridle at the sly comment. The *Bigi,* the "Grays," was the name given Piero's ardent followers. For a long time, those still favoring the rule of the outlawed Medici had prudently avoided exposing their views to the light of day, and discretion was still advisable

"Even Piero is better than Savonarola and his *Piagnoni,* his 'snivelers,'" Laudomia said, defying Antonio, though her husband flapped his huge hands in distress, vainly attempting to shush her. "Under the Friar's rule we would be yoked and driven like cattle to serve the common horde."

"You may find that while the jeweled golden yoke of the Medici is more aristocratic and aesthetic, its weight is far greater than the simple wood and leather collar of the *Populari,*" Antonio said, using the polite name of Savonarola's party only to annoy Laudomia, Veronica was sure. Then, obviously unwilling to commit himself to the Friar's leadership, Antonio added with a certain vicious delight, "Of course, Savonarola may opt for lead harness and steer us all with flagellants' whips."

Veronica suddenly suspected Antonio was in a bad mood indeed. He had angered Maria now, as well as Laudomia. Dorotea looked close to tears. Maria turned on him, snapping, "Indeed, spiritual sins weigh heavy as lead on the conscience. Fornication and murder are the yokes of damnation." Antonio smiled as if she had complimented him.

"Piero reinstated?" Stefano asked, diverting them from the growing tension. "Do you even think it is possible? He betrayed us to the French. The city would never accept him again."

Antonio turned back to him, "In Florentine politics anything is possible, especially with such disaffection among the people. But no, the odds are against Piero. The man has a genius for failure, and I think that is what awaits him here in Florence."

"We shall see," Laudomia declaimed. She was about to say more, but her husband took her arm and bent over her, murmuring urgently. Jerking her arm from his grasp, she turned and stalked off. Embarrassed, her husband lumbered after her, casting a despairing look at them over his shoulder. The restless stirrings of departure seized the group, and Veronica was happy to see Daniele appear with Roberto and Benito at his side, all happily devouring slices of *panforte*.

"Allow me to accompany you," Stefano said, attaching himself to their little group. He turned his glowing smile on Daniele, "I have long admired your paintings. Would it be possible to see what you are working on?"

"Of course," Daniele beamed at him. Veronica felt a wave of dismay. She did not want company today, she did not want to encourage Stefano. Then she smiled. Stefano had a certain quality . . . the sprite, the green-eyed faun. He was just Daniele's type, and he was being just as charming to Daniele as he had been to her. Cecco had wounded Daniele's heart, a shallow but painful graze of Cupid's arrow. Stefano might be just the one to heal that wound. If not, he would at least provide a pleasant distraction. Once home, she would escape quickly and let Daniele do the entertaining.

"I've always wanted to do a *Judgment of Paris*," Daniele was saying. "Would you consider posing?"

"But of course, how delightful," Stefano laughed, linking an arm through each of theirs, as if he had known them for years. "Today I am to be immortalized by one of the great painters of Florence."

Yes, he was charming, warm and uncomplicated, but he was not who she wanted. Filled with longing, Veronica cast one look back.

Caught off guard at last, Antonio's eyes met hers. One look that burned across the space between them, reaching from the dark sexual vortex of his center to her own inner melting core. One look that riveted her where she stood, saying he knew the desire she felt and shared it. Saying everything he wanted to do to her then and there, in the crowded piazza. It lasted no longer than a single, all-encompassing second, then it was gone, his eyes black and dead. He shut her out utterly, then turned away, leaving her cold and empty.

The message was not *later*. The message was *never again*.

11 *The Rescue*

"TOMORROW," Veronica whispered. "I will see him tomorrow." She sat in front of the mirror, staring sightlessly at her reflection, keyed up with an excitement, an anticipation so intense it bordered on fear. She did not know how she knew, only that it was true. "Tomorrow."

There were times when she thought something might happen, and nothing did. Times when things of import came and went with no forewarning. Sporadic and capricious, the psychic undercurrent was often so subtle she could only wonder after the event if her apprehensions had been some unheeded omen. Seldom did a premonition come with this sense of excitement. Most often, it preceded disaster, but never with time or clarity enough to alter it. Except the once, the day of her parents' death, with Mama Lucia's cards, she had never seen exactly what was to be. Instead, her mind was teased with tremors of anxiety or overwhelmed with dread. Like a waking dream, images of those she loved were suffused with a sense of delight or danger or horror. Mama Lucia was right, it was not a gift she desired, if gift it was.

Except, perhaps, tonight. Tonight she was certain—and that certainty filled her with urgency, a hectic fever simmering in her blood. She pressed a hand to the coolness of her forehead and laughed unsteadily. An inner heat only, fueled by an inner hunger. *Antonio*. For good or ill, she must see him, talk to him, finally. She did not know if he would be alone, but she would make certain she was. The rest must be conjured from the situation itself. She was not certain where to look, but she would set out for the Duomo and let impulse guide her from there.

She had waited too long to act, trapped in a quagmire of anger, confusion and lost opportunities. All these weeks she had waited for Antonio to come to her . . . waited for the moment to be right for her to approach him. But he had not come and the time was never right. Tomorrow she must seize the moment and make it right . . . .

Veronica was running, running, trapped in a reality as disoriented as any dream or vision. The air cut sharp as glass in her lungs, but fear drove her blistered feet forward. Dazed with fatigue, she tripped and fell in the street. She lay a second, bewildered and exhausted, then forced herself to get up. Stumbling round the nearest corner, she saw a deep-set doorway halfway down the street. It was a shelter of sorts, and she pressed herself into its protective recess, taking a moment to quiet her gasping breaths. Hot from running, Veronica wanted to rid herself of the gray cloak she wore, but it was less conspicuous than the lavish dress it covered. The silvery brocade she had worn thinking to see Antonio—fool that she was. Her prophetic certainty had been no more than a giddy dream. Why had she not foreseen this trap?

"Palle, palle!" The cry rose sudden and shrill out of the dull roar in the distance. Other cries followed the first, shouts for bread, for freedom, for blood, for death. The poor demanding vengeance for their poverty. The grain crisis had worsened, and with it their desperation and their anger. Frayed tempers had snapped, and now a frenzied mob swarmed through the streets of Florence, wreaking violence on whatever and whoever fell into their grasp. She had fled both the mass destruction of the mob and the roving gangs that splintered off from it, bent on looting the empty streets.

The sound was closer. They must be coming back this way again. Veronica knew she must move, but she had no idea where she was. Forced from the known streets to ones that were safe for a moment, she had lost her way in the dark and tangled warren. There was no visible landmark. Looking down this street, she could see nothing but peeling walls and lines of flapping laundry that stretched from window to shuttered window or lay, trampled by the mob, in the clogged and reeking gutters. The way before her was empty now, that was what was important. She must find a familiar road that would lead the way back to home and safety.

Drawing the cloak close about her, Veronica stepped from the doorway onto the crumbling footpath by the gutter. There was an alley midway down the street, and she approached the shadowed gap cautiously. She was not aware of any sound, but her sense of danger escalated. The very air around her shivered with it. Her nerves prickled with fear, and the heat drained from her body. Sweat shrouded her skin with a cold, clammy film. Instinct screamed at her to turn and run back the way she had come, but the mob and all its fury waited there. Her breathing shallow and harsh in her own ears, Veronica forced herself to the edge and glanced down the narrow passageway. At first there was only a splash of red, vivid in the shadows. Then she saw it all complete—like some gruesome staged tableau or an obscene painting, clear in every grotesque detail.

The red was velvet, the rich red velvet of a woman's gown, bright against the lurid white of her splayed legs. The red was blood, spilling from her slashed throat down across the paleness of her exposed breasts. Her head fell sideways, her eyes staring wide. An old man, his skull crumpled, his white hair matted with blood and brain matter, lay discarded in the corner. A pack of street thugs were gathered around the bodies, a crude array of weapons scattered on the ground about them. Two stood over the woman's corpse, one tying up the front of his hose while the other opened his to erect flesh. A man in a leather apron sat by the old man, tossing gold coins in the air, a satin purse upended on his head like a cap. Another knelt beside the dead woman, gripping her wrist, hacking at her fingers with a sword to cut free the rings she wore. Behind him, in the shadows, a small man stood, drenched in blood, his hand slowly caressing the blade of his knife. A sixth, more boy than man, crouched in a doorway vomiting.

"Puking brat," the last man muttered, a heavy brute with bulging belly and arms thick as hams. "If you haven't any more guts than a woman, we'll put you to a woman's use." He reached out a booted foot and poked between the boy's buttocks, then shoved him forward into his own mess. The man laughed and the dazed youth looked up at him, forcing a sickly, placating grin. Edging away from his tormentor, the boy glanced down the alleyway, straight into Veronica's horrified gaze. For a moment she stood, frozen, while he stared at her, mouth gaping. She lifted one hand, warning him to silence, but he raised his arm and pointed at her, a choked garbling noise coming from his throat. Tracing the gesture, the big man turned and saw her.

"Another one!" he yelled, snatching up the iron bar he'd discarded.

The first word released Veronica. She raced across the alley and up the street. Rounding the corner, she glanced sideways to see the first man in close pursuit, the others hastily emerging from the alley, weapons in hand. Ahead of her, a half-full slops bucket sat abandoned in the gutter. Veronica grabbed it and spun around, heaving its foul contents into the face of the man in the lead. He flung up his hands, cursing, and she hurled the heavy bucket at his feet. He tripped and fell to the ground, slipping in the spilled muck. She whirled and ran once more, his shout following her. "Hurry, you fools! Catch her!"

Veronica plunged through the streets, ducking down one alley after another. She tried to lose them in the maze, but they were gaining on her. They could run faster, and the maze was theirs. They knew all the twists and turns, the secret passage-ways, the false leads and dead ends. Heart pounding against her rib cage, she damned the heavy skirts and fragile shoes that slowed her down. She caught a glimpse of the Duomo as she rushed past one street and paused at the entrance to the next. There was only a second to decide.

A dead-end alley, long and narrow. The brick walls were too high to climb, set with doors all locked against her. All but one. In the far corner, the back entry to some poor dwelling, a heavy wooden door opened to a dark corridor. An old woman knelt in the doorway, gathering up the shattered remnants of a collection of flowerpots that had decorated the ledge of a small barred window. Seeing Veronica, the old woman rose to her feet, clutching a clump of broken dirt and roots and broken stems to her breast. Veronica sprinted towards the door, but even as she ran, the old woman looked beyond her to the head of the alley. Fear warped her features, her mouth opening in a silent wail. Dropping her plant, she scuttled back within the doorway, slamming it shut just as Veronica reached it.

"No!" Veronica cried out, pounding on the door. "Oh no, please open the door. Help me. Help me, please!"

Instead there was the sound of a bolt sliding home. "No more trouble," a frightened voice whispered. "You go away now. Go away." Footsteps retreated from the door. Veronica spun around. Six men waited, blocking the mouth of the alley. Only the boy had not followed.

"Not so clever as you thought you were." It was the thick-set man who spoke, his voice grating with anger. She could smell the reek of slops on him from where she stood. Another man stepped forward, small and taut, with a narrow, pointed face and tiny black eyes that glistened with a feverish light. A weasel's face. Blood coated his arms to the elbow, and his knife performed a tiny jerking dance in his hand. The heavy man held out an arm, staying him. "You don't kill this one first. I've got something better than a knife ready to stick her with, and I want to feel her squirming on the end of it."

The men laughed, all but Weasel. "Quick or dead, get there soon enough and the meat's still warm," he said, his face twitching. "Why put up with all that screaming and kicking?"

"We did the last one your way, this one's mine," the heavy

man said to Weasel. The restless knife wove in his direction, but he hefted the metal bar he carried and Weasel backed off. "When I've finished with the bitch, I'll hold her down for the rest to have their chance. After that, you can do whatever you want." Swinging the iron, he moved forward. The others halted halfway, standing back to watch him take his revenge.

A thick coarse-bristled broom stood by the old woman's doorway. It was all there was, and she grabbed it. The man before her grinned, showing rotten stumps. Laughing, he feinted to the right, then left, making short, rapid slashes at her with the iron. Veronica could tell from the fixed glare of his eyes the moves were only meant to threaten her, to terrorize. Something—his stance, his taunting cruelty, the weapon he bore—flashed Luigi into her mind. Rage rushed through her, and she welcomed the strength it gave her. When she did not cower before him, he snarled at her, brandishing the iron rod at her head.

"Knocked out's no better than dead," Leather Apron called to him.

He glanced over his shoulder. "Just battered a little . . . ." he began.

Gripping the broom handle, Veronica sidestepped and jabbed the stiff bristles into his face, once, twice, driving straight for his eyes. Bellowing, he staggered backwards, one arm flying up to protect himself. She swiveled the broom around and brought it down as hard as she could, splitting the wooden handle over his head. The blows did no more than daze him. He staggered forward again, striking out blindly with the iron. Veronica swung her cloak off her shoulders and flung it over him. He cursed, pawing at its folds, while behind him his cohorts laughed at his plight. In the corner, one flower-pot remained unbroken amid the rest. She grabbed it and smashed it over his head, dirt and crockery scattering everywhere. With a muffled groan, the man slumped to the ground and lay still.

The glow of victory was fierce but brief. It vanished when she raised her head to confront the other five men. No longer laughing, the pack moved forward, Weasel and his bloody knife in the lead. Backing off from the slumped body of their ally, she saw the end of the iron bar protruding from the tangled folds of her cape. She tugged it free. Weasel paused, then gestured two of the others forward. A cold spasm twisted inside her as she focused on their weapons. There were too many of them, and what good was her iron bar against the long wooden stave or the prongs of the pitchfork? They were going to rape her, then kill her. The most she could do was to inflict some damage before she died.

"Veronica!" The cry rang through the alley.

Hearing his voice, seeing him spur the sweating stallion towards her, Veronica's relief was instant and total, despite the danger that waited between them. All the anger, the fear, that coursed through her brightened, intensified into a vivid excitement. "Antonio," she said, no louder than a whisper, but it was a shout of triumph. He was here, and that was all that mattered. She met his eyes, smiling, and saw the fearful darkness there flare to the same blazing excitement. He drew his sword and urged Ombra forward.

The five thugs ignored her now, turning to face this new threat. Antonio and his glittering blade were formidable enough. His mount was a dreadful weapon. The men spread out across the alley trying to surround their opponent, but the quick-stepping animal thwarted their intentions. With the longest reach, the stave and pitchfork moved forward. On the farthest edge, a third man approached with a richly embellished sword. *Some treasured prize of the riot,* she thought, *snatched from the hand of the dead.* He grasped it awkwardly, but with fervor, holding it out before him like some religious talisman. Weasel held only a knife. Veronica saw his eyes dart from the iron bar to her face, a look filled with venom. Catching her gaze, he sneered at her. His bloodstained blade rose up, pantomiming slitting her throat. She lifted the bar higher. Deciding the reward was not worth the risk, he skulked in the background, covering himself behind Stave and Leather Apron, who sported a hatchet.

The man with the sword made a dash to Antonio's left flank. His own *estoc* drawn to guard his right, Antonio pressed his steed to the left wall, protecting his exposed side. Trained to battle, the animal obeyed instantly, surging forward to crush the man against the alley wall. Screaming, he fell beneath the trampling hooves. The man with the stave rushed forward, and

Antonio swerved Ombra to meet him, reining the stallion back to rear. The flashing hooves struck out, knocking the weapon from the man's hands and driving him backwards. Squealing, he tripped and fell, rolling across the flagstones, arms wrapped about his head in futile protection. The lunging horse thwarted Weasel's hope of retrieving the abandoned sword. Dodging both horse and rolling body, he scuttled back into the shadows.

The fallen man scrambled to retrieve his stave. Shielding his companion, Pitchfork made a quick jab at Antonio's right flank, hurriedly retreating as Antonio wheeled to meet the new attack. In the midst of the fray, Veronica saw the man with the hatchet pull back from the others. Avoiding a confrontation at close quarters, he hovered on the edge of the fight, weapon drawn back in his arm, hunting for a clean throw at Antonio. As he poised to fling the hatchet, Veronica darted up behind him. Firming her grip on the iron bar, she swung it against his head. There was a dull, sickening thud as it connected with his skull. He let go of the hatchet and collapsed in a heap at her feet.

The thug with the stave returned to the fray, but his terror kept him dancing beyond the reach of the deadly hooves, and far beyond the length of his own weapon. Pitchfork made a desperate attack to the right, trying to impale the soft underbelly of Antonio's mount. Swerving and sighting in one impeccable motion, Antonio rose in the stirrups and drove his sword down into the man's heart. He pulled out the blade and the man pitched to the ground. Seeing four of his accomplices lying dead or unconscious, the man with the sword panicked and fled up the alley.

Without warning, a hand closed in her hair, jerking her backwards. Before she could catch her balance to struggle or kick, a wiry arm circled from the other side, locking her against the man's chest. She stilled instantly as she felt the tip of a knife pierce her throat. A trickle of blood ran down her skin. The arm that held her was corded with muscle and reeking with gore. Weasel.

"Drop the iron," he spat, and she let it fall. Facing Antonio, the man dragged her towards the mouth of the alley. *Estoc* pointed at the man, Antonio closed in on them but halted when the Weasel spoke. "Stop there, if you want this little bitch alive. You're letting me walk out of here. When I'm far enough that you can't catch me, then I'll let her go.''

Antonio did not back off. He raised the *estoc*, regarding the Weasel narrowly. Veronica could see he did not believe the man, but he was unwilling to put her life at hazard. She felt the arm around her throat tighten, tugging her backwards.

Antonio's eyes met hers, and she said to him clearly and with total certainty, ''Do as he says, and he will kill me. He is in love with death.''

''Shut your mouth, bitch,'' Weasel hissed.

The point of the knife dug in deeper. Veronica drew in her breath at the sharp pain, the feel of the thin line of blood trailing down her throat to her breast, but did not cry out again. She had told Antonio what she wanted, had asked him to risk her life to set her free. Aware of the peril, she did not want to hinder him with her fear.

Antonio was utterly still, his face expressionless. Only his eyes widened, searching hers in the silence that was not silence, but the relentless drumming of their heartbeats. Veronica held his gaze unswervingly, even as his eyes went dark, black and fathomless as death. She did not flinch from that darkness, accepting it. She knew the abyss that waited between them. There was no way across but to leap—or fall.

Slowly, deliberately, Antonio brought his steed forward, blocking the retreat up the alley. He extended his sword, sliding it across Veronica's shoulder so its point, she knew, must touch the throat of the man behind her. She felt Weasel jerk as the steel pricked his flesh. ''No, we will not do it that way,'' Antonio said to him, his voice implacable as the weapon he held. ''You will let the lady go. Now. Do as I say and I will not kill you.''

''How do I know that?'' his voice was shrill. Veronica was his protection, but if he was going to die, he wanted to take her with him.

Antonio bared his teeth, too cold a grimace for a smile. ''How indeed, since your own word is worth nothing? Mine is, unfortunately. Your life for hers.''

''You're lying.'' Weasel began to tremble, fear and hatred oozing from him in a foul miasma. The knife quivered in his hand. Veronica could feel the pulse of her artery beating close to its edge. Weasel did not believe Antonio would spare him, and he wanted her death with all the twisted lust that was in him.

"Drop the knife," Antonio said, each word hard and distinct. He pressed forward, a fraction of an inch, his eyes a black void, cold and empty enough to consume even Weasel's hatred. "Drop it. Or die."

Still clutching her hair, Weasel let go of the knife. Veronica heard it clatter onto the paving stones. Antonio sheathed his *estoc*, and backed his mount away the barest fraction. Weasel thrust Veronica forward against the horse and bolted down the alley. Relief crumbled her defenses. Legs trembling, she swayed on her feet while the world around her dissolved into a swirling mosaic of light and darkness. She did not see Antonio dismount but he was beside her swiftly, his arms hard around her.

"Do not faint now," he commanded.

"No. I will not faint." Closing her eyes, she clung to him, drawing deep breaths until her head cleared. When she opened them again, she rejoiced to see the spark of light, of life, burning in the depths of his own eyes once more.

"There are not many men who could have asked what you asked of me," his voice grated with tension.

"I wanted to live," she said simply. Without thought, on the deepest impulse within her, she put her arms around his neck and kissed him. His mouth was cold and hard under hers, then suddenly open, hot and ravenous, devouring her. Desire flared within her, a rush of flame igniting her blood. His hand covered her breast, and she felt her nipple harden and thrust out to meet his touch, the fabric of her gown a frustrating barrier between his flesh and hers. He kissed her face, the line of her jaw, the throbbing pulse of her neck. His lips sought hers again and his tongue delved into her mouth, the flavor of him sharp with the metallic taste of her blood.

Drawing away from the kiss, he stared down into her eyes. She could see all his urgency at war with his fierce protectiveness. Pressed against her, his sex, every muscle in his body was rigid with arousal. His eyes devoured her, needing life with death all around them, and she knew the same need for him. He pulled her closer for a second, but what he said was, "This is madness. It is not safe here."

Releasing her, Antonio retrieved the iron bar, handing it to her with a ceremonious flourish, "Your weapon, Madonna." He mounted his stallion and leaned down to help her up behind him. Fitting her foot to the stirrup, she gathered her brocaded skirts and swung up astride, as she preferred to ride. Looking over his shoulder, he raised his eyebrows slightly but made no other comment at her scandalous posture. Veronica wrapped one arm tightly about him and kept hold of the iron bar with the other. Antonio drew his *estoc* from the scabbard. Nudging Ombra forward, they moved cautiously to the head of the alleyway and paused. The road was no longer empty before them, but the few solitary men lurking in doorways did no more than glare, spitting in the street as they rode past.

"The worst is over, I think," Antonio said, and Veronica, too, sensed the main force of the riot was spent. He guided Ombra back to the street where she had glimpsed the Duomo. The footpaths filled as they rode on, more and more stragglers making their way homeward. "It was mere chance that I found you," he said. "I only came this way to avoid a knot of rioters."

Veronica laughed softly, hugging the warm solidity of his back. It was not chance but fate. She started to speak, but then there was a sudden pain in her thigh. Glancing behind them, she saw they were being followed by a few boys armed with stones. The next throw narrowly missed Antonio's head, and Ombra shied, struck in the flank. Antonio quickly took the next turning, leading them through another alley, then onto a broad and familiar street that opened into a great piazza. Hundreds of people were gathered in scattered clusters and all was commotion and chaos. A low buzzing hum of anger filled the square as they entered. Veronica hoped stoning would not occur to this mass of people. Antonio sighted the clearest path across the piazza and trotted forward, the horse's hooves clattering on the flagstones. Halfway across, she saw two groups of men detach themselves and move to close off their exit. There were fifty perhaps, banded together, their thicket of wooden staves raised high in the air. Fighting the new onslaught of fear, Veronica adjusted her grip on Antonio and raised up the iron bar. Antonio did not hesitate for an instant.

"They will scatter," Antonio said with absolute assurance. "Hold tight now."

Her certainty fused with his. They would pass unscathed through this danger, as they had through the other. Ombra gathered power beneath them, anticipating his master's command. Antonio spurred his mount forward, charging directly for the gang of ruffians. Veronica felt the last of her fear vanish in that headlong plunge, and in its stead came elation, a reckless abandon. The men held their ground no more than a second before scattering like chaff to either side. They drove through the mob, but Antonio did not stop even with the way clear before them. They galloped through the streets of Florence and across the river, the rushing wind, the speed exhilarating, intoxicating as some heady wine. Antonio laughed aloud and Veronica joined him, at one with him and the hot bright excitement that coursed through him.

This is what I foresaw last night, not danger, but but triumph.

Their pace did not slow until they reached Daniele's house. Avoiding the stable, Antonio cut along the tree lined side street to the garden wall and drew his stallion under the trailing branches of the great willow. Veronica's heart was still racing as Antonio dismounted and held up his arms to her. She slipped into them and he lifted her down slowly, her body sliding the length of his. Like her own, his breathing was fast and shallow. His hair was disheveled and there was a wild light in his eyes. She felt herself trembling in his arms, whether from aftereffect of the adventure or the present effect of his closeness she was not sure.

"Usually the hero rescues the maiden from a dragon. I only managed to drive off a few mangy rats," he said, his voice a rough purr. She clutched him harder as the sound of it shivered through her, prickling her nerves with its cat's tongue caress. "Still, you are a better catch than the last rescue I made from horseback. I trust you have no fleas?"

Veronica laughed at the image, not knowing what adventure he referred to. "I was washed in rose water and picked clean this morning," she answered in kind, her voice unsteady as the rest of her.

"I am glad to hear it," he murmured huskily, his mouth seeking hers and finding it. Her lips parted to the questing pressure of his tongue. Leaning against the trunk of the great willow, he drew her against him. The cascading leaves formed a soft, rustling green curtain around them, shielding them from view. His lips savored hers with deliberate and leisurely intent, then slowly moved to nuzzle her cheek, her neck, his warm breath a whispering caress. "*Dolcezza*," he murmured the endearment into the hollow of her ear and then, "*Selvaggia*."

"Yes," she answered, for she felt wild, savage, and yet drunk with sweetness.

"Brave," he whispered. "You are far too brave, *Selvaggia*."

Antonio's fingers loosened the laces of her bodice, slipped within it, his hand sliding down the delicate silk of her shift so her breast was naked to his touch. She moaned as his hand enclosed the soft round contours, her nipple stiffening against his palm. Arching her backwards, he lifted her to him, his lips covering the tight drawn peak. She shuddered with pleasure, feeling his hot tongue stroking within the relentless suction of his mouth. His hands cupped her buttocks, stroked the back of her thighs, molding her to him. This tree was haven enough for Antonio, the house secluded, the side street empty. He wanted her here and now, and this time he would not stop. Even knowing they would be invisible beneath the boughs of the willow, Veronica felt completely exposed. Excited as she was, a measure of caution had returned with safety. She hesitated now to offer what she would have given in the alley, without thought for safety, much less propriety.

"No," she whispered, confused and shocked by her own wantonness.

He let her go, though she could barely stand. "No, *Selvaggia*?" he queried, the question more tender than taunting. There was no malice in it, only a burning hunger as his eyes searched her face. His gaze lowered to her uncovered breasts and his fingertips reached out, barely brushing one swollen tip. She felt all the fierceness, the power of him, restrained behind that one delicate caress. The touch sent a streak of fire coursing to the very center of her. Desire pulsed from that molten core, spinning out through every vein and nerve, a tracery of flame enveloping her body. Everything in her yearned towards him. His hand rose, fingertips caressing her cheek. She thought she would faint as the sweet fire threaded through her mind. "No?" This query soft-voiced as the first, was soft as any challenge could be issued.

Shame flushed her, but not as hotly as passion. Staring into those burning eyes, there was only one answer for him, as there had always been. "Yes," she said, answering her lover's challenge. "Yes, yes, yes."

Let her be wanton then, let her give way completely. An image from the portfolio rose in her mind, and Daniele saying "That is something all men desire." She found she desired it too, wanting to taste him, to drink the very life of him. Aching with desire, she sank to her knees before him, feeling the length of him throb and swell, hard against the softness of her cheek. His hand twined in her hair, gently urging. Turning her head, she pressed her lips to him, feeling his arousal press through the taut cloth that enclosed it. He moaned now, deep in his throat, the aching sound filling her with power and tenderness. He was hers, her Prince of Cups. She had known he would come for her, and he had.

"I knew you would be here," she whispered, rubbing her cheek against him and then, not what she had planned to say to him but what said everything, "I love you. I love you. There is no one for me but you."

He gasped, his whole body tensing beneath her touch. Veronica lifted her head. His face was like a death mask, utterly still. Looking in his eyes, she saw something akin to horror. He pulled away from her so abruptly she had to catch herself from falling. In a second he had mounted his horse again. "Antonio . . . ?"

"I believe you can reach your door from here without further assistance," he said, the courtesy more savage than violence.

Veronica could not believe he was abandoning her again. She scrambled from the ground as he backed the black stallion away from her. She saw him reach into his money pouch and a wave of total fury swept over her, paralyzing her where she stood. The gold flew through the air, cold and glittering, to land at her feet.

"You arrange such unique amusements, Madonna," he said. Then he wheeled his mount and was gone.

She scooped up the coins and hurled them after him, but he did not even see. In that moment she hated him utterly. "So much for your bravery, Antonio. You have just proved yourself a coward." With sudden resolve, Veronica walked forward and reclaimed the two golden ducats, clenching them in her fist. "You will have them all back again," she vowed, "just as you have given them to me."

12 *Disturbances*

"Palle! Palle!"

Antonio laughed aloud as the cry of the crowd rose in the air. It was not an evocation now, but a jeer designed to harass the small army of soldiers huddled outside the walls of the city.

Jostled, Antonio clung to his hard-won perch, one among the hundreds of Florentines crowded onto the crenellated ramparts. Within the walls, thousands more gathered in the streets to hear the news passed down from above. Piero di Medici had at last returned to Florence, and his rebellion had proved an utter fiasco. Heavy rains had delayed his march and he had arrived not at dawn, in secret, but at high noon. The warning had long been given, and he and his army of mercenaries arrived to find the eleven gates of the city barred against him. Gazing over the wall, Antonio smiled, entertained by the absurdity of the situation. Occasionally, fate dealt out justice.

The rain, which had diminished to a drizzle for a few hours, began again in earnest. The spectators on the wall cheered and added a cascade of rotten vegetables to the downpour. Antonio wrapped his cloak about him and drew up the hood. Then, impulsively, he abandoned his prize vantage point and crossed to the far side of the battlement, overlooking the crowded streets and fields below. With deliberate casualness, he scanned the vast throng, searching the upturned faces, the figures dancing in impromptu celebration. An exercise in futility. Even if he could recognize Veronica among the masses, what would he do? Nothing. If she were here, like as not she would be with Daniele, or Stefano, or both. She had ignored him at the Duomo, cultivating his pretty cousin instead. Had she and Daniele taken Stefano home and bedded him that afternoon? Probably. They had strolled off together quite cozily.

It was best to leave things as they were, best for both of them. True, he had made that decision before the grain riots, only to defy it in the fervor of the moment, but he doubted there would be another event powerful enough to destroy his resolution. He had regained control of himself and would keep it.

His resolve had not been tested yet. Twice since the March grain riot, he had seen Veronica in the marketplace. Both times she had turned away from him, deliberately, as she had the day of the bonfire. Her decision appeared to be the same as his own, but she had not been by herself. His cousin was obviously paying court. Had she been alone, had he followed her, Antonio wondered, could he have turned her round, roused her once more, his sweet *selvaggia*? He doubted she could restrain her passion, her promiscuous nature. Or did he only hope she could not? After the way he had treated her this last time, why should she bother with him? Especially when she had Stefano, with his winning smile and gracious easy manner.

"And you, Antonio, were a bastard," he muttered under his breath. "A perfect bastard."

Why could he not resist the compulsion to toss her those final gold coins? He remembered the look on her face as they fell glittering at her feet. The memory still made him flinch. There had been nothing in that shared adventure that warranted his action, no falseness to be repaid. The first time, after all, he had presumed she would expect payment. The second time she had deserved it, playing her manipulative games with him. But the last time, there had been no point. Nothing except the sudden impulse to cruelty.

True, he had promised himself to have no more to do with

her, but that was not the reason. The circumstances had been extraordinary, he felt no need to punish either himself or her for the lapse. The fighting had stirred him, and more than the danger, she had aroused him with her daring, her laughter, her wild beauty, her ardor . . . . Had Veronica meant what she said, kneeling before him? Perhaps it was the truth, and she was infatuated with him.

But why had she said what she had, in just that way? For a second it was Beatrice before him, her breath hot against his loins, while his brother lay dead but a few feet away. He could not endure the obscene echo of that moment, could not endure Veronica's touch. So he had thrust her from him and flung the gold at her feet, a whore's gift.

Well, he had wanted to hurt her, and he had succeeded. The affair was unwisely begun and wisely ended. He only wished now he had not ended it so discourteously, so painfully. If he did not want to play her games, she had still given him great pleasure and deserved better from him than he had given. But what choice was there? Ended so swiftly, the very brevity must prove painful. The desire had not been burned out, only contained. It smoldered within him still, so that he searched for her face amidst a sea of thousands.

"You are surveying the wrong side of the wall, are you not?" a curious voice asked him. "It is over there, beyond the ramparts of Florence, that history is waiting."

Welcoming the distraction of conversation, Antonio turned and greeted the stranger, a thin man of about his own age with an earnest, ascetic face. The turn in the weather had diminished the crowd, so Antonio managed to recapture his old position on the battlement. Pointing, he showed his new companion a glimpse of Piero himself, sheltered as well he was able behind the wall of fountains in San Gaggio. "History waits in the rain, thoroughly bedraggled."

"It's a pleasing sight, is it not?" the other asked. "Almost a fitting end for Piero."

"What could be more fitting than total defeat? The man is a fool, and has found a fool's end."

"Only an ignominious death could surpass it," the stranger said vehemently.

"I cannot imagine any other awaits him," Antonio said politely. He had not lived in Florence under Piero's tyranny. He despised the man on principle, but he did not hate him enough to anticipate his death. "Yet today's outcome might well be different if he had arrived at daybreak, as planned, and his 'Grays' had opened the gates to him. A mercenary force within the city would have been another matter entirely."

"Then there would have been hatred held in the heart of Florence, and vengeance waiting its chance." The stranger's voice was tight with emotion, but then he shrugged. "As it is, the rain has done our work for us."

"I confess I find this downpour infinitely preferable to a bloodbath."

The man laughed. "I am already drenched to the skin. Let us go down. There is an inn not far down the road. We can sit before a fire, share a bottle of wine, and not miss out should anything new occur."

"An excellent idea, but we had best be quick about it. The crowd here is thinning, and conversation, rather than observation, will soon be the rule. If we are to drink together, I must introduce myself. I am Antonio di Fabiani."

"Niccolò Machiavelli."

As Antonio feared, the closest available establishments were packed full. Men of all classes, old friends and acquaintances of the moment, gathered to celebrate Piero's folly and argue the future of their city. It was a quintessentially Florentine event, and as he watched, its boisterous enthusiasm filled him with delight and an overwhelming nostalgia. Even in the midst of this excitement, he remained detached. He still felt a deep affection for Florence, but Antonio doubted he would ever again belong to this city completely. He had traveled too widely, homeless, to reclaim this one entire.

At last they snatched a vacant table, ordered a bottle of wine, and settled into their discussion. Antonio found he was enjoying his chance companion thoroughly. Machiavelli possessed a sharp inquiring mind and a wry wit that appealed to him. For all his sarcastic humor, the man took himself very seriously. He had a secretarial position at the moment and political ambitions for the future. Niccolò inquired of his own ambitions in that arena, and Antonio shrugged. "I will represent my family interests, indirectly, of course."

Machiavelli smiled. "Our conversation suggests a certain liberality in your nature that does not coincide with what I know of your family. Your father is not noted for his avid support of the Republic. He pays lip service, but what he desires is a return to an aristocracy."

"I have been known to disagree with my father." Antonio leaned back wearily in his chair. He was proud of his noble heritage, but his banishment had changed many of his basic assumptions. "Although I have great sympathy for the ideals of the current movement, I believe it is doomed. As individuals, we are too self-centered to sustain a Republic, serving our own glory above that of our city. This is true of Florence, and the city is a microcosm of Italy herself. The country is so rife with violence and so internally divisive that unification is essentially impossible. And while we war within ourselves and with our neighbors, the surrounding countries unify themselves and turn that united front to our borders."

"What you say echoes my own fears. As Dante said, the political system of Florence is like a sick man tossing about in bed, who can find no comfortable position. What we need is a powerful prince, one who can guide the future of Italy, fuse our disparate states into a whole before the French or Spanish decide to fatten themselves on us piecemeal."

"We all envision such a leader at one time or another," Antonio said. "A man of noble lineage and character, brilliant and courageous."

Machiavelli shook his head. "If his character is too noble, he will not survive. There is too much distance between how men live and how they ought to live. Saints are martyred. A ruler must meet evil with evil to vanquish it. But the true prince cannot succumb to cruelty, any more than he can indulge his virtue. To him, terror and mercy are both tools of rulership, to be used as necessary to achieve the desired end, control of the state. He must display all the courtly virtues, of course, but honor must be laid aside as need shall require."

"You still envision a paragon, although a pragmatic one, if you think a man of great power will not succumb to tyranny if he sees no inherent difference between terror and mercy. It is not so easy to turn aside from violence if it serves no greater goal than expedience. What is necessary soon becomes what is simplest, and terror is the simplest way to rule. Necessity demands hard choices, and sometimes the worst effects evolve from the best intentions. But lay aside honor too easily, or simply too often, and you will not retrieve it when you need it. Nor will men of honor deal with you.''

"If they must, they will, but probably not honorably,'' Niccolò said.

"Perhaps not,'' Antonio laughed, challenged by these views that echoed his own so closely, yet were more extreme than he could accept. Machiavelli lived too much in his mind, he thought, and envisioned a leader of the same intellectual detachment. "I do agree that an astute and benevolent tyrant such as Lorenzo di Medici might be the most practical if not ideal solution to the unification of Italy. My fear is that we will have a tyrant who is neither. I have every reason to believe that the Pope plans to promote his son Juan in just such a role as you describe. His ambition for his son is boundless.''

"Ah, the Borgias. They fascinate me. From what I have heard of Juan, he is quite a glamorous figure.''

"Despite his glamour, I think you would quickly come to despise him. Juan's character bears a striking resemblance to Piero di Medici's. Both are vain, arrogant, stupid, vicious, and cowardly.''

"What of Cesare? He is the elder. Does he not attain even his brother's caliber?''

"On the contrary, Cesare has courage and intelligence, though the other faults apply well enough. For some reason, his father sees Cesare's martial abilities in Juan where none exists, and has shuffled his eldest son into a Church career.''

"But Cesare would make a military leader, given the chance?''

"Perhaps,'' Antonio said. "Both brothers are utterly egotistical, and the vicious streak in Cesare's character has been aggravated by his father's slights.''

"But I think you like Cesare, even though you despise Juan,'' Machiavelli remarked. "The Borgia glamour has not tarnished so much there?''

Antonio considered this. "I have a fondness for cats, great and small. I admire their beauty, their elegance and power, knowing that it is inseparable from their deadliness. Cesare's

presence can be exhilarating, for it is my nature to be excited
by danger. Because of this, I like to be with him but, no, I do
not like him. Cats are innocent in their cruelty, men are not.''

"*Palle! Palle!*" the mocking cry arose once again in the
streets outside. Word spread swiftly through the inn—Piero
and his mercenaries were withdrawing, slinking off into the
rain like whipped curs. Immediately, they both rose to watch
the final retreat, then subsided into their chairs, laughing, as
every man in the place rushed for the door. The crush inside
was too fierce to penetrate, the streets outside chaotic. Even if
they made their way back to the wall, there was no hope of
regaining a view. Better to remain inside, where warmth and
wine prevailed.

"This bloodless victory will restore the city's spirits," Machiavelli said, refilling their cups.

Antonio nodded. "It is the end of Piero. He has too few
supporters and no money to buy more. He has been barred
from all the courts of Europe. This was an act of desperation,
and it failed."

"It's a failure for Piero, and another triumph for Savonarola, the wily fox. This morning, in total panic, the Signoria
sent a messenger to the Friar. "Tell the Signoria," Savonarola
answered, "that we will pray to God for the city, and that they
should not fear Piero, for he will come right up to the gates
and then turn back without doing anything at all." Yet another
prophecy validated," Machiavelli said with a sneer.

"He does have an uncanny talent for it," Antonio commented. "Much of his current power arises from his earlier
predictions."

"Common sense, nothing more. Piero's force arrived too
late for surprise, and without it he had no hope of success."

"You think it is calculated then, this fervor of Savonarola's?"

"But of course. It is the perfect political ploy, don't you
agree? Savonarola is an educated man, but although he has
followers from even the most sophisticated strata of Florentine
society, his primary support is from the masses. Greater numbers give him greater power. The poor are intoxicated with the
mixture of incense and brimstone that wafts from his pulpit.
He uses their faith to attain his own ends."

Antonio shook his head. "You are not alone in your opinion, but I do not share it. I think Savonarola craves power more than he admits, but it is not his primary obsession. The Friar is exactly what he appears, and he is the more dangerous for it, finally, both to himself and to others, for I doubt he will compromise."

"You say that Savonarola is what he seems. Do you believe him to be a holy prophet, then, however obsessed?"

"I think that Savonarola believes he speaks God's prophecies. That does not necessarily mean I think that God speaks to Savonarola. The Friar serves his obsession first, the Church second, and Florence last. He makes a tyranny of virtue, and Florence will not long tolerate a tyrant."

Regretfully, Machiavelli rose from his chair. "Antonio, I must go. It will take hours to get home in this madness. I have enjoyed our conversation."

"And I, also. Tell me your address, and I will send you an invitation to my wedding. It takes place on the seventh day of May."

"You have little more than a week, then, as a free man," Niccolò grinned.

Antonio smiled, though the words chilled him. Machiavelli told Antonio his residence, then made his way through the crowd. Antonio leaned back in his chair, sipping the wine that tasted harsh and sour now. His aversion to the marriage was still strong, but he wanted the wedding over and done with. His reconciliation with his own family would not be complete without it.

There were things to look forward to. After the wedding, he wanted to host a salon each month, cultivate some of the more interesting minds and talents of the city. Niccolò looked to be a provocative guest. He wanted to invite Daniele, and wondered how much the painter knew of the affair with Veronica. Antonio enjoyed Daniele's company and hoped he had not alienated him. He sighed. There were other complications as well. He would prefer to host the gathering in his home, but that was impossible. Aside from his mother's illness and his father's antagonism, Dorotea would never have the grace to handle such an assembly of free spirits.

Bianca could hold the salons at her house. That was the best

solution. He would speak to her about it tonight. The rooms
there were small but elegantly appointed. Once or twice, he
had considered installing her in a larger house, only to reject
the idea. There was no other courtesan in the city to equal her,
but he did not really want to establish Bianca as his exclusive
mistress—presuming she would even agree. Antonio had the
feeling that she also preferred her freedom. Really, they suited
each other perfectly.

He could not believe he was dissatisfied, but he was. He
wished vehemently he had never laid eyes on Veronica. If it
had not been for his brief affair with her, he would be delighted with his liaison with the courtesan. Bianca possessed
extraordinary beauty, a calculating intelligence, and a sexual
appetite to match his own, and yet no matter how avidly she
responded, part of him still compared her calculated skill with
Veronica's ardent passion. To do Bianca justice, it was not all
calculation. The feral wildness he had found so provocative
was real enough. Her flame burned bright, so blinding bright it
plunged him into darkness. Yet for all its brilliance, it was a
flame that gave no warmth. Bianca could burn, but she burned
like ice.

I should have bought her the rubies, he thought. Fire to burn
on her ice. Blood to gleam bright on the snow of her skin.
Antonio frowned, disturbed by the ominous image. What
pretty phrase had he used when he promised them to her? Rose
petals—not blood.

He thought of Bianca wearing the necklace he had given her
instead, the cascading collar of green gems he had bought
impulsively. It was equally expensive and exquisite, the emeralds brilliant as rain-soaked grass, the peridots the tender
shade of unfurling leaves. She had been well pleased, but as
soon as he placed it around Bianca's throat, Antonio knew it
had been a mistake. He had not chosen it for her.

Antonio sighed, weary of himself, of the unrelenting hunger
that consumed him. Bianca was the most accomplished, the
most responsive courtesan he had ever enjoyed, yet he went to
her not to savor her favors, but to prevent himself seeking out
Veronica.

13 The Wedding Night

A MANDOLIN player struck a sour note. Standing with Dorotea to greet the line of well-wishers, Antonio paused as the sound plucked an echoing chord along his nerves. He smiled, a brief sardonic smile. Annoying as it was, the dissonance matched his mood far better than the mincing romantic melodies the other musicians were playing.

Well, it was done. He was married. Few here would understand his discontent. Beside him, Dorotea looked beautiful, exquisite even—in the fashion of a delicate painted doll. Topping her underdress of fragile gold tissue, she wore a *giornia* of heavy cream-colored silk, lavishly embroidered with gold and silver thread and strewn with pearls and moonstones. She had removed the consecrated veil, keeping the wreath of white roses entwined with gilded leaves and trailing gold ribbons. The six rings he was required to give his bride gleamed on her small, cold hands. Her oval face was still and pale, the rouge glowing like fever patches on her cheeks. No doubt, Dorotea would have preferred sackcloth and ashes to her wedding finery, but she had performed as well as Antonio thought possible, considering how reluctant she was to wed him.

His bride was full of fears. Dorotea's youth aroused his pity, but he found little else to touch him. Her piety was intense but shallow, a religious obsession without a shred of Christian compassion. He had taken Dorotea to his mother the night before last, to receive her blessing on their marriage. He tried to prepare her, but Dorotea had not seen her for months, and his mother's decline had shocked and disgusted her. Understandable as Dorotea's reaction was, it did not endear her to him. She had made no effort to disguise her fear and repugnance, shrinking from the sight of the wasted body. Dorotea flinched away from his own touch, and Antonio had abandoned her at the doorway rather than try to urge her forward and risk hysterics. He sat down on the bed and took his mother's hand.

Shamed, Dorotea had crept up to the bedside. The imminent
marriage touched his mother's pain-filled days with joy, and
Antonio was grateful her eyesight was now too weak to notice
Dorotea's response. The girl managed a semblance of composure as his mother spoke to her, and whispered her thank you
to the blessing.

Because his mother was too ill to attend the marriage ceremony, the festivities were held at his father-in-law's palazzo.
Oblivious to the gloomy mood of the bride and groom, their
wedding day was glorious. A fresh breeze skimmed the clouds,
leaving pure blue skies and a brilliant disc of sun rising to its
zenith. All of Florence had come forth to revel in the spectacle
as the wedding party paraded to the sound of flute and mandolin. Antonio was garbed in crimson and gold, the traditional
Fabiani colors. The Della Montagnas were dressed in gold and
cream. The entire entourage was clad in combinations of these
shades, down to the fringed trappings of the horses and the
wreath-twined wheels of the floats. The combined effect was
opulent, an extravagant mélange of plush silk velvets, gleaming satins, embossed brocades, and shimmering metallic tis-
sues. Banners fluttered in the breeze above them, and dancing
girls cast handfuls of flower petals before the gilded hooves of
the horses. Following the processions, hired *zanni* cavorted for
the amusement of the crowd.

Given the attempted assassination of Savonarola and the ensuing Ascension Day riot, not even a week past, Antonio had
feared some incident might disturb the morning's procession
through Florence. The Signoria had expressed their gratitude
to both houses for providing the city with such a marvelous
distraction, and the effect was all the families could have
hoped for. Antonio would have enjoyed the spectacle himself,
if he had been an observer rather than one of the principal
performers. He felt stiff as a puppet and had to force himself to
relax as he rode Ombra along the petal-strewn streets. He had
actually felt embarrassed when the crowd cheered as he broke
through the symbolic garland of blood red roses stretched
across the pathway separating him from his bride. He was glad
that, out of respect for the sacrament, it was against custom to
consummate the marriage on the first night. Antonio was not at
all eager to deflower his fledgling bride.

On the pretext of checking the wine supply, Antonio left Dorotea and moved through the crowd. These guests were the first of a long succession that would arrive during the three days of banqueting and entertainment. Three days of supposed jubilation and definite excess. Antonio's lips quirked ruefully as he surveyed the extravagant culinary offerings. Savonarola had made little dent in the Florentine conscience where gluttony was concerned. The city had long had sumptuary laws limiting just this sort of prodigal display. Weddings in particular were severely limited—in law but not in practice. The magistrates in attendance showed no inclination to arrest anyone, or to order the removal of any of the rich dishes the servants bore to the already heavy-laden tables.

There were bowls of *maritata*, the wedding soup of chicken broth, cream, brandy, and the thinnest of pastas combined with grated cheese. Raviolis were plump with *porcini* mushrooms and truffles, or filled with minced vegetables aromatic with *dragoncello* and other herbs. There were all manner of fowl: roast peacock, pheasant, quail, duck, and thrushes, goose livers, capons' tongues, and glistening chicken galantine. There was suckling pig with apple and a roast kid stuffed with sausage, tender veal, rack of lamb, and rabbit with a sauce of wine, tangy *mostarda* and *romarino*. At the far end were plates of fish and seafood, trout stuffed with ground hazelnuts, pastry shells filled with pink shrimp brought from the coast, swimming now in a sauce of heavy cream. Breads abounded in all shapes and sizes. On a separate table, platters of gold and silver were heaped with crunchy *biscotti* and flaky pastries filled with fresh berries. Enameled dishes were heaped with preserved chestnuts and sugared almonds. Twin cornucopias spilled forth miniature fruits and flowers shaped from tinted *marzapane*. Duplicating the bridal garland, a wreath of red roses twined with gilded leaves and trailing ribbons surrounded the traditional centerpiece, a tender jelly of almond milk, eggs and sugar, golden-tinted with *zafferano*. In his present mood, just looking at the display gave him indigestion.

At the far end of the room, Antonio glimpsed Niccolò Machiavelli involved in fervent argument with Daniele. No doubt they were discussing the Ascension Day riot, a spectacle in itself. The vicious young *Compagnacci* had raided Santa Maria

del Fiore, where Savonarola was to preach. They had draped
the skin of a dead donkey over the pulpit and smeared it with
offal and filth. They had also driven nails upward through the
wood, their points protruding around the edge where Savonarola, lost in his fervor, often pounded his hands. The desecration had been cleaned up by the time the Friar came to preach,
but for once the sound of his voice was drowned out by the
raucous voices of boys in pay of the *Arrabbiati*. Fighting broke
out and the crowd panicked. As the Friar's followers hustled
him through the church, there was an attempt on Savonarola's
life, but the men were fought off and the Friar escorted safely
to San Marco. The assassins vanished in the crowd. The effect
on Savonarola's cause appeared to be mixed. The *Arrabbiati*
were generally condemned for the excess, but the Friar's charisma was diminished. Before the incident he had seemed in-
vulnerable.

Curious about their views, Antonio moved to join Daniele
and Machiavelli, but then the crowd parted and he saw that
Veronica was there as well. Her back was turned to him, so he
could not read her expression. She had been gesturing when he
first saw her talking, but now she stood quite still, as if she
sensed his gaze on her. Throughout the day she had always
been as far away from him as courtesy allowed. Never once
had she met his eyes. Watching her slim attentive figure, Antonio felt the urge to stare at her until she was compelled to turn
round. That was a childish impulse. What point was there? He
forced himself to turn away, to continue his rounds among the
guests, to smile and speak cordially to all those who had come
to celebrate his wedding day.

—

It was long past midnight when Veronica let herself out of
her room and moved silently down the dark corridor. She tried
to walk naturally, so she would not look suspicious if she were
seen. She had no good reason to be up and about. Antonio's
room was not near any other that she could visit with impunity. The kitchen, where she might pretend to beg food or
remedy for headache was in the other direction. But she saw
and heard no one as she made her clandestine journey to his
door.

She stood outside for a moment longer, her heart beating wildly with anger and fearful anticipation. *It is madness, madness to come here,* she thought. Part of her loved Antonio, craved him, cared nothing for shame or the danger of discovery if only she could savor this passion, bitter as it was. Part of her hated him, that he could sweep her into this insanity. She had to end it. The anger made her strong, if she could only hold on to it, wield it against him. She had come here for a reason, to take him as he had taken her, to ravish him and leave him. She meant to reclaim the pride that had been the first casualty of this war between them.

She put her hand to the latch and had the sudden heart-stopping realization that it might be locked against her. Or that he had taken one of the guests, or one of the little serving maids to his bed for tonight's amusement. It was entirely possible, and she did not know if she could bear the humiliation of that discovery. The door was not locked and she slipped inside without a sound, seeing with relief only one figure sprawled on the moonlit bed. She pressed her body back against the door, and the well-oiled latch slipped into place with the faintest click. Yet even that light noise was enough to wake Antonio, for he rolled off the bed in an instant, plucking a dagger from the table as he went, to land in a fighting crouch facing her. It was something she had not considered, that a man trained to war would suspect an assassin in the night.

Almost as quickly as he had reacted to her entry Antonio recognized who she was and stood up. He laid the knife back on the table and lit the candle. He held it up, not to confirm her identity but to read her expression more clearly. He smiled, the small ferocious smile that was like a slap, then blew out the candle, the ghostly line of its smoke lingering, a wavering stripe in the air. Antonio set the candle back on the table and lay down on his back in the middle of the bed. He was naked now, as he had never been those other times, the pattern of hair on his body a darkness sketched against the paler skin, lightly on the chest, a line trailing down to the wilder triangle framing his manhood, which stirred restlessly even as she watched, and began to rise.

Veronica felt her anger grow with her desire. He read her intentions and submitted to them, yet his submission was a dare, a challenge, an affront. Why not, when he had controlled her so easily, so completely before? He had reached inside of her, touched the essence of her being and twisted it to his desire. *Take your revenge,* he offered now. *See if I care.* He reached his hands behind his head and grasped the carved wooden headboard, offering her his body as if he were a slave chained there for her dalliance. He smiled again, a smile no slave would dare. His manhood was hard now, jutting out from his body.

When he took her before, clothes had armored him, except for that one essential nakedness that he had thrust into her. She could do the same now, though she longed to feel the embrace of his skin all along her own. She shed the cumbersome robe and went to the bed in her nightgown of supple white silk. It felt cool and smooth as water flowing over the pulsing heat of her skin. Cool, and blue white as the moonlight that poured over his waiting body.

Climbing onto the bed, Veronica knelt between his legs, pressing open his thighs, wanting him to have that sense of exposure, of vulnerability that she had known. She leaned over him, her face close to his, saw his eyes narrow then close, his mouth tilt up toward her own. But she could not let herself kiss him. Not now. For her the gesture held too much sweetness, too much tenderness. The simplest yet the greatest intimacy. It would be too easy to begin loving him if she kissed him. To-night she wanted to conquer him, as he had conquered her. So she did not touch her mouth to his but traced the sculptured outline of his lips with her tongue, gliding across the inner edges till they parted. The tip of his tongue grazed hers, a bright shock that flashed through her and through him as well, for he gasped at the moist, tantalizing touch. Veronica pulled away from him then. Whatever she gave him tonight, she would leave him wanting more.

She gave him kisses, but not on his mouth. Her lips, her tongue nuzzled his face, his ears, his neck. These soft, wet touches were interspersed with sharp tiny bites, with the ca-resses of her hands smoothing along his cheek, his jaw, or sliding through his hair to draw his head back sharply so her teeth could play along the pulse line of his throat. He was so sensitive there his breath hissed through his teeth, neck arching

to her touch. She had to keep moving. She could not allow
herself to linger too long on any one place, or she would lose
herself in the pleasure of pleasuring him. She plotted each new
movement, following the general design of this fantasy of revenge, modifying her touches to each newly discovered response of her lover, her enemy.

She moved down to his shoulders, his chest, her hands
stroking through the fine, springy hair. Her fingertips, her lips
claimed his nipples, which puckered and hardened in response,
the tiny nubs almost as sensitive as her own. Drawing down the
low neck of her gown, she used her breasts, her own taut
nipples, to tease him now as well. Used the loosened flood of
her hair to stroke the length of his torso. His body stretched
and strained beneath hers. She felt his emotional resistance
even as she took him to higher and higher physical peaks.

Her hands, her mouth, her tongue caressed him intimately
everywhere. Her mouth gathered the hardness of him, her
hands caressed the rounded softness below. One hand explored
beyond, her fingers teasing inside of him so he would know
her touch within his body as she had known his. The triple
stimulation shattered what reserve remained and he arched up,
thrusting, moaning his pleasure, wordlessly demanding completion. He moaned again in disappointment and frustration
when she withdrew her touch.

Veronica straddled his body, the silk of her gown spilling
cool around her thighs. She was ready, more than ready for
him, but she teased him again, drawing his hardness back and
forth against her swollen labia, letting him feel the wet welcome between them, drawing back as his hips raised, trying to
reach her. He was panting and shivering beneath her, his head
thrashing in soundless negation. She could see the strain, the
knotted muscles in his arms as he tightened his grip on the
headboard. He wanted to take hold of her, of what was happening, take control. But the rules were his own and he would not
break them.

So that became her goal. Antonio groaned aloud as she took
him within her, the harsh sound drowning her own quick-
drawn gasp. She rode him hard, shifting her rhythms, searching for the angle, the strokes that would drive him beyond

reason, break his control. She bent her whole being to ravage him body and soul, as he had done to her.

He groaned again and thrust into her savagely. She drove down as he drove up, their bodies attacking each other fiercely, wantonly, trapped in an erotic fury. With a wild cry, he took hold of her, unable to stop himself, his hands bruising, his voice cursing her as he plunged his body deep inside hers. There was triumph in that, but danger too. She had driven him over the edge, but his shuddering passion was pulling her with him. She was losing herself in him once more, his need meshing with hers, overpowering it. He would feel that surrender within her, and be the victor yet again. She could not let it happen. There was only one denial powerful enough to equal his own.

She fought her own response, cutting herself off from the ferocious ecstasy, though the severance ripped her flesh like talons. Sensing the loss, Antonio cried out in protest, but he could not hold back the explosion of his own climax. The pulsating tremors that wracked his body coursed over her, through her, but did not reach her core. Trembling with the effort of her denial, she watched as he arched beneath her, moaning as the last throbbing pulses shook him, then collapsed back onto the bed. For a moment she could do nothing but lean over him, hearing the echo of her tortured gasps in the harsh, rasping breath he drew into his lungs. Abruptly, Veronica lifted herself from his body and slipped off the bed.

His hand reached out to her, then fell back on the covers, the fingers curling inward. "You are not satisfied, Madonna," he said, a question hidden within the statement.

"On the contrary," she lied, "I am supremely satisfied. I cannot imagine any greater pleasure you could offer me."

Her robe lay in a crumpled heap on the floor. She picked it up and slipped it over her nightgown. Hidden deep in one pocket were the six gold coins he had given her, placed there for this moment. She pulled them out and tossed them onto the bed beside him. He glanced at them, silent and motionless, then raised his eyes to her face. "All for one night," he said, his voice hoarse. "How generous. Or are you paying in advance?"

"Two for tonight's performance—the rest as a parting gift," she answered, and then she left him.

Closing the door behind her, Veronica did not even bother to look down the corridor. She heard nothing, saw no one on her return to her room, though she was beyond caring if she were seen. Back in her own small chamber, she lay down on the bed, staring sightlessly at the ceiling. For a moment, she felt nothing. She might lie thus, cold and empty, in her tomb. Then sobs wracked her, and she wept and wept until the excruciating tension in her was released. Exhausted, she lay sleepless on the bed, waiting for dawn. It was no good, trying to sate herself on revenge. To conquer him, she had denied herself far more than her own physical pleasure. There was no release for the pain in her heart. She had won her first and last victory in the war Antonio had declared between them, and it was more bitter than any of her defeats.

14 *The Consummation*

ANTONIO surveyed the ring of faces surrounding the marriage bed. Some were kind and concerned, but most were lascivious. Beside him, Dorotea sat up stiffly, her back not even touching the stack of pillows. He felt her shiver and her eyes looked glassy with panic. A bride's maid with a vixen's sly face leaned over Dorotea and kissed her cheek, slipping one hand into the edge of her own bodice and fingering the erect nipple while her eyes searched Antonio's crotch expectantly. Luigi himself was licking his lips, and Antonio felt revolted by the man, by a nature so carnal, so base, he would want to watch his own daughter deflowered. Maria's actions might be superior in principle but seemed little better in practice. She offered her daughter no support, no comfort, but stood like an effigy at one corner of the bed, her fingers telling the beads of her rosary, lips moving in silent prayer. Searching the assembly, he saw Veronica by the door, her face pale and drawn, her eyes dark-shadowed. A sudden flicker of candlelight showed them bright and glittering, as if they were brimming with tears. Illusion or reality? He found he could not bear to look at her.

"You will all leave us," he said quietly. He had no intention whatsoever of providing erotic entertainment for the wedding party. He was thankful that Florence was civilized enough that such amusements were only hoped for nowadays, not expected. There were groans and protestations and lewd remarks, but he did not have to repeat himself, and not even the most drunken gallant tried to kiss Dorotea. The girl's delicacy and obvious fear had their effect, and in a few moments he was left alone with his bride.

She turned her pinched face up to him, her eyes gleaming feverishly in the wavering candlelight, her skin as waxen pale as the tapers. Without a word, she laid herself down on the marriage bed, a thin tense little figure in her beribboned nightgown, perfumed with the fragile scents of lavender and lily. She had no visible breasts in this position. Her eyes were shut now, her arms stiff, and her small hands clenched into fists. She winced when he laid a gentle hand on her shoulder, trying to comfort her. He sighed, and she shuddered again.

Antonio felt not a shred of desire for Dorotea, and it would be difficult to rouse himself to consummate their union. More than anything he wanted it over and done with, but it would be a crime to rush a girl so inexperienced and frightened. She should learn this first night that there could be pleasure for a woman in the act. Pleasure enough to help ease her over the first pain. He wondered if the candlelight would reassure her or if she would prefer the anonymity of darkness. She had drunk a good deal of wine at the banquet, but perhaps a few more sips would relax that fearful rigidity.

"Dorotea," he said, pitching his voice low and soft.

She squeezed her eyes shut tightly and whispered, "You are my husband, you may do your will."

Her lips moved silently and he saw that she was praying. He saw then, superimposed over her face, her body, a vision of her mother. Maria lay there before him, cold and tight and unyielding of spirit, hating the body, what passion she possessed twisted inward into an hysterical spirituality. Suddenly, the situation felt unutterably futile to him. Only the irony of it all was a sort of bleak consolation. Antonio almost laughed, but he could only make the smallest sound, a weary little snort of disgust. He could not believe the stupidity of this contract to which he had tied himself. He pitied the poor girl, but suddenly he knew that he would never be able to bring himself to touch her. If God wanted her, He was welcome to her. Antonio would have none of her, now or ever.

"Do not be afraid, Dorotea," he said quietly. "I am not going to . . . claim my marital privileges. You may sleep unmolested."

Her eyes flew open, and one hand reached up to clutch his nightshirt. "It is my duty to endure your lusts. A Christian wife offers her body to her husband so that his animal urges are sanctified in the marriage bed and his seed takes root in her womb. In this way the bestial is transformed to the celestial. My pain and suffering will birth new souls to glorify God."

She had been terrified of the sexual encounter, and Antonio had expected gratitude. Instead she was affronted, resentful — even in her fear she craved her martyrdom. His first instinct had been right. No matter how carefully he wooed her physically, even if he could bring himself to try, he would win no response from her. She would not permit pleasure to corrupt the ugly bliss of mutual abasement. He watched, horrified, as she raised the skirt of her nightgown above her hips, exposing her childish loins to him, the little mound marked with only a few sparse curls of hair. It was pathetic and obscene, this reluctant display which was supposed, he realized, to drive him wild with lust. Quietly, he took the delicate fabric from her hands and pulled it down to cover her again.

"You are very young, Dorotea, to be a bride, much less a mother. I can control myself in your presence until you are a bit older," he equivocated. He hoped by that time she would be used to this celibate state of affairs and prefer it.

"You will not seek gratification elsewhere?" she demanded with a dreadful fervor that already knew it would be denied. When he would not answer except with silence, she glared at him then turned away, curling herself up into a resentful ball.

She had her martyrdom, now she would be content, he thought cynically. Rising briefly, he extinguished the candles, then stretched out next to Dorotea, careful not to brush against her, and arranged the covers over them both. *Sotto voce,* the prayers began again, a lisping mumble that droned on and on until, finally, the heady wine numbed even her overwrought nerves, and she fell into a fitful slumber.

For an hour, Antonio lay beside his new wife, staring sightlessly until the darkness faded to a dim gray pallor. Finally, he slid silently out from under the covers and stood up, for a moment surveying the sleeping form of his bride, still curled into a tight knot of denial. His wedding night with Beatrice, he remembered, had been a fever dream of ecstasy. A dream that had become a nightmare. "Rewarded at last," he murmured bitterly, "with a virtuous wife." He did not know why he felt so overwhelmingly sick and weary of both the world and himself. Most marriages were arranged to enhance the fortunes and status of the families involved. His reasons for consenting to this bond had not changed. Certainly, he was not imprisoned in the relationship. A wife and husband, once united to their family's mutual benefit, could lead their own lives within reason. He would leave his bride to her religious fanaticism and pursue his own interests elsewhere.

Tonight's decision assured that there would be no children to quarrel over, not of her body in any case. There was the question of an heir, but he could beget a bastard son and legitimize him. Choose some suitable wench—yet another complication. At the moment he was desperately sorry he had taken such care in the past to prevent any such conception. Except, foolishly, with Veronica. He had hoped to simplify his life by returning to the bosom of his family, following their wishes. Now the path of the future seemed to have become ridiculously torturous.

He could not stay any longer in this bridal chamber with its pervasive scents of candle wax and wilted flowers, stale wine and sanctity. He drew on his robe and slippers, then crossed to the door. It opened quietly enough and he stepped out into the empty hall, grateful to have no one there to question his wandering. There was faint noise echoing in the hallway, sounds of the revels still being celebrated in the main hall. He walked the other way, remembering the steps that led to the far tower. Stifled by his oppressive emotions, he felt hungry for the cool of the night air.

He paused at the foot of the stairs for a moment, looking down the corridor that led to Veronica's room. He felt a sudden compulsion to go speak to her. The impulse baffled him in that there seemed to be no sexual element in it, only a longing for her presence, the sound of her voice. The memory of its husky timbre brought passion back with an elemental rush. Images of her filled his mind now, in all her contradictory manifestations, and his aching spirit viewed them with yearning. He pictured her lovely willowy body, remembering how those long limbs twined about him when he first embraced her. Her face gazed up at him, her lips parted, the gray eyes smoky with desire. He sighed dejectedly, recalling how he had encouraged then scorned her response, thought it wanton, worse than wanton—whorish. Perhaps it was. But how pure that flaming passion seemed now, compared with the frigid chastity of his marriage bed.

Antonio gave a harsh laugh and turned his face away from Veronica's door. She would not be waiting inside. No, she had had enough of his presumption. Last night she had paid him back, in full, for his arrogance. Veronica would be at the hall with the other revelers, laughing, dancing, choosing her lover for the night—Stefano, or someone equally appreciative of her favors. He had another image of her then, standing in his bridal chamber, her shadowed eyes brimming with tears. Perhaps she had withdrawn from the revels after all. But even if she was within her chamber, she would not welcome him tonight. She had made that plain. Antonio turned and climbed the stairs, the amber marble steps lit by candles flickering in their sconces. At the top of the stairs he opened the paneled door onto the moonlit sanctuary of the tower.

Before him the airy archway of the window framed a great full moon and a single standing figure, its slender form limned in opalescent light. That pale, bright edging revealed the dark dusky red of the hair that cascaded over the figure's shoulders. Veronica. The straight lines of her garment were those of a night robe, not the lavish gown she had worn earlier. Another restless soul grown weary of the night's revels, come seeking comfort in the vast, indifferent beauty of the stars.

But that was not what he said. What came from his mouth, unbidden and edged with ugly sarcasm, was, "Expecting company?"

It could, of course, have been true, but he knew it was not. She did not even flinch at the accusation, only stood there facing him, immobile, her position concealing her expression even as his features were revealed to her in the flooding lunar light. He came forward then, standing even with the arched open window of the tower, and she turned to him, her face no longer veiled by her own shadow.

He stood transfixed, gazing into her eyes as if gazing into a mirror, seeing reflected there all his emotions. His own vaulted pride was there, fixing her face into a pale mask, behind which seethed a sea of pain. All his own futility and despair stared up at him. He closed his eyes, shutting off the vision of her face. Within that chosen blindness, loneliness echoed and re-echoed unbearably.

Standing there, enclosed in his own darkness, he felt her arms come around him gently, in comfort, and his body tensed in protest even as his spirit longed to surrender to that proffered tenderness. He knew then whatever emotions they shared at this moment, the mirror was not exact. She had a generosity of spirit far beyond his own, a giving heart that reached out when his would shut itself away. With that realization every judgment he had made about her was suddenly meaningless.

I love her, he thought, *and she loves me. I have betrayed her and myself.* With that acknowledgment the emotion welled up inside him, a sweet tide rushing to the furthest reaches of his being. It seemed to Antonio that he could not bear the sense of vulnerability that came with it, and every self-protective instinct he had cultivated over the past dozen years rose to attack it, conquer it, imprison it deep within himself. Every instinct except love's desire to express itself. Every instinct except the one which recognized this woman as a kindred spirit. To yield to what he felt now was terrifying, to attack or retreat the basest cowardice. With one shuddering gasp he surrendered, his arms encircling her in turn, yielding himself to this breath-taking sweetness.

Gentle, he is so gentle, Veronica thought as Antonio gathered her to him. But it was not surprise she felt, only affirmation of what her heart had known. As his arms enfolded her, the aching bitterness she felt fell away, leaving a relief so profound she knew it as joy. They moved together as if in a dream. He kissed her face softly, his mouth caressing cheek, temple, forehead, drifting down to nuzzle her ear, the curve of her jawline, the extended length of throat and its nestled hollow. She murmured his name, and his mouth returned to envelop her lips, the wet tip of his tongue tracing their contours, then teasing across their inner edge, seeking deeper intimacy. Her lips parted to receive him within her mouth, intoxicated with the wine rich flavor he brought her. The intimate muscle of his tongue explored her slowly, its movements languid, sensuous, and utterly intent, searching out the secrets of this first portal to her body.

Veronica opened her eyes as he stepped back from her for a moment, his gaze holding hers in silence. Slowly, he drew off his robe, then hers, and cast them to the floor, the dark velvet shapes falling like shadows on the patterned marble. Another layer veiled them, filmy white. Antonio lifted off his nightshirt and slipped the shift from her shoulders to pool at her feet. They were naked now. She gazed at him and found him beautiful, lean and elegant, skin taut over cleanly defined muscles. His skin was moon washed pale, the hair a darker wildness against it, smooth and silky as wild grass on his chest, curling in a coarser thicket at his loins, framing his arching manhood.

Later she might reach out, caress him, draw him into the warm wet center of her body as she had welcomed him into her mouth. Now she only smiled and waited, open, expectant. He had denied her emotionally and now he must come to her, both body and soul. It was not a conscious decision she made, only a certain inner knowledge that he must choose her as she had chosen him.

His arms claimed her again, and he lowered her to the velvet covered floor. She sighed as his mouth drifted over her body, covering her with kisses. His lips trailed along her shoulders, down between the valley of her breasts, across the concave plane of her belly, his tongue teasing the miniature cup of her navel. His hands, then his mouth traveled up to her breasts. She cried out softly as his lips captured her nipples, fire sparking within her as he sucked each aching peak in turn.

His hands stroked her with soothing gestures, sliding over belly and hips, down the long smooth length of her flanks. Her own yearning opened her body to his touch, her legs parting helplessly even before his fingertips glided inward, caressing the satin of her inner thighs. His lips followed his hands along her legs, the moist warmth of his mouth moving along that smooth inner flesh to seek her pulsing center, claiming her with a kiss. His lips pressed gently to her tender, swollen nether lips, then delved between them. His hot tongue touched her, laving, licking, probing the secret pulsing heart of her. Transfixed with pleasure, she could barely move, only sob in response to the touches he gave her, opening to him, unfolding. His mouth settled there, lips, tongue, the delicate touch of his teeth embracing that tiny throbbing bud, coaxing her, urging her rapture. Joy blossomed in her, a burning flower that exploded into a billowing cloud of flame, her flesh, her consciousness dissolving into a million particles of shimmering white light.

Passion ebbed, its lapping retreat leaving Veronica dazed and drowsy with euphoria. Antonio had drawn up next to her, his arms encircling her. She leaned into his embrace, her fingertips idly tracing through the soft, crisp hair of his chest. As her languor faded a little, her awareness of him grew, and now she could feel the corded tension of his muscles within his cradling arms. Pressing her body closer, she felt the straining hardness of his arousal graze against her thigh. He shivered at that skimming touch. His need vibrated through her nerves like some sweet, aching music, awakening a pang of longing within her body. He had not been inside her tonight, and she wanted that fulfillment. He had given her exquisite delight, but he had not yet given her himself. She heard her voice pleading with him as she had not before, calling to him softly, her hands coaxing. "Yes, come into me," she whispered. "Now, Antonio, now."

He moaned and rolled onto her. His hands closed on her, pulling her body closer. She felt her legs opened, shaped to contain his, her hips lifted and tilted. He leaned forward, and she cried out in wonder as his sex touched hers, intense desire sparking anew at the touch. He pressed himself against her, but he did not enter her. Their bodies still and trembling, they held each other for a long moment, then he pulled back slightly, so he could look at her.

His eyes were all pupil, black as onyx in the moon drenched night, passion igniting their depths with dark intensity. But it was not the passionate fury she had seen burning there on the other nights when he had taken her so ruthlessly. Tonight it was the hot flare of pain, a glittering flicker of fear. He had given her his tenderness, his gentleness, but there was this dark suffering still inside him that he withheld from her. From the beginning she had felt it in him, loved it with every other part of him. She had surrendered all her pain to him, all her pride, given way to the deepest, most vulnerable point of herself. She stared into his eyes, into that inner darkness where he locked himself away from her. "My pain for yours," she said, asking for an exchange of gifts.

Antonio's breathing quickened and she felt him tense. Even if his mind did not fully comprehend, his spirit understood her request. He gave way to her suddenly, completely. Abandoning all control, he plunged into her, the driving force of him not brutal but desperate. His hands clutched her hair, bruised her as they grasped her shoulders. She moaned, not for the little hurt he gave her, but for his own deeper pain. At the sound, the wild lunges suspended themselves, shifting to slow and torturous thrusts as he writhed against her, wrestling against an inner barrier of his own, his body wrenched and racked with shudders. The struggle went on and on until Veronica felt she could not bear the agony of his passion. Blindly her spirit reached out to him, reached through the black flaming darkness to touch the even more deeply hidden flame of light burning at the core of him. Antonio groaned as if something had broken or torn itself open inside him, then he cried out her name, his voice filled with fearful ecstasy. She sobbed his name in turn as the aching pleasure of his release spilled into her, hot and bright as tears.

He lay beside her, gasping, almost sobbing, while she stroked his sweat drenched body. Eventually, the harsh breathing quieted and he nestled closer with an exhausted, contented murmur. They lay like that for many moments more, drifting in the bittersweet aftermath. "I love you," he said finally, his voice muffled against her shoulder, rich, mellow notes she'd never heard before reverberating through its drowsy tones. And then, still drowsy but insistent, he repeated himself softly, forestalling any possibility of denial, ever again, to her or to himself. "I love you. Love you. Love you."

"Yes," she said. "Yes, love." Completely at peace at last, her hands moved over him delicately, with hardly more pressure than the tremulous night breeze.

Sighing, Antonio rubbed his cheek against hers and breathed in the rose and sandalwood scents of her hair. *I am in love,* he thought. The emotion that had poured forth from him seemed to have merged itself with the very night, and it now surrounded, embraced them both. Or perhaps the love that he felt for Veronica, that she felt for him, had connected with Love itself, universal and all-encompassing. He smiled faintly at his own philosophizing. The perfect Florentine gentleman, spinning treatises on the nature of love while lying in his mistress' arms. The smile took on a faintly bitter curl to one edge, and Antonio found his old world-weary cynicism had not entirely departed but lodged itself uneasily next to his bliss, muttering dark warnings, annoyed and yet protective of this foolhardy rapture.

Even as they lay there the night wind grew sharper, a chill reminder of reality brushing their naked flesh. Antonio roused himself, but only to draw their robes around them then lean himself back against the stone wall, pulling Veronica against him. The majority of his peers would have laughed at his scruples with a carnal contempt. He had acquired a rich wife and a passionate mistress all on the same night—so much the better. Why should he be concerned? Simply enjoy with appropriate relish and due caution his good fortune. But he felt in his soul that it was his wife he held in his arms. To live out this other sham seemed more than ever a pointless obscenity.

Below them there was distant laughter, a shout, torches, the sound of horses' hooves. Some of the wedding party were dispersing. Veronica withdrew from his arms and rose to her feet. "I must go," she said.

He stood up, gathering her tightly against him. "I'll make you mine." He swore it.

"I am yours," she said, then dropped her eyes before the intensity of his gaze. "As much as I can be."

Turning swiftly, she was gone and he stood alone, the sharpened chill of the night wind making him shiver.

15 *The Confession*

 His mother was dying. The doctor said she would not last the night. As soon as they returned from the wedding, she had given way, as if that event were all that still held her to life. The priest had administered the last rites hours ago. It was five in the morning now, the candles guttering in their sconces, the air chill and heavy with impending rain. A few of the most devoted servants kept vigil in the hallway outside his mother's room. Dorotea was upstairs, asleep by now, Antonio assumed. He was grateful for her absence. Her pious prattle wore on everyone's nerves, and her obvious terror and disgust at his mother's condition made her useless in the sickroom.

Haggard with sleeplessness, Antonio stood in the doorway, gazing at the candlelit tableau before him, a silent duet of grief. His mother lay stretched out on the bed, little more than a skeleton now, a stark outline of bones thinly clothed in pale, yellowed flesh. His father sat in a chair by the bedside, stroking his wife's hand. Unaware of his son's entrance, he lifted it, pressing the fingers against his lips. After a moment, he laid her hand back on the coverlet and clasped his own as if he were praying. Antonio's heart ached for his father. Giorgio di Fabiani did not care easily, but cared deeply and irrefutably when he did. As far as Antonio knew, only Alessandro and his mother had ever had his father's absolute love.

Antonio moved forward quietly to stand behind his parents.
His mother was sleeping fitfully, each shallow uneven breath
an effort. His father stared at her blindly, unmoving. Greeting
him softly, Antonio rested his hands on the tense shoulders,
but even that slight gesture was intolerable. His father jerked
away from his touch, rising swiftly. He glanced briefly at Antonio, his face grim and withdrawn, "You may sit with her
now," he said coldly. "Call me if there is any change."

He left the room. Antonio sat down in the chair by the
bedside. His father could not accept his comfort in this shared
pain. And if he could not accept that, then her death would
drive them even further apart. *I still care for my father,* he
thought, *but he will never absolve me. It is simple and un-
changeable.* The words reverberated within him, a dull, aching
echo. He felt not their meaning, but his own bleak hollowness
in response to them.

"Antonio?" The whisper was barely audible.

"Yes, Mother." He took her hand between his own, stroking
it as his father had done. Had she not been sleeping after all, or
had their terse conversation awakened her?

A quiver of pain flickered across her face, distorting it, and
he felt his own facial muscles wince in empathy. When she
spoke, her voice was thin and rasping, "I should not have
called you home. But I wanted to see you again, Antonio. I
love you. I had to see you again."

"Of course you should have called me back. I wanted to be
here with you. I love you too, Mother."

"I had so many hopes," she sighed.

So many hopes. Well, she had lived to see him married,
barely, but she had no more strength to sustain her. The grandchildren she longed to hold in her arms were an impossible
dream now, at least by Dorotea. But she would never know
that.

"So many hopes," she repeated. "But I was afraid, for you
have not been happy."

He wished desperately that she were less perceptive, or more
so. "How could I be happy when you are so ill? When you are
well . . . ."

She frowned at him and shook her head, silencing the lie.
Her eyes searched his face. "Since the marriage things are

better, are they not? I can see the change in you. You are happier now, aren't you?''

Was Veronica's effect on him so apparent then? It must be, for his mother to perceive it through the bleak misery her imminent death engendered in him and the overlying oppression of his ridiculous marriage. He hated deceiving her, but the truth would be pointlessly painful. What was important was that he had found some joy, some solace, even if it was not with the inhibited child bride she had chosen for him. He smiled and answered gently, ''Yes, it is better now.''

''Antonio.'' Her eyes were huge, pleading. ''Antonio . . . I beg you.''

''Yes, Mother, what is it?'' he responded hesitantly, full of foreboding at this sudden terrible intensity. What more could she ask that he, loving her goodness, her love for him, could not deny her?

''You must forgive your father, Antonio. You are too much alike.''

Her words chilled him. He had never thought he was like his father, except in certain features, certain superficial mannerisms. There was much to admire in Giorgio di Fabiani, nonetheless they were very different. He was not so cold and removed, so autocratic, so proud. Well, proud perhaps, and guarded. Definitely not so conservative. Antonio prided himself that his view of the world was far more flexible and progressive than his father's.

''There is more warmth in you, more lightness, more compassion. But you are like him, Antonio. That is why it is so difficult for you. Neither of you loves easily. Everything runs so deep. Alessandro was heedless, all emotion and no thought. You brood, you carry your pain in darkness and will not let the light heal your wounds.''

''There is no need for me to forgive him, Mother. I accepted my exile as just, and he has rescinded it.''

''No, not for that, not the banishment. Not that. You must forgive him,'' she said again, her hand clutching weakly at his. ''And you must forgive me, for lying to you. I feared for his life and yours. Now I fear for his salvation. He will not repent. Murder is a sin—a grievous mortal sin.''

''What,'' Antonio whispered. ''What?''

"I beg you."

"What murder?" he asked her again, although he knew now, as he should have known then. It had always been too perfect a coincidence.

"Beatrice," she said. The syllables were halting, and her lips quivered with distress or fear. "I never told her you would send her away. She did not kill herself. Your father killed her, because of Alessandro."

He had been a fool, taking his mother's word. Trust had blinded him, trust and guilt. Beatrice's death had not been accident, nor suicide, nor divine retribution. Judgment was much closer to hand. Oh yes, it all fell into place now.

"Antonio. Antonio, please. Do not laugh so," his mother begged. "Antonio, you are hurting me."

He released her. There were bruises on her arm, marking the grip of his fingers. Clenching his hands into fists, Antonio swallowed the dark laughter, though he did not know how else to release the swelling wave of rage and grief and futility that rose in him. "How long have you known?"

"Since the night it happened. If I had told you then, you might have killed him, Antonio."

"Perhaps." Yes, perhaps he would have. He had loved Beatrice, even knowing she had betrayed him.

"I wanted her dead too, Antonio. She was beautiful, beautiful as an angel, but her soul was corruption. She was destroying us. All of us." His mother was sobbing. "I was glad she was dead, glad."

He gathered her wasted body in his arms, holding her close, rocking her. "So was I," he said, for that had been true then as well. Hating Beatrice and loving her. Wanting her dead. Wanting her even in death. Her spirit lingered still, a succubus haunting him.

"Promise me you will forgive him."

"I will not kill him," Antonio said. He could promise nothing more. All those years, believing her death was on his head, as well as his brother's. All those years, wishing he were dead himself, courting his own destruction on the battlefield. Hating himself, hating life.

Shivering, Antonio closed his eyes. Would it have been so different, if he had known the truth? Perhaps not. He knew only that his father's deception seemed worse than Beatrice's. And to think, now, how deferential he had been when he returned here. How he had hungered for some sign of his father's forgiveness, some shred of affection.

"Please . . . ." her voice was full of fear.

"No," he said, not knowing or caring what more she wanted. He could make no more promises. "No more."

"Antonio, help me," she gasped, her nails scraping his hand. He looked up to see the blood running from her mouth, her nose. "Antonio." The word choked off in a terrible liquid rattle.

"No. Mother. No!" he cried out.

But it was already too late. She arched and stiffened against him, then collapsed, a limp weight in his arms. Antonio laid her body back down on the bed. Her eyes were open, their gaze fixed and blind. He closed them. The bedside table was cluttered with bottles of medicine, towels, a bowl of water. Dampening a cloth, Antonio wiped the blood from her face. He lifted her hands and folded them across her breast. He wanted to say a prayer, not out of any belief of his own, but for her sake. His lips moved, as if to form the words, but none emerged. Abruptly, he shook his head. What was the point? She was gone.

He heard a noise and turned. His father stood behind him, staring down at the body of his wife. "Leonora?" his father whispered, though it was obvious there would never be an answer.

"She is dead," Antonio said bluntly, too numb with grief to compose his response.

"Dead?"

"A few moments ago."

"I told you to call me," his father said.

"There was no time."

"I told you to call me," he insisted, an accusation now.

"It happened suddenly. We were talking . . . ." Antonio began, then stopped, remembering with vivid clarity exactly what they had been saying.

"I should have been with her! It was my place beside her, not yours. Mine!" his father cried out. Turning on Antonio, he struck him with all his might.

Staggering backwards, Antonio tripped against the table and knocked it over. Glass and crockery shattered on the tiles. Water and medicines spilled all around him as he fell to the floor. The air reeked with alcohol. Shocked by the blow, Antonio stared up from the debris. It was incredible, absurd. His father was jealous. So jealous he wanted solitary possession even of his wife's death. The dark laughter welled up in Antonio again, uncontrollable. Even as it poured out of him, his mother's voice echoed in his mind, the words she had spoken when he first saw her again: *"Only once did I defy him, for your sake."*

"How dare you!" Visage contorted in rage, his father dragged Antonio to his feet and thrust him against the wall. He slapped him back and forth across the face. Antonio felt a streak of pain as his father's ring slashed open his cheek. "How dare you laugh!"

Rage rose up in Antonio, black and consuming. His own arm came up in a backhanded blow that sent his father stumbling away. Still lost in fury, Antonio lunged after him, grabbing hold of him. Off balance, they grappled together for a moment, then toppled to the floor, struggling in the chaos of spilled liquids and broken glass. Antonio was barely aware of the rain of blows falling on him, the fierce thrashing beneath him that grew weaker and weaker. He did not know what brought him to himself—some choked sound, the very lack of resistance. He looked down to find his hands at his father's throat, strangling him slowly and inexorably. His father glared up at him, his eyes wide with fury and terror. A shudder ran through Antonio, and he felt his hold tighten around his father's neck. Sucking in a deep breath, he forced his hands to open, forced himself to stand up. Taking hold of the front of his father's robe, Antonio pulled him to his feet.

"I gave her my word I would not kill you. Don't make me break my promise to her," he said coldly, his face inches from his father's. Then he shoved the other man away from him.

Choking, panting, his father backed away, watching Antonio intently. "Your promise?" he asked, his voice hoarse.

Antonio smiled grimly. "She told me about Beatrice."

"Beatrice. Do you know she tried to seduce me, that little whore you brought to our house?" his father hissed at him.

"That night, I went to the stairway where Alessandro fell, and I found her there. The son I loved was dead because of her. I wanted to kill her then, but I would not have. Perhaps she saw it in my face, for she looked frightened. But she didn't run away, your Beatrice. Your witch. She put her arms around my neck and kissed me on the mouth. Kissed me. I broke her neck. I felt it snap in my hands. When I let go, her body tumbled down the stairs as if she had fallen or jumped. I was not sorry. She should have died. You should have killed her. Instead you killed your brother. You and your lust have destroyed our house."

Stunned, Antonio stared at his father's face, contorted with rage and grief. But it was the other man's gaze that dropped first, shadowed with a guilt. *"She was destroying us. All of us,"* his mother's cry echoed in Antonio's mind. "You wanted her too," he said flatly, seeing the truth his father would never have admitted. "That's why you killed her."

His father turned away from him and walked over to the bed. "Get out of here," he whispered. "Leave me alone with my wife."

Antonio went. Ignoring the fearful, questioning glances of the servants waiting in the hallway, he walked upstairs. In the sitting room they shared between their separate bedrooms, he found Dorotea. Without his consent, she had erected an altar there, candles and incense burning before a statue of the Virgin. She knelt before it in prayer, enacting her sanctimonious rituals for a woman for whom she had felt nothing. Hearing him enter, Dorotea glanced over her shoulder then stood up hastily. Rosary beads clutched to her chest, she backed against the wall, staring at him. He hated her utterly at that moment. Her cringing terror made him want to hit her. "Get out," he snarled at her. "Get out now." Dorotea dropped her rosary and ran out the door.

Antonio restrained the impulse to smash the altar and the entire room as well. Tugging off his soaked doublet, he flung it away and sank into the armchair by the fire, gazing blindly into the flames. After a while, Giacomo came into the room. He padded about, opening the curtains and snuffing the candles. Antonio wanted only to be alone. He was going to order Giacomo out, but when he looked up, his servant was crying si-

lently, tears running down his face. So he said nothing, turning
back to the waning fire. After a time, Giacomo reappeared
beside him, soft rags and a dish of hot, herbal water in hand.
Antonio realized his cheek was still bleeding, and there were
cuts on his legs from the broken glass. He held up a hand,
warding Giacomo off. He could not bear to be touched now.
The damp cloth was placed in his hand. Crumpling it in his
fist, Antonio pressed it to his face. Quietly, Giacomo went and
curled up in the chair by the window. They sat that way, without speaking a word, as the cold light of dawn slowly filled the
room. After a while, it began to rain.

16 *The Storm*

 LIGHTNING flashed through the window, a sheet of
white illuminating Veronica's bedroom. Thunder
rolled in the distance, its deep bass rumbling under the liquid clatter of the rain. It had poured all
day and all night. Unable to sleep, Veronica
slipped out of bed. Draping her velvet robe over
her shoulders, she knelt on the rug by the fireplace. The log
glowed a dull scarlet, and she tossed in sticks of kindling to
revive the blaze, adding another small log once they caught.
The growing flames gave the only light in the room till the
lightning flared again. The thunder sounded, much closer this
time. Nerves on edge, Veronica rose, wandering restlessly
about the room.

Usually thunderstorms exhilarated her, and that keyed-up
excitement was rising in her now, but the interminable bleak-
ness of the day had oppressed her as well. All morning she felt
laden with inexplicable sorrow, even before the messenger had
arrived at noon with news of the death of Antonio's mother.
Tomorrow, today by now, they would inter the body in the
Fabiani mausoleum. Her family would attend the funeral, so
she would see him then. She shared his grief, but the comfort
she could offer would be constrained by the bounds of propri-

ety. She paced, the knowledge of that constraint chafing her spirit.

Impulsively, Veronica opened the door and walked barefoot onto the balcony overlooking the garden. She gazed out at the rain, its fall a silver transparency against the midnight blackness, the trees and plants spectral glittering shapes below. Somewhere beyond the wall, a horse neighed. It could be anyone, any stranger passing in the night, but Veronica felt her whole body tense with anticipation. Antonio, it could only be Antonio. The robe fell from her shoulders as she stepped forward to grip the railing. A moment later she saw movement at the far end of the garden, and a cloaked figure scaled the top of the wall. He crouched there, staring across the garden to where she stood, clothed only in her thin shift, outlined by the faint light of the open doorway. From the wall, he leapt into the branches of the pear tree, then climbed onto the far side of the balcony, beside the model's dressing room. He ran towards her and Veronica rushed around the balcony to meet him, flinging herself into his arms.

Lifting her, Antonio kissed her once, fiercely, then buried his face against her neck. She felt each motion vividly, the strength of his arms raising her up, the slender solidity of his body pressed to hers, the coldness of his lips followed by the hot thrust of his tongue within her mouth. But more intense than any physical sensation was the feeling of being seized by an emotional maelstrom, swept into a dark swirling whirlpool of fury and sorrow, of hunger and desperate joy.

"Veronica," Antonio whispered harshly. Then; "I must be mad, coming here like this. I did not know how I would find you."

"I was waiting for you," she whispered back, so caught in her response to him she only now realized the truth.

He laughed, a short breathless gasp against her throat. Veronica knew he did not believe it, not literally as she meant it, but his mouth sought hers, kissing her again and again as if he could not bear to break the contact. He was drenched to the skin. Shivers coursed through his body, though he did not seem to notice them. She was trembling too, and he felt that reaction, drawing her even closer, trying to warm her against his own chilled flesh. Releasing her lips reluctantly, Antonio carried her back around the balcony towards her room. Dazed with shock and arousal, Veronica clung to him tightly. Lightning flickered again, and the thunder echoed the pounding of his heart and her own.

Face pressed to his chest, Veronica was aware of the strong aroma of saddle leather mingling with the wet wool of his cape and the clear, cold fragrance of the rain overlying the deeper musk of his body. That scent was warm and spicy, like incense smoke rising from some buried ember. She inhaled the musk, heady and intoxicating. She laid her head back against Antonio's shoulder, looking up into his face. His cheek was cut, an angry, diagonal slash raking down towards his mouth. Concerned, Veronica raised her hand, her inquisitive fingertips touching his skin just below the wound and tracing its path along his cheek. His eyes met hers, dark and haunted.

''Antonio, tell me . . . .'' she began, but he stopped her mouth with another kiss.

''No more words,'' he begged her. Then, ''I need you. I have to be inside you.''

''Yes,'' she whispered inaudibly, the words sending a throbbing pulse through her. It was what she needed too, to have him lose himself in her and find himself again.

Bearing her through the open door, Antonio edged it shut behind them then carried Veronica across the room, laying her down on the rug in front of the hearth. She raised herself on her elbows to watch him. Stepping back toward the fire, he unfastened his cape and tossed it aside, his hungry gaze traveling along her body. In the glowing crimson light, she saw that the thin linen of her shift was wet from his clothes. Damp and filmy, it clung to her, displaying the swollen circles of her nipples, the tiny hollow of her navel indenting the smooth plane of her belly, the soft triangle between her legs.

Veronica knew what he felt, for she experienced the same erotic surge at the sight of his chest only faintly veiled by the pale rain-soaked silk of his shirt. The hair showed, a soft black tracery against his skin. The nipples were smaller and darker than her own, not pink but translucent red. Thinking of caressing him, tasting him, she touched her own breast and felt the tip already drawn up taut and thrusting in the middle of her palm. She gasped as pleasure shot out from that one point, streaking along her veins like lightning. As he watched, she reached down and lifted up her gown, revealing what it had barely concealed.

Drawing a sharp, hissing breath, Antonio stripped off his soaked garments, impatiently casting them aside. He stood naked above her, already aroused, the flushed shaft straining, the pendant shapes below drawn tight and round. In the darkened room the firelight illuminated him from behind, staining his skin with crimson light, the blaze casting wavering shadows like wings beating all around him. His eyes searched hers, the impenetrable blackness drawing her to him, into him. Here was her demon lover, more fearful, more melancholy than the one Veronica had once conjured in her dreams. He was a wild, doomed creature of the night, an elemental being of wind and rain and flame, and the sight of him ignited every elemental emotion within her. She shivered as his wet hair dripped on her body, and each icy burning drop seemed to blister her skin. Fire radiated from the heart of her, shimmering along every nerve of her body, a sweet anguish. She opened her legs to him, offering.

Swiftly, Antonio knelt between her thighs. Leaning over her, he kissed her face, her throat, her shoulders, his caresses traveling down breasts, belly, and thighs. Her hands twined in his hair, urging him closer. Wrapping his arms around her hips, Antonio lifted her to his mouth. His lips opened the lips of her sex. Mouth, teeth and tongue plundered the wet swollen center of her. His mouth was urgent, begging, demanding, to taste her flesh, devour her essence. Pleasure coursed through her, and craving for more. He drank from her as if parched, his hunger, her excitement fusing in ravenous passion.

Veronica cried out when his mouth abandoned her, leaving her throbbing with desire. She reached up to him and Antonio came into her arms. Face to face again, his mouth fastened on hers, his tongue tasting of her juices. She felt drunk, dizzy with the liquor of passion, his ravaging kiss sucking her into a reeling vortex of sensation.

She wrapped herself around him, grasping the reality of his flesh. Veronica felt the back of his thighs and buttocks warm from the fire, the length of him still cool where he lay against her, except for the hot, hard maleness of him seeking the open heart of her. As his tongue thrust into the hollow of her mouth, his thrusting sex found her entrance. He moaned as he plunged inside her, the low sound filling her, deep, deeper than his tongue, his sex. She clasped him to her, moaning in answer. His need was a scorching darkness that drenched her, consumed her. Flame and flood mingled and melted into a fierce rhythm that moved through her, rushing through blood and muscle, through mind and soul, until she writhed with the same violent, grieving passion that possessed him.

Release would not come. He was fighting again, but not against her. Some new inner barrier shut him from her. Some dark secret caged his heart. "Tell me," she whispered again.

"I love you," he told her. "I love you."

But those were not the words she must hear. Not the words he must speak. "Antonio . . . ." she begged, but he kissed her again, his mouth, his tongue commanding her silence.

Their passion would not mesh. Caught in the turbulent cross currents of his desire, their bodies struggled against each other. Antonio reshaped their position again and again, lifting, turning, twisting her, searching for some ultimate sensation to release them both. Nothing seemed enough. Kneeling, he took her astride his thighs. She sank onto him, sheathing his sex as he impaled hers, moving on him in a slow moaning yearning dance. But that was not enough. Tilting her back, Antonio rose above her and took her legs over his shoulders, driving himself deep within her. Each plunge was a sharp jabbing rapture that she keened to him, a rising note of pleasure and need. But not enough. He lowered her once more, turning her over onto her knees, her face pressed to the soft roughness of the rug, her hips raised high to his entry. That was quick and hard, the force of his hips strong against her, a relentless barrage of pleasure. Not enough, not enough. He leaned over her, panting. Still in counterpoint, her own breath came in harsh, painful sobs. The rain lashed at the windows, a storm of tears.

Groaning with frustration, Antonio turned her face to face once more, pulling her close. His body was hot and wet now, slippery not with rain but with sweat and she locked her limbs around him. Veronica felt his grip tighten, felt his teeth sharper in each new kiss as their acute, nerve-flaying pleasure edged closer and closer to pain. Reckless, her mouth found its own target. Head flung back, he gasped as her teeth sank into his shoulder. His hands tightened on her, a bruising demand. She bit deeper, feeling the flow of his blood, hot and salty on her tongue. Her mouth drinking the pain of his flesh as her heart drank the pain of his spirit. Pressing her back, Antonio's hips drove against her, a single desperate thrust, burying his sex deep within hers. Lightning engulfed them in bright white flame. Thunder crashed behind it, a vast dark wave rolling over them. Antonio's moan sounded within it, long and shuddering like the tremor that racked his body. The hot liquid of his seed burst inside her, and that scalding ecstasy brought her own shattering release. Crying his name, Veronica clutched him to her as the tremors shook her in turn.

Exhausted, their bodies still quivering, they lay entwined, listening to the sounds of rain and fire blurring with their ragged breath. Sighing heavily, Antonio rested his head on her breast. He did not seem demonic now, only sweetly, sadly mortal. The smudges under his eyes were not cast by the fire's shadows. Despite the signs of strain, he looked oddly young. She could see the child and the youth within the man, as well as the marks that age would carve deeper and deeper with the years. And each face was beautiful to her. She wondered at the unexplained slash along his cheek, the small cuts all over his body. After a minute, he roused himself and raised his face to look at hers.

"You've been weeping," he whispered, concerned. "Have I hurt you?"

"I was weeping for you," she answered. She had not known, had only been aware of the power of his emotion, his rage and torment pouring into her. The pain in him was so intermingled with the pleasure, she could not separate them.

He shook his head, frowning slightly. "It's joy I want to bring you." His fingers glided down her arm, pausing to match themselves to the marks that showed dark against her pale skin. "I did hurt you." His voice grated with self-reproach.

"The bruises are nothing."

His eyes met hers again. "It is like this with me sometimes, when death comes too close."

A warning. He did not understand that his own pain hurt her more deeply than these passing bruises. "You must have loved her deeply, your mother."

"Yes," he answered, and that grief he showed her, moisture welling in his eyes. "She wanted so to live, despite her suffering. Her love for us held her to her agony. At least she is beyond that now. If there is a God, he will take her into his light. If not, even the darkness offers peace."

Liquid spilled over, ran down his cheek, but he did not turn from her. His eyes closed for a second and he drew a deep, shuddering breath. When he opened them, the tears were checked. Her fingers reached out and stroked the glistening track, then lifted to trace the stark line of his wound once more. "How . . . ." she started to ask him, but at the single word he tensed, and all that was open in his face was suddenly shadowed, the answers veiled within it. As the silence continued, he smiled, an ironic twist of the lips, but he bent his head and kissed her delicately. Closing his eyes, he buried his face between her breasts once more, the tension easing from his body. She stroked his hair, and in a few moments he was asleep.

Veronica sighed. She had wanted to understand so she could comfort him, but silence was the understanding, the comfort he had asked from her. Not explanations but the solace, the oblivion of flesh. Her questions had only evoked the same pain he had come here to escape. But it was not escaped, only eased. The wound in his spirit was far deeper than the one in his flesh. Already, sorrow had returned to cloud their peace, and alongside it a sharper frustration that was all her own. To demand explanations was to deny Antonio's need. Not to demand them was to deny her own. Their bodies had never denied each other, but still he held his emotions back from her. Would he never trust her? Never express himself wholly, words and thoughts as well as the language of the flesh? Well, trust could not be demanded. He had only just learned to love her . . . or to recognize he had loved her from the first. Their mating tonight had been more fierce than tender, but it had been a battle they shared, not a war they fought against each other.

The log collapsed in the fire, casting sparks. Antonio gave a start, then sat up beside her. She saw the brief rest had only made him more haggard. "Go back to sleep, my love."

"I must go now." He ran his fingers through his hair, pressing his palms to his temples as if he had a headache.

"Stay," she encouraged, seeing how urgently he required rest, knowing how much she longed to hold him for a night. "Stay a little longer. I will keep watch and wake you close to morning."

He took her face between his hands and kissed her, savoring the tenderness. Then he picked her up in his arms and carried her to the bed, laying her down on the cool, crumpled linen. "I want nothing more than to sleep in your arms," he whispered, meaning it. "But it would be too easy for you to drowse as well. And that is a scandal neither of us wants to deal with."

Veronica was going to say she did not care, but she remembered that today was his mother's funeral. Blankets drawn up to her chin, she held her tongue once more, watching silently as Antonio searched around the hearth for his discarded garments. He seemed remote when he returned to her, wrapped up in the heavy folds of his cape. His eyes were troubled as he bent over and kissed her.

"Good-bye, my love," he whispered.

———

The storm had abated to a gray drizzle when Antonio reined in his horse at the gates to the estate. The cypress trees stood like waiting mourners. Black against the paler blackness of the night, they swayed back and forth, keening faintly in the fitful wind. Shivering, Antonio drew his cloak tighter about him. Sodden as it was, the wool offered some warmth, unlike the cold clammy silk adhering to his skin. He wished he'd had enough sense to lay his clothes out by the fire before succumbing to his passion. Veronica had been all he could think of then, the glowing, melting light of her, beckoning him like a slender flame. She had warmed him, taken the icy chill from his body and soul. But the chill had been waiting to reclaim him. He had to leave or risk compromising her. Warm and drowsy, he had confronted the immediate results of his heedless frenzy, a heap of wet clothes. It had been singularly unpleasant to put them on again.

Well, he would be in bed soon enough. He would have a few hour's sleep, three perhaps, in as many days. It would have to do. He must rise at dawn to tend to the final arrangements for the funeral. Only respect for his mother could bring him back to the estate today. He could not bear to remain here much beyond that final ceremony. Tomorrow he would search for apartments within the walls of Florence and make plans for his future. The house which had nourished his childhood would never be anything other than a crypt for him now. The deaths outweighed the lives. His mother, Alessandro, Beatrice. What was left for him here? His wife's affection, his father's? His love for them? He would leave Dorotea here. She would no doubt prefer it. Let her comfort his father. They deserved each other.

A shudder of fury ran through Antonio. Leaving the estate was the only course open to him now; remaining would not only be difficult, it would be dangerous as well. The atmosphere between his father and himself was fraught with violence. The social ritual of the funeral was the only buffer remaining between the two of them. Without it, that violence would soon erupt. Antonio wondered how long this hatred for his father had lurked, hidden in some murky lair within him, waiting for the power of this revelation to unleash it. His own guilt had not permitted him to feel it before. Guilt and hope. How he had hungered to return to Florence, and now it was no better than a gilded prison. His marriage was a travesty. The heritage he had so longed for, so treasured, was dust. Dust and ashes. He had sold himself to attain it, and it was all worthless. If it were not for Veronica, he would disown it all tomorrow and return once more to Venice—or Rome.

Suddenly, Antonio laughed aloud, a giddy relief washing over his bitterness. "Well now," he said to the darkness, "that would be a solution to it all."

He had bought this future dearly, but it was a future that could yet be redeemed. In the years he spent in exile, he had earned his freedom. Now he would buy it back again. He had saved Cesare Borgia's life once, in a tavern brawl the young Spaniard had started over some foolish point of wounded vanity. They were never close, and that kind of debt was as likely to breed resentment as gratitude in someone as proud as

Cesare. Wary of the man's volatile personality, as well as the political snares involved in dealing with the Borgias, Antonio had never taken advantage of the exploit. Well, now he would. Dorotea was still virgin. Since he had not consummated the marriage, it should be possible to have it annulled. Especially if the Borgias supported his cause. Rumors of the Pope's proposed annulment of Lucrezia's marriage had proved valid. Would her upcoming divorce help or hinder his own petition?

It would be expensive in any case, perhaps more than it was worth. The Borgias were totally avaricious. The debt Cesare owed him would be worth no more than a few words whispered into the Pope's ear. To pressure the Cardinals in Antonio's favor, the Borgias would want a small fortune, and would probably demand certain personal favors as well. If he were granted the annulment, Dorotea's dowry would have to be returned to her family along with Dorotea. There was where the greatest cost lay, and it was not in coin. Gold would not redeem wounded pride or broken alliances. The price would be high in the anger and bitterness it would create between the families. The danger of enmity would be greater if he stayed in Florence, but he would not be staying. Having made this resolution, no matter what the outcome of the annulment, he now had no intention of remaining for longer than it took to untangle his affairs. There was the rest of Italy, the rest of Europe, in which to build his own world. Banished, he had learned to live without family, had begun to learn to like it. Returning to his old life would not be difficult now.

Except for Veronica. He did not want to leave Veronica. She was the only thing of value he had found here. He wanted to take her away with him now, to Rome, but that would be insane. The scandal would destroy both her good name and his chance for the annulment. But later, when he moved permanently, it could be arranged with more discretion. Her reputation must have some protection—though everyone would know she was his mistress. These hypocrisies were so stupid.

Would she even leave Florence and come away with him? He felt certain she would, but his certainty could be presumptuous. He knew so little about her. They had hardly talked. Tender or violent, passion had dominated their every encounter. He did not know what she would want, what she would need to be happy elsewhere. Well, if necessary, they could recreate her entire household in Venice or Rome. Perhaps Daniele could be persuaded to open a studio there. She seemed very protective of the poor fool to whom they'd married her. Antonio supposed he would make arrangements for him and his servant. And the dog, of course, and the cat. No doubt she would want that sharp-eyed Gypsy grandmother as well. What a motley menagerie of man and beast he was suddenly acquiring with his new mistress.

And if Veronica would not leave Florence? She had told him she loved him, but that did not mean she would sacrifice the established life, the status she had now, for an uncertain future with him. What if she thought him a fool for meddling with things as they were, where a hundred easy excuses could be found to meet and continue their clandestine affair? Thought him mad for going to such extremes to cast off a shackle another man would regard as no more than a meaningless symbol? Could he bear it if she did not come with him? Could he bear to stay here if she did not want to leave?

Antonio swayed in his saddle, his head spinning. He felt weak and queasy. There had been too many sleepless nights, too many emotional crises. This speculation was ludicrous. Tomorrow, after the funeral, he would see Veronica and talk to her. Then he must make arrangements to leave for Rome. The annulment must be arranged, and the chances for success were a hundred times greater if he presented his petition in person. Knowledge of his desire for an annulment would create an uproar in Florence, perhaps interference as well. Except for Veronica, he would say nothing to anyone until he saw how his suit was received by the Pope.

The estate came into view and Antonio drew his horse to a halt, staring at the house. Weary as he was, a black pit of disgust and rage opened inside him at the sight of it. Leaving was the right decision. Tomorrow, he would ride into Florence and find out when the next caravan left for Rome. He could not endure another week under this roof.

17 Dark Visions

FEVER and chills wracked Antonio, leaving him weak and shaken, his body aching and drenched with sweat. The sickness flayed his nerves, exaggerating everything, distorting physical proportions, distorting emotion. Lucidity came and went. He was not sure, sometimes, what was reality, what was dream, and what hallucination. All of it was nightmare.

He dreamed of death stalking him and opened his eyes to see his father standing in the doorway, watching him. Without moving, he seemed to loom before Antonio, the shadows on his face carving the skull beneath. Within the hollowed sockets, his eyes burned, bright and implacable. Then he was a thousand miles away, a figure of blackness framed in a coffin of light. Yet even across that distance his eyes still burned.

Antonio had thought there was only his father and himself and the gulf of hatred between them. But there was more. Shadows surrounded him, whispers sibilant within the shifting darkness, but he did not dare turn. He was only sure he was not still dreaming when Dorotea's voice rose, quavering with panic. "You are sure it isn't the black plague?"

"Yes, yes, yes," the doctor reassured her, his voice sharp with irritation. "I have told you, there are no buboes. I cannot say that it is not contagious, but no one else has contracted it yet. The immediate danger is to your husband. Let us worry about him for the moment. He must be bled."

"No," Antonio formed the word, but his throat was too parched to voice it. His father smiled, baring the teeth of the skull. He turned and walked from the doorway, leaving not light but darkness in his wake. Shuddering, Antonio sank into the void he left behind.

When he woke again, the doctor was bleeding him, the knife blade slicing the vein in his arm. He struggled, but two of the servants were there to hold him. He watched the life drain out

of him into the bowl they held to catch it, vivid red against
white.

"Your fever is dangerously high," the doctor chastised.
"You must be bled to cleanse the evil humors. Your good wife
is wiser than you in this. The fever disturbs your reasoning."

"Your father agreed," Dorotea hovered at the edge of the
bed. She reached out, dabbing at his forehead with a wet cloth
that dripped icy rivulets down his face and neck.

"Where is Giacomo?" he demanded, his voice a grating
whisper. Giacomo knew he detested bleeding.

"You sent him to the city hours ago—on some secret errand." Dorotea's voice was thin with anger.

"Errand?" That was right. He could not go to Florence, so
he had insisted Giacomo find out about the caravans. Giacomo
said he was mad, but he had gone. Did Dorotea guess his
purpose? How could she? But why should she care what service he sent his valet to perform? She fingered her rosary, her
lips pinched, her eyes averted from his draining blood.

Perhaps it was only that she did not want to tend him. Well,
that desire was mutual enough. He could not bear her fluttering
about him like some black moth, dressed in mourning she did
not mean. He could not abide the nervous touch of her hands,
cold and damp with fear.

They took the bowl with the blood away. The doctor said he
would return tomorrow. Antonio tried to orient himself, hating
the chaos in his mind. It was two days now, no, three, since the
sickness had taken him. It had begun the morning of his
mother's funeral. He had struggled through the ceremonies
and the gathering afterwards, where the parade of relatives and
neighbors offered their condolences. He had not known what
was happening, only that everything felt wrong. Then Veronica
had come up to him, looked into his eyes, and said, "You are
ill."

He had known then that there was a physical source to his
disorientation, something beyond his own bitterness and grief
warping the world around him. She had touched his forehead.
He could feel his fever, the heat radiating against the cool
smoothness of her hand. He closed his eyes, bathing in the
comfort of her presence. The touch was too brief. He opened
his eyes to find hers clouded with compassion and concern.

Maria appeared at their side, scenting impropriety in that tender gesture. She looked thoroughly annoyed when Veronica informed her that her son-in-law was burning with fever.

An acrid steamy odor assailed Antonio's nostrils. He looked up to see Dorotea beckoning to a servant, who set a tea service on the table by the bed. The smell nauseated him. It was different from the last *tisane* she had brought, but just as vile. Weakly, he turned his head away. "No."

"You must drink this," Dorotea persisted, ignoring his refusal. "It will be good for you." Awkwardly, she tried to lift his head and set the cup to his lips.

"No," he gritted his teeth and jerked his head away, dreading the *tisane* irrationally.

"It is specially made for you," she insisted querulously, pushing the cup at him.

"I told you I wanted no more of your odious brews."

Her lips trembled. "I did not make it, since you do not like my mother's fever remedy. This is brewed from a special packet of herbs, kindly sent by the Lady Laudomia."

Dorotea shrieked as he knocked the *tisane* from her hand, the liquid splashing both of them and the cup shattering on the floor. A servant rushed in, his father's man, obsequious and hostile, glancing at him apprehensively as he gathered up the broken shards of porcelain.

Would Laudomia poison him? Why not? Perhaps it would not be detected. The fever would be thought to kill him. And if she were caught, would not his death be worth the price? Her hatred of him was the greatest passion in her life, his murder its perfect consummation. Did Dorotea know what she carried, bringing him Laudomia's evil brew? It would be such an easy step from bride to widow. No, Antonio thought, she might hate him already, but she treasured her religious commandments. That obsession was greater than any animosity towards him. She would not knowingly give him poison, but her heart might well suspect what her mind did not acknowledge. In that way, she would be the perfect accomplice. And his father . . . Antonio looked up and saw that his father was there once more, standing in the doorway. He was surrounded by enemies—his father, Dorotea, even his father's resentful servant, casting dark looks from the shattered crockery. Chills racked him again, but he struggled to sit up. All he wanted was to escape.

Giacomo appeared in the doorway, squeezing past Antonio's father to hurry to his master's side. He smelled good in the stifling air of the room, clean scents of rain and trees. Antonio let Giacomo press him back down onto the pillows, felt a cool hand test his forehead. Not Veronica's hand, but one he trusted. "Get them out of here," he whispered. "You take care of me."

Giacomo shooed away the servant and turned to Dorotea, solicitous but insistent. "I'll tend to him now, Madonna Dorotea. It would be best, if you don't mind. He's difficult when he's sick, my lady, and I'm used to his moods."

"You are insolent," Dorotea said, glaring at him, but she showed no reluctance to leave the room. Antonio's father had already disappeared from the doorway.

"The caravan?" he asked Giacomo.

"There's one going today—without us, I trust, my lord. The next leaves in six days, the third a week after that. I reserved us places on both."

He was trapped here now. There was nothing to be done but wait.

Giacomo picked up the pot of *tisane* and sniffed. He wrinkled his nose, "That's more likely to make you sick than cure you. What does she put in it?"

"Laudomia sent it," Antonio said.

Giacomo whirled about, his eyes wide, then he said, "Well, at least the mistress didn't send her up for a visit."

"She'd have let more blood than the doctor." Antonio smiled grimly. "You'd best get it out of the kitchen before someone else samples it. Don't throw it away."

"I don't think anyone will drink it by choice." Giacomo set the pot on the table and went to retrieve the basin and cloth. "It's too bad Madonna Dorotea tried to make you swallow this and tossed out those Gypsy herbs."

"What?" he asked.

"You lie down again." Giacomo scurried back, carrying the basin with him.

"Has anyone else called?" Antonio asked, taking hold of

Giacomo's arm. Giacomo stared down at the gripping hand, perplexed, then covered it with his own and patted it.

"Well, not everyone you'd like to see can properly come to visit," he said, sympathy and reproof mingled in his voice. "Signore Daniele came by again this morning, with your cousin, Signore Stefano, and the lady Veronica. She's the one brought you the *tisane* from her great-grandmother, but Dorotea tossed it away, saying she'd have no Gypsy potions here. We told them all the doctor said no visitors, of course."

"Of course," he repeated tonelessly. Veronica had come. With Daniele and his cousin. Regret at missing her flooded Antonio with cold despair. The corrosive flame of his jealousy fused with the rising heat of his fever. Shivering, he lay back among the pillows, hot and cold flashes racing through his veins.

Frowning, Giacomo laid a hand on his brow again. "Damn."

Antonio knew it was bad, for no admonitions followed that muttered curse. Giacomo's hands were gentle and deft, tucking the covers around Antonio's shoulders, but he could not bear the sense of confinement. "Leave me be." He pulled away, curling into himself. He could feel the rising fever hazing his mind, and snarled his curses at the spinning dark.

He was fighting. Sweat poured off him, his breath came short and sharp from his lungs. Panting, every muscle aching, he struggled against the weight bearing him down. Antonio felt the knife cut into him, saw the blood red on the blade. He kicked out, felt the body fly from him, heard the cry as his rival tumbled to his death. Then he was on his feet, stumbling to the balustrade once again, looking at the body. But it was Stefano who lay twisted below him. He turned away, and Veronica came to him, knelt before him, vowing her love while her lover lay bloody and broken on the marble. He wanted to thrust her from him, but he could not, his need was too great. Her breath burned his loins, the fire threading every vein in his body, rushing molten through his blood. Her hair was flame in his hands as he pressed her face to him, unable to stop himself. The touch of her hands scorched his skin. Her tongue darted

out, a red flame licking his sex. He screamed as the fire swallowed him, consumed him entirely, flesh and bone melting to
nothing. All that was left was his heart, burning in the darkness. Then that was gone too, leaving only blackness and
ashes.

———

"Daniele is not at home?" Stefano asked, disappointment
obvious in his voice.

"No, he will be gone today and tomorrow. But come up to
the studio anyway. I know Daniele was eager for you to see the
beginning of *The Judgment of Paris*." Stefano came in, and
Veronica told him about Daniele's trip. "He finished the last
of the Aristi portraits. The family have moved early to their
summer estate in the hills, and he has joined them there. He
thinks they may want some small changes."

"Ah yes, the finicky ones, who wanted a velvet pillow on
the tiles, a dog on the pillow, a jeweled collar on the dog."

"A second painting might be easier than their small
changes," Veronica laughed. At least they were paying generously. With that fee in hand, Daniele would feel free to devote
himself to *The Judgment of Paris*. They would never starve, of
course, but the commissions made life easier.

"Would you like to go riding with me, after we have looked
at the sketches?" Stefano queried. "I have a few hours before
I must return home. The afternoon is warm and sunny, and the
rains have brought new blossoms to the hillsides."

She was tempted to suggest they ride out to the Fabiani
estate and try to visit Antonio, but they had already been
turned away once, despite Stefano being Antonio's cousin. Antonio had been ill a week, but the crisis was past and Veronica
no longer fearful. Perhaps now Antonio was recovered enough
to choose his own visitors. If that were true, she would much
rather see him alone. But today was impossible in any case.

"I am waiting for Mama Lucia," Veronica told Stefano.
"This is one of our days to visit the convent hospital."

"Shall I come with you? I know little of the healing arts,
but I can bathe fevered brows, and I have a certain skill for
holding hands."

Veronica paused at the foot of the staircase. Stefano spoke

lightly, but she knew he was serious. For today, at least, he would come with them and do whatever was asked of him with perfect composure and cheerfulness.

"All right, then, if you would enjoy accompanying us. The sisters will not mind your presence in the hospital. Mama Lucia should be here within the hour."

"I am surprised your great-grandmother does not stay with you. Her spirit is young, but she is too old in years to live alone."

"The tower is Mama Lucia's home," Veronica said as they climbed the stairs to the studio. "My aunt and uncle insist on sending a servant in the morning, and again at night, to see that she is well and to tend to any needs she may have. She hates being waited on, but she lets the woman do a bit of sweeping and such, before sending her back. On days like today, a groom comes to saddle the mule for her."

"I have been meaning to visit Lucia Danti and have my fortune told."

Stefano always had plans, but Veronica had learned he did not enjoy solitary endeavors. "We could ride out together next week . . . ." she began.

"Yes, when Daniele returns," Stefano added blithely, before she had even finished the same suggestion.

Veronica smiled. The slowly budding romance was at last beginning to flower. Stefano's initial attraction had been to her, but she had not lost his friendship when she failed to respond to his advances. Daniele, obviously attracted to Stefano, had been reluctant to approach him. Even though her cousin's sources around Florence indicated that Stefano dallied with both sexes, Daniele doubted it could be true, given the other man's indiscriminate praise of Savonarola. Captivated by both man and model, Daniele did not want to chance rejection from either.

To clarify the situation for her cousin, Veronica had set herself to probe Stefano's attitude, gently questioning him while he modeled for Daniele. It proved to be Savonarola's ardor that he admired, rather than his stifling morality. While admiring Savonarola's seemingly absolute integrity, Stefano still seemed to think that many of his attacks were merely for show —that his threats had no real bearing on Daniele or Mama

Lucia, on anyone Stefano might care for, or on Stefano himself
for consorting with them. In some ways Stefano's naïveté annoyed her, but his generosity and kind heart were genuine.

Ironically, the romantic streak in Stefano that idealized the
Friar was what drew him to Daniele and their unconventional
household. He was as enamored of Daniele's passion for his
art as, Veronica suspected, he envied Savonarola's passion for
his preaching. Once or twice, Stefano had told them how he
would have liked to be a troubadour. Sometimes, while
Daniele painted, he played songs for them upon his lute and
sang in a dreamy, melancholy tenor tales of far travels and lost
loves. His creativity was not a strong enough drive in him to
break with his family, nor did he even seem unhappy to be the
dilettante he was. But in their company, Veronica knew his
fantasy blended with reality.

"Which pose has Daniele decided upon?" Stefano asked as
Veronica opened the door to the studio.

"He has done several studies," Veronica answered. She
spread the small paintings out on the table. "This one is my
favorite." The brushwork was loose, without the meticulous
care Daniele would devote to a finished work, but it had life
and vibrancy. There was no figure in it but Paris, holding out
the fateful apple.

"I am not so handsome," Stefano murmured, clearly flattered.

"Almost," Veronica teased him. She knew the picture was
done by a man falling in love. A golden light gilded the figure
and seemed to pour forth from it. Daniele seeing Stefano
through the eyes of desire.

"Daniele told me he thought that Paris saw not simply the
beauty of Venus, or Helen, but Love itself when he offered the
apple," Stefano mused.

"This is the one he has chosen for the large painting," she
said, handing him another study.

"How strange," he said, examining it. "This is so bright
and yet so ominous. A sun-drenched afternoon, yet the shadows stretch out to the figures. They make a shiver run up my
spine."

"Daniele will be pleased you responded to the shadows,"
Veronica said, laughing. "He calls them the fingers of fate,

they show the death and destruction that love would bring to Paris.''

''And to Troy. Think of it, a whole city, a whole civilization destroyed for love of one woman.'' Stefano paused, staring at the image of the Trojan prince for which he had modeled. ''I think Paris made the right decision. Everyone scorns him for choosing love over power, over wisdom. But since any choice doomed him by evoking the wrath of the rejected goddesses, I believe love was the best choice he could have made. Surely it was the most precious. What would you have chosen, Veronica? Not power.''

''No. But wouldn't wisdom be the best choice, finally?''

''Wisdom, or your heart's desire?''

Antonio, she almost said aloud. Given how he had treated her at first, it would have been wise not to love him. But she believed now that her heart had been wiser than her mind. ''I do not know if love without wisdom has value, but wisdom without love seems no better. I don't think it was that depth of wisdom Athena offered, only knowledge.''

''Minerva does not appear so wise in this myth, does she?'' Stefano asked. ''Squabbling with Hera and Aphrodite over the prize.''

''The Apple of Discord, what a cruel offering . . . .'' Then, in an instant, the world spun into darkness.

''Veronica?'' Stefano's voice called her, a faint echo from the world outside.

She raised one hand, warding him off, all her attention turned inward. First there was only the sense of impending danger, her skin prickling, the coldness filling her belly. Then the image formed: Mama Lucia riding her mule. A solitary figure descending the incline of a street, a blur of cobblestones, a wall, a smudge of sky. But she was not alone. Malicious eyes watched her. Minds bent on harm. *Where, where,* Veronica cried in her mind. She saw a curving wall of a house she recognized, a plum tree, a faded cobbler's sign.

Abruptly as it had come, the vision vanished. She staggered forward and Stefano caught her, her hands gripping her shoulders, his eyes wide. ''What is it?''

''Mama Lucia,'' Veronica gasped, wondering when Stefano

had taken hold of her. "Hurry, hurry. There is still time. I think there is still time."

Her horse was saddled in preparation for the ride to the convent. As they mounted, she called out where they were going, then whipped her horse through the streets. Her burst of speed was forced to slow almost at once, for there were children playing and old people in the way. She turned the horse toward less crowded streets. The ride seemed endless, a nightmare maze. Suddenly, Veronica cried out as her body was engulfed by a ghostly barrage of pain, a muffled echo of what she knew was Mama Lucia's agony. Desperate, she lashed her horse harder.

Ahead was the cobbler's sign, the rising road curving around the stone wall. Riderless, Mama Lucia's mule stood in an empty square, braying hoarsely. Then she saw them. Saw the gang of Savonarola's youth with their rocks and, beyond them, the crumpled heap by the wall that she knew was Mama Lucia. She drove her horse at them, as Antonio had done to the thugs. They scattered, not even realizing at first her charge was aimed at them rather than through them. Only when she wheeled her horse around and Stefano reined his mount in beside hers, did they realize they were now the target. Hurling what stones they held in their hands, the boys broke and ran down the side streets or climbed the walls. Veronica let them go. Mama Lucia was important, not this vile pack of adolescent zealots.

She dismounted and knelt beside her great-grandmother. Mama Lucia was unconscious. Her face was bruised and bloody. Quickly, carefully, Veronica's hands examined the fragile body. She shuddered as she discovered one arm was plainly broken, the bones shifting beneath her fingers. She feared shattered ribs as well, but could detect no other significant injuries. That did not mean there were none, and she felt too distraught to judge the situation clearly. Veronica looked up as Stefano came to stand beside her, "We must take her back to Daniele's at once, and call a doctor. She trusts Doctor Solomon."

"We should take her to the Della Montagna palazzo," Stefano said. "It is closer."

"No, not there." Luigi would not want them there, unless

he could twist it to his advantage. Maria would not want them there at all.

"I don't like them either," Stefano said unexpectedly, "but Daniele's house, or mine, is three times as far from here. We do not know what her injuries are. We should take her there first. Tomorrow we can move her farther, when we are sure it will not cause greater damage."

Looking at Mama Lucia's frail body, the bruises and the blood, Veronica knew Stefano was right, though the thought of dealing with Luigi and Maria filled her with misgivings. She felt dazed, queasy with fear. Mama Lucia was so old, her bones brittle. Knowing there was still danger, she nodded abruptly. "Yes, we will take her to my father-in-law's home."

"Stay here, I will get a stretcher put together." Stefano ran down to the square. Veronica could hear him knocking, yelling, "Open up, you cowards." For a few moments there were only indeterminate sounds, muffled voices; then Stefano reappeared with an older man in a cobbler's apron, carrying rope, poles, and blankets.

"They'll come back and stone us for helping," the cobbler said, but he worked with Stefano to lash together the stretcher and fix it to Veronica's saddle. He took the coins Stefano gave him and crossed himself. "Go away, go away quickly," he said, and hurried back to his shop.

"He's right. We must act quickly," Stefano said, an urgent note in his voice. She glanced at him, and he indicated with a slight jerk of his head that some of the youths had returned. Veronica saw four moving stealthily down an alleyway and another on the roof of the house nearby. Would they dare attack the three of them? She thought not, but there was no mistaking the threat of their presence. And Mama Lucia would be so vulnerable, laid out on her stretcher. Stefano drew his sword and went down the side street. The two boys ran off, but another rain of stones came from a nearby roof. Veronica protected Mama Lucia's body with her own, trying to cover her without putting any weight on her.

Stefano returned. Quickly, gently, they lifted her great-grandmother onto the stretcher. Veronica moaned with each of Mama Lucia's moans, afraid her help might injure the older woman further. Stefano mounted his horse, and she climbed into her own saddle. They moved slowly through the streets, searching for the smoothest path. The boys trailed behind, though Stefano found a route that blocked the boys on the roof from continuing their pursuit. They could not find a watchman, but Stefano went into a tavern and found one man to send ahead for Doctor Solomon, and a ruffian only too happy to earn a few ducats chasing off the boys that followed them. She thought they had gotten rid of them all, but by the time they reached Luigi's palazzo, two of the boys had found another route over the rooftops.

Maria came out into the courtyard, openly hostile. At first, Veronica thought she would turn them away. If Stefano had not been with them, Veronica doubted they would have been accepted. But Stefano's presence shamed her mother-in-law. Veronica pleaded that they need only stay the one night, time for a doctor to examine Mama Lucia and to let her rest, and that was all Maria would agree to. She told Veronica she could have the usual rooms, the shabby ones beneath the far corner watchtower.

"Good, we will not have to lift her up any stairs." The men carried the stretcher inside. Veronica and Stefano moved Mama Lucia into the bed. Two servants brought in a pallet for Veronica and laid it close by on the floor. Stefano told the ruffian to watch at the gates until he returned. "I have to talk to my family, but I will come back soon. I can take a message to Daniele's house for you on the way. That is better than hearing ill news from a stranger."

"Yes, they need to know what has happened. Ask Benito to tend to Roberto tonight. Roberto will want to come and help, but he would only be in the way. Tell them I should be home tomorrow. Once I've talked to the doctor, I'll send news to Daniele at the Aristi estate."

Stefano took his leave of her. While she awaited his return and Doctor Solomon's arrival, Veronica went down to the kitchen to see what herbs were available and set the maid to brewing a cleansing solution and a soothing *tisane*. They were discussing simple remedies together when Maria appeared. One glance at her mistress' irate expression, and the servant made a hasty exit, leaving Veronica alone with her mother-in-law. "You presume on our kinship," Maria proclaimed. "I will endure much, but I will not endure a Jew in my home. I have sent that foul man away.''

Doctor Solomon had been dismissed, without ever seeing Mama Lucia. For a moment Veronica thought she would strike Maria. Shaking, she clenched her hands into fists, nails digging into her palms, the pain cutting against her anger. There was nothing to be done, not unless she wanted to drag her great-grandmother out into the street again, with the Savonarola youths waiting. When she could trust her voice, Veronica said only, ''You should not have done that. He is the best doctor in Florence.''

''Do not dare to send for him again. Savonarola has done his best to drive the accursed race from the city. You may be certain I will drive him from my door.''

Here was yet another way in which Savonarola had diminished Florence. The Jews were the bridge between the Christian and Ottoman empires. Their training encompassed both worlds, and Arab knowledge of medicine was far superior to Christian. But Maria would not care about that. Her mother-in-law looked as if she were about to embark on a tirade. To forestall her, Veronica asked. ''Will you send for your own doctor, then?''

Puffed up with self-righteousness, Maria deflated with a sputtering breath. ''Very well.''

Maria departed and Veronica sat down on the kitchen stool. The maid reappeared and offered to serve her supper. Veronica accepted the offer. She was not hungry, but knew she would feel less irritable if she ate. She had a bowl of soup and a bit of bread while her brews were steeped and strained. Bearing clean cloths and her two preparations, she returned to her great-grandmother. As gently as possible, she cut the torn dress away. She decided to leave the shift, lifting it when necessary to bathe and dry Mama Lucia's cuts and bruises.

The doctor arrived while Veronica worked, and jostled her aside. He seemed to be knowledgeable about bones and reassured her that the injuries were no worse than they seemed. His touch was far rougher than Veronica's, and Mama Lucia regained consciousness. That in itself was a good sign, but she was in a great deal of pain. Veronica had only the *tisane* to offer, which was not strong enough to ease her pain or put her to sleep. The doctor produced his own elixir but refused to tell them what was in it. When they insisted, he finally agreed. It proved to be a crude but potent distillation.

"I will take it, but the dosage is far too strong," Mama Lucia told him.

"You will need it. I have to set your arm. Take what I tell you, and you will sleep through it."

"Sleep through it and never wake again," she snapped. "Set the arm, and then I will take the drug."

"Very well," he said, though his resentment was obvious.

Veronica watched to see he did not retaliate when he set the bone, though there was no way for it not to be painful. When he straightened the arm Mama Lucia screamed aloud, but she did not lose consciousness. She made it through the binding of the splints with gritted teeth, and insisted he change the angle of her hand, which he did with great annoyance.

"I've earned my potion now," she said. "I want half the dose you suggested."

"Add it to my *tisane*," Veronica told him, and watched to make sure he mixed the medicine as Mama Lucia had asked. He sniffed at it and pronounced it nothing special, an ordinary housewife's brew. That was true enough, so Veronica made no comment. She carried the drugged cup to Mama Lucia and helped her drink it.

"I used to be braver in my youth. Now I want only to sleep and wake up healed." Her great-grandmother laughed at her own foolishness, but her laughter pained her. She drank down her *tisane*.

As soon as Mama Lucia was asleep, the doctor announced he wanted to let her blood. A nasty argument ensued, full of hissed arguments back and forth, though even yelling would probably not have awakened Mama Lucia. Infuriated, the doctor finally declared that without the proper authority and respect due him, he would not treat Mama Lucia at all. Veronica thought he had already done the best of which he was capable and it was no loss to order him away.

It was a relief to see him go, but Maria reappeared immediately, equally outraged. "You ask for my personal physician, and then treat him as if he knew no more than the stableboy.

After the way you have treated him, he may not return when we need him.''

"I could not let him give Mama Lucia treatments I knew she would disapprove of, Maria. I know you can understand that. Surely he will not hold my peculiarities against you.'' Veronica doubted the minor injury to his pride would keep that man from the fat fee he would earn.

Maria stormed out the door, but Luigi entered it in her wake. Veronica felt besieged. Steeling herself, she ignored his glower and thanked him for taking them in.

"You know you aren't really welcome,'' Luigi responded. "First you compromise us by bringing the Gypsy here, and then you do nothing but stir up chaos all around you. I am not sure whether my house has been turned into a hospital or a fortress. I don't want you dragging your whole household over here to tend that old wretch.''

"I've already asked that Roberto be kept at home. I was waiting to send for Daniele until I had spoken to the doctor.'' She stumbled slightly on the last few words, then raised her chin in mild defiance. "He will want to help and can sleep in the room across the hall. We will stay out of your way.''

"Yes, that is a wonderful idea, send for your sodomite cousin. With the mood those boys are in, he is as likely to get stoned as the Gypsy,'' he sniggered at her. "And don't ask me to waste my guards to protect him. Any more trouble, and I'll toss you both out on the street.''

"I'll tend to Mama Lucia myself, then,'' she said. "I'll send a note to Daniele telling him not to worry. I will try not to be a problem.''

"You had best not be,'' he warned her.

"I won't.'' Veronica felt queasy, anxiety and animosity mingling uneasily within her. Here she was, groveling to a man she despised. She sat down to try and compose her thoughts. Should she ask Daniele to come after all? Would the Savonarola youth stone him too? Surely Stefano's men could protect him? Would flaunting two obvious targets double the chances of a later attack? Closing her eyes, Veronica reached for some image, but she found nothing within but color-speckled darkness and the jangle of overwrought nerves. Sighing, Veronica opened her eyes again. She could not summon a

vision at will. Well, she need not put Daniele at risk. Stefano
had promised to help her tomorrow. Veronica asked for paper
and pen and wrote a hurried note to Daniele.

My dear Daniele,
  *Mama Lucia was stoned by Savonarola's youth. Luigi's
house was closest, and Stefano and I brought her here, the
boys trailing us all the way. She is sleeping now, but she
woke and spoke to me earlier. I will bring her home tomorrow, with an escort. If you feel you must come here, do not
come alone. It is not safe.*

  *Tend to what you must and do not worry about me. I do
not need you. Stefano is with me now and is most kind. It
would be better if you do not come here. Mama Lucia's
injuries are not as severe as I feared, and the doctor says
she will mend. I will see you tomorrow if I can.*

                                           In haste,
                                           Veronica

"Can you spare one of your servants to deliver the message
to Daniele?" Veronica flushed as she begged the favor. "The
man we brought with us should stay on guard."

"I'll find someone to take it. Better that than having him
parading about here," Luigi said grudgingly. He held out his
hand for the note. With an odd sense of reluctance, Veronica
gave it over to him. He took it away with him, closing the door
behind him.

Veronica sighed, fighting off tears of exhaustion and lingering fear. Another sheet of paper lay before her, and what she
wanted at this moment, more than anything, was to write Antonio and beg his help. To have him gather her in his arms,
protect her, and comfort her. She picked up the pen and laid it
aside again. That was utter selfishness—he needed protection
and comfort as much as she did. She certainly did not want
him to drag himself out of bed to help her. He was still recovering from his illness and might easily have a relapse. She
would write him tomorrow, when she felt less distressed.

There was a knock at the door, followed by Stefano's voice.

Grateful for his company, she opened it to let him in, but he hovered in the hallway. "I have to go talk to my family, Veronica. I cannot stay any longer tonight. Tomorrow, I can come in the morning, but I must attend to family business in the afternoon. I am sorry to desert you."

"I will be grateful for whatever time you can spare, Stefano. It is good of you to help as much as you have," she reassured him. "Tomorrow will be easier. I do not know what I would have done alone this afternoon, without you. I was frantic."

Stefano paused by the door, his expression a mix of admiration, curiosity and apprehension. "I never knew that you were like your great-grandmother, Veronica. That you possessed Gypsy gifts."

Veronica started to tell him that her gift was more of a curse, but she did not speak the words. The visions were maddeningly inconsistent, no more than teasing whispers one time, then like today, overwhelming, almost crippling. But she found her feelings about them had begun to change. "This is the first time that I have seen some dire thing and been able to prevent it. Today, I am grateful for the sight."

For some reason the admission broke her control. She covered her face and wept, the sobs shaking her. She felt Stefano's arms go around her, and she leaned against him, accepting the support he offered. After a moment, she was able to regain control. "I am all right now."

"You are very brave." He kissed her once, on the forehead, and then on the lips, comfort and compliment rather than passion. "I will see you tomorrow."

Stefano turned to walk away. Veronica saw Maria scowling her disapproval, Luigi smirking behind her. "I will escort you to the door," Maria announced. With a rueful grin, Stefano accompanied her. Luigi did not go with them but strolled over to her instead. For some reason, he looked inordinately pleased with the situation. Was he going to order her to leave?

But all he said, before he sauntered off again, was, "I thought you weren't going to be any trouble, Veronica?"

Disturbed, Veronica closed the door, then locked and barred it behind him. The old leering note was back in his voice. Had that one chaste kiss roused his lust once more? Her skin prickled with alarm. She had tried to avoid ever being isolated again in Luigi's household. But she wasn't alone. Tonight she would sleep with Mama Lucia. Luigi had access to all the keys, but he could not break through the bar. Even if he could, sneak and coward that he was, he would not dare risk the noise nor leave the evidence. Nor would he chance a witness.

18 *The Breach*

"FEELING better?" Giacomo asked cheerfully. Tray in hand, he settled himself on the bed beside Antonio.

"Possibly," Antonio replied, eyeing the tray mistrustfully. The fever had waned, but he still had no appetite.

"You slept late. Now what you need is a bit of nourishment." With a flourish, Giacomo uncovered a large bowl of bouillon and a basket of small, tender crusted rolls. Antonio counted six of them and sighed. He knew he must eat to recover his strength, but Giacomo was far too optimistic. Hoping to stir his hunger, he closed his eyes and inhaled the aroma of the rich broth. When he opened them, Giacomo had the spoon halfway to his mouth. "Open wide."

"You do not have to spoon feed me," Antonio snapped. "I am not a swaddled infant."

Giacomo lowered the utensil and grinned. "You've recovered your temper—that's good. Gave me a scare, you did, my lord. Shivering one minute, burning the next, then both at the same time. Leave it to you to manage that."

Antonio could remember little of it, except that it was highly unpleasant. When the fever was at its worst, he knew Giacomo had tended him, his hands quick and gentle. His voice quiet and blessedly brief. His valet's relief was far worse than his concern. Giacomo's spirits had revived along with Antonio's health, and his solicitous murmurs had given way to chattering, clucking, and scolding.

"If you ask me, a fever is just what you deserve. Sneaking

out in the middle of the night like that—galloping about in the rain and getting drenched to the skin. All to go off whoring . . . ." Giacomo moved back quickly as Antonio sat up, the soup sloshing precariously. ". . . . with that Bianca," he finished in a squeaky voice.

Antonio sank back among the pillows, while his valet continued to stare at him, his eyes round with amazement. Giacomo assumed his midnight ride had been to see the courtesan, not Veronica. Now Giacomo would think Bianca was the cause of that surge of anger. Better to let him, Antonio thought, lowering his gaze. Antonio still felt intensely protective of his secret affair.

"You should look guilty," his valet chastised tentatively. Antonio said nothing. He knew Giacomo was annoyed that his master had managed to elude his vigil that night. He regarded Antonio's escape as a personal failure. "Now you've spilt the soup, and I had the cook make it specially. Beef simmered down for hours, the broth beaten with a fresh laid egg and a bit of good red wine. It's your mother's recipe." Giacomo bit his lip at that slip, and mopped unhappily at the small splash on the coverlet.

"There's plenty left," Antonio said, picking up the spoon. "I can feed myself perfectly well." He finished the entire bowl of soup and three of the six rolls.

"When you eat them all, then I'll know you're recovered," Giacomo smirked.

Stuffed, Antonio eyed the remaining rolls balefully, wondering if the effort was worth it. No, it was not. Nor was he falling into the trap of letting Giacomo lay down the rules. "I'll be fine by tomorrow. I want you to ride back into Florence today and confirm our presence on the next caravan to Rome. We must have missed one already."

"We'd never have caught the first caravan, even if you hadn't taken sick, my lord, and the next is leaving the day after tomorrow. Then there's another in a week. We will be joining that?"

"No. We'll take the one leaving in two days. I'll be well enough to ride then. I won't wait another week." The aversion to the house was gnawing at his guts. If anything, it was worse since his illness. No doubt, that was the result of feeling so disgustingly helpless.

Giacomo opened his mouth to argue, and Antonio narrowed his eyes in warning. Giacomo narrowed his right back. "You still have a fever, you look sprightly as a corpse, and now you're wanting to leave for Rome in two days. Your brains are boiled in your skull, to be even thinking of such a thing. If you want to die, I can fetch Madonna Laudomia's *tisane* back again. It did for the rat fast enough."

Antonio glared at him. The memory of the contorted rat Giacomo had shown him yesterday sat ill with this morning's breakfast. There was little to be done with Giacomo when he got in one of his presumptuous moods. Antonio contemplated his valet's advice. Certainly, he could move into town for a week. If he did that, he would be able to spend more time with Veronica before he left. The temptation was so strong he almost gave into it. Some wavering must have shown on his face, for his valet's lips began to curl into a smug smile. "Unless you want me to ride into Florence and settle things myself, Giacomo, you will confirm our reservations today."

Giacomo glowered. Antonio prayed he wouldn't have to make good his threat. Fortunately his valet knew his threats were seldom idle. The only thing that would stop him leaving Florence was if he couldn't get out of bed in two days. He did not dare delay. The magnet of Veronica's presence was too strong. If he stayed, his resolve would waver. Wanting to be with her, he might put off his decision another week, a month, two. The longer it was postponed, the more chance of complications. It would take weeks or months for the final decision as it was, though he doubted he would have to remain in Rome once things were under way.

Giacomo still had not budged. Impatiently, Antonio tossed aside the covers. Giacomo squawked and tossed them back over him. "No, you don't. I won't have it. You'll faint and fall off your horse and crack your skull open. Then no one will have me in service. I'll die a starving pauper through no fault of my own."

"I take it you will do as I ask?"

Giacomo sniffed.

"Good. Complete the arrangements for both of us. For additional protection, we will also contribute two of our own guards to the caravan.''

''We'll be done in by brigands,'' Giacomo sulked. ''They've been very bad on the road to Rome.''

Antonio ignored that. ''After you talk to the caravan leader, I have another errand for you. A note—notes I want you to deliver. Bring me a quill and paper.''

Materials in hand, Antonio dealt with business first, sending instructions to his Florentine *legale*. There was also the unpleasant issue of the poison *tisane* to deal with before he left. Next, he wrote a note to Machiavelli, who was the best person he knew to keep him abreast of developments in Florence, and would appreciate news of Rome in return. Then Antonio began to compose a courteous farewell to Bianca. He should give Giacomo money for a final gift as well. This journey offered the easiest way possible to break with the courtesan. It was always best to part gracefully if one could manage it, especially with a woman of her pride. He was not so foolish as to underestimate her value simply because she was not, after all, what he desired. He would express a properly elaborate regret at leaving her, and simply not resume the liaison when he returned to Florence. Following that was a note for Daniele. He had wanted to say good-bye to the artist, and it would make the letter to Veronica less suspicious. He hesitated now, fighting his own need to confide in her. He did not want to commit his plans to paper.

Madonna Veronica,
I must leave on Friday's caravan for Rome. Name the hour and place where I may meet you tomorrow and say farewell. Your kindness warrants more than this note. I must speak with you in person.

Antonio di Fabiani

He stared at it in distaste. It was graceless, but the convoluted flowery phrases he had addressed to Bianca would be worse. He hoped the very brevity would convey his urgency to her. The note was not important, their meeting was. He had to learn her reaction to his plans, positive or negative. Would absence sharpen her hunger for him or diminish it? The thought of even a few weeks without her presence seemed intolerable to him. Perhaps she could, after all, arrange to visit him in Rome? Would she come? Would she even be willing to wait for him?

Swearing under his breath, Antonio sealed all the notes with wax. His head ached abominably and he suspected his fever was up again. Perhaps his brains were boiled, just as Giacomo suggested. He called his valet back and handed him the letters, and money to buy a gift for Bianca. "If I am asleep when you return, wake me and give me the responses."

Giacomo left and Antonio lay back among the cushions. He had given Veronica no gift—except those cursed gold coins she had flung back at him. He wanted to give her some remembrance of him to keep while he was gone, but nothing he could think of seemed significant enough. He fingered the ruby he wore, his mother's ring. It had been part of him for a long time. If he gave Veronica this, she would know he meant to return for her.

Exhausted, Antonio slept on and off the rest of the afternoon. It was dusk when Giacomo finally reappeared. Since Antonio was awake, he began to relay his adventures before the door closed behind him.

"I've spent the whole day riding about, first one place then the other. Except for your *legale*, nobody was where they were supposed to be. Madonna Laudomia's husband was inspecting a new building, but I tracked him down. Here is his answer." Giacomo handed Antonio an envelope, then felt his forehead, clucking noncommittally before rambling on again. "The lady Bianca was out, so I left the note and the present. I bought her a pair of gloves, red leather scented with patchouli and fancied up with an inch of silver bullion round the cuffs. Signore Danti was gone, and the lady Veronica too, though at least the servants knew where she was, what with the trouble and all." Giacomo paused significantly.

"The trouble?" Antonio asked politely, restraining the urge to throttle him.

"You remember the beggar you rescued from Savonarola's youths? Well, it seems Madonna Danti, the Gypsy lady, had a run-in with those same nasty little street rats this afternoon. Stoned her good and proper, though Madonna Veronica managed to chase them off. They took the poor lady to the Della Montagna palazzo, since it was closest. So I took her note there. I didn't see Madonna Veronica, but I brought you back her answer at least.

It was the one that mattered, though Antonio managed to receive it as if it were of no consequence, frowning as if disappointed. He asked Giacomo to bring him a light supper, and opened the note when he left the room. It was short, and he read it through quickly, frowning in earnest by the end. He felt a stab of apprehension that he tried to subdue. She was upset about her great-grandmother, after all. And his own missive had been even shorter than her answer. He read her note again.

Tend to what you must and do not worry about me. I do not need you. Stefano is with me now and is most kind. It would be better if you do not come here. Mama Lucia's injuries are not as severe as I feared, and the doctor says she will mend. I will see you tomorrow if I can.

In haste,
Veronica

"In haste," Antonio muttered. The note was scribbled on a torn bit of paper, without a salutation even. Not that she would have written *amoroso* or *caro mio*. But even "Antonio" in her hand would have been intimate. Mama Lucia's injuries must be more severe than she wrote, to account for such a hurried response.

He would have gone immediately to offer her protection and comfort, but she asked him not to. Why was that? Was she concerned because he had been ill? Would his presence be nothing but a distraction? True, he wanted to give her more than comfort, but he was not so selfish he could not put those desires aside. He did not even know if he had the strength to act on them. Their plans for the future were more important than the chance for a moment's passion.

Stefano is "most kind." Could she possibly imagine his cousin's presence would reassure him? Did she mean to make him jealous? She seemed unconcerned that he was leaving Florence. She must be covering her anger, her hurt, with this curt message. Unless this was meant to tell him their affair was over. "I do not need you." Was that anger or dismissal?

Antonio crumpled the note and tossed it away. Something was askew. He hoped it was no more than her distress at Mama Lucia's suffering. If she did not send word to him tomorrow morning, he would go see her.

———

"Why can't you wait for the next caravan, my lord? Why go traipsing into the city today? You'll make yourself sick all over again, rushing around like this," Giacomo moaned, helping him on with his shirt. "Next time it will attack your lungs, I know it. I might as well be helping you into your shroud."

"Enough, Giacomo." Antonio knew he could not stand an entire day of this. "I am going into Florence this afternoon. I will take one of the guards with me. You stay here and arrange the packing. We are leaving tomorrow as planned."

"Yes, my lord." Giacomo subsided into an injured silence. That respite would last two minutes at best. However, Antonio would be dressed and out of the room in that time, and the valet could address his remarks to his master's wardrobe.

Antonio spent a tense morning going over business with his father, extricating as much of his independent fortune as he could. He gave no indication of his true intent in going to Rome, but he made it clear he intended to resume his old life as soon as possible. The current arrangement was intolerable to both of them and his father was as much relieved as angry at his departure. Antonio knew that would change when his petition for annulment became known. No matter that his father wanted Antonio out of his house as much as he longed to be gone, such an extreme breach of convention would be viewed as a betrayal.

By noon, there was still no word from Veronica. Antonio bade the briefest possible farewells to his father and Dorotea, then rode into Florence. He went directly to his father-in-law's palazzo. He was handing his reins to the groom when Luigi came outside to greet him, full of false joviality. "Antonio, what a pleasant surprise. What is it that brings you here?"

"I've come to pay my respects before leaving," Antonio said. "I am going to Rome tomorrow."

"To Rome!" Luigi exclaimed. "What can draw you away from your bridal couch so soon?"

"Business that cannot wait."

"Ah yes, the ducat rules us all," Luigi sighed.

"I heard about the unpleasant incident involving Madonna Lucia," Antonio said. "Does she fare better today?"

Luigi shrugged, "Still alive. Badly bruised, and there are broken bones, which will be slow mending at her age. She is lucky to have escaped. With her fortune-telling and her Gypsy brews, the old woman has been asking for trouble. What she does is against God and law."

"From what I have heard, she does more good than harm, which one cannot say of Savonarola's followers," Antonio commented, regarding his father-in-law curiously. Luigi's last statement sounded as if he were mimicking his wife. But to what purpose? Luigi had no love of Savonarola nor his confederates, so Antonio had no reason to think he believed what he was saying. Probably he was merely resentful at the imposition. Maria's petty retaliations would cause far more trouble than Mama Lucia's brief presence, he was sure.

"You should take more care whose talk you heed," Luigi said, and smiled unpleasantly. Antonio wondered if the warning was against Savonarola or Veronica, but then Luigi added, "Savonarola does not take kindly to criticism."

"Have you heard of any plans he might have to move against his critics?" Antonio questioned, but Luigi shook his head. Turning to the point of his visit, Antonio said, "Daniele and the lady Veronica called while I was too ill to see them. I wanted to say good-bye before I left. I thought they might be here today."

"I haven't seen that foppish artist at all," Luigi said scornfully. "As for Veronica, there are some herbs the old lady wants, and Veronica has gone hunting for them. Your cousin went with her, I think, but whether it was to the apothecary or off to the woods, I do not know," he added with a leer.

Antonio schooled his face to show nothing, neither his dismay nor his anger. If Veronica could go hunting herbs, she could have spared the time to bid him good-bye. At least sent him another note. Obviously, he had made a mistake in sending such a short letter himself. But he had made it clear he wanted to explain further. If she felt abandoned, it should be easy enough to reassure her that he meant to return for her. Unless she had already decided she preferred another lover, one who would stay close at hand? Was Luigi's perception of Stefano the truth, or only a reflection of his own lecherous and malicious nature? Only Veronica could give Antonio his answers.

He recalled his stallion from the groom and mounted. "I will return this evening after supper, if there is time," Antonio said, hoping he sounded sufficiently casual. There was no reason for him to return, except Veronica. Would she arrange not to see him?

"You should spend what time you have with your bride, Antonio. She will sorely miss your company while you are attending to business in Rome." Luigi smiled lewdly.

Antonio said nothing in answer to that, knowing Dorotea would treasure his absence far more than his presence. Bidding good-bye to his father-in-law, he rode to Daniele's, hoping to find Veronica there. She was not, and the artist was out as well. His best hope was to return when he had said he would.

Antonio turned Ombra back toward the heart of Florence, wishing he could avoid the next task he had set himself. He thought of the dead rat Giacomo had shown him, that had been fed some of Laudomia's gift. He had no wish to harm Laudomia, but his charity stopped short of collaborating on his own murder. His plans for retaliation did not include her death, and even her abduction could lead to a blood feud. There was one other course open to him. While Laudomia would not respond to threats or blackmail, her husband might. It was a risk. It was obvious she was an embarrassment to Aldus, but he was a weak man. If that weakness outweighed his alarm over his wife's murderous proclivities, Antonio would have exposed his intentions to no avail and opened himself to further retribution. Aldus might discount everything he said. Antonio had the *tisane*, but no proof that he had not doctored it himself. He had no motive, where Laudomia did, but that might not weigh against what her husband would prefer to believe.

Aldus met him in the courtyard and led him into the palazzo, his giant bulk quivering with apprehension. The situa-

tion was as sanguine as Antonio could have hoped. Aldus
heeded his story and eagerly sought his advice. He did not love
his wife, and the virulence of her obsessions had brought him
to the edge of panic. Laudomia had become a volatile liability.
Aldus had been looking for an excuse for action, and someone
to bolster him. Antonio provided both. The other man was
malleable as clay in his hands, but Antonio could only hope
Aldus would hold to the framework he was given. Antonio
suggested a certain discreet and secluded convent, whose reputation had been built on the delicate handling of problematic
ladies of rank. The convent's discretion encompassed a wide
range of social sins, from simple sexual indiscretions to violence and madness. Antonio knew it also served the criminal
greed and vindictive boredom of male relatives wanting freedom from their women. Many of the women confined there
were guilty of no more than inconvenience, but Laudomia, at
least, would have brought her fate upon herself.

"A prison," Aldus mumbled, beating his curled fists in a
nervous tattoo on his thighs.

"Yes, a prison, but one where she will be treated with courtesy and kindness. And her wardens, reliant on your continuing
generosity, will not succumb to any bribes she may offer
them."

"I expect it will cost a good deal?"

"Yes, but her confinement is likely to cost you far less than
her continued freedom," Antonio said, and then disclosed the
convent's exorbitant fee.

"Yes, yes indeed," Aldus nodded, in the tone of one who
found the service cheap at the price.

Aldus begged Antonio to stay, saying he had his own test he
wished to perform. When Laudomia returned a half-hour later,
her *tisane* was brewed and waiting. Silently, her husband offered her a cup of the deadly concoction. Staring at Antonio
from across the room, Laudomia took it and raised it to her
lips. Antonio thought she would drink it. Relief warred with
disappointment when she smashed the cup on the marble floor.

"That was my judgment on it, as well," he remarked sardonically.

Laudomia flew at him, a streak of fury, her nails reaching
for his eyes. He caught her wrists, holding her off. Shrieking

incoherent curses and obscenities, she struggled in his grasp, trying to blind him, claw him, kick him, bite him. Anything to inflict on him some of the pain she had suffered—and treasured—for the past twelve years.

"Call your guards," Antonio snapped at Aldus, who had done no more than hover in the background, bleating and fluttering his hands. Responding to the order, he ran outside. Hissing, Laudomia stretched forward, foam flecking her lips, her teeth snapping. Grabbing her wrists in one hand, Antonio clipped her hard across the jaw. For a second she stared at him, bewilderment clouding the loathing in her eyes. Then her eyes rolled back in her head, and she collapsed at his feet.

Antonio stared down at her, his pity tainted with disgust. Aldus returned with two men, casting a look of dismay at his wife's unconscious body and wounded reproach at Antonio. Curtly, he gave instructions to the guards, not trusting Aldus to do it, then left Laudomia to their tender care. In the courtyard, a wave of exhaustion swept over Antonio, and involuntary chills rippled up his spine. Mounting Ombra, he rode to one of the better inns and took a room for the night, having neither the energy nor the inclination to return to his father's estate. He sent the guard back with a polite version of that message, plus one asking Giacomo to send back a change of clothes. The ones he wore were sweated through with the recurring fever. He might have the maid launder them, but he did not want to be without something to wear, in case of emergency. Antonio draped them over the chair to air as best they could, asked the landlord to rouse him at seven, and went to bed, hoping a few hours' sleep would quell the cursed fever.

It was Giacomo, of course, who woke him, bearing a tray of the best the kitchen had to offer. Antonio ate what he could of the feast while Giacomo alternately spouted assurances about the safe arrival of the baggage the next morning, and dire warnings about his master's recalcitrant behavior. The fever was gone, hopefully for good, so Antonio could easily dismiss his valet's mutterings. He put on his clean linen and told Giacomo that he was going out, alone.

He returned to the Della Montagna palazzo at eight, certain Veronica would have returned long ago. A servant showed him into the sitting room, but it was Dorotea who met him there.

She assumed he had come to see her, and Antonio did not disabuse her of the notion. She dropped a curtsy, then sat in a chair across from him, her fingers nervously working her rosary.

What now? He could wait for hours on the pretext of spending time with Dorotea, but if Veronica had any reluctance to see him, a meeting would be impossible. He could hardly cause a scene here. The idea was to protect her reputation, not to create discord within the family. That would come soon enough, if he had success in Rome. Observing Dorotea's nervousness, he hazarded a guess that fit both the circumstances and her demeanor. "Do you plan to stay with your parents while I am in Rome?"

"Forgive me, my husband. I did not have time to speak with you this morning," she said, her lowered eyes casting him a brief resentful glance. "Then you sent word you would not be returning. My mother begged me to stay and keep her company, and your father gave me permission to come."

"Of course, if that will make you happy."

"My happiness lies in yours, my husband," she answered, a lesson learned by rote.

Antonio wondered if she had ever been happy in her life. What little joy there was in her nature had been crushed by her overbearing parents. Religious hysteria was the closest she came to passion. She did not want to be married to him, but it would be the humiliation of the annulment she embraced, not her own freedom. Not that it would be freedom, only an anxious interim. Luigi was sure to force her to marry again, and the next husband he chose might prove even worse than himself. He pitied her, but he could offer no comfort, no civility even, that did not reek of hypocrisy.

Maria entered and greeted him. "You still look ill, Antonio," she observed. "I will have *tisane* brewed for you."

"No, thank you. I have just dined."

"This is not for your pleasure but for your health." It was an order, not an offer, and she sent her servant off to prepare the remedy immediately.

"Is Madonna Lucia recovering from her injuries?" He felt compassion for the old Gypsy, along with his unsatisfied curiosity. He had not wanted to use her misfortune to arrange a confrontation with Veronica, but if he had to, he would. In normal circumstances he would have visited Mama Lucia, so there would be nothing strange in his request. "Would you show me to her room? I would like to speak with her."

"I believe she is mending," Maria said tersely, "but she has been forbidden any visitors. Fra Domenico da Pescia came today himself, to apologize for the fervor of the boys. Even he was not admitted."

"He apologized?"

"The boys acted from a sense of righteousness," Maria said defensively. "However, Savonarola believes in the justice of man as well as the justice of God. He does not want violence on the streets of Florence."

Then he should do more to control his roving packs, Antonio thought, but he did not want to antagonize his mother-in-law further. "Who is tending to Mama Lucia then, Daniele and Veronica?"

"At the moment, no one but the nurse. Veronica, as usual, was more trouble than she was worth, constantly interfering, criticizing the doctor's treatment, demanding this, refusing that, dragging in all sorts of undesirable persons. At last, even my husband would put up with no more of it. He told me he would tell Veronica that she must go home, or he would send her great-grandmother there ahead of her. Presented with that choice, she has removed herself. Hopefully, her relative will be well enough to leave tomorrow. In this case, I do not know if it was more unchristian to refuse help or to proffer it. It is spiritually unsettling to have such a person visit our home, much less stay here for days on end. I have not allowed Dorotea near her, nor will I besmirch myself by touching her."

"I am sure your charity will not go unrewarded," he remarked. Veronica was gone already? Antonio doubted either of them would lie about it. He would try Daniele's then. Perhaps she was waiting for him there.

"Veronica was concerned, at least. Daniele never bothered to come. But what can you expect? He is a shallow man, bent only on his own perfidious pleasures. When Veronica brought her great-grandmother here, it was your cousin Stefano who accompanied her. Whether the young man offered his assistance from feelings of chivalry or bewitchment, I cannot say. I think you should warn your cousin that she is a bad influence. It was repulsive, the way she was flaunting her . . . association . . . with him in our very hallways.''

Flaunting her association with Stefano? What had Veronica done to provoke that remark? How could he believe her innocent when her conduct was so blatant that both Luigi and Maria commented on it? But then, Maria's mind was as odious in its way as Luigi's, seeing lechery in innocence.

"They are both naturally affectionate," Antonio began.

"She kissed him. On the mouth." Maria's lips writhed with disgust. "I will not tolerate such licentiousness in my house. Before my very eyes."

Before Antonio could think of either response or question, a noxious odor filled the room. A servant appeared in the archway, bearing Maria's special *tisane*. His mother-in-law looked at him expectantly, a small spiteful smile tucked into the corners of her mouth. Antonio vowed he would be damned before he allowed a drop of the vile fluid to cross his lips. There was nothing more he wanted to say to either of them. Rising, he bade the two women an abrupt farewell, saying there were still many details to attend to before morning.

Leaving the house, Antonio rode straight to Daniele's. There was still no one at home but the servants. Although he had never visited Mama Lucia, he knew where she lived. He went there next, thinking Veronica might choose to be among her great-grandmother's things, for comfort and to guard them. It was a long ride and the tower was dark when he got there. There was no answer to his knocking, no sign of habitation, but he could not be certain. Remounting Ombra, Antonio stared up at the shuttered windows until a wave of dizziness made him sway in the saddle. Shivering, he turned his horse back toward the city.

He did not know where else to look for her—except, of course, where it was obvious she must be. With his cousin. Antonio went to Stefano's parents' palazzo, though it was unlikely he would bring Veronica there for an assignation. He was told Stefano had been out all day and was not expected to return until tomorrow. Antonio did not know where to look for them, nor what he would do if he found them together. Nothing, he supposed, however murderous his current thoughts. He wanted no more blood feuds, and experience had taught him that the pleasure of breaking Stefano's neck would be all too brief. But if their own affair was over, he wanted Veronica to say so to his face. It was torture to suspect but not to know. He smiled bitterly. Of course, it would be torture to know as well. He did not imagine he would stop wanting her simply because she was not worthy. Love, travesty that it was, could never be so simple.

The only recompense for Antonio's search was exhaustion. He told Giacomo to wake him at dawn, and fell asleep as soon as he slid between the sheets. The sun was long up when he woke, Giacomo belligerently insisting he needed the rest. Antonio dressed hurriedly, then forced down a reasonable portion of the obscene breakfast his valet had ordered. Giacomo fretted and fussed, contriving such obvious delays that he snapped, "I am well enough to ride. That is all that matters. I am leaving in two minutes, with you or without you."

They arrived at the caravan site with twenty minutes to spare. As promised, the guards were already there, guarding the luggage. Giacomo was clinging to him like a leech, worry pleating his features. It made Antonio tired just to look at him. He ordered his valet to check their things, then walked quickly about the square, searching the crowd for Veronica. The caravan was easy enough to locate, if she wanted to find him. He hated himself for still hoping this was all some ridiculous misunderstanding, that she had not spent the night in Stefano's arms. That she would come to say good-bye.

The final call was given, and Antonio returned to his men and mounted Ombra. He found himself wondering if he should cancel this trip and take next week's caravan. Force a confrontation and leave no doubts lingering to taunt him. Anger flared and he stoked it, for it was far better than the crippling anxiety. He had sworn he would be no woman's fool ever again, and look at him. His heart was no longer his to command. Veronica had it on a leash, to jerk about like some trained pet. It turned somersaults for her amusement and begged the crumbs from her table. And she, of course, ignored its slavish antics.

She had lied when she said that she loved him, or else told

the truth of the moment. Whatever she had felt for him, it obviously was not strong enough to overcome her pique at his leaving. If his feelings were that much stronger than her own, the relationship was entirely too dangerous. Why cling to a hope that promised only more pain? His mind could not command his feelings, but it would command his actions.

Beside him, Giacomo gave a squeak of dismay. Looking up, Antonio saw Bianca approaching them on horseback, with that oiled eunuch of hers trotting behind. Had she come to bid him good-bye? Then he noted that both Bianca and her servant were dressed for travel, not show. Antonio felt a renewed rush of anger at her effrontery, that drained in a backwash of fatigue. There was nothing to be done now but travel with her or not go. As Bianca came closer, he noticed that she was more practically dressed than he would have supposed, in a handsome habit of fine gray wool. The only extravagance was a pair of red gloves, lavishly embroidered in silver. Ah yes, the parting gift Giacomo had chosen in his stead. His valet had done well, especially since Giacomo's own choice would have been a necklace of nettles or some similar object of affliction. At the moment Antonio concurred.

Bianca smiled at him brightly, but he saw the tension in her face. His own expression was hardly welcoming. "Antonio, I hope you will be pleased that we are traveling together to Rome. I have property there, and a legal question has arisen that requires my presence. I knew of your recent bereavement, and your illness, and I did not want to leave Florence without some word of farewell. I had planned to take a later caravan, and then your note suggested this opportunity to me. I thought it would make the journey more pleasant for both of us. Perhaps we can even return together, if you are planning on returning?"

"I am, but I do not know when," he said flatly. At his cold response Bianca's chin went up. Obviously, she had hoped for more enthusiasm. Perhaps another time he might have been flattered that she had arranged her plans to accord with his. There was defiance in her pose, but something else flickered in her eyes that made him look again, intently. Fear? Vain as she was, the courtesan knew her action was presumptuous. It was not like her to risk her pride in this fashion. Just how much of her ploy was motivated by convenience or greed, and how much by desire? The tension that permeated the coolly elegant figure gave him an unexpected answer. Bianca was in love with him. Professional to the core, the courtesan masked her feelings well, but now that he looked for it, he could see the secret hidden in her eyes. He looked down, so Bianca would not read the dismay and pity in his own. *How perfectly ironic,* Antonio thought, wearily. *The one I love spurns me, while the one I pay comes hunting for me.* He felt both touched and strangely uneasy, as if the sultan's tamed cheetah had taken an unnatural fancy to him.

"Forgive my rudeness," Antonio said, raising his head to meet her questioning gaze. "As you have noted, I have been under strain. I do not think you will find me an amiable companion on this journey." He did not want to hurt her, nor did he want to encourage any expectations of intimacy.

"I can see you are not quite recovered, Antonio," Bianca said, studying him. "You look tired. My Dimitri is very skillful with herbs. I will have him brew you a special *tisane*."

Abruptly, Antonio laughed, though there was little humor in it. The Devil himself must be having sport with him. Bianca raised a quizzical brow, so he told her, "I have been stewed in *tisanes*, these last few days, Madonna. I doubt if I can survive another cup without drowning."

"I assure you, Antonio, that this *tisane* will be pleasing to your palate as well as restorative." She smiled provocatively. "You know that I am most anxious for you to recover your strength."

Antonio managed to keep the remnant of a smile on his lips, but he did not return the banter. Beautiful as Bianca was, he felt not one iota of attraction. At the moment, a life of celibacy was tremendously appealing. If only it were that simple. Antonio knew his ravenous sexual appetite would reassert itself with the return of his health. But it would be Veronica he craved. His hunger for her was a hunger of the heart, not to be sated by another.

"I will try your *tisane*, Madonna. But I must tell you that I am dubious of its ability to revitalize my spirits."

"I have great faith in my remedies, Antonio. They have not failed me yet."

The assurance in her voice chilled him. He hoped Bianca would accept his illness, his depression at his mother's death, as excuses to avoid her. They were real enough. In pain himself, he did not want to hurt her in turn. Antonio found he dreaded the thought of rejecting the courtesan, but he did not see how he could avoid it. Having acknowledged his love for Veronica, he would find little pleasure now in Bianca's embraces, skillful as they were. No doubt it was foolish to refuse even that small pleasure, since he must rid himself of this obsession. But Bianca had just priced herself beyond his reach. Money he could give her. Emotionally he was a pauper.

The head of the caravan called out the order to leave. Against his will, Antonio's gaze searched the crowd once more. It was not Veronica he found but his father, mounted on a dappled gray, watching his conversation with Bianca. No doubt his departure with the courtesan would be a gossip morsel to be savored throughout Florence, but he no longer cared what his father thought of him. They stared at each other across the plaza. He could feel the other man's scorn and hatred like a wall shutting him away, bidding him not goodbye but good riddance. Summoning his strength, Antonio met the gaze and outmatched it. His father turned away first. Such a petty triumph, and the effort left him exhausted and bitter. There were no battles of any worth to be won now in Florence. In Rome lay victory and freedom.

19 The Escape

"Six of Swords," Mama Lucia murmured, almost too low for Veronica to hear. The sleeping potion the doctor had given her was too strong, leaving her dazed. "Journey."

"What is it, Mama Lucia?" Veronica asked.

"Seven of Swords," Mama Lucia said this time. "The cards warned of danger."

"The danger is past, Mama Lucia," Veronica assured her, though she did not know if it was true.

"The Seven," her great-grandmother repeated. "Have to use your wits. Have to outsmart the Devil."

The Devil seemed an appropriate enough symbol for Savonarola at the moment. The Devil and all his nasty young demons.

"My cards. Where are my cards?" Mama Lucia asked plaintively.

"I am going to the tower now. I will bring them back to you, I promise. The nurse will stay here with you while I am gone. Sleep." Veronica did not like to leave her, but it would only be for the morning.

Leaving the nurse to watch her great-grandmother. Veronica went down to the courtyard, where Stefano was waiting with the horses. He had come, as promised, to help her. "It was dreadful," she told him as they left the Della Montagna palazzo. "The doctor who came this morning was worse than the last one. I got into another argument. He walked out, but at least he left the nurse to watch over Mama Lucia."

If her great-grandmother was no worse when they returned, Veronica hoped to move her to Daniele's. One day removed from the terror engendered by her vision, Veronica felt the transfer would be all right if done carefully. She did not want to stay here a day longer than necessary. Stefano accompanied her home to say hello to Benito and Roberto. She told them she would be returning that afternoon, or the next day at the latest. Then the two of them rode out to the tower. Veronica unlocked the door and searched upstairs and down, coming away with packets of fresh and dried herbs, a bottle or two of prepared sleeping draught, and the *Tarocco* cards in the blue velvet bag Veronica herself had embroidered.

Returning, both Veronica and Stefano kept a watchful eye for any sign of Savonarola's youths, but they were nowhere to be seen today. A servant from Stefano's palazzo was waiting for them when they arrived back at Luigi's, asking him to come home immediately. Although she was unhappy at losing him, Veronica did not let it show on her face. She would have liked Stefano's assistance, both to help move Mama Lucia and as a buffer between her and the hostility of the Della Montagnas. But that was selfish of her, to impose on his kindness when he had family duties to perform. Yesterday, disturbed by the power of the vision, she had been too frantic to organize what was needed, but she could manage well enough today. She would send for Benito and hire some guards to protect them when they moved Mama Lucia. Nevertheless, Veronica watched Stefano ride off with a sense of dismay.

She turned to enter the palazzo and found Luigi looming in the doorway. He scowled at her, "There's no end to the trouble you bring here, is there?"

She felt her sense of alarm intensifying, "What is it? Has something happened to Mama Lucia?"

"Because of you, Savonarola has cast his shadow on us. Fra Domenico da Pescia was here while you were gone. He wanted to interrogate your Gypsy relative."

Veronica knew Fra Domenico had first formed the Savonarola youth groups. She also knew he was even more zealous than the leader he worshipped. "You didn't let him see her, did you? It is too dangerous. Mama Lucia is too ill to be questioned."

"Her injuries are less dangerous than her magical dabbles, are they not?" he sneered. "But you need not worry, I refused to have the questioning done in my house. I put him off for today, but he will be back. I want the old witch out of here by then. In the meantime, I have moved her out of sight."

"Moved her?" Veronica cried out. "Where? You should not have touched her."

"She is well enough," Luigi shrugged, avoiding her eyes.

"Take me to her. Now!"

"Don't give me orders in my own home. I told you she is well enough. She is down below. The nurse is still with her."

"Down below? Where? Show me," she demanded, distressed by his obvious evasions.

"Follow me," he growled. He led her down the passageway beyond the kitchen and the servants' quarters. There were three doors, for storage she had thought. She had never lived long enough in the Della Montagna palazzo to become familiar with it. The center door was the heaviest. Luigi opened it and stood aside. Veronica looked down rough-hewn stone steps into a murky, torchlit darkness.

"A dungeon?" she asked, though they were common enough. She hesitated at the threshold.

"Go on down," Luigi urged her, moving out from the door. Veronica looked up, catching the twist of smile at the corners of his lips. She turned to run, but he grabbed her arm and thrust her forward. Veronica grabbed the doorframe to keep from falling, but another shove sent her plummeting down the steps. She struck her head and lay at the bottom, bruised and stunned. After a moment, she heard Luigi beside her. He lifted her under the arms and dragged her along the narrow passageway. She struggled, but her efforts only made the darkness swirl in her brain. He fumbled with the keys, unlocked another door and dragged her inside.

"Scream all you want, no one will hear you," Luigi said, then shut her in darkness.

Dazed from the fall, she fell asleep and woke to the sound of a key in the lock. The door opened a crack. She could see him standing there, torch in one hand, sword in the other, gloating with triumph.

"Open it the rest of the way, then stand back," Luigi ordered, gesturing with the sword.

Shaky, Veronica did as he asked. She decided to save her uncertain energy for a better chance at escape. If there was one.

"Good," Luigi said when she had complied. He came only

a step into the room, setting the torch in the metal wall socket. The flame illuminated what she had discovered by touch, the bed, the table and chair, the chamber pot. Stepping back outside, he nudged a basket through the doorway with his foot. "Food, and light to eat it by. Bread and cheese. Wine. Have a cup of wine, Veronica."

"No," she said. She was ravenous and her throat was dry, but she wouldn't give him the satisfaction. Nor did she trust the food he brought.

"Why make it more difficult? There's water and a towel too. Clean yourself up a bit. I'll be back. This time, I'll leave you the light."

"Wait! What about Mama Lucia? Tell me how she is."

"Oh, she is all right, for the moment. Safe in her room. If you want her to stay safe, you will be more agreeable when I come back. Have some wine," he prompted again, then shut and locked the door.

Alone in her prison, Veronica reconsidered Luigi's bounty. She sipped some of the water, then dipped the cloth in it and cleansed her face and hands. She ate a little of the bread, enough to take the edge off her hunger and give her a sense of stability. Her head was clearer too. Mama Lucia had been right this morning when she warned of danger. It looked as if Luigi embodied the Devil, rather than Savonarola. Veronica wondered how long it would be before her father-in-law returned. Next time he would do more than gloat. Veronica stared at the wine bottle and the two cups that came with it. She considered smashing it, but she did not want the reek of it filling the room.

After a while, she opened the bottle and filled one cup.

It was two or three hours later before Luigi reappeared. Night, Veronica presumed, and the house asleep. He slipped inside, locking the door behind him, then sheathing his sword. He stank of alcohol.

"You will not get away with this," she challenged him.

"Oh, but I can," he jeered. "I have."

"I cannot just disappear."

"You can disappear for tonight."

"I am expected at home," she began.

"No, you're not. I sent word for your servants not to expect you until tomorrow." Luigi smiled one of his nasty smiles, his voice already slurred with wine.

"Daniele . . . ." She faltered when the smile broadened.

"Daniele doesn't even know anything's wrong. I tore up the note you wrote him. Tore it right in half," he snickered at that, as if at some private joke. "Your pretty Stefano has left Florence and you aren't expecting anyone else, are you, Veronica?" When she did not answer, he added, "Don't worry, it's just one night. I won't ask any more of you."

"You are not asking, that I can see," she hissed at him.

"No, I'm not, am I?" he smirked. "So, let me tell you how it'll be. You spend the night with me, here. You do what I tell you to do. In the morning I let you go. You take your crazy witch with you and leave, free as a bird."

"No," she told him. "I will fight you. How will you explain the bruises on me, the scratches on you?"

"There won't be any. I'll have you, and I'll have you willing. If not, I'll turn both you and the old witch over to the Church for the good of my soul."

She was afraid, and fear was clouding her mind. Luigi was bluffing. If she brought a charge of rape against him, he would attack her in turn, but he would not initiate such an outrage. "No, you will not do it," she challenged him. "You do not want a scandal, Luigi. Think how it might rebound on your house, on you. If they torture me, I promise you my confessions will include your name."

"The accusation of a vengeful witch? They won't believe it."

"Can you buy all the belief you will need, Luigi? Can you buy Savonarola?"

All the sadistic delight faded from Luigi's face, and he leaned against the wall, glowering. He had counted on her terror, her submission. Attacked in turn, he looked as befuddled as he was angry.

How much truth was there in his threats—were they nothing but a ruse? "Fra Domenico was never here, was he?"

"Oh yes, he was here," he said sullenly.

She did not know why, but she did believe Luigi, though the monk's visit could not have been as significant as he wanted it to seem. Still, there was danger. Mama Lucia had become too visible in Florence.

"Please," she begged him, "I said nothing about the time before. Let me go now, and I will say nothing about this."

"No!" His voice rose, angry and petulant. "You think I don't know about you. You think I can't see, but I do. All these young gallants sniffing at your skirts. They're the ones who're getting a piece of you, but I'm the one who gave you the taste for it. Me. Now I'm claiming what I should have had before."

"You are crazy. I do not want you. I have never wanted you."

"You'll want me when I've got it inside you. I'll be better than any of the others. Bigger." Pawing at the fastenings of his hose, Luigi leered at her expectantly, as if this argument must finally win her over.

Veronica thought she was going to be sick. Her disgust penetrated Luigi's alcoholic euphoria. For a moment, there was only his fury. "You'll do it," he snarled. "You'll do it as sweet as you can, or the old Gypsy won't last the night. She'll fall out of bed and break a few more bones. She'll smother in her sleep. She'll hang herself for fear of Savonarola's bonfire. Whatever—I promise you, she'll be dead come daybreak."

Words would not save her, nor Mama Lucia. There had never really been any hope she could convince Luigi to let her go. He had conceived and carried out his scheme. Now he wanted his reward. The only reason he did not simply take it was that he did not want to leave evidence of his abuse. If she resisted any longer, he would turn vicious.

"Wait," she pleaded, if only to soften his mood. "Give me your word. I do what you ask tonight and you will let me take Mama Lucia and leave in the morning."

He grinned at her. "I give you my word. You do what I ask. Everything I ask. Same as you do it for your pretty boys."

Veronica had thought Stefano's presence would help protect her, but it had only stirred up the obscenities slumbering in Luigi's mind. How ironic, when it was Antonio who was her lover. *Antonio*, she cried out silently. But it did no good to summon him. He would not appear this time, sword in hand, to rescue her. Here and now, there was only herself.

"I need some more wine first," she told Luigi, and picked up her cup.

"Yes," he encouraged her. "Get drunk, Veronica. I'd like you to be very, very drunk."

"You are drunk enough for both of us." Her voice was full of scorn.

"Oh, no I'm not." Luigi poured himself a cup from the bottle and drank it down. She watched as he filled the cup again. Catching her glance, he taunted her, "You hope I'll pass out, don't you? But I won't. I can drink all this and another bottle too." He drank down the second cup.

She took a sip of her own.

"Drink it down. All of it. That's better." Luigi took the empty cup from her hand, filled it from the bottle. He thrust it into her hands, the wine sloshing over the rim. "Have some more."

"I can't," she said, putting the cup on the table. "It's making me dizzy."

"It's supposed to make you dizzy." He laughed, pushing it back at her.

"It's the fall down the stairs," she said, "more than the wine. You don't want me to get sick all over you, do you?"

For a moment, she thought Luigi would hit her. Nausea was not part of his lurid fantasies. He tottered towards her, his face contorted. "You're playing games with me, witch. Get your clothes off. I want to see you naked."

Veronica backed away from him. She retreated into the far corner of the room, fumbling with the laces of her bodice.

"Thas right," Luigi mumbled, "see you naked." He staggered forward three steps then pitched forward onto the floor in front of her. He twitched and muttered for a minute, and then lay still.

The Seven of Swords Veronica could hear the old lesson in her mind. *A direct confrontation will avail you naught, but you may yet succeed through cunning. Know your enemy's weak points, and so disarm him.*

Veronica knelt beside him and felt his pulse. It beat sluggishly but steadily against her fingers. She would not be here in an hour or two to see if he was still all right. She took one of the vials of sleeping potion from her pocket. Not knowing how much of the wine she could get him to drink, she had emptied half of it into the bottle. And Luigi had drunk half of the wine. Enough to sleep like the dead. Enough, even, to kill him? Hopefully, it was only enough to simulate the worst alcoholic stupor of his life. Happy as she would be to see him dead, Veronica did not want to be held accountable for his murder. But she had made her choice and taken the risk. There must be time to get Mama Lucia out of the city. Veronica emptied the rest of the wine onto the floor but kept the bottle as a weapon. The sword she left, but she took Luigi's knife as well as the keys from his belt and unlocked the door.

The stained glass of the lanterns cast eerie pools of light in the darkened hallways. Veronica moved silently from amber to emerald, crimson to cobalt, pausing in the shadows to search each empty corridor. No one was awake in the house besides herself, but Veronica did not know how she would get Mama Lucia past the outside gate. Luckily, Luigi had wanted his sordid little scheme kept secret. As he had set no guard in the dungeon, perhaps he had not thought it necessary to warn the night guards against her possible escape. But leaving so late would be suspicious. If Luigi was sent for, they would be trapped. Veronica supposed she would have to find herself a poker to deal with the guards. First, though, she must get Mama Lucia onto the stretcher. She had the half-empty vial of the sleeping potion, and one more for traveling. And this morning she had thought she was being overcautious in taking two.

The door to Mama Lucia's room was unlocked. Veronica opened it quietly and slipped into the room. She gasped with fear as two shapes loomed up in the darkness and one huge form rushed forward to clutch her and lift her off the floor.

"Veronica!" Roberto squealed with delight, swinging her about in circles, squeezing her breath away. "Veronica!"

"Hush, hush," Benito whispered urgently as he tried to stop the reckless spinning. "Be quiet, Roberto."

"Yes, please, stop. Stop, Roberto, dear," Veronica gasped. He set her down and she sagged against the wall. Her heart was hammering, her stomach queasy with excitement, but she had a moment to recover while Benito shushed Roberto.

"What is wrong, my lady?" Benito asked. "What has kept you away?"

"I was unwillingly delayed, by Luigi," Veronica said, deciding it was time to name their enemies. "He is now unwillingly asleep in his own dungeon. But he told·me he had sent you word that I would not be coming back tonight, Benito."

"The message just didn't sound like you, though I thought it might be only the rough way of the guard. Roberto wanted to see Mama Lucia, and I wanted to know what had happened. No one paid us much attention. We came in the back gate, then through the servants' quarters. I found Mama Lucia here with the nurse. I knew something was wrong when the nurse said she hadn't seen you for hours. She was angry because she was supposed to have gone home. I had enough money to pay her. I knew I could watch over Mama Lucia as well as she could, and I thought the family wouldn't send us away if the nurse was gone. Only then I couldn't look for you, Madonna Veronica, because I didn't want to leave Mama Lucia and Roberto all alone."

"Well, it is good you stayed here, Benito. Now that we are all together, we must get Mama Lucia out of this house as quickly as we can. Luigi is threatening to accuse her of witchcraft. I don't think he will, but Fra Domenico was here today too. Florence is no longer safe for her. I want to take her to the Gypsies. But I don't know if she is well enough to travel, or if we can find them."

"Veronica." Mama Lucia was awake. Veronica moved swiftly to her, lighting the candle by her bedside. "I heard you. I want to go to my people. I know there is a band near Siena. Luigi della Montagna will not find us there, not if the Rom do not want to be found."

"If that is what you want."

"The cards gave me warning. The Devil, the Seven of Swords, the Six. Danger and then a journey. Travel away from trouble. We should leave Florence, Veronica."

"Yes, we shall then." But they could not go as they were. They must get a wagon to carry Mama Lucia and disguises for all of them. Veronica looked at Roberto with dismay. There was no way to disguise him to any but the most casual scrutiny. But he must come along. If they stayed behind, both he and Benito would surely be questioned, along with the nurse. Roberto could easily remember, and give away, their plan to visit the Gypsies.

It was a problem, but first they must find a place to hide till morning. Who could they trust? They could not take Mama Lucia to the nuns for sanctuary, not when the trouble was with the Church itself. Stefano would want to help, but his family, like Antonio's, was far more conservative than he was. She could not impose so on either of them, bringing strife within their households, even danger. It was bad enough that Daniele would be at risk. His house would be safe for a few hours, no more. It was the first place Luigi's men would come looking. "I'm afraid to go back to Daniele's, but I don't know where else to go."

"We can go to my Elizabeta," Benito offered. "I know she will help us. She does not like Savonarola, my lady, and no one will suspect her."

Yes, if they came to her, Benito's Elizabeta would be willing to take the risk. It was unlikely she would come under suspicion, though Veronica was not so certain she would escape all the consequences. It depended on how hungry for revenge Luigi was, and how hard he would search. But it was the best alternative so far. "Yes, all right," Veronica said. "Now we must get out of here."

Veronica opened the second vial of sleeping potion, added a little to a cup of water, and helped Mama Lucia to drink it. As she waited for it to take effect, Veronica considered the best way to make their escape with as little commotion as possible. Leaving Benito to watch Mama Lucia, she crept into the kitchen and opened the door to the wine cellar with one of the keys from Luigi's ring. She stole a fresh bottle and brought it back to the room. She poured a cup for Benito, and wasted more of the precious sleeping potion to drug the wine in the bottle. "Take it to the guards, Benito, and share it around. Here is an untainted cup for you."

Benito set out for the courtyard. Veronica bade Roberto stay where he was and guard Mama Lucia. He would be safe for a few minutes. She went as far as the dining hall, set the empty bottle of drugged wine on the table, and dropped the keys on the floor there, as if Luigi had forgotten them there. It would be best to leave the keys beside him, but she did not want to risk passing the servants' quarters again—nor to look at Luigi. If all went well, he would fabricate his own story in the morning to cover the events of the night. It was all slipshod, but it was the best Veronica could do in the circumstances. She went back to the room, where Roberto still sat, upright and endearingly vigilant, beside the sleeping Mama Lucia. Together, they waited for Benito.

It was half an hour later when he returned, a bit sheepish. "The bottle has put them all to sleep, my lady. The stableboy and the first guard drank from it. The second guard I had to tap on the head. He would not drink, and the other two were starting to nod off."

"They are unconscious, that is what is important. Now we can get through the gate. You and Roberto help me move Mama Lucia."

Together they lifted Mama Lucia's pallet onto the stretcher, then Roberto helped them carry the stretcher and its fragile burden out to the stable. Veronica quickly saddled her horse, and Benito attached the stretcher. He opened the gate for her to guide the stretcher through, then wedged it shut behind them. Veronica found she could breathe more easily, think more clearly, now that they had made their escape from Luigi's palazzo. She hoped to be well on the road before Luigi could organize a search . . . presuming Luigi survived. Veronica found she was certain he would, and accepted that certainty. It was Luigi's revenge she must escape now, not the law of Florence. Except, perhaps, for Savonarola's law.

They moved slowly through the midnight streets, Benito and Roberto trotting along the footpaths beside the road as they made their way to Elizabeta's. It was the seamstress' son, Tommaso, who warily answered Benito's late night knocking. He let them into their tiny home, and Elizabeta welcomed them gladly. Quickly, Veronica explained their situation, trying at the same time to impress upon her the danger and to reassure her, "We only need a place to stay and change into disguise. At sunrise we will leave for Siena."

"I would hide you here if you wished it. My life won't be

ruled by that stingy-spirited monk,'' Elizabeta bristled with disdain. Short, with a plump voluptuous body and dark eyes, her soft looks and manner belied her bold spirit. ''I've had trouble enough from him as it is.''

She had started as a servant, helping a dressmaker. She had a talent for fine design as well as fine sewing. Skill, perseverance, and luck with rich patronage had established her in a small shop of her own. The past few years had been a struggle, however. All the luxury trades had suffered during the Friar's reign, and her business had diminished as well. ''Under Savonarola's rule, Florence has grown smaller, tighter, like a shoe that pinches with each step you take,'' Elizabeta commented, and Tommaso gravely nodded his assent. ''Give him his way and we will all be cripples, hobbling through the streets, praising the Lord for the afflictions Savonarola has laid on us.''

''It is good of you, Elizabeta, but you do not need to hide us. It will be safer if Mama Lucia is out of Florence. Neither my father-in-law nor Savonarola will put much effort into a search beyond the city walls.''

''Whatever you wish, Madonna Veronica. You are right about disguising yourselves,'' Elizabeta declared. ''It would be easy to dress you as a servant girl, but I don't know if that would be clever enough to fool them, if they bothered to look for you.''

''I think not,'' Veronica said. ''They will be searching for two women, one injured. Instead, Mama Lucia will be dressed as an old man, and I a young one. I can think of no way to disguise Roberto.'' Veronica pondered the problem again. There was no good solution. Benito and Roberto could ride around by a separate route and meet her in Siena. They would be just as conspicuous, but they could travel a little faster, although Roberto was not a good rider. Or they could try to hide him in the back of the wagon if they saw anyone; but any activity like that was likely to be noticed, the wagon searched, and all of them taken. ''Benito, I think it is best if you and Roberto hire a guard and ride first to San Gimignano. Keep checking to see if anyone is on the road behind you. If there is trouble, try to escape and hide. When you reach the city safely, find a room for the night. Tomorrow, hire a different man and come to Siena. I will meet you at sunset inside the Duomo.''

"And you will hire a guard, my lady, or two, for protection."

"No, I do not want to risk it. At such close quarters, the guard might see through our disguise or become suspicious later. Luigi may offer a reward for our whereabouts, more than I could offer for silence. It is dangerous enough to go directly to Siena, when it used to be my home."

"But it is too dangerous for two women to go alone on the open road. I cannot let you do it, Madonna Veronica."

"It is a lesser risk, Benito. A poor young man will not be the target that a young woman, wealthy or poor, would be. I cannot take Mama Lucia on the stretcher, though. Will you sell me your wagon and horse, Elizabeta?"

"I will gladly loan you my wagon, Madonna Veronica, and we will come with you as far as Siena, Tommaso and I. You can hide there in my father's house until you find the Gypsies." Elizabeta looked to her son, and he nodded agreement.

"That is kind of you, but I can manage alone, Elizabeta. It is only a day's journey."

"If they search, they will be looking for two people. Better if there are three or four, a family traveling together. And if you are questioned, Madonna Veronica, you may give yourself away. Your voice is deep, but you do not know the speech of the streets. It will be difficult for you to sound like a common youth. Better if I am the mother, you my younger son, and Madonna Danti my old grandfather."

It was a good plan, but Veronica hesitated to accept it. "I have to go, Elizabeta, but I do not want to put anyone else at risk."

"I want to help," Tommaso said simply.

"You have been good to Benito, Madonna Veronica, and he has been good to me. I want to do this for you."

It was a declaration, not a request. To refuse would be a discourtesy to her generosity. She looked at Benito, but the pride in his face outshone the concern. So Veronica said simply, "Thank you, Elizabeta."

That settled, they began to deal with the practicalities. They planned their costumes from what was available at Elizabeta's and Daniele's. With warnings to be cautious, Veronica sent Benito back to Daniele's for money enough for travel, the two beards from the trunk in the studio and oddments of clothing; also for paper, pen and wax for notes. In the meanwhile, Elizabeta sat Veronica down on a chair and proceeded to cut her hair, clucking her tongue as she did so. Veronica found it an alarming sensation. Her head felt much lighter, as if it were about to float off her body. At the same time, watching the shearings pile up about her feet, she felt so bereft she wanted to weep. She chastised herself silently for such silliness, and sat motionless as Elizabeta finished her work. Next the seamstress dyed Veronica's hair to a dark brown, and stained her skin as well. "The color will fade out slowly, over the next month or two," she said, then combed Veronica's eyebrows down and smudged her face with charcoal.

Benito reappeared. He looked horrified at her shorn locks and grubby face, but offered her his package without comment. "The money was where you said it would be, my lady. Here are the two beards, and the paper and such. There's some clothes of mine in there for you. Tommaso is too big."

Thanking him, Veronica opened the bundle. Slipping behind Elizabeta's dressing screen, she stripped, bound her breasts, and put on Benito's clothes. She smiled, seeing he had given her his best. When she was finished, she sat in the chair again to complete her transformation. Elizabeta devised a glue to hold the beard in place and rubbed more charcoal around the edges. "The color matches close enough. You will have to renew the glue. If I make it stronger, it will burn your skin."

She showed Veronica the result in a mirror of polished metal. "It is believable in this light, Elizabeta."

"You're a pretty young fellow, but I think you will pass, even in the sunshine, Madonna Veronica."

They began on Mama Lucia, as gently as they could. Only lightly sedated, she woke. Groggy from the potion and crabby with pain, she regained her spirits when they told her their plan. Together, Veronica and Elizabeta helped her to stand and to use the chamber pot. They dressed her in the disguise, cutting and stitching her into the man's shirt to protect her injured arm. Veronica tied the velvet bag with the *Tarocco* cards to the rope belt, while Elizabeta attached the bushy gray beard and pulled a cap over her head. A tattered old cape was added to cover the sling.

They arranged Mama Lucia as comfortably as they could in the wagon. Veronica mixed a fresh cup of the sleeping potion and gave it to her. While Mama Lucia nodded off, they loaded the day's food and water. Veronica wrote a hurried note to Daniele, giving a brief explanation and arranging for a meeting. With a pang of longing, she wrote an even briefer message to Antonio and enclosed it within the first. Elizabeta had a quiet moment with Benito while Veronica hugged Roberto good-bye. He was in tears, begging to come with her, but she had to refuse him. She could not even let him come as far as the gates, for fear someone would notice them. Veronica got in the back of the wagon with Mama Lucia, and Elizabeta and Tommaso got in the front. He clucked to the horse, and they set off through the streets of Florence as the sky paled with the coming dawn. There was the usual early morning hubbub at the gates, wagons and riders wanting an early start. Benito and Roberto set off to find a guard for their journey. Veronica hired a messenger to deliver the letter to Daniele at the Aristi estate. She paid what he asked, and told him Daniele would pay the same again. She presumed he would deliver it, though he might well ask for double the fee. After that, there was nothing to do but wait the few minutes that remained. Veronica climbed in the back of the wagon with Mama Lucia. Tommaso flicked the reins at the horse, and set off on the road to Siena.

The Six of Swords. Travel away from trouble, Mama Lucia had said. The Six was also an obstacle overcome, but not vanquished. Well, safe for the moment was good enough. All Veronica asked was to get Mama Lucia to safety. Savonarola was still there to be dealt with, but she would not be so afraid of Luigi if he had no hostage to hold against her.

20 *Rome*

"WELL, here we are in Rome, Feet—scheming, plotting, and spending our nights with the Borgias. Two weeks now, and I've no more clue of just what we're plotting than when we left Florence. But Florence is what this is all about, I know it is." Giacomo heaved a giant sigh, and proceeded to clean his toenails with a nut pick. "You should listen to me more often, Feet. I told you that this marriage would come to no good, didn't I? Here in this very room, I remember it quite clearly. And I was right, wasn't I? Our old mistress is gone, dear soul. Antonio's father hates him worse than ever, and I don't know if it's good or bad that he's finally letting himself hate back. I swear, Feet, I thought the master was ready to strangle his father, and how could he live with that?" Horrified, his toes curled up defensively.

"All this misery, and what's he got to show for it all but the tender affections of Mistress Dorotea? That skinny bit of a thing is no solace to him. There's no woman to her, she's child and crone all rolled together. Since she's dressed in mourning, you can see just what she'll look like as an old woman, when the bit of bloom she's got has gone. All pinched and dried up and spiteful. You could see she was relieved the master was leaving Florence.

"To Rome, Giacomo. Day after tomorrow, Giacomo. Never mind that I'm half dead with fever, Giacomo, just do what I say. Now, Giacomo! Yes, master. Certainly, master. Whatever you want is fine, master, but don't say I didn't warn you. How do you think it makes me feel, watching you grit your teeth and sway in the saddle? I'm supposed to take care of you!

"Didn't please Mistress Bianca much either, did it, Feet? She was expecting much more of a pleasure trip, though she got nothing, not even after that *tisane* she sent over helped to revive his energy. The way that Dimitri looked at the master, I wasn't sure his brew was any safer than Laudomia's. The eunuch's probably in love with Bianca himself, not that he could do anything about it. Or could he? Gives me the creeps, he does, and not just because I don't like to think about some Turkish cutpurse getting my own sweet jewels, either. There's more to him than meets the eye. Herbal cures, and a mean hand with that whip, he had, when the brigands attacked.

"Bianca was full of surprises too, wasn't she?" Giacomo asked, and his toes twitched in agreement. "That one brigand ran straight for her— thought she'd be easy prey, and she got him right through the heart with that little dagger of hers. Damned clean thrust it was too, not just a wobbly bit of luck. The master was as impressed as I was. Renewed his interest, I can tell you that. I thought for sure he'd forgive her then, for turning up without asking like she did."

Bianca had gone as coy and blushing as Giacomo had ever seen her when Antonio praised her marksmanship. He supposed that a more typical patron than Antonio would be put off by a fancy lady with a man's skill with a weapon. Dimitri had puffed himself up and announced that not even gentlemen were always gentle men, and his mistress had to be able to protect her honor. Well, Bianca hadn't much honor, but her skin was pretty enough and worth a goodly bit besides. Giacomo supposed it was natural enough she'd learned a bit of dagger work to discourage men who figured they'd get a piece of her for free.

The encounter with the brigands had cost the caravan four guards. They'd made it the rest of the way to the inn just before dark, and had a hell of a celebration. Antonio had bought a lavish feast for them all, and enough good wine to get them all happy but keep them sharp for the next day's ride into Rome. He told a few tales too, but Giacomo saw the way his eye kept sliding to Bianca. Giacomo recognized the feverish glitter that burned on him, and what heat ignited it. A brush with death always did stir up the survival instincts in Antonio. In Bianca too, apparently. The look the courtesan gave his master before she went upstairs was hot enough to make every man in the room stand up in the middle.

Giacomo figured that was it for sure, when Antonio followed her up not long after. Giacomo trailed behind just to make certain, and he practically tumbled back down the stairs when he saw Antonio pause for a moment outside the open door of Bianca's room, then walk on to his own. Antonio's door closed, and then Bianca's. Giacomo was glad that neither of them had seen him in the hallway. Totally bewildered, he'd scurried after his master, determined to see he got what he needed. If Antonio was still angry at the courtesan, Giacomo did have a toothsome alternative. Helping Antonio disrobe, he mentioned that the landlord's daughter, a shy and buxom brunette, had been casting longing glances at his master as she passed out the wine. Antonio had only looked askance at the thin wall between his room and Bianca's and shaken his head.

That put Giacomo into a fine fret. If it was the courtesan that Antonio wanted, why not bed her? If he didn't want her, why should he care what she thought? If he didn't want her to know, why not just sneak down quiet to the rooms below? Giacomo was used to Antonio's secrecy, but he was also used to making sense of it. When he had persisted about the maid, for Antonio's own good, he'd felt a tremor run through his master. Turning to face him, Antonio had suggested Giacomo service the wench himself, if he found her so irresistible. The look that accompanied the suggestion had Giacomo out of the room in a thrice.

"No sense, no sense to it at all, Feet," Giacomo moaned. He knew he'd missed some vital clue in his master's affairs, but he'd too much wine in him to be tracing it down that night. Afterwards, he'd made his way to the downstairs and tapped on the buxom maid's door. When she opened it, it was obvious it wasn't him she'd been hoping for, but he'd been lucky. She'd been willing enough to accept a bit of consolation, knowing bedding the servant was the closest she'd get to his handsome master. It wasn't the first time he'd gathered a fine windfall that way, and Giacomo was properly grateful. He knew he'd had a few sweet, juicy bites of sin's sweetest apple that he'd not have tasted otherwise. He preferred to be wanted for himself, of course, but he usually managed that quite nicely once he got under the sheets. His fingers were clever at finding hidden secrets, and his tongue had a use or two other than talking. When the landlord's daughter woke the next morning, her blushing smile was for him and him alone.

Neither Bianca nor Antonio had been smiling that morning.

Neither looked as if they'd slept all that well. Giacomo almost wished the master had let go of whatever was holding him back and taken up with her again. "Never thought I'd say it, Feet, but I'd rather he'd bed with that bitch Bianca than go out night after night carousing with the Borgias. Not a family I'd want to do business with, I can tell you that, Feet. You can't say no to a Borgia and keep the blood in your veins. Whatever it is he came for, I don't think he's got it yet. He's been coiled tight for days. I can't stand not knowing what it's all about, Feet," Giacomo moaned, and his toes waggled in a frenzy of frustration. "I'm steaming open letters again. That's how desperate I am. And not a shred of useful information do I get for all the risk I'm taking. The master would skin me alive if he caught me at it again, as if it wasn't all his fault. I just hate it when he does this to me, Feet, scurrying about inside his brain and leaving not a single trace of what he's plotting."

Giacomo heard the clatter of Ombra's hooves in the courtyard. Antonio was back, earlier than usual. It was not even three. These late hours were ruining Giacomo's health. "Well, Feet, I suppose I shouldn't complain," Giacomo sighed, pulling on his slippers. "Things could be worse. Things can always be worse until you're dead and roasting on a slow spit in Hell."

——

" . . . . And so I escaped!" Laughing, Cesare Borgia raised himself up on his couch. "I made total fools of the French. It took no effort to do it, merely a semblance of good behavior. For two days I drank with them, bested their wrestling champions, told them tales of war and women. I charmed them, and they quickly grew careless. The muleteer's garments were already secreted away. It was easier than I had dared hope to make my way through the midnight campfires. My men had my horse waiting for me in the hills outside Velletri." He gestured expansively towards Antonio, who raised his wine in a toast. "By dawn, we were miles away, leaving the French to slosh through the Pontine marshes alone. They could not believe I had vanished, leaving seventeen velvet covered wagons filled with the riches of my household. Then they opened the chests and found them filled with stones. They knew then I'd planned it all along. The wagons were a pittance to pay for the pleasure of duping them.''

There was applause and laughter from the surrounding couches. His face alight with pride, the Pope beamed at his son and guests in turn, then added his own commentary. ''King Charles was rightly outraged and demanded the immediate return of his hostage. Of course, I was deeply shocked at Cesare's dishonorable action, but what could I do? I was not a magician, to know where he had gone. I told them so, but for some reason they did not believe me.'' He spread his hands in a gesture of mock wonder, and the gathering laughed on cue once more.

Antonio sipped his wine, smiling politely. The escape had happened little over a year ago, and he still enjoyed hearing the tale. It had been one of his best adventures with Cesare. The Spaniard told the story often. So did the rest of Rome, for that matter. Italians loved a tale of deceit.

Cesare basked in father's pleasure, for once stealing his attention from Juan. Had it been five years now, Antonio wondered, since he first met Cesare? Yes, in 1492 Roderigo Borgia had been coronated as Pope Alexander VI. He had been a scandal even then, this rich Spanish cardinal who had bought himself the highest office in Christendom. It had been the end of August, the air boiling with heat and excitement, Rome draped in splendor. Every triumphal archway in the city was decorated with epigrams praising the might and glory of the Borgias. Banners decorated with their emblem hung from balconies and rooftops, the great red bull grazing on its field of gold. Everywhere you looked, the Borgia bull declared its presence. It was there in miniature, as little sugared sweetmeats and gilt ornaments sold by the hawkers to the crowd. Colossal, it was carried through the streets, a gigantic gilded creature pouring bloodred wine from its horns. Dressed in glittering cloth of silver, twelve pages led twelve perfect white horses bridled in gold. The Church paraded itself from the bejeweled cardinals to the humble, barefoot friars.

Antonio had simply been one of the crowd then, though his vantage point was better than most—the balcony of one of the better brothels. He had not known the Borgias except by reputation, which was already tarnished. Cynic that he was it had amused him, even as he reveled in the spectacle, the vast parade of pomp and glory, of power and glittering riches. He looked at them again now, with the deeper cynicism of experience.

Alexander VI was not the first Pope to be a libertine. He was less a hypocrite than others about it, which was a virtue in Antonio's eyes. A contradictory man, he openly flouted many of the most obvious proprieties, but in a few corners of his life he appeared to be truly devout, even abstemious. He offered gluttonous feasts to his guests, but ate only one frugal meal a day himself. Crafty and practical, Alexander VI might still prove a good leader for Italy, if only he could restrain his ambitions for his brood. Antonio doubted that he could. His love for them was obsessive. Looking at the man, with his strong fleshy features, Antonio could see only bits of his visage passed on to his children— the arched brows to Cesare, the full lips to Juan. They were all more finely built than their father, with lighter coloring, and they all possessed his personal magnetism and rapacious sexuality. Yet, despite his overt carnality, the Pope seemed naïve beside them. The great Borgia bull had bred a trio of prowling cats, of sleeker build and far more perfidious temperament than his own. Young, with scant tempering from time, the heady wine of power intoxicated them far more than it did their father.

Antonio wondered why the Pope continued to promote Juan over his elder brother. Alexander VI was a fool to encourage Juan in the military arts and shove Cesare into the Church. With his craving for glory, Cesare was not a man to live for long off old exploits like the French escape. Lately, the rivalry between the two brothers had intensified. There was a knife edge to their banter now, a viciousness to which only the Pope appeared oblivious. That blindness in him was disturbing. Cesare excelled his brother in everything but beauty, and his father's favoritism gnawed at Cesare's pride. Even Lucrezia preferred Juan, enamored of the golden glamour he possessed, spurious though it was.

The Pope's daughter was giddy tonight, full of a frantic gaiety that Antonio suspected hid a troubled spirit. Alexander VI was finally pressing her divorce suit. Her husband had not taken the charges of impotence with the desired grace, and was countering with accusations of incest. From certain covert glances, it was obvious to Antonio that Lucrezia had a secret inamorata, a tender young Spaniard named Pederito. Antonio was pleased to be spared that amorous complication. But if Lucrezia was no longer a problem, there were others who were.

Juan, ignoring the voluptuous courtesan at his side, was competing with Cesare for the attentions of a married lady of rank. Earlier, Juan had suggested that he and Antonio bed the courtesan together. It was not the first time such a proposition had been made, though this woman was the most beautiful so far. Antonio suspected Juan offered to share his women only as an inducement to the men who refused to bed him alone. Antonio had declined courteously, making it clear that neither offer had any interest for him. Juan's eyes, his lips, had thinned with anger, but he covered the reaction with a theatrical sigh of despair, chastising Antonio for his mundane habits.

Antonio hoped Juan would let it go at that. Once he heard that Antonio wanted an annulment, Juan might be tempted to try blackmailing him into bed. Then Antonio would be forced to consider if he valued his annulment more than his virtue— presuming a man of his experience could still be said to possess such a thing. Sex was a common coin at any court, but it was one with which he had never yet had to pay. Antonio hoped the night he had spent with Lucrezia might do him some good, but it had been a folly of the moment rather than a calculated bribe. There was no point in hypocrisy. Antonio had accepted that Lucrezia might demand a repeat performance of him, and was prepared to respond accordingly. But Juan . . . .

Refusal would not necessarily cost Antonio the annulment, but it was possible. He wondered if the supplementary services the Pope or Cesare might demand from him might not prove equally, if more subtly, demeaning. He hoped that apprehension was unfounded. Cesare owed him his life, after all. He should be content to rid himself of that debt by presenting Antonio's petition to his father—and by collecting his percentage of the annulment's price.

A page appeared by his side, offering more wine. Antonio had him add some to the gold goblet he held, though he had barely tasted it yet. The appearance of indulgence suited him better than its actuality. The musicians took up a sprightly suggestive melody, and the night's entertainment began—a lascivious burlesque devised by Lucrezia for her father's amusement. A door opened and a group of male servants appeared, carrying small gilded baskets filled with roses and other flowers. They walked the perimeter of the circle, doling out the baskets to the guests, each guest receiving flowers of a different hue or shape. When the baskets were distributed, they moved back to the walls, waiting. Next, a bevy of naked whores emerged from the door, sliding between the couches to stand in the center of the room. The Pope, and others who had played the game before, tossed their flowers out onto the floor. The nude women dropped to their knees and began to crawl about, gathering the flowers in their teeth. The flowers were carried back, to be exchanged for rubies, gold coins, or nothing at all, depending on the generosity of the giver. From her couch, Lucrezia raised her hand and beckoned to the group of male servants waiting in the corner. The men moved forward, opening their hose and swiftly readying themselves to mount the women from behind. They lifted the whores by their hips and impaled them, then stumbled along behind as the women scrambled after the precious roses, collecting treasure, now, for both themselves and their riders.

Bored, Antonio lay back among the cushions. He had seen erotic performances he found arousing, but the mercenary excess of this one was distasteful. However, given a choice, he preferred it to watching the Borgias stand on their balcony and shoot condemned prisoners released into the courtyard below. Cesare had shown him a newly arrived load of Spanish arquebuses, and he had feared a more bloody entertainment than this debauch. Weighted with lassitude and contempt, Antonio tossed a few of the flowers and paid in gold for their retrieval.

He had a sudden, unpleasant vision of the coins he had tossed Veronica. Emotion welled in him, a twisted morass of despair, anger, and longing, cut through with aching physical need. Was there no exorcism that could force the memory of her from his mind, the longing for her from his flesh? Antonio had known it would be like this, but that did nothing to alleviate the torment of wanting her. Since his arrival in Rome, he had tried a dozen new women, searching for a carnal attraction strong enough to supplant the emotional power Veronica still wielded, hoping at the very least, that novelty would distract him. Each experience had left him more unsatisfied than the last. If he ignored his hunger, however, his temper, his control, grew precarious indeed. Tonight, tired of the futile hunt, he had brought no one with him. There were always beautiful women available at such entertainments, and one was as much or as little good as another at the moment. Feeling conspicuous alone, he surveyed the bejeweled courtesans stretched out on their couches, the whores naked on the floor, and felt no desire for any of them. But desire itself he still felt, a throbbing insistence in his loins. Their availability aggravated a need that only Veronica could appease.

Faced with that impossibility once more, Antonio found himself wishing Bianca were here, then cursed himself silently. There was no point in adding to the emotional entanglements that cluttered his life. He had made the right decision, refusing to resume his relationship with her, despite the temptation. His sexual hunger had reawakened early during the trip to Rome, but he had avoided the courtesan until their confrontation with the brigands. He had almost given in then, to his physical craving. A brush with death made the stricture of celibacy seem utterly foolish. Bianca wanted him. He wanted. She would accept him on any terms he chose. And his terms would be generous, as always. Hounded by his mutinous lust, he had gone upstairs to her.

Bianca's door had been open. She was waiting for him, sitting and brushing her pale hair, her own fine mirror set on the rough table of the inn. She wore a clinging silk shift of deep magenta. That, and the last necklace he had given her— the emeralds and peridots that should have gone to Veronica, their vivid colors evoking the newborn brightness of spring. In the flickering candlelight the green gems glittered like drops of poison set in gold, casting an eerie light upon the courtesan's pale skin. Poisonous. Venomous. With Bianca, such images came to mind often. Strange, his passion for Veronica had driven him into darkness, yet he still thought of her as life. Bianca brought only these insidious images of death. He met the courtesan's eyes in the mirror, and for a moment that blacker darkness within her was the most compelling thing of all.

He had turned away then, how he hardly knew, only that he must and had. Turned and walked to his own room and listened to Giacomo prattle about the landlord's daughter. Antonio knew what it would have taken to satisfy him that night, and no bashful young girl could have provided it. He sent Giacomo away before he struck him, and sought what bleak release he could in the solitary vice. From his valet's smug smile the next morning, Giacomo had shown the wench more pleasure than she would have had at his hands. Someone, at least, was happy.

Arriving in Rome, Antonio had been relieved to bid Bianca farewell, had scarcely thought of her until tonight. But none of the women he had bedded since had appeased his physical hunger, much less helped to erase Veronica from his thoughts. Climax brought a brief physical exhaustion, without satisfaction, and the emotional craving cut all the deeper. His body stilled for a moment, his mind was cast adrift into the void within him, seeking Veronica and finding only his own emptiness. She seemed to float before him, her luminous eyes promising everything the others could not give, pleading for him to give it in return. Antonio shivered with longing, wanting to reach out and touch the beckoning phantom. *Impossible.* Forcing his attention back to the festivities, Antonio discovered that the lingering image of Veronica, however false the sweet fiery perfection she promised, revealed the utter obscenity of this world to him, a light falling on the seething darkness.

Even as he watched, a murmur swept the room, a small sucking gasp of arousal. Juan had exposed the breasts of his courtesan of the evening and was kneading them, pinching the nipples. She was flustered but quickly recouped, displaying her beauty with pride since she had no other recourse. The guests watched avidly, for this was a breach of the unwritten rules. This party was not so private that the observers had come expecting to be participants, even with their own partners. Just six months ago, etiquette would still have forbidden direct involvement in such an entertainment. There would have be a bit of discreet fondling, and rooms provided for whatever more wanton indulgences were desired thereafter. As Juan's power grew, so was the level of depravity in the Vatican rising ever more swiftly.

Suddenly, Juan released his hold of the woman, only to push her out into the midst of the sexual fray. He tossed out one of his scarlet roses, demanding she bring it back to him. The woman was one of the most famous courtesans in Rome, but she dared not refuse him. She carried the flower in her teeth, dropping it at his feet. For reward, he exposed himself to her and bade her service him with her mouth. As she knelt between his legs, he summoned one of the servants to mount her. The man came forward eagerly to claim his prize, tossing her heavy skirts over her buttocks. As she sucked Juan, he detailed exactly where and how he wished the man to penetrate her. Antonio looked at the faces of the other courtesans and saw fear, arousal, malicious pleasure. Would Bianca delight in seeing a rival humiliated so? Probably. But she would know that it could as easily be herself. When both Juan and the servant had finished with the courtesan, the Pope's favorite son took out a half dozen rubies and fed them to her, making her swallow them, one by one.

Antonio turned away. This debauchery was wearying . . . .

No, it was not weariness, not that jaded boredom he had felt only a few minutes before. It was disgust. When he had first been involved with the Borgias, he had been drawn as well as repelled by their excesses. Now he felt glutted, surfeited and sickened with vice. What had happened to his detachment, much less his former arousal and amusement at these lascivious displays? It had begun to vanish the day he ceased to be a bystander at this court. Supplicant now, he had entrapped himself within its noxious atmosphere. A prisoner by his own devising.

Across the room, Juan fed the courtesan the last of the gems, then directed her face once again to his crotch. Raising his head, Juan saw Antonio watching, and smiled. He did not smile back. He held the gaze coldly till Juan dropped his eyes and returned to tormenting his prey. Juan was a coward at heart, but Antonio wondered if his own reputation as a swordsman or his alliance with Cesare would do him any good once Juan heard of Antonio's petition. With his seductive offerings spurned, would Juan be able to resist sexual blackmail? The

Pope would expect Antonio to comply with whatever small personal requests his children might have, of course, as part of the unwritten price of the annulment. It was, after all, such an insignificant favor . . . .

Could he do it, even once? Antonio tried to think of the act cold-bloodedly, but the aversion he felt was so powerful, he knew he could not force himself to submit to such a bargain. To couple with a man went against his own sexual nature but he had refused other suitors without this accompanying sense of revulsion. If they were not insistent, he took no offense. With Juan, it was far more than his maleness that repelled Antonio, it was his depravity. He had heard enough of Juan's taste for debasement to know he could not endure his touch. The thought brought unbidden images of venomous snakes, clawing demons, and animated corpses oozing corruption. Antonio shuddered. The extremity of his reaction was ridiculous, but there it was. Already there was a price he would not pay to obtain what he had thought he wanted above anything else. He could not submit himself to that man, not of his own choice. And if it was not by his own choice, the Spaniard would have to kill him. If Juan were fool enough to try and stage one of his abductions, Antonio would slit his throat. Before, if he could. If not, after. And it would cost Juan his manhood, as well as his life.

The revelry had begun in earnest now. The Pope had left by a separate door. Lucrezia had vanished too, probably at her father's insistence. Everyone else was granted the license to join the emerging orgy. One of the whores crawled to his couch. Antonio shook his head, but she reached out and laid her hand between his legs. Arousal and rage leapt in him. The whore cowered, licking her lips, excited by what she saw in his face. Her degradation, perhaps, and his own? She waited, sure he would offer it to her, let her drink her fill.

Only the whore and Cesare noticed when he left the room.

21 *Murder*

JUNE 27th, 1497
Dear Niccolò,

By now the news of Juan Borgia's mysterious death will have reached Florence. Since it follows close on the heels of the Pope's excommunication of Savonarola, I can well imagine the uproar in the City of the Red Lily. Although the murder is obviously the result of human passion, no doubt the Friar's advocates will proclaim it to be an act of God. The coincidence is certain to strengthen the Friar's position, at least for a time. He will need it, as the Pope has not rescinded the excommunication. I cannot foresee anything but a disastrous end for the Friar now that the Pope has committed himself to this course. Savonarola's spiritual pride is too great to bow down before the unholy idol he perceives the Pope to be. I do not think Savonarola can serve his God in silence, and for him to preach against the Pope now is to sign his own death warrant. Florence may continue to worship the Friar for a while, but in the end it will prostrate itself before the temporal power of the Church. I know you view Savonarola as a more purely political creature than I do. I am curious to hear your views on the situation when we meet again.

When we talked in Florence, you expressed a fascination with the Borgia family, so I will relate to you what I know of the recent events, as I was involved, if only indirectly, in some of them. On the evening of the 14th of June, Cesare invited me to dine with him at his mother's country home. Cesare was animated as we rode out to the estate together, and I was in a good mood as well. Certainly there was no sense of impending doom. The ride to Madonna Vanozza's villa was quite beautiful. The bridle path we followed led through lush orchards and beyond to the pastures and fields surrounding the ancient Colosseum, then up to the summit of the Esquiline.

It was a small party, mostly family. Juan was there, but not Lucrezia. As all Italy knows by now, the Pope is seeking an annulment for his daughter's marriage. She has gone into seclusion at a convent until the cardinals convene. The evening passed swiftly. The table was heavy-laden, the dishes particularly fresh and appetizing. We feasted, drank the fine wines, and told stories until after midnight. Then Cesare called for our mounts.

For the past month, rumors of Juan's masked companion have been a favorite item of gossip and speculation. As we were preparing to leave, the elusive figure appeared, stepping out of shadows of the surrounding trees and beckoning to Juan, who went to speak to him. They talked for a moment or two, then Juan pulled him up behind him in the saddle. All was good humor as we descended the hillside, the servants bearing the torches. Cesare kept the wineskin passing round, and the laughter and song of our raucous group seemed all the louder as we reached the silent streets of Rome. Juan's friend was silent all this while. Curious, I tried to guess his identity, but he was both cloaked and masked. He seemed vaguely familiar, but I could tell little about him except that he was of less than medium height, slender and broad shouldered. There was a grace about him, also a tension, a sense of expectation. This is not a case of creating a memory to fit the tenor of the events, for I noted it at the time. Most likely the man's expectations were amorous. Since he has now disappeared, we will probably never know. He may simply have been frightened into running away. If he was involved in the murder, was it as instigator or victim?

In Rome, our group parted company near the old Borgia palace and crossed over the bridge into the Borgo. It was dark, the only illumination the small lamps burning before the holy images set at each street corner. Juan dismissed all his servants except for one groom. Although Cesare warned him that the narrow streets of the Jewish quarter were dangerous so late, Juan only laughed and set off into the night, *his masked companion still riding pillion, and the groom trailing behind. I rode with Cesare in the opposite direction.*

Juan did not appear the next morning. The Pope's anxiety escalated throughout the day. By evening, the alarm was given and the search begun. Juan's mount was found riderless, and then the groom was discovered, mortally wounded and unable to impart any information before he died. The Pope's fear became frenzied, and his Spanish guards began a house-to-house search of the Jewish quarter, taking the opportunity to wreak havoc on both the people and their property. There was fighting in the streets, with friends and enemies of the Borgias joining in the fray.

Despite the mayhem, the search at last yielded a witness, a wood-seller who plied his trade along the Tiber. He was loath to talk at first, but the threat of torture produced the following tale: During the darkest hours of morning, he saw two men check out the nearby bridge, then signal to someone waiting. A rider on a white horse appeared, carrying a dead body slung across the animal's rump. They pulled down the corpse and, holding it by the head and heels, flung it into the river, then vanished back the same way they had come. His inquisitors made much of the fact that he had not reported the murder, but he told them that he had seen a hundred such corpses thrown into the Tiber. This was the first time anyone had deemed the event of enough importance to come asking questions of a riverbank wood-seller.

They dragged the river then, and Juan's corpse was found at last. It was covered in weeds and river scum. The hands were bound, the throat cut, the clothed body badly marred by the eight wounds it bore. There was no attempt at robbery, for his purse still held at least thirty ducats, and a rich collar of gold and jewels was set about his neck.

For three days and nights, the Pope succumbed to a frenzy of grief. Feeling cursed by the crime, he vowed to relinquish all temporal concerns and devote himself to the reformation of the Church. He said that if he possessed seven Papacies he would give them all to bring his son back to life. His grief is still great, but I believe his religious zeal has waned as he begins to look once more to the future. The future, now, is Cesare . . . .

Antonio paused, laying his pen aside. He wondered again why he bothered to write to Machiavelli when he would be leaving so soon for Florence, but he had the urge to sort out his memories on paper. The events of that night continued to disturb him. It was more than his anger at Cesare. He was convinced that he was overlooking something. But what? Antonio wished he had drunk less during the first part of the evening. He had carefully stayed sober at the orgies Cesare had dragged him to, but that night he had been in a celebratory mood. The countryside was beautiful, and it was a relief simply to have escaped the unending debauchery of the Vatican. Cesare had just assured him that the Pope would support his petition before the cardinals. That assurances meant nothing now. Aside from the possibility that the Pope might take an entirely different stand on the annulment or his son's support of it, Antonio doubted if Cesare's promises had been anything other than a ploy to disarm him.

Although he had been about to list a dozen other prominent suspects for Machiavelli, Antonio was certain that Cesare had arranged Juan's murder. The exact how and by whom hardly mattered. By now the men had fled Rome or been murdered in turn—unless Cesare had secreted a few select assassins he trusted with such commissions. Was it the masked stranger? If stranger he was. Antonio was sure he had met him under more normal circumstances, but he could remember no one associated with Juan who fit his memory of the mysterious figure. Antonio had presumed he was a young aristocrat whose family would have disapproved of his liaison with Juan. Now he was not so certain. There was something odd about him, something beyond the obvious contrivance of the cloak and mask he wore. And there was the heightened tension Antonio had noted at the time, the sense of waiting. Was it only hindsight that now insisted that tension was not sexual but sinister? That the young man was not Juan's fellow victim but Cesare's accomplice? Antonio knew now that the cloaked figure was the key to what troubled him. Possessing the key, however, did not tell him what lock to fit it into.

Nor, knowing that there were a multitude of men and women with reason and resources enough to kill Juan, could Antonio say why he was so certain that Cesare had sent his brother to his death. There was nothing obvious, nothing except an expression Antonio had glimpsed on Cesare's face just as they were leaving the party. For a second, a calculating glitter had flashed behind the showy exuberance of that night. He had known then that Cesare was up to something, and struggled to clear his head, refusing the wine that continued to pass among them as they rode down the hillside. At the time, Antonio had assumed the look meant the Spaniard was going to ask an extra price for his help with the annulment, or assistance in some scheme he knew Antonio would never agree to otherwise. Only Cesare had claimed his price without asking. As soon as the cry went up that Juan was missing, Antonio knew that Cesare had sent his brother to his death.

Claiming Antonio as witness to his innocence was nonsense. Antonio was not Cesare's only companion that night, and he was a dubious witness, at best—a man soliciting favors from the Borgias, a man responsible for the death of his own brother. Why then the unexpected invitation, asking Antonio to a family celebration? Why Cesare's insistence that they celebrate till dawn, while his assassins did the deed for him? There was an answer, though it filled Antonio with revulsion.

It was nothing but a trick, a twisted joke, a bit of gilt embellishment on Cesare's triumphant night of treachery. Was the joke meant to be shared? Had the Spaniard expected admiration, vicarious pleasure even—two Cains toasting each other in blood? Or had Cesare only wanted to infuriate him and force him to suffer that fury impotently? Was one response as good as the other, as long as Antonio remained in thrall, dependent on Cesare's assistance?

Antonio loathed being no more than a whimsical pawn in Cesare's murderous game. He did not regret Juan's death. If anyone other than Cesare had instigated the assassination, he would feel nothing but relief. But he had neither conspired in nor condoned the crime. Now, in accepting Cesare's help with the annulment, those unvoiced suspicions, his personal aversion to Juan, made him an unwilling accomplice. As the personal price Cesare had exacted, it was less demeaning than what he had feared from Juan. But Juan's price he would not have paid, and Cesare's he would. So his honor played whore to the Borgias after all . . . .

His honor? Looking back, Antonio found it a rather tarnished commodity. He had killed men in duels, fighting over
women he did not love. He had killed men in battle, fighting
wars he did not believe in. Whatever the common conviction,
he had found no honor in those useless deaths. But at the
moment, at least, it had been life or death, fighting against an
opponent who had made the same choice. Circumstances had
never demanded he commit a premeditated murder, but he had
imagined more than one, Juan Borgia's being the most recent.
If necessary, he would have carried the action through without
compunction, and done his best not to be captured. But Juan
was not his brother, and that was where his revulsion with
Cesare lay.

Antonio did not know what he would have done in Cesare's
place. Ambitious as Antonio was, he had never craved power
as Cesare did, never had someone as odious as Juan standing
in the way of achieving his aims. The Pope had loved Juan, as
did Lucrezia, and Antonio had thought them fools to dote on
such human garbage. Should he now condemn Cesare for removing the garbage? If Antonio had had such a brother, perhaps he would have killed him as Cesare had killed Juan—
without guilt or regret or anything but pleasure in the deed.
Why scorn Cesare for qualities he respected in himself? It was
his own cunning, his ability to calculate, Antonio most valued.
What had his passion ever brought him but destruction? Because of it, he had married a whore. Because of it, he had
killed his own brother. Only a month ago, he had almost strangled his father. Did his blind rage really have more virtue than
Cesare's deliberate plotting? To judge by their victims, the
answer was no.

Cesare felt triumph now, where Antonio felt only regret.
What good was regret? His guilty conscience would not bring
back the dead, yet Alessandro's death would be with him all
his life. He would feel the loss, as old soldiers felt their severed limbs still aching. But he had loved Alessandro. Would
Cesare have loved Juan, have spared him, if he had been valiant and generous? Perhaps. That Cesare possessed courage
and charisma made Juan's murder more palatable, but disguised the essential truth. Cesare would kill a man of virtue as
easily as a worm like Juan.

Antonio might despise Cesare's treachery, but he did not let his emotional reaction blind him to reality. The Spaniard was not unique. Intrigue and murder were the way of life at every court in Europe, interwoven with the struggle for power. Roderigo Borgia reigned in Rome and looked to do so for many years to come. If the Pope must promote one of his sons, better the rogue than the fool, especially a vicious fool like Juan. But just how much better, Antonio now doubted. Cesare's cruel streak, coupled with his total ruthlessness, was a frightening prospect. Rome, the whole of Italy, was only beginning to see the treachery, the cruelty, of which Cesare was capable.

Still, Antonio had no intention of exposing Cesare. Even if he had, there was no proof. If through some magic he acquired proof and brought it to the Pope, no doubt both he and it would magically vanish in turn. Roderigo Borgia was willfully blind where his children were concerned. Even without the hushed rumors, the Pope must suspect his eldest son, but Antonio doubted he could bear to acknowledge that suspicion. He would call the most damning proof deception . . . and swiftly remove the threat. Presuming Antonio ever reached the Pope. If Cesare suspected Antonio was taking action against him, there would be another set of assassins stalking Antonio. Laudomia's minions had been quite sufficient.

Even as simple an act as withdrawing his request for the annulment could be dangerous. Whatever excuse he gave, Cesare would take it for the condemnation it was. The gesture might give Antonio a measure of personal satisfaction, but it would cost him his freedom and, he suspected, his life. With careful planning, he might kill Cesare first and escape undetected. That thought obsessed him briefly, but disgust had outweighed anger finally. What he could and would do was leave Rome. He had enough to contend with without tangling himself further in the machinations of the Borgias. At the moment he devoutly hoped the entire family would dispatch each other in an orgy of hatred.

Antonio gave a bitter laugh. Living in Rome, less than a year ago, he thought he had worked out his accord with fate. For a man with no family he could claim, he had done exceptionally well. He had wealth and pleasure at his fingertips, enough power to achieve his objectives without drawing undue attention to himself, and an emotional detachment he had struggled to obtain and prized more fiercely than any other possession. Then his mother's letter had arrived and shattered that detachment. He had set out for Florence, brimming over with guilt and sentiment, longing to rebuild the shattered dreams of his youth. Instead, he had unleashed a chain of events that wrenched the control of his life out of his own hands. Everything he did to regain control caught him in a new tangle more knotted than the last. Since his arrival in Florence, passion and rage had directed too many of his actions. And, if he were honest, directed them still.

Strangely, one note of grace sounded amidst his discordant emotions. Faced with Cesare's cold, virulent hatred like some distorted mirror of his own, the rage he felt against his father had diminished. But not his desire for freedom. The marriage was a shackle, binding him to both Dorotea and his father. As long as it existed, he was a prisoner. Whatever his current antagonism for the Borgias, it did not rankle as much as that invisible chain. Because of it, he would carry through as he had begun. Supposedly the annulment would be accepted, but it would be months before the final judgment was made. He would begin now to rebuild his life to his own desire, with or without the annulment. With or without Veronica.

Fool that he was, Antonio had let hope awaken in him, cradled it close while it cut its infant teeth on his heart.

Even before Juan's death, he had decided to return to Florence. Whether he waited there for word of the annulment, or moved on to Venice depended on Veronica. Their relationship remained an unanswered question. He was sick of mysteries. Tales of Stefano, the strange note Veronica had sent him, and his own hurried departure from Florence—all had continued to plague Antonio. An inner voice kept insisting something had gone wrong. He did not know what it could be. To all appearances, Veronica had taken the simplest way possible out of their affair. But it was the coward's way out. Whatever else she might be, she was not a coward.

And she had said she loved him.

Then a letter had arrived from Dorotea. Brief and obviously dictated out of duty, it sent her greetings and brief descriptions of the activities of both families. Amidst the other news, Dorotea expressed her relief that Mama Lucia had left both the Della Montagna's palazzo and Florence, and Veronica with her. There was no more explanation, but the single sentence sent him into a whirlwind of pointless speculation. It seemed more likely now that Veronica had not been avoiding him, but had not been able to come. His fever had affected his judgment, he knew, exaggerating his anxieties. He must find Veronica. He could not be sure what had happened until he spoke to her. If his initial surmise were correct it would be an unpleasant confrontation, but it would settle the matter between them, once and for all.

And if he had been wrong, he had abandoned Veronica when she needed his help.

"Hurry," Bianca urged.

Cesare laughed softly, pinning her to the bed with one hand, the other searching between her legs. His fingers teased her inside and out, spreading her wetness. As if she were not ready for him now. As if she had not been ready the second she arrived. Cesare had smuggled her into the heart of the palace to celebrate their success before he was forced to leave Rome. For Bianca, this meeting was a greater risk than the killing itself, but it was worth it, worth as much as the gold Cesare had paid her. The danger had already aroused her almost unbearably. Within the locked room, inside the curtained bed, they caressed each other secretly, while all around them the corridors of the Borgia palazzo rang with howls of rage and grief.

"Hurry," she demanded, throbbing with excitement.

He laughed, his teeth a faint glitter in the darkness. Kneeling between her thighs, Cesare took hold of her legs, opening them wide. His sex grazed her swollen nether lips, poised at her opening. He held her like that, totally exposed to him, till she felt a faint twinge of fear. He knew, of course, for he chose that moment to thrust into her, quick and hard.

"Bastard," she gasped, laughing now too.

"My brother once had a man killed for those words,"

Cesare said. "Do you embrace death so easily, reminding me of my sinister birth?"

Bianca wrapped her legs about Cesare, drawing him inside her. "Unlike your puling brother, you are not afraid of the truth."

"Bitch," he challenged her. "Bloody-handed bitch. Killer whore."

"Yes," she said, "that's right." She spread her legs again, wide apart. Cesare drew back till they barely touched.

"Do it," she hissed at him.

"Tell me," Cesare demanded, staring down at her. "Tell me everything, all the details. I want to feel the knife in my hand."

Bianca gave them to him, describing each of the eight wounds she had made in Juan's body to Cesare as he penetrated her. When she reached her peak, he covered her mouth with his hand, to muffle her cries of pleasure, while he whispered in her ear, "Scream. Yes, scream. Scream again."

When she went limp beneath him, he plunged into her in a frenzy, pumping until he exploded in release. Bodies satisfied, they lay side by side reviewing their plot, pleased with how smoothly everything had gone. The commission had excited Bianca from the first. She had despised Juan. He had always been obnoxious in bed, delighting in obtuse cruelties, in humiliations both small and great. She had spared herself as much as possible this last month by playing pimp to his fetishes, finding virgin morsels to tempt him. That was where Juan had thought she was taking him that night. He had never suspected she was leading him to his death. It had been a pleasure to see his smugness dissolve into surprise, his surprise into horror. An even greater pleasure to destroy him.

"I don't know why you insisted on killing the guard I bade you take with you," Cesare chastised, biting her earlobe.

"Didn't you want me to?" Bianca asked testily. "I presumed he had become troublesome. Why else send him along? You know I alone will choose who knows my true identity."

"Would you kill your handsome lover, then, if he guessed you were the assassin? Would you cut Antonio's throat from ear to ear, and toss him into the river?"

So that was why Cesare had brought up his superfluous guard—she had suspected as much. She kept her voice cool as she answered, "I was well disguised." It was, in fact, one of her best costumes: the mask and the cloak, plus the black wig, padding to broaden her shoulders, gloves, even special boots. "If I had not had to speak, even your guard might not have guessed until Dimitri joined us. He heard a woman's voice; he knew Dimitri. So I dispensed with him. Antonio has no suspicion of my other life."

"Perhaps not. Even I did not recognize you." Cesare smiled, cupping her breast, pinching the nipple.

She gave an appropriate whimper of pleasure, but Bianca was furious that Cesare had exposed her to Antonio's suspicion. He had done it deliberately, inviting Antonio to the supper party without telling her. Cesare did not love her, but he was resentful of rivals. The Spaniard presumed she would not dare to bed Antonio while she was servicing him, and Bianca did not disabuse Cesare of the notion. The fact that Antonio had not sought her favors since they left Florence was not something she would admit.

Although he had Bianca to himself in Rome, still Cesare was toying with Antonio's life, trying to create a situation that would force her to destroy his competition. Of course, if she thought it necessary to kill Antonio of her own accord, Cesare would be angry. He liked Antonio and considered him a friend, as much as he could be friends with an Italian. Or with anyone. He certainly did not want to kill Antonio himself, although he was sure Antonio knew he'd arranged Juan's death. It amused him, knowing Antonio was angry at being used. Another minor bit of revenge, she supposed. Cesare disliked owing his life to anyone.

"He suspects me, but he is himself the witness to my innocence," Cesare said. Idly, his hand slid over her hips to squeeze her buttocks. "He is annoyed when he should be grateful to me. I might have saved myself all this trouble and let Antonio kill Juan for me. My brother was determined to have him, but Antonio has no taste for such things."

A memory flickered in Bianca's mind, of Antonio and Daniele's model in Florence, but she kept silent. Except for that single episode, it did not seem to be his predilection. Annoyed, she wondered why Antonio had risked their alliance for that meaningless encounter. She squirmed as Cesare's fingers probed between her cheeks.

"Juan was getting tired of hearing no for an answer," Cesare continued, smiling lasciviously. "It would not have been the first abduction he had arranged to insure a yes. No one had challenged him yet, and Juan mistook his luck for invulnerability. He was a fool. Antonio di Fabiani is hardly the green boy he usually favored. If Juan didn't kill him after taking his pleasure, Antonio would have killed Juan. If he had, I would have felt nothing but gratitude."

"I doubt that," she said coolly. "If you couldn't kill Juan yourself, the next best thing is to have arranged the murder."

"You are right as always, my silver bitch. But perhaps I could have arranged that as well—arranged to help Juan abduct Antonio, and then rescue Antonio myself. Would he have restrained himself from killing my brother out of gratitude? That would have been an ironic twist. No, he does not trust me, he would have seen through the subterfuge. Then he would want to kill me too."

She found herself growing angry at the thought of Antonio forced to be Cesare's plaything. Antonio belonged to her.

"It was a test really," the Spaniard said, thrusting his fingers inside her. "I had hoped Antonio would be more appreciative. We fratricides should band together. It's a pity his honor is so prickly, he'd be the perfect accomplice if he had just a few less scruples. It limits what services I can ask him to perform. Of course, for some services you want a man with scruples, rather than one without. Unfortunately, it may even have ended his willingness to perform any more services for me." There was a note of hostility, as though this were a betrayal on Antonio's part. "If you have to kill him, Bianca, remember to wait until he pays me for the favor I'm doing him."

"And how will I know when that is?"

"Oh, it will be obvious" He chuckled to himself.

Obvious? Just what favor had Antonio asked of Cesare? Money for some venture, she supposed. Though why he would keep that silent she could not imagine. She did not question Cesare. He would only refuse to tell her, not because he didn't trust her to keep silence, but to annoy her, as his probing fingers now purposefully annoyed her. Now was not the time to draw attention to Antonio.

To free herself and diffuse his jealousy, Bianca began to arouse Cesare again. As her hands stroked him to hardness, her lips told him what he wanted to hear, enumerated all the ways that he was better in bed than Antonio. Pretty lies. Good as the Spaniard was, there were none—except the one. Cesare knew who she really was, and shared her pleasure in the kill.

"Your mouth," Cesare demanded, and Bianca bent to his pleasure. Hips bucking wildly, he held her head against him as he climaxed. He gave a triumphal shout and collapsed amid the tangled linens, his ragged breathing slowing to normal. "No one stands in my way now," he whispered, staring upward, as though he saw his fate woven in gold within the tapestry of the canopy. "If anyone tries, I shall destroy them as I destroyed Juan. *Aut nihil* will be my motto. 'Myself—or nothing.' "

Abruptly, Cesare turned away, telling her to wake him before dawn. In moments he was asleep. Wide awake, unsatisfied, Bianca caressed herself secretly, thinking of Antonio. Once again, she found herself wishing she could tell him all her secrets. It would be so exciting to share these pleasures with him. Sometimes she imagined whispering in his ear, and in her fantasy, he only laughed that rough laugh of his and said, "Tell me more." But she doubted the fantasy would match the reality. True, he had killed his brother. But to kill for revenge or even for passion was not the same as to kill for pleasure. From what Cesare said of Antonio's reaction to Juan's murder and Antonio's adamant silence about his past, Bianca did not think his own brother's death was a memory he relished. It was worth her life, or Antonio's, to be wrong, and she did not want to have to destroy him.

She wanted to possess him, utterly.

Bianca acknowledged her mistakes. She should not have indulged her impulse to accompany Antonio to Rome. It had not gained her anything, rather the reverse, though it was impossible that the loss was permanent. She had offered herself twice, joining the caravan and opening her door to him at the inn. The first was a serious miscalculation. The second, she was not so certain. She remembered Antonio's face, the look in his eyes as he watched her in the mirror. The bottomless darkness in them drinking her in. It had been close that night, so close . . . . But he had turned away. The only thing that made her humiliation tolerable was the certainty that it was love that drove him from her door.

She had ensnared him with her beauty, with her passion as intense, as violent as his own. Antonio loved her, but he was struggling with all his will against it. He did not want to love at all, she suspected, and certainly not a courtesan. His pride was writhing in agony. That agony was his tribute to her, just payment for making her wait so long. And she wanted full measure. When he admitted he loved her at last, she would torture him with uncertainty, just a little, so that she could see the pain in his eyes. In the past he had given her only glimpses of his torment, but she would not let him look away then. He suffered so exquisitely, her Antonio.

The image of Antonio's face, the sensation of her own fingers stroking between her legs, brought her release. Bianca bit her lip, shivering with pleasure. She had not let herself cry out, but Cesare stirred, then woke. Obviously ready for other things, he rose and began to dress. Bianca watched him without interest, still savoring her fantasy. He turned to her, tying up his hose, "There is a servant who will get you out without being seen. I want you to prepare yourself to travel to Naples with me."

"To Naples? But this will be a crucial period in Savonarola's control of Florence."

"I do not think he can maintain his power in the face of the excommunication, but who knows—the Medicos survived it. I will make do with one less spy in Florence for the time being. There is someone I want you to seduce in Naples."

"Oh? Who?"

He grinned at her. "I do not know yet."

Bianca did not protest. It would be useless. There were others who could serve him far better as a spy in Florence and they both knew it. Cesare was testing the power of her attraction to Antonio as much as anything else. It was too dangerous to deny Cesare, and she was not prepared to risk killing him. Not yet. "Whatever you wish," she told him.

"You can return to Florence when I am finished with the mission to Naples," Cesare said magnanimously.

Perhaps it was for the best, Bianca thought, ignoring the cold hollowing in her belly. Her abrupt departure would shock Antonio. Let him visit every courtesan from Rome to Florence in her absence—they had not satisfied him yet. When she returned to Florence, he would return to her, the misadventure of the caravan long forgotten. His hunger for her would be all the greater because the others he had sampled would be unable to sate it. She would have him at her mercy then. Yes, the trip suited Bianca's own devices. It was drastic, but she felt something drastic was called for. Antonio was fighting himself, and she must wait until he had finally lost that battle. She could endure that wait, knowing he would at last come begging.

But the longer she waited, the more she would make him suffer.

22 *Crossroads*

VERONICA saw the figure hurtling toward her. As his hands reached out and grasped her, she fell backwards, letting the force of his movement bring him down over her. As she hit the ground, Veronica bent her legs and thrust her feet upward as hard as she could, catching his body and sending it flying over her. Turning her head, she tracked his landing with her eyes and heard the solid thud of his body striking the ground. Swiftly, she sprang to her feet, drew the knife hidden in her boot, and knelt over him, pressing the point to his throat.

"Yes, good, I am dead," Carlo announced. She lifted the blade and let him sit up. He rubbed his neck and examined the smear of blood on his fingers. "You nicked me, Veronica. You are too zealous."

"Last time you accused me of hesitation. Zealous is an improvement."

Carlo, *voivode* of the Gypsy band, laughed, his tanned face creasing into a hundred wrinkles. "I didn't know it was so

dangerous to criticize. I must be more careful in the future."
He clapped an arm about her shoulders and they headed back
toward the camp. "You did well today. That kick is an instinctive move, but to do it well takes practice."

She was pleased with the bout, also. "Yes, I felt the balance
better."

"That throw will work best against someone like me, close
to your own size. Too big, and he may end up on top of you."
Seeing the frown on her face, he asked, "He is big, this man
you fear."

"Yes, big," she acknowledged. "As big as Roberto, but
meaner."

"What is simplest of all, Veronica, is to make him dead.
There are men here who would do this for you happily, without price."

"No," she said. Learning what Luigi had planned for her,
Daniele and Stefano had already offered to have her father-in-
law killed, or do it themselves. Practical as the solution was,
Veronica could not bring herself to order murder. She hoped
she would not regret the decision. "I don't expect I'll have to
use what I've learned against him. But I feel better, learning
new ways to protect myself."

"As you wish," Carlo said. "You tell me if you change
your mind. Meanwhile, you are safe here among us."

Escaping Florence, they had been stopped on the road by
two men, one of whom Veronica recognized as Luca, Luigi's
pock-marked brute. He did not recognize her though, nor
bother with more than a cursory glance at "Grandfather" Lucia and the others before galloping on. When their group met
Benito in Siena, he could not say if he and Roberto had been
followed, for they had kept off the main road for much of their
journey. Roberto was trying his best to be brave, but he was
obviously upset by this sudden upheaval in his peaceful existence.

Safely hidden with Elizabeta's parents in Siena, Mama Lucia had sent Benito out in search of the Gypsy camp. She told
them the signs to look for, and Benito had found, or been
found by, a young Gypsy who led them to the camp. Mama
Lucia had spoken to the *voivode*, who had agreed to shelter
them. Since then, they had moved twice to new locations, al-

though no word had come to the Gypsies of guards searching for them.

Soon after their arrival at the camp, Veronica had begun to look for someone who would train her. Not wanting to impose on the *voivode*, she asked the younger men first. They had either laughed at her or eyed her body smugly—or both. So, finally, she had approached Carlo. His hair was streaked with gray, but he was as lean and tough as any of the other men in camp. "I want to practice fighting, not grappling," she had told him.

"I will help you, and I swear I will not take advantage. But you will not always be disguised as a youth, Veronica. The fighting you do will most likely be because some man is eager for just such grappling. Unpleasant as the thought may be to you, that eagerness is a weakness you can use against him. You must learn to control your panic when someone touches you too intimately. Learn how to gather your anger so the force of it will add to your strength."

The training was as practical as the *voivode* could make it. He insisted she work with staves, a weapon that might be readily to hand in one form or another and good at keeping an attacker at a distance. She had wanted to swing it like the iron bar Antonio had once dubbed her weapon, but Carlo had shown her that the greater length of the stave was put to better use as a kind of blunt spear. "Like this—jab and jab again. With the stave you can hold off an opponent, or fight close in, driving up like this. If you start to whirl it around, the man will come under the swing, and the weapon will be useless."

He had shown her the best places to conceal a knife: inside her men's clothing, a boot, or strapped to her leg underneath a gown. "I will teach you how to kill or how to disable a man quickly. This is what you must do if your life or your honor is at stake. Surprise is as much your weapon as the knife, for you will not have the experience nor the strength to intimidate him. If he takes your blade away, your throat will be the one slit."

When she did well, he rewarded her with one of his Gypsy tricks—a kick or a toss like the one they had practiced today. He also knew certain pressure points that caused extreme pain or loss of sensation. "Grappling work—for when they get too close," he teased, giving her a grin.

Veronica saluted him with her knife, then sheathed it to mark the end of their lesson.

"You know it is not only I who respect you. The others have stopped snickering. Your great-grandmother is *phuri dai* here now, the wisest of the wise ones. We have taken her back among us, though she abandoned us to marry a *gadje*. We would welcome you among us too, Veronica. Though the Gypsy blood runs thin in your veins, our spirit is strong within you."

She shook her head. They had had this conversation before. The Gypsy ways appealed to the adventurer in her, and Veronica knew she could remain here if she must, and find pleasure in it. Life among the Gypsies had its own richness. They had no written language, but they told their tales, their history, around the campfire, weaving their world from memory. Still, Veronica was fiercely homesick for her old life, with its civilized pleasures, the paintings, books, and ideas that brought so many other worlds within her grasp.

"This Roberto is no husband to you. He is a child. A woman like you should have a man to warm her bed. Any of the men would pay a high bride price for you, if you would become one of us."

"My heart is not here," Veronica said, for it was more than life in Daniele's villa that she missed.

"My heart belonged to another country entirely, but it cast me out to wander. So I make my happiness here." Carlo gestured to the wagons gathered under the trees. "You must recapture your wandering heart, and keep it with you."

"Tomorrow we ride to Siena." Her reminder was unnecessary, but Veronica did not know how to respond to the *voivode's* comment. "The day after, I would like to work with the knife again."

"All right. Only this time, not so zealous." He pantomimed cutting his throat, then strode off to tend to the horses.

Veronica watched him go, hoping he would not press his offer again. She had escaped the perils that threatened her, and the tasks she set herself gave her confidence and held her loneliness at bay, at least briefly. She must forget Antonio, as he had forgotten her. If that were even possible. She could see the whiplash beauty of the young Gypsy men as she could appreciate Stefano's sunlit charm, but it did not draw her to them. She wondered if she would ever desire anyone but Antonio.

Getting a change of clothes from her wagon, Veronica went down to the stream to bathe. Finding a secluded spot, she stripped off the sweaty practice clothes. She tossed them into the water and jumped in after, washing first the garments and then herself. The dye had faded from her skin and hair, leaving them their natural color again. Climbing out on a grassy bank, Veronica wrung out the wet clothing and laid it out over the bushes to dry. She enjoyed the freedom of men's garments and continued to wear them in the camp, but she lamented the old luxuriant weight of her hair, for all the ease of the shorter cut. Refreshed for the moment, Veronica strolled back to the camp for her herb lesson with Mama Lucia. It was only early morning and already the July heat was rising. It would be sweltering by noon. The hills of Siena were cooler than Florence, but the earlier they saddled and rode, the more pleasant the ride would be. She still loved the city of her birth—the hilly streets swooping down to the open fan of the Piazza del Campo, the facades of blue, rose, and gold that mingled with the earthier tones, the elegance of their Duomo . . . An image came to her of Antonio waiting for her within the sheltering magnificence of the cathedral. Clenching her fists, Veronica thrust the image from her mind, stilled the leap of joy in her heart. She had hoped for the same meeting the first time she went to meet Daniele in Siena. Then it had almost as much expectation as desire. She was certain her cousin had given the note to Antonio and that he had accompanied Daniele on the ride. But Antonio was not there. His absence had stripped half the joy of seeing Daniele again, but she had gone to her cousin and embraced him and heard his news.

"All the family has been told is that you have taken Mama Lucia to another city for safety. It is good you left, Veronica. Luigi had guards prowling about my home and Stefano's for a week. He has given up now, I think. Neither of us has been followed for several days, and I took care that no one trailed me here. The money for Roberto's care came as usual," Daniele added with relish. "I was afraid Luigi would refuse to send it and deprive me of the pleasure of throwing it back in his face. You are my family now, I will take care of you."

There were other problems than theirs in the city. As expected, the first cases of the plague had arrived with the summer heat. This was not the dreaded Black Death but a sweating sickness, perhaps the same one that had infected Antonio. "I am lucky to be one of the survivors," Daniele said. "The disease is usually lethal. So far, there are only a few new cases each day, and no one else we know has taken ill."

Veronica asked after Antonio then, and what she heard destroyed the rest of her good humor. Antonio had left Florence and taken Bianca with him to Rome. He had not received her note, nor had he sent one to her, only a simple farewell to Daniele. No one knew how long he would be gone. His departure was a minor scandal in Florence, Daniele said, considering that he had been married to Dorotea for so short a time.

Antonio had gone, without a word to her . . . . Veronica was stunned. Yet she had had no sense of whether he was well or ill. When her spirit had reached out to him, some barrier had forestalled her. She had told herself it was distance. It seemed now the obstacle was Antonio himself.

"It is better he is gone, Veronica. He would not be good for you. Try to forget him."

Veronica remembered little of the rest of her conversation with Daniele. She had returned to the Gypsy camp full of apprehension and gone straight to Mama Lucia for a reading, asking for news of Antonio. Veronica shuffled and cut the cards and Mama Lucia had dealt them one by one with her good hand. But the *Tarocco* had no comfort to offer, only a wretched tangle of reversed swords and overturned cups—the ill-omened Moon the single card of the Major Arcana.

"Self-delusion, lack of faith." Mama Lucia tapped the Moon. "It exaggerates and distorts his vision. But the blindness is not all his own. Darkness surrounds him, deception and betrayal are everywhere."

"And the outcome, the Eight of Swords?" Veronica asked.

Mama Lucia shook her head. "Things are bad at the moment. The outcome is uncertain. The cycle of adversity may be drawing to a close, but if things are to change, it is he who must change them."

Meeting Daniele the second time in Siena, she had again asked after Antonio, flushing at Daniele's gentle pitying glance. But he told her the truth. No communication had come from Antonio, but there was gossip that he was spending much time with the Borgias, reveling in a life of decadence. Veronica asked no more. She told Daniele a little of her life among the Gypsies, and they spent the rest of the time talking of what was happening in Daniele's world. With the advent of the summer plague in Florence, all the wealthy families had moved to their country villas, Stefano's included. Daniele was spending a good deal of time there. Discountenanced at the thought of his son posing for the ill-fated Paris, Stefano's father had commissioned a more conventional portrait of Stefano's sisters as the three Graces. Daniele's acceptance was not without ambivalence. He felt that Stefano's father was trying to be gracious to his son's friend, at the same time seeking to underscore Daniele's social inferiority by commissioning the painting to be done at their home. "In his world, gentlemen may dally with each other to their hearts content, so long as they beget the proper heirs. But, in his world, gentlemen do not paint," Daniele said. "Therefore, I am not a gentleman."

"And Stefano?" Luckily, a gentleman should sing and play, even if he should not entertain thoughts of becoming a wandering troubadour. "How difficult does he find this? I know his family is dear to him."

"His two worlds do not mesh as he would wish them to, but he is more adept than most at weaving them together with nothing more than his own charm. An ephemeral substance, yet it suffices for our social gatherings. He must attend to his duties, so if I wish to see him often, I must go to the villa. It is anything but a hardship. The gardens are cool and fragrant. I want to include them in the portrait of his sisters."

"I did not think you could put off *The Judgment of Paris*."

"I cannot. The sisters, as you can imagine, are quite beautiful. I will enjoy working on the portrait, but it does not compel me the way the other painting does. So I will spend time in Florence as well, despite the summer heat and the sickness. Anyway," Daniele added, "the frequent riding back and forth will discourage any lingering watchers. I have seen no one for two weeks now, but I make sure I have a guard with me when I ride."

"I am glad to hear it, Daniele. Next time we meet, look for

a youth but not a bearded one. The glue on this thing leaves
my skin itching for a week.''

"I prefer you without it, though the tights are most fetch-
ing.''

That was the second visit. Back at the camp, she had asked
another *Tarocco* reading of Mama Lucia, feeling trapped
within some strange circling nightmare as she watched card
after card fall into place.

"He is wandering in darkness, with only the illusory Moon
to light his path. He must find his own way through the laby-
rinth of doubt and deception. It is a time of choice, Veronica.
The outcome is uncertain. You must wait." Mama Lucia's
gaze was piercing as she added, "If he is worth waiting for."

She had waited for Antonio all her life. When he had finally
come, he had denied her, again and again. Could it be that he
had not loved her as he said? *Too much,* her heart cried out, *not
too little but too much.* She cursed it to silence. Did it matter
finally which it was? In the end it was the same. If he had left
her, he loved her too little.

She swore she would not ask again, neither the cards nor
Daniele. She would not beg. And so she waited.

At the last meeting, early in July, Stefano rode into Siena by
Daniele's side. Loving horses, he had come for the first running of the *palio.* Savonarola had long since banned such races
in Florence, for which Stefano actually criticized him. Their
own group was large, for Roberto and Benito went to see the
race too, along with several of the Gypsies. With thousands of
others that day, they gathered in the Piazza del Campo for the
opening ceremonies. Everything was ready, the bricks of the
piazza spread with earth, the special Mass said for all the
participants, both man and beast. As they watched, the pageant
began, the standard bearers of the *contrade* paraded around the
piazza, whirling their vivid banners to the music of trumpets
and drums.

Picking up the excitement in the air, Roberto was in a tizzy
of anticipation. His delight was contagious, but Veronica
needed no encouragement. She was as eager for the *palio* as
the others. Growing up in Siena, she had watched it almost
every year of her life. Of the seventeen *contrade* in the city,
only ten ran in the *palio,* but she did not even care that her old

district had not drawn a winning lot. They would race next time. Today, along with Stefano and the others, she looked at the rippling colors on parade before them, trying to decide which *contrada* to champion. Not that the choice mattered. With so many in their group, one of them would "win" the race. She hesitated for a moment over the ice and night banner of *Lupa* the she-wolf, before choosing the smoke and flame device of the *Pantera*, for the image of the panther reminded her even more of Antonio.

At last, this year's *palio* was brought forward, the hand-painted silk heavy with gold fringe. The gleaming standard hoisted above the judges' stand. At this signal, the horses were led into the courtyard and each rider was handed the traditional crop made from the desiccated phallus of a bull. This provoked some ribald comments from Daniele and Stefano, and it was true enough that the men would be whipping each other more than their mounts. Lots were drawn for position. Garbed in her boy's clothes, minus the fretful beard, Veronica cheered and shouted the circling horses and their battling riders without a thought to feminine decorum. She was totally hoarse by the time the winning steed galloped across the finish line. No matter that the mount's saddle was empty. Unhorsing your opponent was not necessarily a winning maneuver, for it was the steed, not the rider, that won this race. The victorious *contrada* came forward to accept the *palio*, and their own colors of green and gold were raised to fly from the walls of the palazzo.

The winner was Roberto's choice, *Bruco*, the caterpillar. They were all exhilarated by his triumph and ready to celebrate. Squeezing through the chanting throng to slightly less crowded streets, they finally found a shady table where they drank wine and devoured bread, cheese, fruit, and chunks of *panforte*—the best in all Italy, rich with nuts and spices. They talked of horses as the excitement wound down. After an hour, the Gypsies left them—gone while the thieving was still good, Veronica expected. Daniele and Stefano told them the latest news of Florence. Savonarola had just been excommunicated, and the Pope had not revoked the ban despite the murder of his oldest son.

"Has he defied it and preached?" Veronica asked.

"No, Fra Domenico da Pescia has been preaching."

Daniele said, then added with grudging respect, "Savonarola has been busy enough treating the plague victims. The pestilence grows worse with the heat. There are sixty cases a day now, and hundreds already dead. Savonarola and his monks have been tending the sick day and night, fighting dauntlessly against the spread of the disease."

Stefano smiled, as pleased to have a word of praise for one of his idols as Daniele had been to hear Stefano's criticism. They smiled and clasped hands across the table. Roberto begged for more *panforte*. The wine was passed around again and it was late when they took themselves off to bed. Siena was crowded for the *palio*, but Stefano's wealth had managed to procure a room for himself and Daniele. The Gypsies had friends who put the rest of them up for the night. The next morning, they met for breakfast at the inn. All was pleasant until it was time to leave, when Roberto demanded they return to Florence with Daniele. Veronica had thought he would be happy living in the wilds of the Tuscan countryside, but she had been wrong. As much as he loved nature, there was too much of it for him, and too many strange new people. Overwhelmed by all the changes, he had been unhappy ever since they left Florence. And Benito, she knew, missed his Elizabeta.

"Roberto can come back with us," Daniele said. "It is safe now, I think, especially with the guard. Benito and I can look after him till Mama Lucia has no more need of you."

Mama Lucia had the whole of the Gypsy camp to tend to her needs. It was more Veronica who needed to spend time with her. Once she returned to Florence, she did not know how often she would be able to see her great-grandmother. And there was the simple feeling that she should stay here. "The *voivode's* birthday is at the end of July. I could come back then."

"Or when we all come back for the second running of the *palio*."

Roberto was upset again, hearing she would not come back with him. But he wanted to go back more than he wanted to stay with her. She kissed him good-bye, promising to return soon, and made her next appointment to meet Daniele. In all this time, he had said nothing about Antonio, and Veronica had sworn not to ask. Then, looking in her eyes, Daniele simply shook his head, an almost invisible negation. So Veronica had only smiled and kissed him good-bye, as well. She felt terribly lonely, watching her friends and family ride out of Siena. That loneliness deepened the even greater one.

Antonio . . . .

Three more weeks had gone by, and he was more in her thoughts than ever. Not that he had ever been totally absent, but his image was more persistent. Perhaps it was presentiment rather than wishful thinking, and there would be news of him today? Her heart lifted then sank again in a deluge of misery and confusion. *I should have chosen wisdom,* she thought, bitterly. *Wisdom does not tear your heart out.*

Giacomo heard a splash downstream, where the master was washing off the dust of the road. Unless, of course, Antonio had tossed in a large rock as a ruse and was now sneaking off on some new adventure, undoubtedly perilous. Barefoot, Giacomo padded through the grass to the bank and checked, just to make sure, but Antonio was swimming naked in the river, for once seeming simply to enjoy himself.

"You can't be sure. He's a tricky one, Feet," Giacomo muttered, plopping down by a tree and stretching out his legs. "It's been one secret after another, and I, personally, am sick of it. I feel like a dog that's chased my own tail too long.

"Well, it's peaceful enough now," he sighed, settling back against the tree truck to watch the lazy flow of the river. The rippling surface reflected the still vivid turquoise blue of the sky, and the metallic light of the setting sun gilded the clouds and glittered like golden coins cast on the waters. For the moment all was well with the world. Giacomo had set a nice rabbit stew cooking over the campfire, then he'd had a bit of a bath, and now a bit of a bake in the lingering heat. He hoped the two guards back at the camp could hold off any brigands that might pop up out of the bushes. They weren't looking very rich on this ride, but it didn't take much richness to attract a brigand. Giacomo had his sword with him, but he was feeling so lazy they'd have him in pieces before he could reach it.

"I'll tell you one thing, Feet, I'd rather be sitting here talking to you than playing spy. Then again, I'd rather be lounging in the sun than bashing brigands. I'm a peaceable man. I like my creature comforts, and I prefer a flagon of wine to a sword in my hand any day. If they'd play the game fair, I'd as soon drop my sword and let them have the money. The thing is, you give brigands what they say they want and they're just as likely to run you through anyway, so you better skewer them before they skewer you. I don't like blood, Feet. My own, especially. Makes me sick every time.''

There had been even more trouble coming back from Rome than on the way to it. Traveling with just a few guards for protection, they'd been waylaid by brigands again, a whole nasty lot of them. The fighting was merciless, and there had been one second, seeing a descending knife blade, that Giacomo was sure he'd die unshriven. Knocking him aside, Antonio had taken a knife thrust that was meant for him, which was backwards of how things were supposed to be, but try explaining that to a brigand. Antonio's wound wasn't looking any too well, either, so he'd gotten the master to stay a few days at the nearest inn. He'd fretted and fumed the whole time, despite Giacomo's remorseful ministrations. The master was wanting to leave, and the wound was wanting to fester. Antonio took great offense that his valet sided with the wound.

''It was to be my wound,'' Giacomo told him, ''I won't have you dying of it.''

''If it had been yours, you would be dead already.''

''You will be yet, if you don't put on your poultice and get some sleep—say a week's worth.''

''Two days.''

''Three.''

Antonio glowered agreement, which meant the wound hurt three times as much as he was admitting. Still, that concession was the best Giacomo had hoped for, since Antonio was slightly more sensible about incapacitations from weapons than from rheums, phlegms, and fevers. In the end, he'd gotten four days, but only because there was a caravan due, which they rode with the rest of the way back to Florence.

''So what does he do, Feet, as soon as we arrive? Visits his father's estate for two hours. Pays a call on his wife for one. Goes to see Signore Daniele for another hour. Tries to find his cousin. Hires some guards and sends them off, only the saints know where. Then he finds us rooms in town and sleeps like the dead. And there he stays for a week, not even bothering to grace his wife's bed for one night. One morning at breakfast a guard appears, whispers in the master's ear, and we're off on the road to Siena, me and the master and the guard. And who are we following? Signore Stefano, who you'd think would be happier if we kept him company and helped ward off brigands! The master's gone mad, Feet. What will he do next?''

But his feet were asleep, both of them. He had quite a time waking them up to get them back to camp so he could put the finishing touches of wine and herbs into the rabbit stew.

23 *Turning Point*

Cor Magis tibi Sena pandit. ''The heart of Siena opens to embrace you,'' read the city's gates. The irony was not lost on Veronica as she trotted into Siena with the *voivode* by her side. The cool dewy breeze of the morning had evaporated into a sweltering noon, and she was glad she had simplified her disguise, discarding the itchy beard for smudges of red clay and charcoal. From a distance the reddish shadow imitated a downy beard and mustache. Close at hand, she was just another grimy youth. Atop her shorn hair she wore a floppy cap, the curling plume obscuring half her face and tickling her nose. Although she felt safe, both she and Carlo kept sharp watch as they rode up the hill to the Duomo. As the street opened into the piazza, Veronica saw Stefano waiting outside, alone. After the first glimpse, she ignored him, circling the piazza as if looking for someone else entirely. She saw no familiar faces, and no one showed them any unwarranted attention. Completing the circuit, she saw that Stefano had vanished. She rode down one of the side streets with Carlo, left her horse in his care, then walked back to the square and up the steps of the Duomo. Pausing in the doorway, she pulled off her cap, perusing the interior before she entered.

Inside it was cool and shadowy, the air perfumed with frankincense and summer roses. Veronica had always loved this cathedral. The walls were as dramatic within as without, the interior striped horizontally in black and white marble. The floors were marble too, etched and inlaid with scenes both religious and historical. Walking across them to the center of the Duomo, she looked up and was enveloped in a dazzling vertigo. The wide stripes seemed to ripple and swirl as they ascended in tiers to the coffered and gilded dome. Still slightly giddy, she turned to her most beloved piece, a carousel of parading beasts bearing the intricately carved pulpit upon their backs. Here Stefano stood, waiting for her. She went to him and they embraced briefly, friends-well-met. Still cautious, they moved to the side slightly, out of direct line of sight from the doorway but with a good view themselves.

Quickly, Stefano assured her that Daniele was all right. "Since Roberto's return, he has stayed at home and worked on *The Judgment of Paris.* But three times this past week, he glimpsed the same man loitering about the house. It might mean nothing, of course, but it made Daniele uncomfortable. I offered to make the trip in his place. He sends you his love and says to tell you Roberto is fine."

"Do you think it was Luigi's guard?"

"I don't know. If the house was being watched, it must be by him. But perhaps there is some other, less sinister explanation. Do not worry, I sent over a guard of my own."

How depressing. Their lovely home was becoming a fortress. To change the subject, Veronica asked, "How is the painting progressing?"

"It is becoming quite a sensation. Hearing its praises sung in the street, my father is even reconsidering buying it. Dozens of people have come to the studio to see it." Stefano paused and added, "A week ago, Daniele had a brief visit from Antonio."

Veronica felt herself go very still, so still she stopped breathing for a moment. Antonio was back in Florence. "Yes?" she asked, not trusting herself with more than the single syllable.

"My cousin has just returned from Rome, as mysteriously as he went." Stefano said it lightly, as if it were no more than the latest gossip, but it was obvious to Veronica that in their new closeness, Daniele had told him that she was enamored. She felt a blush rise to her cheeks, wondering what Stefano thought of her—and of Antonio. Any impressions of him were precious. When she looked at Stefano, his eyes were gentle as always. Feeling more secure, she ventured her question, "What do you think of your cousin?"

"I do not know him well. When I was growing up, Antonio was rather a romantic figure for me—the tragic love affair, mysterious deaths, banishment. I never thought he killed Beatrice. I don't know why, but I was quite convinced of his innocence, even after I comprehended the rumors whispered behind the family fabrication. Perhaps it was his stunned grief at the funeral, which mirrored my own. Though still only a child, I was a little in love with Beatrice. I can still remember the first time I saw her. She was so delicate, so fair, I thought she must be princess of the fairies. And she kissed me. It was my first kiss from a woman I felt to be beautiful." He shrugged, smiling. "Now? I should like to be Antonio's friend, but I doubt he will open himself to me. He seems such a solitary creature. I admire his intelligence, his style, the drama of his presence. When he is about, the very air crackles with excitement."

When he paused, hesitant, Veronica asked simply, "But?"

"If one of my sisters told me she loved him, I should understand . . . but I should warn her. Caring for her happiness, I should wish her someone kinder."

Not feeling able to defend Antonio's kindness as once she might have, Veronica turned the conversation back to Daniele and Roberto. She had meant to stay for the *voivode's* birthday, but with this new trouble perhaps it would be best for her to return to Florence sooner. Stefano told her he was far more concerned about the summer plague than about further problems with Luigi. He said there was still room for company in his family's villa in the hills, and that they could all stay together there. Veronica could not imagine encumbering his family with Daniele, herself, Roberto, and Benito. She knew Daniele's house was an escape for Stefano, and it would be a

shame if their family became a burden instead, by invading his
own home. Stefano asked after Mama Lucia. "She is doing
well, though her arm is mending slowly. She has decided to
remain with the Gypsies." It was what her great-grandmother
wanted, and it freed Veronica of her chief fear of Luigi.

As they talked, Veronica felt her nerves prickling. At first
she ignored the sensation, but it only grew stronger. They were
being watched, she was sure of it. She tensed with the realization, but there was no fear. Why was she not afraid? Senses
finely honed, she scanned the other people within the Duomo,
both the penitents and the priest. There, half turned away and
obscured by a pillar, a figure lingered near the side altar,
cloaked and hooded despite the heat. The man had not been
there when they arrived. Smoothly, the muffled form moved
out of sight. Veronica gave a short, pained gasp of surprise.
Involuntarily her eyes shut, denying what they had seen, but
the dark form burned behind her closed eyelids. "Wait here,"
Veronica told Stefano. She strode directly towards the altar.
She did not need to see his face to know who stood beside the
flickering candles. All this time, she had hungered to see him.
Now she had found him—lurking in the shadows, watching
her secretly.

Seeing her approach, Antonio stepped forward. He threw
back the hood of the cloak and leaned against the pillar, waiting. He showed no discomfort as she confronted him, his
facade as smoothly polished, as cool as the column of marble
he lounged against so casually. His very coolness inflamed the
heat of her anger. "You are spying on me." Fury seethed
within the low-pitched words.

"To see the truth with my own eyes," Antonio countered
the denunciation evenly, though he felt a faint flush rise to his
cheeks. It was difficult to maintain his composure when caught
skulking like any common villain—and to be caught by this
rakish youth he knew in another guise entirely. Beneath the
smudges, her beauty, her blazing presence, beat against him
like a flame, and his only shield was to draw deeper into coldness.

"You might have asked me for the truth. I would have given
it to you." She saw the icy glimmer of distrust in his eyes.
What had she ever done to warrant it but love him too ar-

dently? ''What good is your spying if you see only what you wish? You will not see the truth any more than you will hear it.''

''Very well. I ask you now if Stefano is your lover,'' he responded. The tone made it more statement than question.

''There is nothing but friendship between Stefano and me,'' she told him. ''Nor has there ever been.''

''Nothing?'' Antonio's voice was flat. ''Ever?''

''Nothing,'' she insisted.

''You kissed him.''

''What?''

''Do not deny it,'' he said wearily. ''You were seen.''

''I kissed him?'' Veronica did not remember for a moment, then she recalled the day of Mama Lucia's stoning, Stefano's tender parting salute, and Luigi and Maria watching. ''He kissed me. Once. It is not what you would have it be.''

''I would not have it be what it most obviously is, *dolcezza*.''

The ''sweetness'' was pure acid. Stung by the caustic tone, her temper flared again, her voice rose. ''You claimed you loved me, and bedded your courtesan all the while you were in Florence. You took her to Rome with you—and you judge me faithless for one kiss given in friendship? What a hypocrite you are!''

Veronica glared at him. Before Antonio could decide what to answer, he was distracted by a movement behind her. Drawn by Veronica's outburst, his golden cousin had decided to join them. Stefano approached, his expression both curious and wary, his hand resting lightly on the hilt of his sword. Antonio restrained the impulse to mirror the gesture. His wrath was too close to the surface, he would not reach for his weapon unless he meant to act on the threat. Once he acted on it, he could not guarantee he would spare Stefano's life. Carefully, he studied his cousin's face. Obviously, Stefano was ready to defend Veronica. Antonio saw a protectiveness there, but it was not the protectiveness of passion, not jealous and possessive as his own feelings were. Still he had often wondered if Stefano's innocence was as guileless as it seemed, or merely a clever facade.

Stefano looked from one to the other. For a moment no one

spoke. "I do not want to interfere," Stefano began pleasantly enough.

"But you must needs protect your interests, cousin?" Antonio asked, deliberately goading him.

"My interests, cousin, are disinterested." The words were bantering, but the edge in his voice could easily sharpen. "You misunderstand the situation if you think me your rival here. At first, I was as interested as you, but the lady gave me no encouragement beyond the warmth she bestows on all her friends. I found, after a time, that her cousin's interests coincided with my own, and his consolation made me happy. It is not Veronica, but Daniele and I who are lovers."

Antonio's eyes widened in surprise. The possibility had occurred to him, but he had not expected an open declaration.

Stefano smiled, pleased to have startled him. "If you think the lady unworthy, cousin, perhaps you value yourself too highly. Your honor is somewhat tarnished, and hers gleams pure and unblemished as a pearl."

"Leave us alone, Stefano," Veronica interrupted, disconcerted by his praise. "You need not worry. I am in no danger."

"Lady, I think you wounded already," Stefano said softly. "I only hope your cure is as close to hand as your hurt."

"Please," she repeated.

"I will wait for you in the piazza outside. If you need assistance, you need only call," Stefano said. Then he paused, turning back to Antonio. "I did not see you following me, cousin."

"No, you did not," Antonio replied, taking a certain pleasure in Stefano's obvious annoyance.

"I let any pass who seemed to follow too closely. How did you manage? Did you disguise yourself?"

"No, though my valet was the tinker you let pass by. You watched your back quite well, cousin, but I followed before you, and my other men well after. It seemed likely that Siena was your destination, so I had only to keep watch over the crossroads to make sure you did not turn off. When you entered the walls of Siena, I fell in behind you and trailed you in this direction. When I was sure the Duomo was your goal, I had a man watch each of the surrounding streets while I came in here. Through there." He nodded to a back entrance reserved for the priests. "The price of exclusive entrance was minimal, and will be put to God's work."

Stefano awarded him a rueful smile, "A cunning twist, cousin. I shall remember it in future." They watched him walk outside, leaving them together beside the candlelit altar. They were alone in the Duomo now, except for the priest.

Veronica turned to face Antonio. "Do you believe now that Stefano is not my lover?"

Disconcerted, Antonio turned back to her. Stefano could be lying—to avoid a duel, or because she had asked it of him. He could be lying, but Antonio believed his cousin, and he wanted to believe in Veronica's honesty. Still, too many unanswered questions remained.

Veronica saw his hesitation, and it cut her to the quick. "Shall Daniele witness my virtue next? He has been father and brother to me. But you have been cavorting in Rome with the incestuous Borgias. Therefore, he must be my lover as well?"

"No, I do not think that." Though he had accused her of it once, Daniele had long since faded from his jealousies.

"Who then—Frederigo, Benito?"

Antonio shook his head, but his eyes searched hers, dark with suspicion. Veronica turned away from him. The suspects had vanished, but the doubt remained. It did not matter how many denials there were. It was herself he doubted. Would it be this way always? No matter how faithful she was, would he always look to be betrayed, misjudging even comradeship as rivalry? Could she endure that, to give herself to him totally and yet never be seen for who she was?

But he had seen, had believed. Love had dispelled his doubts, for a time. What had gone wrong? "You did trust me," she entreated him. "Why do you distrust me now?"

How innocent she looked, pleading with him, how distressed. But if she had not wanted him jealous, why had she praised Stefano to him? If she wanted him, why had she bid him stay away? "What of the note you sent me?" he demanded abruptly.

"The note?" Why would the simple message she wrote chill his voice with winter frost? "Telling you why I must leave Florence? I thought it a bitter joke when I found you had already left, with Bianca."

He frowned, perplexity and indignation mingled in his expression. "Not that one. I received no note saying you must leave. My first news of that came from Dorotea, when I was in Rome."

Veronica was baffled. "Then what note do you speak of? There was only the one, which I gave to Daniele to give to you, but he did not, since you were gone already. I thought he must have given it to you when you returned, since you mention it now."

"He gave me nothing," Antonio told her, remembering Daniele's reluctance with him, the sense of something withheld. The artist had not forgotten the message; he had chosen to keep it back, not knowing how Veronica would feel about it with two months gone by since she first penned it.

"It was you who left without a word," Veronica accused.

"I left . . . ?" He stared at her. The whole conversation was bizarre. A tangle of absurdities.

Looking at his face, Veronica's ire vanished. "Did you send word?"

"What game is this?" he began sharply, then stopped. He would play the game, nonsensical as it was. "Two days before I left for Rome, I sent you a note."

"I did not receive it."

"I received an answer."

"I sent no answer," she asserted. "Could it have been a forgery?" Then the memory came suddenly, Luigi's drunken words, slurred and insinuating; "*you aren't expecting anyone else, are you, Veronica?*"

"I told you I was leaving and that I wished to see you," Antonio continued. "You answered tersely, saying you did not need me, that Stefano was with you . . . ."

The coldness was back in his voice, and the hollow echo of betrayal. Veronica raised her head and met his eyes. "That was in the note I sent to Daniele about Mama Lucia. Luigi told me he had torn it up."

"It was torn," Antonio said slowly. "There was no salutation."

"Nor warning for you to stay away from Luigi's, to avoid Savonarola's youths?"

"No."

"Luigi intercepted both our notes. You were sent half of what I wrote to Daniele, and I received nothing at all. He must have suspected you were my lover and tried to deter you from seeing me."

"Luigi." Yes, he could believe that.

"He was quite pleased with himself," Veronica recalled. "He wanted me isolated and did his best to make certain there would be no interference."

"He is so desperate to have you once more," Antonio asked scornfully, "that he will risk such measures?"

Stunned, for a second Veronica could only stare at him. They had come full circle. Returned to jealousy, mistrust, and accusation. And all this ugly suspicion was not for gentle beautiful Stefano, but for Luigi, with his fetid breath and pawing hands, his vileness. Rage pulsed through her, red waves that welled up inside her, obliterating everything else. Passion driving her forward, Veronica struck Antonio hard across the face. He took the blow without defending himself, the force of it whipping his head to the side. He turned back to her, his eyes blazing, the mark of her hand stark on his face.

"I have loved you from the moment I saw you," she whispered furiously, "but you will teach me to hate you yet!" She glared at him, tears of pain and wrath streaming down her cheeks.

Horrified by the confrontation, the priest hurried toward them. Antonio held up his hand in warning, and the priest halted a few feet away. "Gentlemen, I beg you, no violence here," he exclaimed, scandalized. "Take your quarrel elsewhere."

"You need fear no duel, Father," Antonio assured him, never taking his eyes from Veronica's face. The priest wavered for a moment, then withdrew, muttering prayers for deliverance.

She glared at him, the tears still falling unheeded.

"Weeping now?" he snarled it, for her tears scalded his heart. "Is that not the oldest trick of all?"

"For a clever man, you are a fool." She turned away from him, her hands gripping the back of a bench. She closed her eyes to shut him out, fighting each sob that shook her.

Antonio tried to stoke his anger against her and failed. If it was a ruse, it worked well, her small choked sobs knotting his guts with pain. But he knew it was no ruse. He could see now that she was trembling, a fine shivering along the tensed muscles of her arms, her hands, her white-knuckled fingers. Could feel the tremors coursing through her as he laid his hand on her shoulder.

"Do not touch me!" She jerked away from him, her eyes flashing warning.

For once, he heeded her rage. "I only want the truth," he said at last.

"You do not want the truth," she challenged, wiping the last of the tears from her cheeks. "What you want is to be free of me. You do not want to trust me. You do not want to love me. That is your truth. And for it you will believe any lie."

"Not quite," he said at last. "When I left Florence, I wanted to be free of loving you. Yet I am here now—as much because I doubted myself as because I doubted you."

"I have no proof to end your doubting," she said defiantly. "There is only my word."

"Luigi forced you?" he asked, step by step crossing the breach between them.

"It was his second attempt," she answered harshly. "Did you think I would go to him willingly?"

Antonio flushed. When she said it, he saw the impossibility, yet he had taken it for granted. He remembered Luigi's hand on her, the lewd caress trailing over her breast. "At the betrothal, I watched while he fondled you, and you permitted it."

"Permitted it," she repeated tonelessly, a shudder running through her.

"It was obvious you detested him," he admitted. "Why did you allow such an intimacy?"

"He has threatened to accuse both Mama Lucia and me of witchcraft, if I exposed him. Whatever acquiescence you have seen has been fear of that."

"And what acquiescence has there been?"

The question held pain but no blame. Her own anger fading, she saw that he sought now to believe her, his eyes black and fathomless, gazing into her own. "No more than you have seen. I told you he has tried twice now to rape me. The first time, I hit him with a poker from the fireplace. The second, I drugged him with a sleeping potion, and so escaped from the room where he had imprisoned me and then from Florence.''

"Luigi,'' he repeated. He had wanted to kill him even then. But loving Veronica had been the greater threat, and he had protected himself instead of her—warded off love with rage, nurtured every suspicion. "I thought you wanton. I heard tales of your wildness before I met you—to know your true identity. And when I met you . . . .''

"You knew me wanton already. And so I have been, with you. Only with you. Ever. I have had no other lovers.''

Antonio did not take his eyes from hers, but he shook his head helplessly. She could see doubt overwhelming within him, bleak as despair. The final truth, and it was too simple to be believed. Veronica did not even blame him anymore. She sank to her knees by the altar, and he knelt beside her. She felt him willing himself to accept her words, but he could not make her a gift of his trust. Tears welled up, and she fought them. Veronica had no proof to offer him. Only the devotion of her heart. Without thinking, she said, as she had said once before, "There is no one for me but you.''

His head went back as if she had struck him again. Face pale, eyes dark and wide, Antonio stared at her as though the declaration itself had condemned her, not an offering of love, but a curse. Then Veronica knew it was not herself whom he saw. An image came, pale gossamer hair, melting eyes, a fragile, unearthly beauty.

"Beatrice,'' she murmured. "She said those words to you once.'' And what could he think them now, except the most fearful warning?

"Yes,'' he responded at last, his voice hoarse. "She lied. She was a liar.''

"Look at me, Antonio. See me. I am not Beatrice. It is the truth I speak.'' *And because it was the truth for me*, she thought, watching the struggle within him, *I thought it must be so for you as well. But perhaps she wounded you so deeply the hurt will never heal.* "Did you trust her so utterly then, that you can trust no woman ever?''

"Yes,'' he said, and then, frowning, "No.''

"Yes and no,'' she smiled bitterly, and so Antonio trusted her, yes and no.

"I loved her—desperately," he answered, as if that explained it all.

"And did you trust her so desperately as well?" she queried.

Startled, Antonio lifted his eyes to meet her questioning gaze, gentle and clouded with her own pain, pain he had brought her. Then he bent his head, closed his eyes, and looked to the past. It was a dozen years ago, and held from his mind for most of that time, yet it was clear to him what he had felt, the ecstasy and the torment of it. He remembered the shock of Beatrice's infidelity, never guessed and yet known, as one may know one is dying without knowing the name of the disease. "I adored her, I worshipped her—but something was wrong. Almost from the beginning there was fear, like a dark chord sounding in the joy she brought me. I did not understand it. She was my first love, and I did not look to be betrayed."

"She was very beautiful." A beauty that could hold men in thrall, even from the grave.

"Her beauty was too good to be true. I think not even Beatrice could endure it. It created a madness in her, as it did in all the men who loved her."

She heard sadness in his voice, but not hunger, nor anger. "You have forgiven her. It is yourself you have not forgiven, for loving her." And then, "You do trust me. It is your own heart you do not trust."

Looking at her, her eyes so direct and honest, he knew it was true. If it were not, he could not have told her all that he just had. All these months, he had been battling not Veronica, but himself. His heart and mind at odds. But it was his heart that had known the truth, as it had known it before. With Beatrice, his mind had not known how to admit his heart's fear. With Veronica, it had refused to heed his heart's hope. Once before, she had opened the prison he had made for his emotions, only to have him lock it against her again. Now, the dark fortress he had locked himself within had dissolved, his prison of shadows vanished, and he was free, standing in the shining sun of her presence.

Antonio took her face between his hands. Looking into her eyes, he acknowledged the simple and ultimate truth of her. He kissed her, tenderly, tasting on her lips the last salt sweet traces of her tears.

"I love you," he said to her. "There is no one for me but you."

24 Celebration

"THESE are not for eating, not yet," Veronica warned Antonio as she handed him the rounds of *panforte* she had bought. "I promised them for supper tonight."

"I am too virtuous, and Giacomo is too full," Antonio protested. He passed the package on to Giacomo, along with his own warning; "Do not crush them."

"You're more full than virtuous," Giacomo muttered happily, packing the rich cakes into his saddlebags with meticulous care.

Gorged on sweetmeats, they had left Stefano inside the confectioner's shop, selecting yet more delectable treats to bring back to his sisters and Daniele. Since their roads would take them in opposite directions, Stefano preferred to spend the night in Siena and return to Florence tomorrow at a leisurely pace. Before they parted, Antonio had entrusted Stefano with a message to his *legale*. Honored with the confidence, Stefano had promised to search out one of the Sienese street Gypsies if there were any news of import to pass on before the next agreed meeting. Their farewells given and the *panforte* secure, the three of them mounted their horses and set out with Carlo to rejoin the Gypsies.

"You made one mistake," Antonio said lightly as they left the gates of Siena behind.

"Yes?" Veronica queried.

"Your boots are too small," he told her. "Those are not the feet of a youth. Other than that, it is not a bad disguise, though rather grimy. But I have always liked you with charcoal smudges."

"Better smudges than the false beard I wore escaping Florence. You missed the full effect."

"I do not know if the priest was more relieved or scandalized to discover you were a woman in boy's clothes, Madonna," Antonio laughed, relishing the irony.

———

The journey was a pleasant one, a cool breeze rising to gentle the heat. They arrived at the Gypsy camp as the late summer dusk faded to silvered blue, the silhouettes of the trees gathered like clusters of black filigree against the veiled light of the sky. The moon floated above them, pale and luminous as a chipped pearl. Seeing them approach, the Gypsies came forward to greet the newcomers. Among the men, Veronica detected a certain rivalry as well as curiosity, overt but not hostile. Antonio and Giacomo were disengaged from their party and led off for a bit of inquiry and initiation. Since the *voivode* only grinned at the incident, Veronica did not worry about Antonio.

"Well, I have my wish," Carlo said as they dismounted, "if not exactly as I wished it. Your heart is here among us now, even if it will not stay."

Veronica hugged him, too happy for words. Rescuing the *panforte*, she delivered the package to the *voivode*'s wife, borrowed some clothes from one of the younger women, then set off for the river to wash away both smudges and trail sweat. Refreshed, she slipped on the skirt and blouse of gauzy white linen, brightly embroidered at neck and hem, and wound a fringed crimson sash about her waist. When she walked back in the deepening dusk, she saw Antonio sitting by one of the campfires amid a circle of young Gypsies, freshly scrubbed and dressed in borrowed finery as well. They had given him raiment for a wedding, dressing him in their precious silks and velvets. The full sleeves of a sapphire blue shirt were visible beneath an exotic vest stitched with gold thread and glittering bits of mirror. Antonio's back was to her, but his face was in profile. He threw back his head and laughed. A pang of delight vibrated through Veronica at the sound. She had never heard him laugh so freely before—laughter that rose not in response to clever wit, but in the simple joy of being alive.

Giacomo appeared at her side with a handful of wild basil he had picked. He offered the dark green leaves to her like a bouquet to sniff. Veronica breathed in the aromatic fragrance of the herb, clean and sharp. Giacomo nodded at Antonio, bantering with the other young men. "Like a cat the master is, at ease amid princes and beggars . . . and Gypsies." She smiled at him and he grinned in return, his expression mingling pleasure and something like relief. Giacomo left her to sit by Carlo's wife, consulting over the herb blend in the stew.

Veronica moved closer to the campfire. Sensing her presence, Antonio turned. He rose from among the young Gypsies and came toward her, smiling. "I have been approved, tentatively, but the terms are somewhat uncertain. Opinion is divided on whether I should follow you about on hands and knees, declaiming my abject unworthiness, or beat you daily, for your own good and mine."

"Neither, I trust."

"I would not dare the latter, for I hear you have become quite deadly."

"Not as deadly as I would like," Veronica said, only half bantering, "but the *voivode* has taught me to handle a knife and stave with some competence, at least."

"This I must see."

There was no mockery in his tone, though she did detect a lascivious gleam in his eyes. "You may grapple before or after, but not during," she warned him, both annoyed and enticed by his reaction to her serious endeavor.

"Perhaps both?" he answered. "Before, in anticipation of watching you, and after, in response. But in between I promise to be the soul of courtesy, observing sedately from my grassy tussock."

"You had best," she told him. "Come with me, I have not greeted Mama Lucia yet."

"And I have never met her."

Veronica took Antonio to the wagon of the new *phuri dai*. She knocked at the door, and Mama Lucia welcomed her inside. "Antonio is here, Mama Lucia," Veronica announced as they clambered into her wagon.

"Well, it took him long enough, didn't it?" Mama Lucia

commented acerbically, scrutinizing Antonio as he settled himself beside her.

"Too long." Antonio took her hand in his and raised it to his lips.

"Don't think your charm will win you any favor with me." She eyed him mistrustfully, but permitted the courtly compliment before withdrawing her hand.

"So I see," he responded gravely, though his eyes gleamed. "But if my charm avails me nothing, you must tell me how can I win your favor. I most earnestly wish it."

"As long as my great-granddaughter looks like that, I have no complaint." Mama Lucia glanced from Antonio to Veronica, and then back to him again. Mama Lucia leaned forward, her face intent. "Her heart is open to you. Do not close yours off from her, even to protect her. You cannot keep your darkness from her, only your light."

He met the intensity of her gaze. "Her happiness is my one desire."

"Remember that," she said severely, then leaned back into her nest of cushions, thumping them into order about her. "If you forget, I've a curse for hives to remind you of your promise. Veronica has refused it once, but I shall try it out myself if I hear any further ill of you."

Antonio's eyes widened in alarm, even as his lips quivered with suppressed amusement. "A dire threat indeed. I shall not risk your displeasure, Mama Lucia."

"See that you don't. I've never tried the curse, so who knows what would happen?" She pondered the possible consequences, "I might even get the hives myself."

"I see I must thank Veronica twice over, for sparing both myself and you such a dreadful bane." Casting a wide-eyed glance at Veronica, he pressed one hand to his breast and murmured fervently, "Thank you, Madonna, thank you."

"You are most welcome," she said graciously.

"But what of my fortune, Mama Lucia?" Antonio asked, turning back to her. "I have never had the *Tarocco* read, but I am told you are very good at it."

"So I am, and so I should be," she answered imperiously. "I will read for you, but not now. I'm too hungry, and you wouldn't remember one word, unless it was about that chit of a girl beside you. When you are ready to leave us, then I'll read for you."

"It will be difficult to wait, but I shall accept your judgment."

"I'm famished," Mama Lucia announced. "Let's eat now."

Tantalizing odors of roasting meat and savory wood smoke greeted them as Antonio and Veronica emerged from the wagon. Hungry after the long ride, they helped Mama Lucia down as well and joined the Gypsies around the campfires, sitting together beneath the glittering canopy of the night sky. Tonight the simple repast had become a feast. The abundance was freely shared—roasted game birds, freshly caught fish, rabbit stew, fried cheese, and bread were followed by luscious juicy berries, and spicy *panforte*. Skins of rich red wine were passed from hand to hand during the meal and after. When the platters emptied, the campfires were extinguished, but torches lit the darkness in their stead. The spirit of festivity permeated the camp, flowing from the impromptu party that had sprung up in their honor. Instruments appeared, the lively music of strings and bells filling the air as the Gypsies leapt up to dance.

In the first burst of excitement, Antonio pulled Veronica to her feet and led her, laughing, into the circle. Her hands clasped about his neck, they danced recklessly, giddy with wine and love. Music, flame, and stars swirled around them as he spun her amidst the other dancers, the swift pace of song matching the quickened beating of their hearts.

After a time, the wilder edge of gaiety was burned away, but the dancing continued. The exuberant tunes of the early evening shifted to ballads of loves won and lost, haunting melodies whose sadness was one with their sweetness. For Veronica, even the exuberant revelry had the entranced quality of a dream. Now she floated on the seductive currents of sound, lost in the music and Antonio, the rhythm of the yearning songs one with the soft, insistent pulse of desire throbbing between them. Their own passion weaving the spell that bound them, they moved slowly and ever more slowly, until they paused with the last note, suspended in the poignant silence between the sighing ballads.

Antonio's eyes held Veronica's, his husky whisper only barely audible. "I want to be alone with you."

"Yes," she answered him. Without another word, she took his hand and led him away from the circle of dancers, across the grassy field to the trees that sheltered her wagon.

The musicians began again, and the song followed them, a melancholy ballad, aching with tenderness. Antonio felt the music speaking for him, its tremulous joy tinged with penitence. Standing outside the wagon, he turned Veronica towards him, his hands cupping her face as he had by the altar in Siena. Her eyes caught the gleam of starlight, their clear depths shining with a warmer light.

"I do not deserve you," he said quietly.

"You have only to love me to deserve me. We were made for each other's happiness."

Antonio lifted her through the door into the wagon and followed her into the night-shadowed interior. Perfume enveloped them, for the Gypsies had scattered tiny, deep blue wildflowers there like fragrant stars, their darkness bright against the expanse of clean white linen. Secluded as their wagon was from the rest, he did not close the door behind them, but left it open to the breeze and moonlight, to the hushed whisper of the song, a sighing scarcely louder than their breath. Kneeling, Antonio drew Veronica down before him on the flower-strewn pallet. He felt desire resonating between them, a subtle and all-pervasive music.

He raised his hands to Veronica's shoulders and paused gazing into her eyes. Then, gradually, he began to undress her and she mirrored his gestures. Reverently as in some sacred ritual, they opened each garment in turn, lifted it off, and laid it aside. With every revelation, they praised with word and touch the sculptured contours and supple shapes that lay beneath. Velvet, silk, and linen fell away until there was only the intimate beauty of skin beneath their caress. Intense as their longing was, they did not hurry a single gesture or slight the most trifling discovery. Both of them knew that only through this infinite leisure, this slow, tender searching, could they recapture the time lost between them.

For months Antonio had denied Veronica, denied his own heart. But the dark fury, the bleak desperation of that time was behind him at last. Realizing that, he left the craving of his body unsatisfied, welcoming the sweet pain of his hunger. For the moment, anticipation and expiation were satisfaction enough, the pleasure of pleasing its own fulfillment. He bent his head down to her, his lips gliding from the arch of her throat to the soft mound of her breast, tongue and teeth coaxing the rosy center to a tight crest. His hands went on their own quest, rediscovering the treasures of the long, lithe body. As he caressed her, Veronica's sighs deepened to sobs of passion. He heard his own low moans echo her responses, urge them anew. Her ardor would be his absolution. She had forgiven his rejection, but he knew the pain of it lingered, invisible bruises in her flesh, her spirit. Words would not heal that hurt. Only touch could convey his repentance.

But his atonement was brief. With each caress he felt her delight swell, washing over him like a soft wave of light that banished all else. Their fading sorrows were no more than thin, dark veils to be cast from their spirits as their garments had been slipped from their bodies. Enraptured, they worshipped at the altar of each other's body with unclouded joy.

As Antonio's hands explored Veronica, seeking out all her beckoning curves and hollows, so hers began to explore him, finding all the contradictory strength and gentleness of his being revealed in his body. Her fingers roamed freely, sampling the manifold textures they found. She was fascinated with the fine, grassy silk of hair shadowing his body, with the alluring smoothness of satin skin drawn taut over the hard muscle. She watched his face as her hands moved over his body. His eyes grew more intent, his lips softer with each new discovery. His breathing grew more ragged as she ventured down chest, belly and hip to the firm rise of his thigh. With exquisite deliberation, Veronica slid her hand down, stroking the vulnerable tenderness of the inner flesh, slowly moving up to cradle the twin spheres encased within their tight-drawn sac. Silently, he urged her to continue. Releasing that soft taut treasure, her fingers moved up, hovering for a moment, letting his expectation build, then closed around the blazing thrust of his shaft.

Antonio gasped aloud, again, and again, the sharp note of

breath trailing to a shuddering sigh. With each compelling stroke she offered him, desire flared brighter, hotter, but the intensity of that fierce flame was suffused throughout his body transformed by some alchemy to a vivid radiance that warmed rather than burned, filling every corner of his being. He cried out in wonder, even that cry sounding no louder than a sigh.

"Love," Veronica whispered. The one word naming the gentle sorcery that enthralled him.

"Yes," he answered, gathering her to him, kissing her lips, her cheeks, his mouth soft against the softness of her skin. "Oh, yes. Love."

His kisses moved across her face, her throat. She felt his lips part, his moist tongue brush against her, taste her. Slowly he traveled downward, lavishing delicate washes of sensation along the angle of neck and shoulder, tracing the rounded curve of her breast. The delicious torture ascended the aching peaks of her nipples, fastened there briefly before sweeping across belly and navel and thighs. Parting her legs, Antonio nestled there, his laving tongue delving between the secret folds of flesh to discover the sensitive bud hidden within. The hot, flickering touch of him flashed sweet lightning to the heart of her.

He journeyed down the length of her body and up again, returning to reclaim her lips in an all-consuming kiss. As their mouths joined in moist probing intimacy, his hands continued to stroke her. His cherishing caresses urged her to rapture, his touches shaping her flesh only to dissolve it in bliss. Pleasure built upon pleasure, delight on unendurable delight, as his gentle fingers moved over her and then within her. She cried out softly as his penetrating touch raised her to a throbbing pinnacle and released her into ecstasy. Sighing, Veronica drifted for a time on the muted echoes of that fulfillment.

Beautiful as it was, the first release was not completion for her but a new beginning. Craving total union she lifted her arms, and Antonio came within their circle. Looking down at her, his eyes were an absolute blackness, drawing her to a burning inner light. He embraced her in turn, guiding her closer as his aching hardness sought and found her yielding softness. He paused there, questioning, tempting her with his searching gaze, his probing flesh. Liquid with longing, Veron ica opened herself to him utterly. Controlled still in the fierceness of his yearning, Antonio entered her slowly, sheathing himself in the deepest recesses of her body. Encased within the fluid warmth of her, he did not thrust but pressed infinitesimally deeper, and deeper still, undulating against her, his whole body caressing hers over and over again. She moved with him, melting into oneness, flesh, sensation, emotion fusing. Softly, in the starlit darkness that enfolded them, he moaned her name and she called to him in turn, naming him even as she lost herself in him, drowned in him. Her love flowed out to him as his poured into her, suffusing them both with heart-wrenching sweetness.

Afterwards, Antonio drew her into his arms, cradling her against him, his cheek pressed against the tumbled mass of her hair. "Tell me. Everything."

And so she told him her tale, from the death of her parents and her own marriage to her escape from Luigi's dungeon. Antonio held her, kissing her lightly as she spoke, murmuring his quiet responses to her tale, asking questions.

"You can foretell the future? Is it a voice, such as Savonarola says he hears?"

"No, it comes in images, or sometimes simply knowledge, as one may know something in a dream. It is not as impressive as it sounds. I have little control. I still mistake fear, or hope, for premonition."

"Can you read my mind?" he asked, with a twinge of uneasiness.

"No, not as you mean it. I knew today when you were near. Sometimes I know what you feel."

"You feel what I feel?" It was difficult enough to live with himself at times, to bear his own darkness. How could she know that darkness and still love him? And yet she did.

"Does it frighten you?" she asked, a faint catch in her voice.

Looking into her eyes, Antonio shook his head. "No, I am done with fearing you."

A moment later, he was thoroughly bemused by her description of the Prince of Cups. "A *Tarocco* card with my face? I must see this phenomenon."

"And will you be jealous?" she teased.

"It is no better than I deserve, with the paper figures I chose to battle."

When she spoke of her marriage, Antonio frowned and repeated, "Roberto is impotent?" But he was not surprised. Antonio had never been jealous of him. Something within him had perceived Roberto's essential innocence. He had trusted that feeling as he had not trusted his feelings for Veronica.

When she revealed Luigi's first attempt to rape her and his clumsy violation of her body, Veronica felt Antonio's body tense with rage. He kept silent, letting her tell it all, perhaps not trusting himself to speak. "You see," she whispered against his chest. "You are my first love. My only love."

He held her close while she told him her perception of their confused affair, and her pain at his departure from Florence. His arms tightened painfully when she explained how she had escaped from Luigi's dungeon.

"I will kill him," Antonio said coldly. "I will not have you at risk again."

"No. I wish he were dead, but I do not want his death on your hands, nor on mine through yours. Blood follows blood. I do not want responsibility for the feud that would follow."

"Would it? Who would bother to avenge him? Is there one person who wants him alive?"

"Perhaps not. Certainly Frederigo would do nothing. But Luigi has brothers, uncles, cousins who would avenge their honor, if not his life."

"At the betrothal, when he touched you, I wanted to kill him even then, but I felt too much for you, too soon, and so I turned away."

"It does not matter. You are here with me now." She finished by telling the tale of her escape from Florence with Mama Lucia, and a little of her life among the Gypsies. When she was finished, there was silence for a moment, Antonio's lips nuzzling tenderly on the curve of one bare shoulder. Then, still cradling her in the circle of his arms, he turned her to face him.

"I want to marry you."

She smiled. "We are both married, in law."

And so he told her of Rome, all of it. "I am waiting to hear of progress on the petition. I do not expect to hear for some weeks yet, but if a letter comes, my lawyer will contact Stefano and he will find the *voivode's* man in Siena."

"Even if your marriage to Dorotea is annulled, I am still wed."

"Once I am free, we will begin a petition for you. Roberto is impotent, so there should be little difficulty in obtaining a divorce for you. Then we can marry. There will be a furor, but the effect of the scandal will be mitigated if we are not living in Florence. We can keep Roberto with us, since you feel responsible for him."

Veronica desired it and yet she resisted. A dark knell sounded within her, and she heeded its ominous note. "Do you have enough money, enough influence, to procure two annulments from the Borgias? Because a petition will not be enough. Do you think Luigi would let you best him twice in such a fashion without a fight?"

"But Roberto's impotence is not a fabrication, like the Pope's charge against Lucrezia's husband."

"What if the doctors were paid to say nay instead of aye? Luigi could buy them easily enough."

"It can still be proved," he said, though his voice roughened.

"Have Roberto perform like a trained animal before the judge, but only to show his lack?" The thought appalled her.

"He would fail the test. It would be terrible, but he would not fully understand it. In time he would forget." Antonio did not want to torment a simpleton, but he did want Veronica's freedom.

"He would not forget the betrayal. I cannot let him be subjected to such a thing."

Antonio thought for a moment then said, "It need not come to that. It is obvious that Luigi despises his son. I think Roberto's lack reflects on Luigi's sense of his own manhood, and he would probably withdraw his objections rather than permit a public examination, especially one doomed to failure. He is too selfish to imagine that you would not permit Roberto to be treated so."

"Perhaps. It depends on which he hates more, the scandal of a second annulment, or us for causing it. I do not want to risk this." Veronica felt the weight of forces balanced precariously. A wrong move, and they would fall to crush those beneath.

"Why are you so set against the effort?" he asked, but there was no accusation in the question, only puzzlement.

"I do not know exactly why. I only know Luigi will fight it if we try and something terrible will happen. Perhaps if we succeeded with the annulment, he would reclaim Roberto, and I cannot let them take him back. Luigi is weak and lazy, but anything within easy grasp he will torment. Push him too far and he will fix his energies on revenge. It is that revenge I fear."

"We will not talk of it for a time," Antonio said, sensing how upset she was. "When my annulment is granted we can consider it again."

"I am your wife, in heart and spirit," Veronica told him. "The law's bond is not as deep."

"No, but so it should be." He took his mother's ring from his little finger, the only one he always wore, a cabochon ruby simply set in gold. Even in the moonlight it glimmered, the red clear and pure as the heart's blood of a rose. He slipped it on her hand. "It is a covenant I would make with you."

"And I with you," she whispered, wondering if it could truly be possible.

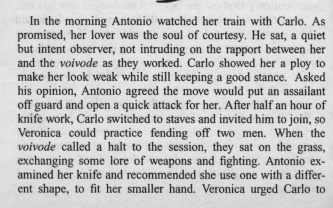

In the morning Antonio watched her train with Carlo. As promised, her lover was the soul of courtesy. He sat, a quiet but intent observer, not intruding on the rapport between her and the *voivode* as they worked. Carlo showed her a ploy to make her look weak while still keeping a good stance. Asked his opinion, Antonio agreed the move would put an assailant off guard and open a quick attack for her. After half an hour of knife work, Carlo switched to staves and invited him to join, so Veronica could practice fending off two men. When the *voivode* called a halt to the session, they sat on the grass, exchanging some lore of weapons and fighting. Antonio examined her knife and recommended she use one with a different shape, to fit her smaller hand. Veronica urged Carlo to show Antonio the knife he used for throwing, so the *voivode* demonstrated a toss or two.

"I am impressed," Antonio said, and asked to examine the knife.

Veronica lamented. "I wanted him to teach me to throw, but he says there is no point."

"A knife good for fighting is not good for throwing," Antonio acknowledged, "and it is far more difficult to do well."

"The skill makes me money at the fairs," Carlo shrugged, "but I would not want to stake my life on it. You miss, or the knife glances off the bone and your opponent is still alive while you are now weaponless." They talked awhile longer of balances between blade and hilt, then Carlo said good-bye to them and returned to the camp.

Veronica led Antonio down through the winding path to the river. Antonio watched as she slipped off her clothes and dove into the deep pool beneath the sheltering trees. Then he stripped and joined her. Surfacing beside her, he shook the water from his hair in a glittering spray. They swam, naked in the sunlight, the river a transparent green glaze flowing over their bodies. Above them, clouds light as meringue were piled high in a sky of pure azure. The gentle silence of the morning was broken only by the chirrup of birds and insects, the flutter of wind ruffled leaves, and their own soft splashes.

Finding a shallow spot by the riverbank, Antonio stood up. Hands on Veronica's waist, he lifted her above him, licking the bright droplets from her breasts. She sighed at the touch, his tongue deliciously hot after the water's cool caress. Tilting his head back, Antonio smiled at her, the darkness of his eyes warmed to lustrous mahogany, his fair skin spangled with water and light. Last night's moonlit lover, her brooding demon of storms and dreams, had transformed into a creature of trees and grass and glowing sun. Laughing, Antonio lifted her even higher above him, then slid her down the length of his body into a breathtaking kiss.

A surge of joy filled Veronica, and an eager rush of desire. Slipping from Antonio's embrace, she climbed onto the bank, then held out her hand, drawing him up to lie beside her beneath the trees. All the old pain was banished, and she felt totally free with him at last, without fear or shame. The only shadows cast upon them now were from the spreading branches of the trees overhead and the wind stirred dappling of the leaves. Eagerly, Veronica pushed Antonio onto his back in the plush grass. She straddled him, her legs encompassing his thighs. He reached up, cupping the softness of her breasts in his hands, his thumbs brushing nipples already taut and puckered. Veronica shivered, bliss threading its way along her nerves with each delicate touch. Caressing him in turn, her fingertips skimmed over the clear red of his flat nipples with their tiny bud of hardness, the pliant, silky growth of black hair that spread across his chest and down to the wilder patch at his loins. Flushed, his manhood lifted to nestle amid the springy softness of her own dark red bush. Her hands shaped the rampant length of him, her fingertips spreading the gleaming jewel of moisture at the tip over the crown and flaring ridge. Raising her hips slightly, she shifted forward to tantalize him with the moist parting of her nether lips. At the intimate touch of her sex against his own, Antonio's eyes closed and he drew in his breath in a soft hiss of pleasure.

"*Selvaggia,*" he murmured, opening his eyes to smile at her, his palms stroking the length of her enclosing thighs. "That was the first I heard of you. The wild girl who rides astride."

"I will show you how wild I am." She laughed, raising her hips higher and drawing him through the moist folds to center at the hot, open heart of her.

Antonio gasped and his body tensed in anticipation, but he made no other move. The game they had played once before, in enmity and denial, he offered her now for their shared delight. Teasing, Veronica held herself poised above him. His eyes glittered, and his chest rose and fell with his quickened breath. His sex throbbed in her hands, nudging her blindly, but Antonio waited, giving her the power of their joy without resistance, his capitulation sweet where it had been bitterly won before.

"Show me," he urged her, dared her. "Show me."

Antonio's eyes went wide as she slid onto him, sheathing his straining hardness within her own welcoming wetness. Never taking her eyes from his face, from the racing expressions of elation and hunger, Veronica raised up till they barely touched, then thrust down, recapturing the penetrating sweetness of his entry again and again. Once begun she could not stop, the need for him driving her on, reckless and unrestrained. His eyes locked with hers, Antonio moaned his response, lifting his hips to meet the wanton drive of her body. Her swift movement spun the pleasure for both of them, a dizzying whirlpool of desire that melted them from within. Their bodies fused, dissolving into one molten core. From the hot depths, Veronica felt a rush of ecstasy rising, a burning wave, sudden and bright. Saw the expectation of its glory blazing in Antonio's eyes.

"Go," he whispered. "Go and I will follow you."

Veronica plunged into that radiant wave, her whole being submerged then lifted the shattering crest of passion. The brightness released her into the gleaming sunlight, her cry of rapture one with Antonio's. Joy shimmered all around them, opalescent and glistening bright as water droplets sparkling in the air. Fulfillment pulsated within them, a glowing inner light.

They lay in the rustling shade for a tender, languid time, lazy with sunshine and happiness. Their hands and lips wandered in bemused caresses, full of wonder at the wealth of beauty shown to them in the open day. Finally, Antonio rose to his feet. Veronica watched as he stretched, the movement carving new reliefs and hollows into his torso. Arching back, his arms lifted to the sky, fingers reaching for the sun, and lowered again with an accompanying sigh of contentment. Smiling, he pulled Veronica to her feet and kissed her thoroughly. Then, scooping her up in his arms, he carried her to the river's edge, tossed her into the water, and jumped in after her with an enormous splash.

A month found them lying once more beneath the trees by their riverbank.

"Perhaps, we should just stay here," Antonio mused, drowsy and sated with love. "Build a bigger wagon and live among the Gypsies forever."

"Forever and a day," she murmured, stroking the river-

damp tendrils back from his forehead. Pretty thoughts, suitable
for a gilded afternoon, but not seriously made by either of
them. The time had gone by quickly as they basked in the
simple pleasures of their pastoral refuge, but they both knew
their time here was only an interlude, and that interlude was
drawing to a close.

There had been breaks in their idyll. At the end of July they
met Daniele in Siena, and Antonio rode back with him to
Florence. He was gone almost five days and returned moody
and withdrawn, though he did his best to disguise it. He told
her there was still no word from Rome, but she suspected it
was the ongoing conflict with his father that troubled him.
Veronica did not question him but lured him from his mood
with love and laughter. In August, they all went as planned to
the second *palio*. This time Veronica's *contrada* was one of the
ten to take part in the race. Antonio laughed when she pointed
out the banner to him—*Selva*, the forest, with its device of a
branch in leaf—and said he should have known she'd been a
selvaggia from birth. They were convinced their cheers were
the ones that urged both horse and rider across the finish line.
After the evening meal they all celebrated their win with more
wine and *panforte*, as fireworks dazzled the night sky.

"A new tradition," Stefano toasted, "to be celebrated every
year in Siena."

"Every year that Siena is not at war with Florence," Antonio suggested, with amiable sarcasm.

"Every year that Savonarola rules in Florence, at least,"
Giacomo had grumbled, refilling everyone's cups.

It had been a wonderful time, but Roberto had cried again
when he found Veronica was not coming back with him. She
promised to return soon, and he sobbed she had promised
"soon" before. And so she had. The birthday of the *voivode*
had come and gone, and now the last *palio* was run. She felt
guilty, knowing she was neglecting him, but she would make it
up when she returned. These days of happiness were precious
to her. But they could not last forever.

"We must return soon," Antonio said, perversely echoing
Veronica's thoughts.

"Yes," she agreed. Her regret was tempered with the anticipation of returning to the more complex and civilized plea-

sures that Florence had to offer, and the joy of sharing them with Antonio.

"Many things have been in abeyance these past weeks. If I am to rebuild my finances after I pay the Borgias what they will demand for the annulment, I must watch my affairs more closely."

"If it is time to return, then it is time for your reading with Mama Lucia."

Mama Lucia watched, amused, as Antonio spent some time examining the figure of the Prince of Cups. "It is disconcertingly like me," he admitted.

"Place him in the center, then, to signify yourself." She indicated the piece of black velvet she had spread out for the reading. "Now shuffle the cards, slowly."

"For how long?"

"Until they feel ready in your hands. Concentrate," Mama Lucia scolded Antonio, whose gaze was wandering to Veronica. Chastised, he turned his attention back to the *Tarocco*, giving the cards the focus they deserved as he finished shuffling them. "Good. Now cut them in three, left to right."

When he had done as she asked, Mama Lucia restacked the deck and began to deal. Convinced that the cards would repeat certain messages that had revolved around the lives of the two lovers, Mama Lucia chose a layout of her own devising that would reveal the pattern of the year ahead. Many of the cards she expected appeared, set in a new and illuminating context. Mama Lucia studied them for a moment, then began to talk to Antonio of what she saw, emphasizing the significant points of the reading. He listened with respect and interest but not with the devotion and concentration that her great-granddaughter would bring to a reading. She wanted him to remember.

"Here you see the past, the forces that are waning. Here is the Ten of Coins. You made a choice—for tradition, wealth, for ties of blood and family. But the card is reversed. Your choice has not proved to be what you expected. These things have operated for ill in your life, and you are severing yourself from them."

Antonio nodded silently, and Mama Lucia continued.

"Even more important is the passing away of the obscuring influence of the Moon. For a time, you were your own worst enemy, were you not?"

"Yes, that is true."

"The Six of Swords shows that you have overcome one major obstacle, but not the problem itself. You have left your troubles behind you for a time and traveled to more harmonious surroundings."

"So I have." Antonio smiled, his eyes seeking Veronica once more.

"That is past, or passing. The future comes to you with the blessings of the Magician. He is a powerful card of the Major Arcana. His energy manifesting within you will bring new vitality of will and imagination. You are open to life again, in ways you have not been for years. This is the beginning of a new cycle of life for you. This energy will find its way into all parts of your life, but here The Four of Wands suggests that some endeavor in the creative world would bring you great satisfaction."

"I had thought of starting a salon in Florence, a monthly gathering of the artists and writers. The idea has even more appeal now, if Veronica and Daniele would help me host it." They both looked at Veronica, who nodded her confirmation, then returned their attention to the *Tarocco*.

"There is much that is positive in the Cups and Wands, but you must take heed, there are dark forces gathering in the future. Here is the crux. The Three of Wands indicates a venture of great importance to you, one you have already taken steps to achieve. There will be attempts to thwart you, but help as well, from unexpected quarters, the Knave of Coins."

"A helpful knave? Giacomo, perhaps?"

"No, he would be the sprightly Knave of Wands. This help will come from unexpected quarters."

"And will my venture succeed, Mama Lucia?"

"If you take care, it will be successful, but that very success will bring danger in its wake. See, the dark force of the Devil is here. He has two minions, the Prince of Coins and the Queen of Swords, both reversed. A powerful man and a woman, dark of coloring—or dark of heart. She means you evil."

"Laudomia, I suppose, my brother's widow. A tiny, malignant queen. She tried to have me killed, more than once. I do not think she will try again. She has been placed where she can do no harm."

"The cards say your life is still at risk."

"I will look into it, if you say so, Mama Lucia."

"There is an ominous array of Swords—the Two, the Three, the Ace, all upside down. The swords are in the hands of your enemies. It is a time of great enmity. They will use both treachery and violence against you."

"How does the *Tarocco* say I should fight them?"

"On this side, the energy and spirit of the Wands are in your favor. The Eight shows a journey that will hasten the outcome of your venture. Beyond it is the Five. You must use your wits and your courage to defeat those who threaten you. You cannot avoid these conflicts. There is violence in the future, against you and those you love. If you are to win your prize, you must fight for it. Fail, and you will lose it, and perhaps your life as well."

Antonio's lips quirked. "So much for promises of love and riches."

"You want riches? There are other Coins here, the Three and the Eight. Later in the year, the time will be favorable for new ventures which will build your fortunes. As for love . . ." Mama Lucia regarded him indignantly ". . . I trust your eyesight is better than that."

Antonio looked over at Veronica, then reached out to touch the figures in the Lovers. "This is very beautiful. But should it not be at the end of my reading?"

"It is a card of choice, and you have chosen wisely and well. The Two of Cups follows it, bringing you the love and harmony you have been seeking. You have attained what you desire. Fight your way through the Swords and you will have it to keep."

"And this is the outcome? It appears as promising as the Lovers."

"Yes, the Three of Cups is a card of joy. It promises you great happiness in love, in marriage."

"That is the outcome I desire. And it will be worth fighting even the forces of the Devil to win," Antonio told Mama

Lucia. Then, with another quick glance, he asked, ''But what of Veronica? Does she not need a reading also?''

It was perfectly true, Veronica would want a reading. Mama Lucia was also aware that Antonio was curious to see how similarly or differently the cards would fall. She handed the *Tarocco* to Veronica. Her great-granddaughter, well aware of the same thing, took a long time shuffling the deck, first to mix the cards well, and then to attune herself to them. Satisfied, she laid the deck down and cut it. Mama Lucia stacked the *Tarocco* and dealt the same layout she had chosen for Antonio.

Mama Lucia smiled as Antonio drew in his breath, amazed at the number of cards duplicated in the new reading. There was no Moon for Veronica, of course. The waning cards were two overturned Cups, the Five and the Eight. Since they were both reversed, Veronica would be happy to be free of all the misunderstandings, the worries, anxieties, and separations they represented. The same two Cups of good fortune that Antonio had drawn were there, but as Mama Lucia had feared, the Devil had also returned, and with him the same reversed Court cards, the same treacherous and deadly Swords—with the Eight added for good measure. Some kind of isolation or imprisonment awaited her great-granddaughter. The other differences were intriguing. Justice was there, and the Hermit. How strange, or perhaps not. Summoning her concentration, Mama Lucia began the reading. Veronica nodded as the reversed Cups were dispensed with, and smiled at the affirmation of love promised in the other two. She frowned as Mama Lucia came to the next three cards.

''The Fool.'' Glancing over to Antonio, she explained, ''In my readings the Fool has always been Roberto.''

''The reversed sword shows some physical threat to him. Danger—no, it is an illness.''

Distressed, Veronica stared at the card. ''I should have returned to Florence sooner, but I felt nothing wrong.''

''Perhaps the danger will pass.''

Veronica nodded, unconvinced, then returned her attention to the *Tarocco*, ''Here is the Hermit, beside the Eight of Swords. How strange. I have never had the Hermit before.''

''In your readings,'' Mama Lucia said, ''The Fool has been Roberto. In mine, the Hermit has always been Savonarola.''

25 Turmoil

"DAUGHTER, would you pray with me?" Savonarola asked as he knelt at Roberto's bedside. He looked up at her, the heavy bones and coarse features of his face an odd contrast to the long elegant fingers clasped before him, as the frail body was a strange contrast to the implacable will that ruled it, and all of Florence as well.

"With all my heart," Veronica answered. She was aware that the question was a test as well as an appeal, but it made no difference. She would gladly pray for Roberto, lost in pain and fever. Kneeling across the bed from Savonarola, she swayed, then steadied herself. She had hardly slept in the three days since her return, but Roberto had been ill for twice that long. Pushing tiredness aside, she concentrated her strength, her hope, in her plea for Roberto's recovery. When she raised her head, Fra Girolamo still prayed quietly, fervently, for the life of the innocent before him.

Daniele told her the Friar had appeared the day before her arrival, after a convoluted series of invitations. Simona, the cook, had told Roberto that the Holy Friar's prayers would heal him—a claim Savonarola never made for himself. Roberto had begged to see him, and Simona too afraid herself to ask Daniele or approach the Friar, had told Maria of his request. Maria had gone to Savonarola. It had been a great triumph for Maria to bring her saintly scourge into the den of inequity she envisioned Daniele's household to be. Given their errand, Daniele had not turned them away, though he avoided them whenever possible. Intimidated, Stefano had disappeared for two days after Savonarola had given Daniele and him a single scathing glance, then reappeared this morning, subdued but defiant. There had been a similar glance for Antonio and herself, condemnatory if not as contemptuous. Adulterers, it said. It was unsettling because of its keen perception—Savonarola had looked at them and had known, though there had been no overt intimacy between them at that moment—and because he could perceive the power of their love and still judge it shameful.

Then there were his veiled questions, testing Veronica for heretical beliefs. Who knew what Fra Frederigo and Maria had said about her? Or Simona the cook, who had overheard her tell Daniele that the *Tarocco* had warned her Roberto was ill?

And yet, despite these glimpses of the censorious judge, the fanatic, Savonarola had not been what she expected. If he had failed to completely conceal his disapproval and suspicion, he had treated her with unfailing courtesy. He had examined her medicines with less prejudice and more knowledge than Maria's physician had done, and had praised her remedies. To Roberto, he had offered such kindness and selfless care she could not help but be grateful.

What she did not understand was how his unsparing devotion lived side by side with his condemnation. *He hates sin,* she thought, *but not the sinners. Neither does he truly love human souls, only the enthralling possibility of their redemption.* Still, if he loved more with his intellect than with his heart, he served his concept of God with purity and unfailing commitment, at times with true compassion. To her mind, he would be a better man, a better monk, if he never returned to preaching. Savonarola had found power there and succumbed to its temptation. He still believed that through that power he led others to the light, but Veronica thought he only led himself into darkness.

Watching him now, she felt a cold prickling run along her limbs. It was not the first time this sense of dread had touched her in his presence. There was an aura about him, invisible yet palpable to her, of danger. Flame danced in his eyes A scent of smoke clung to him that had no spice of incense to it. The bonfire of the vanities might have impressed itself on her memory so that it fused these images. Or might these images be the first fragments of a dire warning? Savonarola spoke of having visions himself. He, of everyone in Florence, she should have been able to talk to of her gift. And he, of all people, must not know.

Savonarola finished his prayer and raised his head. Their eyes met briefly. For the space of a heartbeat, something reverberated between them, like the ominous echo of a great iron bell sounding in her very flesh. It dizzied her so that she closed her eyes. When she opened them, Fra Girolamo was staring at her, but the feeling was gone as if it had never been. The Friar rose to his feet, and bent his gaze to Roberto. "I think tonight he will live or die."

"I am afraid you are right," she whispered. Despite all their efforts, the fever mounted higher and higher.

"Our prayers may yet be answered. But if he is to die, let us hope he wakes, that he may confess and prepare to face God."

"There is no sin on Roberto's conscience graver than a stolen *biscotti*."

Savonarola smiled faintly, then looked stern again. He spoke in the deep, carefully modulated voice she knew he had worked to attain. A voice of quiet command that he never raised, except when he mounted his pulpit. "If he does recover, Madonna Veronica, the boy's mother has told me she wishes to visit him more often."

"Maria is not Roberto's mother, Fra Girolamo, neither in flesh nor spirit. What she wishes is to impress you with her piety. I will not have her do it at Roberto's expense." She stopped abruptly. Savonarola unnerved her because he seemed to compel the truth from her, when she would have chosen more politic answers.

"You are uncharitable. She has made many efforts on his behalf."

She decided to follow her instincts and speak plainly. "When Roberto lived with her, she treated him with no more than tolerance, though it was better than the terrible abuse he had at his father's hands." She put her hatred of Luigi from her mind. There had been no trouble from him, so far. "My mother-in-law has never been turned away from our door, for she never came to see Roberto until it was an opportunity to curry your favor. When you cease to come here, so will she."

"Her reasons may not be God's reasons, yet they may lead her hence. Your anger helps neither of you."

Was she still angry? Yes, she was. Vividly, Veronica remembered the last time she had spoken with Maria, here in this room, in Savonarola's presence. "It is your fault your husband is ill," Maria had proclaimed, pointing a bony finger. "You chose to spirit a heathen fortuneteller beyond the reach of justice, and leave your defenseless husband to be tended by a heedless pervert. God has inflicted Roberto with the plague to punish you.''

The insult had infuriated Veronica for Daniele's sake, and hurt because of her own remorse for neglecting Roberto. Memory gave her that image as well. Roberto, feverish and aching, staring up at her with frightened, tear-filled eyes. "Where were you?" he had asked her. "Why didn't you come?"

"I couldn't until now," she had lied, knowing she would not have done it differently, except to return a few days earlier.

Guilt and fatigue had loosed her anger on Maria. "How can you worship a God you believe to be so spiteful?" she had demanded. Maria had hissed, pointing at her as if she had committed some foul blasphemy, challenging God's existence rather than Maria's petty vision of him. Veronica suspected it was just the sort of dramatic eruption her mother-in-law had hoped for in bringing Fra Girolamo into their midst. If Maria had hoped the Friar would act as a pious scourge, flaying Veronica on the spot, she had been disappointed. He had only studied them both in silence, keeping his judgments to himself.

As he does now . . . , Veronica thought, emerging from her memories to find him watching her intently. "You are right. My anger does not help." It would not change Maria. It did not lessen her own guilt. And if the fire she saw in Savonarola's eyes was meant for her, she had only given him fuel.

There were voices. Groggy, she listened for a moment only half comprehending.

"Let her sleep," Antonio murmured urgently. "She'll fall ill herself if she gets no rest."

"Only for a moment," Daniele said. "Roberto is asking for her. She would want to come."

"Yes." He sighed. "Yes, she would."

"Roberto," she gasped, sitting up in bed. Her own bed.

"You fell asleep kneeling at his bedside," Antonio said, sitting beside her. "I brought you in here."

"Daniele said Roberto is asking for me. Is he dying?" She

knew Antonio would not rejoice if Roberto died, but he would not grieve either, except for her pain. He wished her free, but he had done everything in his power to help her.

"No," he assured her. "The fever has broken."

Jumping out of bed, Veronica hurried to Roberto's side. Pressing her hand to his forehead, she could feel the fever waning. Opening his eyes, Roberto smiled at her wanly but with an effort at his old cheerfulness. She stroked his damp hair. "You are going to get better."

Roberto nodded, wide worshipful gaze fixed somewhere beyond her. "Yes, I will live. Savonarola saved me."

—

When Veronica emerged from the Duomo with Roberto, she found Daniele waiting for her, bundled against the December chill. He had not come alone—Benito and Bombol were cavorting in the piazza behind him, looking far warmer than her puffing, stamping cousin. Forgetting his prayers and devotions, Roberto ran forward to join them. Veronica turned to Daniele, asking, "Has Antonio returned yet?"

He shook his head. "I am as nervous as you, waiting, but there will be news of the annulment soon." Taking her arm, he led her away from the Duomo. "I wish you would not chance bringing yourself to Savonarola's notice."

"Every time Roberto hears one of the rumors that the Friar will preach again, he begs me to bring him here. You know I have not the heart to always send him with Benito instead. He did not appear today, so I have escaped his notice once again."

Daniele grumbled, "The gossip is that he will enter the pulpit again at Christmas, but who knows what it is worth."

"Eventually he will defy the Pope's command not to preach. His vision of God, his vision of himself, will demand that he speak."

Beckoning to the others, they made their way homewards along the Arno. She hoped their brisk pace would not leave them pacing the floors once they returned. "Perhaps Antonio will be there when we arrive," she said to Daniele. "It should not take him long to announce the news of the annulment. He is not planning to stay and argue with either Luigi or his father."

"But who knows how different the two confrontations will be from what he has planned," Daniele replied, echoing her own anxiety. "It is well the guards are still with him, but he should have waited until tomorrow. Why go the same morning he returns from Rome?"

"He wants it over and done with." *Only it is not over, not done with. Now it is just beginning.* Three weeks ago, the Pope had finally summoned Antonio to Rome. He left immediately, not knowing if his petition was accepted, but presuming the Pope would not have him make the journey for a refusal. On his arrival, he found that Cesare had returned from Naples, his star ascendant at last. The Borgia prince now had his father, and so the whole court of the Vatican, under his sway. He was reveling in his burgeoning power. Antonio had been certain it was Cesare who wanted him kept waiting a week for his audience, but at last it was granted and the news was good. The Pope had agreed to support Antonio's petition.

Daniele frowned. "How long till he has paper instead of promises?"

"Lucrezia is to receive hers in two weeks. Antonio was told to expect his own a month or two later, January or February at the latest."

"More waiting," he said. Then, after a moment, he adopted a cheerier tone. "Well, now that Antonio is back, shall we plan another salon?"

"Yes," she agreed. "Right before Christmas?"

"No, just after, I think. If Savonarola does defy the excommunication, I would rather listen to reactions than conjectures."

"I will send out the invitations. Let me know if there is anyone new you want to come."

"We do not have to invite people anymore. They will come on their own. We may be crushed beneath our own success."

"I am afraid you are right." The salons had been everything they hoped, exciting, amusing, challenging. Word had spread quickly, and the number of guests had doubled from one dozen to two between the first and second. Veronica had enjoyed the intimacy and intensity of the first gathering the most, but Daniele had liked the variety of people and ideas at the second. They all hoped the numbers would grow no bigger.

"Perhaps we should be less lavish with the refreshments? Dispense with the musicians?" Daniele suggested. "Antonio did not tell me if the Borgias had left him a ducat to call his own."

"I think we may continue our modest feasts and retain a lute player or two. Antonio said the payments to the Pope and Cesare were not as exorbitant as he feared. A hundred thousand ducats leaves him diminished but hardly destitute. If his ventures go well, he expects to recover what he has lost in the next two years."

"He did not pay in advance, I trust."

"Half now, and half when the petition is granted."

"A hundred thousand ducats. His family's fortune is worth ten times that, and all he need do to assure it was not seek this annulment. He could have moved to Venice until his father died, left Dorotea behind, and taken you with him."

Veronica stopped walking and turned to face him. "You could have ten times your income as well, Daniele, if you had become a silk merchant instead of a painter."

"I am sorry," he said, meeting her gaze. "Such piles of gold glitter brightly in the mind as well as the hand, but you know it is not the money concerns me. Life would have been simpler and safer if Antonio had not defied custom in this way. I am afraid the cost of this will be in blood as well as gold."

"I am frightened for him too, Daniele."

"Safer for you." Daniele said, taking hold of her hands. "I am growing to love Antonio, but there are few people dearer to me than you."

"Thank you," she whispered, wrapping her arms about her cousin and hugging him. "But do not worry for me, Daniele. The annulment changes nothing. The only one who might harm me is Luigi, and he already knows Antonio is my lover." She believed it when she said it, then wondered if it was true. Would Laudomia, or Antonio's father, strike at her out of fury at him?

"I suppose you are right," he sighed as they began walking again. "But it will be ugly for a while. When news of the annulment spreads, there will be renewed speculation about Antonio and everyone around him, just as there was when he moved into his apartments in the city instead of returning to his father's estate. It is a miracle there have been so few rumors about you and Antonio so far.''

''Not quite a miracle,'' she said wryly.

Protecting their relationship as best he was able, Antonio had come often to Daniele's, but outside those sheltering walls they had never appeared alone together. Always Daniele or Stefano accompanied them. It was Antonio and Stefano who were most often seen in the streets of Florence. A friendship was developing, and along with Antonio's discovery that Stefano had a talent for business as well as lighthearted pleasures, the possibility of a partnership as well. ''I will deal with Rome and Venice, and Stefano can develop the market in Florence—honey and furs from Russia, certain rare spices from the East. This trip I found a new source for amber, musk, and other pure essences,'' Antonio had told her, then added, ''Stefano has good sense—albeit he is too trusting.''

Veronica smiled at that memory, and then at another, ''I told him what you had said, that you overheard rumors coupling him with Stefano.''

''How did he react?''

''Outrage and amusement.''

''I am the one who should be outraged,'' Daniele said, but he smiled. ''Well, now that he is back, perhaps I can begin my next painting.''

''You could have begun with me,'' she laughed. ''I am here whenever you wish.''

''No, no, it is not the same. I must have you both together to capture the mood I want, the inner light. Later, when it is under way, it will not be so important.'' He grinned at her, ''Besides, while he was gone, I have finished four more *Tarocco* cards.''

''Four? How wonderful!'' she exclaimed. She missed Mama Lucia, and she missed working with the cards. She knew it would take Daniele many more months, but she would have her own deck at last.

Antonio was not awaiting them when they arrived back at the house. They shared a simple lunch of lentil soup, fresh baked rosemary bread and tangy, golden *limone* tarts. After the meal, Veronica tucked Roberto into bed for a nap, then went to the studio to help Daniele. Half an hour later, she heard Antonio ride into the courtyard.

"He is here," she said, hurrying to the door. "Are you coming down?"

Daniele shook his head. "No, see him alone first. I will hear it all later."

Veronica blessed his discretion, knowing how his curiosity would torment him. She went out to meet Antonio, waiting at the top of the stairs. He looked grim, but not as bad as she had feared. Silently, she led him to her room and closed the door. Antonio came into her arms, embracing her without words or kisses, only holding her. She felt his sorrow, a darkness heavier than the desired weight of his body pressing against her.

"Tell me what happened." When he said nothing, she asked again, "Tell me."

He shrugged and drew away from her, smiling lightly. "Savonarola must wonder at the sudden lightening of his spiritual burden, for I am, at the moment at least, the most hated man in Florence. As I expected, Luigi threatened to kill me."

"And your father?"

"I am once again disinherited. That too was expected," Antonio said, though a shiver ran through him. Quickly, he changed the subject. "Only Dorotea is pleased. Her pleasure at the prospect of spending the interval within the walls of a convent far outweighed her distress at the annulment. She even accepted the necessity of the physical examination, when I told her it could be performed there."

"I would not think you would be required to supply proof, given what you are paying for your freedom. No one in Italy believes Lucrezia Borgia's marriage was unconsummated."

"I am not the Pope, or even the Pope's bastard, and so cannot perjure myself with the same impunity. Alexander IV told me that I must supply documents attesting to Dorotea's virginity. I want the most impeccable sources, in case the Cardinals decide to salve their guilty consciences by attacking my petition instead of Lucrezia's."

"When will you take her to the convent?"

"I will send an escort to bring her to my apartments tonight, and we will ride tomorrow morning. I do not relish the thought of her company, but we can endure each other's presence for one evening. I still think it is the best solution. My father bears her no ill will, but it is unsuitable for her to remain there. Staying with her family is equally impossible. Luigi would find some way to use her against me.''

In the pause that followed, Veronica gathered her courage to ask, ''What did your father say to you?''

There was another pause before Antonio answered, ''He was, if possible, angrier than Luigi. He wants the forms of tradition preserved, even when they are meaningless. He had hoped, I think, that I would go back to Rome with Dorotea and trouble him no further.''

''Are those his words?'' she asked again, sensing evasion.

Veronica felt his body tense, then deliberately relax. He shrugged with forced casualness. ''He was somewhat more emotional than I expected. First he accused me of breaking my mother's trust in having this marriage annulled. He said the mark of Cain was on me, and everything I touched would come to ruin. Then he told me I was disinherited and ordered me from the estate. I left.'' He turned to her, drawing her into his arms. ''I thought I might find a warmer welcome here.''

Tentative, famished, his lips sought her own.

Dusk was fading into early winter night when Daniele rapped on their door. ''My apologies if necessary, but Antonio has visitors below—Dorotea and her brother.''

Basking in the comfort of afterglow, they disentangled from their embrace, staring at each other in dismay. ''Two minutes, Daniele,'' Veronica called out. They hurried from the bed and made themselves presentable.

''Our lives are being overrun by monks,'' Daniele muttered when they emerged, raking anxious fingers through his hair.

''I suppose Fra Frederigo wants to lecture me on my sins,'' Antonio said.

''Our very mutual sins,'' Veronica amended.

''I do not think he is here to proselytize. To me, it smells of trouble,'' Daniele told him. They went to the head of the stairs together, where Daniele gestured to Fra Frederigo and Dorotea. "I will leave you to them," Daniele said, and made his escape.

At the sight of them Dorotea burst into sobs. Veronica went to her, but she twisted in the offered embrace, flinging herself on her brother. Fra Frederigo offered little physical comfort, though he was obviously angry in her behalf. "You were not in your apartments," Frederigo accused, turning on Antonio.

"So you thought to find me here," he answered coolly. "And here I am. I gather Dorotea has informed you that I am seeking an annulment, or was it your father?"

Frederigo bristled. "Neither. I learned of it this morning from my own sources."

"Ah, yes," Antonio said. "Savonarola will have his spies within the Vatican, even as the Pope has his in Florence."

"When I heard the news, I went to speak to my father. To inform him of this slight to our honor."

"And found him already informed."

"Yes," he answered tersely. Dorotea's sobs suddenly increased in intensity.

"He threatened your sister?" Antonio asked. He knew his own life was at risk, but why would Luigi harm Dorotea?

"He threatened your wife," Fra Frederigo began, then halted, speechless with outrage. "My father said that there would be no evidence of virginity to provide you with your annulment, even if he must deflower Dorotea himself."

"Frederigo says he was drinking," Dorotea gasped out, though whether this was accusation or excuse was unclear.

Veronica opted for accusation. "Then he is all the more likely to carry out his threat."

"He was drunk and getting drunker when I left his house," Fra Frederigo said scornfully. "It allowed me time to reach your father's estate before him and bring Dorotea here. He passed us on the road, but we hid in the trees and he did not see us."

"My father . . . ." Antonio began, then stopped. His father would never permit such a despicable act. Lesser reprisals and deterrents would be accepted without question, but Giorgio di Fabiani would never suspect such baseness unless Luigi were fool enough to reveal himself. And murder? If Luigi killed Antonio, would his father feel bound by honor to seek vengeance for a death he so obviously desired? Antonio smiled bitterly at the thought of such a difficult quandary.

"You are the one who must protect Dorotea," Frederigo said. "Until the annulment is granted, her chastity is in danger. If you have no feeling for my sister, I assume you would want to protect your own interests."

"You assume correctly. Nor would I want any woman under my protection to suffer at the hands of Luigi della Montagna."

"If my father cannot stop the annulment, he will try to arrange a new marriage, but my sister wants no husband but Christ. She wishes to be a nun. She says that you yourself have perceived this to be her true vocation, and that in seeking this annulment you are but the selfless instrument of Our Lord." Frederigo paused, eyeing Antonio dubiously.

Dorotea came forward, wiping the tears from her face. Trembling, caught between hope and fear, she knelt in front of Antonio. "After you spoke to me, I saw it was all part of a great design leading me to my destiny. I will enter the convent as your wife and under your authority. If you are granted the annulment before my father can reach out to reclaim me, I will take my vows. I will remain there for the rest of my life, doing God's work."

"Well now," Antonio said, smiling his wolf's smile. "Why not?" It was the perfect solution. He did not believe Dorotea had a true vocation, but he did believe she had more chance of happiness within the cloister than as a wife and mother. And thwarting Luigi della Montagna in such a fashion would only add to Antonio's satisfaction.

They rode that afternoon, while there was still some confusion to cover their departure. As far as Antonio could tell, they had not been followed. Perhaps Luigi's threats were hollow, but Antonio had no intention of putting them to the test. They spent the night at an inn, leaving at dawn to arrive at the convent before noon. Despite her fear and fatigue, Dorotea was as happy as Antonio had ever seen her. This was her perfect romance, and she the chaste and pious heroine. The girl was glowing when he introduced her to the abbess. Antonio hoped that her pleasure would not fade too quickly.

Once Dorotea was safely installed within the convent's walls, Antonio asked after Laudomia. The abbess looked at him askance, then lowered her eyes and murmured, "Why, she is gone, my lord."

"Gone? Do you mean she is dead?" He realized he was hoping it was true, that his duel with her was finished at last, even as instinct warned him it was not.

"Why no, my lord. It is her husband who has entered the great sea," she said, offering the Florentine euphemism for death. "I assumed you would have heard."

"I am just returned from Rome."

"There were no provisions in his will to keep her here. In fact, she inherits all his wealth."

"When did she leave?"

"The *legales* came for her but a few days ago."

The convent was but a day's ride from Florence, supposing she was there. There had been no word of her return to the city. Had she gone into hiding?

"We had no choice but to give her into their care," the abbess continued, "however misguided we might feel that decision to be."

"And it was misguided?"

"Oh yes, my lord. She was quiet enough with the *legales*, and there are periods of lucidity still. But Laudomia is quite mad."

26 Detection

BIANCA lay in bed, naked, her legs open, her hand stroking lazily between them. She shivered with anticipation, delicious ripples of pleasure spinning from her teasing fingers.

Antonio appeared. He stood at the foot of the bed, smiling down at her, carnal fires flickering in his eyes.

"I was thinking of you," she told him. "Now I don't have to amuse myself."

"Ah, but that would amuse me," he said, his voice husky with desire. "Show me."

Dimitri, others, had told her how pretty it was. The lips pink as rose petals, framed in delicate white-gold floss. She opened her legs wider. She had performed thus, occasionally, for a patron, stimulating herself in the ways she knew would most excite him. Antonio she showed what she did to excite herself, her most secret rituals. He appreciated her artistry, but it was her growing arousal that roused him in turn, the flicker of desire in his eyes burning hotter, darker. As he watched, she brought herself close to the edge, whimpering for the very release she denied herself. He sat beside her on the bed, his hand sliding hard and smooth down the soft inner slope of her thigh.

"Antonio." The one word was plea, dare, and demand.

"Like this?" he asked, his fingers opening her, moving over her with the same strokes, the same rhythms she had shown him. The same, yet different, with the touch of his hand instead of her own.

"Yes," she moaned.

"Like this?" Antonio asked, dipping within her. "Tell me," he insisted, and she told everything she wanted, in every detail, and he did it exactly as she asked, his fingers moving ever more swiftly. He brought her to the edge, again and again, till she wanted to scream at him. But it was what she wanted, this torment. The exquisite suffering of his touch.

"Now," she hissed. "I want it. I want it in me."

Throbbing with anticipation, Bianca watched as Antonio undressed. He had taken a long time pleasing her, and his erection thrust from his body, red and swollen. She came to the edge of the bed, staring at him, her tongue moistening her lips.

"Does it hurt?" she asked him.

"Yes," he said, and smiled at her.

"Good," she said. "I want it to hurt you."

"I know," he answered, offering himself. The moist tender tip of him brushed her lips, the driving power of the shaft held behind. Bianca licked him slowly, slowly, until he gritted his teeth, groaning, thrusting his sex at the welcome wetness of her mouth. She pulled away from him, lying back down on the bed. He waited, his gaze scorching her, his eyes slitted with lust and sweet tantalizing fury. She opened her legs wide for him, held them apart.

"Do it slowly," she demanded, wanting the torment to last, inseparable from the ecstasy. "Make it last."

He slid between her legs, his thighs forcing hers wide apart. The tip of him touched her, but just barely. Moaning, he slid the tender head of his sex back and forth across the swollen bud of hers. A final torture he offered for her delight. Antonio paused, his gaze meeting hers. His eyes were black flame, burning with hunger. She opened to him, wider, wider, and he plunged deep within her, the pleasure of him piercing her, filling her.

"Bianca!" His cry was an agony of release. At the sound of it, Bianca began to come, Antonio's name a wail rising to her lips . . . .

And bitten back to a wordless scream. Even as she writhed in the throes of her climax, Bianca did not want Dimitri to hear her cry out that name. She collapsed back on the bed, her hand lying limp between her legs, shaken by the power of the fantasy. Her own hand, her own mind had wrought the pleasure, but only the thought of Antonio could bring such devastating intensity to her climax. It amazed Bianca how much she still craved him. She had thought time would diminish the craving and increase her power over Antonio when he returned to her. But her desire grew more insatiable. She had lived on her fantasies of Antonio all the while she was in Naples. Fantasies were sweet, but they could not content her forever. Not when their source was so frustratingly close.

Abruptly, Bianca rose and went to her dressing table, sitting naked before her mirror of Venetian glass. When she had returned to Florence two weeks ago, Antonio was still in Rome, paying off Cesare and the Pope for his annulment. The Spaniard had been right—the mystery of his bargain with Antonio had been solved as soon as she heard of the petition. Bianca was shocked and intrigued. Seeking an annulment seemed such an emotional thing to do, and she had thought of Antonio as far more calculating. It was both, she had decided. The gossip Dimitri brought back informed her that Antonio had

moved from the family estate into apartments within the walls
of Florence and lived there exclusively. There was no denying
that it was an extreme action. Obviously, the healing of the
breach between his father and himself had not survived the
death of his mother. But why bother with the scandal and
expense of an annulment? Why not leave the unwanted wife in
Florence and move back to Rome or Venice? That must be it—
for all the wealth and influence it brought him, the marriage to
Dorotea della Montagna benefited him far more if he remained
in Florence. He wished to be rid of the brat because some even
more influential liaison awaited him in another city. For now it
remained secret, but no doubt he would leave Florence as soon
as the annulment was granted.

Could this new marriage be contrived by the Borgias?
Cesare, or even Alexander, might choose such a course to bind
a man of Antonio's talents even closer to them. It would be
clever of them, but they tended to save such favor for their
fellow Spaniards. If they were involved, it would be doubly
dangerous to interfere. Bianca confessed she was tempted to
try. Antonio would be free, and courtiers had married courtesans before this . . . . It was a pleasant daydream, but a foolish one. Better to remain his mistress. He would be wealthier
by far with a rich wife, and his passion would still be hers. It
would be too difficult to live under his roof—and under his
perceptive gaze. She wanted Antonio, but she wanted her clandestine life as well. Bianca gazed into the mirror, smiling.
Love and death, she would have them both at her command.

There was a discreet knock at the door, and then Dimitri
entered. Bianca was sure he had been listening. He had always
had a scent for sex, and considered his silent voyeurism as
much his right as the pleasures she requested of him. There
had been little enough of that lately. She would have to be
more attentive to him, she knew, but it was difficult. Even his
talented mouth did not fully satisfy her any longer. Aside from
her own fantasies of Antonio, her victims were her best release. The secret knowledge heightened her pleasure. But she
could not indulge that pleasure indiscriminately.

Dimitri set the silver tray on the table beside her. Today,
along with the pot of fragrant *tisane*, was a plate laded with
flaky apricot and almond pastries, and a bowl of winter pears

poached in spiced red wine and drizzled with fresh thick cream. "That is too much rich food for breakfast," she chided him.

"You are too thin," he complained in turn.

"It suits me," she answered, contemplating the more pronounced flare of her cheek and collar bones. Dimitri preferred her too plump.

He pursed his lips in disapproval but said no more. He poured a cup of *tisane* and she sipped it, nibbling at one of the pastries. "There have been two new callers this morning."

"I told you, I am taking no new patrons yet," she snapped. Considering how he hated her lovers, Dimitri had been promoting them far too assiduously.

"You need to know who has approached you, for when you do decide to resume your profession."

"I am practicing my profession. Making them wait will only increase their rivalry and anticipation." It was true enough, but they both knew the greater truth. She was waiting for Antonio to call, and he had not, though he had been back in Florence for a week. "I will make some social appearances."

If she needed jealousy to spur Antonio, then she would take a patron. At the moment the thought of such mercenary fumblings only aggravated her. She did not need a new lover, she needed an assassination to focus her concentration, alleviate her restlessness. Cesare had given her no further instructions except to learn what she could of Savonarola. A well-paid Judas within the Friar's own flock had informed Cesare that Savonarola was contemplating defying the excommunication and preaching once more.

Observing Savonarola was a pointless assignment, but Bianca had been glad to take it. Luckily, Cesare had made good use of her in Naples. There had indeed been someone he wanted her to seduce, subvert, and then dispatch. The man had proved fiendishly possessive, and Bianca had lived with him for the months she was in Naples, passing her messages to Cesare at social functions. It had been an excellent excuse to avoid Cesare's bed. She had been spared the hazard of refusing him after he contracted the pox. The *mal francese* had left him scarred, and if she was any judge, of far more uncertain temper. Her beauty was her life, she would not risk it to keep his favor. But she had managed to avoid the dreaded confrontation. The illness and his own political and sexual maneuvering had kept him occupied. They had not had occasion to celebrate the victim's death. After Juan's brazen murder, Cesare had not wanted to be in Naples when she carried out the assassination, so she had waited until he departed for Rome. She and Dimitri had done well that night. Both the killing and the sex afterwards had pleased her eunuch.

That work accomplished, she was free to return to Florence . . . and Antonio. A week now, and still no word. She knew there was no rival courtesan installed in Antonio's new residence, nor did he seem to have a current favorite in the city. The rumor she had heard linking him with his younger cousin, Stefano Simonetta, she had dismissed as absurd. Despite the incident at Daniele's studio, Bianca was convinced Antonio's passion was for women. And there was no woman to equal her in Florence. She would wait a week more for him to come to her. If he did not, she must devise a way to meet him. Supposedly he had arranged the salons being held at Daniele Danti's studio. She could easily secure an invitation to one of those. Already they were gaining a certain renown, and nothing would be more natural than an appearance by the most fabled courtesan in the city. She would be certain to appear accompanied by a suitably impressive rival, with her beauty most lavishly displayed. Her new white velvet, she thought, dressed with pearls and diamonds.

When her meeting with Antonio finally came two days later, it was by accident at a small, exclusive jewelry shop on the Ponte Vecchio. The encounter was not what Bianca had expected. Though she had imagined a hundred ways it might occur, she had never imagined that she would be disconcerted. Entering as another woman left the shop, she had but the briefest moment to collect herself. Bianca drew a deep, uncertain breath, and waited for him to notice her. Vivid as her memory of Antonio was, she had not thought to be so struck by his insolent beauty. Despite the rumors, she had not expected to find him with his cousin, their heads, dark and fair, bent together over a piece of jewelry. Bianca cast a glance at that and saw it was a heavy brooch of gold and gems, a design to be worn by a man, not a woman.

He was as she remembered, and yet different. A subtle tension that she had thought an inseparable part of him was simply no longer there. He looked younger, the harder edges of his face softened. Was it the pretty Stefano who brought out this new ease in him? His cousin said something to him and Antonio laughed, lightly, without the cutting edge that had characterized his humor. She sensed no passion between them, only an air of casual intimacy. But the change in Antonio was so obvious that Bianca had to wonder if the rumors were true. Dread hollowed the core of her, like a foul dungeon within the perfect fortress of her facade. If the rumors were true, was there any hope? No woman could equal her, of that she was certain. But if Antonio had hidden the strength of this penchant from her, even from himself, and had only now discovered its power, that would explain why he had not returned. Would never return.

The perceptions, her reactions, encompassed no more than a moment, and then Antonio raised his head, aware of her regard. In that fraction of a second his expression shifted. The smile remained, but it was now a social smile. He straightened, and she could see the fluid ease of his body transmute to a more heedful posture.

"Madonna," he said, inclining his head graciously, presenting a surface smooth and cool as marble.

"Antonio," she murmured, too faintly. No, this was not what she had imagined. There was no widening of his eyes as the flame of hunger ignited within them, no sudden tension as desire permeated his body. He was guarded, but not from suppressed passion, nor from fear of any inner pain. This was no more than a slightly awkward social encounter. He had never left her thoughts, but he had forgotten her until she appeared before him. Anger swept her and she seized it. She had never allowed herself to lose her temper, except for effect. But anger was better than the queasy weakness of fear.

"You are looking as exquisite as always, Madonna," Antonio began, offering her the prosaic compliments that courtesy demanded. "Your gown . . . ."

"Not exquisite enough, it seems," she interrupted, hearing

the acid sting of malice in her voice. "I see now that a woman, however beautiful, will lack what satisfies you. You can love only your own image and so must fiddle with your own kind."

Antonio stared at her with simple astonishment. "You think I . . . ." he began, then again. "*You* think that I . . . ."

He burst out laughing with such genuine amusement that Bianca was convinced she must be wrong. She did not like being made a fool of. Her eyes narrowed. "Was it only the once then, when you dallied with that little catamite that Daniele Danti keeps, while I waited on your pleasure in the garden?"

He stopped laughing abruptly, staring at her. The first frown of confusion faded quickly, and then he slowly flushed. Oh, it was lovely to see him disconcerted at last.

"You mistake me," he said coldly. "But it is not something I care to discuss. I bid you farewell, Madonna."

He turned and left, Stefano close behind him. Bianca could not believe she had allowed it to happen. She wanted to believe he would come back, but she knew he would not. He had been too cold, too polished. She had left no wound in his heart. Nor even in his manhood. Bianca looked over at the jeweler, agog with curiosity. Catching her gaze, he took a step back in alarm. Smiling, Bianca approached him, and he retreated even further. She pointed to the brooch, a lavish swirl of gold and rubies displayed on a pillow of black velvet. "What a handsome piece," she commented, her voice crusted with sugar now. "Tell me, which of the gentlemen was interested in purchasing it?"

"Signore Simonetta, Madonna, the fair-haired gentleman. It was to be a birthday gift for his father." He frowned then, realizing he had lost a most lucrative sale. "Can I show you something, Madonna? Pearls, perhaps?"

"No," Bianca said, and left the shop. The brooch was not a love gift then. That proved nothing, but he had not responded to her taunt about Stefano. It was only the mention of Daniele's model. If Antonio would not tell her the truth of it, perhaps the catamite could.

A pretty young man answered her knock. His eyes were dark and liquid, his hair a mass of tousled curls, his lips full and tender. A succulent morsel, but insufficient to cause such a stir in Antonio, surely? Bianca lowered the hood of the simple cloak she had worn and he gaped at her, the tip of his tongue moistening his full lips. Whatever his proclivities, they included her sex.

"Cecco?" Bianca asked.

She had not remembered the model's name but, asking among her artist acquaintances, she had found that Daniele tended to use a particular one repeatedly. The first man she visited was obviously not the one she sought. He was far too ordinary and, although he had worked for Daniele on the painting she remembered, it was not until after Savonarola's bonfire. He had, however, known the name and dwelling place of his predecessor.

"Yes, I'm Cecco," the boy gulped, but said nothing more.

Was this the right one? Her memory, vague as it was, had conjured an impression of a fineness that this boy lacked, for all his attractiveness. And something else was wrong. His height? Or perhaps it was just that the beard was gone now. Nonetheless, she proceeded on a note of familiarity, "Don't you remember me? I am . . . ."

"I know who you are, Madonna Bianca. You're very famous. But I've never met you. How could I forget?"

"At Daniele Danti's," she reminded him. "Can't you ask me inside?"

He cast a desperate glance behind him, bit his lip, then opened the door. Bianca thought his poverty embarrassed him, but he said, "My mother is buying bread and oil, Madonna. I do not know how much longer she will be gone. She will be very upset if she finds you here. She worships Savonarola." This last he confided in a whisper, like a secret sin.

"I see," Bianca murmured sympathetically. "Has she made it difficult for you and Daniele?"

He lowered his head, blushing. "I have not seen him in months."

"You had a quarrel, over another man, perhaps?" A courtesan could ask outrageous questions as if they were ordinary.

Cecco blushed wildly. "No, no, that is all over for me,

Madonna. I liked Daniele, but I am not like that, not anymore.''

Was it just the one time, or had Antonio told him to keep
their relationship secret since then? Bianca did not think so.
She doubted this boy could keep a secret. She slipped off her
plain cloak to reveal her provocative gown, letting her beauty
work its magic on him. It had the desired effect. ''No?'' she
asked softly.

''No!'' he exclaimed with a burst of masculine pride. ''My
mother says I should not go with women either, but that is too
much. I have given up one pleasure for her, but I will not give
up everything.'' Cecco eyed her shyly, aquiver now with hopeless lust. ''Why did you think you knew me, Madonna?''

''You did not model for a large painting of *The Adoration*
that Daniele did last February? I saw it right before the bonfire
of the vanities, and I thought you must be the model. You had a
beard then and posed as a monk holding a cross.''

Cecco shook his head. ''It's true I posed for that painting, as
a monk even, but I've never had a beard.''

And if he had, it would be curly. The young monk she
remembered had worn a simple pointed beard. It was not this
boy who had lured Antonio away. ''Do you know who that
model could be?''

''I did not go back to pose for Daniele, but he came here
once to bring me the money he had promised—and to see me.
That was right before the bonfire of the vanities, I remember. It
was the last time I saw him.'' Cecco hung his head, and nibbled at his lower lip again. ''I told him I was sorry I hadn't
ever returned. He told me it was not a problem, Madonna
Veronica had taken my place. I remember he said she put on
the monk's habit. Daniele had false beards in his trunk, and
maybe she wore that too. She liked to put on costumes.''

''Veronica,'' Bianca whispered. Not a boy, but a young
woman disguised? A young woman whose name Antonio
wanted to protect? If this was the truth, he would have to
protect far more than her name.

''Madonna?'' Cecco's voice was suddenly apprehensive.

She gave him a blinding smile, and he smiled back. She
wondered if she should kill him, but decided against it. She did
not want to alert Daniele's household in any way. From what

he had said, Cecco would not seek out Daniele to inform him of the visit—though he was likely to babble about it to his friends. His mother might also appear most inconveniently. Letting him live was the lesser risk, if not the more appealing one. "It's all a silly misunderstanding," she told him, and slipped him some silver. It was not what he wanted, but better than he might have received at her hand.

———

"This is marvelous, Daniele," Bianca enthused, sweeping into the hallway, ablaze now with candles. "I had not imagined so many people were attending the salons."

"Too marvelous, I fear. They have grown alarmingly since we began. Conversation is better with fewer people. We did not want the formality of a dinner party, but now we have the informality of uninvited guests."

"Indeed?" she queried, linking arms with her companion of the evening.

Daniele gave her a quick uneasy glance at that. Bianca smiled at him. She knew he had not meant her specifically, just as she knew he wished she had not appeared at his doorstep. But she was officially escorted. Rather than a patron who would demand too much attention, Bianca had graciously offered the favor of her company to one of Daniele's fellow artists, who had eagerly accepted the privilege. Saving face, Daniele nodded as they passed two pedants lost in passionate argument. "They were not invited, but fortunately they have found each other."

"Your translation is inaccurate," Bianca heard one declaim.

The other puffed himself up to the greater insult; "Your style is graceless."

People were gathered in small groups throughout the house. As they walked through the crowd, Bianca caught snatches of conversation, listening all the while for the husky cadences of Antonio's voice amidst the others.

"They say Savonarola will preach at Candlemas."

"Rumor said the same at Christmas, but he did not return to the pulpit then."

"At Christmas he celebrated Mass and gave communion."

"It is his sermons against the Pope which brought on the

excommunication. Savonarola would be mad to defy that prohibition."

"Would he? At Epiphany, the Signoria knelt and kissed his hand. Alexander may be Pope in Rome, but Savonarola is Pope in Florence."

Politics gave way to art, as a young man in the next group said earnestly, "Donatello was the first man in centuries to sculpt a free-standing nude. How can this Michelangelo equal such genius?"

Daniele led them past the interior staircase, towards a table spread with wine, fruit and pastries. "There are refreshments upstairs as well, aren't there?" her escort asked, and Daniele nodded. "Then let us go up to the studio. That is where the best conversation was last time."

At the foot of the stairs, they passed between the arts of war and medicine. *"Horrendis machina bombis!"* came an exclamation from the right. "I was at the battle, and I tell you that artillery is a weapon invented by demons, not men." On the left, another voice rose; "But it has been proven, I tell you, by Vesalius of Padua. There is no bone in the heart!"

The open door to the studio led them past more political gossip. "Lucrezia's divorce is final. A magnificent accomplishment. She paraded herself before the Cardinals and declared herself to be *virgo intacta,* when the word is that she is six months pregnant by some unknown lover."

"She is the Pope's daughter. Perhaps he has asked God for a miracle and it is the truth she tells." There was much smug laughter over that. The mention of the Borgia annulment was like a goad, and Bianca had to restrain the impulse to search for Antonio. She forced her attention back to her host.

"Oil is the medium of the future," Daniele was saying to her companion. "True, there is some work for which I still prefer tempera, but the texture, the luster of oils I love."

"To me, tempera is more refined, and I shall continue to work in it. In fact, I have a new subject." He paused dramatically.

"Yes?" Daniele prompted.

"You had your chance, Daniele. Bianca said you had spoken of painting her as Venus, but done nothing about it. So I have seized on the project myself."

"I wish you luck. I did consider it once. Bianca would be a perfect Venus, of course." Politely, Daniele paused to acknowledge her once more. "Alas, as chance would have it, other work has demanded my attention."

"I loved the concept you described to me last week. I think the finished work will be greater than *The Judgment of Paris*. Especially if Fabiani will pose for it."

"Antonio has agreed to pose? What is this fabulous painting you've chosen to do next, Daniele?" Bianca asked archly. "Mars, I believe, was the role you saw him in, but for that you wanted Venus."

"No, Antonio is to be Pluto," Daniele said tersely, obviously reluctant to talk of the painting.

Her escort, perhaps thinking Daniele too modest or grasping for some vicarious credit, continued to expound; "It is the idea that is brilliant—Pluto, lord of the Underworld, transfigured by love. A figure of darkness radiating light. *Pluto and Persephone* is to be the next painting."

"And who is to pose for Persephone?" Bianca asked, knowing what the answer must be.

"Veronica, of course," her escort said. "Who else?"

Who else indeed? Bianca thought, watching Daniele pluck nervously at his hair. He knew why she was curious and he was trying to protect his little bitch of a cousin. She smiled at him, then turned to her companion. "I have never met Veronica, you know. Will she be as perfect a Persephone as Antonio will be Pluto?"

"You've never met her? She is right over there, talking to Machiavelli in the corner. Ah marvelous, she is wearing her Persephone costume."

Not knowing Machiavelli either, Bianca simply looked where he pointed. She could not see her quarry at first. A severe but animated man, who must be Machiavelli, and Daniele's easel both conspired to block her view. "Antonio agrees with me," the man was saying. "If Cesare wishes a kingdom in Italy, he must carve it now, while the Pope reigns, for Cesare will not inherit the throne on which his father sits."

Then Machiavelli moved, and a young woman came into sight. Fighting the first blinding surge of jealousy, Bianca forced herself to study Veronica with the practiced calculation

of a courtesan. The girl was not the exquisite, classic beauty
she had expected, but she was interesting. Her hair was totally
unfashionable. Blond was the correct color, of course. Courtesans and princesses alike spent hours perfecting their herbal
treatments and spreading their hair to bleach in the sun. But
perhaps Veronica would start a new fashion in Florence. However correct blond might be, it would not have suited her as
well as the dark red mass tumbling about her face, setting off
the translucent porcelain skin. It was a striking face, Bianca
admitted, the brows, the features, strongly marked and yet refined—large wide-set eyes, a full sensual mouth. She was tall
with a loose-limbed grace of gesture that probably carried into
movement as well. Falling in gentle folds of muted mauve silk,
the Grecian costume set off a slender figure.

"Perfect," Bianca's companion enthused. "Innocence and
sensuality combined."

Just then, Veronica lifted her head and smiled. It was smile
given only to a lover, radiant, dazzling. Seeing it, Bianca perceived her beauty. Knowing who the smile was for, she turned
and saw Antonio on the other side of the room—saw him
return the smile in all its sudden joyous intensity.

Standing motionless, her body gowned in white velvet encrusted with crystals, her throat bejeweled with pearls and diamonds, Bianca might as well have been buried in a snowbank,
frozen, immobile. Seeing Antonio in love, Bianca knew now
that however potent bedding her might have been for him, he
had felt nothing for her but lust. Then a shiver ran through her,
releasing her.

"Pluto, Lord of the Underworld," she murmured soundlessly. "Yes, I will see you there yet, I promise you. You and
your Persephone."

27 The Attack

 THERE had been no forewarning, not even a vague creeping sense of unease. Antonio had told her he would be late. He had business to attend to, accounts to review, business correspondence to encode for delivery to Venice and Rome. Since she had been waiting for his knock, Veronica was at the door ahead of Benito. She opened it to reveal Antonio leaning against the door, drenched in blood. She cried out, reaching to help him.

"It's not mine," he said quickly. "At least, not all of it." His voice grated with pain, but he shook his head at her offered support. Studying her face, he said, "The cuts are simple enough. There is no need of a surgeon, if you are willing to treat them."

"Of course I can," she answered. She had helped treat enough wounds in the convent hospital. But now it was Antonio's flesh the blade had cut . . . . Benito appeared in the hallway and looked to her for orders. The necessity for action subdued the shock of fright. Grateful for the task, Veronica sent Benito for the hot water, bandages, and medicines she required. Then she turned back to Antonio. "There is a fire in my room, or I can treat you here," she said, carefully not asking if he was able to walk that far.

"Upstairs," he said.

"Tell me what happened?" she asked as they walked up the interior stairway. She did not want to go through Roberto's room to reach her own, so she took him along the balcony.

"We were attacked near here, my guards and I. They are both dead. Two of the men who attacked us are dead as well. The third ran off." He hesitated. "I did not want to disturb you, but it seemed best not to try to make my way back to my apartments alone."

"I should have been more disturbed if you had not appeared tonight."

"I know, but a neat bandage is easier to face than ripped flesh," he said.

"I should have demanded to see anyone else's handiwork, so it is best you let me do it."

He gave her a rueful smile. "At least you do not scold me, as Giacomo would."

Pausing outside her door, Veronica asked, "Shall I send Benito to fetch a watchman?"

"Unless I file a complaint, they will let it pass for a street brawl between the guards. And I have no intention of calling any more notice to myself."

Inside her room, Veronica drew a bench in front of the warmth of the fire. The metallic reek of blood pervaded the air as she helped Antonio free himself from the saturated doublet and shirt. She cast them aside and examined the wounds carefully. There was a vivid red slash across his chest, cruel but shallow, and a second deeper cut to the flesh of his arm that posed more danger of damage. "Can you move your fingers?" she asked.

"Yes," he said, drawing them in one by one to form a fist.

"Then infection is what we must fight." Benito knocked, and she had him set the tray he carried on a table nearby. She told him she needed no further help and he withdrew. Veronica set about treating Antonio's injuries, beginning with the arm. He braced his body slightly for the new pain but made no sound as she cleaned, stitched, and salved the wound, then bound it with clean strips of bleached linen. Finished with her first task, Veronica paused. Around her feet, the floor was a welter of bloodstained cloth. The second wound waited to be treated, a vicious red line etched between his nipples. The mark of a sword tip deflected from his heart.

A surge of fear swept through her veins. *I should have known. Why did I not know he was in danger?* After she had rescued Mama Lucia, she had hoped her visions would bring warnings she could act on. But it was the *Tarocco* that had told her of Roberto's illness, and now this attack on Antonio had come with no premonition. Her gift had always been erratic, but had she lost it entirely? Wishing it gone for so long, why did she now feel so bereft, so helpless without it? Veronica remembered the horrifying vision of her parents' death, but she was no longer sure that ignorance was preferable to a warning that came too late. Both were intolerable. Her hands began to quiver. Thrusting everything from her mind but the task before her, she steadied herself and began again, bathing and treating the wound, then binding the linen about Antonio's chest.

Only when she was finished did Veronica become aware of Antonio's tension, the stillness of his body counterpointed by his quickened breathing. It was not the tension of withheld pain, not any longer. Beside them, the fire crackled and leaped, staining his skin in colors of flame and blood and molten metal. Looking into his eyes, she saw darker fires smoldering there. *It is like this with me sometimes,* he had told her, *when death comes too close.*

The front of her robe was open. Antonio's hand slid beneath it to caress her belly, the thin silk of her shift the only barrier between their skin. His fingers slid down to cup the soft triangle beneath, the heat of his hand pressing against the heat of her sex. The strength of sinew and bone was restrained, but all the intensity of his need was conveyed in that one questioning touch.

Desire desperate as her hidden fear shuddered through Veronica. She longed to plummet into his darkness. The blazing oblivion he offered would consume her own fears. Involuntarily, she closed her eyes as another shudder ran through her, cold then hot. Misunderstanding, Antonio withdrew his hand, but she reached out and caught it with both her own, holding it to her even as the shudders racked her again.

"You are shaking," he said, his voice low. "Are you afraid?"

Fierce as his hunger was, Veronica saw he would curb it to match the gentleness she might need from him. But it was not gentleness she needed now. She shook her head, gasping, half sobbing. "Not of you. Never of you."

He started to speak, but Veronica lifted a hand to his lips to silence him. Jerking away abruptly, she unfastened her robe and shrugged it off. Antonio watched, unmoving, as she loosened the ribbons of her shift with trembling fingers, sliding it over her shoulders to join the robe on the floor. She shivered as the coolness of the air prickled her arms, puckered her nipples, even as the warmth of the fire licked up her legs with invisible flickering tongues.

Rising, Antonio stripped off *braghetta* and hose to stand naked in front of her. The haunted angles and hollows of his face, the planes and muscled curves of his body, were sculpted in shadow and flame. The linen bandage was stark white against the fine black hair of his chest, the crimson light flickering across it like a visible heartbeat. His sex rose as she watched, flushed and straining with need.

Stepping forward, Antonio pulled her to him, her breasts crushed against the freshly bound sword cut. His eyes narrowed and he drew in his breath sharply, pain and arousal mingled in the sound. The grip of his hands tightened, his erection probing blindly at her hip. She reached between their bodies, drawing him against the softness of her belly.

"Yes." Harsh with passion, the whisper commanded her. "Touch me. Harder . . . harder."

Her fingers closed tight around him, feeling the life of him pulse and leap at her touch. She stroked upward, her hand as demanding as his words had been. Antonio moaned, a harsh, helpless sound. The desperation in it echoed within her, compelling her on. Veronica slid to her knees, pressing her face to the curling thatch at his loins, breathing in the musk of him, heady as incense. The scent of arousal mixed with the tang of sweat the deadly struggle had left on his skin. Veronica licked at his thigh, tasting the sharp salts of excitement and fear. Antonio's hands twined in her hair, guiding her closer. She turned, opening her lips to the thrusting shaft. Antonio moaned, bracing against the onslaught of pleasure as she sucked, her mouth filled with the surging power of him.

She would have ended it that way, drinking bittersweet ecstasy from his body, but Antonio pulled away from her, groaning at the anguish of separation. Veronica looked up at him. The darkness of his eyes devoured her. She felt the answering darkness within her. Fear had hollowed a void that would be filled only when she felt the pulse of his life inside her. Pulling him down with her, Veronica lay back on the floor, opening her legs to receive him. Antonio knelt between her thighs and paused, motionless. Control carved his face like a mask, only his eyes black and burning within it. Her hunger had usurped his own, and Veronica could feel him reining the force of his craving to serve her need. Slowly, too slowly, he came to her. Veronica sobbed as she felt the first touch of him against her, like satin cased steel. He moaned in response as the blunt head of his sex parted her lips, gliding through the welcoming wetness to poise at the entrance to her body. She was ready, throbbing with desire. "Yes," she begged him. "Yes, now. Hurry. Hurry."

Antonio thrust into her abruptly, drew out and thrust again. He whispered her name over and over, each murmur a demand as he plunged into her. Opened to him utterly, Veronica sobbed wordlessly in answer. The darkness was inseparable from the passion now, her fear inseparable from her love. Desire devastated her, but the only escape was in more. "Harder," the demand, the frantic plea was hers now. "Harder. Deeper."

With a wild cry, Antonio drove into her, the last restraint discarded. It was what Veronica needed, to feel him as out of control as herself. "There," she gasped as he touched the depths of her. "There. Ah yes, there." Beyond words then, she let his passion engulf her, as hers engulfed him, the shattering pleasure annihilating all fear.

They lay by the fire, curled within the quilt Antonio had tugged from the bed. He cradled her against him, his lips gently grazing over her neck, her ear. "*Selvaggia*," he whispered, neither taunting nor teasing now. The word was a murmur soft as he would use to comfort a weeping child, a wounded bird.

"I should have been able to protect you," she said, knowing it was absurd as soon as she spoke. There was no protection, for either of them. Only life, and death. And love. Antonio laughed softly, sadly, and drew her closer.

"I love you," she said.

"Yes, I love you too."

Comforted, Veronica drifted for a while on the edge of sleep. But she felt no relaxation in Antonio. She wondered if the pressure of her body was causing him pain, and disengaged herself to lie beside him. He turned away from her then, facing the door. For a long time, she lay watching him in the glimmering firelight. His breathing was slow and even, but she knew he was feigning sleep. The demands of passion were answered for both of them, the raw assertion of life in the face of death. But an aura of darkness lingered like smoke about Antonio, its presence subtle and pervasive.

"You cannot sleep," she said to his back.

Antonio tensed, then turned over, drawing her into his arms again. But she did not need comfort now, only honesty.

"What is wrong?"

"Nothing."

"You do not think the attack was robbery," she said at last.

"No" was the only syllable he would give her.

"Who do you think sent them?"

"There are too many suspects and too many motives—honor, wealth, vengeance."

That told her no more than she already knew. It was becoming the pattern between them. Sexually, he gave himself completely. And emotionally . . . as long as no words were necessary. When they were, he withdrew into himself. Veronica wanted his trust as a gift, and so she had never challenged him. But it was not a question of trust any longer. Antonio did trust her. It was pain that he held within himself, and fear, letting them gnaw at him.

"Have you forgotten Mama Lucia's warning?"

He turned to look at her, a faint spark glittering in the bottomless depths of his eyes. "In the *Tarocco* reading? Which one? As I remember, there were far too many." His voice played at lightness, but he waited intently for what she had to say.

"Not when she read the cards, but the night you first met her. She told you then that you cannot keep your darkness from me, only your light."

After a moment's silence, he answered, "I remember. I promised her that your happiness was my one desire. Are you unhappy, my love?"

"At your unhappiness, yes. Share it with me, and it will be lessened for both of us."

"Or doubled, burdening two?" he said sharply. Then he sighed, and rolling onto his back, he began to converse with the ceiling. "There are many who would be pleased to see me dead, but fewer who would pay to see it done. At least I no longer suspect Stefano. I doubt my complacent uncle would go so far to increase his son's fortunes, but I have not totally dismissed the possibility. He is at the bottom of the list, along with assorted old friends of Alessandro who would have acted before now if the urge for revenge still stirred in them. Then there is Bianca. She has not forgiven me the wound to her pride, and the pain is still fresh for her. Encountering her at the jeweler's and then at the salon was unsettling. Still, it is doubtful she would go as far as hiring guards to dispense of me, though she will certainly join in the celebration if someone else accomplishes my demise.''

"So those are the unlikely possibilities. Who is next on the list?"

"Two nights ago, I thought I saw someone following me. It was only a glimpse, but it adds a somewhat unnerving suspect —Cesare Borgia. It was not enough to tell for certain, especially in a cloaked figure, but the man reminded me of Juan Borgia's mysterious friend and possible assassin. Now that Cesare has taken my money for the annulment, perhaps he finds it convenient to take my life as well.''

"Do you really think so?"

Antonio shrugged. ''No. He was friendly enough in Rome. I was not encouraging the relationship, but neither did I antagonize him. The edge has gone from my anger. I do not think we are actively enemies. I hope not, for I have little recourse if the Borgias want me dead.''

"And who is left?"

"I have had no luck in tracing Laudomia. She may have sent them from wherever she is hiding.''

"But you think not? Why?" she asked.

"There were only three of them, well placed but not expert. I would have expected a battalion of professionals from Laudomia at this stage. But the abbess said she was mad, so who knows what she will do. Still, the Queen of Spades is highly suspect,'' he said, casting her a quick glance before surveying the ceiling once more. When he spoke again, his voice had hardened. ''And then there is the Prince of Coins.''

"Luigi.'' The most obvious choice, and the man Veronica believed was behind the attack.

"Probably," he said tersely, but a shudder ran through him. Some unease in Antonio's voice that warned her this was not all. There was something else, someone else. And Veronica knew then who it must be.

"Say his name." It would be worse locked away.

"My father," he said flatly. "He hates me. He has hated me since Alessandro's death. I suspect he is the one who hired the guards."

"There is much bitterness between you, but why do you think he would go so far as to order your murder? Because he refused to pay your ransom?"

"Is that not enough? I almost died then, rotting away in that foul cell."

"No." She shook her head. The story of that trial he had already given her. There was something else hidden within him.

"Because I know what he is capable of," Antonio said finally. "Because it was he who murdered Beatrice."

There, at last, was the heart of it. "How do you know?"

"My mother told me . . . the night she died."

When he had come to her, full of torment and secrets.

"I hated him then. But hating him is not enough to free me." The words seemed not to be spoken but bled. Veronica ached for him.

"You hoped your hatred would release you from your love, but it will not. If he cannot let go of his hatred, you can let go of yours."

"And leave only love? Not the most useful emotion to have for a man who means to kill me."

"No. Your father did not hire the guards," Veronica said, with certainty so absolute that Antonio turned to her. "You are forgetting the *Tarocco*. Reversed, the Prince of Coins is the weakest of the four. From what you have told me of your father, I would make him Prince of Swords. You were promised unexpected aid from the Knave of Coins—that was Frederigo, bringing you Dorotea. Luigi is the Prince of Coins. It is he who is behind all this."

"If you say so." His smile was faintly mocking, but Veronica did not care. That he could smile meant his heart was eased.

Wrapping his arms about her, Antonio held her to him, simple comfort for a time. After a while he began to kiss her, softness mingled with a growing urgency. Veronica felt herself stir to his kisses, but she wondered if it was really physical intimacy he needed. Looking in his eyes, she saw the need to share the solace she had given him, and the rebirth of hope.

If the fierceness had been burned away in their first desperate mating, the intensity of the new intimacy was even greater, summoning a tenderness more devastating than their frenzied violence. Soft lips murmured love between moist, tantalizing kisses. Questing fingertips traveled each other's bodies, evoking delicate ecstasies. Beyond surrender, Veronica opened herself to Antonio, and he came into her gently, slowly, making his entry a pleasure too exquisite to be borne. He held nothing back, the lingering sorrow giving resonance to the joy. Trembling in his arms, Veronica sobbed with the sweet grieving, giving pleasure of him.

28 *Schemes*

"LUIGI della Montagna is downstairs," Dimitri announced from the doorway.

Preparing for bed, Bianca paused. She had met him only a few times and had not thought him interested in her, except in the general way of male curiosity. From what she had heard, his taste ran to wine-soaked serving wenches. Now he had appeared at her door, late at night and unannounced. He was one of the wealthiest men in Florence, reason enough to accept his suit—if she had intended to take a new patron, and if he had presented himself courteously. She had not, nor had he.

Rude as Luigi's arrival was, there was no question of sending him away. Antonio was married to his daughter, and some useful information might be had from the man. Useful enough to make bedding him worthwhile, if she must. Bianca grimaced with distaste. Although he retained the last vestiges of a dissipated handsomeness, he was crude and overbearing, a despoiler. He might have sought her out tonight for the pleasure of purchasing the brutal debauch of a woman his son-in-law had possessed. Still, desiring no one but Antonio, Bianca found it easier to contemplate taking a man she despised, rather than one she might have found attractive in the past. If nothing else, Luigi's seed could fuel her hatred.

Dressing sedately in a *camorra* of deep blue velvet trimmed with ermine, she fastened the sapphire necklace Cesare had given her about her throat and added the matching earrings. They were still her most expensive jewels. If Luigi della Montagna was to have her, he would have her dear.

Downstairs, he was waiting on a chair in the *salotto*. His vermilion silks were garish amid her muted tones of gray and silver, ivory and gold. The insolence of his greeting was overt, cooling her welcome to him even more. Still, since she had chosen to make her appearance, the courtesies must be observed. Bianca sat on the couch and poured the wine that Dimitri had set out on the table into the goblets. The third best red, she noted. Even that was probably wasted.

Luigi settled back among the cushions and leered at her. "Do you remember Ugolino Villani?" were the first words out of his mouth.

Bianca continued pouring steadily. "Of course, I remember him. His appalling demise . . . ."

"Was a great relief to someone," Luigi finished for her. Saying nothing, Bianca handed him the wine and poured a second goblet. Luigi went on, "I was with him the night he died. But you know that already, do you not?"

She took a sip of her wine. "No one informed me of it. I do know he was fond of gambling, and I hear you are as well." She smiled coldly. "Apparently his love of risk cost him his life."

"I do not think mine will cost so much." Luigi grinned, a flash of feral teeth. He set his wine down, then leaned forward, licked his lips, and whispered. "I know you killed him."

"You believe I was in some way responsible for his death?" Her voice was scornful. "If you suspected such a thing, why did you not report it to the authorities when he died? Or did you fear such an accusation would make you appear a total fool?''

''As I said, his death was a relief to me as well as whoever hired you. I know he liked to beat his women now and again, but I do not think you did it just for spite.'' He paused, surveying the riches on display in her room. ''Nor for the gold he carried. What I saw looked professional enough. So who bought his death, his son or the grieving widow? Whichever it was, Villani's death spared me the repayment of a large debt. As to the rest, it seemed to me that my knowledge might prove useful one day. Well, that day has come.''

''Useful?'' She took another sip of wine, excitement prickling every nerve.

''I have a proposition for you. I will even pay you, though silence should be reward enough. In fact, you might want to do it for free.''

There could be no question now of what he wanted. Bianca had to fight not to laugh out loud, jubilantly. It was too perfect! Examining the fine gold chasing on her goblet, she managed to keep her voice even as she answered, ''If there is something you want done for free, you will have to do it yourself.'' Then she met Luigi's eyes in full acknowledgment. ''My professional services are as expensive as they are expert.''

''That is better,'' Luigi said settling back among the cushions. ''If you succeed in removing my problem, I will pay you well enough. I know Antonio has rejected you for that redheaded witch, but you might still be able to arrange a way to get close to him. That is why I am hiring you. Once he is separated from his men it will be easier to take him. I have already sent a pack of guards after him, and it was the guards who ended up dead.''

Bianca felt a flare of rage. She knew she was not the only one with reason to kill Antonio, but already she felt his death belonged to her. She contained the ferocity of her response behind an icy smile and commented, ''Confrontation was hardly the best tactic. Do you not know his reputation with a sword?''

He shrugged, ''Every young gallant has a reputation with a sword and few deserve it.''

''I hear you are good yourself,'' she remarked, testing him.

Luigi puffed up as she had suspected he would, boasting his skill. *Antonio would cut you to bloody laces in a minute,* she thought. What expertise Luigi once possessed was as dissipated as his looks. But she parted her lips and widened her eyes to convey her admiration. A boor, a vain, stupid boor. But it was not a stupidity that could be relied on, the man was crafty.

"You will do it for me, then?" Luigi asked.

"Of course. My price will be six thousand ducats, half now and half on fulfillment of the contract."

He was outraged. "I hired all five guards for less than half that!"

"They failed."

Sulking, he sank back in his chair. His beefy fingers kneaded his lips as his glance flicked over her with cold, avaricious lust. "Just what is included in that price?"

Bianca had been expecting this part of the bargain, and had already weighed her alternatives. She must take control of the situation. Submission would weaken her position but outright refusal might endanger the commission. "The money is for the murder," Bianca told him, enunciating each word clearly. Luigi pursed his lips, his expression belligerent. Before he could protest, she smiled lasciviously. "When it is done, then we will celebrate."

He was crude—crudity would appeal to him and aggression would give her the upper hand. She lifted her skirts and spread her legs. The sudden sight of her nakedness changed his cold lust to hot. His thick tongue lapping at his lips, Luigi rose from the chair, fumbling at the crotch of his hose. "No," she said sharply, though she did not cover herself. Luigi stared at her still open legs, and she thought for a moment he would try to force her. She realized that the prospect of this murder had aroused her almost unbearably. Only the touch of the man who had hired it would be more unbearable. Then he met her eyes and remembered why he had come, and exactly what she was capable of. He dropped his gaze, lust and anger warring with fear.

"The money goes over there." Bianca indicated a box of carved ivory on a shelf. It did not matter where he put it, only that he followed her orders. Luigi did as she asked, slipping

the ducats into the box, staring over his shoulder at her unchanged posture. Bianca smiled. He would have tried to cheat
her of the second payment; now he would not be satisfied until
he had bedded her.

There was only one problem left, and she had little control
over it. "Did you tell anyone you were coming here tonight?"

"Of course not," he said sullenly, bewildered by her detached manner played against the brazen display of her flesh.

"I am a famous courtesan, you need have no other reason."

"No, I tell you. I did not want Antonio to hear of us together."

He had that much wit. And, since she had not submitted to
him, there would be nothing for him to boast of in his cups.
"Good. Do not risk coming here again until our business is
concluded," she told him.

"And when it is?" he asked, his eyes fixed on her lap.

"Then I promise I will demonstrate all my skills to you."
She enumerated, in obscene detail all the acts she had no intention of performing. When she was done, she could see his
erection bulging against his padded *braghetta*. Satisfied,
Bianca lowered her skirts and dismissed him. Drugged with
anger and lust, he hesitated and then left, whispering curses
under his breath.

Taut with excitement, Bianca sat alone within the *salotto*,
the entire scope of the plan already formed in her mind. She
had brooded on her revenge too long. The same pride that
demanded satisfaction had postponed action. Well, now she
would act. The money sanctified her revenge. She would kill
Antonio, as she had been hired to do, and she would kill the
girl. As soon as Luigi had paid her, she would kill him as well.
He could not be trusted to keep her identity secret.

She knew Dimitri was waiting, curious to hear what Luigi
had asked of her. Fanning the fires of his jealousy. She should
call him, for he would want to share this ecstasy. But she did
not.

In the past, with Dimitri, with Cesare, she had celebrated
her kills. It should have been easy enough to do the same with
Luigi tonight. Knowing she would kill him in turn should only
have enhanced her pleasure. There had been practical reasons
not to, but none had been as important as her body's fierce

denial. Luigi would have nothing from her but a knife. Anticipation sent a hot rush of lust through her body, but still she did
not call Dimitri to give her release. He, too, would have to
wait.

This murder would be her final duet of love with Antonio.
What sex there was in it would be between them and no one
else. She trembled with anticipation. Could she arouse Antonio
before she killed him? Taste the pleasure of his body before
she cut the life from it? If he submitted to her, she would kill
him as he came, his death throes one with his orgasm within
her. Veronica would be obliterated from his mind. Bianca's
fatal passion, her hatred, would be his last memory—not his
Veronica. Sliding a hand beneath her skirts, she closed her
eyes and let her fantasy claim her.

—

Standing back from her, Dimitri regarded his handiwork in
the mirror, then leaned forward to apply another layer of
shadow beneath her eyes, under her cheekbones.

"No, no," Bianca declared. "That is too much."

"Not from a distance, with the hood of a cloak about your
face."

"If he comes close, he will see it is nothing but makeup. I
do not think he will confront me, but it must bear such scrutiny."

"The first time or two, you can risk it. Choose your position
well. Let him see you only briefly, and then vanish," Dimitri
insisted. "He must see death in your face, if he is to believe a
suicide attempt. You must play on his pity."

It was the best of the plans she had devised after Luigi della
Montagna had hired her two days ago. A way to catch Antonio
off guard and lure him within her grasp. Bianca moved back
from the mirror to examine Dimitri's handiwork. The eunuch
was right—from a distance, this was exactly the effect she
wanted. The vision of a woman hollow eyed with despair, her
obsession with love consuming her from within. A woman
abasing her pride to snatch a stolen glimpse of the lover who
had rejected her.

Bianca shivered. She had told herself this was no different
from the role of repentant sinner she had played to seduce

priests. But it was. There had been no chilling undercurrent of
reality in that masquerade, no corroding shame eating away at
the pleasure of that calculated scheming. Only for Antonio
would she demean herself in this way.

She turned back to Dimitri, and practicalities. Antonio's
apartments were lavish but small. They were also secure. At
night, he had only his servants on guard. The additional men
he had hired met him in the morning and escorted him home at
night. "I am concerned that Luigi's attempt to assassinate him
will spoil our plans. Even if he does not suspect me, he is
wary. He may well insist on sending for his guards before he
comes here. If he does that, we cannot kill him undetected.
You will have to be very convincing, Dimitri, to lure him here
with no protection."

"Do not worry. You know how he hates being encumbered
by them, and he will not want to call attention to such a situation. I will persuade him there is no time to lose. Antonio will
believe me, mistress. He will follow me here alone or, at most,
bring his valet. When we are done with them, we will throw
the bodies in the river. Even if it is discovered they came here,
they will think he was attacked after he left you."

It would work. It must. She wanted Antonio here. Wanted
him at her mercy.

"Bianca," Dimitri wheedled, "let me cut Antonio. Let me
kill him."

"No!" She forced her voice to an even level. "You will not
touch him. His life is mine. You can have the valet, and Luigi
as well, for whatever you wish."

Dimitri pouted, his lower lip trembling, his eyes accusing
her. Aggravated, Bianca wondered if she should have forced
herself to fornicate with Luigi della Montagna. Dimitri would
enjoy killing him far more if she had. As it was, he felt
cheated. Sex would mollify him, but she did not have the patience to placate him now. Once Antonio was dead, everything
would return to normal. She would reward Dimitri then.

"What if Antonio does not come?" Dimitri asked, petulant
and resentful now.

"Then we will devise some other plan!" Bianca snapped.
Antonio had to come if he heard she was dying. *I will kill him
if he does not,* she thought, then bit back a hysterical giggle at

the absurdity. She turned back to Dimitri, taking the offensive. "What about the poison?"

"It's all ready," Dimitri grumbled, his expression still sullen.

"Tomorrow I will go to Daniele's, dressed as a beggar. You know it is one of my best disguises. If their cook is as religious as you say, she will offer me a bit of bread and soup."

"Not in the kitchen," he said. "She will bring it into the yard. Even if she did let you into the kitchen, she would not leave you there alone."

"You yourself told me she is a devotee of Savonarola. The eunuch of a famous courtesan will not get as far as the yard, no matter how prettily you praise her pastries." At least they were in agreement that the sugar should be poisoned. "The very fact that you visited the house would arouse suspicion."

"I can play the beggar," he insisted.

"Nonsense." Dimitri was too plump and sleek to arouse sympathy. Not even skillful makeup could disguise that. And if he feigned some disease as the source of his poverty, he certainly would not be allowed in the kitchen. It was unlike Dimitri to refuse to accept sense, but he was piqued that his role was so small.

He tried once again. "I will be a friar then. A humble friar on pilgrimage to visit Savonarola. I will beg alms, a bit of bread. Then I will beg her to tell me all she knows of the Holy Friar."

Bianca stared at him. The new plan was feasible, especially if the cook was coaxed to lead the conversation. Bianca realized she was reluctant to let go of any part of the plot, but her relationship with Dimitri was too strained. She would make this concession. "Very well," she agreed, and watched him break into a smile.

"This is best, mistress. A friar she may trust alone in the kitchen. If I can poison the sugar when she is not looking, so much the better. If not, I'll be able to see the arrangement of the household, and we can plan a way to break into the kitchen when they are asleep. One way or another, the sugar will be poisoned, and a wasting disease will claim the whole household." Dimitri giggled, propitiated for the moment at least. He performed a gruesome pantomime for her benefit.

Bianca had envisioned many deaths for Veronica. The first ones involved a great deal of blood and pain, and were always carried out before Antonio's eyes. But she wanted nothing to interfere with the final intimacy between Antonio and herself, not Veronica's death, nor even the knowledge of its possibility. Next she had relished an ever-burgeoning fantasy of Veronica's sexual violation. First, a *trentuno*, a rape by thirty one men—the revenge visited on whores by vengeful patrons. No, a *trentuno reale*, seventy-nine men all ravaging her rival's body. Best of all was the plan to abduct her and sell her to the brothels of the Ponte Sisto, the worst hellholes in Rome. Years of degradation and abuse would be a worthy fate for having stolen Antonio from her.

These elaborate revenges were pleasant fantasies but foolish. Bianca realized an unobtrusive death would be simplest and least suspicious, poison that would simulate a slow illness. She could savor the knowledge of Veronica wasting away slowly, painfully, and none the wiser. Tomorrow, with luck, Veronica's death would begin.

But Antonio would be gone long before her.

29 *Snares*

IT was after midnight when Giacomo woke him. "That crazy eunuch is at the door."

"Dimitri?" Antonio asked, though the image that came to his mind was not the eunuch but Bianca as he had last seen her.

"He's begging to talk to you, master." Giacomo squirmed uncomfortably. "I wanted to send him off, but I wasn't sure. I was afraid if you didn't see him, he'd start howling in the street."

"I had best find out what he wants first," Antonio said. "What time is it?"

"Two in the morning."

Giacomo brought him a towel and water. The cold dampness against Antonio's face and neck cleared the remnants of his grogginess. He slipped into the quilted satin robe Giacomo held up for him, tying the sash with the absurd sense of girding on his sword for battle. Giacomo following close behind, Antonio went down into the tapestried *salotto* where Bianca's eunuch waited. Dimitri was agitated, his face pale and sweating, his hands clasped at his breast, kneading and wringing each other in a frenetic prayer.

"Can we not talk alone, my lord?" he pleaded.

Antonio signaled Giacomo to make himself unobtrusive in the hallway, knowing full well he would listen to the conversation. Dimitri spared the valet a spiteful glance but saw that he would get no further concessions. Licking his lips, the eunuch slid closer to Antonio and mumbled in a nervous undertone, "Please, my lord, you must come with me. To see my mistress. She is very ill."

"The liaison between your mistress and myself is finished," Antonio said. He kept his tone distant, but his sense of apprehension was growing. He hoped this was no more than a vulgar bid for his attention. Yet he paused, unable to believe that Bianca, of all women, would lower herself to such crudities. "If she is ill, it is a physician you should summon, not I."

"She refuses a doctor. You are all she wants." Casting a desperate glance at the hallway, Dimitri gasped out, "She is dying."

"Dying?" Antonio said incredulously.

"Poison, she took poison. She is in agony, my lord. Take pity. Come with me now."

Antonio shook his head, refusing not Dimitri's request but the idea itself. But it could not be dispelled. He remembered Bianca swathed in a cloak, pale and hollow eyed, haunting the shadowed alleyway near his lodgings. Three times he had seen her there, the last only yesterday. Each time he had turned away, refusing to approach her. The theatrical play for his sympathy angered him even as he was appalled that she would expose herself so. Bianca, who had been so proud. Did not the fact that she was reckless enough to make such a display show she was unbalanced? Unbalanced enough to attempt suicide? Could she truly love him so much that losing him made her despair of life? Before those ominous visits, he would have said no. But he would never have imagined her loving him in the first place, and she had. He remembered the passion burning in her eyes as she stared at him from the alleyway, desperate, devouring. He realized now that it was not only anger that eerie figure had evoked in him, but also a thin edge of fear.

"You must come," Dimitri was trembling, sweat beading his forehead. "It is too late for the doctor to save her. You alone can ease her journey into the great sea. What will a few minutes matter to you, once she is gone? Let her see your face. Say some words of kindness. If you never loved her, surely she was beautiful, desirable. You took pleasure in her. Her pain is all for you." Dimitri knelt in front of him, tears streaming down his cheeks, the pudgy hands pawing his knees,. "Have you never loved, never suffered? Will you let her die with no word of comfort?"

The spectacle both disgusted and disturbed Antonio. Could Dimitri be so overwrought if it were not a matter of life and death? Antonio suspected he loved Bianca himself, as much as he was capable. As he hesitated, Dimitri screamed at him, "She is dying! Dying for love of you!" then collapsed in a frenzied weeping heap at his feet.

Turning away, Antonio walked to the fireplace, though no flames were burning to give him warmth. Leaning against the mantel, he thought of Beatrice and her deceptions, of Lucrezia Borgia's machinations, of Laudomia's virulent hatred. Thought again, of his past cruelty to Veronica, tormenting her for offering him her love—and how she had loved him enough to endure it. "Very well, I will come with you," he said quietly.

Instantly, Giacomo scurried forth from the hall. "The streets aren't safe at night. Let me send for the guards, master."

"There is no time!" Dimitri cried, beating his fists on the floor. "There is no time!"

"Do not bother, Giacomo," Antonio said. "The distance is short. I doubt anyone will bother us." He hated having the pack trailing after him, and the chances of an attack were minimal. No one would be expecting him to leave his apartments so late at night. Giacomo was no guard, but he was resourceful in a fight and had a nose for trouble. Dimitri himself had some fighting skills, he remembered. He eyed the eunuch warily. It was not impossible that Bianca was conspiring with his enemies. But somehow he could not imagine her abandoning her pride in someone else's service. If it was a trap, it was probably the courtesan's.

"Hurry," Dimitri begged him. "Hurry, or she will die."

"Dimitri, go wait in the foyer below. Giacomo, get dressed. I will take care of myself," Antonio ordered, then returned to his bedroom, glad to escape the eunuch for the moment. Dimitri was pathetic, but there was something abhorrent about him, an abnormality that went beyond his physical condition. Dressing himself quickly, Antonio then had to snap at Giacomo, who was obviously procrastinating. They armed themselves and set out for Bianca's, Dimitri in the lead, bearing the torch. They went with both speed and care, watching for ambush, but no one met them. When they reached Bianca's house, Antonio drew his sword, as did Giacomo. His valet insisted on going in first, to check the *salotto* and the other downstairs rooms.

When Giacomo started for the stairs, Dimitri rushed to block the way, renewing his outraged wails, "What are you doing? This man must not be permitted to see my mistress. It is humiliating!"

"Giacomo comes with me as far as the door. He can go downstairs when I am sure it is safe."

Dimitri cast him a glance of undisguised disgust. Pushing past Giacomo, the eunuch led them to the door to Bianca's room. He demanded to go in alone first, and Antonio nodded his acceptance. Dimitri opened the door and went inside. The room was lit only by firelight, and Antonio ordered the eunuch to light all the candelabra. Chaos emerged from the shadows. Usually exquisitely kept, the room was in disarray, clothing scattered about, the scent of spilled perfumes mixed with the sharp medicinal smell of alcohol. The eunuch went about the room, making a great show of opening the cupboards and curtains. Antonio spared enough attention to assure himself there was no one secreted within. Empty. Feeling both foolish and ashamed of his lingering sense of suspicion, he dismissed his apprehension and focused his attention on the figure lying wretched within the silk-draped splendor of the bed.

"Fetch a doctor," he commanded Dimitri.

"No," Bianca whispered, her voice weak and hoarse.

"Do it, or I will send Giacomo," Antonio told him. Perhaps it was hopeless, but he could not comprehend why the eunuch had permitted Bianca's wishes to overrule basic common sense.

"I will go, my lord. Right away." But still Dimitri hovered

"Presto," Antonio urged. "Go alone, or take Giacomo with you, if you will feel safer."

"Thank you. We will go now. I will leave you alone with my mistress," Dimitri said in a hushed voice, closing the door behind him.

Sheathing his sword, Antonio started to approach the bed, horrified at the change in the courtesan. Bianca raised one arm, gesturing him to stop. "Stay there," she begged. "Let me look at you for a moment."

The plea discomfited Antonio, but he did as Bianca asked, using the time to recover from his first shock and to steel himself for the ordeal that still awaited them both. In the flickering light of the tapers, the exquisite courtesan looked like a corpse already, some pitiful creature drowned then cast up by the river. Her hair was damp and matted, clinging to her face and shoulders like pale, slimy weeds. Her overbright eyes stared out at him from hollows of dark bruised flesh, and her complexion was tinged with an evil greenish pallor.

"Why?" he asked her.

"You know why!" she cried.

Bianca had been so vain of her beauty, so proud of her erotic skills. She could have had any man in Florence groveling at her feet—almost any man. Antonio had once thought her incapable of love—perhaps because love had never touched her before and so left no traces of its joy or pain. If she had never known love, perhaps she did not know she could survive its loss? Or did not care. He knew that feeling well enough. Exasperated, aching with a bitter sadness, he went to her side. At his approach she turned her face away from him, burrowing into the pillows. *Shame or vanity?* Antonio wondered. Did she really believe she would look any worse at close range? Or that it could possibly matter now?

Bianca moaned as Antonio sat beside her on the bed. Even as he gently spoke her name, laid a hand on her shoulder, he

recognized an off note in the setting. The smell of alcohol and
herbs gave the air the scent of a sickroom, but there was no
odor of vomit. The poison she had taken might not have in-
duced that reaction or Dimitri might have cleaned the mess
away, but the waxy green hue of her skin suggested unrelenting nausea. Then, as he stroked Bianca's hair aside, he saw
something else. Beneath the damp weedy strands, the skin on
her back was its usual delicate, rose tinted ivory.

Antonio froze as the image struck him, coalescing all the
other fragments of wrongness. The elaborate chaos of the
room looked staged now. Bianca gasped his name as he pulled
her around to face him. She clung to him, her eyes wide and
pleading, carrying through the game, but this close the sickly
tints of her face were obviously nothing more than skillful
paint. Disgusted, he shoved her away from him. The courtesan
buried herself amid the pillows again, sobbing, imploring him
not to abandon her. Was this show the cheapest possible ploy
or was it something more sinister? Whichever it was, it was
time to leave, and with even more caution than he had arrived.
Antonio drew his sword.

The rest happened within the space of a few seconds. Somewhere below, there was a cry and an ominous thump. *Giacomo*. Even as he whirled around, Antonio knew it was a mistake. He felt the impetus of Bianca's lunge, but he was not
quick enough. Something struck his head, and he fell to the
floor. As darkness swallowed him, the last thing he felt was
fury at his own stupidity.

Regaining consciousness, Antonio realized he was bound
hand and foot to the bed, his clothes stripped from his body.
Cautiously, he scanned the room, finding only Bianca in the
far corner by the door, dropping a bundle onto a chair. His
clothes—and his sword. Was she the instigator or only the
lure? Antonio remembered the cry he had heard before she
struck him and wondered if Giacomo was alive. He jerked the
bonds to test them, but he could tell they would hold. He
subsided then, loathing the confinement, but not giving his
captors the pleasure of his struggle.

His movement brought Bianca to his side. One look in the

courtesan's eyes convinced Antonio that she wanted his death. More than Luigi did, and more than his father did. Only Laudomia had looked at him with such obliterating, hate-filled passion. But there had been no lust in Laudomia's hatred, while Bianca's reeked of it.

She smiled. "You are awake."

"So I am."

Incredibly, Bianca had cleaned the sickly makeup from her face and repainted her lips and eyes. Her hair still had its slimy look, but she had twisted it back from her face. The satin shift she wore flowed like liquid silver over her body, gleaming cool and poisonous as mercury. Studying her, Antonio saw that the effect she had created earlier was not all the deceit of cosmetics. Bianca was thinner, her cheekbones pronounced, with deeper hollows beneath them. They gave an austerity to her features that had not been there before. More than ever, she was an ice queen. The ice still burned, hotter than ever.

"I am grateful that you came when I called you," Bianca murmured as she sat beside him on the bed. "I have missed you. We have not yet had our proper farewell." She kissed him on the lips, then began to caress his body with her hands, her mouth, the blade she held so lovingly.

———

Gasping, Veronica woke from nightmare into vision. Antonio was in danger. The scent of death was like a sick black perfume clouding her mind, and through that dark cloud, fearful images came reeling. A glimmering knife etched fine lines of pain across his chest. Blood ran bright across his skin and stained the long, pale fingers toying with his sex. Above him was a mocking, avid face, beautiful and vile . . . . The Queen of Swords had not been Laudomia after all.

With a choked cry, Veronica tossed back the covers and stumbled to the wardrobe, pulling out the men's clothes she had kept since the Gypsy camp. Frantically, her body drenched with cold sweat, she tugged on the hose and doublet and thrust her feet into the boots. Strapping on her knife belt, she ran down to Daniele's room and flung open the door. "Wake up!" she yelled at him. "Daniele, wake up. Wake up!"

He came awake with a start, springing naked from the bed. "What is it? What is wrong?"

"Antonio is in danger." She managed to say that clearly. "Fetch a watchman and bring him to Bianca's house."

"Bianca?"

"Yes. Hurry, hurry." Veronica turned and rushed out of the room and down the stairs. She heard Daniele crying for her to wait, but she ran headlong from the house into the street, racing down to the Arno and across the nearest bridge. She knew Bianca's street. Daniele had pointed out the house to her once. Like their own and unlike those closer to the center of the city, the houses in this neighborhood were set apart from each other. But she could remember no distinguishing features from that casual glimpse. A hanging lantern, a wrought iron gate like all the others along the way. Could she find it again in the dark? Yes. She must. Whether her eyes recognized the place or not, her fear would know its source.

Reaching the street, Veronica forced herself to stop, catch her breath, move forward slowly. She must be cautious. There might be guards about, or Bianca's fabled eunuch standing guard. She recognized the house immediately, her heart racketing in her chest at the first glimpse of it. She moved along the wall to the gate. No one was watching the front of the house, and the gate was unlocked. Carefully, not wanting to be heard within, Veronica tried the front door. It was locked. The front windows were barred with wrought iron. The draperies were drawn, no glimmer of light showing through.

Upstairs. It was less a thought than her own voice speaking to her. Looking up, Veronica saw more windows, not barred but adorned with an ornamental balcony of iron scrollwork. There was a light above, a glow she perceived not only with her eyes but felt pulsing in her heart. *Alive. Antonio was alive.*

She made her way round to the back door, but it was locked as well, and all the back windows barred. One, shuttered instead of draped, she took to be the kitchen. The window that showed thin cracks of light, and there were faint sounds coming from within. The eunuch, a guard, Giacomo? She did not know, and it was the upstairs she must reach. That left the wall. Jumping from the top, she could probably reach one of the tiny balconies outside the windows. Veronica had found no trellises to climb, no tree close enough to be of use. She ran back to the wrought iron gate and found enough grips there to clamber up to the wall, and from the wall back to that window that showed the pale beam of light through its curtains. Choosing the best angle, she leapt from the wall and caught hold of the wrought iron, cursing silently as it creaked against the stone. No one rushed to the sound, so it must not have been heard within. As quietly as she could, Veronica got a foothold and pulled herself over the balcony and onto the wide bottom ledge. She could grasp the upper ledge as a brace to kick in the glass. But first she concentrated on the narrow crack opening in the curtain, shifting back and forth to peer into Bianca's bedroom.

"*Inferno,*" Veronica swore under her breath, and her heart seemed to double its pace, hammering against her chest. Antonio was there, alive. He was tied to the bed, Bianca sitting beside him, running her hands, her knife across his body. But they were not alone. The eunuch was oozing in the doorway behind them.

Antonio was not cooperating. At least, not as Bianca wished. Given his perverse response to danger, it would not have surprised him if her efforts had aroused him. Once he had been drawn to her darkness, but now he was repelled by it. His senses were heightened, but there was no heat in his fury, nothing tantalizing in the delicate pain she inflicted, nothing stimulating in her most intimate, expert caresses. Revulsion blunted every erotic sensation she tried to evoke in him. Antonio was glad not to give her the satisfaction of a reaction. On the other hand, when she drew away from his limp cock, he saw that her rage was swiftly rising, which brought death one step nearer. Death prefaced by torture.

Yes. Now the knife cut deeper. Antonio showed no reaction to that either. This time. He could endure the pain for a while, but he did not doubt she could drive him beyond his endurance. His refusal to respond to Bianca would cost him far more than his life. His manhood would probably be forfeit as well. When he saw Dimitri looming like a bloated wraith behind her, Antonio was sure of it. He met the eunuch's anticipatory gaze as scornfully as he had met Bianca's.

Dimitri's approach had been soundless. It was Antonio's shift of focus that alerted Bianca. She whirled around, her face suddenly distorted, her voice a menacing hiss. "I told you not to interrupt me. He is mine. You can have his servant for yourself."

"You know it is not the same," Dimitri whined. "You know it is better when we kill them together."

Them. When we kill them together. An idea took shape in his mind, too bizarre to be believed, and yet it brought everything into place. He was certain now why Juan's masked friend had seemed so familiar.

"Not this time," she whispered vehemently. "I will share Antonio with no one, not even you. Now, go back downstairs and enjoy what I have given you. Unless you have finished with him already?"

"No," Dimitri mumbled. "I haven't begun yet."

Giacomo was alive. For the moment at least. Antonio's lips twitched in a small grim smile. The eunuch was a fool to leave him alone. Giacomo could wiggle his way out of almost anything.

"You mean you crept up here instead, to listen."

"Mistress, please," Dimitri begged, cringing before her.

"Out," Bianca ordered. "Get out now!"

"Yes, mistress," Dimitri whispered. His face puckered, drawing up into an aggrieved pout, but he went to the door. Pausing there, he turned back and the look he gave Antonio was pure venom.

Losing patience, Bianca stalked to the door, and the eunuch scuttled down the stairs. She closed the door and slid the carved wooden bar across it, then listened, waiting for Dimitri to go downstairs. When he was gone, she returned to stand beside the bed. Antonio could see the confrontation had done nothing to improve her temper. Her forbearance was at an end for himself, as well as Dimitri. Bianca smiled, promising him many unpleasant things.

"You can scream all you want," she told him. "My patrons often scream in the extremity of their pleasure."

Suddenly, from a window across the room came the splinter

of breaking glass. Bianca whirled as the sound came again and again. Knife extended, the courtesan dropped to a crouch at the foot of the bed as a figure hurtled through the curtain to land in fighting stance in the middle of the room. *Veronica*, Antonio thought, joy and fear locking the breath in his throat.

Bianca looked stunned, but only for a second. Then she laughed. ''The bitch comes sniffing out her master. How did you track him? By the scent of his blood?''

Antonio gasped as Bianca's knife slashed across the soles of his feet. Veronica cried out, her gaze caught the vivid redness of the welling blood. The courtesan darted forward, making her first deadly jab. Veronica leapt back, but if Bianca had been a few inches closer, the knife would have found its mark. Antonio gritted his teeth, cursing himself. He could have borne the pain of the cut, but Bianca had taken him by surprise.

Now there was more trouble. The eunuch had heard the crash and was thundering up the stairs. He tried to open the door and found it barred against him. But the bar and the door itself were light, and Antonio knew Dimitri could break through it in a minute or two if he set his weight to it. Now he only pounded with his fist, crying out, ''What is wrong, mistress? What is happening?''

''Stay where you are,'' Bianca called out, never taking her eyes from her quarry. ''Our pretty Veronica has joined the party. She is about to find out what happens to uninvited guests.''

Antonio watched as Bianca circled lightly, a vicious smile on her lips, her knife flashing out in quick cunning jabs. Moving warily, Veronica managed to stay out of reach, but despite her Gypsy training it was obvious that the courtesan had more skill. It confirmed Antonio's suspicion that she was a trained killer. The only hope was that Bianca would be overconfident in her ability. The courtesan struck and dodged. Veronica struck back, but Bianca countered then moved in swiftly, her blade slicing Veronica's left arm.

''First blood to me, bitch,'' she spat, then darted forward again. Veronica parried the new thrust, but Bianca cut her again, a shallow wound on her knife hand. ''Second blood,'' she jeered. ''When I am done with you, you will be nothing but pretty red ribbons to drape on Antonio.''

Bianca circled left, mixing rapid stabs with taunting jibes, trying to lure Veronica closer. Antonio could see the defiant light of anger in Veronica's eyes, could see her fighting the reckless urge to attack. She held back, circling, waiting for an opportunity to strike. Terrified for her, Antonio willed himself to lie soundless, motionless, but Veronica cast another desperate glance at him. Seeing her distracted, Bianca lunged. Veronica leapt back, staggering as she landed. Unable to catch her balance, she tripped and fell backwards on the rug. Certain that was the end, Antonio felt horror smother him. Then, as Bianca leaped for her, he realized the whole maneuver was a feint. Veronica grabbed hold of Bianca's knife arm and her feet came up, catching the courtesan in mid-lunge and tossing her overhead. Bianca crashed against the bedroom door and lay there. She was not unconscious, but the impact had jolted her. After making a feeble effort to rise, she sagged against the wall once more.

"Is it over, mistress?" Dimitri's voice asked, then after a pause, he called out on a rising note of panic, "Mistress? Bianca? Bianca!" When no answer came this time, Dimitri began to hurl himself against the barred door.

Veronica had already regained her feet and run to Antonio's side, her knife sawing at the rope that bound his wrist to the bed. She cast a glance over her shoulder to make sure Bianca was still too stunned to be a threat, and that the barrier was holding against Dimitri's pounding, then returned to her work. The first rope gave and she straddled Antonio, the fastest way to reach the other bond. Perverse indeed, his body responded instantly to that contact, all the arousal Bianca had failed to provoke rushing through his veins, fierce and hot. Feeling the sudden thrust of his hardness beneath her, Veronica turned back to give him a look of only half-amazed outrage, then reached for the second rope.

"I told Daniele to bring help," she told him as she worked the blade against the bond.

There was a great crash and clatter, not outside the door but downstairs, as if every pot and bottle in the house had come down at once. "Giacomo is stirring too, I think," Antonio said. Then he saw Bianca was on her feet, running forward, a gilded chair lifted above her head. He cried out, "Behind you!"

Veronica whirled around, but it was too late. Bianca swung the chair full force, the fragile wood shattering over Veronica's head. Antonio felt her go limp, and she fell from the bed onto the floor. The battering at the door stopped for a moment, and Dimitri called out, "Bianca! Bianca, are you all right?"

"Yes," she snapped, and the eunuch fell silent. Swaying, the courtesan stood at the foot of the bed, her mad eyes traveling from his face to his erect sex. There was only one thing that could have enraged her more, and his treacherous body did it, withering under her gaze. Bianca glared at him, her face a livid mask of hatred, contorted, grotesque. He thought she might rip him apart with her own hands. Veronica moaned, and Bianca's gaze shifted down to her, then back to him again. "She will die before you after all," she snarled at him. "And you will watch as I do it."

Bianca grabbed a silk scarf from the strewn clothing. Stretching and twisting it between her hands, she knelt behind Veronica and wrapped the scarf about her throat. Waking to her danger, Veronica began to struggle, but Bianca was already tightening the silken garrote. "Watch carefully," she said to Antonio.

He saw Veronica's fallen knife lying by his foot at the bottom of the bed. Lunging, his arm straining in its socket, Antonio still could not reach it. Bianca laughed as Antonio began jerking frantically at the half-severed rope that bound his other hand to the bed, but the laughter stopped as the shredded strands began to give way. The courtesan began dragging her victim backward, out of easy reach. Catching her foot in her gown, she stumbled, loosening her hold for an instant. Veronica doubled her efforts to escape. Bianca renewed her grip, screaming for help. "Dimitri! Dimitri!"

"Bianca!" came the answering cry, and the battering of the door resumed.

Veronica was gasping for air, her body arching in agony as Bianca drew the scarf tighter and tighter. Wrenching free of the bond, Antonio grabbed the knife and went for the rope that bound his left foot to the bed. He hacked at it, cursing the weakness of his numbed wrist. Then the air was filled with the sound of splintering wood as the door split open and Dimitri burst into the room. There was a whip crack and a slash of pain along Antonio's hand. The knife flew from his grip to fall beside Bianca. Dimitri struck again, aiming for his eyes. Antonio threw up an arm to ward off the whip, jerking his left leg against the frayed strands binding it. Dimitri's arm drew back, and then the lash cut through the air. This time Antonio turned to it. The flaying leather striped his arms, but he managed to catch hold of it, trying to wrench it from the eunuch's hands. Caught off guard, Dimitri quickly shifted his grasp on the whip and yanked it forward. Antonio's grip held, but now the shredded rope at his foot gave way and he fell forward. The whip was torn from his hands. Before he could raise himself, Dimitri had grabbed hold of his hair and was dragging him backwards. Trapped by one bound ankle, Antonio struggled against the eunuch.

"Yes! Hold him, hold him!" Bianca yelled at Dimitri. "Make him watch."

But Dimitri had his own plans. Antonio felt the whip loop round his neck. He managed to thrust one hand under the coils, but the eunuch strengthened his hold and the whip tightened around Antonio's throat. "Together," Dimitri told Bianca. "We will do them together."

"No!" The piercing scream was Bianca's.

"Yes! Together!" Dimitri cried.

There was a moment of stunned silence. Bianca seemed mesmerized, her gaze fastened on his throat. Antonio could see her hands loosen their grip on the scarf, even as he felt Dimitri jerk the whip tighter. Wrestling against the pressure, he could see Veronica was still alive, though her movements were feebler. The knife was on the floor beside Bianca. If Veronica could reach it . . . . Snarling, Antonio drove back with his free arm, smashing his fist into Dimitri's face. But it did no good. Dimitri grunted in pain, but the stranglehold tightened inexorably. Antonio gasped, struggling for air, his lungs seared with pain.

"No!" Bianca shrieked. Snatching up the knife, she leaped forward.

Blood, hot and reeking, splattered Antonio as Dimitri squealed, a shrill cry abruptly choked off into a bubbling gurgle. Bianca leaped back from the bed, her hands empty. Antonio felt the eunuch release the whip, and he pulled free of both the strangling coils and Dimitri's weight. The eunuch swayed back and forth, his hands clutching at the knife hilt protruding from his throat. He gazed in horror at the woman who had stabbed him. The ghastly noise went on and on as the blood gushed between his fingers.

"He is mine!" Bianca was screaming over and over. "I told you he is mine!"

Antonio saw Veronica roll away, unnoticed. Quickly, he switched his gaze away from her, back to Bianca. She was silent now, but her eyes were crazed as she watched Dimitri crawl toward her on his knees. Choking in his own blood, he hovered for a second on the edge of the bed, then toppled forward onto the floor. Bianca's gaze followed his fall. When the last of the noises, the twitches, ended, her eyes lifted to Antonio, still bound by one foot to the bed. He had the whip now, but she did not notice or care.

"You are mine," she said, a whisper as mad as the screams had been.

"No," Veronica said, rising from the floor. Her voice too was a croaking whisper, but sane. "No, he is mine."

She came to her feet with his sword in her hand and raised the extended point level with Bianca's heart. The courtesan's gaze fixed on the weapon, and Antonio saw the fever of her insanity chill to icy calculation. Veronica was almost close enough. A lunge would drive the blade home, but she was unsteady on her feet. Slowly, Veronica approached, and Bianca retreated before her, out of easy reach of the deadly blade. Urgently, Antonio bent over his ankle, working the knots with his fingers. They were too tight. He looked about the room, trying to discover where the other knife had fallen. He needed it, but he did not want Veronica to lower her eyes or his sword from the courtesan for one instant.

Bianca was almost at the wall. A few more steps, and Veronica would have her pinned. Then the courtesan turned and snatched the candelabra from the table, thrusting the burning tapers into the gauzy silk hangings at the head of the bed. The delicate fabric caught with a rush of flame. Bianca dodged out of the way as Veronica lunged with the sword, grazing her back. Bianca hurled the candelabra at Veronica and ran for the door.

"Chase me, or save your lover," she cried, then fled down the stairs.

The canopy was ablaze, its fragile curtains transparent sheets of flame enveloping the bed. Tongues of fire sprouted from the pillows, the mattress. Veronica ran to the burning bed, quickly slicing through the last bond on Antonio's ankle. He staggered off the bed, wincing in annoyance as his slashed feet hit the floor, and looked around him. Already the fire had leaped from the bed hangings to the closest draperies. Now it sought out the piles of clothing scattered about the room. "We cannot put this out," Antonio said. He saw his own clothes untouched in the corner, grabbed them, and headed for the stairs. "We have to find Giacomo."

"Bianca will escape," Veronica said as they descended. "We will never catch her now."

"If she is wise, she will get as far from Florence as she can. She is mad, but I think her own survival matters more than revenge. What I do not know is if she acted entirely on her own tonight or if someone hired her."

"Hired her?"

"You are not the only one who fancies men's clothing, *selvaggia*. After tonight's performance, I am convinced Bianca was the assassin who killed Juan Borgia. I will never prove it now," he said, glancing back at the flames licking the upstairs door and smiling ironically. "Not that proof would have done me any good, had I found any."

Giacomo appeared in the kitchen doorway, severed ropes dangling from his wrists and ankles, a broken bottle clutched in one hand, a knife in the other. He looked up at the fire, then turned back to the survivors. "If you'd waited another minute, I'd have rescued you," he declared in an injured tone.

There was shouting in the front yard. "That is Daniele with the watchman," Veronica said.

"If this is going to be an official scandal, master," Giacomo suggested, viewing Antonio's nudity, "you should at least put on your cape."

They sat in Daniele's studio, sipping *tisane* and eating pastries. Antonio, who had less taste for sweets, was lost in the new shipment of books from the printers. Roberto was on a walk with Bombol and Benito, but Marco Polo was with them, playing with a feather. It should have been a perfect morning, but Veronica was feeling weak and achy again. Was it only a month ago that she had raced through the streets to save Antonio? Today even sitting seemed a chore. Veronica sighed. She wanted to see *Pluto and Persephone* finished, but she hoped Daniele would not ask them to pose this afternoon. He did not look well, either, and he was in an even crankier mood than she was.

"I hope that yesterday's bonfire of the vanities was Savonarola's last," he complained. "The air stinks of smoke, even inside the house."

"I think it will rain later today. That will clear away the smell," Veronica said. Trying to placate her cousin, she offered him her remaining almond tart.

Daniele took it and nibbled around the edges of the flower petal crust, before sinking his teeth into the sweet filling. Mouth full, he muttered, "You would think the excommunication would have more effect."

"Stefano said the mood was far more subdued, even before the *Compagnacci* tried to break up the ceremonies," Antonio offered from his chair. "They were snatching crucifixes from the hands of children."

"I am glad I did not go with him," Daniele said. "The first time was troublesome enough." None of their household had gone, except Roberto, accompanied by Benito and Simona, the cook.

"Excuse me," Veronica said, feeling abruptly nauseous. She made it almost to the door with dignity, then broke into a run to reach the *latrina* in time. When she emerged, Antonio was waiting for her on the balcony. "I am all right. You need not look so worried."

"Are you pregnant, *dolcezza*? I have been more careful, but not as careful as I should."

"No, I am not. Not unless Daniele and Roberto are pregnant as well," she reassured him then smiled, despite her queasiness, at the mixture of relief and disappointment in his eyes. "I think I have caught some illness from them, or they from me. Or perhaps it is only indulgence, for Simona made my favorite pastries this week and I ate too many for breakfast again.''

Antonio was about to say something, then was abruptly still. He led her to the edge of the balcony, turned her face to the sunlight, and studied her with an intensity that had nothing to do with his usual passion. ''What is it?'' she asked, alarmed.

''Show me your hands,'' he commanded. She gave them to him and he studied her fingernails. She watched as the color drained from his face.

''You are being poisoned,'' he said, his voice harsh. ''If you take no more, I think you will recover. We must find the source and determine, if we can, if Bianca was behind it or someone else.''

''The pastries!'' Veronica ran back into the studio, where Daniele was about to pop the last bite of the tart into his mouth. ''Do not eat that,'' she cried.

''Why did you offer it, if . . . ?'' he began perplexed. Antonio came in and Daniele looked from one face to the other. He blanched and dropped the tart to the floor. Marco Polo promptly rushed it and was outraged to have it snatched away again.

''Bombol would eat it,'' Veronica said. ''Marco Polo just wants to bat it across the room.''

''And lick his paws afterward,'' Antonio commented acerbically.

''You must excuse me while I go make myself sick,'' Daniele said, and departed hurriedly for the *latrina*.

''How long have you felt ill?'' Antonio asked Veronica.

''A week or two.'' Then thinking on it, she said, ''No, three.''

''Is it always the pastries that make you feel ill?'' Antonio asked.

''I do not know!'' she exclaimed, trying to quell the sickening panic within her, her horror of this invisible penetration of her body like some insidious rape. Antonio put his arms around her, coldly calm though she felt the tension in his muscles. Veronica leaned on him until she felt in control herself, then turned to face him. ''It must be something we eat all the time, must it not, since it has been getting slowly worse? And something that we eat but the servants do not, since none of them are ill?''

"Not the well water, then," Antonio said. "Do you share the flour?''

"Yes, and the salt, and the herbs for our *tisanes*.''

"The sugar," Antonio said, abruptly. "It is in the sugar.''

She nodded. "There is nothing else that is not replaced or used too infrequently to be effective.''

"Unless Simona is the poisoner, adding it to whatever she chooses.''

Veronica shook her head, "She would not do that.''

"Not for money, perhaps. But her life or her family might have been threatened.''

"If so, she could not have concealed her fear, her guilt from us.''

Wide and dark, his eyes gazed at her, and Veronica saw fear and guilt there, plain enough. "Bianca implied that she planned to kill you as well as me, but I did not think of this.''

"No," she whispered, seeing him hate himself for failing her. "How could you know?''

"Because I saw the evil in her and the madness. I knew that if she could, she would find a way to strike at us. But I thought we were safe from her.''

"You have had word of her?''

"Not long after she vanished, an informant in Rome sent me word of a beautiful woman confined within the brothels of the Ponte Sisto. They called her "the white one." From his description of her face, her body, it is Bianca. I think she was desperate enough to go to Cesare Borgia for help, and he was swift to realize she was now a danger to him. It strikes me as the kind of revenge Cesare would find amusing.''

"And you pitied her, hearing it," Veronica said.

"I had considered that death might be better," Antonio answered her, "but I did not attempt to obtain even that mercy for her. I am glad now I did not.''

Daniele rejoined them, and Antonio told him of their deduction. "Ah, *Jesu*," Daniele moaned. "All my friends troop in and out of the kitchen, stealing Simona's pastries.''

"I do not think anyone will take ill from one or two. The poison was meant to be cumulative, to imitate an illness,''

Antonio said. "It is too bad Marco Polo keeps you free of rats, or we could test our theory."

"Let us see what Simona has to say," Daniele suggested.

They found the cook in her kitchen preparing an herb pasta. Was it only her imagination, Veronica wondered, or did Simona appear more nervous than usual? More likely it was their own odd manner that was flustering her. Trying to appear casual, Daniele asked her if anyone other than the usual members of the household had been in her kitchen in the past month or so.

"Visitors? There are always visitors."

"Not visitors who are friends, Simona. Strangers. A peddler? A beggar? Some kind of messenger?"

"Messengers come to the front, and I would let no peddlers or beggars in my kitchen—your kitchen, master. There has been no one here except your own friends, no one at all," Simona declared, then paused and added, "except the Holy Friar."

"Savonarola? Savonarola eats my pastries?" Daniele exclaimed. He looked outraged and then, for a moment, grimly pleased.

"Not Fra Girolamo, master, but a friar from the south, on pilgrimage to see our great prophet."

"What did he look like?" Antonio asked. "Tell us everything you can remember."

"He was a large man, my lord, a man who appreciated good food. That was the day I made *marzapane*, I remember, and he was very helpful. As for his looks, well, he wore his hood up, but his hair was dark and curly. His eyes were dark too. He had the face of an innocent, a cherub, with plump cheeks and a soft little mouth. His skin was smooth and pretty as a girl's."

"And his voice?"

Simona frowned. "A high voice, my lord, with an accent I'd not heard before."

"There is our source," Antonio said bitterly.

"Fra Dimitri," Veronica tried for lightness.

Daniele turned to Simona. "I want you to bring me all the sugar."

"The sugar?" Simona sounded so guilty that Veronica had a sudden qualm of doubt. She saw Antonio's eyes narrow in speculation and Daniele's grow round with surprise. Seeing their expressions, Simona cried out, "Forgive me, master. I did not mean to do it! I could not help myself! I see now that it was a wicked sin."

"What!" Daniele exclaimed, horrified.

"Forgive me, master, please. I promise I will pay you back, and I will never steal from you again."

"You stole the sugar?" Antonio asked.

"How much did you eat?" Veronica exclaimed.

"I ate none of it. I gave it all to Signore Roberto," Simona said, moral affront mixing with guilt. "It is precious, a luxury dear to him. He wanted to make a sacrifice to God, so I gave him the sugar and told him not to let Benito see it. Forgive me, master. I let him throw it all into the bonfire of the vanities."

30 Accusations

"FIRE is a strange element, and I am against employing it," Filippo Giugni was saying to the salon guests clustered in the studio. "I told the Signoria that we should ask Savonarola to walk into water instead. If he does not get wet, I will be the first to ask his pardon."

Veronica had to smile at the image of Savonarola drenched and dripping. But the test was fire, not water, and that thought erased the smile from her lips. Strange, it was always Savonarola she saw, Savonarola the others talked of, though it was not he but Fra Domenico da Pescia who had accepted the test of the flames.

Declaring that he had not been excommunicated by Christ, Savonorola had finally returned to the pulpit in February. Fearful of papal interdict, the Signoria had forbidden him to preach barely a month later. He had accepted their ban. "My Florentines' faith is like wax," the Friar had remarked. "A little heat and it melts."

Now, as March neared its close, Savonarola's chief rival, Fra

Francesco di Puglia had challenged to an ordeal by fire anyone who affirmed the truth of Savonarola's doctrine and contested the validity of his excommunication. Fra Domenico da Pescia, preaching in Savonarola's stead, had taken up that challenge. The Signoria had set the date of the trial for the seventh of April, and few attending Daniele's latest gathering were talking of anything else. Even the recent arrival of Antonio's annulment was old news.

"Three orders are involved now, the Minorites as well as the Dominicans and Franciscans," Stefano was saying. "Fra Mariano Ughi has taken up the challenge, and asked if one of the Minorite friars will oppose him in the ordeal. They are at odds with Savonarola as well and have accepted."

"But Savonarola himself still refuses the test?" Daniele asked.

"He has been heard to say that it is tempting God, but what else has he been doing for the past decade?" Machiavelli answered scornfully.

"There is no escape for him now," Antonio said. "His enemies want the ordeal in hopes that its failure will destroy him. His followers want a miracle to validate their belief in him. If he did not ask for this trial, he has asked for just the sort of faith that has engendered it."

"Now he has no choice but to support his credulous brethren and watch them walk to their deaths in the flames," Machiavelli agreed.

"If he is trusting in faith, perhaps he believes theirs is stronger than his at the moment." There was sadness in Stefano's voice.

"Stronger than that of the Franciscan brethren certainly," Fillipo Giugni remarked. "Fra Francesco promised three or four of his friars to the ordeal, but none came forward. When the Signoria pressed him, he gave them Fra Giuliano Rondinelli, who was not present to protest."

"He protested loudly enough when he heard," Antonio remarked.

"But he signed the agreement nevertheless."

"I have heard that Fra Francesco has been assured he will not have to go into the flames," Fillipo confided.

Antonio was dubious. "By whom, the leader of the *Com-*

pagnacci? What good will the 'bad companions' do against the vast horde that will be there? The crowd may well set him afire if he refuses."

"No matter what the outcome of the ordeal, the *Arrabbiati* will rid Florence of Fra Girolamo," Machiavelli said smugly. "They have control of the Signoria now. It has already been announced that if Fra Domenico burns, Savonarola will be declared a rebel and must leave the city within three hours. Even if both friars go up in smoke, still only Savonarola will be banished, though it was the Franciscan who issued the challenge. The only way for Fra Girolamo to triumph now is to pray very hard for Fra Domenico to emerge unscathed from the flames. If he has God's ear as he claims, a miracle should not be so difficult to produce."

"I could almost wish for it," Daniele said. "I want Florence rid of Savonarola, but not at the price of burned bodies."

"Show that man mercy, and it is you who may be condemned to the flames, Daniele," Machiavelli retorted. "He is your enemy and, I believe, the enemy of Florence. We will all be well rid of him."

Veronica woke to her own sobbing. She found Antonio's arms already around her, his voice soft but urgent. "What is it? Tell me what you were dreaming."

Shuddering, Veronica curled against him as the images, the sensations, assailed her. "About the day Mama Lucia was attacked. I was riding to her. I could feel the stones as they struck, as if it were my own flesh." She sat up in bed, fingers pressed to her temples, trying to recall the details of the nightmare, but they had already vanished. "I hope it was not a warning that Mama Lucia is in danger. I cannot tell."

"It may only have been all the talk of Savonarola at the salon," Antonio said gently.

"Perhaps, but it has been too long since I have seen her. I am worried." Veronica lay back in his embrace. Whatever horror she felt in the dream had dissipated quickly, leaving only a vague oppressive uneasiness.

"I will send a messenger to our Gypsy contact in Siena.

When he finds out where the *voivode* is camped now, we can go for a visit.''

"Yes. Soon." She would visit the convent tomorrow. Tending the patients there would make her feel closer to Mama Lucia.

"Would you like to live in Siena again, Veronica?" Antonio asked. "Now that the annulment is final, we should decide where we want to live, for next year if not forever."

Veronica nestled against him, welcoming the distraction he offered her. "Could we not just travel? For a few months at least? I have seen so little of the world."

"See the fluid streets of Venice gilded by sunset? Circle the green waters of Lake Guarda beneath the purple shadows of the Alps? Visit France in the spring, with fruit trees in bloom and the fields scarlet with poppies?"

As he murmured of enchanted places, Antonio began to caress her, all gentleness. His lips nuzzled her neck, her shoulders, traveling slowly to her breasts. He cupped their softness in his hands, sucking each nipple in turn to a tender aching peak. His desire was real, as was his hope of easing her away from fear. Veronica murmured her pleasure, her gratitude, going gladly into the release he offered. Her hands carded the dark silk of his hair as his kisses descended the arch of her ribs, the slope of her belly. His hands parted her thighs and she opened herself to him, moaning as his warm mouth, his slow insistent tongue, lured her into rapture. Her soft gasping breaths released into a trembling sigh of fulfillment.

"You taste of spices," he whispered and kissed her, his lips, his tongue, sharing her flavor.

Veronica felt the yearning hardness of him pressed to her thigh. A hardness she could melt. Smiling, she drew him inside her, moist with welcome. Enthralled in the same spell he had woven, Antonio moved gently within her until he came with a soft, broken cry, as if he could not bear the sweetness of the pleasure.

Borne on the lingering glow of pleasure, Veronica floated towards sleep. A shiver of memory ran through her just before she drifted beyond the edges of consciousness . . . the stones, the jeering voices. *I have had that dream before,* she thought. But she had gone too far, and darkness enveloped her.

—

"Witch!" The cry rose up all around Veronica. Stones hurtled through the air.

It was her nightmare, but it was real, not a dream. She saw her guard fall, his sword clattering on the street, blood streaming down his face. She tried to run, but the boys closed their ranks, cutting off her escape. She backed up, but there was only the wall behind her. Once more Savonarola's youths had lain in wait for their victim, but their stones were for her, not Mama Lucia.

"Witch! Witch!" The stones hurtled at her, struck with pain fiercer than any dream barrage. Was she going to die with no more warning than this? Anger filled her—at her own flawed gift, at the vicious, taunting boys with death in their hands. She crouched against the wall, curling as small as she could, wrapping her arms about her face and head.

"Stop!" she heard someone cry. "In the name of God I command you to stop."

The jeering stopped. After a moment, Veronica lowered her arms. A stone struck her forehead, and she fell unconscious.

"How do you feel?" a voice asked, concern edged with nervousness.

Veronica opened her eyes and recognized the face of Fra Domenico da Pescia, the very friar who had formed the groups of Savonarola youths. A wild energy rushed through her, urging her to leap up and run, but she forced herself to lie quietly. His hands were gentle as they tended her, but there was an anxiety about him, as if he were afraid of her. Surely he must have treated other women in the time of the plague, so it was not her sex. It was the taunt the boys had hurled at her with their stones, *Witch, witch.* Veronica shuddered. When the friar moved back from her, she tested her arms and legs. She hurt all over, but nothing appeared to be broken.

"Where am I?"

"Within the walls of San Marco," Fra Domenico replied. "In the infirmary."

"Where is my my guard? Is he all right?"

"Yes. He has been dismissed."

Dismissed? "I want to go home. I can be taken care of there."

"Later, perhaps," he answered, and the *perhaps* sent a new shiver of fear through her. "Fra Girolamo wants to question you."

Witch. She was trapped. Was this the same band of boys that stoned Mama Lucia? Was it their own idea, or did someone put them up to it? It must have been Luigi. Dorotea had just sent word she had taken the veil, and Luigi must have gone out seeking vengeance.

The door opened. Veronica tensed as Savonarola entered the cell. He stood looking at her for a moment, his face an unreadable mask, his eyes intent. Fra Domenico joined him, whispered a few words, then went out the door, leaving them alone together. "We meet again, Madonna Veronica," Fra Girolamo said in his quiet voice. "I was certain we would."

"I want to go home," she repeated, but it was a test more than a demand.

"Certain accusations have been made against you."

She took a deep breath. "They are not true. Nor do I believe that the youths who stoned me acted of their own accord. Question them, and I believe you will find they were bribed to attack me."

"By Luigi della Montagna," Savonarola said. "A few of them used to be with us, but they have turned away from our teachings. One not yet fallen warned Fra Domenico of their plan. He has spoken to those who stoned you. Some have learned shame and confessed."

"They have reason. They tried to murder me."

"' Thou shalt not suffer a witch to live,' " he quoted.

"I am not a witch. You have already discovered that Luigi paid my attackers. This was a way for him to have me killed with no blame attached to himself or his family."

"But the accusation remains."

"Luigi will retract it. He will never accuse me openly."

"He refuses to lay the charge before the Signoria, but his

cowardice does not absolve you. It is not the first time you have been brought to my attention. This summer, you spirited your great-grandmother away from Florence—a Gypsy, who sins against God by telling fortunes with the Devil's playing cards.''

"Mama Lucia is wise and kind. She means no harm to anyone. Ask at the convent hospital. The nuns will tell you of her goodness.''

''I know that you and your great-grandmother used to tend the sick. The sisters speak highly of your care. It may be that you are misguided rather than evil. Do you also use these cards to tell fortunes?''

''I have studied their meaning, but I have never read anyone's fortune,'' she answered, glad for the first time that Daniele had never finished her *Tarocco* deck.

''Nevertheless, I think it best you be handed over to the authorities for questioning.''

Terror swept over her. Trembling, hardly knowing what she was doing, Veronica knelt before him, a supplicant. His compassion and mercy were for the weak. ''Father, I beg you to question me yourself and release me if you find me innocent.''

''I will be a harsh judge,'' he warned her.

''I fear your harshness less than the greed of these other unknown judges. I do not want my guilt or innocence determined by the weight of Luigi della Montagna's purse.''

Savonarola studied her, his moss green eyes gleaming in the dim light of the cell. ''Very well, I will question you.''

What had she done, laying her life in the hands of an implacable fanatic, who would see evil where she saw good, the work of the Devil where she saw the mystery of life? She was shaking, afraid to speak and condemn herself further. But transfixed by his gaze, Veronica knew that she could not lie to him. Lies would trap her in a web from which there would be no escape.

As if he read her mind, Savonarola said, ''If you are innocent, you need not fear the truth.''

''I do not think my truth and yours are the same.''

''There is but one truth.''

''May it not be reached by more than one path?''

He studied her, then said quietly. "You must tell me your truth then, as you know it."

"I do not know what to say to you. I know that you will not think me good, but I try to be."

"That is hard to believe, living as you do in the midst of licentiousness and depravity."

"I live with my cousin, who is gentle and protective of my welfare. Both my virtue and my soul were more at risk in Luigi della Montagna's palazzo."

"Your father-in-law says you are a dangerous wanton—and that you practice the black arts."

"I am neither a witch nor a wanton, only a woman who has thwarted Luigi della Montagna's lust. Twice I fought him when he attempted to rape me. Twice I could have killed him and did not."

"He says you enthralled him with your powers, but he grew fearful and spurned you. In revenge, you have bewitched his son-in-law, Antonio di Fabiani."

Choked with fear, she whispered, "There is no bewitchment but love, which we share."

"You speak of lust. Lust is the tool of the Devil, luring the weak to break the sacrament of marriage."

"I speak of love, as well as desire," she insisted. "As for our marriages, both his and my own were unconsummated. Roberto will never be husband to any woman, and Dorotea is now the bride of Christ."

"If, as you say, Roberto cannot be a husband to you, why did you not seek an annulment when you were first wed? The Church would have granted you one on those grounds."

"I loved Antonio in my heart already," she said, not daring to mention the Prince of Cups. "Not knowing him, still I knew I wanted no other husband. Roberto protected me from a worse fate, I thought, as I tried to protect him from his father's abuse. If I sought my freedom now, Luigi would punish Roberto in my stead."

His mouth thinned to a grim line. "Your father-in-law says that you plan to murder his son so that you can marry your lover. He suggests it was not plague but poison that almost killed Roberto last summer."

Veronica swayed, rage and nausea swirling within her.

"That is not true! You have seen me with Roberto, seen how I tended him—prayed for him. You have examined my medicines. I have never wished for his death. Roberto is as dear to me as a brother."

"Under God's law, Roberto is still your husband. Nor do you deny that Antonio di Fabiani is your lover. You are an adulteress."

"Adultery is not witchcraft." She could confess to that but not repent of it, nor believe loving Antonio to be a sin.

"Is it because of you that Fabiani has renounced his marriage vows?"

"I do not know what he would have done if he had not met me. But it was not for love of me alone that he sought the annulment. When he went to Rome to seek it, he was angry with me and did not mean to return. He and his father have a dark grief between them. For that alone, Antonio would have renounced both his marriage and his inheritance."

"And what is this grief?"

"The secret is not mine to tell," Veronica said. Then looking into his eyes, unable to stop herself, she added, "But you know it."

"How do I know it?" he demanded. Glowing hot as embers, his gaze burned into hers, compelling her to speak. She felt now the power that ruled his order, that ruled Florence itself.

"Not his father—he would not speak of it to anyone. His mother confessed it to you before she died."

"How did you know this?"

"I saw it in your eyes," she replied, knowing herself trapped at last.

"What else do you see there?"

Even as she stared at him, the embers ignited. Flame filled her vision, a conflagration that blotted out all else. Then Savonarola appeared at its center, for a moment a figure wreathed in flames, then a dark twisting thing enveloped and consumed. Veronica gasped, knowing it was not her death she had long sensed hovering about him, but his own.

"You see it too," he said.

Trapped in the power pulsating between them she could only answer, "Yes."

"The fire," he whispered, his fear edged with a terrible

hunger. "Is it to be a joyous sacrifice, my martyrdom? Or is it only the just abasement of my pride?"

"That is between you and God."

"Is it the ordeal? Shall I offer myself to the trial by fire?"

"I do not know!"

"You are lying!"

"I am not lying. You say yourself that you see the fire, but you do not know."

"You must tell me what you see," he commanded.

"I do not think it is the ordeal. But I have no certainty. You are suspended in the flames, not walking through them. I have nothing else to offer you."

He whirled on her, his eyes slitted. "You say you studied the cards. I will bring you a deck of the *Tarocco*, and you will read it for me."

"No!" she exclaimed. "No, I will not!"

"You want to show me your truth, now is your chance. You say there is no evil in these cards."

"I do not believe there is, but you do. You will not trust me or them! If the *Tarocco* told you what you wished to hear, you would fear it tricked you with false hope. If not, you would claim it tempted you to doubt your faith. Even if everything evolved as the cards said, you would say it was the Devil working through them."

"And so he would be."

It had been a test to trap her. "Then you see that I will not tempt you to do what you think is evil."

"Nor prove yourself a witch in my eyes. But it is not only the *Tarocco*," he accused. "What you have seen is more than intuition. You possess supernatural powers."

"Not as you mean it."

"How then?"

"Sometimes," she choked on the words, "sometimes I see the future. I have visions."

"Visions," he repeated with deadly quiet.

"I do not say they are from God. I do not say they are not. I do not know where they come from except that they are not from the Devil."

"How can you know that?"

"They have never been wrong. They have never tempted me

to evil. At worst, I have suffered them, unable to do anything. At best, I have been able to help those I loved from danger.''

"Yet who knows what wickedness to which they may yet lead you? They might be part of a cunning design.''

She shook her head helplessly. "I cannot think that way. It is difficult enough to deal with that reality when it overtakes me.''

"You are only a woman, and weak. You cannot judge.''

"I cannot judge? I know good and evil when I meet it in men. I know kindness and cruelty. If Satan has laid some snare for me, I confess I have not seen it, unless it is to be falsely condemned.''

"For your own salvation, you must submit yourself to the Church.''

"Whose Church must I submit to?'' Veronica challenged him, anger breaking through her fear. "Yours or the Pope's?'' The light in his eyes flared in warning, but she rushed on recklessly, "You fight over what you believe, but I must choose one of you and be damned by the other. I must choose rightly, yet I will be damned by all if I try to see the truth for myself. You rule through fear, but fear is a weapon that can be passed from hand to hand. What of wisdom? What of love?'' She stopped, gasping, and covered her face with her hands.

When Savonarola spoke, his voice was controlled, "What I have of either, I have offered in the service of God to this city and its people.''

Raising her head to look at him, Veronica saw his face stern but thoughtful. The path he trod was a narrow one, narrow enough that he might still cast her into the abyss if he felt she barred his way. But it would not be from spite. "I know that. Forgive me. I am afraid.''

"And angry,'' Fra Girolamo said. "But I told you to speak the truth as you see it, and you told me you would submit to my judgment.''

"Yes. But I cannot stop my visions, nor beckon them at will. If they revealed that someone I loved was in danger, I would have to act on them . . . as you have acted on yours.''

"As I have acted on mine,'' he repeated.

She saw, suddenly, how tired he was. And how full of doubt. "You must be a messenger, but whether from God or the

Devil I do not know.'' His gaze swept over her, but Veronica saw his attention was turned inward as he spoke. ''I saw God's glory blossoming in Florence and thought I would be the one to nurture it. I thought I walked in the paths of righteousness, but now I am wandering in the wilderness. I believed I wanted the power to do good. Now I wonder if I have come to desire power for my own sake rather than His. Why else is He silent now, when I so desperately need to hear Him? I listen for His voice and hear only the echo of my own, preaching to the multitude.

''I wanted to live in Him and die in Him,'' Savonarola whispered, agonized. ''Now this test has come, but I have not been called. Perhaps God tests my humility in summoning my brethren to walk in my place. I fear for them, but if I protest too loudly I may cripple the power of the faith that must bear them through the inferno. They offer themselves in all purity to His glory. Surely He will lead them through unharmed.''

Savonarola turned, becoming aware of her once more, though he still spoke almost to himself. ''Like you, I do not believe tomorrow's fire is the one I am called to enter, though this pyre may ignite the other. Since he has not yet summoned me, I must stand aside and offer my prayers to those who have been chosen. His will be done, amen.''

He stood for a moment in silence, his head bowed, then walked to where she knelt on the stone floor of the cell and lifted her to her feet. ''Whatever doubts I have about you, I do not doubt that Luigi della Montagna bears false witness. You are a misguided sinner who has yielded to the temptations of the flesh, but I feel no evil in you such as you have been accused of. I do not know if you are a witch, but I find I cannot condemn you without condemning myself. Today I say unto you, go in peace and sin no more. I cannot say what will happen if you are brought to me again.''

———

One of the younger monks was assigned to escort her to her home. Outside San Marco, Antonio appeared and told the friar he could return to the monastery. Intimidated, the young man hurried back within the walls. Antonio stared at her, relief still at war with the grim tension in his face. Briefly he reached up to touch the cut on her forehead. "You are hurt?"

"Only bruises."

"And Savonarola has released you?"

"Yes. You knew he was questioning me?"

"We were not allowed to see you. Da Pescia said the Holy Friar would have to talk to you first." Antonio's voice grated with anger. Taking her arm, he led her down the street. "Was it difficult?"

"It was difficult, but I am no longer in any danger." Despite his parting words, the only fear she felt now was not for herself but for Savonarola.

"You are still in danger." Antonio's face hardened into a mask of cold fury. "I questioned some of the boys. They did not act on their own."

"Luigi did not like Dorotea's news."

"That is unfortunate. For him."

Looking into the implacable blackness of his eyes, Veronica wondered if she could dissuade Antonio from seeking Luigi's death, or if she should even try. She did not want him to risk himself, any more than he wanted her at risk. Before she could speak, Daniele and Benito joined them. Glancing down the street they had emerged from, Veronica saw her guards and three others. "Stefano is ahead of us, with half a dozen men," Daniele said. "We thought they might try to transfer you to the *bargello* under guard."

If they did not die trying to rescue her, they would be outlawed and excommunicated, hunted. The guards could fade into anonymity, but not aristocrats. "You should not have risked so much."

"We love you," Antonio said. "You are worth any risk."

31 Fire and Rain

 A GREAT platform had been erected in the Piazza della Signoria. Ninety feet long, sixteen feet wide, and seven feet high, this was the stage, the battleground on which the opponents would meet their trial by fire. To prevent the flooring from burning, the surface had been topped with bricks covered over with dirt. All that was left of this surface was a single narrow pathway, heaped high on either side with piles of wood. When the trial began, the friars would stand opposite each other at the far ends. The pyre would be lighted, and the challengers enter the inferno.

"The wood is saturated with oil, resin, and gunpowder," Antonio said. "It will burn fast and hot."

"And the friars with it," Machiavelli said. "How many in this vast crowd, do you think, actually expect one or the other of them to emerge alive?"

"More than half," Antonio conjectured.

"Presuming, of course, that any of the holy orders other than the Minorites put in an appearance today," Machiavelli gibed. "They look uneasy, don't they, waiting all by themselves in the Loggia della Signoria, staring across at the pyre?"

"I am certain Savonarola and the other Dominicans will appear after he conducts his morning Mass. Whether the Franciscans emerge from the palazzo is another question entirely."

Even as they spoke, silence swept over the crowd like a wave. As their voices were stilled, others were revealed, lifted in song. Antonio and Niccolò watched as two hundred and fifty Dominican friars made their entrance into the square. They proceeded two by two, singing psalms as they walked. After them came Fra Domenico, robed in a cope the color of flame, and then Savonarola, carrying the Host in a silver monstrance. Following the orderly procession of the friars was another far more vast—thousands of men, women, and children all bearing lighted torches or candles. Still singing, Fra Girolamo and his brethren approached the loggia. The Minorite and Franciscan brethren were already awaiting them, seated on their own side of the partition with their own altar. The thousands that had followed Savonarola mingled with the even greater crowd already gathered in the piazza.

"Phenomenal, is he not?" Niccolò asked, rhetorically. "Savonarola always knows how to achieve exactly the effect he wants."

"An impressive entrance," Antonio agreed, "but I doubt the crowd will walk through fire for him—no matter what they said when he preached at San Marco."

"It is Savonarola's vanity which has led him to this bonfire," Machiavelli said, contemptuously.

"Perhaps if Fra Domenico walks through unscathed, the crowd will rush to follow him. If he performs such a miracle, in God's name or Savonarola's, even I might be swept away by faith." Antonio laughed. "As it is, not even his challenger has appeared for the test."

"Fra Francesco is a coward. I think the plan was for Savonarola to answer his challenge. That accomplished, he would have retreated as he has done today, and left Savonarola to face the ordeal alone. No matter that Francesco started it, the Friar's claims are the ones on trial."

"But the Franciscan offered his challenge to anyone, and he got da Pescia. Fra Domenico may believe Savonarola is the voice of God, but he has made no such declaration for himself, and the same sort of pressure cannot be brought to bear upon him," Antonio pointed out. "However eager he may be to undertake the ordeal in the Friar's name, Savonarola does not want him to be put to the test, and he will defend Da Pescia's rights as he would not defend his own."

"And so?" Niccolò queried.

"And so we wait. The next move is the Franciscans'."

"What is it this time?" Machiavelli snapped as Antonio squeezed his way back through the crowd. "We have been standing here for hours."

"More objections from the Minorites. Fra Domenico has now consented to lay aside his supposedly bewitched crucifix, but he has raised up the monstrance that Savonarola carried in the procession. The outcry is louder than ever."

First it was the scarlet cope. The Minorites had protested that the garment might be bewitched by spells that would guard it from the flames. Fra Domenico had removed it. Then it was suggested that his simple undergarments could also have been bewitched. Fra Domenico agreed to enter the palace, strip naked, and don whatever clothes the Minorites deemed acceptable. He disappeared within the doors and reemerged some time later dressed in a chasuble from the palace chapel. Then the complaints switched to the crucifix, and now the monstrance.

"This is ridiculous!" Machiavelli exclaimed. "The Franciscans are still hiding in the chapel, and the Minorites are making fools of themselves with this quibbling."

"Better fools than scorched meat," Antonio said coldly. "Delay is their only hope, and it may well work. Look at the sky."

"It was clear half an hour ago," Niccolò complained, studying the dark clouds rolling in over the piazza. Even as they spoke came the first growl of thunder, a sharp flash of lightning. Machiavelli pointed to the loggia, "Look. The Signoria is dismissing the Minorites."

Amazingly, there was no demonstration in the crowd as the friars quickly and quietly made their escape. Then Savonarola and his followers departed as well. There was some effort to interfere with him, but his escort got him safely out of the piazza. With almost no warning, the roiling clouds unleashed a fury of rain and hail upon the gathering, drenching both the crowd and all the preparations for the ordeal by fire.

"Another fiasco!" Machiavelli exclaimed as the rain soaked them to the skin. "Do you think Savonarola's followers will proclaim this storm the will of God?"

"That is what they will say now. If he is lucky, the rain will hold. If it relents, the people will have time to grow discontented. Then no matter what anyone claims, they will blame Savonarola for not giving them their spectacle."

"They are sounding the bell at San Marco," Daniele said, raising his head from his sketch pad.

It is his death knell, Veronica thought, but she said nothing, only sat motionless in the fading light. The tolling echoed in her heart, a dull throbbing pain.

"Stefano said that at Mass this morning, Savonarola offered himself as a sacrifice to God, declaring he was ready to die for his flock. He may finally be called to fulfill his promises."

"Yes, he knows," Veronica murmured. "He said yesterday's pyre would ignite this one."

"Do not tell me you believe in him too!" Daniele leapt from his chair, his face livid with sudden anger. Veronica stared at him, shocked. Wordlessly, she shook her head. He collapsed back in the chair, his hands snarled in his hair. "I am sorry."

"I believe he has some ability to predict the future, as I have," she said quietly. "And what he saw or heard revealed was wedded to his own harsh, exacting faith and called divine prophecy. Or if the voice was God's, Savonarola heard it as all humans must—imperfectly."

"You are weeping," Daniele said.

"Am I?" She brushed the tears away with her hand.

"One may weep even at the death of an enemy," Daniele said. "It is his death you see?"

She met Daniele's eyes. "Yes. He will die. By fire. He knows that it awaits him, and this time he will walk forward to greet it."

They sat in silence, motionless in the fading light, the muffled clamor of San Marco's bell the only sound in the room. Then after a moment or two, the sound of a horse, a door slammed, footsteps running up the stairs. Antonio appeared at the door to the studio and paused there. "It has begun," he told them, grim and glittering, as he was whenever danger brushed him. "They are rioting in the streets."

Too grim, Veronica thought suddenly. "What is wrong?"

He smiled at that, a sharp mirthless grin that faded abruptly. He came into the room and walked not to her but to her cousin. "Yes. Something specific is wrong. Stefano has been hurt. Sit down, Daniele. He was knifed in the back, but he will survive.

In that he is lucky—one of the few to suggest to the mob that their violence is ill mannered who will survive to tell of it.''

"What happened?" Daniele asked, mastering his distress. "Were you with him?"

"We saw it happen. I had been walking about Florence—a tour of impending chaos. Giacomo was with me, and one of the guards. There have been incidents against Savonarola's followers all day, taunts, abuse, beatings. The *Piagnoni* are most unpopular after their master's failure to be fried to a crisp. The riot began at Santa Maria del Fiore, at evensong. Apparently, some of the *Compagnacci* began hammering on the benches, cursing the *Piagnoni*, then driving them from the church. Outside, there was a gang of boys waiting. They stoned everyone who tried to leave.''

"It was planned," Veronica said flatly. She had no doubt.

"Oh yes, it was planned. The *Arrabbiati* and the *Compagnacci* have been fomenting the discontent of the city and gathering their own forces. There will be no better time for them to strike at Savonarola.''

"What happened?" Daniele's voice was hoarse.

"I am sorry," Antonio said. "I assure you Stefano is not in danger. He was inside the church. When he came out, he tried to reason with some of the men.''

"He is gentle," Daniele said, "but he is not foolish.''

"He had his sword drawn," Antonio said, "but he was taken from behind. We were close enough to reach him before they inflicted any more damage. We took him home and then I came here. I have left Giacomo there, with instructions to bring news later tonight.''

"Thank you," Daniele said.

Antonio inclined his head in the direction of the monastery and its tolling bell. "Most of the attackers are gathering at San Marco. There have been at least two murders already. Another knifing outside the doors of San Marco, and a young boy who was foolish enough to be praying as he walked. The mob chased him through the streets. When they caught up with him, they ran him through with a lance.''

"Animals," Daniele whispered.

"Yes, a mob is a mindless beast, thirsty for blood. But I have no doubt there will be calculated killings tonight as well.

Even with yesterday's fall from grace, Savonarola still has too many supporters in high places. They must fall too. Tonight will end Savonarola's rule of Florence, one way or another.''

"Veronica says that Savonarola will die by fire," Daniele told him.

Antonio turned to her, his eyes black and unwavering. "Tonight?"

"I do not know."

"If so, he will die as he wished. For his sake, I hope he is not disappointed."

"What is that sound?" Veronica asked suddenly. "Is someone crying?" For a moment it seemed there was nothing, and then the muffled sob came again. Veronica froze for a second as cold chills raced along her spine, shivered her body. Then she ran to the door, Antonio and Daniele following behind her. They discovered Simona climbing the stairs to the studio, pressing her apron to her mouth to stifle her sobs. "Simona what is it? Are you hurt?"

Simona stared at her, terrified, then burst into a loud wail. Crossing herself, she knelt before Veronica. "Madonna, it is terrible. I went to San Marco for vespers. I wanted to show my devotion to the Holy Friar."

"Is he dead then? I am sorry, Simona," Daniele said.

"No, it is something else," Veronica said, the chills coursing through her again. At the moment she did not care if Simona thought she was a witch. "Tell us what has happened, Simona."

The terror in the cook's eyes was what she would show an avenging angel rather than a devil. "I went alone, Madonna. I went alone to San Marco, but Roberto knew I was going and he followed me there."

"Where is he?" She had left Roberto asleep in his room. He had cried half the night and most of the morning. They had refused to take him to the ordeal by fire yesterday. No one had wanted him to see Savonarola go up in flames.

"We were praying, a thousand of us," Simona sobbed, "praying inside the church. Then the mob came. They threw stones at the church. One of the men went out. He spoke to them, told them they offended the house of God. They fell on him, Madonna, and cut him to pieces."

"Where is Roberto!" Veronica cried.

"He is still inside San Marco. They made me leave. All the women had to leave. The good friars escorted us out by a back door of the monastery," she told them. "Roberto would not come with me. I could not make him. I saw *Fra* Frederigo, and begged him to find Roberto and bring him outside. Some of the men came out after us, too cowardly to stay with the Holy Friar, but Roberto was not with them."

"Frederigo will not put Roberto's safety before Savonarola's," Veronica said. "I must go find him."

Even as she started forward, Antonio's hand closed on her arm. "I will go. You stay here with Daniele."

"I must go too. He will listen to me."

"No. You are not going," Antonio said with such fierceness Veronica knew there was no arguing with him. It did not matter that she had proved her skill saving his life, he would not let her risk her own if he could prevent it. Without a word, she pulled her arm free and left the studio. She went to her room and lay down on her bed. After a moment Antonio appeared. He came over to where she lay and kissed her.

"I will find him."

Veronica nodded. When she did not soften, he turned and left. When she was certain he was gone, Veronica rose and went to the cupboard. Opening it, she pulled out her men's clothes and quickly dressed herself in the doublet and hose, tugged on the boots and stuffed her hair inside the cap. Dressed, she retrieved her knife, tucked it inside her boot, and set out for the monastery of San Marco.

32 Destruction

 By the time Antonio reached it, the square in front of San Marco was already packed. The mob grew larger by the minute, urged to join the assault by the jubilant *Compagnacci* or by their own feverish lust for destruction. Antonio forced his way through the press to the open area surrounding the walls of the monastery. Above him, the great brass bell rang on, summoning help that would not appear. The tide had turned against Savonarola, and few of his followers would risk their necks to save their fallen idol. The monastery would have to make do with what protectors it had already. Antonio estimated two score men were staggered atop the walls, guarding them as best they could from the attackers swarming below. Despite their vigilance, a pile of straw had been heaped in front of the main doors and set alight. The fire burned, scarlet and orange in the darkness, the smoke billowing with the shift of the wind. Skirting the edge of the crowd, Antonio saw an opening and made one attempt to scale the walls quickly, but he was spotted and driven back by a hail of tiles from above. He withdrew unscathed and went searching for a better position.

Passing an alley, Antonio heard a muffled sound. He turned down the narrow passage, and found a man huddled in a doorway, weeping. The man cowered when he took hold of him, afraid that the Friar's enemies had seized him. As Antonio suspected, the man had been inside San Marco and left, but had not been able to bring himself to desert the square. Not knowing what information might prove useful, Antonio got an account of what had happened before the man had fled.

"First we heard that the Signoria had ordered Savonarola to leave Florence within twelve hours, as if he, not his challengers, had failed the ordeal yesterday. We could not believe the command was real. We thought it must be a trick to lure the Holy Friar into the hands of his enemies. Many of the friars grew angry and sought to arm themselves. Savonarola discovered what they were doing and forbade it. He told them to put aside their weapons and take up a cross.''

"He is doing nothing to help them protect themselves?"

"Fra Girolamo prayed for them. He raised up the sacraments and led his brethren in procession around San Marco, singing psalms," the man answered shakily.

Antonio felt a rush of anger. The mob would slaughter the unarmed monks. But if Savonarola were what he claimed, he would not forsake his vows to defend himself, and the monks would also view the attack as a test of their faith.

"The Holy Friar was terribly distraught," the man continued. "He told us that it was because of him that this terrible storm had arisen in the city. He took up his crucifix and went to give himself to the crowd. But we begged him not to go, for what would we do without him? He told us that we were resisting the will of God, but he did not abandon us.

"We waited, listening to the noise, smelling the smoke of the fire outside the doors. Then another order came, demanding that all ordinary citizens within San Marco leave or be declared rebels. Half of the men left then, deserting the chapel and the defense of the walls." The man burst out sobbing. "I too am a Judas. I should not have abandoned him, but I could not bear to be outlawed from Florence. I believed God would protect Savonarola. I believed He would protect me for serving him."

Antonio said nothing. He thought the man had made the right choice, but he did not believe in Savonarola's sainthood, as this man did or had once done.

"Those who remained will die," the man moaned, separating himself a step further from his former compatriots. He started to pull away, but Antonio tightened his grip long enough to demand the best place to scale the walls. The man quailed, not wanting another betrayal on his conscience but too frightened to resist.

"I mean no harm to the Friar, or to anyone within San Marco," Antonio said impatiently.

"By the cloisters," the man replied, cringing. Antonio released him and circled around the wall in the direction the man had indicated. It did look to be the best access, and he was only one of many attempting the climb. The hail of tiles pelted the attackers here as well, but the angle was difficult, and more got over. Even as he plotted his approach, Antonio saw a familiar figure dart ahead and scale the wall—Veronica. He froze for a moment in pure disbelief, then cursing furiously, he ran forward. Ducking the worst of the barrage, he found the hand and foot niches to follow her up and over the wall into the grounds of the monastery.

Hearing someone stalking her, Veronica whirled, knife in hand. Antonio glowered at her. "You promised to stay with Daniele."

"No, I did not. I said nothing, and you believed as you chose."

Antonio was seething with anger, but who had misled whom was a pointless question. It was too late now to do anything about it. He had as much fear of ordering her back through the mob as of keeping her with him, and far less chance of achieving it. "Will you promise not to go off without warning?" he asked.

"I will promise—so long as you are within warning distance."

He did not much like that answer either, but at least it was honest. "Come on, then."

He led her through the grounds of San Marco. Most of the attackers who had made it over the walls were looting the cloisters and infirmary, but a small crowd had reached the sacristy and were intent on ramming the doors of the chapel. Above the racket the friars could be heard inside, singing. Sometimes the hymns would falter with the pounding, but always they resumed. Antonio could imagine Savonarola bidding them to continue their psalms to the Lord.

Then the singing ended, and caught in the grip of anticipation, the battering stopped as well. After a moment the doors opened, and the crowd fell back. A friar Antonio did not recognize appeared before them, his face stern and his voice unwavering as he commanded, "Savonarola bids you to be quiet. Go and cease to disturb this holy place."

The silence lasted the space of a breath, then a great cry went up and the mob rushed the doors, knocking the friar aside and bursting into the church. Antonio grabbed hold of Veronica as the rush swept them inside. Once there, he thrust her behind him into the most obscure alcove he could find, watching as the plague of human locusts descended. Many of the monks remained kneeling, singing once more, but others rose up to fight back. Some struggled barehanded against the attackers, but others seized crosses, torches, or whatever weapons came to hand to fend off the enemy. Antonio saw a monk hurl himself into the midst of the attackers and wrench an arquebus away from one of them. Mounting Savonarola's pulpit, he began to fire the weapon into the midst of his enemies, singing out with each shot, *"Salvum fac populum tuum, Domine!"*

Within minutes San Marco was a miniature inferno. Small fires flickered everywhere Antonio looked, and the chapel was filled with plumes of acrid gray smoke. Above them in the choir, still beyond the reach of the mob, Savonarola and a handful of friars continued their chanting. That melancholy cadence was an eerie backdrop of sound shredded by the screams and groans of the wounded, the grating clash of weapons. He had seen worse hells of blood and death on the battlefield, but none had possessed this crazed and nightmarish atmosphere. Perhaps it was no more than his concern for Veronica that exaggerated his perceptions, stringing his muscles with tension and tainting his mouth with the metallic edge of fear. Scanning the smoke filled interior, Antonio estimated there were already a hundred casualties.

"Can you see Roberto?" Veronica asked beside him.

"Not yet. Could he be on the roof, hurling tiles?" Such violence would be unlike him, but who knew what Roberto would do in defense of his beloved Friar.

"I think he is more likely hiding," Veronica said, with the same uncertainty he felt.

"Look up, Savonarola is leaving the chapel."

The stones and shot that had been sent aloft into the choir had done no visible damage, unlike the carnage below. The friars carried no wounded with them as they filed out. Antonio and Veronica recognized Fra Frederigo among them and ran forward, calling his name. They did not know if the monk heard them in the midst of the riot or if their movement caught his eye, but he paused, recognizing them, and gestured them to a doorway below. Obscure as it was, the door was already under siege, two men hammering at it with a bench. Sword drawn, Antonio warned them off. They backed away long enough for Fra Frederigo to let them through and bar the door behind them.

"Roberto . . . ." Veronica gasped.

From his startled look, Antonio realized Frederigo had not recognized her, only himself. His disapproval of her disguise was obvious. "Do you know where Roberto is?" Antonio asked him.

Fra Frederigo turned his disgusted gaze on Antonio now. "Sheath your weapon," he ordered. When Antonio reluctantly complied, he told him, "Roberto is safe. He is locked in my cell. I will take you there, but not Veronica. She must wait here. Women are not permitted."

"She is coming with us," Antonio said.

"Frederigo," Veronica pleaded, "you know Roberto will listen to me. You must let me come with you."

For a moment, Fra Frederigo glared at them, but at last he nodded and beckoned them to follow upstairs. He kept them at a discreet distance behind the procession that Savonarola was leading down the corridor. Unlike the elaborate interior of the church, the dormitory they entered was austere, but it maintained its air of serenity despite the chaos surrounding it. One or two cell doors were open, revealing the frescoes of Fra Angelico that adorned the walls, their severity and grace one with the architecture of the building. Frederigo stopped outside the door to his cell. The faint sounds of weeping could be heard within.

"Is Roberto hurt?" Veronica asked.

"No, only upset by the disturbances." Fra Frederigo then unlocked the door and turned to them. "I am going to rejoin Fra Girolamo. He is leading us to the library to seek solace in the midst of this madness."

They watched as he walked down the corridor to rejoin the procession, then opened the door to Fra Frederigo's cell. Antonio let Veronica go into the tiny room alone. He could hear her soft voice murmuring to Roberto, but the weeping did not stop, and Antonio suddenly heard those sobs overlying those of the man he had spoken to in the alleyway, that memory mingling with all the unseen, unheard weeping happening at this instant in thousands of households throughout Florence. The faithful were mourning the fall of hope.

"Savonarola has brought this on himself," Antonio muttered under his breath, dismayed at the surge of pity that cut through his defenses. He did not want a fanatic like Fra Girolamo controlling Florence, but he could not rejoice in his downfall. Fra Girolamo had striven for goodness as well as for power. If only he had not been so rigid, so obsessed—Antonio sighed wearily. If Savonarola had been the saint so many thought him, he would probably have been martyred sooner, and for less cause.

At last, Veronica led Roberto from the cell. Not knowing if the way they had entered was the safest way to exit and not wanting to leave that door unbarred behind them, Antonio suggested they find Frederigo. At the cross corridor the sound of voices led them to the open door of the library, a large airy room graced with two rows of columns. Their entry was noticed, but Fra Frederigo quickly spoke to his superiors and no one sent them away. They moved to the far side of the room, trying to remain as inconspicuous as possible. It was not difficult, for there were already two agents from the Signoria within. They announced to Savonarola that he was to accompany them to the palazzo. Fra Domenico stepped forward and demanded that they present a written order and a safe conduct. Conferring with each other for a moment, the emissaries agreed to these terms and said they would return shortly.

"We should try to follow them out. They are probably our safest escort," Antonio suggested, but Roberto had caught sight of Savonarola and refused to budge.

"No one has ordered us away yet," Veronica whispered. "Let us wait awhile longer."

"We will stay until they return, then," Antonio agreed, sensing that the Signoria meant to impose some order on the violence. Curious about their reactions, he returned his attention to the monks conversing among themselves.

"We should find a dark spot and lower you down from the walls, Fra Girolamo. You must escape from the city," one of the friars told Savonarola.

Another monk protested, "Should not the shepherd risk his life for his flock?"

Savonarola gathered the man in his arms and embraced him, then turned to the others and said, "It is the essence of the Christian life to do good and suffer evil. I shall suffer these tribulations gladly." Then he gave each of his followers a kiss.

Fra Domenico returned his kiss and said, "I too would come to this feast."

Savonarola accepted Fra Domenico by his side, but when another monk also begged to come, Savonarola told him, "Brother, if you would obey me, do not come, for Fra Domenico and I are going to die for the love of Christ."

Antonio gestured to Veronica when the envoys of the Signoria returned bearing their written order. Roberto was willing to follow Savonarola, so the three of them trailed the friars and their escort through the ruined chapel. The fires had been extinguished, and they opened the doors into the square. Outside the mob waited, as well as hundreds of armored soldiers from the Signoria, complete with artillery. The friars came forward and gave themselves over to the guards of the Signoria, who bound them and led them out of San Marco into the square. A great howling rose from the crowd when they appeared. Faces distorted with hatred, the mob sneered, cursed, and spat upon Savonarola. The saint had become a pariah. As they led Fra Girolamo down the steps, a man rushed out, thrusting a lighted torch at his face. Another man kicked him from behind, jeering, "There, that's where the Friar keeps his prophecy." Obviously, the guards were protecting him only enough to ensure he reached the palazzo alive.

Roberto had been stunned into silence by the mob, but now he began to sob again, ignoring even Veronica's attempts to calm him and struggling to follow the captured friars. His protests could easily make him, make them all, a target of both the guards and the mob. Swiftly, Antonio maneuvered them out of the crowd and down one of the less populous side streets. Out of sight of San Marco, Veronica was able to quiet Roberto a little. He stopped resisting, though tears continued to stream down his face. Even that short a distance from the monastery they were much safer, for the mass was following Savonarola's journey to the palazzo.

"With luck we will make it back to Daniele's with no more incidents," Antonio told Veronica as they began their journey homeward.

She shook her head, her body radiating tension. "There is still danger. I can feel it. I was not afraid before, but now I am."

Antonio's skin prickled at her warning. Rapidly, he scanned the faces in the few groups scattered along the street. Loitering on the corner ahead of them was a thin, dark man. The stranger's glance grazed the three of them almost aimlessly, then he turned and walked up the street. The casualness was studied—that alone would have warned Antonio—but there was something familiar about the thin, bitter features as well. The prickling sensation came again, apprehension edged with the anticipation of danger. He blanked his mind for a second, letting the image rise to the surface. *Canino*, he thought. The Sicilian was a famous assassin, known to be a lethal swordsman. The bravo worked mostly in southern Italy, though enough ducats would draw him anywhere. Canino could have many reasons for being in Florence, but murder was the most likely. There would be many unexplained deaths tonight. The killer would be very useful to anyone who wanted to use this opportunity to dispense with a few enemies.

"What is it?" Veronica asked.

"A Sicilian dog, sniffing for blood," he answered.

"Our blood?"

"He is here now, when we are. I do not like the coincidence." He paused briefly in the shadow of a wineshop, examining some fictional problem with his boot heel as he asked her, "Do you see anyone you recognize?"

Veronica did her search casually enough, as though she were keeping watch rather than hunting. She gave no indication that she saw anyone, but her lowered voice told him another story, "Behind us. It is too dark to be sure, but I think the man standing by the alley is Luca, Luigi's guard."

Antonio knew the man—thin reddish hair, pockmarked, brutal—but when he flicked his gaze in the direction she had indicated, he saw no one. That was no reassurance, for it meant he had most likely ducked into the alley. Turning back to Veronica and Roberto, Antonio drew his *estoc* and moved forward slowly, leading them through the narrow streets, scanning each cross street before they passed it. Antonio moved his sword in small circles beside him to keep his arm loose, his wrist limber.

Veronica stopped to pull a wooden pole loose from the makeshift awning of a storefront. The improvised stave gave her another weapon besides her knife. Antonio did not want her to risk herself, though he knew full well that Veronica's instinct would be to protect them even as he intended to protect her. "If there is trouble, keep Roberto as calm as you can," he said.

A dead-end alley tempted him. If he stationed them there, no one could attack them from the rear, but he did not know how many men he would have to hold off, and Veronica and Roberto would be trapped if he were killed. Antonio passed the alleyway and then regretted it. There was nothing else, nothing but empty streets with high walls and shuttered windows on both sides. They were caught in the open, and all they could do was go on.

The street curved out of sight ahead of them. Antonio led them cautiously around the turn. Suddenly three men were rushing toward them with swords raised: Canino, another man beside him, and Luigi following. Roberto wailed as Veronica thrust him against the wall, quickly shifting to guard Antonio's back. "Luca is running this way," she warned him.

Hoping she could hold Luca at bay, Antonio focused on the three approaching. Luigi was trailing behind, and Antonio blessed his cowardice. Swiftly, he feinted a charge at Canino. The Sicilian shifted back, bringing his sword more to the front to cover himself. The other guard thought he had a chance to come at Antonio from the side and started forward, but committed himself a little too far. In a single fight Antonio would have maneuvered this man into a worse position, but there was no time—this might be his only chance. Keeping track of Canino peripherally, Antonio wheeled and lunged at the second guard. The swirling action of a sword fight confused most men, but Antonio was trained to see it all happening at once. He could see the opening in the downward slash of the guard's sword, savage but clumsy. Antonio went through the opening and stabbed him in the heart.

Antonio saw Canino moving toward him. He had a dark heartbeat of fear that he wouldn't be able to pull his sword back out of the guard's body in time. He jerked, and as his sword came free, stepped back. Canino's sword just missed his head and nicked his shoulder. Antonio countered, but he was still off balance and the Sicilian dodged out of reach.

"Clever of you, Antonio, to take out an easy one before facing a real threat," the assassin sneered at him, even as he beckoned to Luigi, trying to reposition him closer to Antonio. "But it will do you no good. You are no match for Canino."

"I have dispensed with all the other dogs that Della Montagna has set on me," Antonio told the Sicilian. "Dogs and bitches both," he added, glancing at Luigi in time to catch the flicker of recognition in his eyes. He was right. Bianca had been his hireling as well.

Antonio heard a flurry of movement behind him, shuffling feet followed by a bass grunt of pain. Not daring to turn, Antonio guessed Veronica had landed Luca a blow with her stave. Frightened by the fighting, Roberto shrieked even louder.

"Shut up that bawling," Luigi bellowed at him, and Roberto lapsed into cowed silence.

There was more scuffling behind Antonio. He could hear Veronica's harsh breathing. He wanted to swing around and cut down the red-headed guard, but he saw that Canino was waiting for exactly that, pausing longer than he had to, tempting Antonio to try to protect Veronica. As soon as Canino saw that he was not succumbing to the lure, he attacked again, his sword lashing like a razor edged whip. Antonio parried Canino's slashes, retreating back as he learned the timing of the strokes—only there was little distance left to give. Veronica and Roberto were too close behind him.

Holding his ground, Antonio parried thrust after thrust from the assassin. They were fast and powerful, but Antonio sensed that Canino was not yet striking with all his force. Peripherally, he saw Luigi sidling in closer, trying to find a vulnerable spot on the side. Leaping back out of Canino's range, he made eye contact with Luigi, sending him scuttling out of reach. Antonio knew Canino had wanted him to repeat himself, to try to shorten the odds by striking at the weaker opponent, but he had expected Luigi to hold to his attack. If Luigi were less craven, the chances were that Antonio would be dead by now. But if it were only Canino and himself, the Sicilian was the one who would be dead. The assassin was not as good as he thought he was. Skillful and swift he might be, but Canino had a flaw in his approach. He was too much the hired professional. Canino kept playing the odds, using misdirection. He favored the strategic when a daring strike might have earned him his killer's fee.

Trusting his instincts, Antonio stopped thinking, pouring his force strictly into the movement itself. Cut, parry, thrust, dodge. Letting the instant of his counterattack be a complete surprise to himself, he suddenly found himself stepping forward right under the arc of Canino's sword, slashing up at the deadly swordsman. Canino leaped aside, stumbling as he landed. Moving in for the kill, Antonio heard a cry of pain from Veronica, heard the stave she had used to hold Luca at bay clatter to the flagstones. He sacrificed his momentum against Canino in order to snap his head back to look at those behind him. What he saw in that second almost paralyzed him. Weaponless, her arm drenched with blood, Veronica was totally vulnerable, and Luca was thrusting his sword straight for her heart.

"No!" Even as the Antonio cried the word silently, Roberto cried it aloud. He plunged past Veronica, both arms out reaching for Luca, and took the driving thrust of the sword in his own belly. Impaled, screaming, Roberto reached out to grab the guard's wrist. Veronica snatched her knife from her boot.

Antonio turned and parried just in time, Canino's sword grazing his neck. Recovered, the Sicilian attacked fiercely, his blows whipping faster and faster. Antonio countered and slashed back at him. From behind him came another scream, Luca's voice crying out in mortal agony. Antonio could not turn to see, but he felt a rush of relief and pride, knowing Veronica had dispatched Luca. That death freed Antonio of danger from behind. He could finally focus on what was in front of him. Luigi, seeing the odds vanish, found his courage and attacked as well. Fighting off thrusts from both men, Antonio tried to draw them away from Veronica. He had let his relief show too obviously. "Leave this one to me," Canino ordered Luigi, smiling at Antonio all the while. "You kill the woman."

Luigi drew back. Antonio knew Canino's command was meant to unnerve him. The Sicilian was expecting him to try a desperate feint followed by an attack on Luigi. That would be Canino's moment to follow Antonio in and take him from the side. His blood shimmering with icy fury, Antonio gave the assassin the feint he was expecting, but he didn't turn for Luigi after it. Canino was already lunging in anticipation. Antonio parried and bored forward again, full force directly at Canino. The Sicilian tried to counter, but the calculating professional had out-manipulated himself. Antonio's thrust struck home. Canino stared at the sword impaling him, then tumbled to the ground without a sound.

Antonio whirled. Luigi was harrying Veronica, but she had reclaimed her stave and was holding him off, despite her wounded arm. The silence warned Luigi. He turned to find himself trapped—his guards, his paid assassin were dead. With a moan of dismay, he began backing slowly down the street. Implacably, Antonio followed him. As long as Luigi lived, Veronica's life was in danger. Luigi's gaze turned to her, beseeching mercy where he had given none. Antonio would not have stopped—but she did not even try to stay his hand. Not with Roberto dead. In desperation, Luigi tossed his sword away.

"Pick it up," Antonio said, his disgust as cold, as merciless as his hate. "Pick it up, or I will kill you anyway."

"No!" Luigi exclaimed, his eyes widening in terror. Shaking his head, he sank to his knees, blubbering, "No, no, no."

Antonio put the sword to his heart and silenced him forever.

He pulled out his blade and wiped it clean and sheathed it. Turning, he found Veronica watching, her face as expressionless as he had ever seen it. She met his eyes briefly, then walked slowly over to Roberto's body and knelt beside it. Tears slipped from her eyes, rolled down her cheeks, but it was as if he watched a mask weeping. Not looking at him, she said, "If I had found the courage to slay Luigi, Roberto would still be alive."

"You are not a killer."

"I let you do it for me. Wanted you to do it. Too late."

Antonio felt her futility. He did not know what to say to ease her guilt. "You could not know what would happen. Not knowing, you did not take Luigi's life—did not risk what evil might have followed from that act. The world is full of those who slay heedlessly; we do not need more of them. It was your gentleness Roberto loved you for, Veronica, as we all do."

"My gentleness cost him his life."

"You would have given yours to save him," he said, thanking God she had not. "Roberto knew that. Instead he gave his life to save you. It was his right, the right of love."

"He did not understand," she said woodenly. "Of all of us, he was the only one truly innocent."

"He understood well enough. I do not think he would take his sacrifice back again. Innocent as a child he may have been, but he chose a man's death. Honor him for that."

Veronica gave a choked sob, and another. The blank mask of controlled pain dissolved, the grief that twisted her features twisting Antonio's heart. Kneeling beside Veronica, he took her in his arms and held her while she wept.

33 *Fire and Ashes*

ONCE more a vast crowd had gathered to watch a bonfire in the Piazza della Signoria. This time there was no doubt of the outcome of the spectacle. Today, at last, the waiting throng would have their burnt offerings. Savonarola, of course, was the centerpiece, but on one side would be Fra Domenico and on the other his third in command, Fra Silvestro, who had been found hiding inside San Marco the morning after the other two had been arrested. Stretching out diagonally from the terrace of the Palazzo della Signoria, a long wooden platform six feet high led out into the square to the waiting pyre. From the center of the great mass of straw and wood rose a towering post. A ladder led to the top, which was set with a crossbar. From that dangled three nooses and three iron chains with rings to hold the bodies once the ropes had burned away.

"It looks like a crucifixion," Veronica said.

Antonio heard the strain in her voice and moved closer to her. He did not urge her to leave, knowing it would do no good. Veronica had shunned the trial by fire that had been the beginning of Savonarola's destruction, and Antonio was shocked when she said that she intended to come to the execution. When he asked why, she told him that she feared suffering the horror of the reality less than the horror of the vision seizing her. Veronica was convinced she must watch Savonarola burn, one way or the other. Whether that conviction was foreknowledge or merely fear, Antonio accepted the necessity that drove Veronica here. He stood beside her, offering his comfort and his protection.

"You are not the only one to notice the resemblance," he said in response to her comment, keeping his own voice calm and level. "The Signoria shortened the arms of the crossbar to diminish the effect, but with little success."

"They will make a saint of Savonarola yet," Machiavelli said with disgust.

"Whether or not he is a saint, he is a martyr to his faith," Stefano said. His face was ashen, but his stance was resolute. Only the four of them were there to witness the burning. Daniele, equally resolute, had refused to come with them.

"They could simply tie the Dominicans to stakes," Machiavelli said, choosing to ignore the last comment. "As far as mercy goes, they should be throttled instead of hung before burning."

"Mercy?" Stefano asked bitterly. "What mercy has the Signoria shown Savonarola? The trial is a travesty. I have seen terrible things in Florence, but never have I been so ashamed of my city."

"He was dead from the moment of his arrest, Stefano," Machiavelli snapped. "Once the Signoria seized him, they had to find him guilty or lose control of Florence. As it was, there was almost a rebellion."

"Yes, I know. I was in San Marco the day they came and told us to disperse or be declared rebels."

"And you left, did you not?"

"Yes. The threat was wearing thin by that time, but I was not willing to risk my citizenship to aid the Friar."

"You, like the rest of Florence, have forsaken Savonarola, even as his God has forsaken him."

"You may understand the politics of the city perfectly, Niccolò, but I doubt you know the mind of God," Stefano said sharply.

Antonio wished his two friends liked each other better, though this was the first time the friction had been so obvious. Machiavelli thought Stefano frivolous. He was not charmed by Stefano's gaiety and had no experience of his goodness and generosity. Neither could Machiavelli see that the other man understood the political realities. Stefano was not a fool, but he was idealistic, and he needed to voice his moral outrage. From the other standpoint, Stefano did not know that Machiavelli's cynicism masked a great deal of unadmitted anger at the blatant injustice of the Friar's trial. But Niccolò was unlikely to share any of that indignation with him. Anxious as Antonio was for Veronica, both the cynicism and the idealism were grating on his nerves, but losing his temper would help none of them. So he only said, "Ugly as it is, this is the death the Friar has chosen for himself, Stefano."

"The Signoria have made grounds where none existed. What little confession they managed to wring from Savonarola cannot justify his death. They tortured him every day for weeks, hauling him up by the ropes of the *strappado* and dropping him again and again from a great height. Fra Girolamo recanted anything false he was brought to say through that agony."

"If he is, as you say, a martyr, it matters little that Savonarola is unjustly accused. Like Socrates, he would much prefer to be innocent of the charges," Machiavelli said. "And the Friar has admitted that he now doubts that his visions came from God."

"Yes," Stefano said. "But even Christ felt doubt on the cross. What else do they have, besides the doubts of a tormented man?"

"Savonarola has admitted to several heresies . . . ." Machiavelli began.

"Such as the belief that the Pope should not keep concubines, nor the sacraments be bought and sold like fish in the marketplace," Antonio remarked caustically.

For once Machiavelli looked apologetic. "I know it is flimsy. This mockery disgusts me, but it is necessary. Savonarola has the makings of a despot. He must be destroyed if Florence is to regain her strength as a republic."

Antonio shook his head. "Savonarola was head of the *Populari*, as well as his own religious campaign to scour the sin from the city. His death will strike a heavy blow to the liberal movement. The *Arrabbiati* will control Florence now."

"Your father should be pleased with that outcome," Machiavelli commented, returning to his sarcastic tone.

"No doubt," Antonio answered, refusing to be drawn.

The crowd murmured uneasily, and the four of them turned their attention to the palazzo. It was not Savonarola and his fellow monks who appeared, but Remolino, the Pope's despised envoy, planning to finish questioning the Signoria had begun and to give sanction of the Church to the trial.

"The Signoria were fortunate that the Pope agreed to send Remolino when they refused to surrender Savonarola," Machiavelli commented when the envoy appeared. "As laymen, they had no right to question the monks. If Alexander VI were not so pleased to be rid of the Friar at last, he might have excommunicated them all. He had already threatened to interdict the entire city."

Antonio smiled grimly, "The Signoria could not afford to relinquish him to Rome. The Holy Friar knew too many of the unholy secrets of Florence."

"Remolino is a disgrace," Stefano said, watching the envoy strut along the terrace. "The man did not even bother to be discreet about his orders—he boasted that he carried the verdict with him inside his doublet. He said the Pope had declared Savonarola must burn, though he be another John the Baptist."

"And so he shall," Machiavelli said.

Veronica shivered slightly, and Antonio moved closer to her. He only half listened to Stefano, who still would not relent, "All of Florence knows that the confession that was read out in court was a forgery. They would not allow Savonarola to be present, for fear he would refute it, as he did all the earlier ones. They gave up the torture, for they could never break him.''

"The Friar has many flaws," Veronica said quietly, "but cowardice is not one of them."

Machiavelli quickly turned to her, but whatever he saw in her face tempered his response. "Fra Girolamo is a fanatic and so a fool for all his cleverness, but he is brave. I was wrong about him, and Antonio was right. Savonarola might have survived this if he had been the political maneuverer I thought him to be."

A wave of agitation ran through the crowd as the three friars were brought forth under guard. Dressed in white tunics, they stood on the terrace of the palazzo. They appeared calm, although their faces, their bodies, showed signs of the ordeal they had undergone. They were stripped of their tunics, and for a moment, Savonarola clung to his own, a last talisman of the Church he had served; then he let go of the garment. Stepping forward to face them, a friar who had once belonged to San Marco had been given the task of final excommunication. He did not look as if he welcomed his duty when he said, "I separate you from the Church militant and triumphant."

Savonarola lifted his head, his voice clear and steady as he said, "Not the Church triumphant. That is not in your power."

Then the Pope's man, Remolino, proclaimed their sentence, that they would be hung and their bodies burned. Smiling, he added, "In his generosity His Holiness frees you from the pains of purgatory, giving you absolution for your sins and restoring you to innocence. Do you accept this indulgence from his hands?"

For whatever they might think of its worth, the three Dominicans accepted the Pope's generosity. At Remolino's command they began the walk to their deaths. Some of the youths broke through the crowd and ducked under the platform. Drawing knives, they stabbed up through the cracks in the planks at the feet of the three friars, following their progression along the platform to the waiting cross. Silently, the three friars fought to retain their dignity, even as the new pain caused them to stumble and limp. Their knives bloody, the boys squirmed back into the mass of spectators to watch the hanging.

"Now is the time to do miracles!" The same taunt rose from various places in the crowd.

When the condemned men reached the base of the looming gallows, Fra Domenico began a psalm of thanksgiving. The executioner led Fra Silvestro forward first. Though his fear was apparent, he went forward without protest to have the noose set about his neck, the chain bound about his body. Then the executioner thrust him from the platform. The drop was too short to break his neck, and he strangled slowly, begging Christ for mercy. When he was dead, Fra Domenico walked forward, still singing. Halfway up the ladder, he called out to the crowd, assuring them of the truth of Savonarola's prophecies. Then put his head in the noose, and the executioner thrust him forward. His fate was mercifully brief. Finally, Savonarola came to stand calmly in the central position. The hangman fastened the rope about his neck and pushed him from the platform. Even as he choked, the executioner grasped the waiting torch and tried to thrust it into the waiting pyre. In his hurry, he fumbled. Antonio hoped the Friar was dead by the time he recovered, for the straw caught fire immediately. In a moment, the whole bonfire was ablaze.

As they watched, a sudden powerful wind blew the flames away from the hanging bodies of the friars. From all over the square cries of "A miracle!" rose and hundreds of people fled in terror. But the flames returned quickly, and most of the watchers with them. For a moment Savonarola was wreathed in their shimmering scarlet halo. Stirred by the scorching breath of the fire, his right arm lifted, the palm open and two fingers raised in a last blessing on his flock. As one being, the watching throng drew a gasping breath, but vision was brief. A dozen youths ran forward, armed with stones that they flung at the uncanny figure till the arm dropped and the flames engulfed the Friar. The bonfire burned, incinerating flesh and rope. The chains held the blackened bodies for a time, but at last nothing was left but a heap of charred bones.

Antonio and Veronica made their way homeward slowly. "Was it truly less horrific to see it this way than within your mind?'' Antonio asked her gently, trying to understand her gift.

She turned to him, pain tightening the composure of her face into a pale mask. "Yes," she said. "Had I seen him burn within my mind, the need to help him would have tormented me unbearably. This way, for all my pity, I knew there was nothing I could do." She smiled wanly. "It sounds selfish, does it not? I went to spare myself that desperation, that despair."

"Not if you could not save him," he replied. Then he asked, "Would you have, if you could?"

Her eyes were dark and clouded, staring into some possibility he could not see. "I do not know. I do not think he wanted to be saved. As you said, Savonarola chose the means of his dying. Whether his death was what he hoped, only he can know."

———

"Rumor says they found Savonarola's heart whole amid the ashes," Machiavelli laughed.

Seated beside them in the wineshop, Frederigo della Montagna snorted derisively. "Yes, I have heard that tale. My mother is most distressed. She disguised herself as a servant collecting ashes so she could ferret amid the wreckage. Soldiers drove her off, of course, but not before she found a blackened finger bone. It is being set in a silver reliquary, encrusted with jewels."

"Do not scoff, Frederigo," Machiavelli said mockingly. "Think what a priceless heirloom it will be to your grandchildren."

Antonio had met Machiavelli in their favorite wine shop to celebrate his friend's election as chancel of Florence. Niccolò would enter his first office next month, and he was in an expansive mood. Even Frederigo della Montagna's uninvited appearance at their table did not dampen their spirits.

Fra Frederigo's faith had not survived Savonarola's death. He had expected a miracle from his idol, and when none occurred, he had renounced his vows, certain the Pope would grant him a dispensation. Abandoning the monastery, Frederigo had returned home to take control of the Della Montagna property—apparently only a few days before Maria planned to turn the entire fortune over to the Dominicans. Frederigo had put a stop to that plan, and he was already searching for a bride whose dowry would expand the estate. He would marry and carry on Luigi's line. Unexpectedly, Antonio found he preferred the zealot to the skeptic. It seemed what little heart Frederigo possessed had burned with Savonarola.

Reluctantly, Antonio decided to confide his own news. Frederigo was here, and he must inform the Della Montagna family sooner or later. He smiled ironically, since his news was joyful, however reluctant he was to impart it to his former relative. "I have an announcement of my own," he said to the two men. "Veronica and I have decided to marry at the end of July."

Smiling, Niccolò leaned forward to congratulate him. Frederigo drew back in his chair, his face settling into familiar lines of prim disapproval. "Only three months after Roberto's death? It is disrespectful." Apparently, his disillusion with religion had not altered his character extensively.

"No disrespect is intended," Antonio responded. There was no mention of Luigi, he noticed. No one missed him or cared to probe too deeply into the circumstances of his mysterious death. Veronica was still mourning Roberto, but not as a wife. After the darkness and violence of the last few months, she and Antonio both wanted to pledge their vows to each other.

"My mother will be outraged. Florence will be scandalized."

"Another scandal will do us little harm here," Antonio said wryly, "and we will be leaving Florence immediately after the wedding."

Piqued, Frederigo bade them an abrupt farewell. Antonio conversed awhile longer with Machiavelli, then made his own departure. He found Giacomo in the courtyard with the horses, staring into his cupped palms. Seeing him coming, his valet extended one hand. "See what I have found."

Antonio looked at the tiny offering. "A caterpillar?"

"Not just any caterpillar. These are most strange. Look at the markings."

Antonio took the creature into his own hand, where it wavered about, blindly seeking some escape. On closer view he could see that the body of the caterpillar bore the mark of a cross. Stranger still, it seemed to have a miniature face surrounded by a wispy halo.

"Savonarola's followers—what's left of them that will admit it—say these caterpillars have never appeared before and never will again, for they do not become butterflies."

"It is a curiosity," he agreed, returning the soft-skinned thing to Giacomo, who put it inside his pocket with a sloe leaf. Its markings were uncanny and, if what Giacomo said was true, its nature even more so. Antonio found himself curiously sad that this poor creature would never transform, never take flight. Irrelevant as the life and futile death of a caterpillar were, it seemed an ill omen for his next visit.

Mounted on Ombra, Giacomo a faithful shadow, Antonio left the city and took the road to the Fabiani estate. Having told Niccolò and Frederigo of the wedding, the word would spread quickly now. Antonio did not know if his father would see him, but he did not want the news of the marriage to reach him as gossip. As he approached, Antonio felt a tumult of emotion stirring in him at the thought of the coming confrontation. He recognized anger, apprehension, and with a bleak smile, hope. With all that had passed between them, some part of him still yearned for his father's forgiveness.

Hoping to forestall a dismissal, Antonio told the servant who met him in the courtyard that he had important news. The man bade him wait outside and vanished into the house. A few moments later, the servant reappeared and led him to the *salotto*, where Giorgio di Fabiani sat in a chair in the sun. Antonio was shocked. His father had aged ten years since he last saw him a few months ago. Everything about him and thinned and faded, grayed. He was clothed in arrogance still, but it now seemed a tattered pauper's garment rather than the princely robe it had seemed before. Facing the brittle shell before him, Antonio wondered how long his father would survive his mother's death.

"Whatever your news may be, say it and be done," his father said waspishly. "I want you out of here."

"I am to be married at the end of next month. To Veronica della Montagna."

His father stared at him in amazement, "The *selvaggia?*"

Despite himself, Antonio smiled. "Yes, to the *selvaggia.*"

"I do not know why I am surprised." His father's voice was caustic. "Your taste has always run to . . . ."

"Do not say it," Antonio said harshly. His father stilled, and they stared at each other for an interminable moment. His father looked away first, defeated but unrelenting. Antonio's heart thudded painfully once, twice, then he continued evenly. "I came to give you the news and to invite you to the wedding."

"Do you actually expect me to come?"

"No," he answered quietly.

"It is well that you do not."

"Nonetheless, I wanted you to know you are welcome to attend the ceremony. It will be very simple, and we will be leaving Florence soon after."

"So you have brought me news of import after all."

"So I have."

"I suggest you take the first steps of your journey now," his father said.

There was nothing to say, no way to bridge the gap between them, but still Antonio hesitated.

"Go, and when you are gone, do not return. For any reason." To leave no doubt, his father added, "I can think of nothing worse than to see you appear beside my deathbed."

"If I know, I will come. If you cannot forgive me, you may have the pleasure of banishing me once again," Antonio said quietly, then turned and left the room.

On his way out Antonio passed the corridor leading to his mother's bedroom. He had no intention of visiting it. He had said his farewell to her, and the room would not evoke the memories he cherished. But he saw old Paolo emerge, bearing a tray, and curiosity gripped him. Turning aside, he made his way to the door, which was locked from the outside. He heard the servant call out but he ignored him. Even as he turned the key and opened the door, Antonio knew what he would find within.

Head bowed, Laudomia sat in a chair. Antonio waited for her to lift her head and recognize him, but her posture did not change. He went forward cautiously, until he was standing, then kneeling, before the last of his enemies. Her eyes were unfocused, her face, her body, plagued by restless twitches and tics. Hands plucking at the silk of her skirts, Laudomia mumbled an inaudible litany. He could not understand what she was saying, but it was obvious she would not be sending any more assassins after him.

Hearing footsteps, Antonio glanced over his shoulder as his father and Paolo appeared in the doorway. The servant waited outside, but his father came in, his face livid with rage. "Get out of here," he hissed. "Have you not ruined enough lives, Antonio?"

At the sound of his name Laudomia started screaming. He turned back to her, but his father thrust him aside to gather her in his arms. Laudomia hated Antonio still, it seemed, though she was so lost to madness that she could no longer recognize him. It was not him that her clawed hands attacked but her own cheeks, her own breasts, and his father's hands as he tried to restrain her fierce, pathetic frenzy. Antonio reached out to help.

"Do not touch her!" his father cried out. "Go. Leave us. Leave us be."

Paolo appeared at his side, whispering in his ear, "Your father is the only one who can quiet her, Signore Antonio. He holds her and talks to her of her dead husband."

Sick with pity, Antonio left them alone together. Giacomo was waiting in the courtyard, his eyes round and questioning when he saw his master's face. As he mounted Ombra, Antonio told him, "There is nothing more to fear from Laudomia."

In silence they rode back toward Florence, Antonio brooding on the wretched scene he had witnessed. Giorgio di Fabiani had loved his mother for her open heart, her goodness, had loved Alessandro for his fire and joy. Now his father had embraced Laudomia, her madness, her thwarted malice, and made her the emotional center of his life, shutting his son further away than before. His father would nurture his hatred to deny his fear. He would never forgive Antonio—to do so would open the possibility of love, and his father would never risk that pain again.

Abruptly, Antonio reined in his horse, stopping in the middle of the road. That realization was the death of hope, and with it the last of Antonio's anger flickered and died as well, all its fervor burned to ashes. He drew a shaky breath and urged Ombra forward, filled with a strange freedom that was as much sorrow as relief. He accepted, at last, that his father was lost to him in bitterness as finally as his mother was in death. The only forgiveness that would ever be given between them was his own. He gave it now, without hope of return.

His mother had told him he was too much like his father. Antonio saw it clearly. Neither of them loved easily, and love possessed them fiercely. His passion for Beatrice had held him in thrall for years, as his father's love for Alessandro possessed him still. Love fused with hate and fear, the emotions twisting within them both until they crippled. Like his father, the path Antonio had set himself on led into darkness. If he had not found Veronica, at best his heart would have shriveled and died. At worst, it would have embraced the madness Bianca had offered, as his father embraced Laudomia's.

But he had not. He had found Veronica and with her light and love. He would follow that path as long as he lived.

34   *The Lovers*

"WELL, Florence was not such a catastrophe after all, Feet," Giacomo said, slipping on his nightshirt. It had been a day of hectic preparation, and all his feet wanted was to get off themselves. Settling into a chair by the window, Giacomo lifted them up onto a stool to catch the night breeze while he sipped his wine. He could hear them sigh blissfully.

"I'd say Madonna Veronica was worth the trouble. Isn't she

exactly the sort of lady I told you the master needed?'' Giacomo began, breaking off as the door opened without warning.

Antonio paused at the threshold, managing to widen his eyes and frown in perplexity at the same time. ''Who are you talking to?''

Giacomo gulped. ''To my feet.''

''To your feet?'' Antonio repeated with delicate incredulity.

Giacomo was aggrieved. ''Well, they listen, don't they? And they don't interrupt private conversations either.''

''I assure you, if I had known you were engaged in a discussion with your extremities, I would not have interrupted.''

Giacomo followed his master's gaze to his toes, which were writhing in embarrassment. ''You've got them all upset,'' he accused.

''My apologies.'' Hand pressed to his heart, Antonio bowed slightly. ''I meant no offense.''

''Just so it doesn't happen again,'' Giacomo conceded. Tomorrow being Antonio's wedding day, he could afford to be magnanimous. ''What is it you're wanting?''

''I cannot find my doublet,'' he said then, noting his valet's altered expression. ''What have you done with it?''

''Rescued it,'' Giacomo replied with great dignity. ''Marco Polo chewed off two of the big gray pearls, but he only swallowed one. I've got a maid sewing the one I saved back on, moving one from the shoulder to the front to cover the other and rearranging the loops of silver bullion to cover that gap. No one will notice.''

''No one will notice . . . ?''

''You can't even see the tooth marks—unless you look,'' Giacomo assured him.

The valet watched as his master started to swell with outrage. Mid-swell, his lips began to quiver and he burst out laughing instead.

Giacomo's toes tingled with pleasure at the sound. Grinning, he indicated an extra goblet on the table. Accepting the offer, Antonio perched on the bed, and extended the goblet. Giacomo filled it to the brim with the rich red wine, then extended his own cup in toast: ''To love.''

"To marriage." Giacomo, curled in the willow tree, toasted the moon with the last of his wine. He was alone for the moment and, for the moment, content to be so. He slipped off his fancy slippers and set them in a branch overhead.

"The wedding went perfectly, Feet, if I do say so myself, which of course I do. It was anything but traditional, at least in Fabiani terms, no fuss, no fanfare, no parade through the streets on horseback with flower petals strewn before and *zanni* cavorting after. A big gaudy ceremony wouldn't have been right anyway, but I think the master has had his fill of them. There were just the people who cared there to hear the vows: Stefano, Niccolò, Mama Lucia and the *voivode*, come specially from the Gypsy camp. Benito with Elizabeta and her son.

"Not that it wasn't lovely, Feet. We held the ceremony outside by the little fountain in the garden, and draped the balcony with garlands of roses and silver ribbons. Daniele gave the bride away. Beautiful she looked too, all glowing in that dress she wore for the painting, like ripples of pale purple water flowing over her, and her hair falling like fire under the silver net of the veil. Did you know Antonio asked her to wear that dress specially? He wore the mauve and silver doublet, looking young the way he does when he's happy. And if you hadn't been told, Feet, you'd never guess the loop of bullion on the shoulder was supposed to be a gray pearl.

"After the ceremony there was music and good food and wine. The master and his lady celebrated with us throughout the afternoon. We watched the sunset together, one of the prettiest I've ever seen, Feet—it's a shame you were still in your shoes then. The clouds blossomed like giant flowers along the horizon, rose and gold and coral. After that, they left us to our pleasures, while they went to take their own. There they still are, Feet, and I wish them joy."

"Giacomo?" Feminine laughter rose from the ground. "I can hear you up there, chattering like a squirrel at the moon."

Caught twice in as many days, but he was too happy to care. "Do squirrels chatter at the moon?"

"You do," was the saucy reply. "Giacomo, I've brought some more wine. You'll have to help me up."

"Right away, *carina*." He finished off the last of his goblet and helped Daniele's new serving girl up beside him. He smiled at her and she smiled back, drawing a bottle and second cup from her apron. Settled among the branches, they sipped their wine happily. She was very pretty, and had noticed right away what nice brown eyes he had. She was clever too, she laughed at all his jokes. For that matter, she laughed at all his complaints as well. Giacomo leaned forward and kissed her. She kissed back. He sighed. She sighed.

"Aren't weddings wonderful?" she asked.

Before he could wonder just how dangerous it was to agree, she kissed him again.

—

Dusk, an almost invisible veil of diamond spangled darkness, drifted over the glowing aquamarine sky. Arms linked, Antonio and Veronica circled the garden, saying good evening to their guests. Then he led her upstairs to the bedroom and closed the door behind them. Inside, the room was fragrant with the lush heady scent of summer roses, and the delicate notes of recorder and lute trickled through the quiet air. Smiling, they faced each other, dazzled with wine and happiness. For Veronica, traces of sorrow lingered, but its faint presence was a low note that deepened her awareness of the day's wonder.

Lovers, friends . . . and now husband and wife. They had claimed each other before the world in peaceful, radiant surety, their marriage both celebration and communion. Alone now, they embraced with the same serene elation, the same expectation of joy. Entwined, they kissed with languid fervor, exploring the satin surfaces of each other's mouths before their lips parted, their tongues plumbed for deeper sweetness, savoring tastes of honey and wine. Hazy with pleasure, Veronica looked up into his eyes. "Let me go for a moment," she murmured. "I want to light the candles."

The blue light of dusk was fading, its silky transparency deepening to velvet, dense and glossy black. As the night embraced them, Veronica went about the room, lighting the multitude of candles she had placed there. She wanted to see Antonio. See the beauty of his body revealed in the flickering glow of their flames. See the fulfillment of passion illuminate his

face. Antonio stood, content to watch her at her task. When
she was finished, the room shimmered with golden candlelight.
She set the final taper in place and returned to the enfolding
circle of her husband's arms, his delectable kisses, the gentle,
vivid power of his presence.

After a moment, he tugged the veil of silver net from her
hair, then reached for the neckline of her gown. "I love you in
this dress," he murmured, "but I shall love you even better out
of it."

Veronica caught his hands. "We must start with you," she
chided, laughing. "Your clothes have three times as many
ties."

She unfastened all the bindings of his doublet and pushed it
off, uncovering the cool gossamer silk of his shirt. Lifting it
over his head, she sought the living warmth of his skin. Her
palms glided smoothly over the elegant rise of muscle, her
fingers riffling through the soft fur of his chest. She bent her
head to kiss each rose red nipple in turn, a tender salutation.

"Now you," Antonio said before she could delve any further.

Veronica turned around, raising the tumbled weight of her
hair from the back of her gown. Antonio pressed his lips to her
neck, just below the tendrils curling at the nape. She tilted her
head to the side, so his lips could follow the line of her throat,
shivering as his lips tarried over the quickened pulse beat.
Drawing back, he deftly untied the first delicate cords that held
the dress at neck and back. He slipped the finely pleated silk
from her shoulders, kissing the smooth flesh as he slid the
fabric down, freeing her arms and baring her to the waist.

Antonio paused there, his hands reaching around her to cup
the swell of her breasts, her pink nipples drawing taut as he
brushed them, the eager peaks nudging his palms. Sighing her
pleasure, Veronica leaned against Antonio, her arms reaching
back to encircle his head, her fingers carding the thick fine
hair. She sighed again as one of his hands slipped within the
silk. His warm palm planed down over the curve of her belly
and through the springy hair below, shaping itself to the
mound of her womanhood. His fingertips ventured deeper,
parting the soft cleft to find the sensitive inner folds already
moist and swollen with anticipation. He found the pulse there

as well, his touch centered on the hidden bud of flesh. She felt herself throb against him, a tiny heartbeat of desire.

They stood for a moment in that embrace. Veronica's arms twined about Antonio's neck, his hands pressed to the warmth of her sex, the tender lips enfolding his questing fingertips. He withdrew his hands, but only to unfasten the last ties, letting the gown slither over her hips to pool like moonlit water at her feet. He turned her to him. His eyes were dark and luminous, the golden light of the candle flames reflected in his gaze. "I love you," he told her.

"I love you," Veronica answered. She kissed him, and kissed him again, relishing the pliant sculpture of his mouth. Then she began to move slowly down his body, her eyes reveling in the beauty of him as her hands, her lips, discovered all the tactile pleasures he offered her—the carved lines of neck and shoulders, the square masculine planes of his chest, darkly shadowed, the taut-muscled belly. There was a glimpse of the hollowed cup of the navel, but the rest was hidden from her view beneath the clinging gray silk of his hose.

Antonio had enticed her with his questing fingertips. Now Veronica knelt before him, to tantalize, to ravish him with delight. Stroking up his legs, her hands modeled the sleek-muscled curves of calf and thigh, the tight swell of his buttocks, the narrow hips. Then, eager, unhurried, Veronica took down the hose and freed his sex from the confining *braghetta*. Leisurely, she fondled the sensuous shapes and textures she had exposed to view. The crisp abundance of the thatch at his loins that framed all the rest. The plump round jewels of his manhood enclosed in their velvety sac. The swelling shaft that lifted eagerly to her touch, its rose satin surface embossed with pulsing veins of amethyst. Glimmering like a liquid moonstone, a drop of moisture crowning the head intrigued her erotic curiosity. Antonio gasped as the pointed tip of her tongue licked the droplet, the tart flavor of him mingling with the fruity tang of wine. With deliberate, dreamy leisure, Veronica's tongue traced the length of him from base to crest and back again, while Antonio shuddered and moaned at each luscious stroke. The moans contracted to a single sharp cry as she enveloped him in the heat of her mouth. Antonio stood, his body rigid as the straining sex in her mouth as Veronica caressed him over and over with the fluid velvet of her tongue. She felt tremors coursing through him, felt his hands tugging her away.

"No more, or I shall die of pleasure here and now," he whispered, his voice husky with desire. Drawing Veronica to her feet, Antonio tilted her face up as his mouth descended to cover hers, his supple tongue a welcome invader. Parting from the kiss, he smiled at her. "Now you again, *dolcezza*," he said.

Lifting Veronica in his arms, Antonio carried her to the bed and lay down beside her. Softly, his lips, his hands, grazed the length of her, as gently provocative in their quest as hers had been in their amorous wanderings. She could feel his need simmering beneath the surface calm. His breath had quickened. The searing hardness of his arousal pressed itself to her thigh—but there was nothing rushed in his seductive wooing. Knowing his choice was to prolong his passion and rouse her own, she let herself float on these slow-stirred currents.

At first, Veronica was content with this drifting sensual languor. It seemed she would never want, never need, more than this endless tenderness, these melting kisses, the slow certain exploration of his hands that rediscovered all the secret wonders of her body and revealed them to her anew. But the sweet warmth that streamed through her blood grew hotter. With knowing caresses, Antonio coaxed the rising heat into flame. Beneath his skillful, impassioned fingers, his searching tongue, the sinuous movements of her body grew more urgent, more ardent, seeking, demanding more, when more only swelled the sea of fire that coursed through her veins.

They had taken turns guiding each other on their voluptuous journey. Now, Veronica sought to be one with Antonio in this incandescent fever of desire. Her hands drew him over her, her thighs parting to receive him, the heart of her open and wanting. She moaned as she felt him enter her, fill her, felt the leashed power of him pulse within her. Antonio held himself poised so for a minute, his throbbing hardness buried deep within her molten aching softness. He murmured her name, the dark velvet of his voice caressing her. "Yes, love," she whispered in answer. "Yes, Antonio. Yes."

He withdrew, slowly, and slowly thrust again. And again,

surging forward through the liquid, gliding heat of her. Each stroke drove swifter and harder, until he was driving into the yearning core of her. Sobbing with the sweet desperation of her pleasure, Veronica wrapped herself around him, drawing him deeper and deeper still, molding their bodies together until nothing separated them but the same fierce plunging that joined them. With each burning stroke, their passion intensified, sensation merging with emotion, possession and surrender fusing to shared rapture. The sweeping force of their longing lifted them to a shimmering pinnacle, then dissolved them, melting flesh and spirit into purest ecstasy. They cried out in one voice, lost in the glory of their tender, excruciating joy.

One by one, Veronica began to turn over the Tarocco cards. Their jewel colors gleamed, vibrant against the deep ultramarine blue of the velvet. As the layout unfolded, she was acutely conscious of Mama Lucia, Daniele, and Stefano standing behind her, watching—and of Antonio seated before her, waiting to see what his next card would be.

"The Priestess looks like you," he said the instant she was revealed. "Her face is older, wiser, but it is your face."

Veronica was honored, but still somewhat disconcerted, that Daniele had chosen her face for such a powerful card—one of the Major Arcana. Her visage was not the only familiar one. The Prince of Cups still resembled Antonio, and Veronica had seen similarities to Stefano and Benito and Giacomo in the faces of various figures throughout the deck. It endeared them to her, and the likenesses did not seem to interfere with the unique identity of the cards. Except, perhaps, for the Priestess. She contemplated it a second, then turned over the remaining cards.

With inspired effort, Daniele had finished painting her *Tarocco* pack and presented it to Veronica a week before the wedding. She had spent time alone with them, examining the beauty and spirit of each card in turn. They were so alluring that they begged to be used, and she had done an initial layout or two for herself. Her sense of connection, of communion with the cards was immediate and strong. What little awkwardness there had been would pass with time. The wonder and

delight of them would never fade. Alone, Veronica was not
hesitant to use them. Still, she had not planned to read for
anyone else for a long time . . . .

But the five of them were sitting in the garden, on their last
day together in Florence. Daniele had asked about the cards,
obviously longing to see her use his gift. Antonio had
promptly asked for a reading. Veronica turned to Mama Lucia,
expecting her to be critical of such an early debut, but her
great-grandmother seemed eager and curious. So she had
fetched the cards, wrapped in the square of silk Antonio had
given her to keep them in, embroidered with clouds and flying
dragons. When she returned, Mama Lucia had another chris-
tening present for the new *Tarocco*, her own cherished cloth of
blue velvet. Seeing this gift emerge, Veronica suspected the
innocent suggestion was a conspiracy but was too touched to
resent it.

"You have taken command of your life in all but this,"
Mama Lucia said, reading her as clearly as always. "Come
fledgling, try your wings."

Veronica knew she would not have Mama Lucia's skill, her
wisdom until she had Mama Lucia's years, if then. But neither
quality would come to her without practice. She need not demand perfection of herself, and no one else here would demand it of her. There could be no easier or more loving initiation for her and her deck.

And so, a table was set up, the velvet laid over it. Her family, her friends gathered round. Perhaps because Daniele had
designed them, the cards were a gregarious pack. They wanted
to be out in the world. Veronica felt their eagerness, separate
from her own uncertainty. She held the deck quietly for a
moment, to find a sense of calm and connection. Then she
gave the cards to Antonio, bidding him to do the same. When
he was ready, she asked him to shuffle and cut the deck in
three. She restacked the piles and laid out the *Tarocco* . . . .

The reading was perfectly clear to Veronica, except for the
Priestess. She understood the meaning of the card but not in
this placement. The Priestess had appeared in both the readings Veronica had done for herself. Now she wondered if
these cards were meant for her instead of Antonio. It might

well be too early to attempt to read for anyone else. It was difficult to tell. Given how closely their lives were interwoven now, the layouts might easily look similar, with the happy Cups and the journey shown by the Eight of Wands. But no, the enterprising energy of the second Wand, the financial promise of the Coins—those cards were for Antonio. So the Priestess was his as well. But the placement still confused her.

Well, she had Mama Lucia here to help her in this first venture. "I can read all the other cards, but I am not sure of the meaning of the Priestess in this context."

She spoke to her great-grandmother, but it was Daniele who answered, "Why not the obvious, Veronica? The Priestess represents your influence in Antonio's life."

Startled, Mama Lucia stared at him. "Hummf," she said, slightly piqued, "that's just what I would have said."

Veronica realized they were right. However flawed and uncertain her gifts, they partook of the power and mystery that the Priestess represented. It was time to put aside her own denial of that connection. The card had appeared like a beacon in her own readings. That power was awakening in her, more strongly than ever now that she had begun to work with the *Tarocco*. Touching her, its influence would reach out to Antonio.

"Yes," she said, accepting. She looked at the layout again, drawing her thoughts together.

"Many of these cards look familiar," Antonio said. "I cannot be certain, since Daniele's designs are different from the ones in Mama Lucia's pack."

"Yes, several of the cards are the same as the last readings," Veronica answered, "but the dark shadow of the Swords is gone. There is no strife here, no deceit or violence."

"No use looking for trouble where there is none," Mama Lucia clucked her tongue. "You were promised the possibility of this happiness, and you have struggled with yourself and the world to attain it. Now it is yours."

Veronica saw Antonio's lips curl as Mama Lucia added her comments. Veronica smiled openly, not minding at all. It seemed a perfect benediction to begin her reading.

She indicated the first card of the layout: "The Three of the

Cups was the outcome promised in the reading Mama Lucia gave you—a marriage that brings joy in abundance. The Ace of Cups, your second card, the wealth of that love overflowing all around you.''

"It seems an embarrassment of riches," Antonio commented, gesturing at the array of golden Cups, though his tone indicated he was well pleased to have them.

"And then the Priestess . . . .''

"Whose presence has been illuminated," Antonio said, reaching out to caress the card with a fingertip.

"It seems I am to have some beneficial effect in your career. The presence of the Priestess links the emotional joy of the Cups and the adventure and enterprise promised by the next grouping.''

"I am certain that is correct," Antonio said, his eyes glittering with delight.

"The Eight of Wands indicates a journey." *Travel*, she thought, *to Venice, the Northern Lakes, to France.* "The Eight is followed by the fiery creative energy of the Ace of Wands. Your journey will lead you to new enterprises, new connections, new opportunities. And after them, the opportunity to create success offered by the Wands is developed in the Eight and solidified in the Nine of Coins.''

"That perfume recipe I gave you will make your fortune," Mama Lucia told Antonio. "I've had it for fifty years, and you're the only one who could gather all its ingredients. Only the best, of course.''

"Love, adventure, and riches," Antonio said, laughing. "I hope such fortune will not spoil me.''

"The cards say not. The material success and comfort the Coins bring you will not dull the pleasure of love. Your emotional contentment will match your physical. The Ten of Cups promises you the perfect fulfillment of love.''

"And what of the World?" Antonio asked. "What else is left to be won?''

This card of the Major Arcana was the last of the reading. Looking at it now, Veronica saw it could be the first as well. The mystic energy of its circle embraced all the others.

"The World shows the culmination of a cycle of destiny. A

search ended, a goal attained. Union perfected. Within its circle, those in love are one with each other and with all of creation," Veronica said, smiling into Antonio's eyes. "It is the perfect end—and so the time of new beginnings."

Author's Note

 THE Prince Of Cups has been extensively researched. Of course, selection, interpretation, conjecture, and dramatic license are all involved in creating my own version of the time. One of the Borgia brothers was completely deleted, and the complex political aspects of Savonarola's downfall have been slighted in favor of the religious conflicts that are more central to the story I chose to tell. While I could not agree with those who view Savonarola as a saint, I have tried not to dismiss him as nothing but a fanatic.

The mystery of Juan Borgia's death has never been solved. While modern historians tend to favor one of several other candidates, Cesare Borgia was the best dramatic choice. He was long the favorite contender, and I perceive nothing in his character to indicate he would have had any difficulty committing fratricide.

The Tarot packs of the day had descriptive pictures for the Major Arcana and simple depictions of the number of Wands, Cups, Coins, and Swords on the Minor Arcana. Mama Lucia's and Veronica's decks foreshadow the modern custom of fully illustrating all the cards.

My apologies to whichever Sienese *contrada* actually won the *palio* in 1497.

For those interested in the period, three books which I found particularly helpful in giving vivid detail as well as general history were Roberto Ridolfi's *Savonarola*, Joan Haslip's *Lucrezia Borgia*, and Lucas-Dumbarton's, *Daily Life in Florence in the Time of the Medici*.